בס"ד

MARIENBAD
& Beyond

THE LEGACY OF THE LEITNER FAMILY FROM MARIENBAD

A Fascinating Journey of Eighty Years Around the World

DOVID LEITNER

MARIENBAD AND BEYOND

teleshop@talk21.com

ISBN: 978-1-5272-8873-7

Layout and cover design:
Devorah Englard
devorahenglard@gmail.com

ACKNOWLEDGEMENTS

From the day I undertook to begin writing this book, I have witnessed open Hashgocho Protis (Divine Providence) at every stage. When I first told my brothers about the idea, I received their immediate approval, encouragement and offers of help. I am very grateful to my older brother Micha, who organised the translation of some of the family letters that were written in Italian, providing all the details of the "Santiago Experience" and Santiago Mikvah, the photos of the Kokisch Kevorim, and undertook to enhance some of the Leitner photos from Marienbad. My brother Aaron, with whom I sat for many hours in his home sifting through numerous files and boxes of family photos, letters and documents, and records of some of the minutes from the Machzikei Hadass Office archives.

Aaron has also undertaken to research the state of the Marienbad Cemetery with the hope of being able to replace the relevant Matzeivos there, or at least to erect a plaque commemorating those who are buried there, but whose exact locations cannot be verified.

My thanks to my brother Binyomin for supplying all the correspondence that Opa received from Reb Aaron of Belz and other pertinent information.

I thank my nephew, Meyer Eichler, for transcribing the Belzer Rebbe's letters.

To my nephews Avrumi and Akiva Leitner, who provided some interesting family photos. I am very grateful to my cousin Sarita Abelson (-Kahan), who shared with me many details and information pertaining to the Kokisch side of the family, and to Golde Kahn (-Winkler) and Yerit Shapiro (-Winkler) for their input.

My thanks also to my cousins Getty Kahan and Harry Leitner who shared with me more detailed information about their parents.

To Avrohom Yehuda Leitner for his expertise in compiling the 'Family Tree', and to my granddaughters Shani Prijs for her skills in putting the family tree in order, and Reizy Heimann for her help with some typing.

A special thank you goes to Hirshel Tzig of America for providing extra quality photographs and relevant details, who has been a tremendous help. A very useful contact was Family Adler of Zurich, as Reb Schmuel Adler lived in Marienbad from 1933-38, and his son Shlome supplied the photos of Gottlieb Leitner.

A special thanks to my sons Mordechai Meir for his help with the letters from Belz, Eliezer for his constant assistance with the computer, and Yossi for his photographic expertise.

Part of the Hashgocho Protis was that shortly before we completed this work, my oldest son, Moishe, made contact with a neighbour who supplied me with some interesting additional photos.

A special thanks to my daughter Esti for proofreading the manuscript and for her practical suggestions.

A very special thanks to Mrs. Devorah Englard for her beautiful design and layout by transforming my simply typed words into this appealing book. Her expertise and talents are evident on every page.

Much credit and thanks, however, goes to my wife, Mirjam, who spent many hours painstakingly translating letters, documents and newspapers about the Kenessio from their original German into English, and for proof reading the manuscript with her natural Swiss perfection.

Dovid Leitner
10, New Hall Road
Manchester M7 4EL
England

APPRECIATION

Soon after this project started, my son Eliezer surprised me with an unusual gift: he handed me a sealed envelope which I opened in his presence. He had organised that our immediate family, my wife, me and all our children would visit Marienbad shortly after Purim 2018, to see this famous resort that we had heard so much about. The envelope contained our boarding passes for the flights and details of the itinerary. We would all meet in Prague on Sunday afternoon, with flights from London, Newcastle, Tel Aviv and Manchester, all scheduled to arrive at similar times. All arrangements had been pre-booked in Marienbad and ב"ה we accomplished a lot in the short time that we spent there. Eliezer had asked Yechezkel to organise the entire itinerary, which was meticulously arranged. On arrival in Prague we drove to Marienbad, where the children had organised a grand supper and full program before retiring for the night. After davening and an early Israeli buffet style breakfast, we proceeded to the Hotel National and Leitner Haus. There we met Mr Borsky and his interpreter, who gave us a guided tour and made us 'feel at home', after which he presented us with a framed photograph of the hotel as it was in 1927, to commemorate our visit. From there we drove to the cemeteries in Drumol and Marienbad to daven at the Kevorim, and were shown around by Mr. Fred Chavatel, the curator of the Tachov Museum. Our next stop was a visit to the Kursaal where the 3rd Kenessio Gedoloh was held. The manager had prepared a welcome pack for each of us and gave us an extensive tour of this magnificent hall. Our final visit was to the local Museum in Marienbad, which is normally closed on Monday, but the Tourist Office requested that the curator, Mr. Bardosh, make an exception for us, as the Leitners were part of the history of the town. He had prepared copies of the Marienbad Newspaper of 1937 with a full report of the Kenessio, and also presented us with a 246 page book written by Dr. Huttenmeister, listing all the gravestones in Drumol, together with a CD of the cemetery. The curator then gave us a copy on a USB stick containing a detailed History of Jewish Marienbad. This was true Hashgocho Protis, as I now had plenty high quality material for the book.

When referring to family names, I have incorporated an identification number, which refers to their specific place in the detailed Family Tree which is to be found at the end of the book.

I would be grateful to receive any further photos relating to Marienbad that any member of the public would like to share with me. Simply forward them to my email address at **teleshop@talk21.com.**

A separate booklet with additional family photos is available on request from the author.

All photos in this book are available for purchase in digital format.

CONTENTS

MARIENBAD AND BEYOND

A FASCINATING STORY OF EIGHTY YEARS AROUND THE WORLD

INTRODUCTION

My parents are referred to throughout this book as Opa and Oma, as they were fondly called by all their grandchildren.

I often asked Opa ז"ל to write down his rich life history so that his children and future generations would be inspired by the special Hashgocho Protis that saved him and Oma ע"ה from the Nazis, and also to leave a legacy of their tremendous Mesiras Nefesh for Yiddishkeit throughout their lives. This would also serve as a reminder to us of the numerous social activities that Opa was involved in, in organising the 3rd Kenessio in Marienbad, his involvement in the numerous organisations of Hatzolo work in London during WW2, establishing an Orthodox Jewish community in Santiago de Chile, and finally being instrumental in helping with the rebuilding of the Orthodox Jewish community in Manchester.

Additionally, Opa grew up in Marienbad, the town that was famous for hosting a large number of Chassidishe Rebbes, Litvishe and Yekkishe Rabbonim as well as many influential business people. There was no other town in Europe that would attract such a large and varied range of Orthodox Yidden on an annual basis, which gave Opa the opportunity to become personally aquainted with all of them. He would often remark that he was personally familiar with all the pre-war Gedolim of Europe, apart from the Chofetz Chaim, whom he never met. He also related that he not only knew these Rebbes and Rabbonim, but that they knew him too by his first name. Opa would always add a personal story that had occurred to a certain Rebbe, or the achievements of a particular Rov, etc. Unfortunately, I am unable to supply these personal anecdotes. Although he spoke openly about his experiences, he never actually documented them, but left sufficient information, so that I, together with the help of my brothers, have taken on that job on his behalf. I am one generation further down the line, but have tried to piece everything together as accurately as possible.

We are taught that although throughout the ages the Jewish People had over 1000 prophets, but only the prophecies of 24 of them were written down, as only these few had profound lessons of relevance to future generations. Similarly, although Opa and Oma lived a full life, it is impossible and unnecessary to write down every detail and occurrence. I have tried to select those that I feel are relevant and can provide us with much inspiration.

However, this is not just another book about two Holocaust survivors, who not only survived physically but also spiritually, and remained steadfast in their commitment to every detail of our rich Mesorah despite everything that they went through. This is a unique story of a couple who had the energy, conviction and enthusiasm to rebuild their lives and that of their Jewish brethren, for the benefit of the wider Jewish community in four different countries.

I have named this book 'Marienbad and Beyond' because it was the unique Yiddishe life that all the Leitner family witnessed and absorbed in Marienbad on a regular basis, by personally meeting and attending to the varied needs of the large spectrum of Gedolim, learning from them, their ethics and personalities, that ensured that they each could take these lessons and further their own Yiddishkeit. Then, during and after the Holocaust each member of the family was able to export these lessons from 'Marienbad and Beyond'. This is true for all the Leitner members, whether Opa in his eighty year travels around the world, or Sima Kokisch, who as a young widow managed to educate and navigate her four daughters through Nazi Europe, moving to the other side of the world and setting up a kosher home in the 'spiritual desert' of Santiago, without deviating from the personal pride in Yiddishkeit, just as she had witnessed at home in Marienbad. Similarly too, Aunty Ernestine (Winkler), as a young widow, continued to lead the Machzikei Hadass Community in Copenhagen with wisdom, pride and dignity, transporting that which she had seen in Marienbad and Beyond.

Opa and Oma and their parents lived in a generation that witnessed much spiritual destruction brought about by the Haskala, Reform and the birth of the Zionist Movement, who were all determined to destroy authentic Judaism, and unfortunately were very successful with their propaganda and efforts. With the growth of anti-Semitism in Europe it was very easy to sell these ideologies to the masses. They would preach that having our own homeland would solve all our Jewish problems and it would replace our obligation for Torah observance. They propagated and wished to be 'a nation like all other nations', and thought that this would solve all the problems that have plagued the Jewish People throughout the centuries. They refused to acknowledge that the Jewish People are unique and are not governed by the same laws of nature that govern 'all other nations'.

The large devastation that was caused by the Haskala Movement in a period close to the arrival of Moshiach was already revealed to Yaakov Ovinu in a truly remarkable way. Shortly before he died he commanded his son Yosef to take the trouble and bury him in Chevron, together with his ancestors. He then explained to Yosef that "I did not trouble myself to bury your mother Rochel even in the nearest town, but purposely buried her on the road side on the way to Beis Lechem. You must appreciate that this was done so that your mother could plead and advocate on behalf of her children at the time of their exile from Eretz

Yisroel on the way to Bovel. They are destined to pass this very spot of her grave, where the Jewish nation will pray and רחל will intercede on their behalf receiving a Divine assurance that ultimately ' ושבו בנים לגבולם – 'Your children will return to their borders'.

The opening Possuk of Tehillim reads:

אשרי האיש אשר לא הלך בעצת רשעים ובדרך חטאים לא עמד ובמושב לצים לא ישב

'Praiseworthy is the man who did not walk in the counsel of the wicked, did not stand in the path of the sinful, nor sit in the sessions with the scoffers.'

The Chassam Sofer points out that the acronym of the three types of people mentioned in this opening Possuk, namely, רשעים חטאים לצים spells out the name רחל! It is the descendants of רחל that represent that section of Yisroel that, through the difficulties of exile throughout the centuries, fall away from their Mesorah and are 'buried along the road of time', becoming the wicked sinners and scoffers of our sacred Heritage. It is for these unassociated Jews who are spiritually dead and buried, having perished spiritually along the long passage of time, that רחל prayed for and was assured that they would ultimately return to the correct path of authentic Yiddishkeit.

The Chassam Sofer of Pressburg (1762–1839)

The only way that Orthodox Yiddishkeit could survive and remain vibrant is by following the teachings of the Chassam Sofer who established the principle of an 'Austrittsgemeinde', a self sufficient Orthodox Jewish Community that would be protected and insulated by not being affiliated with other non-orthodox organisations. The Chassam Sofer, being Rav of Pressburg, left an indelible legacy to the world, and especially to the Czechoslovakian Jewry, and that is the legacy that the Leitner family followed. It was with this in mind that the Torah leaders of the 20th century established Agudas Yisroel in 1912, to procure support and strength to Orthodox Jewry, providing a little light that will dispell much darkness.

Opa would often explain the difference between the ethos of the Aguda Movement and that of the Zionist Organisation. The Zionists used false ideologies with which to fight against the Truth, whereas in contrast, Agudas Yisroel uses the Truth to fight against falsehood.

Avrom was told לך לך 'Go and leave your homeland' but was not told where to go, only' אל הארץ אשר אראך' – to the land that I will show you. How did Avrom know in which direction to go? The Baal Haturim explains that a 'cloud' appeared and he followed this cloud as a Divine indication of his destination. In our case too, as we relate this amazing story of Opa and Oma's lives, the cloud that showed them the correct path was the teachings of the Torah and directives as dictated by the Chassam Sofer – make yourself an 'Austrittsgemeinde' wherever you go.

Rabbi S.R. Hirsh

Opa was a very keen student of the teachings of Rabbi S.R. Hirsch and was fond of saying that 'Hirsch you cannot just read casually – Hirsch one has to study'. It is on this very same possuk of לך לך that Rabbi Hirsch writes:

'Avrom heard Hashem's call לך לך 'Go for yourself'- go your own way. Do not concern yourself with what others will think. Do not fear isolation if it means separating yourself from a society that is bent on destroying everything sacred in Yiddishkeit. We have survived the millennia because we are imbued with Avroms courage to be a minority. Stand up for what is just and correct and do not 'go with the flow'. It takes courage, resolution, conviction and strength. But ואעשך לגוי גדול – I will make you into a great nation, not a large nation but rather a great nation, as we are measured by quality and not by quantity. We stand alone as a minority, singular in our belief, proud of our heritage, and strong in our relationship with Hashem and His Torah. What could be greater than being an active member of the nation that was made great by Hashem Himself!'

The ethos of life that they received was to be the transmitters of the unaltered Torah, our Mesorah. Their occupation was focused not on material gains but on nurturing a calm happy family that fostered Torah principles and adherence to them at all times and in all circumstances. Opa was a keen follower of Rabbi S.R. Hirsch, whose famous motto was תורה אם דרך ארץ as it was the תורה that always took preference, and even the דרך ארץ that followed was always to be within the guidelines of the תורה.

This is the path that Opa and Oma followed, and I hope this small tribute will help portray their legacy and encourage all of their descendants to continue in their ways.

The last century has seen a profound change in electronic, scientific and technical 'advances' or perhaps it would be more accurate to term them 'changes' rather than 'advances', and it is often hard to appreciate the physical situation that existed 100 years ago. Can we imagine a world where telephones, cars, washing machines etc. were luxury items? So I make no apology for sometimes describing what life was like just one or two generations ago, to help the reader better understand and appreciate the Mesiras Nefesh that the previous generations displayed for keeping every single Mitzva.

CHAPTER 1
The Development of Marienbad

A SHORT HISTORY OF CZECHOSLOVAKIA

Czechoslovakia has had a very turbulent history, and for the purpose of this book it is worthwhile to learn a little bit about its past two centuries. Czechoslovakia is part of Central Europe and is surrounded by Germany to the West, Poland to the North, Austria and Hungary to the South and the Ukraine to the Eastern frontier. Marienbad, a subject discussed at length in this book, is situated in the Bohemian district of the country, bordering onto Germany. This became known as Sudetenland which was annexed by the Germans in September 1938, whilst the remainder of Czechoslovakia was occupied by them on March 15, 1939.

In 1620, at the defeat of the Bohemians at the battle of the White Mountains, an Austrian monarchy ruled, known as the Habsburg Dynasty. Hence until 1918, Marienbad belonged to the Austrian Empire, and on October 28 of that year witnessed the foundation of the independent state when Czechs and Slovaks merged, thus forming Czechoslovakia. This became know as The First Republic. The Germans occupied Czechoslovakia from March 15, 1939, until the end of World War II, and left on May 9, 1945, which became known as The Second Republic. Their freedom was short lived as in February 1948 the Communists came to power, and the Russians invaded in August of the same year, which became known as the Third Republic. The Communist regime collapsed in November 1989 and on the first of January 1993 Czechoslovakia split again into two separate Republics, namely the Czech Republic and Slovakia.

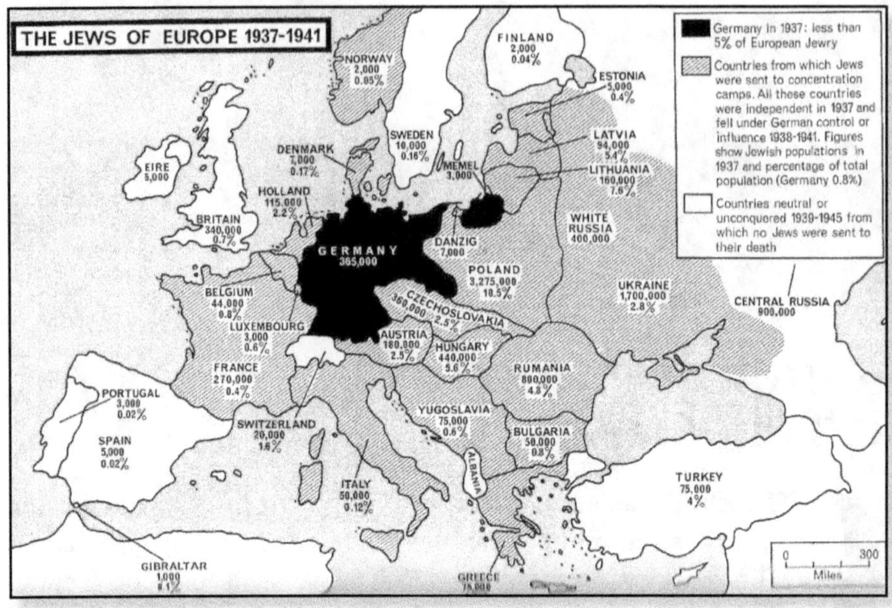

The Jews in Europe - taken from the Jewish History Atlas by Martin Gilbert

The foundation of the independent First Republic of Czechoslovakia in 1918, with its multi nationals and different faiths being combined into one single country, brought with it much social tension that resulted in anti-semitic clashes in the early years. The first president of Czechoslovakia, Mr. Jan Masaryk, together with his loyal colleague Mr. Edvard Benes, made great efforts throughout their lives to promote a peaceful existence between all faiths and ensured that the Jewish population was well treated. They accomplished this by putting much effort in making official visits to Jewish establishments, all of which were well publicised in the local and national media. This included a visit to the Leitner Hotel in Marienbad by Mr. Edvard Benes where he enjoyed a good kosher meal, and was happy to sign the visitors' book and hotel stationery, in addition to an official State visit of Mr. Jan Masaryk to Palestine as shown below, when he met with Rabbi Yosef Chaim Sonnenfeld.

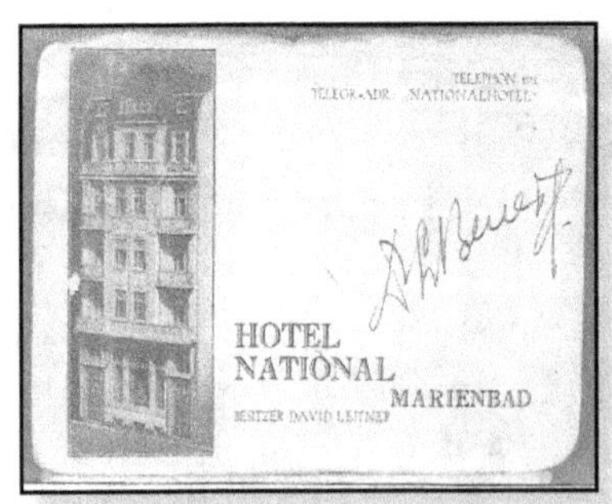

Mr. Edvard Benes signed hotel stationery during his visit

Czechoslovakian President Masaryk in Jerusalem 8th April 1927 with Rabbi Yosef Chaim Sonnenfeld זצ"ל.

Mr. Edvard Benes also made an official visit in 1933 to the Jewish Community in Piestany, (presently in Slovakia) and in 1934 met the Munkatcher Rebbe at the Goldenes Schloss Hotel in Marienbad, owned by Gottlieb Leitner (1.2.1).

Gottlieb Leitner

President Edvard Beneš meets with the Munkatcher Rebbe, Rabbi Chaim Elozor Spira in Goldenes Schloss 1934

When the Germans entered Czechoslovakia in 1938, the entire Czech government escaped to London, and continued their efforts to help the Jewish Refugees from there, as will be explained more fully in that section of the book. In London they organised themselves as the 'Czechoslovakian Government–in-Exile', where they obtained international recognition from the United Kingdom (approved by the Foreign Secretary Lord Halifax on July 18, 1940, and in July 1941, by the United States and the Soviet Union too.) Their Foreign Minister in exile

Opa with Thomas Masaryk (Czech Foreign Minister) January 1940 after a reception in London

was Thomas Masaryk, who was extremely friendly and used his diplomatic connections to help the Jewish cause whenever possible. After World War II, in 1948, the entire government returned to Czechoslovakia where Thomas Masaryk, the then Foreign Minister, secretly negotiated and sold arms to help the Israeli War of Independence effort.

Opa kept up his connections with members of the Czechoslovakian Government even whilst in London during the war, and is seen escorting the Czech Foreign Minister, Mr. Tom Masaryk, after a reception in London.

SHORT HISTORY OF JEWISH LIFE IN CZECHOSLOVAKIA

Carlsbad, Marienbad and Franzensbad are the three 'spa' towns that developed in Czechoslovakia in the late nineteenth century, where Jewish life flourished and the population increased. Carlsbad was by far the largest spa town, about 100 square kilometres in size, followed by Marienbad which was half the size of Carlsbad, a distance of approximately 55km. They both attracted many Chassidic Rebbes and guests, but also a large number of Zionist leaders, as well as many unaffiliated and affluent Jewish people. They found these towns with their kosher facilities an ideal place to relax, as they were conveniently situated between Eastern and Western Europe. Carlsbad became the choice for the large Zionist Conference in 1921 and again in 1923, whilst Marienbad was chosen for a Conference of Chassidic Rabbis that took place in July 1928 with the object of unifying the work of Orthodox Jewry in Poland, the preparatory Kenessio Mechino of 1936, and the subsequent World Aguda Conference, the 3rd Kenessio Gedoloh which took place in 1937. Whilst Carlsbad was referred to as simply a nice town, Marienbad was classified as 'magnificent' in comparison.

The 3 spa towns

The entrance to Marienbad (Marianske Lazne in Czech) in 1890

A Marienbad to Carlsbad shuttle servie

Marienbad is a town in western Bohemia in the Czech Republic, not far from the German border and some 175 km from Prague. The first Jewish people settled in Marienbad in 1820, prior to which Jews were only allowed to enter Marienbad during the 'health cure' season in the summer, as they provided the locals with much needed revenue. They inhabited neighbouring villages, including Drumol, some five miles away, where the Leitner family lived until they eventually settled in Marienbad permanently.

August 22, 1899 postcard showing Jewish visitors drinking the spa waters in Marienbad

An early scene of Marienbad's main road,
on a postcard from 1900 as seen from the Kaiserstrasse

DRUMOL JEWISH CEMETERY

A monument of a Shul that was established in 1724 and was in use until 1938, when it was destroyed by the Nazis, stands close to the Drumol Jewish Cemetery which is surrounded by a forest. Four ancient tombstones connected with the Leitner family are found in this old cemetery, and are highlighted on the cemetery site map below. Located at number 19 is that of Avrohom ben Chaim Aryeh, number 22 for Yechezkel Leitner, number 23 for Chaim Aryeh ben Avrohom and number 135 for Mirel Leitner.

Drumol Jewish Cemetery

Records held at the Jewish Museum in Prague confirm other members of the Leitner family being buried there, but sadly no other tombstones have been found.

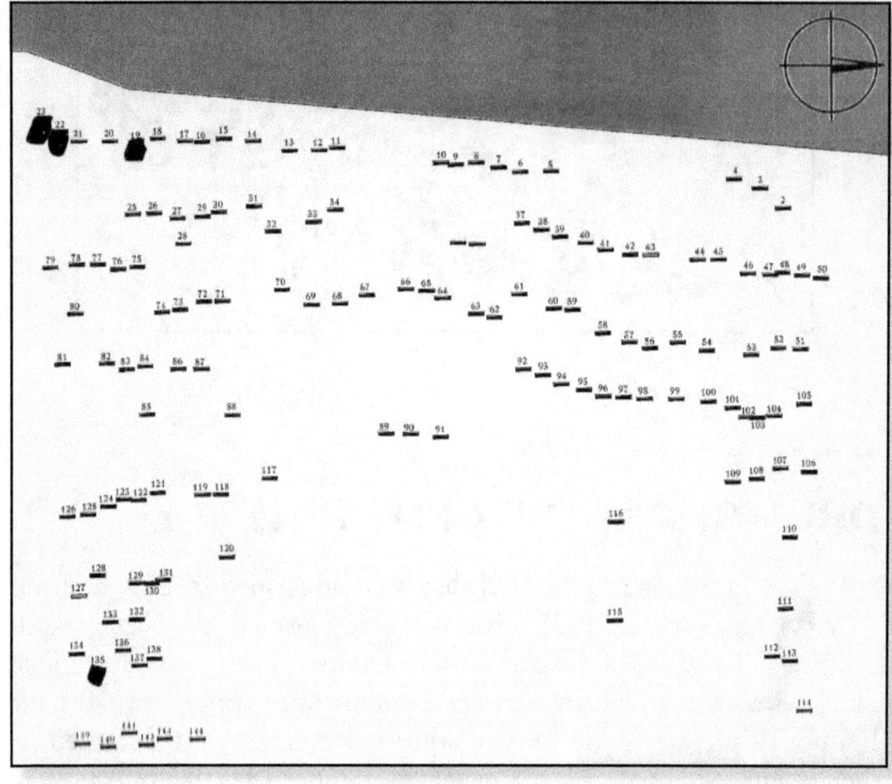

Site map of top part of Drumol Cemetery with four relevant tombstones highlighted

The Leitner Matzeivos in Drumol

NUMBER 19 - אברהם בן חיים אריה ז"ל

The inscription reads:

פ"נ
איש תם
וישר הולך תמים
ופעל צדק ירא אלקים
וסר מרע הי' מנעוריו עשה
צדקה וג"ח כל ימיו הי' פאר
עדתו וראש קהילתו ועסק
בצרכי צבור באמונה ה'
אברהם ב"ה חיים אריה ז"ל
נפטר ביום ד' ונקבר ביום
ת.נ.צ.ב.ה

Avrohom ben Chaim Aryeh

d. November 14, 1822.

[Although this tombstone does not mention the name Leitner, it is fair to assume, due its proximity to grave 23 and the similarity of their names, that it may well be another Leitner relation.]

NUMBER 22 - ר' יחזקאל לייטנר ז"ל

The inscription reads:

נפטר ביום ש"ק ונקבר ביום א'
י"ד טבת בשנת תקצ"ג
פ"נ
האיש הישר כ"ה יחזקאל לייטנר
איש אמונים ירא אלוקים
סר מרע עושה צדקות לכל
עניים עסק בצרכי צבור באמונה
נאבל בחצי ימיו חטף אותו המות
הלך לפניו צדקתו
אביו יאספהו ובתוך גן עדן יהי' מושבו
ת.נ.צ.ב.ה

d. January 4, 1833

[13th Teves 5593 grave 22 in Drumol as above] י"ד טבת תקצ"ב

NUMBER 23 - ר' חיים אריה בן אברהם לייטנר ז"ל

The inscription reads:

פ"נ
איש ישר ונאמן
כ"ה חיים אריה בן
אברהם לייטנר
הלך לעולמו זקן
ושבע ימים נפטר
ביום ב' י"ט שבט
ונקבר ביום ד' כ"א
שבט תרמ"ט לפ"ק
ת.נ.צ.ב.ה

NUMBER 135 - האשה מירל אשת ר' חיים ליב לייטנער ז"ל

The inscription reads:

פ"ט
עד הגל הזה ועדה המצבה
האשה החשובה א"ח מ'
מירל ע"ה אשת ר' חיים
ליב לייטנער שהלכה
לעולמה בשם טוב ובמעשים
טובים ביום ש"ק ב' כסליו ש'
תרלד לפ"ק שם אמה יסכא מייער
ת.נ.צ.ב.ה

b. 1811 d. November 22, 1873 [2. Kislev 5634]

On this tombstone the name Leitner is spelled with an extra letter (ע)

Another Jewish cemetery that was used was located in Bad Königswart, some 18km north-west of Marienbad, and had a small Jewish community since 1430, but as Marienbad grew, Bad Königswart's Jewish population dwindled.

MARIENBAD JEWISH CEMETERY

As the Jewish population of Marienbad increased, the necessity for its own burial grounds arose, and a small plot of land was purchased, together with an adjoining house. The upper floor was used by the cemetery keeper (caretaker) whilst the ground floor was used as a Tahara room and mortuary. Max Leitner (1.1.3) is buried there, and although the Nazis removed all the gravestones during the War, his children (the Leitners from Haifa) replaced his Matzeivo after the war. Since he was buried next to a tree with a rather unusual shape (it has a large bulge in the bark) and stands near the entrance of the cemetery, it enabled the family to locate the exact position of the grave. Max Leitner was born on July 18, 1874 and died on Erev Pesach, April 6, 1917.

Max Leitner's (1.1.3) Matzeivo stands alone in the cemetery next to a tree

There is an old fashioned hand operated water pump just outside the gate, to enable people to wash their hands after visiting the cemetery. In the 1860s the entire population of Marienbad numbered 2500, and at the beginning of World War II in 1939 it had grown to approximately 12,000 inhabitants in total.

The entrance to the cemetery in Marienbad and the water pump

It was reported in the J.T.A of January 7, 1948 that a certain Mr Projer, a Czech administrator of a German tombstone company, was found guilty of removing several tombstones from the Marienbad Jewish cemetery. He was ordered to make a full indemnification to the Jewish community for the damage, and was sentenced to one year in prison. [Soon after the Communists came to power and took over the country, this sentence was not enforced.]

In 1875 a Jewish congregation was established in Marienbad, who organised the building of their own large Synagogue. It was completed in 1884 and functioned until it was destroyed by the Nazis on November 10, 1938, during the infamous Kristallnacht, the only building that was physically destroyed by the Germans in Marienbad! Its large edifice was to cater for both the inhabitants of the town and also for the many spa guests and tourists that visited Marienbad annually, and could accommodate 318 men and 170 ladies. However, in 1898, owing to popular demand, an organ was installed and even a mixed choir was allowed to perform, which consisted not only of men and ladies, but even of a mixture of Jews and non-Jews alike. All that remains today of this Reform 'Shul' is a grassy area and a memorial stone.

The fifteen or so Orthodox families that lived in Marienbad, including the Leitners, had their own minyan, their own 'Austrittsgemeinde'.

Reform Synagogue plaque on site of former Synagogue in Marienbad.

One of these local resident Orthodox families was Family Daum, who owned a Delicatessen and Grocery at Hus Strasse in the vicinity of the railway station. Mr. Avrohom Daum, a man born in Marienbad in 1917, told me that he remembers going to the park one Shabbos afternoon in 1927, when he was ten years old. Sitting on a bench nearby, he saw Reb Elchonon Wasserman הי"ד who sat there for three hours, looking straight ahead. He was staring at a large tree opposite, and was completely engrossed in Torah thoughts. Mr Daum relates: "After three hours, Reb Elchonon noticed me looking at him, and asked me what I wanted. [Imagine Mr. Daum, as a young child, had the respect and decency to simply wait quietly for three hours and not disturb - what Derech Eretz]. I answered that I wanted the Rov to test me on my learning. He took me by the hand and we went together to his flat, where he tested me on the Chumash with Rashi that I learnt that week with my father. Reb Elchonon was happy with what he had heard and wanted to reward me, so he took a sugar cube from the dining room table and told me to make the Brocho aloud, and he would answer 'Omen'; that would be my reward! He then blessed me that I should merit a long life. [I spoke to Mr Daum on the telephone in December 2017, when he was 100 years old, presently living in New York].

Emil Gerstel (1.1.8), the father of Oscar Gerstel (1.1.8.3), was the head of another local Orthodox family who ran a bakery in Marienbad, and on Friday the local housewives would bring their 'Cholent' and other Shabbos foods to heat up in his commercial ovens. This was normal practise.

In order to attract more visitors to Marienbad and to ensure that their holiday would be pleasant and relaxing, the Municipality forbade any door to door peddlers from selling merchandise, and likewise no door to door charity collections were allowed. The Jewish community naturally wanted to continue helping the needy, so they established three collection points at local retail shops were people could continue to bring their Tzedoko on a regular basis, and the Community would then distribute these funds to the destitute. One of these collection points was at the retail clothes shop owned by Max Leitner, not far from the main Shul, in a prominent place on the main thoroughfare in Marienbad.

Schnitt-, Manufaktur-, Weiß- und Modewaren

Balázs Marie, Nordstern	**Kohn** Eduard, Miramare, Tel. 374
Basch Irene, Weißer Schwan	**Kohner** Luise, Anker
Dolejš Rudolf, Louvre, Tel. 457	**Kopetz** Anna, Triest
Drozda Henriette, Kolumbus	**Krechtner** Richard, Villa Böhm
Ehrlich Hubert, Bremen	**Kübl** Helene, London
Fantes Ignaz, Schw. Adler, Tel. 161	**Leitner** Louise, Haus Lucker
Feigl Josef, Augsburg	**Leitner** Max, Haus Lucker

Extract from the Marienbad City Register – Max and Louise Leitner lived in Haus Lucker.

Israelitische Kultusgemeinde Marienbad.

Datum des Poststempe

„Der Edle sinnt auf Edles". Jesaja 30, 8.

Euer Hochwohlgeboren!

Die bisher übliche Sammlung von Haus zu Haus zu Gunst der **israel. fremden Armen, die täglich mit Bitten u Unterstützung an uns herantreten,** wird seitens der Behör nicht mehr gestattet.

Die gefertigte Kultusgemeinde ist leider nicht in der glücklich Lage, über hinreichende Mittel zu verfügen, weshalb sie gezwung ist, an das bekannt mildtätige und opferwillige jüdische Herz apellieren und stellt die **dringende Bitte an alle unsere Glauben genossen** um eine gütige Spende, um den vielen an uns gestellt Anforderungen entsprechen zu können.

Der Allmächtige wird es Ihnen gewiß reichlich lohnen.

Hochachtungsvoll

Der Vorstand
der israelitischen Kultusgemein
in Marienbad.

Gütige Spenden werden vom Bank- und Wechselgeschä **Stingl & Co., Haus „Merkur"** gegenüber dem Kreuzbrunne und im Modewarengeschäft **Max Leitner, Haus „Lucker" Kaiserstrasse,** entgegengenommen.

Letter sent by Jewish Congregation informing them of the three collection points for charitable contributions.

This translates:

Hebrew Cultural Community of Marienbad.

Your Honour! Date as postmark

The usual collection from door to door on behalf of Israel's poor, who appeal to us daily with requests for help and support, has been banned by the authorities.

Unfortunately, the Cultural Community does not have sufficient funds, and has been forced to appeal to the well known benevolent and charitable Jewish heart of all our fellow believers, to please act charitably, to allow us to respond to the petitioners who approach us.

The Almighty will surely repay you generously.

Sincerely yours,

The Board of Directors of the Hebrew Cultural Community of Marienbad.

Please send your donations to the Bank Change Stingl & Co, Haus 'Merkur' opposite the Kreuzbrunnen, and to the fashionshop Max Leitner, Haus Lucker, Kaiserstrasse.

Max Leitner's retail clothes shop a few doors away from the Marienbad Synagogue on the main road.

King Edward V11 (centre) with 2 physicians

The city of Marienbad received a lot of publicity due to the fact that the British Monarch, King Edward VII (1864–1910) visited Marienbad a total of nine times for medical treatments, and during his visit on August 16, 1904 he met with the Austrian Emperor Franz Josef. This was well documented in the world press and provided awareness of the excellent therapeutic properties of the 40 natural Marienbad spas and helped the popularity and expansion of the town. Many other dignitaries visited Marienbad, but in a private capacity, that were not publicized in the press.

Austrian Emperor Franz Josef and King Edward V11 of England meet in Marienbad

The Jewish Hospital in Marienbad with patients convalescing on the balconies, enjoying the fresh air.

Marienbad was not only famous because of its therapeutic spa waters but also enjoyed particularly clean air. It boasted a small Jewish hospital, which was jointly sponsored and funded by the Jewish communities of Prague, Vienna and Berlin, and patients from all over Europe were treated there and benefited from the town's relaxed atmosphere. The hospital also had its own Orthodox Shul.

The establishment of the Jewish hospital in Marienbad together with the pleasant and peaceful surroundings that the town offered attracted many doctors and members of the medical profession to settle there. The spa waters of Marienbad have a slightly bitter taste, and special cups were available that allowed people to drink this water in small sips while taking a walk, as this was part of the treatment.

The special drinking cup for Marienbad's Spa Water

Early Jewish holidaymakers in Marienbad 1900

CHAPTER 2
The Leitner Hotels in Marienbad

MARIENBAD

Yoachim Leitner (חיים ארי') lived in Drumol, and had two sons, Herman (1.1 צבי) and Edward (Eduard 1.2 יחזקא'ל). In 1859 Herman Leitner (1.1) founded the hotel in Marienbad that became known as "Hotel National", and bought another property in 1893 at the back of the Hotel, which became known as "Leitner Haus". Edward Leitner also owned a hotel on the same block, known as "Goldenes Schloss", and figures in greater detail below.

Both of these hotels were of course strictly kosher, and the brothers' honesty and strong religious beliefs soon earned them an excellent reputation throughout the Jewish communities of Europe and around the world. The fact that so many visitors were happy to travel great distances to come to Marienbad is a clear indication of its popularity, especially at a time when travel was far more arduous than it is today. For example, from Vishnitz to Marienbad was 1300km, Belz nearly 1000km, Ger about 850km, Baranowitz a journey of 500km, and Frankfurt 400km. A holiday in Marienbad offered excellent Spa facilities and magnificent and numerous forest walks, all combined with outstanding kosher accommodation.

Herman Leitner's son, Moishe Dovid Leitner (1.1.1) married Getty Schopflocher from Fürst (Germany). Initially they helped out in the management until they eventually took over the daily running of the hotel.

The original Hotel Building 1859

The original Leitner's Haus 1893

Zahl der Grundbuchs-Einlage: 16[illegible]

Grundbuchs=Auszug

Katastralgebiet Marienbad Gerichtsbezirk Marienbad

Wohnhaus Nr.199 Leitners Haus. A.

Post-zahl	Parzellen-nummer	Bezeichnung der Parzelle (Hausnummer, Kulturgattung)	Post-zahl	Parzellen-nummer	Bezeichnung der Parzelle (Hausnummer, Kulturgattung)
1	77/2	Bauparzelle mit Wohnhaus Nr.199.			

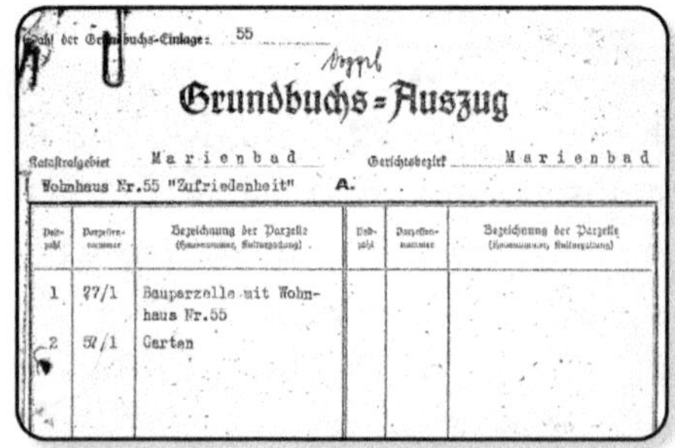

The Property Deeds for Number 199

Zahl der Grundbuchs-Einlage: 55

Grundbuchs=Auszug

Katastralgebiet Marienbad Gerichtsbezirk Marienbad

Wohnhaus Nr.55 "Zufriedenheit" A.

Post-zahl	Parzellen-nummer	Bezeichnung der Parzelle (Hausnummer, Kulturgattung)	Post-zahl	Parzellen-nummer	Bezeichnung der Parzelle (Hausnummer, Kulturgattung)
1	77/1	Bauparzelle mit Wohnhaus Nr.55			
2	57/1	Garten			

The Property Deeds for Number 55

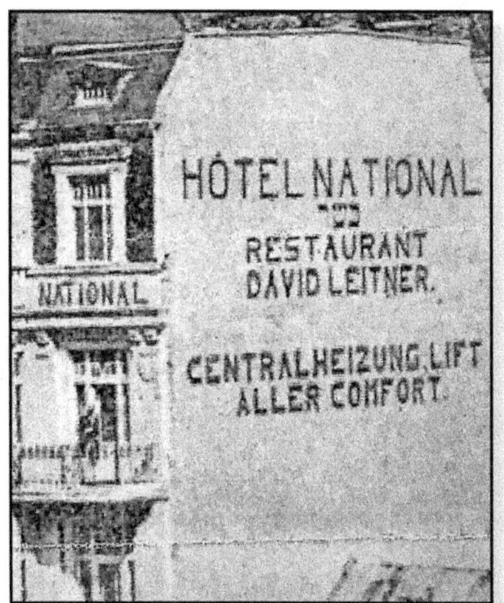

Side view of Hotel National – The Restaurant central heating and all mod cons

Brochure of the Hotel National

TELEPHON 191
TELEGR.-ADR.: „NATIONALHOTEL"

HOTEL
NATIONAL
MARIENBAD
BESITZER DAVID LEITNER

The Dining Room

Betzimmer

Zweibettiges Zimmer

DAVID LEITNER'S
HOTEL NATIONAL

ist das modernste und vornehmste rituelle Haus in Marienbad. Es verfügt über allen modernen Hotelcomfort, wie fließendes Kalt- und Warmwasser in allen Zimmern, Lift, Zentralheizung sowie Privatbäder. Hotelsynagoge und Mikweh.
Das Hotel liegt im Zentrum des Kurortes in unmittelbarer Nähe der Bäder und Heilquellen.
Vorzügliches, altrenommiertes Restaurant. Pensionsarrangements nach Übereinkommen. Frequentiert von der Elite des Kurpublikums. Hotelautobus an der Bahn.

Translated:

DAVID LEITNER'S HOTEL NATIONAL is the most modern and elegant ritual house in Marienbad. It offers all modern hotel comforts such as running hot and cold water in all rooms, lift, central heating, as well as private bathrooms, hotel synagogue and Mikve.

The hotel is centrally situated and in very close proximity to the healing spas and baths.

Excellent, famous restaurant. Boarding arrangements. Frequented by the Elite of health cure guests. Hotel car service at the train station.

The veranda restaurant was also used for guests who stayed at other hotels in town, and just came for their meals to Hotel National, where at the height of the summer season a total of one thousand meals were being served daily! To appreciate what it meant to organise and cater this huge undertaking, I reprint a short extract of the food list taken from the hotel's records, which shows what would have been used over a regular Shabbos during the summer season: 400 kg of fish, meat from 8 cows, and over 300 chickens were required. They employed two private Shochtim and three ladies to kasher the meat, 20 waiters, and 25 kitchen and auxiliary staff.

The hotel had its own Mikve, and a Shul with a beautiful dark blue ceiling decorated with stars, giving it the impression of a night sky, as described by an eye witness.

These modern amenities were advertised prominently on both sides to the hotel entrance, and they were even proud to display the word כשר in Hebrew letters. This five star hotel had an elegant dining room that could comfortably accommodate 120 people, plus a veranda that could seat another 160 people. Apart from the restaurant they also had their own wine cellar, to complement their high class service, and as Rabbi Dr. Shlomo Schonfeld confirmed, 'I recall that when I visited the hotel with my late father, Rabbi Avigdor Schonfeld, that visitors were even able, if they so wished, to select live trout from a fresh-water tank situated on the premises.'

From a close inspection of the official Marienbad Address Book that lists all the residences, it appears that when Herman Leitner first opened his hotel, the address was noted as Postgasse, and even when David Leitner built the large extension it was still listed at the same address, albeit with a different street number. The present street name 'Klicova-Gasse' for the Leitner House appears to have been built after 1915, and hence the two buildings received different addresses and street names although they are attached, back to back. In later entries of the local Directory the Leitner House is listed by the name that appeared on the plaque outside the front door, as 'Zufriedenheit' (Satisfaction).

Even today the town is mainly a summer resort and the hotel was open for approximately 150 days a year. To serve 1000 meals per day to a large diversity of people, each one with their own dietary requirements, and often individual and specific religious customs and requests, was not an easy accomplishment, but thanks to the efficient way that Getty Leitner [Opa's mother] managed the catering staff, that everyone's wishes were respected and satisfactorily catered for. 'Zufriedenheit' (Satisfaction) was therefore a well deserved and appropriate name for this establishment.

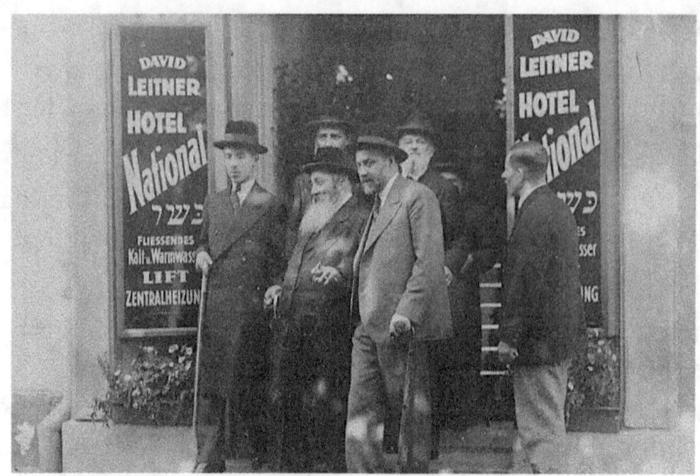

The salient features were prominently displayed at the front door.
The Vizhnitzer Rebbe [Ahavas Yisroel] leaving the hotel

Advert for Leitner Haus – Zufriedenheit

כשר **MARIENBAD.** כשר

„Leitner's Haus" u. „Zur Zufriedenheit"

in nächster Nähe der Brunnen und Bäder.

Anerkannt feinstes und streng rituelles Restaurant I. Ranges

unter Aufsicht eines polnischen שחט

Exquisiteste kurgemässe Küche. — ff. Getränke.

Elegante Speisesäle nebst Garten.

40 hochfeine Zimmer. Separierte Speisezimmer für Familien.

Diner à part und à la carte.

Annahme und solideste Ausführung von Hochzeiten.

Civile Preise. **Aufmerksame Bedienung.**

David Leitner, Restaurateur.

Translated:

כשר Marienbad כשר

"Leitner's Haus" and "Zur Zufriedenheit"

In nearest proximity of the spas and baths.

Known as the finest and srictly kosher 1st class restaurant

Under supervision of a Polish שוחט

Exquisite and healthy kitchen – incl. drinks

Elegant dining rooms and garden.

40 high quality bedrooms. Separate dining rooms for families.

Weddings catered to perfection

Fair prices Attentive service

David Leitner, Restaurateur

	Angemeldet am 1. August:			
15131	Herr **Henoch Liebschütz**, Geschäftsführer	Wichu	Leitners Haus	1
15132	Herr **Kalman Weber**, Rabbiner	Pöstyen	„	1
15133	Frau **Rosalie Kaufmann**, Kaufmannsgattin	Russland	„	1
15134	Frau **Regina Czwall** und Schwester			
15135	Frau **Gisela Ziegler**	Rzeszow	Zufriedenheit	2
15136	Herr **Ignaz Hahn**, Privatier mit Gattin .	Budapest	Leitners Haus	2
15137	Frau **Freida Halberstamm**, Rabbinersgattin	Galizien	Zufriedenheit	2

Extract from guest list at Leitner Haus and Zufriedenheit

This new extension became known as 'Hotel National', and together with the 'Leitner Haus' comprised of a total of 60 bedrooms which were available for guests, apart from the private accommodation used by the Leitner family. Getty Leitner died in Marienbad in 1934, and Moishe Dovid continued running the hotel together with his four sons and daughter.

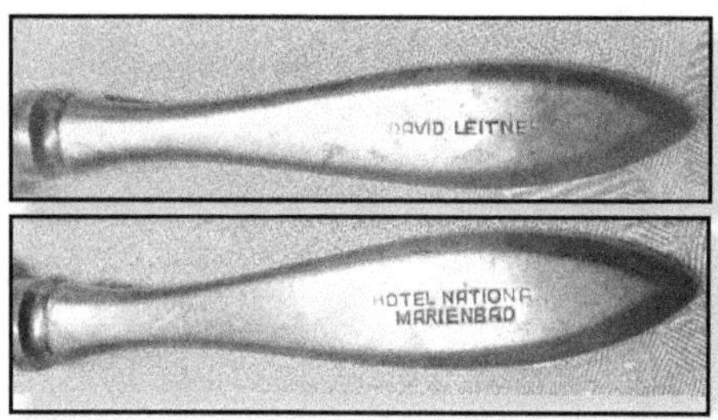

Personalised hotel cutlery.

Edward Leitner (1.2) (יחזקאל.) (brother of Herman Leitner) had also bought a hotel building on the same block as Hotel National, which became known as 'Goldener Schlüssel'. The two Leitner brothers put in a joint planning application in 1906 for a large extension to their hotels, which was finally completed in 1912, by which time Edward had died and his oldest son, Gottlieb (1.2.1) took over the management of the hotel.

Letter headed paper from Hotel Goldenes Schloss

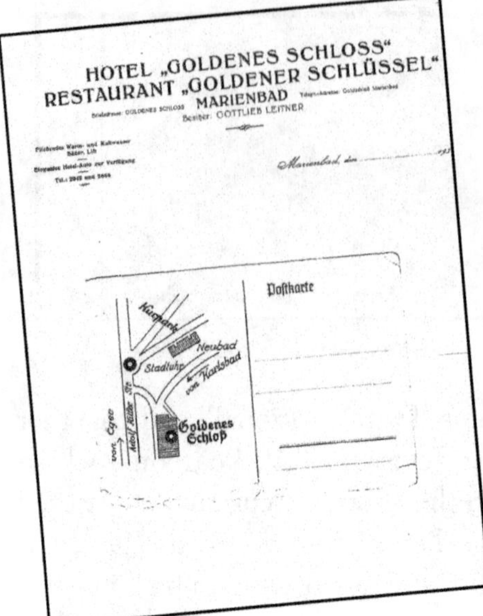

HOTEL „GOLDENES SCHLOSS"
RESTAURANT „GOLDENER SCHLÜSSEL"
MARIENBAD
Besitzer: GOTTLIEB LEITNER

Marienbad, den 193

Goldener Schloss stationery

Číslo vložky 58

Výpis z pozemkové knihy

katastrálního území Mar.Lázně
Wohnhaus Nr 57,,drei Mohren,,
Wohnhaus Nr 56,,Gold.Schlüssel,, A. und 423 Gold Schloss.

Běžné číslo	Parcelní číslo	Poznačení parcely (číslo domu, způsob vzdělávání)	Běžné číslo	Parcelní číslo	Poznačení parcely (číslo domu, způsob vzdělávání)
1	60	B.parc.mit Wohnhaus Nr 56			
2	54	Garten			
3	79	Bp.mit Wohnhaus Nr 57			
4	55/1	Garten			
5	405	Bp.mit Wohnhaus Nr 423			

Běžné číslo	Zápis
	A.
1-3	bezpředmětné

Front page of Property Deeds for Goldener Schloss

Advert for Goldener Schlüssel

Translated:

Marienbad

Goldener Schlüssel

Opposite the Kaiserstrasse

Close to Spas and Bathhouses

כשר Restaurant כשר

Strictly Kosher under supervision of

Mr Leib Neuding, Shochet from Warsaw.

First-rate guest rooms at fair prices.

Newly renovated elegant dining room and garden with electric lighting

Eduard Leitner

Artist drawing of proposed extension November 5, 1906
This is for the Goldenes Schloss (left) together with Hotel National (right)

This major building project involved the addition of a five storey house with an additional 40 bedrooms for the Leitner Hotel National, all tastefully furnished, and included a passenger lift. All the rooms enjoyed private sanitary facilities, central heating and hot and cold running water. Although this might be considered standard in today's society, these amenities were far from the norm in those days, and not commonly enjoyed by people even in their own homes. 'Whatever you do, do it well' was the Leitner motto in life. In 1912, when the extensions were nearly completed, the cousins Gottlieb and Moishe Dovid Leitner requested permission from the Town Council to install an external door near the ground floor window, with the purpose of opening a shop next to the Hotel National, a document that both Gottlieb and Moishe Dovid signed, as illustrated below.

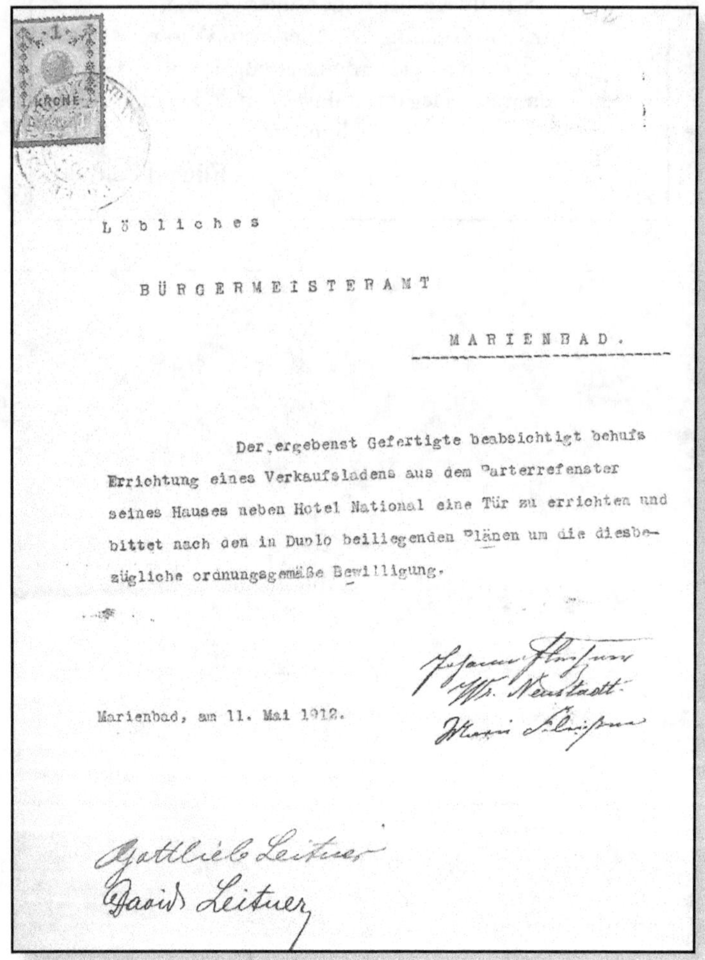

1 KRONE

Löbliches

BÜRGERMEISTERAMT

MARIENBAD.

Der ergebenst Gefertigte beabsichtigt behufs Errichtung eines Verkaufsladens aus dem Parterrefenster seines Hauses neben Hotel National eine Tür zu errichten und bittet nach den in Duplo beiliegenden Plänen um die diesbezügliche ordnungsgemäße Bewilligung.

Marienbad, am 11. Mai 1912.

Gottlieb Leitner
David Leitner

Planning application for the exterior door

A coloured brochure postcard of the Goldenes Schlüssel and Gerer Rebbe as an esteemed guest

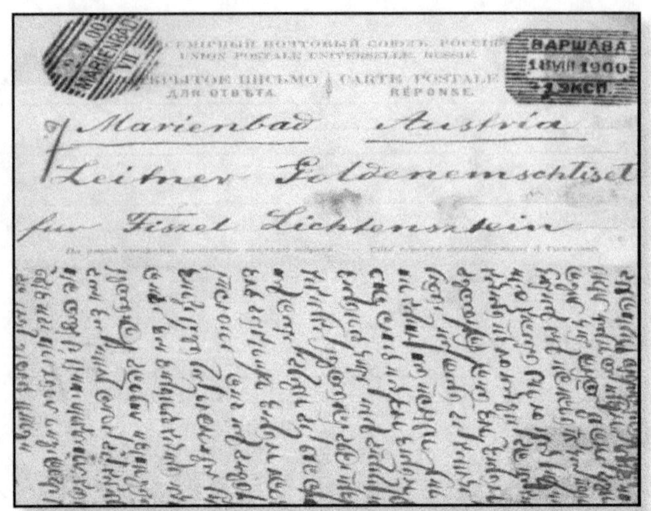

A postcard sent from Budapest on August 18, 1900 arrived in Marienbad (still part of Austria) on September 3, 1900, sent to Leitner at Goldener Schlussel for the attention of Mr. Fishel Lichtenstein, one of their guests

The hotels comprised of several buildings and were registered under different names for tax purposes. Moishe Dovid's hotel remained known by their two separate names: Hotel National and Leitner Haus, whereas Gottlieb Leitner's hotel was known as Goldenes Schloss (golden castle) and Goldener Schlussel (golden key), and Drei Mohren, but were combined in 1928, after the death of Gottlieb Leitner, when they all became know as "Goldenes Schloss".

Both hotels offered a free porter service to bring guests to and from the local train station, using their own cars.

Goldenes Schloss Hotel Taxi service. Reb C.T. Levin, Bendiner Rov (brother-in-law of Imrei Emes) entering taxi

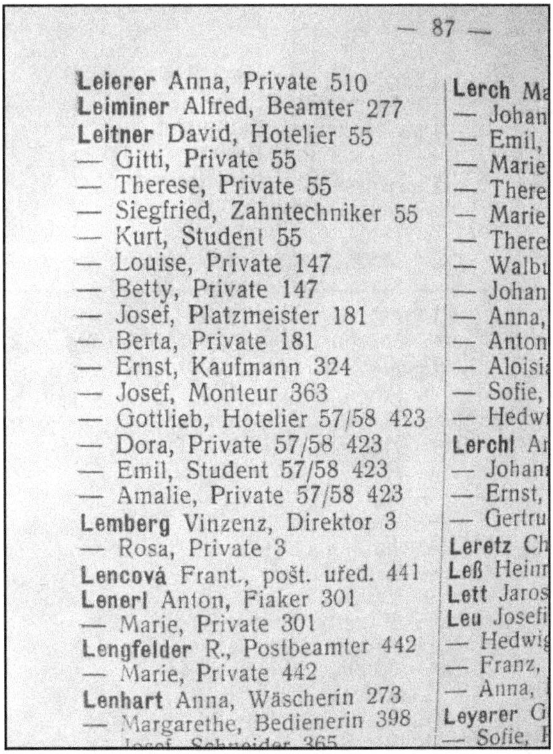
— 87 —

Leierer Anna, Private 510
Leiminer Alfred, Beamter 277
Leitner David, Hotelier 55
— Gitti, Private 55
— Therese, Private 55
— Siegfried, Zahntechniker 55
— Kurt, Student 55
— Louise, Private 147
— Betty, Private 147
— Josef, Platzmeister 181
— Berta, Private 181
— Ernst, Kaufmann 324
— Josef, Monteur 363
— Gottlieb, Hotelier 57/58 423
— Dora, Private 57/58 423
— Emil, Student 57/58 423
— Amalie, Private 57/58 423
Lemberg Vinzenz, Direktor 3
— Rosa, Private 3
Lencová Frant., pošt. uřed. 441
Lenerl Anton, Fiaker 301
— Marie, Private 301
Lengfelder R., Postbeamter 442
— Marie, Private 442
Lenhart Anna, Wäscherin 273
— Margarethe, Bedienerin 398

Lerch Ma
— Johan
— Emil,
— Marie
— There
— Marie
— There
— Walbu
— Johan
— Anna,
— Anton
— Aloisi
— Sofie,
— Hedw
Lerchl An
— Johan
— Ernst,
— Gertru
Leretz Ch
Leß Hein
Lett Jaros
Leu Josefi
— Hedwi
— Franz,
— Anna,
Leyarer G
— Sofie,

Marienbad Electoral List circa 1925 on the Leitner page

The Jewish population of Marienbad continued to expand and by late 1938, over 72 properties belonging to Jewish people were confiscated by the Gestapo in Marienbad alone! These included other hotels owned by Jews, including;- Alexandria, Atlantic, Berliner Hof, Continental, Corfu, Elbschloss, Florida , Goldener Adler, Goldener Anker, Helvetia, Hungaria, Klinger, Leipzig, New York, Nordstern, Rheingold, Riviera, Savoy and Versailles.

Konsk.-Nr.	Hausschild	Straße, Gasse, Platz	Grundb.-Einl.-Zl.	Eigentümer
52	Englischer Hof	Hauptstraße	52	Ernst u. Hans Baruch
53	Neubad	Kirchenstraße	529	Staatseigentum
54	Weißes Rößl	Poststraße	54	Präm.-Stift Tepl
55	Hotel National	Poststraße	55	David u. Getti Leitner
56	Wiener Neustadt	Poststraße	56	Joh. u. Marie Fleißner
57	Drei Mohren	Poststraße	58	Gottl. u. Dora Leitner
58	Gold. Schlüssel	Poststraße	58	Gottl. u. Dora Leitner
59	Gold. Schild	Poststraße	59	Franz Beer
60	Florida	Poststraße	60	Hedwig Frank, Karl u. Christine Gluth
61	Marienb. Mühle	Hauptstraße	61	Norbert u. Ant. Wilfert
62	Villa Kraus	Ferd.brunnstraße	62	MUDr. Eduard Kraus
63	Hotel Klinger	u. Kreuzbrunnstr.	35	Hotel-Klinger-Ges.
64	Haus Römer	Schillerplatz	64	Bernhard und Marie Luise Tratner
65	Nordstern	Schillerplatz	65	MUDr. Max Porges
66	Walhalla	Schillerplatz	66	Karl Löwenthal
67	Buen Retiro	Hauptstraße	67	Ing. M. Mečíř, Marie Gut, Miloš Mečíř u. Antonia Kvěch
68	Glocke	Hauptstraße	68	Karl Franz Josef Hammerschmid
69	Auge Gottes	Hauptstraße	69	Anna Rosner, Ing. Hans und Fritz Lion
70	Hotel Egerländer	Hauptstraße	70	Elise Hammerschmid
71	Villa Schönheim	Ferd.brunnstraße	71	Heinrich Grimme und Marie Lustig
72	Paradies	Jägerstraße	72	Alois u. Wilh. Weschta
73	Pyramide	Jägerstraße	73	Wilhelm Neuberth
74	Sächs. Hof	Jägerstraße	74	Anton u. Marg. Baier
75	Schlüsselburg	Jägerstraße	75	Frz. u. Marie Gleisinger
76	Hotel Wagner	Jägerstraße	76	Josef u. Leop. Wagner
77	Hotel Annaberg	Jägerstraße	77	Rudolf Habermann sen.
78	Frankfurt	Jägerstraße	78	Franz und Marie Habermann
79	Habermanns Haus	Jägerstraße	79	Rudolf Habermann jun.
80	Schloß Windsor	Waldbrunnstraße	80	MUDr. Rudolf und Emilie Reiniger
81	Eiche	Hauptstraße	602	Böhm. Eskomptebank u. Creditanstalt Prag

Konsk.-Nr.	Hausschild	Straße, Gasse, Platz	Grundb.-Einl.-Zl.	Eigentümer
179	Wiesbaden	u.Ferd.brunnstr.	53	Jachetta Brum
180	Synagoge	Hauptstraße	169	Israel. Kultusgemeinde
181	Dampfbrettsäge	Egerer Straße	214	Präm.-Stift Tepl
182	Ebenfurth	Ferdinandstraße	163	Franz und Anna Winterling
183	Hotel Imperial	Alleegasse	187	Franz Beer
184	Lohengrin	Prof.-Basch-Str.	203	Engelbert und Marie Futter
185	Villa Busch	Alleegasse	184	Manfred u. Anna Stöger
186	Neubau Müller	Hauptstraße	148	Wenzl u. Dr. Josef Müller
187	Albion	Prof.-Ott-Straße	199	Josef u. Mathilde Schmiedl
188	AtlanticNebengb.	Hauptstraße	46	Philipp Rosenthal
189	Evang. Pfarrhaus	Kasinoparkstr.	170	evang. Gemeinde A B
190	Requisitenhaus	Prof.-Ott-Straße	764	—
191	Aeskulap	Ferd.brunnstr.	211	Adam und Marie Zimmermann
192	Columbus	Alleegasse	205	Pensionsfond d. Fürst Lichtenstein'schen Angestellten in der čsl. Republik
193	Villa Waldeck	Kasinoparkstr.	452	Dr. Leo Wenzl und Martha Paczowsky
194	Neapel	Moorbadstraße	212	Adam u. Emilie Lößl
195	Villa König	Ferd.brunnstraße	323	Ignaz König
196	Va. Ast, Hofgeb.	Poststraße	165	Aloisie Helmer
197	Villa Kraus, Nebengeb.	Ferd.brunnstraße	62	MUDr. Eduard Kraus
198	Bristol	Alleegasse	219	Luise Skalnik
199	Leitners Haus	Poststraße	162	David u. Getti Leitner
200	Midgard	Karlsbader Str.	336	Julie Wollak
201	Villa Wahnfried	Karlsbader Str.	382	Anna Kraus
202	Villa Lappert	Egerer Straße	399	Franziska, Paul Ernst Lappert
203	Villa Therese	Karlsbader Str.	231	Sofie, Anna, Ernst Wurdinger, Mizzi Klotz, Theresia Ziegenspeck
204	Waldmühle	Waldquellzeile	241	Josef Flauger

Local address book showing Hotel National at No.55 Gold. Schlussel at No. 58 and Leitner Haus at 199

THE HOTEL AND ITS GUESTS

World War I (1914–1918) had an enormous impact on the European Jewish community. More than 1.5 million Jews served in the armed forces, completely out of proportion to the numbers in the general population, whilst hundreds of thousands of Jews were uprooted and became refugees. For example, Bobov which was part of Galicia and part of the Austro-Hungarian Empire, was taken over and re-taken six times between the Austrian and Russian armies, as a result of which over 250,000 Galician Jews fled to Vienna and Czechoslovakia.

General view of both hotels on the block with Goldener Schloss on the left and Leitner Haus to the right.

Hence at the onset of WW1, the Bobover Rebbe, Rabbi Benzion Halberstam הי"ד, together with his family, travelled over 1500 kilometers and came to take refuge in Marienbad. Seeing the distinguished looking guest and his accompanying entourage, the porter instantly invited him inside. The Rebbe declined, asking to see the proprietor. Even when Moishe Dovid ushered him in, the guest refused to step over the threshold saying, 'You don't understand, I have no means to pay you at the moment.'

Reb Benzion [Bobov] taking a walk with his sons Moishe Aaron and Yechezkel Dovid.

The Halberstam family ended up staying for an extended period of time, and it was during this time that the Rebbe composed many of the legendary Bobover 'Nigunim' such as 'ק"ל אדון - לכה דודי לא תבשי - י"ה' רבון עלם etc. Reb Benzion, during his lifetime, inspired many thousands of Yidden to return to Yiddishkeit through his exceptionally powerful songs that he had composed. Opa would often sing these Bobover Nigunim at the Shabbos table, after which he would lean back in his chair and nostalgically travel back in his mind to Marienbad, and relate his memories of the Bobover Rebbe, as he composed these very Nigunim while seated in the dining room of Hotel National.

During this time, Opa found a companion in the Rebbe's charming son, Shloime, who succeeded his father after WW2. Opa played and spent much time together with Reb Shloime, who were both of a similar age, and maintained a very close friendship throughout their lives.

The Kedushas Tzion of Bobov with some Chassidim

Rabbi Benzion Halberstam [Bobov] with his son

The Bobover Rebbe – Kedushas Zion with R` Naftoli Zvi

The Kedushas Tzion of Bobov with R` Shlomo Rubin and some Chassidim.

A picture with over 50 of the famous Rabbonim who frequented the hotel was prominently displayed in the hotel foyer. The rectangular box at the top pictures Herman Leitner (צבי), the original founder, and the bottom rectangular box is that of his son and successor, Moishe Dovid Leitner. The large oval picture in the centre is Rav Yissochor Dov of Belz. The reason why he features so prominently in the picture will become apparent as the history of the hotel unfolds. The smaller oval picture, directly above Rabbi Yissochor Dov, is that of his son and successor, Reb Aaron of Belz.

In order to capture some of the flavour of the broad spectrum of the famous Rabbonim that frequented Marienbad, I have allocated a separate chapter entitled 'The Picture Gallery' which portrays some of them. The reader will gain an appreciation of the exalted atmosphere and holiness that prevailed during their visits, and can let his mind wander and imagine what it might have been like. The attraction of Marienbad reached its climax in the year 1936 when the town hosted the Kenessio Mechino, and even more so in 1937, when thousands of Orthodox Yidden visited Marienbad for the 3rd Kenessio Gedoloh of Agudas Yisroel. [A smaller Kenessio was held in Marienbad in 1947, to discuss what approach should be taken to the Peel Report and the establishment of a Jewish State.]

Photos and index of some of the hotel's visitors as displayed in the hotel foyer. (The spelling of the names are reprinted here as they appeared originally)

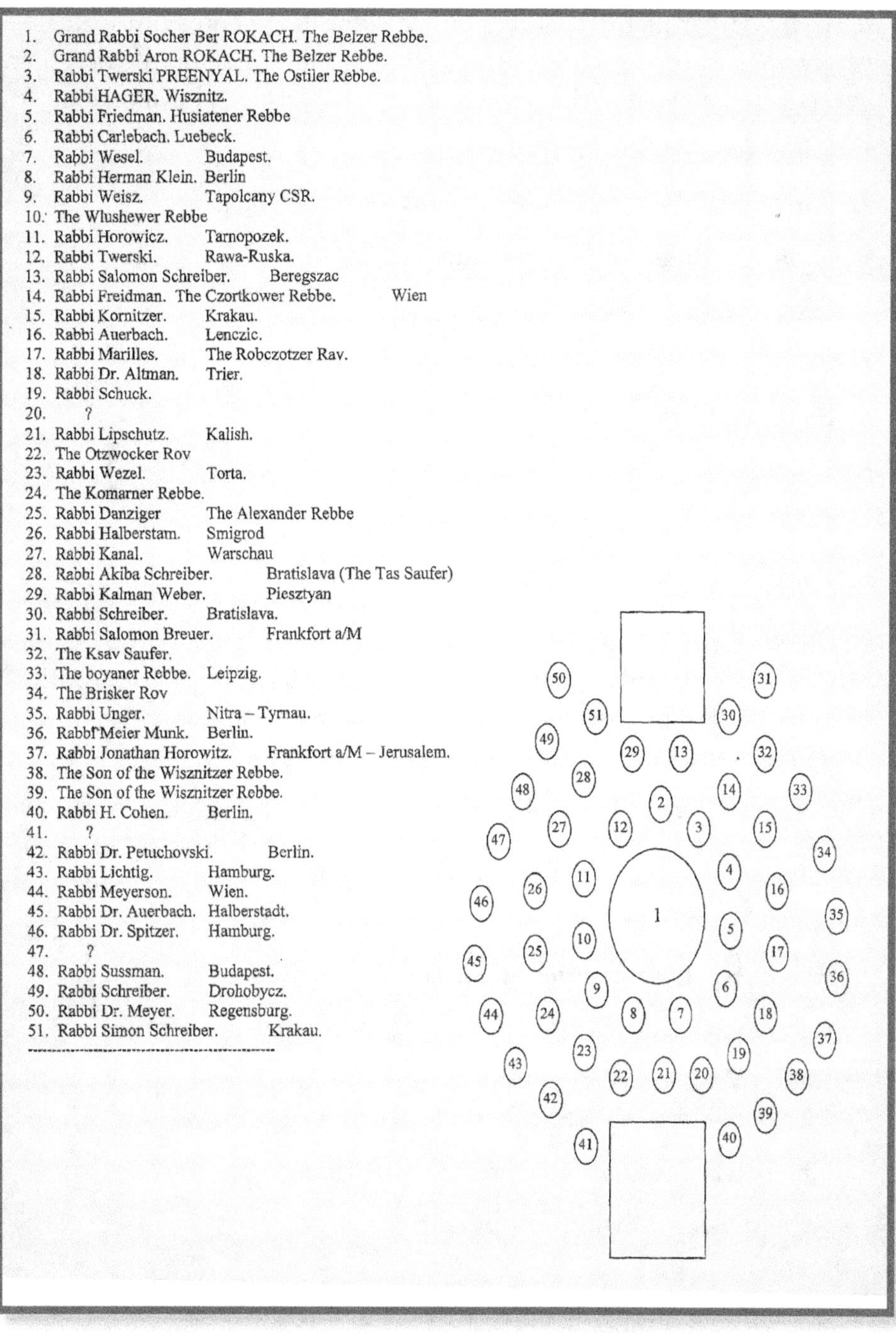

1. Grand Rabbi Socher Ber ROKACH. The Belzer Rebbe.
2. Grand Rabbi Aron ROKACH. The Belzer Rebbe.
3. Rabbi Twerski PREENYAL. The Ostiler Rebbe.
4. Rabbi HAGER. Wisznitz.
5. Rabbi Friedman. Husiatener Rebbe
6. Rabbi Carlebach. Luebeck.
7. Rabbi Wesel. Budapest.
8. Rabbi Herman Klein. Berlin
9. Rabbi Weisz. Tapolcany CSR.
10. The Wlushewer Rebbe
11. Rabbi Horowicz. Tarnopozek.
12. Rabbi Twerski. Rawa-Ruska.
13. Rabbi Salomon Schreiber. Beregszac
14. Rabbi Freidman. The Czortkower Rebbe. Wien
15. Rabbi Kornitzer. Krakau.
16. Rabbi Auerbach. Lenczic.
17. Rabbi Marilles. The Robczotzer Rav.
18. Rabbi Dr. Altman. Trier.
19. Rabbi Schuck.
20. ?
21. Rabbi Lipschutz. Kalish.
22. The Otzwocker Rov
23. Rabbi Wezel. Torta.
24. The Komarner Rebbe.
25. Rabbi Danziger The Alexander Rebbe
26. Rabbi Halberstam. Smigrod
27. Rabbi Kanal. Warschau
28. Rabbi Akiba Schreiber. Bratislava (The Tas Saufer)
29. Rabbi Kalman Weber. Piesztyan
30. Rabbi Schreiber. Bratislava.
31. Rabbi Salomon Breuer. Frankfort a/M
32. The Ksav Saufer.
33. The boyaner Rebbe. Leipzig.
34. The Brisker Rov
35. Rabbi Unger. Nitra – Tyrnau.
36. Rabbi Meier Munk. Berlin.
37. Rabbi Jonathan Horowitz. Frankfort a/M – Jerusalem.
38. The Son of the Wisznitzer Rebbe.
39. The Son of the Wisznitzer Rebbe.
40. Rabbi H. Cohen. Berlin.
41. ?
42. Rabbi Dr. Petuchovski. Berlin.
43. Rabbi Lichtig. Hamburg.
44. Rabbi Meyerson. Wien.
45. Rabbi Dr. Auerbach. Halberstadt.
46. Rabbi Dr. Spitzer. Hamburg.
47. ?
48. Rabbi Sussman. Budapest.
49. Rabbi Schreiber. Drohobycz.
50. Rabbi Dr. Meyer. Regensburg.
51. Rabbi Simon Schreiber. Krakau.

The numbers on the above index correspond to these Rabbonim in Chapter 4 - 'Picture Gallery' for easier identification

A second larger picture that contained some 120 photos unfortunately never survived the Holocaust. Records found of some of the other guests who had visited the hotel and are not pictured above include:

- Baron Freudiger from Budapest.
- Director of the Feuchtwanger Bank from Munich.
- Judge Dr. Breuer from Frankfurt-am-Main.
- Chief Rabbi Dr. Hertz from England.
- Chief Rabbi Lewin from Warsaw.
- Rabbi Halberstam from Bobov.
- Chief Rabbi (Marcus) Melchior from Copenhagen (1897-1969)
- Rabbi Dovid Feldman from Leipzig.
- Rabbi Dr. Avigdor Schonfeld from London.

Marienbad became the No. 1 holiday resort, especially for the Orthodox people. Opa often remarked humorously that any person wanting to enter the Rabbinate could only qualify after having passed the relevant exams and taken a week's holiday in Marienbad!

The August 1927 edition of the Orthodox magazine, 'The Israelit' issue 31, featured an article about Marienbad which lists some of the prominent guests that stayed at Hotel Goldenes Schloss during that summer's season:

- Rabbi Avrohom Mordechai Alter – Gerrer Rebbe
- Rabbi Meir Dov Plotzki (Sokolov) [author of Kli Chemdo]
- Rabbi Wolkin from Pinsk [Rabbi Wolkin would speak at the Goldenes Schloss every Shabbos, attracting a large crowd]
- Chief Rabbi Issaiah Silberstein from Waitzen
- Rabbi I. Meir Lewin from Bendin

And at the same time, Hotel National had the following prominent guests:

- The Belzer Rebbe

- The Tzikover Rebbe
- Rabbi Halberstam from Zemigrod (26)
- Rabbi Dr. Auerbach from Halberstadt
- Rabbi Dr. Spitzer from Hamburg
- Chief Rabbi Jacob Meir [Palestine]
- Rabbi Horowitz fromYerushalayim
- Shlomo and Zalman Levontin [Bankers]

Individual pictures of these celebrities were available in the form of postcards and could be purchased in the hotel lobby.

L. to R. unknown, Lev Simcha, Imrei Emes, Gerrer Rebbe arriving at the station in Marienbad, with Opa (1.1.1.3) to his right and Moishe Dovid Leitner (1.1.1) behind to his left

Dr. Salomonski Kurt, Augenarzt mit Familie	Tel Aviv	St. Antonius	3
Alter Abram Mordka, Oberrabbiner mit Begleitung	Polen	Goldenes Schloß	2
Sonnenfeld Agathe, Näherin	Mannheim	Beamtenkurhaus	1

Copy of town register showing Gerrer Rebbe accommodated at the Goldenes Schloss

L to R: Opa behind Gottlieb Leitner (O) greeting the Imrei Emes (X) at Marienbad station

The Gerrer Rebbe did not stay in the Leitner Hotel National but next door at the Goldenes Schloss, but out of respect both Opa and his father, Moishe Dovid, went to the station to greet him on his arrival in Marienbad – a sincere display of כבוד התורה

The extension to the Leitner Hotel was completed in 1912, and this was accomplished with the help of a large mortgage obtained from the Bank in Prague. Shortly afterwards World War I broke out and lasted 4 years. This was having an adverse effect on the number of visitors on vacation in Marienbad and through no fault of their own, their mortgage repayments soon fell into arrears. Despite many reminders there was simply no money to repay the bank at the moment, and it was in the summer of the early 1920s that the final notice arrived from the Bank on a Shabbos morning, which stated that they had decided to put the Hotel up for Sale by auction!

It must be pointed out that at this crucial time, Herman and Moishe Dovid and their families were all, as they call it, 'Yekkes', and to them the Chassidic Rebbes were very welcome guests who came with their Gabboim and many Chassidim, who provided commercially beneficial and interesting clientele. In fact when the Belzer Rebbe came with his entourage, they could take up to 18 rooms, nearly 30% of the hotel's capacity. Having grown up in the Derech of the Yekkes they were quite clueless of the Chassidic way of life.

The Belzer Rov, Reb Yissochor Dov, and his great son, Rabbi Aaron, travelled nearly 1000 kilometers annually to Marienbad and were honoured guests at Hotel National. They were treated with utmost respect and even the non-Jews had such respect for the Belzer Rebbes, that the station master himself would conduct them over the railway lines rather than trouble them to go downstairs and through the subway in order to cross to the other side.

One amusing episode that occurred at the hotel demonstrates how ignorant the proprietors were of the Chassidic conduct and way of life. Moishe Dovid noticed that the Rebbe was accustomed to eat his fish and chicken without using his cutlery, and divided the 'shirayim' with his hands. Moishe Dovid was puzzled about this and thought that perhaps the Rebbe had some doubts whether the entire hotel cutlery was ever 'toiveled' correctly [immersed in the Mikve] when initially purchased. So he went and bought a complete canteen of cutlery, toiveled it himself, and presented it to the Rebbe. He said to him, 'My dear Rebbe, I purchased this canteen especially for your exclusive use, and I even toiveled it myself **yesterday** morning'. To this the Rebbe simply replied 'I toiveled my fingers **this morning**,' and things continued as before.

On that fateful Moitzei Shabbos when the 'final notice' arrived from the Bank in Prague, the Gabbe came downstairs to fetch some food for Melava Malka to take up to Reb Yissochor Dov, as was customary every week, when he noticed that Moishe Dovid was unusually upset, and enquired as to what was bothering him. After some coaxing Moishe Dovid finally told the Gabbe what the problem was, and he instantly answered, 'Nu, let's go up to the Rebbe'. Moishe Dovid was so unaccustomed to the chassidic lifestyle that he innocently asked the Gabbe, 'Why should I go up, has the Rebbe got money to lend me?' The Gabbe responded and explained that the Rebbe would give him a warm Brocho that everything should be resolved satisfactorily.

With nothing to lose they went upstairs and the Gabbe wrote the appropriate message in a 'kvittel'. The Rebbe asked Moishe Dovid some further details, to which he replied 'the situation is very bad'. The Rebbe however corrected him, and said 'it is never bad – it could perhaps be better, but it is never bad.' The Rebbe then read the 'kvittel' and blessed Moishe Dovid 'Ihr vert bleiben Baal Haboss' (you will remain the owners). With much excitement the Gabbe served some 'lekach and bromfen' and they drank a 'lechaim', and sincere Mazel Tov wishes were exchanged! A bewildered Moishe Dovid thanked the Rebbe profusely for his warm Brocho and left the room, unsure of what to think, as this was his first close encounter of a personal nature with a Chassidic Rebbe.

The next day, on Sunday evening, one of the affluent businessmen who stayed at the hotel, approached Moishe Dovid with a request. "I need a big favour and hope that you would be able to help." He explained that he lived in Prague but had an urgent business meeting in another city, and it was imperative that he catch the connecting train from Prague to this other town. He would, however, ideally have liked to first go home to pick up any post that had arrived in the meantime, before travelling on, but was doubtful whether he had enough time between the two train journeys to do so. He would therefore greatly appreciate if Moishe Dovid could 'spare' one of his sons to accompany him to Prague, who would then take a taxi to his home, pick up the post, and return immediately to the station. "If I'm still there, he can give me the post, and if I have already departed, he can forward it onto me."

Reb Yissochor Dov of Belz

Moishe Dovid was always willing to help out and do someone a favour, so he asked Opa to accompany this gentleman. They left early on Monday morning for Prague, and Opa accomplished his mission. He then asked the station master for the departure time of the next train to Marienbad, but was told that this was not until several hours later that afternoon.

Wanting to make good use of these spare hours in Prague, Opa decided to make an unannounced visit to the bank manager who had mortgaged the hotel. He explained to him what had brought him to Prague, and excused himself for coming without a prior appointment. He then tried very hard to convince the manager that the Leitners were honest people, and could not be blamed for the downturn in business which had been affected by the recent war. Initially the manager refused to listen and informed Opa that it was too late, as the auctioneer was at this moment already in Marienbad in order to arrange the auction. Opa tried to explain that the world economic situation had been adversely affected by the war, and it was therefore very unlikely that the bank would find a suitable buyer, nor obtain sufficient funds from an auction to cover the loan, as the sale of the hotel was unlikely to provide enough capital to cover the mortgage. The bank manager was sorry but explained that he had little choice, as he too had to follow Bank guidelines and protocol.

However, at the last moment the bank manager had second thoughts and told Opa that the auctioneer was staying at the Excelsior hotel in Marienbad, (which was across the road to the Leitner Hotel National) and requested, "Please ask him to phone me when you get back to Marienbad". Upon his return to Marienbad, Opa promptly went to visit the auctioneer, and to cut a long story short, the auction was indefinitely postponed, and in the meantime the mortgage was repaid, as business began to pick up and normalise again!

It appears that they also took on some private loans to help them in the meantime, all of which were repaid. The Leitners remained owners of the hotel, and occupied it until they were forced to leave with the Nazi annexation of Sudetenland in September 1938. It is therefore no wonder that Reb Yissochor Dov of Belz, whose Brocho was instrumental in effecting such remarkable results, features in such a prominent position on the hotel photo!

Opa had a small personal diary where he recorded all family birthdays and anniversaries. In his 1955 diary, nearly thirty years after Rav Yissochor Dov was niftar, he still had his Yahrzeit marked therein on כ"ב חשון , and also that of Reb Yissochor Dov's father [Reb Yehoshua] on כ"ג שבט. This indicates how Opa always remained attached to the Belzer Rebbes, although he was a 'Yekke at heart'.

This episode proved to be a great turning point in Moishe Dovid's appreciation of Chassidus, his connection with the Rebbes of Belz, an impact that continued to develop over the coming years.

The Gemoroh (ברכות ז) teaches us that גדולה שמושה של תורה יותר מלמודה – being occupied in attending to Torah Giants is even greater than learning the Torah itself. Opa was fortunate that for the first thirty two years of his life, he observed, attended, accompanied, cared for, absorbed and witnessed the vibrant Yiddishkeit from the greatest Torah giants of the generation on a very personal level. This taught him a unique way of how to conduct and live a Torah life which remained ingrained within him for the rest of his life, and a legacy that he often spoke about with pride, both in public and in private. With much passion and love he demonstrated to his children and acquaintances this wonderful path of a life of authentic Torah that he personally witnessed, being especially attached to Reb Aaron of Belz, and made it his business that whenever the Rebbe was on his way to Marienbad, Opa would travel to a nearby station and personally accompany the Rebbe to their hotel. Similarly on his departure, Opa would travel and accompany the Rebbe a short distance to the next station.

Opa became so attached to Belz that he even spent one Pesach in Belz, where he observed the Rebbe's Seder and revelled in being in his proximity and absorb his holiness. Being a 'Yekke', who was accustomed to eating 'gebrockts', he was unaware that in Belz they are careful not to do so. But it didn't take long for him to learn about this. It so happened that when he was once in the process of putting a piece of fish onto his Matzoh, he was being observed by one of the Chassidim, and before he had a chance of taking a bite, this Chossid snatched it from him and discarded it as 'chometz'!

The uniqueness of life in Marienbad was expressed eloquently by Rav Schneebalg, the Rav of Machzikei Hadass, himself a Vizhnitzer Chossid, at the Hesped he gave for Opa in 1988. He said, 'Chassidim often have to make long and arduous journeys to travel to their respective Rebbes, and frequently wait in long queues to merit an appointment and receive a Brocho from them, sometimes only seeing their Rebbe for a few minutes. The Leitner family in Marienbad was so unique that the Rebbes would travel to them, and the Leitners merited seeing these great Rebbes in their own home and over an extended period of time.'

PERSONAL EPISODES

Since there was no Jewish schooling available in Marienbad, Moishe Dovid employed a private Rebbe to learn with his children after the formal school-day and during school holidays, and more so during the winter months, when the hotel was closed for business. However, the large influx of so many great Rabbonim during the summer months provided an excellent atmosphere for them to grow in Yiddishkeit. The unique variety of Rabbonim from different sectors and countries provided a special blend and experience that was impossible to find elsewhere. Not only could the Leitner family observe these great Jewish leaders, but similarly, in their relaxed holiday atmosphere, these great Rabbonim would impart them and other holiday makers with much Yiddishkeit and warmth.

In 1864 Rabbi Shloime Ganzfried from Hungary first published his קצור שלחן ערוך 'Kitzur Shulchan Oruch' which became an instant success. For the first time the ordinary laymen had, in one single volume, all the essential laws that he needed to know on a day to day basis, which would enable them to conduct a true Torah life. This was specifically written in simple and easily understood language to make it suitable for all. It became extremely popular worldwide, and during the author's lifetime alone it was reprinted a total of 14 times, as there was hardly a Jewish home that did not possess a copy. During the dispersion of families, a direct result of the two World Wars, it was more likely that people would take a single volume Kitzur with them rather than a complete multi volumed Shulchan Oruch. Additionally, not many could afford a complete Shulchan Oruch and not all could study it by themselves.

The Kitzur proved invaluable to Opa and Oma in Chile too, when there wasn't always someone that they could ask, serving as a quick reference on all relevant matters of Halocho.

Germany in the early 20th century had nearly 800 smaller communities that were scattered throughout the country, each with their own

Minyan, but were too small to employ an acting Rov to lead them, so whenever a question in Halocho arose, the members would simply discuss it amongst themselves and do whatever the majority thought was correct, or what they had remembered from previous generations, but there was no way that enabled them to verify the correct Halocho.

Yom Tov - Yonas Sanger from Frankfurt-am-Main was conscripted into the German army in 1914 as a German soldier. Before he went into active service he vowed that if he survived the war, he would arrange to have the Kitzur translated into German. He ב"ה survived and organised the translation of the Kitzur Shulchan as promised. This new German translation was an instant success too, and all these small communities now had 'an authority' to refer to whenever the need arose. Initially it was printed in one volume and distributed by the Hoffman Verlag of Frankfurt, and later re-printed by Goldschmidt of Basel, who divided it into two volumes.

In the 1920's Rabbi Dovid Feldman from Leipzig published the 'Feldman's Kitzur', which contained the same Halochos as the original Kitzur, but being a very practical person, he appended the sources to all the laws contained in the original Kitzur Shulchan Oruch. He also wanted to make use of the improved printing technology now available, and incorporated many illustrations at the back of his volume, an additional feature to enable clear understanding of some important laws. One example is the illustration of the correct position for donning Tefillin on the head and on the arm. It is often said that a good picture is worth a thousand words, and these pictures certainly had that effect. He also included many charts on a large variety of useful topics, which also proved extremely popular.

Owing to the success of the Feldman's Kitzur and the use of illustrations to explain certain Halochos, Rabbi Feldman compiled a second sefer named שמושה של תורה – 'Shimusho Shel Torah'. In this volume he makes extensive use of photographs to explain, for example, the machinery required for baking matzos, the quality of wheat that is most suited for baking Matzos, the correct way to check the internal organs of an animal after 'Shechita' etc. He writes in his introduction that all the graphic details on these photographs were discussed with many different Rabbonim whom he met when he frequented the spas at Marienbad and Carlsbad. It is more than likely that Opa had seen

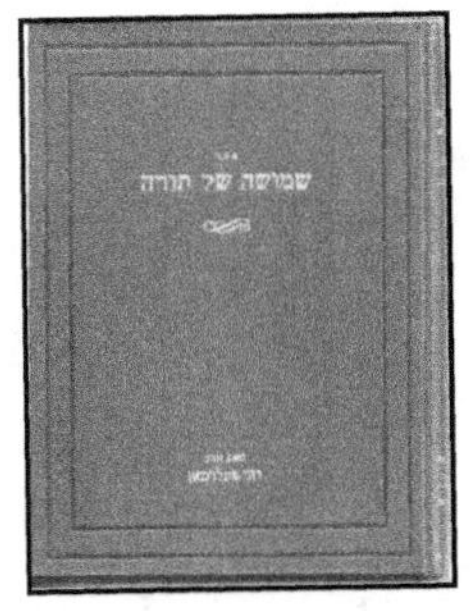

these pictures and was thus able to make use of this knowledge when he later came to Chile. Rabbi Feldman wrote that, unfortunately, some of the original manuscripts and pictures that he possesed in Marienbad were lost en route to Manchester, where he later became the Rov of the Machzikei Hadass Community. Consequently, the שמושה של תורה as we know it today (printed in London in 1951) contains fewer pages and illustrations than the original manuscripts that were available in Marienbad. This is but one example of the great benefit that the Leitner family derived from the visiting Rabbonim that frequented the town and hotel.

The Rebbes also gained from, and enjoyed each others' company during their vacations in Marienbad. The following story I heard firsthand at a Sheva Brochos in Yerushalayim. A certain Mr. Moses from Bnei Brak told me that he had lost both his parents at a very young age, and the 'Beis Yisroel' (Gerrer Rebbe) took him into his household and treated him like a son. He provided him with everything that he required until he eventually got married and settled in Bnei Brak. One day, in the middle of the summer, he saw an announcement on the Shul's noticeboard, advertising an organised coach trip that would be leaving on כ"א אב to Har Hamenuchos, a large cemetery in Yerushalayim, to visit the ציון of Rabbi Aaron of Belz. Anyone interested should call the telephone number given, to reserve a seat on the coach. Mr. Moses took the opportunity to daven at the Kever, and then went to visit his "adoptive" father, the Beis Yisroel.

The Gerrer Rebbe wanted to know what had prompted him to come to Yerushalayim, to which he replied that there was an organised bus going to Har Hamenuchos for the Yahrzeit of the Belzer Rebbe. The Beis Yisroel exclaimed, 'He was a great Tzaddik!' This remark aroused Mr. Moses' curiosity and he asked, 'How does the Rebbe know?' The Beis Yisroel then told him the following:

"Before I got married, I went together with my parents to Marienbad and stayed at the Goldenes Schloss, whilst Reb Aaron of Belz stayed next door, at the Leitner Hotel National. One morning I got up at 3.30am in order to learn before Shacharis, [during holidays!] and when I opened my curtains I noticed that there was a light on in Reb Aaron's room. I was intrigued and went next door and, peeping through the keyhole, saw something fascinating: four wooden chairs were lined up next to each other and Reb Aaron lying on them, asleep, but fully dressed and the light on! Later on that morning I went to the Belzer Rebbe's Gabbe and admitted what I had done, and wondered what the explanation was. The Gabbe confirmed that this was nothing unusual, but rather the nightly habit of his Rebbe, who did not want to enjoy the luxury of sleeping on a comfortable mattress. Yes, he was a great Tzadik who derived minimal worldly benefits!"

Another interesting episode happened with Rabbi Yisroel Friedman, the Tchortkover Rebbe, who also stayed at Hotel National.

In 1932 a wealthy doctor from Hamburg (Germany) was a guest at the Leitner hotel together with his wife and teenage son, Heinz. On the third day of their stay, they were kindly asked to vacate their rooms and move to a higher floor, as the Grand-Rabbi, Rabbi Friedman, always stayed in those rooms during his annual holiday. Grudgingly the doctor acquiesced, and from his balcony observed the awesome reception that Rabbi Friedman received at the hands of the large crowds outside. The doctor was so intrigued that he requested a private audience with the Rebbe, which was granted. The Rebbe then invited the doctor's son, Heinz, to come to him, and asked him about his personal life and aspirations for his future.

Heinz mentioned that his father wanted him to train for engineering and settle in Hamburg. The Rebbe however advised him that a career in medicine would be more beneficial, as that way he would always be helping other people, and also advised that he should rather settle in Palestine. The Doctor, however, was extremely unhappy that the Rebbe had interfered in their private affairs.

It turned out that the only opening at the University was in fact in the field of medicine, and whilst studying there, Heinz became friendly with a group of Zionist boys who all made Aliyah to Palestine. Dr. Heinz Goldhaber is the only member of his family who survived the Holocaust, and became a leading doctor at Bar Ilan University.

The following story happened in Marienbad in 1935:

In the summer of 1935, shortly after Rebetzen Wasserman was niftar, Reb Elchonon's health deteriorated. His entire body was racked with pain, and a specialist in Warsaw recommended that he travel to Marienbad for spa treatment, where he spent a total of five weeks.

Whilst trying to recover in Marienbad, an urgent telegram arrived, stating that the baker and butcher in Baranovich had stopped supplying the Yeshivah with food because of the accumulated debts owed to them. Reb Elchonon's weakened physical condition however rendered travelling impossible in order to raise the required funds. In his distress he turned to the Gerrer Rebbe, Rabbi Avrohom Mordechai Alter, who had recently arrived in Marienbad with a large contingency of Chassidim. He made an appointment and went to the Goldenes Schloss hotel, where the Rebbe stayed. Reb Elchonon began:

"חז"ל have taught that when a person is in distress he should go to a תלמיד חכם for advice, hence I have come here." He showed the Gerrer Rebbe the telegram, and explained that the Yeshivah owed 5,000 zlotys. It was reasonable to assume that if the Yeshivah paid half that amount, the deliveries from the baker and butcher would resume. Reb Elchonon then added that it would be helpful if the Rebbe would summon 10 of his wealthy Chassidim presently in Marienbad, and ask each one to donate 250 zlotys. That same day the full amount of 2,500 zlotys was raised!

MARIENBAD.

MARIENBAD (BOHEMIA).

628 *METRES ALTITUDE.*

SUB-ALPINE CLIMATE. FOREST OF HIGH TREES. SHELTERED POSITION.

Kreuzbrunn, Ferdinandsbrunn, the strongest Glauber salt waters in Europe (five grammes in a litre). Indications: Diseases in connection with metabolic changes, diseases of the heart (fatty degeneration), of the liver, of the intestines, derangements of circulation, &c. **Rudolfsquelle,** prominently large contents in carbonate of lime and magnesia. Indications: Gout, uric acid diathesis, chronic catarrh of the basin of the kidneys, of the bladder, &c., nephritic stone, chronic catarrhs of the intestines, &c. **Ambrosiusbrunn,** strongest pure iron chalybeate water (with 0·177 grammes of bi-carbonate of iron per litre). Indications: Anemia, chlorosis, &c. **Waldquelle,** for all diseases of respiratory organs.

Natural Carbonic Acid Bath in various degrees. Mud Bath from Own Mud Deposits (75,000 per season). Hydropathic Establishment. Steam and Electrical Baths.

Balneological-Hygienic Institution. Zander Institute. Dr. Bulling's Inhalatorium. 30,000 Visitors, 90,000 Tourists. Best Golf Links on the Continent. *Prospectus given by the Burgermeisteramt.*

The Therapeutic properties of Marienbad Spa water as advertised in the medical journals.

About two years later, just before the Kenessio, Reb Elchonon met the Gerrer Rebbe again in a private session and discussed various communal matters. The Alexander Rebbe, Rabbi Yitzchok Menachem Mendel Danziger, who had previously been in disagreement with Aguda policies, had a change of heart and had arrived in Marienbad for the first time, to attend the Kenessio Gedoloh. Rabbi Chaim Eis from Zurich (Switzerland) suggested to the Gerrer Rebbe that, for the good of the cause, perhaps the Rebbe would, as a gesture of goodwill, go personally and invite the Alexander Rebbe to participate fully in all the sessions of the Kenessio. The Gerrer Rebbe agreed to go, but only after discussing the matter with Reb Elchonon.

Gerrer Rebbe leaving the Goldenes Schloss Hotel with his Chassidim

The Gerrer and Alexander Rebbes

In Marienbad contact was made not only between Chassidim and their respective Rebbes, Rebbes with Litvishe Roshei Yeshivah and Rebbes with laymen, as mentioned above, but these esteemed visitors also had an impact on the non-Jewish population.

In 1908 Queen Wilhelmina, the Dutch Queen, was on a private visit in Marienbad with only a few attendants. When she arrived at the train station, she noticed huge crowds who had obviously come to greet someone else. The Queen was curious to know who this personality might be, and was informed that the great Rebbe of Munkatch, Rabbi Tzvi Hirsch Spira, had come, and the large crowds had come to greet him at the station.

Not knowing about Rebbes or their lifestyle, the Queen was informed that a Rebbe is a most pious man, on a very high spiritual level, and possesses great wisdom. The thousands who had come to greet him were hoping to receive his blessing, as these were known to come true. The Queen was fascinated as she had never heard of such people before.

Queen Wilhelmina was childless, and the fact that she was the only surviving heir to the throne was never far from her mind. The queen asked her attendant to arrange a quiet meeting between herself and the great Rebbe, and was delighted when informed that the Rebbe would receive her the next evening.

And so it was. On the following evening, without publicity, Queen Wilhelmina with two of her attendants, and the Munkatcher Rebbe with two Bochurim, met at a designated meeting place in the nearby woods.

Sensing that the personage sitting opposite her was a man of great stature, Queen Wilhelmina was earnest with the Rebbe, telling him of her soul's torment at not being able to produce an heir. The Rebbe eventually told her she need not worry and that her monarchy would continue. The Rebbe used the words כעת חי'ה as part of his assurance, with the clear meaning that the queen would have a child within a year. Amazingly, the Rebbe added מלכותה לא חנתק עד כי יבא שילה. The following year Queen Wilhelmina bore her only child, a daughter, who later became Queen Juliana of Netherland in 1948.

Rabbi Yaakov Tzvi Katz had suffered tremendously in Bergen Belsen, and after liberation applied for a visa to enter Holland, but his application was refused. He applied a second time, and this too was refused, on the pretext that their immigration quotas were full. Rabbi Katz then decided to write directly to the Queen, in Yiddish, as follows (translated):"Surely your Highness recalls the very momentous meeting that took place in Marienbad together with the Grand Rabbi of Munkatch. I was one of the two boys who accompanied the Rabbi and acted as his interpreter, and who transmitted his blessings to you!" He then asked her to reciprocate the favour and arrange to obtain an entry visa for Holland.' Queen Wilhelmina made it her personal agenda to ensure that Rabbi Katz , together with another 80 Rabbonim, obtained their entry visas, and shortly after his arrival, Rabbi Katz was appointed as the Rov of the Nidchei Yisroel Shul.

EDUCATION AND TRAINING

The Orthodox Jewish residents of Marienbad were few, and during the winter months, when the hotels were closed, there were only 15 resident Orthodox families. Jewish schools were non existent, and all the Torah was taught at home by private Rebbes at the end of the school day. More often then not, there was only one Orthodox Jewish child in any class. In those days it was common practice that they had to attend the non-Jewish schools on Shabbos as well. The Jewish children however just sat and listened to the lessons, and on Sunday were busy copying out all the notes that the teacher had dictated on the previous day. After the compulsory school years it was the norm to learn a trade to further one's education. The Leitner children all followed this path, training and practicing in one or more areas of Hotel management, bookkeeping, business studies etc.

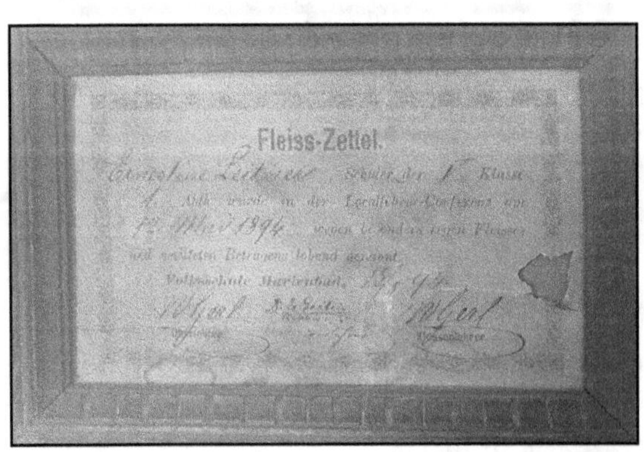
Fleiss-Zettel.

A certificate of Class Merit for Diligence and Best Behaviour received by Aunty Ernestine March 12, 1894

As the hotel in Marienbad was only open during the summer, Opa would find other employment during the winter, to learn and gain more experience. Moishe Dovid was advised by Opa's teachers that 'Opa possessed very special managerial and organisational skills' and would benefit greatly if he were to get experience in as many and varied employments as possible, to broaden his skills and develop his special talents. Although his brothers found local employment during the winter months, Opa travelled to different places to train. In the summer of 1922 he graduated from the Marienbad School of Commerce at the age of 16. Opa is seen in this graduating class photo, standing third from left in the middle row.

1. Abschlußlehrgang der Handelsschule Marienbad 1922 mit Lehrkörper
Untere Reihe von links nach rechts: H. H. Josef Stillip, Prof. Willibald Stelzig, Direktor Heinrich Sedlak, Prof. Josef Tropper, Rechtsanwalt Dr. Josef Steiner, Lehrer Franz Hohler. – Mittlere Reihe von links: Josef Frötschel, Franz Konhäuser, Kurt Leitner, Mendel Ernst, Eduard Thummerer, Hans Becker, Eduard Stopfer, Oskar Arbes. – Obere Reihe von links: Robert Roth, Richard Schwarz, Karl Narhaft, Doktor Norbert, Paul Kohl, Johann Sadlo, Josef Fischer.

A graduation Class Photo for Marienbad School of Commerce 1922

HISTORY OF EMPLOYMENT

From Nov 1922 until May 1923, at the age of 16, Opa worked as a cashier and bookkeeper at the Carlebach Bank in Leipzig, Germany, after which he received a glowing letter of recommendation, praising him for the excellent work that he had performed at the bank. The owner of the bank was also a frequent guest in the Hotel National in Marienbad.

The Bank also sent a separate letter to his father, Moishe Dovid Leitner, confirming their great satisfaction with Opa's employment.

Carlebach & Co. Leipzig

TELEGRAMM-ADRESSE:
CARLBANK „EVTL. BÖRSE"
FERNSPRECHER 4865, 4980.

REICHSBANK GIRO-CONTO
POSTSCHECKKONTO:
LEIPZIG Nº 68988.

MC'M

Leipzig, den 5. Mai 1924

MARKGRAFENSTR. 10.

Zeugnis.
=.=.=.=.=.=.=.=

Herr Kurt Leitner aus Marienbad war vom No= vember 1922 bis Mai 1923 in unserem Hause als Kontorist tätig und wurde hauptsächlich bei uns mit buchhalterischen Arbeiten sowie als Kassenassistent beschäftigt. Herr Leitner besass eine gute Auffassungsgabe und fand sich schnell in die Materie hinein, sodass es uns auch möglich war, ihn zeitweise in der Effekten= und Devisenabteilung zu beschäftigen.

Herr Leitner hat alle ihm übertragenen Arbeiten zu unserer vollsten Zufriedenheit ausgeführt, sodass wir ihm in jeder Beziehung, auch was Fleis, Pünktlichkeit und Ehrlichkeit betrifft, das beste Zeugnis ausstellen können.

Durch sein freundliches und zuvorkommendes Wesen war er ein allgemein beliebter Mitarb iter und können wir ihm nur aufs Wärmste empfehlen.

Wir wünschen ihm für sein ferneres Leben das Allerbeste.

Leipzig, den 5. Mai 1924

Certificate of excellence for his work at the bank which is translated below:

Translated:

Carlebach & Co Leipzig

Telegram Address:
Carlsbank EVTL BÖRSE
Fernsprecher 4865, 4980.
Leipzig
Markgrafenstr. 10

Reichsbank Giro Conto
Postscheckkonto
Leipzig No. 68988

May 5, 1924

Commendation

Mr. Kurt Leitner from Marienbad was employed in our business from November 1922 until May 1923 as a Clerk and worked mostly in the bookkeeping department and as assistant teller. Mr. Leitner was a quick learner who grasped new concepts with ease, which enabled us also to employ him in the Stocks and Shares and Currency department.

Mr Leitner completed all his assignments to our greatest satisfaction, and we can attest to his diligence, punctuality and honesty in every aspect.

We can highly recommend him, having gained the admiration of his co-workers through his friendly and pleasant manner.

We wish him all the best for his future.

Leipzig

May 5, 1924

The following winter, from beginning of November 1923 until end of May 1926 Opa was the Manager of Hotel Bell'aria in Meran, situated on the Swiss-Italian border. This was owned by Yosef Bermann, who also owned Hotel Edelweiss in St. Moritz, Switzerland. Opa was still very young to manage a large hotel, but having received excellent results and training at the 'Hotel Training College in Marienbad', he was very suited for this job.

Family Bermann were also frequent visitors in Hotel National in Marienbad.

Hotel Bell'aria, Merano

Bermann's
Hotels
*
4. Nov. 26.

Hotel Edelweiss, St. Moritz-Bad

From 1926 until August 1938, Opa directed Hotel National in Marienbad together with his father.

However, for a period of six weeks in 1934, before the season began in Marienbad, Opa served as manager of the Ritz Hotel in Tel Aviv. He originally intended to stay for three months but only stayed for six weeks, the minimum possible under his contract of employment, as he was not happy about the state of Chilul Shabbos in Tel Aviv, and it may well have been the main reason why he never wanted to emigrate to Eretz Yisroel from Chile, but chose to come to England instead. Despite his dissatisfaction with his surroundings in Tel Aviv, his honesty and efficiency in performing his job conscientiously was unaffected, a fact which itself is truly remarkable.

Date 25. Mai 1934 יום

PHONE 498 טלפון

Z e u g n i s

Herr Kurt Leidner war vom 9. April 1934 bis 18. Mai 1934 als Maitre D'Hotel bei uns taetig. Herr Leidner hat sich in jeder Beziehung unsere Zufriedenheit durch seinen Fleiss und seine Energie erworben. Sein Austritt erflogt auf eigenen Wunsch, da er in sein elterliches Geschaeft fuer die kommende Saison zurueckkehrt. Wir sind gerne breit, Herrn Leidner, falls er wieder nach Palaestina zurueckkehrt, in seine alte Stellung zurueckzuversetzen.
Fuer die Zukunft wuenschen wir alles Gute.

Recommendation received from Hotel Ritz, Tel Aviv 1934.

Translated:

Date: May 25, 1934

Recommendation

Mr. Kurt Leitner was Maitre D' Hotel by us from April 9, 1934 until May 18, 1934. Mr. Leitner has proven himself in all aspects with his diligence and hard work. His leaving us is by his own volition, as he expressed his wish to return to his family's business for the coming season. We will be only too happy to reinstate Mr. Leitner to his former position should he return to Palestine again.

We wish him all the best for his future.

'Whilst in Tel Aviv Opa met Meyer Dizengoff, the Lord Mayor who had been a guest at Hotel National in Marienbad, who kindly offered to arrange to change his tourist visa to a permanent one, and offered him a first class employment too. A few days later he met Mr. Meyer Berlin (later known as Bar Ilan), another of the Marienbad guest, who likewise offered to exchange the tourist visa. Opa visited the Kosel Hama'arovi, the plaza being much smaller than it is today. Whilst in Yerusholayim, he met Rabbi Moishe Blau, who again offered to arrange a permanent visa, but on all three occasions Opa refused their kind offer, and decided to return to Marienbad. En route, he spent Shabbos by his Aunty (Hedwick Kokish) in Bad Gastein from whom he learned that his mother had been diagnosed with a terminal illness. Immediately on Sunday morning, he travelled back to Marienbad were he still enjoyed his mothers company for the next few weeks, before she died.'

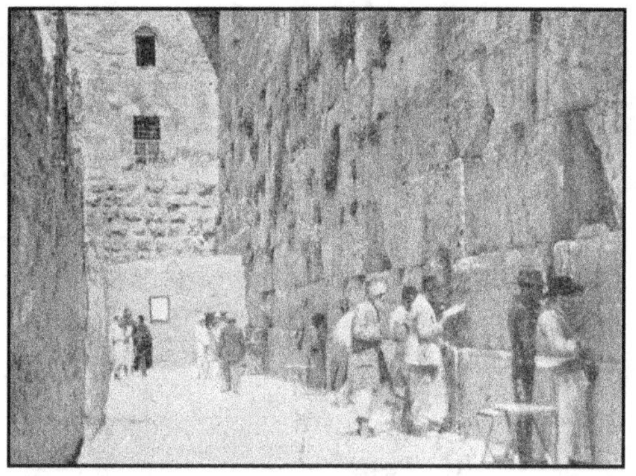

The Kosel Plaza under the Ottoman Empire

In 1936 he was chosen by Rabbi Yaakov Rosenheim to be the organising secretary of the Kenessio Gedoloh which was to be held in Marienbad the following year, during which time Opa was kept busy organising this major world event.

During the war he was employed as general secretary of the Federation of Czechoslovakian Jews and by the Agudas Yisroel World Organisation in London, whilst all other Hatzoloh work undertaken in London was performed purely on a voluntary basis.

In Chile, apart from managing and running the matzo factory during the winter, he had the catering franchise for all functions at the 'Bnei Israel' Jewish Community Centre in Santiago.

On his return to England, between the years 1955 and 1962 he was appointed as the first full time secretary and administrator of the Machzikei Hadass Community in Manchester, and then in 1962 until his retirement, he became self employed, running 'Leitner's Catering' and collecting rent for the Freshwater group of companies.

A BRIEF HISTORY OF JEWISH EUROPE 1912-1939

To try and understand the importance of the 3rd Kenessio Gedoloh that was held in Marienbad in 1937, one first has to view it against the background of the problems that were facing Orthodox Jewry in this turbulent period. During the second half of the 19th century the Haskalah and the Zionist Movements had enticed the masses and made great inroads amongst Jewry. To counteract and attempt to stem this tide of mass assimilation, the Gedolim, including the Chofetz Chaim, Reb Chaim Solveichik (Brisker Rov) and Reb Chaim Ozer Grodzensky, had formed the Agudas Yisroel Organisation in Kattowitz in 1912, just shortly before the outbreak of the First World War. The aim of this organisation was to provide help, structure, support and guidance to Orthodox Jewry, and help them remain loyal to their Torah heritage. It was soon after its formation that World War I erupted, and Europe suffered the turmoil and upheavals that caused havoc and destruction to many Jewish communities. In June 1917, towards the end of the war, and as part of their war efforts, the British sent troops under the leadership of General Allenby to conquer the Ottoman Empire, which had occupied Palestine for the past 400 years. After some initial setbacks, General Allenby dismounted from his horse and entered Yerushalayim on foot through the Jaffa gate, as a sign of respect for the Holy City. He then continued his campaign and conquered most of trans-Jordan and even reached Damascus by mid 1918.

Allenby in Yerushalayim 1917

In a most remarkable turn of events which makes no political sense at all, and can only be explained as a pure and visible act of Hashgocho Protis, the British were heavily involved in fighting a World War and General Allenby was sent to topple the Ottoman Empire, as a result of which he conquered Yerushalayim on December 11, 1917. What is extremely surprising is that on November 2, 1917, five weeks before Allenby had even entered Yerushalayim, the British Government issued a public statement:

The 'Balfour Declaration' in which they proclaimed their willingness to establish a national home for the Jewish people in Palestine. They intended to give Palestine away even before they had it themselves, and to give it to the Jewish people who were then the smallest minority of the inhabitants of Palestine. This is truly an indisputable open Divine Edict, and it is impossible to justify the Balfour Declaration as having been the result of a gesture of friendship towards any Zionist individual.

The text of the Balfour Declaration, issued by the Foreign Office, reads:

'His Majesty's Government view with favour the establishment in Palestine of a national home for the Jewish People and will use their best endeavours to facilitate the achievement of this object, it being clearly understood that nothing shall be done which may prejudice the civil and religious rights of existing non-Jewish communities in Palestine, nor the rights and political status enjoyed by Jews in any other country.'

The Balfour Declaration provided a great deal of hope to the Jewish People, who after two thousand years of exile and persecution anticipated receiving their own homeland. In the year following the Balfour Declaration, over 100,000 new Jewish immigrants arrived in Palestine, causing a backlash from the local Arab population. Their high hopes, however, soon faded once again, as the Arabs and Muslims who comprised of the majority of the inhabitants of Palestine during this period, staged numerous and continuous riots, protests, massacres, general strikes and rebelled forcefully against the British Mandate and their declared intentions. In a desperate effort to try and calm the Arab majority, the British Government enforced a very strict quota, thereby limiting the Jewish immigration into Palestine. Unfortunately the situation did not improve, and any British attempts to get all parties to discuss matters together failed completely, as the Arabs refused to sit at the same table with the Jewish representatives. Out of desperation, the British Government appointed Lord Peel in 1936 to 'investigate the cause of unrest in Mandatory Palestine,' and on July 7, 1937 it published its recommendations as to the 'partitioning' of Palestine, which included the division of the City of Jerusalem itself, but the Arabs were forcefully against the establishment of any independent Jewish State, irrespective of its size. Unable to make any progress, the British Government eventually asked the United Nations in July 1937 to enforce the matter. At the same time, the Jews were deeply upset in the reduction in land that would be apportioned to them, and to the proposed partitioning of Jerusalem, their sacred and holy city. The Balfour Declaration had injected fresh hope into the Jewish population, but at the same time was used by the other nations of the world as a pretext for not permitting extra Jewish immigration into their respective countries before and during the World War II, as they now had the tangible possibility of their 'own homeland'.

Historians have referred to the Balfour Declaration as:

'Only 67 words, on a single piece of paper, that lit a fire in the Holy Land, thereby igniting the most intractable conflict in modern times.'

It was during this turbulent period that Rabbi Elchonon Wasserman published his sefer 'Ikveso DeMeshicho' (Epoch of the Messiah) where he clearly and concisely explains the Torah view point to current events in the period before the arrival of Moshiach.

Although much work continued to be carried out in strengthening Torah institutions throughout Europe after the formation of Agudas Yisroel, from 1917 and onwards the subject of Eretz Yisroel was discussed at length amongst the Gedolim and the population in general, with a full report of this discussion being recorded on the Sunday session of the 3rd Kenessio.

With all these problems facing Jewry, it was imperative that Agudas Yisroel called another Kenessio of the Gedolei Torah that would enable them to discuss and formulate together what action to take.

The Leitner Hotels

CHAPTER 3
Second and Third Kenessio

KENESSIO MECHINO

AUGUST 4-6, 1936 - 16-18 AV 5696

A preparatory Kenessio was held in Marienbad in August 1936 to talk about and formulate the program that was to be discussed in greater detail at the main Kenessio, which was to take place the following year. Almost 100 delegates met at the Continental Hotel Conference room, a hotel owned by Mr. Buxbaum, the deputy Lord Mayor of Marienbad, and included representatives from America, Belgium, Czechoslovakia, England, Germany, France, Holland, Yugoslavia, Lithuania, Austria, Poland, Rumania, Switzerland and Scandinavia.

The Kenessio Mechino with Rabbi Yaakov Rosenheim, President of Agudas Yisroel, speaking in Marienbad 1936

The local 'Marienbader Zeitung' reported on this Kenessio Mechino, which ended with a public session, at which Rabbi Aaron Lewin (Reige) was the main speaker. Rabbi Yaakov Rosenheim, as President of the World Aguda, thanked Rabbi Horowitz from Yerushalayim for his positive input, and also gave a special thanks to 'Kurt Leitner' for his superb organisation of this event. The following day, August 7, 1936, Rabbi Yaakov Rosenheim, Rabbi Horowitz and Mr. Harry (Aron) Goodman (London) were invited to attend a reception in Prague hosted by the Czechoslovakian President Edvard Benes, in their honour.

JÜDISCHE PRESSE

בה

WIEN · BRATISLAVA • 7. AUGUST 1936

כ' אב תרצ"ו

22. Jahrgang / Nummer 29

Redaktion und Administration: Wien, II., Malzgasse 12 a, Telephon A-46-0-15; Tschechoslowakei: Bratislava, Postfach 381 / Erscheint jeden Freitag / Redaktionsschluß: Mittwoch Mittag

Abonnementpreise: Ganzjährig: für Oesterreich S 16, Tschechoslowakei Kč 80, Jugoslawien Dinar 150, das übrige Ausland Schw. Fr. 14. Einzelnummer öst. Gr. 40.

Zahlungen f. „Jüdische Presse", Wien, auf folgende Postsparkassenkonti: Wien Nr. D-93.614, Brünn Nr. 126.058, Budapest Nr. 50.170, Warschau Nr. 190.409, Zagreb Nr. 40.217, Zürich Nr. VIII, 4117, Berlin Nr. 122.619.

ORGAN FÜR DIE INTERESSEN DES ORTHODOXEN JUDENTUMS

Die Kenessio Mechino in Marienbad

Wenn auch die üblichen Formalitäten, die nachgerade schon zur Schablone geworden sind, eingehalten wurden, so ist doch das rein Aeußerliche und Kon-

Und wie auf einen Befehl erhebt sich Schlag 10 Uhr die Versammlung, als der Gerer Rebbe in gebeugter Haltung, gefolgt von den Mitgliedern des

Doch von der Tribüne der Kenessio Mechino muß auch der Ruf nach innen, der Ruf an die Brüder, die sich vom G-ttesglauben abgekehrt haben, der

The Newspaper Report of the Kenessio Mechino 1936

It was provisionally decided to arrange for the 3rd Kenessio Gedoloh to be held in Yerushalayim in March 1937, if circumstances permitted. The Jewish People were contemplating the impending implementation of the Balfour Declaration, and lived with high hopes for their imminent return to the Holy Land. However, when this did not happen as quickly as they had hoped, and the problems facing the Orthodox Jewish people needed to be urgently addressed, it was announced that the 3rd Kenessio would be held in Marienbad from August 18-23, 1937.

The Jewish Telegraphic Agency of July 12, 1937 reported just prior to the Kenessio:

'On July 11 1937, The League of Nations received a request from the British Government to convene and to consider the entire report of the Royal Commission on Palestine (Peel Commission). This was scheduled to take place in Geneva on July 30 of the same year. The Royal

Commission on Palestine published its findings in a 404 page report that sold out within the first hour of publication.

On July 11 1937, the leaders of World Aguda confirmed to the British Government the 'virtual acceptance of the proposed Jewish State in Palestine, with the stipulation that 'the suggested boundaries undoubtedly require revision' and that the Association of Jewry to Jerusalem must be maintained. It is essential to establish the new Jewish Commonwealth on the basis of the Torah, thus enabling Jews to again fulfil their mission in the Holy Land, and that the League of Nations consider the views of **all** Jewry in all future negotiations, and not just those of individual organisations. This was to be ratified at their world conference scheduled for the following month [Kenessio]'.

Novinove výplatné povolené riadit pošt a telegrafov v Bratislave čís. 41572-III-20

V. b. b.

Zeitungen vom Verleger versendet
Journal expédié par l'éditeur

JÜDISCHE PRESSE

ב"ה

WIEN-BRATISLAVA ■ 20. AUGUST 1937

י"ג אלול תרצ"ז

23. Jahrgang | Nummer 27

Redaktion und Administration: Wien, II., Malzgasse 12a. Telephon-Nr. A-46-0-15; Tschechoslowakei: Bratislava, Republikplatz Nr. 37, Postfach 381 / Erscheint jeden Freitag / Redaktionsschluß: Mittwoch Mittag

Abonnementpreise: Ganzjährig: für Oesterreich S 16, Tschechoslowakei Kč 80, Jugoslawien Dinar 150, das übrige Ausland Schw. Fr. 14. Einzelnummer öst. Gr. 40.

Zahlungen für »Jüdische Presse«, Wien, auf folgende Postsparkassenkonti: Wien Nr. D-93.614, Brünn Nr. 126.098, Budapest Nr. 30.170, Warschau Nr. 193.316, Zagreb Nr. 40.217, Zürich Nr. VIII, 4117, Berlin Nr. 122.619; für »Jüdische Presse«, Bratislava: Prag Nr. 53.386.

ORGAN FÜR DIE INTERESSEN DES ORTHODOXEN JUDENTUMS

Eröffnung der Kenessia Gedaulo

(Spezialbericht der »Jüdischen Presse«)

Dienstag, den 17. August, 10. Ellul, um 8 Uhr abends, fand in überaus begeisterter Stim-

In seiner Eröffnungsrede am Dienstag Abend führte Präsident Jakob Rosenheim u. a. aus:

schichtskrisis hineingeschleudert wurde. Soll das jüdische Volk seiner metaphysisch-geschichtlichen Aufgabe genügen, das Ferment des organischen Einheitsaufbaues der Völkergemeinschaft zu werden, so muß es zu allererst selbst dastehen als wiedergeborener, vom G—tteswort als Zentralseele belebter Organismus.

Mag immer der finanzielle und technisch-

The Austrian 'Judische Presse' reporting on the opening session of the 3rd Kenessio

THIRD KENESSIO GEDOLOH MARIENBAD AUGUST 18-23, 1937

Rabbi Yaakov Rosenheim had personally observed Opa's exemplary organisational skills in the way he assisted in organising the Kenessio Mechino at the Continental Hotel in 1936, and appointed Opa to be the 'Organising Secretary' for the 3rd Kenessio that was scheduled to be held in his home town, a challenge that Opa accepted. Much preparatory work needed to be done, all of which will become apparent from the reports on the Kenessio itself, which proved to be the last place where all the pre-war Gedolim met to discuss the enormous challenges and problems facing the Jewish People.

Because of the importance of the Kenessio to world Jewry and the integral part in Opa's involvement as the largest single communal project that he undertook at the prime of his life, I have included three separate reports on the Kenessio, as observed from different viewpoints. The first is a translation of the report that appeared in the local secular daily newspaper 'The Marienbader Zeitung' that gave a detailed daily coverage of the Kenessio. The second one is a combined report that was taken from the 30 page official Kenessio news bulletins edited by Mr. David Turkel and the September and October 1937 editions of the HaPardes Hebrew Monthly Magazine, which reported on the Kenessio in great detail. The third report includes some personal recollections that Opa gave when interviewed by the Jewish Press in Manchester.

Despite the growing nationalistic and anti-semitic feelings, Marienbad became the meeting point for the 3rd World Congress Agudas Yisroel (Kenessio Gedoloh) in 1937, to which the Orthodox Jews rallied. It was no coincidence that this Congress took place in Marienbad, since the 12th and 13th World Congress of its Zionist opposition had already taken place in nearby Carlsbad in 1921 and 1923.

The 3rd Jewish-World-Congress, the Kenessio Gedoloh, was held in Marienbad from August 18-24, 1937, taking centre stage of world media and for all residents of Marienbad. The focal points were devoted to the Jewish emigration overseas as well as the founding of an independent Jewish State in Palestine.

However, Palestine was then under British Mandate. Due to World War II, the Jewish-British conflicts of interest were put on hold, and the project that had been mapped out in Marienbad was only realised in 1948.

Marienbader Zeitung

Marienbader Tagblatt für Marienbad und Umgebung

Schriftleitung und Verwaltung: Marienbad, Schulstraße 427, Fernruf 2025
Herausgeber, Druck und Verlag: Buch- und Steindruckerei Josef Gschihay,
für die Schriftleitung verantwortlich: Dr. Josef Bauschke, beide Marienbad

Folge 189 | Mittwoch, den 18. August 1937 | 64. Jahrgang

Eröffnung des Juden-Weltkongresses.

700 Delegierte der orthodoxen Juden. — 1700 Personen im Kursaal.

Marienbad, 18. August. Gestern abend begann der III. Weltkongreß der orthodoxen Juden (Agudas Jsroel), der bis einschließlich 23. August dauern wird. Der Kursaal, in dem die Tagungen abgehalten werden, hatte bei der Eröffnungssitzung ein ungewöhnliches Gepräge. Im großen Kursaal waren längs der Marmorwände Schriftbänder mit hebräischen Lettern und Aussprüchen angebracht. Im Saal drängten sich 700 Delegierte der orthodoxen Juden aus der ganzen Welt zusammen. Auf der Tribüne saßen die Mitglieder des Großen Rabbinischen Rates und führende Persönlichkeiten der Orthodoxen Judenschaft. Die meisten haben lange wallende Bärte, tragen große, schwarze Hüte oder kleine Käppchen – auch zwei Zylinderhüte konnte man sehen. Die Frauen waren mit vielen Zuhörern und Zuhörerinnen im kleinen Kursaal, wohin die Reden mittels Lautsprecher übertragen

daß die natürlichen Egoismen in das Gefüge einer übernationalen Weltordnung einbaute. Das jüdische Volk ist in die allgemeine geschichtliche Krise hineingeschleudert worden. Aber es ruht auf ihm die prophetische Verheißung: „Ich berufe dich um des sittlichen Ideals willen zum Bunde der Völker". Es ist die geschichtliche Tendenz, daß das jüdische Volk das Ferment der Völker sein werde. Die liberalistisch-individualistische Ordnung hat die Organismen zerrissen oder verleugnet. Die zionistisch-nationalistische Ordnung hat das jüdische Volk seiner Seele beraubt."

Zwei Aufgaben seien jetzt zu bewältigen: die politische, wirtschaftliche und religiöse Zukunft des Volkes Israel in Palästina und der Wandersturm der jüdischen Volksmassen, der heute beobachtet werde. Es gebe nur ein unfehlbares, in der Vergangenheit erprobtes Mittel der nationalen Existenz: die jüdische

Etablissement
Café BELLEVUE Restaur.
Beliebter Frühstück- u. Jausenplatz
Diners Vorzügliche Küche à la carte
Täglich vormittags, nachmittags und abends Konzert und Tanz
Bellevue-Band

Abb.. 29, 30: *Marienbader Zeitung informierte ausführlich über das Kongress-Geschehen*

The Marienbader Zeitung's comprehensive reports on the Kenessio.

The 3rd Jewish-World Congress in Marienbad was organised by the Jewish organisation of Agudas Yisroel, whose headquarters were in London, with several branches in various other European countries. This influential organisation opposed the religious Nationalism as well as the unhindered Liberalism and Marxism Socialism, which had enticed many Orthodox Jews. The aim of this Kenessio Gedoloh was the strengthening of Orthodox Jewish Unity and became the extraordinary meeting point for delegates of different Jewish movements.

Even before the onset of the Congress, Chief Rabbi Yonosson Horowitz from Yerushalayim met with Rabbi Meir Schenkolewski from New York, and discussed various urgent matters together.

The young Kurt Leitner, from the family of the Jewish hotelier David Leitner, owner of the Hotel National in Postgasse, was responsible for the preparation of this huge undertaking. More than 5000 visitors from Europe, America, Asia and Africa were expected, and price reductions for visas, train tickets and Kurtaxe (holiday tax), for use of the spa etc. had to be arranged. After hearing of these price reductions, the number of intended participants began to soar. The Rabbis of Alexander,

Sochatchov and Spink as well as Chief Rabbi Schreiber from Pressburg, together with family and attendants, had already arrived before the Congress began, to make the most of this special place and benefit from the healing spa waters. According to some news reports, a further 70 Rabbis were expected to meet here 8 years after the previous Kenessio, in order to discuss problems concerning Jewry.

At the helm of the Congress stood the Great Rabbinic Council, the Moetzes Gedolei Hatorah, and all the leading West European Rabbis. Rabbi Chaim Ozer Grodzenski from Vilna (Lithuania) was due to open the proceedings but was unable to attend due to ill health. Points of discussion were firstly the founding of the Jewish State in Palestine, as well as the agreement as to the type of Government of the new State. Another theme was the Jewish mass emigration, and uniting of the numerous independent parallel Jewish organisations overseas into one central body. A further debate was reserved for the education of the younger generation.

The imposing Kursaal building, the hall where the Kenessio was held.

Some of the delegates at the Kenessio hall entrance

Kenessio placards prominently displayed

כנסיה גדולה של אגודת ישראל

MERKBLATT

FÜR DIE DELEGIERTEN UND GÄSTE
DER 3. KENESSIO GEDAULO
MARIENBAD

Kenessio program

L. to R. Rabbi Yitzchok Breuer Rabbi Y. Rosenheim and Rabbi Dr. Ehrmann on the way to the Kenessio 1937

Preparing the Hall for the Kenessio

Kenessio stationery

Orazitkuje výdejna jízdenek,
při jízdě do Mariánských Lázní.

Legitimace čís. 1388

pro účastníka sjezdu „3 Kenessio Gedaúlô - Agudas Israel", pořádaného v Mariánských Lážních ve dnech 18. — 23. srpna 1937 pro jízdu tam v době od 11. do 23. srpna 1937 a zpět v době od 18. do 30. srpna 1937 včetně.

Pan(í) Mosi Herz

bydliště v Luzern

železniční nástupní stanice

jest oprávněn(a) požadovati za podmínek a v rozsahu na rubu této legitimace uvedeném na tratích československých státních drah skupiny „A" a „B" vyjma Frýdlantských okresních drah, Hustopečské místní dráhy a lanové dráhy Horní Hanychov — Ještěd tyto slevy jízdného:

a) tuzemský účastník 33⅓%ní slevu jízdného v použité třídě osobního vlaku a na vzdálenosti přes 100 km též vlaku vyššího druhu.

b) zahraniční účastník 50%ní slevu jízdného v použité třídě vozové a druhu vlaku, prokáže-li se kromě této legitimace též zahraničním cestovním pasem.

Vlastnoruční podpis držitele (inkoustem):

Büro der 3. Kenessio G[illegible]
(razítko a podpisy)
Marienbad.

Orazitkuje výdejna jízdenek
před jízdou z Mariánských [illegible]

A Discount Voucher for Swiss representative Mr. Mosi Herz (Luzern), issued by the Kenessio Office and signed by Kurt Leitner (bottom right)

Further reports in the 'Marienbader Zeitung' on the following day read:

The 3rd Jewish World Congress, Kenessio Gedoloh, began on Wednesday August 18, 1937. During this Congress they had strung symbolic strings in the forests around the town (Eiruv), and on Shabbos the Postgasse, where some of the meetings took place, was closed off. A ribbon was draped around all the places where the gatherings were held, and welcome notices and placards were displayed. All houses, hotels, health spas and public buildings were decorated with flowers and flags. There were specially marked buses, taxis and street cars that offered reduced fares to all the participants. An information centre for the Kenessio was located in the Cafe "Stadtpark" not far from the main post office.

A second information centre for the benefit of all participants was opened at the train station. Here a member of the Kenessio staff welcomed each delegate and guest with a snack, and presented them with their programme and timetable, with details of their allocated accommodation. A long row of taxis were waiting outside, ready to transfer these guests to their lodgings. Most of the houses on the block between the Postgasse and the present Klicova Street belonged to the Leitner families, and the leading Jewish representatives were accommodated in Hotels National (Postgasse 55) and Goldenes Schloss (Klicova Street 423), where there were Mikvo'os and most reliable kosher restaurants.

This picture was included in the welcome pack showing available restaurants and Mikvah facilities

For the youth they had prepared large hostels with 500 beds. The post office of Marienbad had produced special Kenessio postmarks in Czech and Yiddish, [as illustrated on page 89] and additional booths were also available at the main post office.

The world Kenessio took place at the Town Hall where 750 delegates and a further 1700 official participants had gathered. 600 delegates were representatives of Jewish organisations from many countries, and 150 delegates represented the women's organisations. Members of the Chief Rabbinical Councils and representatives of Worldwide Orthodoxy were seated on the dais. When Mr. Leitner informed the Marienbad Town Council that the Town Hall was too small to accommodate this large gathering, and that they might have to consider moving it to the nearby resort of Carlsbad, they agreed to build an extension to the main stage at their own expense.

The guests made their way to the Kursaal for the opening session, which was full to capacity some twenty minutes before the commencement of the proceedings. This large and magnificent hall is said to provide the best acoustics available in any public building in Europe. The large stage was draped in a deep red satin cloth and gracefully decorated with many flowers and plants, with red, blue and white ribbons, representative of the colours of the Czechoslovakian flag. The marble walls of the Kursaal were appropriately decorated with large posters to mark the occasion. Rav Yaakov Rosenheim from London, President of the Congress, opened the proceedings. He welcomed the guests and mentioned that the first Kenessio Gedoloh had taken place 25 years earlier in Kattowitz in 1912. He then read out greetings of T. G. Masaryk and the new Czech president, Dr Edvard Benes. The next speaker was Rabbi Y. Meir Lewin from Warsaw, who spoke in Yiddish, and remembered the Yidden who had died in Palestine during the Arab uprising. Mr Harry Goodman from London conveyed a welcome message from Czech President Edvard Benes, the Czech Consul in London, and from Sir Malcolm, the British Secretary to the Foreign Office. He then read out a very warm personal letter of apology from Neville Laski, President of the Board of Deputies of British Jews, who was unable to attend in person. Rabbi Menachem Ziemba was one of the main speakers, one of the few delegates apart from Rabbi Rosenheim, who had also been present at the previous two Kenessio Gedolohs that were held in Vienna.

Rabbi Zirelsohn (Kishinev) in conversation with Opa (1.1.1.3)

The Kenessio organising committee 1937 with Opa 2nd from left and Rabbi Fishel Gelernter directly opposite
37. Rabbi Yonason Horowitz (Yerusholayim) at head of table

L. to R. Rabbi Dovid of Sochatchov with Reb Elchonon Wasserman and Rabbi Aaron Kotler and Opa (1.1.1.3) at the Kenessio, with Rabbi Moishe Blau behind Opa.

Rav Elchonon Wasserman, Rav Aaron Kotler and Rav Moishe Blau, with Opa (1.1.1.3) on the telephone on the right

In fact Reb Menachem Ziemba joined Agudas Yisroel immediately after it was founded in 1912 and took an active role in all its activities. At the first Kenessio he was chosen to be the honorary secretary of the Moetzes Gedolei Hatorah, and at the second Kenessio, Reb Chaim Ozer Grodzenski only agreed to serve as chairman of the Moetzes

Reb Chaim Ozer

Gedolei Hatorah if Rabbi Ziemba would continue in his position as secretary. At the third Kenessio, Reb Menachem was at the height of his fame, where he spoke twice to the full assemblage, and each time was greeted with hushed silence and awe. His second speech, in retrospect, seems almost prophetic, as he spoke at length about the Mitzvah of Kiddush Hashem – the sanctification of Hashem's Name. He was tragically killed in the Warsaw Getto together with his entire family.

Legitimation Nr.

תעודה מספר

Legitimace čís. 1115

Vorverwaltungskomitee der 3. Kenessio Gedaulo Marienbad

Entrance card for Rabbi Eis from Zurich with Opa's signature on the bottom right

The Delegates arriving at the Kenessio 1937

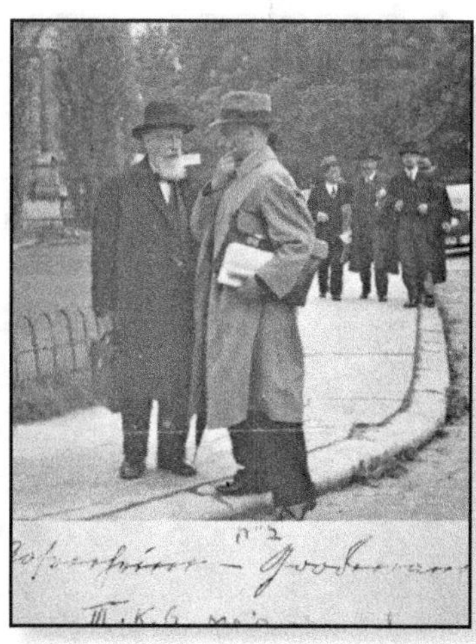

Rabbi Yaakov Rosenheim with Mr. Aron (Harry) Goodman

Rabbi Yaakov Rosenheim arriving at the Kenessio 1937

Polish Representatives arriving at the Kenessio

Delegates arriving at the Kenessio 1937

Discussion outside the Kenessio. Reb Elchonon Wasserman on the left, seen from the back. Central figure, Rav Ungar from Nitra and front right is Rabbi S. Zalman Sorotzkin of Slutzk.

L. To R. Rav Ungar and Rav Sorotzkin in conversation

Rabbi Zalman Sorotzkin with
Rabbi Mordechai Dubin (Latvia) at the Kenessio 1937

L. to R. Rabbi Alexander Zusha Friedman, Rabbi Eliezer Sivkin, Rabbi Fishel Gelernter, Opa, and Rabbi Shlomo Ehrmann in Marienbad 1937

Mr. Fritz Buxbaum, the Jewish Deputy Mayor of Marienbad, welcomed the Congress on behalf of the City Council, and ended his speech with the Hebrew saying "Where there is Torah there is Wisdom". All halls and rooms were fully occupied. Ladies and other delegates sat in adjacent rooms, and could hear and follow all the proceedings and speeches via loudspeakers.

RECHTS

SITZREIHE ____

NR. ____

III. WELTKONGRESS D. AGUDAS JISROEL

MARIENBAD
18.–23. AUGUST 1937
11.–16. ELUL 5697

EHREN-KARTE / כרטיס־כבוד

FUR HERRN ____

ZUR TEILNAHME AN ALLEN OFFENTL. TAGUNGEN

GESCHAFTSFUHRENDER AUSSCHUSS DER AGUDAS JISROEL • KENESSIO GEDAULO ZORO

NR. ____

KURHAUS

Complimentary Ticket issued for 3rd Kenessio for Rav Wolf S. Jacobson, Copenhagen

Fritz Buxbaum

Apart from the main themes mentioned above, they also discussed the need to strengthen and educate married women about the importance of covering their hair correctly, and the urgent need to educate the public in Shemiras Shabbos.

The Congress took centre stage in the world press, and especially in the British papers. The decisions of the Congress from August 24, 1937 were unanimous – an independent Jewish State in Palestine based on the dictates of the Torah.

The opening session of the Kenessio 1937 (everyone standing).

Rabbi Yaakov Rosenheim chairing a meeting at the Kenessio

The dais with the Rabbonim at the Kenessio 1937

Mr. Fritz Buxbaum, the Jewish Deputy Mayor of Marienbad, greeting the guests on behalf of the Marienbad Council.

The venue of the Kenessio with Hebrew postmark.

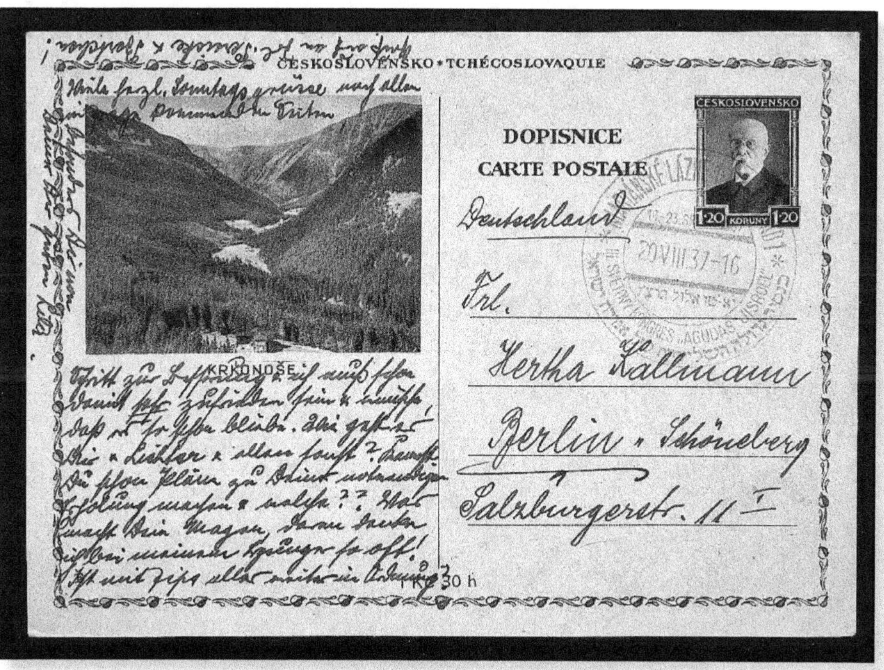

A private postcard with the Kenessio postmark

Partial view of the delegates attending the 3rd Kenessio

The text of the resolution issued at the end of the Kenessio Gedoloh by the Moetzes Gedolei Hatorah read:

'The foundation of the Jewish People's right to the Holy Land is based on the Torah and the Prophets. A Jewish State not based on the principles of Torah is a denial of Jewish origin, is opposed to the identity and the true stature of our people, and undermines the basis of existence of our People. Any relinquishment of the Holy Land given to the Jewish people by G-d has no validity.'

The second Kenessio report is a combination of information contained in the official Kenessio news bulletin printed in German (Die Kenessio Gedaulo) and the monthly Hebrew Hapardes Magazine, from which I have collated the following information.

DIE KENESSIO GEDAULO הכנסיה הגדולה השלישית

HERAUSGEGEBEN VOM PRESSEBÜRO DER KENESSIO GEDAULO

Nr. 3 — Marienbad, 16. Elul 5697/24. August 1937 — ב"ה

Gegen den Peel'schen Judenstaat

Jüdischer Staat nur auf Basis der Thora möglich. — Verzicht auf die vom Weltenschöpfer festgesetzten Grenzen ausgeschlossen. — Verhandlungen können nur im Einvernehmen mit der Orthodoxie geführt werden. — Ein Appell an alle Juden der Welt. — Für jüdisch-arabische Versöhnung. — Ermächtigung der Exekutive zu Verhandlungen mit der englischen Regierung.

The official Kenessio paper – 3rd edition.

As part of the Kenessio arrangements, David Turkel, the Orthodox Viennese journalist, was responsible for printing an official 30 page bulletin entitled 'Die III Kenessio Gedaulo' whose first edition appeared on August 17, one day prior to the opening of the Kenessio, containing the history and goals of the Aguda. Opa was nominated as its official publisher and any articles that were submitted for publication had to be sent to 'Kurt Leitner, Hotel National, Marienbad.' These bulletins proved extremely popular, not only with the numerous delegates and guests attending the Kenessio, but with Yidden worldwide! Over 100,000 copies were printed and sold, as Jews were eager to learn what took place at this unique Torah Conference in Marienbad. It contained a comprehensive program, timetable and details of the topics that were to be discussed at the Kenessio. The timetable was strictly adhered to, with some sessions continuing until 2am, so as not to encroach on the next day's schedule. However, the organisers had to remain long after these sessions came to an end, in order to prepare for the next day.

שנה י"א | (נוסד בשנת תרע"ג בפינסק) | חוברת ד'

חודש אלול תרצ"ז

הפרדס

קובץ רבני חדשי

יוסיע לאור כעת בשיקאגא

ישא מדברותיו להגדיל תורה ולהאדירה בהשתתפות גאוני וגדולי דורנו שליט"א

העורך והמו"ל

הרב שמואל אהרן הלוי פרדס

מחיר "הפרדס" לשנה:

בארצנו: — 3 דולר | בחו"ל: — 2 דולר

Hapardes Hebrew Magazine – Elul 1937

3. KENESSIO GEDAULO, MARIENBAD

5697

K. G.-SELA

Nr. S. 300111 *

Die 3. Kenessio Gedaulo soll der ganzen religiösen Judenheit Gelegenheit geben, geschlossen zu den geistigen und wirtschaftlichen jüdischen Problemen der Gegenwart Stellung zu nehmen und zu deren Lösung beizutragen. Darüber hinaus wird die Kenessio Gedaulo eine machtvolle Willenskundgebung des jüdischen Volkes für Gtt, seine Tora und sein Land darstellen.

Durch Zahlung des K. G.-Sela hat der Inhaber dieses Scheines — unter Anerkennung der Verpflichtungskraft der Tora für das jüdische Volk, insbesondere für den Aufbau Erez Jisroels — das Wahlrecht für die 3. Kenessio Gedaulo im Rahmen der Wahlordnung* erworben.

Name: | Aktivist Nr.

Voting Card for spectators

In this first edition, Mr. Turkel was pleased to report that while walking in the main street in Marienbad he was approached by a non-Jew who asked him the following question: 'Could you please explain to me how come that in the past few days so many Jewish people have come to Marienbad from many different countries, often not even dressed alike, yet they are all very friendly and speak with each other. It is really remarkable!' To which Mr Turkel replied, 'these people have come here for a common goal, and that is what created this special and unique bond between them.'

...'DIE III KENESSIO GEDAULO'

As one entered the Kursaal, to the left was the large Kenessio office with twenty secretaries in attendance, all busy typing. [It is worth remembering that everything had to be typed out on manual typewriters; photocopiers were only invented later.] In the lobby of the Kursaal, visitors could also obtain the following auxiliary services:

- All Kenessio delegates or visitors could get their Kenessio Pass stamped which entitled them to a 20% disount on tours to Carlsbard, Frankensbad and Prague.
- Any spa treatment, baths and doctors' fees were discounted by 20%.
- On Thursday and Friday (August 19-20) flowers were available for purchase in honour of the forthcoming Shabbos.
- All Aguda publications pertaining to Beth Yaskov Movement, Keren Hatorah, Vaad HaYeshivahs, Keren Hayishuv etc., were sold there. For example:

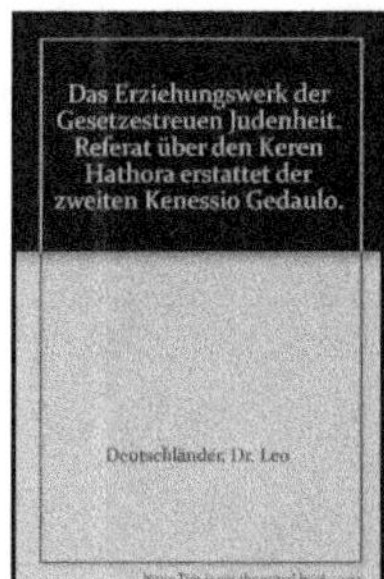

Das Erziehungswerk der Gesetzestreuen Judenheit. Referat über den Keren Hathora erstattet der zweiten Kenessio Gedaulo.

Deutschländer, Dr. Leo

TÄTIGKEITSBERICHT

DER

BETH JACOB ZENTRALE

Dr. L. DEUTSCHLÄNDER

WIEN

DAS ERZIEHUNGSWERK DER GESETZESTREUEN JUDENHEIT

KEREN HATHORA

A Jewish Journal reporting on the Kenessio in pictures.

Souvenir photo album from the 3rd Kenessio

- A large number of photos of the Rabbonim present at this Kenessio as well as at the previous ones were on sale here.
- Specially printed Kenessio postcards and stationery were available, and any letters posted in designated letter boxes would be franked with the unique Kenessio postmark.
- The Austrian National Railway offered delegates and visitors returning home after the Kenessio a 25% discount on train fares, used by transit passengers travelling through Austria.

Whereas the two earlier Kenessios were represented mainly by delegates from Europe and Eretz Yisroel, the third Kenessio welcomed the arrival of an unexpected American delegation, which established Agudas Yisroel as an International Organisation. Rabbi Eliezer Silver, who led the American delegation, travelled via Paris, where it was confirmed that Rabbi Chaim Ozer Grodzenski of Vilna was recuperating from an illness and would be unable to attend the Kenessio in person. Rabbi Silver then travelled especially to Vilna to meet with the Godol Hador, and received guidance on matters pertaining to American Jewry as well as advice on problems that were to be discussed at the Kenessio. Due to his trip to Vilna, Rabbi Silver arrived in Marienbad after the opening session of the Kenessio, but was accorded much honour, as he himself was a great Talmid Chochom, and also because he had brought personal greetings and instructions from Reb Chaim Ozer, which were read out in public and later printed in the Hapardes Magazine.

The daily program of the Kenessio began at 10 am, but was preceded by an hour-long Shiur on Mishna Berura. Many sessions took part as workshops, addressing problems pertaining to individual countries, whilst others were discussed in public in the main hall. On Friday all meetings finished at least two hours before Shabbos.

The first page of the 'Die III Kenessio Gedaulo' contained an article by Rabbi Dr. Pinchos Kohn (Ansbach, Germany), highlighting this unique gathering, which was to continue to build on the foundations that were established by the Gedolim at their initial meeting in Kattowitz in 1912, and the previous two Kenessios of Agudas Yisroel in Vienna. A similar sentiment was expressed by Rabbi Wolf S. Jacobson of Copenhagen, who urged the assembled to continue to work together in unity toward a common goal, and look to the future with hope for continued success.

At a workshop meeting of Moetzes Gedolei Hatorah;
L. to R. facing;- Rabbi Mordechai Dubin (Latvia), unknown, Rabbi Horovitz, Rav Y. Tzvi Dushinsky (with son standing behind him), Imrei Emes (facing away from photo), Rabbi Avrohom Yaakov Friedman (Sadigur), Rabbi Yehuda Leib Zirelsohn, Rabbi Zalman Sorotzkin (obscure), unknown

Rabbi Dr. Shlomo Ehrmann (Frankfurt) pointed out that the Beth Yosef (Rabbi Yosef Caro) finished writing his commentary on the Tur Shulchan Oruch in the holy city of Safed on Wednesday 11 Elul 5302, the same day and date that the 3rd Kenessio began in Marienbad, 395 years later. It is therefore appropriate that all decisions taken at the Kenessio should continue to be made by the present day Gedolim, who follow the same dictates as those laid down by the Beth Yosef in the Shulchan Oruch. The Beth Yosef initially wrote his commentary on the

Tur, which contains a compendium of all the different relevant opinions pertaining to each section of Jewish law. Later on he wrote the Shulchan Oruch, an authoritative work based on the decision reached from all the opinions, as quoted in his commentary of the Tur. Similarly, Rabbi Dr. Shlomo Ehrmann drew a parallel to the first part of the Kenessio, which will be spent with general discussion and debates by different representatives voicing their opinions and recommendations, and during the final two days they will forward the conclusions as decided by the Moetzes Gedolei Hatorah.

The famous Orthodox writer, Selig Schachnowitz (1874–1952), was present at the 1st Kenessio in Vienna and described in vivid details his memories of the opening session there:

'The most remarkable personality at the First Kenessio Gedoloh was indisputably the Chofetz Chaim. The entire Jewish world has been under the spell of his wonder-some personality, and many have come to Vienna only to see this holy sage face to face. Many tales were told about his life and even his journey to Vienna. In the days of strict passport and border controls, he was permitted to cross every border with a passport that was devoid of his picture, because he would not allow himself to be photographed. Now in Vienna one can see the original 'picture'; his small posture, simply dressed and wearing a typical Lithuanian hat. His face was illuminated by his shining eyes that seemed to look onto other worlds. He probably viewed our small world only as transitory, yet always saw the right thing, the thing that really mattered.'

The Chofetz Chaim and Rabbi Yaakov Rosenheim arriving at the Kenessio 1923

'The big moment of the opening arrived. 'The Chofetz Chaim is about to speak!' The tension of the moment was palpable, as this great man of small stature went onto the stage unaided, and will remain an unforgeable experience for all the participants. There he stood at the lectern, gazing into the distance, and his lips moved. What did he say? Although total silence reigned in the hall one couldn't hear a word. Our press table stood directly in front of the stage. I only hesitated for a short moment, and then jumped onto the stage, although I really did not belong there, but my readers were entitled to know what this great personality, the greatest in Israel, had to say. I stood closely behind him, listening intently, a sharpened pencil in my hand. The latter was however totally unnecessary, as his words were etched into my soul forever.

How great he must have been, to convey in such a clear and eloquent way and often with few words, that which was on his heart and of utmost importance. He protested against being given the honour to give his blessings to the assembled Congress. 'I am an old man, what do you want from me? Do you want to receive the priestly blessings from an old man? I cannot deny that I am a Cohen and an old man'. He then told of a great Rov who came to town and was afforded great honour, but when he was asked halachic questions he was unable to answer a single one. All knowledge had suddenly departed from him, the cause being the honour and haughtiness that it had caused. When pride and haughtiness is awakened in a person, his wisdom leaves him…

And then the Chofetz Chaim spoke about the problems mentioned at the Kenessio. And again he told a story. A sick person is lying on the road and the doctors are called in search of a cure. One wants to heal his eyes so that he can see again, another doctor wants to heal his feet so that he can walk again, yet another wants to heal his hands so that he can feel and touch again. Then comes the correct doctor and advises, 'the heart is sick, let's cure the heart and then the blood will flow to all the other parts of the body'. The heart of our life is the Torah, this is where we have to begin the healing process, and then all other problems will be solved.

The Rov continues in a similar manner. "The Torah problems in the West? It says that where the Torah has proven itself through three generations, it will always return to the same "inn", so that it will not budge from later generations. But", asks the old venerated Rabbi, "could there still be unlearned men and scoffers of the Torah amongst Jewry, after the first three generations, Avrohom, Yitzchok and Yaakov have kept the Torah faithfully? The answer is, it says 'the Torah **returns** to its inn, but if they don't let it in" - here the Rabbi weeps as he describes the picture of the wanderer who knocks on the door of the inn, and when refused entry, he recalls the merits of his ancestors who had taken shelter there, but they still won't allow him in. He has no choice but to look elsewhere for lodgings. "A hundred years ago the Torah came knocking on the doors of Germany, but they wouldn't let her in. "But it is my homeland", it begged, "Rashi, the Baale Tosfos!" But there was no room for it, "all full", it was told. "Emancipation, modern schools, secular education, business world..." so the Torah went in search of another place to live, in Poland and Lithuania. And today? The Torah is on its way back, where to? We don't know. Let her in, you men of the West, hold her tight!...

Rabbi Meir Shapiro then repeated the words of the Chofetz Chaim in a loud and clear voice, for all the assembled to hear. These words were heard directly from the holy mouth and sounded very different than the way they could be read in the reports which were later printed in the newspapers.

These are Selig Schachnowitz' memories, from the first Kennesio.

The second edition of the special edition 'Die III Kenessio Gedaulo' appeared three days later and provided detailed information of the progress made so far, with a comprehensive list of all the official delegates who attended the Kenessio, categorised by country, for both the men and women delegates.

This included:

America (6), Belgium (15), Germany (84), England (19), Eretz Yisroel: Yerushalayim (18), Tel Aviv (6), Petach Tikva (2), Tiberias (1), Poalei Aguda (14), France (6), Holland (8), Yugoslavia (6), Austria (20), Poland (80), Romania (48), Switzerland (4), Czechoslovakia (24), Latvia (22). A further list of all the people elected to join numerous working committees in the above countries are also listed, with a similar list for the ladies' representatives.

It lists the great achievements that the Aguda had made since its inception some twenty five years previously and could look back at their great achievements. Some of these included:

KEREN HATORAH: They had established Keren Hatorah, a general fund that gave financial support to many Yeshivah Ketanos in Europe, allowing them to continue operating and supplement their budgets. They were presently funding a total of 267 Yeshivahs with a very large number of students.

VAAD HAYESHIVAHS: Was responsible for printing and distributing large quantities of Gemorohs and other Sifrei Kodesh, supplying these to the public and institutions at cost.

KEREN HAYISHUV: Was a fund that supported the Orthodox establishments in Palestine that funded the purchase of land which was used for Orthodox 'Kibbutzim', allowing new immigrants to earn a living, and also funded many vocational courses to train people for suitable employment.

BETH YAAKOV MOVEMENT FOR GIRLS: The Beth Yaakov Movement, founded by Sarah Schenirer in Crakow in1917 and ably assisted by Rabbi Schmuel (Leo) Deutschlander, had grown to a total of 333 schools. Beth Yaakov schools were to be found in Czechoslovakia, England, Eretz Yisroel, France, Italy, Yugoslavia, Latvia, Lithuania, Austria, Poland, Rumania, Belarus, Bulgaria and Hungary, a truly proud achievement.

HOREB DAY SCHOOLS FOR BOYS: A comprehensive system of 297 Orthodox boys schools.

THE JEWISH PRESS: Much enphasis was placed in printing Orthodox Jewish newspapers and magazines that informed and helped educate the masses with the correct Torah outlook and viewpoints. There were some daily papers, and many more weekly and fortnightly journals, including the Hamodia, Der Yid (in Poland), Hapeles, Darkeinu, Israelit, Hapardes, Digleinu etc.

NOAM AND BNOS AGUDAS YISROEL: Youth groups were organised, Noam Agudas Yisroel for the boys and Bnos Agudas Yisroel for the girls, to provide cultural and social activities, and organising many local events, as appropriate. The Noam youth groups later became known as Pirchim (for the younger boys) and Zeirim for the older ones, whilst the Bnos name was adopted by the younger girls and Neshei Agudas Yisroel for the social activities of the young married ladies.

Dr. Maximillian Landau gave a very comprehensive review of the Orthodox Jewish Press and made some very constructive suggestions, which were later ratified by the Kenessio.

He pointed out that all newspapers are dependent on receiving their news bulletins from the JTA, [Jewish Telegraphic Agency] but unfortunately these were received with an anti-orthodox bias and sometimes even containing anti-semitic ones. He suggested the establishment of a completely independent source of News Agency, with its own central press office. This office would employ professional writers who would produce quality work, and also have these articles translated into the various European languages, whose press would all be able to make use of these same articles. This Central Press Office would also attract adverts from larger companies, as their adverts would receive exposure in many different countries, and these would generate extra revenue for the Press Bureau. All the local individual papers would need to do is allocate a small portion of their paper for the local news. Everything else would be supplied ready from the Central Aguda Press Office. These suggestions were approved by the Kenessio Gedoloh, and Mr. Selig Schachnowitz was appointed to implement them. On his appointment he gave an unscheduled speech, in which he undertook to raise the standard of Orthodox journalism. Later on in the week, Mr. H. Goodman from London, himself an editor of the British Jewish weekly, chaired a workshop that was attended by all the sixty Orthodox journalists who were present at the Kenessio. (Selig Schachnowitz became famous for his historic novels entitled 'The Light from the West', 'Avrohom ben Avrohom', 'The Kusary', 'Fire in the Sky', etc).

Mr. H. Goodman

Rabbi Akiva Sofer, Rav of Pressburg (Bratislava) and a direct descendant of the Chassam Sofer, mentioned how appropriate it was that this conference which has been convened solely for the purpose of strengthening Torah observance, should be held in the same country where his great-grandfather, the Chassam Sofer, had exerted so much effort to safeguard the genuine Mesorah againt the destructive powers of the Haskalah that were prevalent in that period. He then switched from Yiddish and spoke a few minutes in the native Czech language, and on behalf of all Orthodox Jewry, thanked the first President of Czechoslovakia, Jan Masaryk, and his successor Edvard Benes, for having 'created and maintained a haven of democracy in the heart of Europe, where the Jewish people were made welcome and cared for.' These appreciative words were widely circulated in the secular press, and created a great Kiddush Hashem.

Rabbi J. Horowitz of Yerushalayim gave a detailed report about the troublesome situation of the Jewish Yishuv in Eretz Yisroel. There was the ongoing religious struggle with the Zionist majority, as well as the political situation with the Arabs. "We do not want to work in conjunction with them as they have no interest in creating a religious country, but we cannot just simply 'bury our heads in the sand' and ignore the situation." He reminded the public of the 1931 Rabbinic Conference in Vienna, with the object of discussing the above point. They had stressed that the Orthodox people have always maintained a connection with Eretz Yisroel ever since the destruction of the Beis Hamikdosh, and have continued to pray for Yerushalayim ever since, many centuries before the Zionists came on the scene. The Gerrer Rebbe was invited to come to Yerushalayim to discuss these important issues with Rabbi Dushinsky, and observe the situation first hand, and give his valuable suggestions.

Rav Horowitz concluded by suggesting that the British Government must be made fully aware of the existence of the Agudas Yisroel, which is now an international body that represents Orthodox Jewry, and demanded to be consulted on matters pertaining to the future administration of the Holy Land. The Peel Commision had reported of the existence of over 50,000 Orthodox inhabitants in Palestine, and they should therefore likewise be represented in all future discussions. Furthermore, the Zionists' monopoly on immigration quotas must be broken. This recommendation was accepted, and Agudas Yisroel was granted three representatives who attended the Round Table Conference in London.

This conference was chaired by the British Prime Minister at St. James Palace, where they discussed the format of the future 'Jewish State' with Rabbi Yaakov Rosenheim, Rabbi Moishe Blau (Jerusalem) and Mr. H. Goodman, representing the Aguda. Rabbi Horowitz called for an exerted effort to be made to strengthen the independent establishment of Torah institutions, Avodah and Gemilus Chesed in Eretz Yisroel. Financial assistance should be provided to the Poalei Tzion, the Orthodox people who pioneered and emigrated to Eretz Yisroel and were working, but did not earn enough to make ends meet, as these heroes were living in dire poverty. Extensive debates on the topic of Eretz Yisroel were scheduled for the following Sunday. Rabbi Dushinsky urged the Kenessio to establish a Shemitta fund to alleviate the financial hardships of the farmers, and used this opportunity to publicly thank the Chazon Ish of Bnei Brak for providing halachic guidance to all the Shmitta observers.

Dr. Salomon Liebe from Prague wrote an extensive article on the ongoing struggle to maintain Shechita which had been under attack from the non-Jewish population of Europe for many years, and the hipocrisy of those who campaign against 'Cruelty to Animals' whilst they themselves continue to enjoy deer and fox hunting and fishing. This topic was widely debated at the 2nd Kenessio some 8 years previously, but new independent scientific research had recently been published and was made available to provide extra help in the future.

The Chinuch debate was opened on Thursday August 19 by Rabbi Dovid of Sochatchov and was followed by a fiery speech by Rabbi Zalman Sorotzkin, who reminded the Kenessio delegates that only by establishing genuine Torah Chinuch Institutions can we guarantee the future of the Jewish Nation. He bemoaned the drastic fall in Jewish educational standards that was prominent in the 'liberal' schools, and related that he had recently inspected a 'text book' that was widely used in one of these schools. This was a Siddur, but was shocked to observe that it only contained one Brocho in the entire Siddur, and that was the one made before lighting the Menorah on Chanuka. But even this single Brocho was an abridged version of the standard text! Rabbi Zalman Sorotzkin later successfully headed the Vaad HaYeshivahs and 'Chinuch Atzmai', the independent Orthodox school system in Eretz Yisroel.

Other notable speakers on the topic of 'Torah Chinuch' included Rabbi I.M. Lewin (Warsaw) and Rabbi Avrohom Yaakov Friedman (Sadigur). Rabbi Hager stressed the importance of not ignoring 'adult education' as they too needed to continue their commitment to Torah learning. Rabbi Silver (America) requested help in establishing Torah Chinuch on the American Continent, and was appointed chairman of the American Committee for Keren Hatorah, whilst Rabbi Yosef Shloime Kahaneman (Ponevez) demanded that the Torah in Eretz Yisroel be made accessible to all types of Jews.

Rabbi Wolf S. Jacobson (Copenhagen) gave a very detailed report of the achievements of the Beth Yaakov Movement, and praised the success that has been achieved by the recent publication of the 'Beth Yaakov Journal', which was aimed at promoting authentic Yiddishkeit amongst the masses. He reported on his personal visits to the recently established Teachers Training Programs in Cracow and the vocational training schools in various cities throughout Europe, set up by the Beth Yaakov Movement. A 300 page detailed booklet on Beth Yaakov Movement was published. He then mentioned the importance of providing greater and regular financial support to the Chadorim and Yeshivahs, and emphasised the dire need to train suitable teachers and Rebbes who would instruct the younger generation. Young and capable men should be encouraged to train for Shechita, Bris Milo and Rabbonus, with the intention of taking up employment in outlying towns and cities. He asked that financial grants should be offered to encourage these different apprenticeships.

Regarding the proposal to establish Beth Yaakov Seminaries in Eretz Yisroel, it was suggested that Israeli girls should initially attend the presently well established seminaries in Europe, and after graduating, return to Eretz Yisroel where they woud be in a position to teach and train further students.

On Friday morning the Kursaal was packed to capacity as Reb Elchonon Wasserman was scheduled to present the Torah viewpoint towards Eretz Yisroel under the current conditions. He said, "We are fully aware that the British Government will not relent on their recommendations of the Peel Commission, and we are also fully aware that the Jewish People will receive only a small section of the Palestine that was originally offered under the Balfour Declaration, and far less than the official borders stipulated in the Torah. We are powerless and cannot change this. As these borders do not conform to those stated in the Holy Torah, there is no way that the Moetzes Gedolei Hatorah can accept the recommendations of the Peel Commission. Furthermore, the proposed division of the Holy City of Yerushalayim was rejected outright." Rabbi Wasserman made a very powerful statement, and compared this suggestion to the case of Shloime Hamelech, who had to judge between two mothers and their babies, one of which was alive and one had died, where both mothers claimed the live child as their own. Shloime Hamelech in his great wisdom ruled that the live baby should be cut in two and then divided between the two mothers. The true mother of this baby screamed and protested, thereby proving her claim to the live baby. Similarly, Rabbi Wasserman reasoned that as far as we, the Orthodox Jewish People, are concerend, Yerushalayim has always remained 'alive' throughout the generations, even when in exile. Those who suggest partitioning it only prove that they have no real feeling of the vitality of this Holy City. The Holy Land, however, can only remain holy if the Torah is observed therein.

Further reports were given by Rabbi Dr. Issac Breuer and Rabbi Moishe Blau (both from Yerushalayim), who stressed the importance of establishing an independent Orthodox school system, and expanding and supporting more Yeshivahs in the Holy Land.

A special session was held to discuss the necessity of providing a social network for the Jewish youth, as a result of which Rabbi Hirschhorn (Jaworzne) was appointed chairman of Zeirei Agudas Yisroel. This session was enhanced by the presence of Reb Elchonon Wasserman, who also spoke and encouraged them to provide 'club facilities', where Jewish boys could socialize together, and be entertained in a true Torah environment.

The Gedolim at the Knessio expressed the great need for Agudas Yisroel to establish an independent framework, which must not join forces with the Mizrachi or the Sochnut on any matter.

The program for Sunday was eagerly awaited by all the delegates and the hall was full to capacity. The Gedolim are about to meet and formulate their response to the proposals set out in the Peel Commission. The European political situation was very tense, and Orthodox Yidden had for the past twenty years voiced a whole spectrum of different opinions as to how to respond to the British proposals on the establishment of 'The Jewish State in Palestine'.

There were some Gedolim who insisted that we should only accept Eretz Yisroel if it becomes a Land that is governed solely by Torah Law, and if that was not attainable, then we should abandon the idea until Moshiach arrives. On the other side of the spectrum, the Zionists were interested in having their own homeland, where they would be able to create 'a nation like all other nations' and any spiritual element was of little importance. Then there were the Mizrachi, a group of religious Zionists, who sought a Zionistic state with some religious tolerance. And even amongst the Aguda party there were those who favoured the first opinion, of either a complete Torah state or none at all, whilst others preferred to work from within and try and improve the religious situation. A further question arose, as to how the Orthodox Yidden should respond to the Balfour Declaration and the Peel Report. Even though they wanted the establishment of a Torah State, they questioned if it was correct to show disunity between different Jewish organisations when negotiating with the secular British Government, as many felt that discord amongst different Jewish groups would create a big Chilul Hashem ח"ו. These different opinions were voiced by various Gedolim at the Sunday session of the Kenessio in 1937, and Rabbi Zirelsohn, who chaired this session, was eager to find an acceptable solution on this important matter. He turned to the Gerrer Rebbe and asked for his valuable opinion, to which the Rebbe replied in one sentence, quoting a possuk in Yoel (4:2) verbatim that provided the required guidance. He stated:

> הנה בימים ההמה ובעת ההיא אשר אשוב את-שבות יהודה וירושלם:
> וקבצתי את-כל-הגוים והורדתים אל-עמק יהושפט ונשפטתי עמם שם
> על-עמי ונחלתי ישראל אשר פזרו בגוים ואת-ארצי חלקו
>
> 'I will gather all the nations and bring them down to the valley of Yehashofot and I will contend with them there concerning My People and My possession, Israel, that they dispersed among the nations and they divided up My land.'

(This may well allude to the events that took place 10 years later, when all Nations attending the United Nations Meeting on Palestine collectively agreed to partition the Land).

Rabbi Silver was then asked to read out a letter which he had brought from Rabbi Chaim Ozer Grodzensky, providing further guidance on the topic of Palestine and the Peel Commission.

The program for Monday morning was changed at short notice. A surprise announcement informed all participants about a special reception in the Kursaal at noon, in honour of Rabbi Silver and the American delegation, who had to return to America in order to arrive home in time for Rosh Hashono. All delegates attended this reception, at which Rabbi Silver thanked everyone, and expressed how fortunate he was for the opportunity to have met personally with Reb Chaim Ozer in Vilna, and for the hours that he spent on Shabbos in the company of the Gerrer Rebbe and Reb Elchonon Wasserman. A large crowd accompanied the American delegation to the train station. Soon after Rosh Hashono various communities in America made a welcome reception for Rabbi Silver, who gave a full report of his meeting with Reb Chaim Ozer and his experiences at the Kenessio. At the same time he launched an appeal on behalf of Keren Hatorah, Vaad HaYeshivahs and Keren Hashevi'is.

Rabbi Silver with the American Delegation at the Marienbad train station

Anti-semitism in Europe was becoming a major problem. For five years numerous restrictions were imposed on Jewish merchants, barring them from suitable employment, which led to widespread poverty. In an attempt to find a solution, Dr. Maximillian Landau had been instructed by the Aguda to explore different possibilities and options to solve this acute problem. He reported to the Kenessio and suggested that new colonies should be established, and mass emigration from Europe should be made to these new settlements. This should not be viewed as a rejection of their aspirations of the fulfilment of the Balfour Declaration, and their resettling in Eretz Yisroel, to which immigration was strictly limited by the quotas imposed by the British Mandate. The desparate present situation demanded immediate action, and an alternative solution had to be found. Dr. Landau had made some very extensive research, and negotiated with many governments on the different options which included:

- A large number of people should settle in Palestine and help build up the country's infrastructure. Although this was the most favoured option, there was much opposition from the British Mandate who had imposed strict quotas, apart from the fact that all immigration certificates were controlled by the Zionist organisation, who did not favour the Orthodox immigration.

- There was an area of 6,000,000 hectares of marshland in Poland, which the Polish Government was eager to have drained and made arable. They were happy to allocate this for a Jewish colony, if they were prepared to drain the marshland themselves.

- Canada had large areas of unused land that would be suitable for this project, and negotiations were in progress with the Canadian Government.

- Mr. Landau discussed the possibility of using land in one of the South American countries, and detailed plans were discussed with the Governments of Ecuador, Peru, Venezuela, Colombia, Paraguay, Bolivia and Costa-Rica.

- Out of desperation, much thought was given to building such a colony in the African country of Angola.

- The final suggestion was the most favourable: The British Government was approached, as almost a quarter of the inhabited world belonged to the British Commonwealth, and it was hoped that somewhere within the Commonwealth a spare stretch of land would be made available.

Dr. Landau's full speech was later printed in a separate 26-page booklet, which ended with the caption: 'If you desire it, this dream will come true.' This booklet was later widely used as part of the program at the Evian Conference, which is discussed later on.

THE WOMENS CONGRESS AT THE KENESSIO

A special session was held in the Ladies hall on the recommendations of the Belgium Vaad Hapoel of Agudas Yisroel. It was officially decided to open an International Neshei Agudas Yisroel Organisation, under the leadership of Mrs. Flora Rothschild (Antwerp), who outlined the aims and ambitions of this new organisation. Rebetzen Sofer (wife of Rabbi Akiva Sofer, Pressburg) spoke eloquently and provided much practical guidance as to what the Neshei should aspire to. She suggested that the ladies form social groups and organise a variety of fund raising events, to help support other Aguda projects such as Keren Hatorah, Keren Hayishuv and the Beth Yaakov Movement, and other charitable causes. In this way the ladies will earn the great merit of helping support and uphold Torah. This, no doubt, was the catalyst that inspired Aunty Ernestine (Rebetzen Winkler) to subsequently set up the famous JODISK SYKLUB (Jewish Sewing Club) in Copenhagen.

Before the closing session of the Kenessio it was announced that the forthcoming Siyum Hashass of Day Hayomi would take place on June 27, 1938 (28th Sivan) and was to be held at the Yeshivahs Chachmei Lublin.

The final edition of the 'Die III Kenessio Gedaulo' appeared at the end of the Congress, giving a full report of all the resolutions agreed on, and all the various international committees that had been formed, with full details of all their elected members who had agreed to continue and expand with the important work that the Aguda had achieved so far, in strengthening Yiddishkeit in their different countries.

OPA'S RECOLLECTIONS FROM THE KENESSIO

Taken from interviews which he gave in Manchester

'You want me to talk about the Kenessio Gedoloh? If I started now and spoke for a week, I don't suppose I would be able to tell you everything. How does one convey what it feels like to see that huge assembly of ehrliche Yidden? How does one talk about Gedolei Yisroel like the Gerrer Rebbe and the Chortkover Rebbe, the Reishe Rov and Rabbi Meir Shapiro and....and....? I knew many of these Gedolim personally as they used to stay in our Hotel in Marienbad, and many of them also knew me by my first name. Ah, it's terrible to think that they are all gone. It really hurts. But anyway, 'Dor Dor Vedorshov' as they say; so let's get down to the job. I'll probably jump from one point to another, so you'll have to sort it out yourself.'

'MY MEMORIES OF THE 2ND KENESSIO'

I was only a young boy at the time (1929) but I was so fired up by the idea of seeing so many Gedolim together at once, that I just had to travel to Vienna from Marienbad. Agudas Yisroel at that time had already put its name on the map. Since the last Kenessio Gedoloh of 1923, which had been ridiculed as the 'Shtreimel Congress', the Keren Hatorah Chinuch system had been set up, Beis Yaakov for girls was continually growing, 'frum' newspapers were to be found everywhere, the Daf Hayomi was learnt all over, and the Keren Hayishuv was helping the religious settlers in Eretz Yisroel. Now everyone was waiting with bated breath for this new Kenessio.

Representatives at the Kenessio Gedoloh in Vienna 1923.
Rabbi Nathan Birnbaum seated middle of 2nd row

The public hall and dais of the 2nd Kenessio in Vienna 1929

Inside the 2nd Kenessio Hall in Vienna

Of course only delegates could get into the huge hall in Vienna – and there were thousands of delegates. So how was Chaim Aryeh Leitner going to get in? And to get in I was determined! I wandered around the entrance and suddenly I met Reb Godol Heilpern from England in the same predicament. Well, 'a trouble shared is a trouble halved' they say, so we discussed the matter together. We decided to go to one of the big organisers and request his help.

He had a good idea. Reb Godol was to be a press representative for the London Jewish Post and I was to represent the Prague 'Togblatt'. He got us Press passes and we went in. My impression was of a tremendous hall, packed full of 'Orthodox' Yidden with hundreds of Rabbonim at the front, and to my great delight the Press box was situated right next to the speakers' platform. One of the first speakers, who gave greetings from the nations of the world, was the Czechoslovakian Ambassador to Austria. And there I nearly got into trouble. I whispered to the Chief Press Officer sitting near me, 'what's his name?' He looked at me with some surprise. Aren't you supposed to be from the Prague 'Togblatt'? You see, Prague is the capital of Czechoslovakia and I should have known the name of our own Ambassador. I hope I didn't blush too much!

I can still remember Dr. Nathan Birnbaum, the first speaker, speaking for two hours. I can remember the arguments and discussions about how much and how little we should work together with the Zionist Jewish Agency, resulting in a demand that our efforts in rebuilding Eretz Yisroel should be independent of theirs. [Dr. Nathan Birnbaum was initially the vice president of the Zionist Movement at the same time that Theodor Hertzl was its president, but then realised the falseness of the Zionist ideology, and by 1914 developed into a strong advocate for Agudas Yisroel, and became its General Secretary in 1919. Using his prolific literary capabilities he wrote many articles promoting the Orthodox view point and the Aguda ideology. [In a period when thousands of Jews discarded their traditional allegiance to Torah, Nathan Birnbaum has been termed as the first 'Baal Teshuvah' whose reversal from Zionism to Orthodoxy had a profound ripple effect on other people too.] I can remember the Beis Yaakov Congress which took place at the same time which had expanded its influence under the leadership of that great man Dr. Schmuel (Leo) Deutschlander.

Q; Which famous Godol did you see there?

The big surprise was seeing and hearing the Godol Hador, Rabbi Chaim Ozer Grodzenski, who travelled all the way from Vilna. When he gave his Drosho, Rav Chaim Ozer could hardly be heard, so Rav Meir Shapiro repeated it word for word. Rav Shapiro was a profound speaker and the audience was spellbound by his address. Even the American non-Jewish reporter for the New York Times termed him 'the world's finest speaker'. After Rav Meir Shapiro had finished, Rav Chaim Ozer commented, 'I didn't know I was such a good speaker!'

Q; How could you describe the atmosphere?

The atmosphere was very special, it was electrifying. I will never forget the feeling. However, you must remember this was 1929, just a few weeks after the Chevron Massacres, and the situation in Eretz Yisroel was very tense, as the Arabs were going wild everywhere and people were very concerned. The delegation that arrived from Eretz Yisroel included Rabbi Moishe Blau and Rabbi Moishe Porush, but was much smaller than originally planned. Our hopes and Tefillos were for an improvement in the situation there.

Q; What was the highlight of the event?

I clearly remember the most emotional moment. Rav Meir Shapiro stood up and declared in the name of the Chofetz Chaim and the other Gedolim that they had decided to award and bestow the founder and 'engine' of Agudas Yisroel Movement, Rabbi Yaakov Rosenheim of Frankfurt, with the title 'Moreinu'. This was a huge honour for him, and the crowd clapped and applauded. But the ever-humble Rav Rosenheim would not accept it. He stood up and begged for silence, and then declared: 'According to the Aguda contract I signed with the community in Frankfurt, I am not allowed to accept any titles.' Rav Shapiro with his sharp wit did not hesitate even for a second. He answered, 'Where international issues are concerned, the sole decision lies with the Moetzes Gedolei Hatorah. Rav Rosenheim does not belong to Frankfurt alone; he belongs to the whole of Klal Yisroel. Therefore, the decision of the Gedolei Yisroel overrides any other local agreement Rav Rosenheim might have made, and he is expected to accept their decision.' All eyes were turned upon Rav Rosenheim who was contemplating how to react. Eventually he gave in. With tears in his eyes, he stood up and recited the Brocho of שהחינו out loud!

בעזרת י׳ברך שמו

בהתאסף ראשי עם יחד שבטי ישראל בימי
אלול תרפ"ט בעיר וינא אל הכנסיה הגדולה
השניה של אגדת ישראל החליטה מועצת גדולי
התורה בהסכמתם של צירי הכנסיה הגדולה לכבד
את אחד מחולליה ומנהיגיה של אגדת ישראל
העולמית איש חי ורב פעלים גדול התורה
והמדע לוחם מלחמות ה' בעוז

מו"ה יעקב ראזענהיים שליט"א

מפראנקפורט דמיין
בתואר מורנו הה"ב
השי"ת יאריך ימיו ושנותיו ויחדש כחותיו בעבודתו
עבודת הקודש מתוך נחת רוח ושלות הגוף עדי
שנזכה לביאת גואלנו הצדק אמן!
אבע"ה בשם מועצת גדולי התורה

בשם הכנסי׳ הגדולה השני׳

ער היסטארישער דאקומענט פון טיטול מורנו, וואס ר׳ יעקב ראזענהיים ז"ל האט באקו
ביי דער צווייטער כנסי׳ גדולה אין ווין, אין יאר תרפ"ט.

The ' Moreinu' Certificate signed by the Chofetz Chaim, Reb Chaim Ozer Grodzenski, Imrei Emes of Ger, Reb Yisroel Chortkover, and Rabbi Meir Shapiro

Rabbi Meir Shapiro

Rabbi Yaakov Rosenheim

Q; What were your feelings when you came away from this special gathering?

The end of the ceremony was very special. Rav Meir Shapiro made a Siyum on Messechta Zevochim. Daf Hayomi had been established six years earlier by Rav Shapiro himself at the first Kenessio Gedoloh, and now they had just finished Zevochim, where Rav Shapiro spoke very movingly. These were his words, "We have just finished learning about Korbonos and we hope we have finished sacrificing our own Korbonos, and pray that the murdered Talmidim of Yeshivahs Chevron הי"ד be the last of our Korbonos. Now we start learning Menochos and we pray that we will have 'tranquility from all our troubles". He cried as he spoke, and there was not a dry eye in the hall. Following the Siyum, the crowd burst into a lively dance lasting well into the night. I have carried these memories with me for many decades.

But let us get down to the third Kenessio. That is something I really do know something about. You see, I was the organising secretary! But first I must describe Marienbad.

Ah! Marienbad! It brings back so many memories. It is a small health resort in Czechoslovakia, near the German border, surrounded by forests, mountains and streams. For most of the year a quiet town with only about 15 frum Yiddishe families, and then – the season! All the hotels were packed out, private rooms taken, the whole town changed. All the Gedolei Yisroel came there, The Lubliner Rov, Reb Meir Shapiro, who occupied a large room with a balcony in our hotel. Rabbi Elchonon Wasserman regularly had a small room in the house of a widow, which was cheaper and less luxurious than staying at the hotel, and it therefore suited Reb Elchonon better. During 1937, the year of the Kenessio, room prices were at a premium, and Reb Elchonon intended to return home to Baranovich, as the rent was too high, until I intervened and arranged for the Aguda to settle the difference. Other esteemed visitors included the Pressburger Rov, Rabbi Akiva Sofer. People used to stroll through the streets hoping to simply catch a glimpse of a Godol!

I remember in the summer of 1936: a few leaders of Agudas Yisroel with Moreino Yaakov Rosenheim at their head, were sitting on the veranda of the Leitner Hotel discussing a possible Kenessio Gedoloh. When they had finished their deliberations, Reb Yaakov Rosenheim stood up and formally thanked the Leitners for the use of their veranda, and said that they had finally fixed the Kenessio Gedoloh for the following year, and that it would be held in Marienbad, if Palestine had not been returned to the Jewish people.

You can imagine how excited we were. Here in our own town a Kenessio Gedoloh! All those thousands of people who would come to our town, and all those Gedolim too. I was appointed Chief Organising Secretary together with three other Agudists, one from Frankfurt, one from Vienna and one from New York. So you can see how international the Aguda had become by then.

Our first job was to meet the local town council to arrange for halls and sufficient accommodation. They gave us the Town Hall free of charge for the Kenessio, and also a restaurant in the forest for executive meetings, which also belonged to the Council. During the Kenessio that restaurant provided kosher meals. We soon had trouble with the hall, however, as the stage was too small to accommodate all the Rabbonim. There was a lot of discussion about moving the Kenessio to Carlsbad, another health resort, but the Vice Mayor of Marienbad, a Mr. Buxbaum, put his foot down. 'You've got all these great men coming here and you're going to send them away to Carlsbad? No Sir! What's the problem? The stage is too small? Enlarge the stage!' And enlarge the stage he did.

'Everyone who visited Marienbad had to pay a special tax on their hotel bill called a 'Kurtaxe', for benefiting from the good air, but all Kenessio delegates were exempted from this tax. The First Class waiting room at the train station was turned into the Aguda office so that we could be on hand to meet all the visitors. There were posters all over town in Loshon Hakodesh. The post office made a special postmark to be stamped on all stamps in Czech and Loshon Hakodesh, commemorating the Kenessio. If you had a delegation card you could get cheaper rail travel up to the Czech border. There were many stateless Jews who would have to get special visas from the Czech Foreign Ministry in Prague to enable them to come to the Kenessio, which would have taken too long, so I was given permission to tell the local Consul who should be issued with a visa, as they made a secret code so that the Consul would know that it really was authentic.

The great day drew near. The Gedolim, the Rabbonim, the Roshei Yeshivahs and the Great Rebbes started to arrive. Hundreds of delegates and thousands of interested viewers had crowded into our little town.

It was 10 Ellul 5697 (1937), the hall was packed. We all stood in expectation of the entry of the Rabbonim. Then in a hushed silence, Moreinu Yaakov Rosenheim enters, followed by the Gerrer Rebbe, the Tchortkover Rebbe, the Kishinev Rov, who chaired the Kenessio, the Reisher Rov, Reb Elchonon Wasserman, Reb Aaron Kotler, and so many others. You must not forget that behind the happy atmosphere at the Kenessio there was a dark shadow of fear. The Nazi Reshoim in Germany were growing stronger and stronger, spreading their unclean tentacles in all directions. Anti-Semitism was growing daily in many European countries and delegates were terribly concerned about the future. A great cloud of worry hovered over all the proceedings.

Reb Elchonon Wasserman stood up to say Tehillim. But he was too choked up with emotion to be able to speak. The Nitra Rov stepped forward and with a clear but very moving voice began 'Kapitel Yud in Tehillim'. – 'למה ה' תעמד ברחוק'– I am telling you, the walls cried! I can still hear his voice in my ears. What a beginning that was!

Then Rav Yaakov Rosenheim called on the Ponevezher Rov to introduce the first speaker, Rabbi Yitzchak Breuer. The introduction took two hours! But he was a marvellous speaker!

And so the week carried on, meeting after meeting, speech after speech, resolution after resolution; and all with an overpowering feeling of working for a Tachlis. The final 'Rekida', was extremely moving, with Rabbi Moishe Blau from Eretz Yisroel, carried in the air at one end of the hall, and Rav Yitzchak Breuer at the other end. Ah! Those memories! All I can say to finish off with this: if you are going to the Kenessio I wish you as many happy memories for as many years as I have in my mind. Kol Tuv.

K. Leitner, Manchester, December 1979.

Even before the Second Kenessio Gedoloh and more so afterwards, it was obvious that Agudas Yisroel would dedicate a major portion of its efforts to establish a firm Chinuch network. The creation of the Keren Hatorah was a major factor in the rebuilding of the great Yeshivahs which had been displaced, and in some cases destroyed during World War I. Keren Hatorah organised a huge rescue campaign for these Yeshivahs, and more significantly the work of building and maintaining Yeshivah Ketanos.

Rabbi Yaakov Ettlinger (1798-1871) pioneered the medium of journalism and the power of his pen, to teach his generation the eternity of Torah values, by publishing a bi-weekly Torah journal that appeared in both German and Hebrew, and called it "Shomer Tzion Hane'eman." Witnessing the success of this publication, the Rabbonim placed much emphasis on the publications of Jewish newspapers and magazines, which waged an unrelenting campaign for the integrity of Torah and Yiddishkeit. In 1922, the Yiddisher Togblat, (a daily paper), the Israelit and Darkeinu appeared, and were followed by many others in different countries.

77 Jahrgang
Der Israelit
Frankfurt a. M.
Nummer 31
Trost im „Namen G'ttes"
Der Kenessio Mechino
in Marienbad zum Gruß!

JÜDISCHE PRESSE
ב"ה
WIEN-BRATISLAVA • 7. August 1936
22. Jahrgang / Nummer 29
ORGAN FÜR DIE INTERESSEN DES ORTHODOXEN JUDENTUMS
Die Kenessio Mechino in Marienbad

The Israelit, Jüdische Presse and other Aguda Orthodox Newspapers

In May 2013 I met a Mr. Fleischman, originally from Pressburg, who was present at the Kenessio in Marienbad. He remembered going to the woods with some friends when they met Reb Elchonon Wasserman, who observed them just chatting together. He approached them and asked if they wanted to learn a little. They then sat down on a bench, and Reb Elchonon took a מסילת ישרים from his pocket and taught them a complete chapter.

Mr Fleischman never forgot his encounter with one of the pre-war Gedolim.

Rabbi Pardes of Chicago, editor of the Jewish monthly 'Hapardes', was present at the Kenessio and took part in several of its sessions, and reported about Reb Elchonon Wasserman:

'He was distinguished, his slow walk, his head turned downwards... His long beard had turned white...Fear of Heaven preceding his wisdom; he was the centre of attention within the Moetzes Gedolei Hatorah. He spiced his remarks with simple analogies replete with moral lessons which captivated each and everyone on his own level. An outstanding disciple of the Chofetz Chaim, he delivered his remarks with his Rebbe's sagacious similes.'

Reb Chaim Ozer had requested that all delegates to the Kenessio should fast until midday on the opening day of the Kenessio.

Rabbi Pardes describes the opening session:

'The opening session began with the public recitation of Tehillim. This was lead by the Nitra Rov, Rabbi Shmuel Dovid Ungar, with the Rov of Kishinev, Rabbi Yehuda Leib Zirelsohn and Rabbi Elchonon standing on either side of him. The Nitra Rov began, and when he reached the Possuk: עד-אנה י' תשכחני נצח עד-אנה תסתיר את-פניך ממני (תהלים פרק יג ב) he let out a terrible cry and the whole hall wept with him.... The Rav stopped. He was totally choked up and could not continue for several minutes.' This is how the Kenessio began.

2nd Kenessio Vienna – view of front rows of delegates inside the hall

Rabbi Dr. Michoel Sholom Winkler (see 1.1.6)

Menashe Winkler (1.1.6.1) attended the Kenessio together with his mother, Rebetzen Winkler (nee Leitner) and brother, as representatives from Copenhagen, Denmark. He relates the following:

'I was born in Copenhagen in 1919. My father, Rabbi Dr. Michoel Sholom Winkler, was born in Yerushalayim in 1863 and learnt by Rav Yosef Chaim Sonnenfeld, but the poverty in Eretz Yisroel forced him to seek a rabbinical position in Germany and ultimately in Copenhagen, where he became the Rov of the Machzikei Hadass Community in 1914. This community was founded only two years previously, and in 1912 it became officially affiliated with Agudas Yisroel.

Rav Winkler was very involved in communal work on behalf of the Jewish community and had attended the Second Kenessio in 1929, where he spoke and became a member of the Moetzes Gedolei Hatorah. Due to the great depression in Europe after World War I, there was very little money about, and Rav Winkler was sent to America in 1932 to collect funds for Keren Hatorah, a fund that the Aguda had set up to help the Torah students and Yeshivahs. Tragically he died in New York in 1932, and consequently I became an orphan at the age of 13.

When I (Menashe) was approximately 14 years old, a representative from Radin came to Copenhagen to collect funds for the Yeshivah. His name was Rav Yitzchak Grozalsky, an excellent speaker and truly passionate about Yiddishkeit. Owing to the high standard of Kashrus at the Winkler home, he ate all his meals with us. He convinced my mother that she should send me to Radin to the Yeshivah of the Chofetz Chaim, and promised to take full care of my needs. My mother's piety was so great that despite my young age, and the fact that she'd been widowed only recently, she agreed to send me to devote myself to Torah learning. However, she employed my Melamed from Copenhagen, Rav Nosson Tzvi Knoepfelmacher, to accompany me to Radin. We travelled by boat across the Baltic Sea until the Polish port of Gdansk, and from there we continued by train until the Polish city of Lida, and then by bus to Radin. I learned in Yeshivah from 1933-1939.

The truth is that my mother (Ernestine Leitner [1.1.6]) was the matriarch of the entire community and accomplished much on behalf of Chinuch in Copenhagen. Later she also sent my younger brother, Efraim (1.1.6.2) to Yeshivah, and convinced several other boys from the community to travel to the Yeshivahs in Eastern Europe.

Rebetzen Winkler was invited by her brother, Moishe Dovid Leitner (1.1.1), to come to the 3rd Kenessio. My mother and younger brother travelled together from Copenhagen, a distance of some 800 km whilst I joined them in Marienbad from theYeshivah.

I was privileged to speak at the 3rd Kenessio, although I was only 18 years old at the time, as I had been learning in Kamenitz Yeshivah, and when Reb Boruch Ber Leibovitz heard that I was travelling to Marienbad, he dictated a message to me that included his strong opinion about the 'Partition Plan' for Palestine' which I was asked to read out. Reb Boruch Ber was above politics, but he considered support of Agudas Yisroel and its projects an obligation that was also above politics. He often repeated what he had heard from his Rebbi, Reb Chaim Soloveitchik, that Moreinu Yaakov Rosenheim, the chairman of the Aguda, was working entirely for the sake of Heaven. 'The situation would be impossible without Agudas Yisroel, as the Maskilim would otherwise dominate everything.'

During our stay in Marienbad, Rabbi Elchonon Wasserman was discussing an issue with Rabbi Moishe Blau, when a young boy approached them, soliciting Tzedoko funds for 'Keren Kayemet' (a Zionist cause). Rabbi Wasserman refused to give to this cause, but Rabbi Blau took a few coins out of his pocket and put it into the 'pushka' (box). Rabbi Wasserman was surprised and queried this action, to which Rabbi Blau merely replied, 'I am not supporting the Zionists at all; I am teaching this young boy how to give 'Tzedoko'!

I got married in Copenhagen and we had ב"ה four sons and one daughter. They attended the local non-Jewish school there, whilst I worked as a fully qualified accountant. Owing to the difficulties in the public school, my brother-in-law persuaded us to move to New York, where our children could attend good Jewish schools. I, however, had to retrain and study from scratch for my accountancy exams, but it was worth the Mesiras Nefesh for the sake of the Chinuch of our children.

Rebetzen Winkler continued to run the Machzikei Hadass Community in Copenhagen and although her official title was Frau Dr. Rabbiner Winkler, leading the community with wisdom and integrity, and displayed so much care for every individual, that everyone simply called her 'Mutty' - our mother. She formed the 'JODISK SYKLUB', a club for ladies who met once a week. While they were busy with all sorts of needlework, Aunty Ernestine spoke about Emunoh and subjects of general Jewish interest, thus ensuring that the time was well spent and no idle chatter was spoken. All the many handcrafted items created at these social gatherings were prominently displayed at the annual Bazaar, and together with a Chinese Auction, raised a substantial amount of money for the Orthodox communities in Eretz Yisroel. This Bazaar was a well publicized event, which even the Queen of Denmark attended.

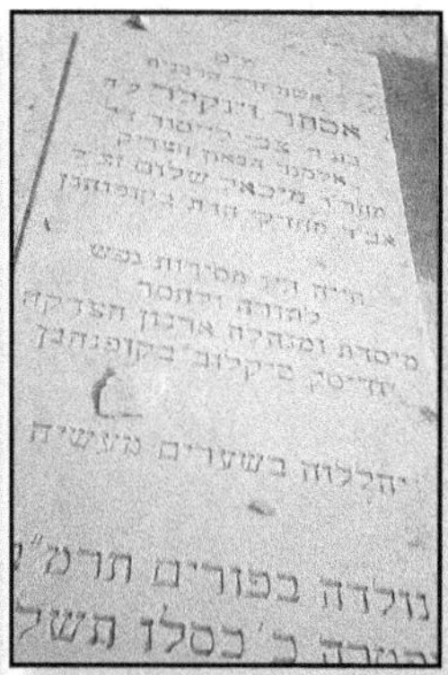

Rabbi Dr. מיכאל שלום Winkler - his Matzeivo in New York. ---
and his wife (Aunty Ernestine, (Esther Winkler) buried on Har Hazeizim

One year the money was allocated to pay for a new classroom in Sdei Chemed, the children's village near Rishon LeZion, set up by Agudas Yisroel. This was in the early 1950s, but there was a shortage of building material in Eretz Yisroel. Rebetzen Winkler arranged to have a complete pre-fabricated building shipped over from Denmark, which is still being used today. A plaque above its entrance makes appropriate mention of this noble deed.

The special affection that the community had for Mutty manifested itself in 1935, when she was suggested as a suitable match for none other than the Torah Leader, Reb Elchonon Wasserman, after the loss of his first wife. Although 'Mutty' seriously considered this suggestion, she eventually declared, 'a mother cannot abandon her children, my place is to remain in Copenhagen', and so Mutty remained the matriarch of the Kehilla for the remainder of her life.

Aunty Ernestine wrote numerous letters, many of them to members of the family, before, during and after the war. Above all, she made it her job to regularly send money and food parcels to numerous people in need. For example, her brother, Isidor Leitner, thanked her on June

18, 1936 for the money she had enclosed in her previous letter, which enabled them to pay for their Pesach expenses!

Uncle Alex Kokisch (2.1.2) received a monthly food parcel from her which was posted to Vienna, for seven years.

In April 1939, Sima Kokisch (1.1.4) wrote to her sister, Aunty Ernestine in Copenhagen, confirming that they had arrived safely in Santiago in Chile, were ב"ה very well looked after, and had managed to celebrate Pesach with a special feeling of freedom this year. Aunty Ernestine replied on May 3, 1939, thanking her for the excellent news, and also emphasizing how they must have felt this Pesach, after having experienced their own 'Crossing of the Sea' [Krias Yam Suf] by having been transported across the oceans of the world to reach their freedom on dry land.

When Aunty Ernerstine was niftar, Opa telephoned her son Efraim (1.1.6.2), and enquired about the funeral arrangements. He was told that they were taking her for burial to Eretz Yisroel, and Opa offered to contribute towards these astronomical costs. Funeral costs are high and transfers to Eretz Yisroel are very high. Efraim Winkler was very touched by Opa's generous and spontaneous offer, which he did not want to accept, and replied, 'thank you very much, but this is my mitzvah, and I would like to honour my mother myself.'

CHAPTER 4
Picture Gallery

14

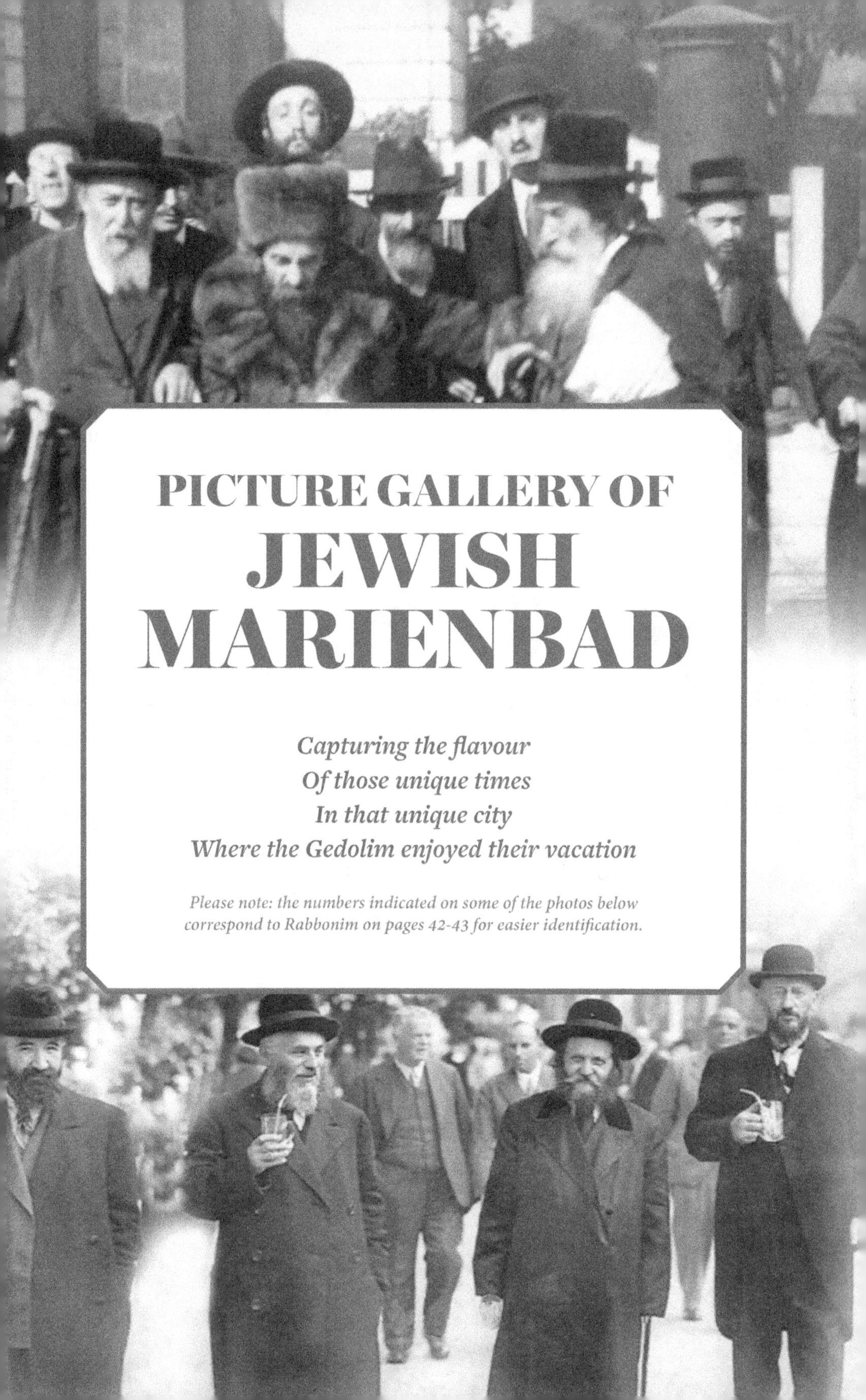

PICTURE GALLERY OF JEWISH MARIENBAD

Capturing the flavour
Of those unique times
In that unique city
Where the Gedolim enjoyed their vacation

Please note: the numbers indicated on some of the photos below correspond to Rabbonim on pages 42-43 for easier identification.

THE BELZER DYNASTY IN MARIENBAD

The Belzer Dynasty comprises of the first Rebbe, Rabbi Sholom Rokach, followed by Reb Yehoshua, then Reb Yissochor Dov Rokach, and Reb Aaron Rokach. The present Rebbe was born in Eretz Yisroel.

1. Belzer Rebbe –Reb Yissochor Dov and Moishe Dovid Leitner (1.1.1) (holding his arm) in Marienbad, with the Gabbe Reb A.Y. Landau on the left and the Rebbe's son, Reb Sholom, in the backround 1915

2262	Herr **Schönfeld** David, Privatier mit Gattin [illegible]			
2263	Herr **Kleinmann** Moritz, Kaufmann mit Gattin Ida	»	Florida	2
2264	Herr **Rokach** Sucher Ber, Grossrabbiner m. Gattin, Familie und Dienerschaft	Belz	Leitners Haus	22
2265	Herr **Rottenberg** Jakob, Rabbiner mit Diener . .	Kozowa	»	2
2266	Frau **Scherzer** Lea, Kaufmannsgattin mit Familie	Stanislau	Goldenes Schloß	3

City Register of Guests: Reb Yissochor Dov of Belz with 22 members of his household and attendants staying at Leitner Haus 1920

1.Reb Yissochor Dov of Belz with his Gabbe Reb A.Y. Landau on the left 1920

L. to R. Reb Mechele Lukman, Reb Yossel Gold (Jarotschever), 1. Belzer Rebbe, household member, Rav Uri Lukman, Marienbad 191

Reb Yissochor Dov of Belz. July 8, 1916 Marienbad

Rav Zev Babad, Rav Simcha Dinter, 1. Belzer Rebbe, Reb Yossel Gold (Jarotschever) holding glass, Marienbad 1916

L. to R. Reb Mechele Lukman, 1.The Belzer Rebbe, Reb Yissochor Dov, Reb Yossel Gold (Jarotschever), Reb Mordechai (Bulgorajer Rebbe), Reb Mendel Landman, Reb Yaakov of Rava. Marienbad 1915

1.Belzer Rebbe on the way to Hotel National 1920
L. to. R. Rav S. W. Waldman, (unknown), Reb Mendel Landman, 1. Belzer Rebbe, Reb S. Eichenstein, Reb Yossel Gold (Jarotschever) holding glass, Rav Uri Lukman

1. The Belzer Rebbe with Isidor Leitner (1.1.7.) to his right, Reb Yossel Gold (Jarotschever) holding stick, Rav Uri Lukman (far right), 1920

1. Belzer Rebbe accompanied by Rabbi Michoel Lukman, Rav Uri Lukman, Y. Friedman, Marienbad 1921

12. Reb Yochonon Twersky, Reb A.Y. Landau, 2. Reb Aaron of Belz

2. Reb Aaron of Belz, Marienbad 1929

L. to R. Reb Yossel Jarotschever, Rav A.Y. Landau,
2. Belzer Rebbe, Rav Mendel Landman,

Rabbi Yossel Gold (Yarotschever), 2. Rabbi Aaron Rokach, Rav Aaron Yehoshua Landau, Marienbad 1931

L. to R: Rabbi Twersky, Rav Shmuel Frenkel, Gabbe Rav Landau – 2. Belzer Rebbe (Reb Aaron) – Moishe Dovid Leitner (1.1.1) and Uncle Fritz (Shlomo Leitner) (1.1.1.2) behind. At Marienbad train station 1929

2.Reb Aaron of Belz and Reb Yossel Gold (Yarotschever) leaving Hotel National 1931

L. to R. Rav Sinai Singer, Reb Berel Karniol, Rabbi Aaron Yehoshua Landau, 2.Belzer Rebbe, Moishe Dovid Leitner (1.1.1) and Kurt Leitner (1.1.1.3) (in bowler hat) Reb Mendel Landman, Reb Yitzchok Friedman, Rabbi Twersky. Circa 1933

L. to R. Rav Sinai Singer, Rav Twersky, Reb Mendel Landman, 2. Belzer Rebbe, Reb Berel Karniol, Reb Yitzchok Friedman, Reb Yossel Gold (Yarotschever)

Insert: Opa standing behind.

A second (clearer) photo with Opa (1.1.1.3) standing behind Reb Aaron of Belz in Marienbad woods.

2. Belzer Rebbe leaving Marienbad 1931 with Opa (1.1.1.3) next to him, travelling to the next station

Departure from Marienbad Station 1932

L. to R. Rav Aaron Lewin (Reisha), Rav Sinai Halberstam, Rav Alter Hurwitz (Dzikov), Rav Yehoshua Rokach, Rav of Jaroslav walking together in Marienbad

THE GERRER REBBE
IMREI EMES

Rabbi Mordechai Avrohom Alter, leader of Polish Jewry and active leader of Agudas Yisroel and was a frequent visitor to Marienbad.

Gerrer Rebbe (Imrei Emes) with Beis Yisroel next to him, arriving at Marienbad train station with Opa (1.1.1.3) behind him 1932

The Gerrer Rebbe (Imrei Emes) with the Beis Yisroel and Chassidim in Marienbad

A popular postcard of the Imrei Emes in Marienbad

The Imrei Emes with his son the Beis Yisroel in Marienbad, walking in the woods

Imrei Emes on Klicova Street, Marienbad on the way to the hotel.

L. to R. Rav Kanel (from Blashki), Reb Meir Rosenfeld, Beis Yisroel, Imrei Emes, Reb M.S. Segal, Reb Meir Alter, Lev Simcha, Reb Dovid Perle, Reb Chanoch Gad, Rav Shimon Shalsbersky, Reb Meir Varshaviak

L. to R. Rav B. Levin, Imrei Emes, Rav Sheldovsky, Reb Meir Alter, Lev Simcha, Reb Naftoli Alter, Reb Yoskovitz,

Gerrer Rebbe (Imrei Emes) with Beis Yisroel and Chassidim in Marienbad

Beis Yisroel, Imrei Emes and Reb Meir Alter

Imrei Emes

L. to R. Reb Itzi Yoskovitz, Reb Meir Yoskovitz, Beis Yisroel, Imrei Emes, Reb Meir Alter, Lev Simcha

The Gerrer Rebbe (Imrei Emes) with Beis Yisroel and Chassidim in Marienbad

L. to R. Beis Yisroel, the Imrei Emes, Reb Meir Alter 1935 Marienbad

Imrei Emes on the way to Kenessio 1937

Imrei Emes arriving at the Kenessio session sitting in carriage at the centre; a popular postcard in Marienbad

The Gerrer Rebbe (Imrei Emes) with Chassidim outside Hotel Goldenes Schloss

L. to R. (unknown), Rav Meir Alter (oldest son of Imrei Emes), Pnei Menachem, Reb Tovia Rosenwasser, Imrei Emes

The Gerrer Rebbe (Imrei Emes) with Chassidim outside Goldenes Schloss Hotel on Klicova Street 1930

The Imrei Emes outside the Goldenes Schloss

Imrei Emes departing from Marienbad 1935 with Bendiner Rov looking on

THE VISHNITZER REBBE (AHAVAS YISROEL) IN MARIENBAD

4. Ahavas Yisroel of Vishnitz with Kopishnitzer Rebbe outside Leitner Hotel, Marienbad

4. Vishnitzer Rebbe (Ahavas Yisroel), 1933

1930. 4. 3rd from Left Vishnitzer Rebbe (Ahavas Yisroel)
11.Rabbi Horowitz (Tarnopozek)

4. The Vishnitzer Rebbe [Ahavas Yisroel] leaving Hotel National with Rabbi Y.M. Heshel {Kopishnitzer Rebbe] to his left, Rabbi Simcha Frankel-Teumim, Rov of Skovin. Opa (1.1.1.3) second from right wearing a dark suit

Kopishnitzer Rabbi Heshel with 4. Vishnitzer Rabbi Hager, Marienbad station

4. Vishnitzer Rebbe [Ahavas Yisroel] leaving Hotel National with Opa (1.1.1.3) to the right in light grey suit

L. to R. Rabbi Simcha Frankel-Teumim Rov of Skovin, 4.Ahavas Yisroel, 2nd Kopishnitzer Rabbi YM Heshel, outside Hotel National 1934

L. to R. unknown, Opa (1.1.1.3), unknown, 4. Ahavas Yisroel, Kopishnitzer Rabbi Heshel arriving at Marienbad station

Second from the left is the 4. Vizhnitzer Rebbe, The Ahavas Yisroel. The Rebbe in the middle is Reb Alter Dzikover, his son-in-law. Next to him is the 'Damesek Elieser' Reb Lazer'el Vizhnitzer walking in Marienbad

Leaving Marienbad

SOME OTHER GEDOLIM WHO VISITED MARIENBAD

Rabbi Lewin (Reisha Rov) on the way to the Kenessio

Munkatcher Rebbe

Rabbi Meir Shapiro and Rabbi Chaim Elozor Spira [Munkatch] Marienbad 1923

4. Ahavas Yisroel with his son 39. R Chaim Meir departing Marienbad 2nd left 5. Rabbi Yisroel Friedman

The Munkatcher Rebbe (Rabbi Chaim Elozor Spira) walking along the Marienbad Collonade

Rabbi Josef Sholom M. Friedmann, with Rabbi AvrohomYaakov Friedmann / Sadigur with Rabbi Nachum Liberson from Jassy

3rd from left Rabbi Menachem Ziemba walks along Collonade

Rabbi Yosef Sholom Mordechai Friedman (Sadigur)

Sadigur Rebbe with his Uncle Reb Avrohom Yaakov (Avi Yaakov) seated on his far left

Friedmann Schulem, Rabbiner	Przemysl (Pol.)	Hotel National

The Rebbe stayed in Hotel National during the 3rd Kenessio

Rabbi Nachum Mordechai Friedman, 3rd Rebbe of Chortkov

L. to R. Rabbi Zalman Sorotzkin with Rabbi Lewin (Reisha Rov)

The Sadigurer Rebbe [Rav Y.S. Mordechai Friedman] in conversation with Imrei Chaim of Vishnitz

10. The Bluzhever Rebbe, Tzi Elimelech Spira (Tzvi LaTzadik) in Marienbad 1930

Centre: Rav Meir Frei of Shuran in Marienbad

25.Alexander Rebbe (Rabbi Danziger) with Opa in the backround

Rabbi Yitzchok Breuer (far right) arriving at the Kenessio 1937

3nd from Left Rav Yoel Teitelbaum, (Rav of Orshiva and later Satmar Rebbe)

Greeting Rabbi Yosef Tzvi Dushinsky, Jerusalem, on his arrival in Marienbad for the Kenessio.

Rav Yosef Tzvi Dushinsky with his son (carrying the walking stick) – Became Head of Eida Chareidis in 1932 in Jerusalem. Seen walking in Marienbad 1937

L. to R. son of Rav Dushinsky, Mr. Blier; Rav Yehoshua Buxbaum (Galanter Rov), Rabbi Yosef Tzvi Dushinsky

Third from left: Rabbi Josef Nechemia Kornitzer (Crakow)

25. Alexander Rebbe, Rav Yitzchok Menachem Danziger in Marienbad

L. to R. 4th Boyaner Rebbe of Cracow, next to Strikover Rebbe

Reb Avrohom Steiner of Kerestir [center] (son of Reb Shayele) in Marienbad 1925

L. to R. 2nd Radzyminer Rebbe, Reb Aaron Mendel next to 24. Reb Yaakov Moishe of Komarna 1930

L. to R. 2nd R Shimon Frankel -Teumim Rov of Skovin 1920

3rd from left;26. Reb Shayele Halberstam of Tchechov with his son Yechezkel Shraga Halberstam (son-in-law) of Reb Ben Zion of Bobov 2nd from left

L. to R. Reb Yisroel Friedman (Tchortkov), Reb Y. Horowitz (Dzikov) with his son Reb Alter Yechezkel

Reb Elchonon in conversation

OR SIMPLY RELAXING

Travelling in style 21st century -
Sadigurer Rebbe in Marienbad for Rabbinic Reunion, 2000

PORTRAIT GALLERY OF JEWISH MARIENBAD

18. Rabbi Dr. Altman

45. Rabbi Dr. Auerbach (Halberstadt)

Rabbi Reuben Zelig Bengiz (Lithuania)

31. Rabbi Shlomo Breuer

Rabbi Yosef Breuer

Rabbi Refoel Breuer

Rabbi Moishe Blau

Dr. Nathan Birnbaum

33. Boyaner Rebbe (Leipzig)

Rabbi A. Yitzchok Bloch (Telse)

Rabbi Eliyohu Meir Bloch

Rabbi Y. Buxbaum (Galant)

Rabbi Dovid Bornstein (Sockachov)

Rabbi Yosef Zvi Carlebach (Hamburg)

6. Rav Carlebach (Luebeck)

Rabbi Moishe Deutscher

Rabbi Dr. Schmuel (Leo) Deutschlander

Rabbi Dubin (Riga)

Rabbi C.Y.Eis (Zurich)

Dr. Shloime Ehrmann, (Vienna)

Rabbi Chanoch Ehrentreu (Munich)

Rabbi Alexander Zusha Friedman

Rabbi Mordechai S. Y. Friedman (Sadigur)

Rabbi Avrohom Y. Friedman

14. Rabbi Yisroel Friedman (Czortkow)

5.Rav Y.Friedman (Husyatin)

Rabbi Eliezer Friedensohn

5 Rabbi S. Fuerst (Vienna)

Rabbi Tzvi Hershel Gottesman

Rabbi Eliezer Gordon (Telsh)

Chief Rabbi Hertz (London)

37. Rabbi Yonason Horowitz

Rabbi Yacov Horowitz

Rabbi Shimon Tzvi Hurwitz

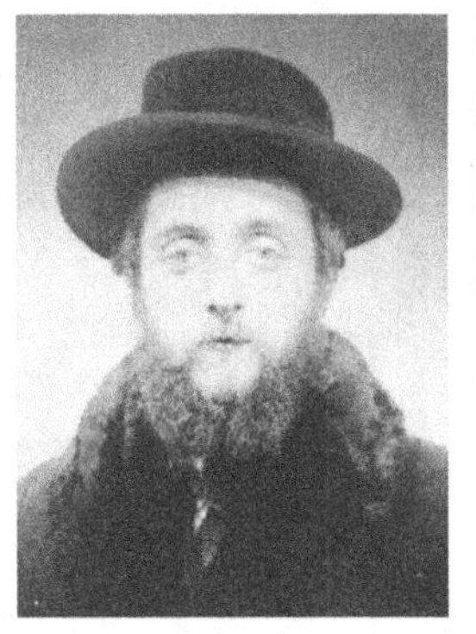

Rabbi Tuvia Horowitz (Sanok)

Rabbi Moisheinu Friedman (Boyaner)

Rabbi Chaim Shaul Karelitz

Rabbi Meir Karelitz

Rabbi Avrohom Kleinhof (Nuerenberg)

Rabbi Yosef Shloime Kahaneman (Ponevez)

Rabbi Avrohom Kalmanowitz

21. Rav Shimon Kalish (Amshinov)

Rabbi Reuben Katz (Chust)

Rabbi Dr. P. Kohn (Ansbach)

15. Rabbi Yosef Nechemia Kornitzer

Rabbi Aaron Kotler

Rabbi Mordechai Langer

Rabbi Moishe Chaim Lau (Pietrokova)

Rav Aaron Levin (Reige)

Rabbi I.M. Lewin

Rabbi Zalman Dovid Levontin

43. *Rabbi Lichtig (Hamburg)*

Rav Aaron Lewin

Rabbi Tuvia Lewenstein (Zurich)

Rabbi Yitzchok Gedalia Liberson

Rabbi Margulies (Premishlan)

50. *Rabbi Dr. Meyer - (Regensburg)*

Rabbi Leib Mintzberg

Rabbi Jacob Meier (Palestine)

Rabbi E Munk (Paris)

Rabbi Eli Munk (Berlin)

Rabbi Yehuda Leib Orleans (Cracow)

Rabbi W. Pappenheim

Rabbi Z.Portugal (Skulen)

Rabbi Meir Don Plotzky (Kli Chemda)

Rabbi Pessach Pruskin

Rabbi Rabinowitz (Biala)

Rabbi Rubin (Sassover)

Rabbi Koppel Reich (Budapest)

Rabbi Yaakov Rosenheim

Rabbi Shimon Schreiber (Erlau)

30.Rabbi Shimon Sofer (Bratislava)

29. Rabbi Akiva Schreiber

28 Rabbi Shlomo Schreiber

13. Rabbi Shlomo Schreiber (Sofer) (Beregszac)

51. Rabbi Shimon Schreiber

32. Rabbi A.Schmuel Binyomin Schreiber

Rabbi Shimon Schwab

Rabbi Avigdor Schonfeld (London)

Rav Selig Schachnowitz

Rabbi Shimon Shkop

Rabbi Eliezer Silver (USA)

Rabbi I. Silberstein

34. Rabbi Yitzock Zev Soloveitchik (Brisk)

10.Rabbi Yisroel Spira (Blushover)

46. Rabbi Shmuel Spitzer

Rabbi Yaakov Snyders

Rabbi Taub (Modzitzer)

Rabbi Lippa Turkel

12. Rabbi Twerski (Rawa-Ruska)

35. Rav Ungar (Nitra)

Reb Elchonon Wasserman (Baranowitz)

29. Rabbi Kalman Weber

Rav M.B. Weissmandl

Rabbi Aaron Wolkin (Pinsk)

Rabbi Yehuda Leib Zirelsohn

These pictures give us a glimpse of many such scenes which were commonplace during the summer in Marienbad, where both the Chassidishe and Litvishe Gedolim of the pre-war era vacationed regularly.

1947 Kenessio postmark

In 1947, after a lapse of ten years, the Aguda leaders met in Marienbad again after the war. Everyone was keenly aware of the vast void left in the wake of World War 2; only a handful of the members who had been present at the 3rd Kenessio remained, as the majority of the Moetzes Gedolei Hatorah who had enhanced that special event… were gone. They tried as much as possible to duplicate all the arrangements from the 3rd Kenessio, and even had a special postmark to mark the occasion.

When the Telsher Rosh Yeshivah, Rav Eliyohu Meir Bloch, stood on the stage to eulogize the Kedoshim who had perished, the entire assembly became a sea of tears, and it was this mood that prevailed at this mini Kenessio. But the leadership soon set a new tone which called for renewed efforts to revive Klal Yisroel.

Rav Eliyohu Meir Bloch took out from his pocket a Nazi newspaper with a picture of the Gerrer Rebbe strolling in Marienbad, with the caption:

EUROPE WILL SEE NO MORE OF SUCH PICTURES

But the Telsher Rosh Yeshiva gave renewed hope and said:

> **'Today the enemy lies destroyed, and we, the Jewish People, are still here, with faith in Hashem, and we must strive to create a renewal and reconstruct our Jewish identity once again.'**

CHAPTER 5

The Miraculous Escape

THE MIRACULOUS ESCAPE OF OPA LEITNER DURING WWII

In September 1938, still before the annexation of Sudetenland, the Leitner family were having lunch in their hotel dining room, when a local police chief entered and told them that they had received secret information, and that they were advised to leave town immediately as their safety could no longer be guaranteed. The police officer gave them a revolver for their protection on their escape, and provided them with a police escort until the outskirts of the town. The family hurriedly packed their essentials, and escaped in cars that belonged to the hotel and travelled to Prague. Shortly afterwards the Germans annexed Marienbad as part of the Sudetenland. It was during this time in Prague that Uncle Fritz became engaged to Malka (Margit) Wiener from Pressburg, and the two were then able to travel to London in January 1939. This was made possible with the help of Dr. Shloime Schonfeld, whom he had first met in Nitra Yeshivah. Uncle Fritz got married shortly before the outbreak of the war.

Uncle Shurl (Yeshaye) escaped to Paris, so Opa was left in Prague together with his father and sister. Opa was already engaged to Oma, his first cousin, Hinda Kokisch, but due to the prevailing war conditions they were prevented from getting married at the time.

For Sukkos, Opa had decided to go to Reb Aaron in Belz, where he stayed in the "Belzer Hoif". The Rebbe made sure that Opa felt at 'home' by ensuring that he always had cutlery with which to eat his meals, the way he was accustomed to, and even instructed him to put on Tefillin in the privacy of his own room during Chol Hamoed, according to his Minhag from home. After Yom Tov Opa went to take leave of the Rebbe, who advised him that 'Shabbos Bereishis still belongs to Yom Tov' and he should stay that extra weekend.

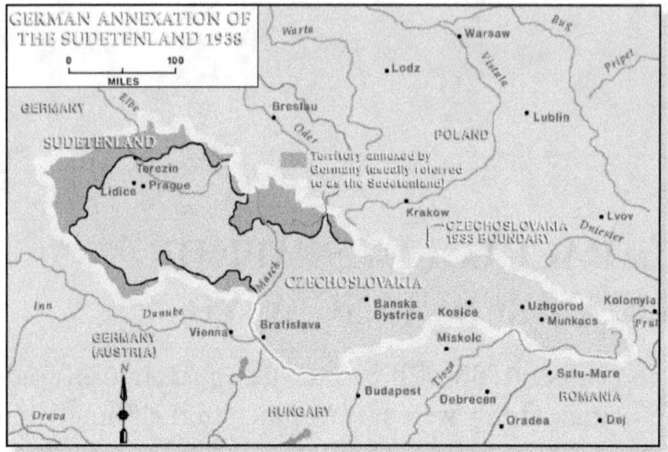

Map showing area annexation of Sudetenland 1938

The Beis Hamedrash in Belz

The present day replica in Yerushalayim

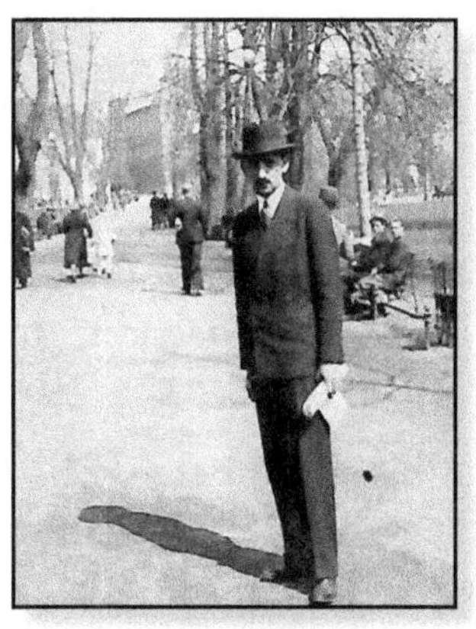

Opa in Prague 1938

After Shabbos Opa again went to the Rebbe and discussed his future plans with him. Reb Aaron told him that 'If you leave, you should all travel together'. He then gave him a Czech coin as an amulet ('kemeiah') which Opa had later attached to a chain and always wore under his shirt, except on Shabbos. He treasured this very much and was very proud of it. The Rebbe then wished him a safe journey, and also sent his warm greetings to his father.

Opa made his way to northern Slovakia and until February 5, 1939 stayed in the kosher hotel 'Pension Schreiber' in Stary Smokovec.

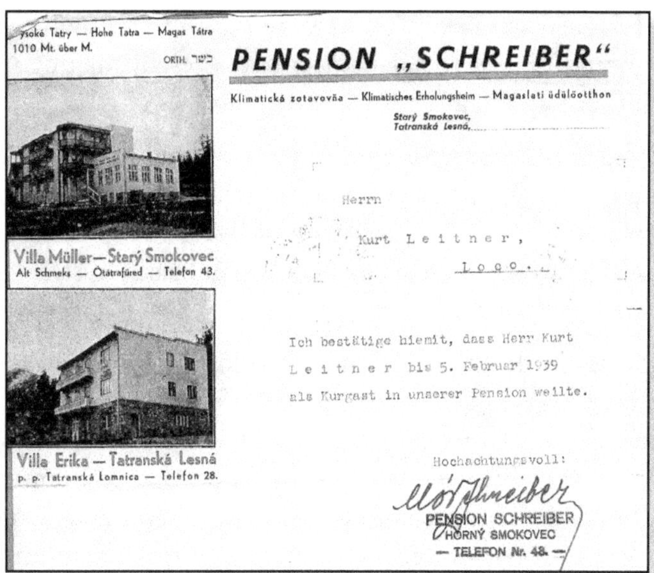

Vysoké Tatry — Hohe Tatra — Magas Tátra
1010 Mt. über M.

ORTH. כשר

PENSION „SCHREIBER"

Klimatická zotavovňa — Klimatisches Erholungsheim — Magaslati üdülöotthon

Starý Smokovec,
Tatranská Lesná, ...

Villa Müller—Starý Smokovec
Alt Schmeks — Ótátrafüred — Telefon 43.

Villa Erika — Tatranská Lesná
p. p. Tatranská Lomnica — Telefon 28.

Herrn

Kurt Leitner,

Loco.

Ich bestätige hiemit, dass Herr Kurt Leitner bis 5. Februar 1939 als Kurgast in unserer Pension weilte.

Hochachtungsvoll:

Mór Schreiber

PENSION SCHREIBER
HORNÝ SMOKOVEC
— TELEFON Nr. 48. —

When the Nazis rose to power, they were looking to arrest prominent public figures and Opa was one of these. His photo appeared on the front page of the venomous Nazi tabloid newspaper "Der Sturmer" on March 16, 1939, as A WANTED MAN, for having brought Agudas Yisroel to Marienbad. From that day on Opa was unable to stay for more than two consecutive days in one place, and was desperately looking for ways to escape. But this too was an open act of Hashgocho Protis, for had his picture not appeared in the Nazi paper, he would have been unaware that he must now be extra vigilant in order to survive. Similar alarm bells were sounded when the picture of the Tshebiner Rov, Rabbi Dov Ber Weidenfeld, appeared in the same newspaper, which forced him to escape. During the war, when the pictures of Reb Aaron of Belz and the Imrei Emes of Ger appeared on the front pages of this tabloid newspaper, it prompted their respective Chassidim to make very urgent efforts to secure their Rebbes' safe escape.

Opa was asked by his father to try and make his way to the Polish border to attempt an escape, but Opa was unable to convince his father and sister to accompany him, however hard he tried. Moishe Dovid asked his brother, Isidor (1.1.7), who had many excellent connections, to establish if Opa was still on the 'wanted' list. In the meantime, Opa together with his cousin, Leopold Gerstel (1.1.8.1) made their way to the train station near the Polish border. A telegram sent to Leopold Gerstel confirmed that Opa was indeed still on the wanted list, and this was the sole purpose of him accompanying Opa, so that no traceable telegram should be sent to a 'Kurt Leitner', thereby making it impossible for the Germans to trace his whereabouts.

They bade each other farewell and Opa made his way to the train station at Mahrisch–Ostrau (Czechoslovakia), hoping to somehow catch a train across the Polish border. Mahrisch-Ostrau is 15 km from the border, and 320 km from Prague. (From Mahrisch-Ostrau to Belz in the Ukraine it is 580km).

The station was full of people, many trying to escape too, but more worrying for Opa was the large number of 'brown shirts' as the Nazis became known. Out of desperation, and wanting to stay out of the limelight, he went into the waiting room and stood facing the wall, to try and avoid being spotted. Here he was, a man with a moustache, who was on the Nazi wanted list, and finds himself standing in a station which was swarming with bloodthirsty Gestapo soldiers. Opa was always proud to be Jewish, and it is really amazing that even under these extreme circumstances, he never even contemplated shaving off his moustache in order to make himself less conspicuous.

It is at such crucial moments that one realises the true meaning of the possuk (Tehilim 121):
הנה לא ינום ולא יישן שומר ישראל - Behold He neither slumbers nor sleeps – the Guardian of Israel.

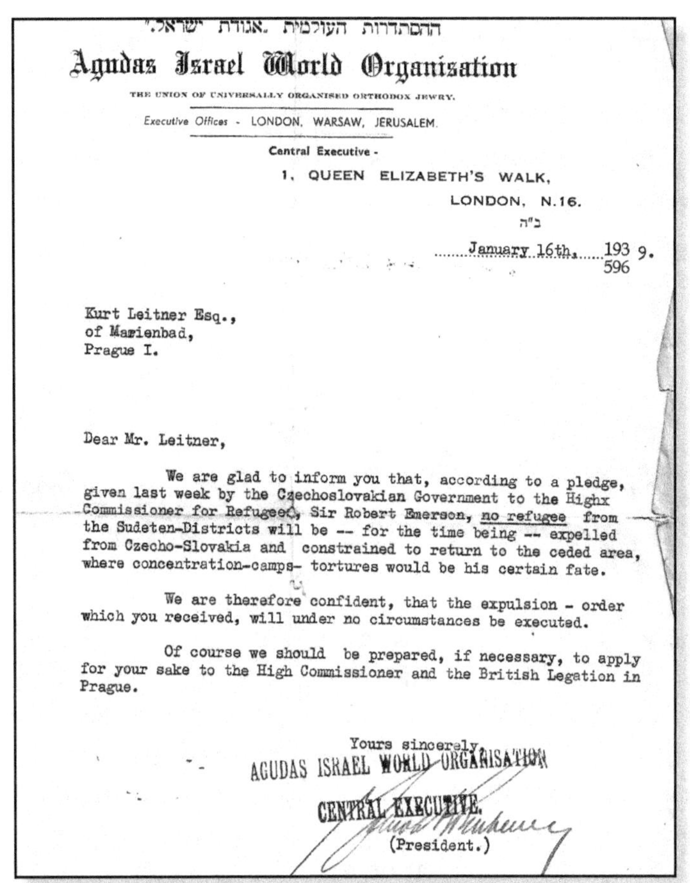

ההסתדרות העולמית. "אגודת ישראל."

Agudas Israel World Organisation

THE UNION OF UNIVERSALLY ORGANISED ORTHODOX JEWRY.

Executive Offices - LONDON, WARSAW, JERUSALEM.

Central Executive -

1, QUEEN ELIZABETH'S WALK,

LONDON, N.16.

ב"ה

January 16th, 1939.
596

Kurt Leitner Esq.,
of Marienbad,
Prague I.

Dear Mr. Leitner,

We are glad to inform you that, according to a pledge, given last week by the Czechoslovakian Government to the Highx Commissioner for Refugees, Sir Robert Emerson, no refugee from the Sudeten-Districts will be -- for the time being -- expelled from Czecho-Slovakia and constrained to return to the ceded area, where concentration-camps- tortures would be his certain fate.

We are therefore confident, that the expulsion - order which you received, will under no circumstances be executed.

Of course we should be prepared, if necessary, to apply for your sake to the High Commissioner and the British Legation in Prague.

Yours sincerely,
AGUDAS ISRAEL WORLD ORGANISATION
CENTRAL EXECUTIVE.
(President.)

Letter received in Prague offered some consolation

Shortly afterwards, a man dressed in a train drivers uniform approached Opa, and asked him 'Where do you want to go?' Opa did not know if this person could be trusted, so he replied diplomatically 'What have you got to offer?' He told Opa that he was a train driver who takes empty wagons across the Czech-Polish border to reload with coals from the Polish coal mines, and then drives the fully loaded trains back to Mahrisch–Ostrau, a big industrial city with a large steel foundry that needed much coal to fire its furnaces. 'Do you want a lift across the border?' Opa confirmed that he was trying to escape, but warned this anonymous driver that he was on the Nazi 'wanted list' and they needed to be very cautious. The driver told him to stay in the waiting room while he went to the store room at the station and fetched a spare uniform for Opa to change into. He told him to come with onto the train and help stoke the coals of his steam engine. [At that time they only had steam engines, which were powered by a coal fire that heated a large water tank. This in turn generated the steam that would push the pistons which moved the wheels, which then powered the train].

The train moved through the winding countyside, and after one and a half hours they had crossed the border and arrived at their destination. The driver then told Opa that they were safely out of German occupied territory, and asked Opa to take him in a taxi to his house, drop him off there, and then he could continue on his journey.

Train station at Mahrisch-Ostrau

Steam Engine

This Opa did, and when they arrived at this train driver's home, he wrote down his name, address and all relevant contact details, and thanked him very much for his great assistance. He then immediately went to the local Post Office and sent a telegram to his father in Prague, giving him the details of this helpful train driver, so that he might also be able to make use of this contact to help him and his sister escape. His father sent him back a telegram, that he had tried to contact this train driver, but the post office returned the telegram with a note, saying that neither this name nor this street existed!

Map showing Mahrisch-Ostrau' the exact place from where Opa crossed the border into Poland

From there Opa made his way to Reb Aaron of Belz, and the Rebbe asked him how he had managed to escape. After relating the entire story, the Rebbe replied, that the reason why his father could not contact this Polish man was only because 'It was Eliyohu Hanovi who took you out'. Unfortunately your father should have been with you in order to be saved at the same time. 'Hashem should help all Yidden.' This is how the Rebbe finished his conversation, an expression that did not offer much hope of salvation for his father and sister.

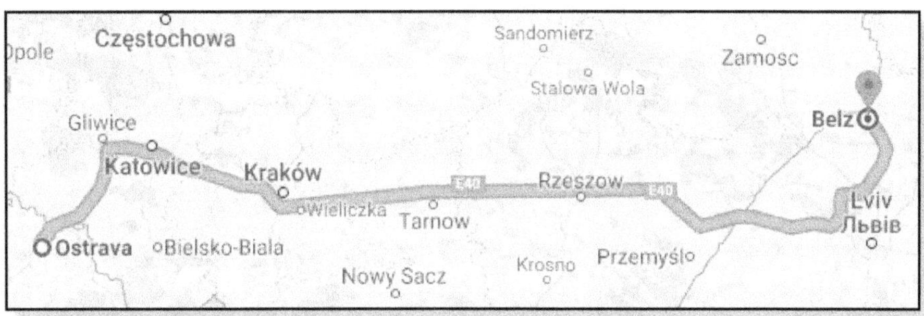

From Mahrisch-Ostrau to Belz

We learn in the Torah how יוסף הצדיק had enjoyed special privileges from his father while he was at home, and then within a few hours had lost all this, and found himself in a pit surrounded by snakes and scorpions. His torment continued for the following 13 years, 12 of which were spent in prison with very unsuitable company. What a sudden and drastic fall and change from his previous lifestyle, but despite all that he remained the same יוסף הצדיק as before, placing his entire trust in Hashem.

Similarly, Opa had only a few months previously been the centre of attention as the organiser of the Kenessio Gedoloh in Marienbad. He often related that not only did he know all the pre-war Gedolim personally but that they even knew him by his first name. And now he found himself away from his home and family, without an income, a wanted fugitive all on his own, and his Kalloh was en route to Santiago de Chile, the other side of the world! It is very hard to imagine how lonely and despondent he must have felt during this very trying period, but being a frum Yid he knew that nothing happens by chance. Every event is preordained and is part of the bigger picture of the Master Planner of the World, as seen in the story of יוסף הצדיק.

They say that it is easy to have Emunah in Hashem when everything is rosy. It is when life throws us an unexpected challenge that we can see who truly believes and has genuine Emunah.

Opa then travelled from Poland to England, and eventually reached London, where he spent the next six years, until after the war. This part of his life is recorded more extensively in a later chapter.

In March 1939, the Germans occupied the entire Czechoslovakia. Moishe Dovid together with his daughter, Theresa, had obtained visas to enter England in the interim, but were not permitted by the German forces to use them. They made their way to Pressburg and in 1942, were transported to the concentration camps, where they perished. It was, however, not until January 23, 1953 that Opa received official notification from the Committee of the International Red Cross in Berlin that confirmed the following:

> LEITNER David, born 1869 in Marienbad, was transported in the second transport on May 17, 1942 from Bardejoy to Naleczow. Enclosed is a list of all Czech Jews on this transport. Signed: I.A. Opitz.

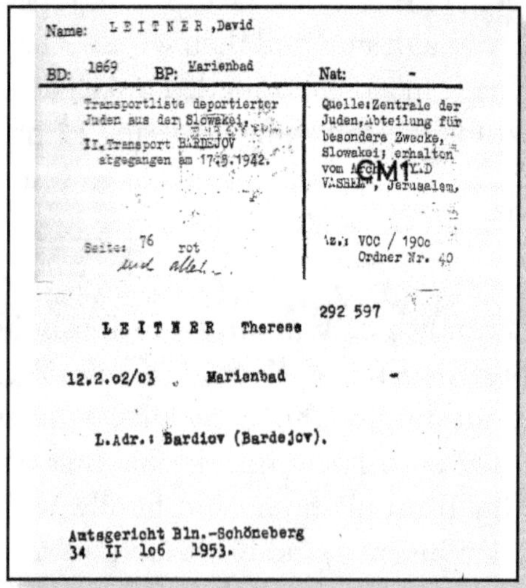

Name: LEITNER ,David

BD: 1869 BP: Marienbad Nat: -

Transportliste deportierter Juden aus der Slowakei,
II.Transport BARDEJOV
abgegangen am 17.5.1942.

Seite: 76 rot

Quelle: Zentrale der Juden, Abteilung für besondere Zwecke, Slowakei; erhalten vom [illegible] VASHEM", Jerusalem,

Az.: VOC / 190c
Ordner Nr. 40

292 597

LEITNER Therese

12.2.02/03 Marienbad -

L.Adr.: Bardiov (Bardejov).

Amtsgericht Bln.-Schöneberg
34 II 106 1953.

Record of transportation of Moishe Dovid (1.1.1) and his daughter Theresa Leitner (1.1.1.1) on May 17, 1942.

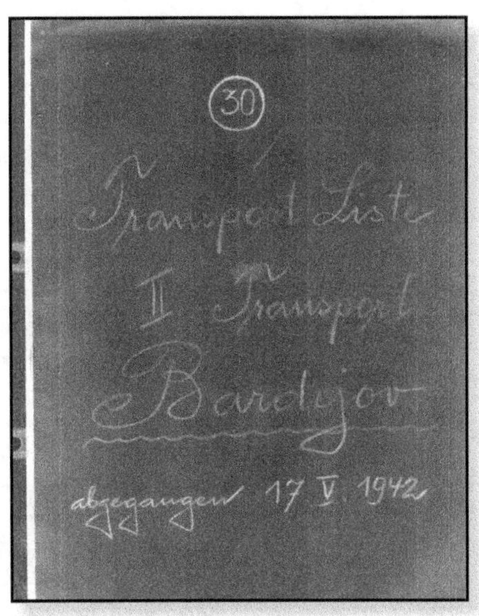

Cover of Transport list

332.		Helena	1881	Bardejov
333.		Israel	1925	Bardejov
334.		Izak	1925	"
335.		Elisabeth	1928	"
336.		Alexander	1931	"
337.	Weil	Regine	1866	Sp. Podhradie
338.		Ester	1904	Červený Kláštor
339.	Leitner	David	1869	Marienbad
340.	Birnbaum	Lazar	1892	Bardejov
341.	Schönfeld	Schaje	1908	Bardejov
341.		Minna	1908	"
343.		Fanny	1937	"
344.		Josef	1939	"
345.		Moses	1941	"
346.	Brandmann	Juda	1928	"
347.	Grünfeld	Lina	1920.	Dortmund
348.		Ernst	1938	Teschen
349.	Weiss	Adolf	1906	Bardiov
350.		Jiďnra	1915	Breclava
351.		Milan	1939	Bardiov
352.	Blau	Eliaš	1901	Mor. Ostrava
353.		Regine	1913	"
354.		Fridrich	1941	Bratislava
355.	Joles	Elza	1903	Brody
356.		Hermann	1920	Košice

Nr. 18999/1942 C[1]

Auschwitz, den 15. August 1942

Die Therese Leitner, ohne Beruf

, mosaisch

wohnhaft Berd.jov. Komanova Nr. 6, Slowakei

ist am 9. August 1942 um 16 Uhr 25 Minuten

in Auschwitz, Kasernenstrasse verstorben.

Die Verstorbene war geboren am 12. Februar 1903

in Marienbad, Sudetengau

(Standesamt Nr.)

Vater: David Leitner, wohnhaft in Marienbad

Mutter: Jetti Leitner geborene Schopflocher, zuletzt wohnhaft in Marienbad

Die Verstorbene war nicht verheiratet

Eingetragen auf mündliche — schriftliche Anzeige des Arztes Doktor der Medizin Thilo in Auschwitz vom 9. August 1942

Der Anzeigende

Vorgelesen, genehmigt und unterschrieben

Die Übereinstimmung mit dem Erstbuch wird beglaubigt.

Auschwitz, den 15. 8. 1942

Der Standesbeamte In Vertretung

Der Standesbeamte In Vertretung Quakernack

Todesursache: Algemeine Korperschwache

Eheschliessung der Verstorbenen am in

(Standesamt Nr.)

Death Certificate (1.1.1.1) *for Therese Leitner issued in Auschwitz. How ironic that the Germans even recorded the cause of death "general weakness" and exact time of death: 16.25pm!*

Records of another three members of the Leitner family were found at the Yad Vashem archives:

Isidor Leitner (1.1.7) who was transported to Theresienstadt on 14th December 1941 and died there on July 27, 1942, together with his wife Regina and their oldest daughter Theresa (1.1.7.1).

Isidor Leitner (1.1.7)

ÚSTŘEDNÍ KARTOTÉKA — TRANSPORTY.

24.503

Leitnerová Tereza

22.5.1912

PŘEŽIL podle knihy „TEREZÍN"

1. transport 14 XII 1941 č. 111

2. transport dne: číslo: do:

Transport Certificate to Terezinstadt for Theresa Leitner -

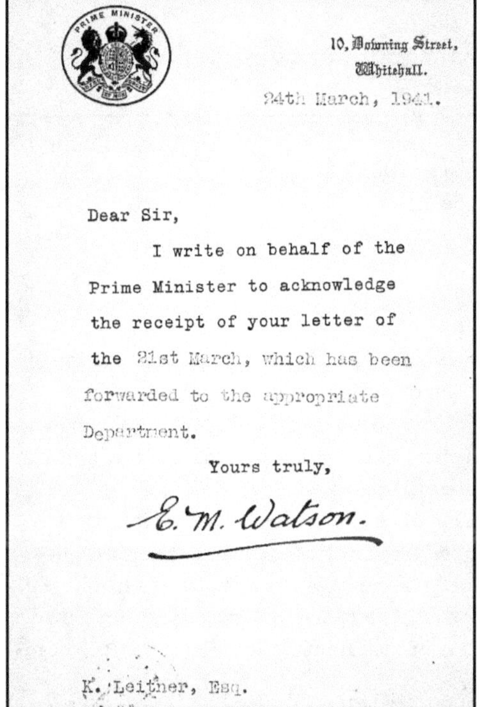

10, Downing Street,
Whitehall.

24th March, 1941.

Dear Sir,

I write on behalf of the Prime Minister to acknowledge the receipt of your letter of the 21st March, which has been forwarded to the appropriate Department.

Yours truly,

E. M. Watson.

K. Leitner, Esq.

Reply from 10 Downing Street

As soon as Opa arrived in London, he made it his top priority to try and secure the safety of his father and sister. We don't have any records of his earlier efforts, but on March 24, 1941 he wrote to the Prime Minister at 10 Downing Street, requesting assistance in obtaining an entry visa for them. When Opa received no satisfactory answer, he continued nevertheless via other sources.

His efforts included a suggestion that originated from Rabbi Y. Rosenheim. Contact that was made via the Aguda office in New York (America had not yet entered the War) to the Consul in Portugal, which was also a neutral country, with a request to obtain 'transit visas to Portugal in order to obtain American Immigration visas in Lisbon.'

August 29, 1941.

Dr. Augusto d'Esaguy,
Comissao Portuguesa
de Assistencia
aos Judeus Refugiados,
Rua Rosa Arauho 12,
Lisbon/PORTUGAL.

Gentlemen,

We are certifying by this letter that

Mr. David LEITNER,

formerly in Bratislava (Chechoslovakia), now somewhere in Hungary, is in possession of a valid and acknowledged Affidavit for the purpose of immigration to USA.

We are now endeavouring according to the new regulations of July 1st, 1941, to obtain in Washington the renewal of the acknowledgement of this affidavit for Mr. Leitner himself und at the same time for Miss Terezie Leitner, his daughter.

As there are no American consulates anymore in Chechoslowakia and it is not certain how long Mr. Leitner und his daughter may be able to remain in Hungary, we should be extremely grateful, in the interest of Mr. Leitner whom we know as a highly respectable personality, if you would try that a transitory stay in Portugal may be granted to Mr. and Miss Leitner in order to get his American Immigration Visa at the American Consulate in Lisbon.

Thanking you in anticipation, we are fully prepared to assist in the matter as efficiently as possible, and remain

Yours very faithfully,

AGUDAS ISRAEL WORLD ORGANIZATION
Branch Office New York,

PRESIDENT.

Transcribed:

August 29, 1941.

Dr. Augusto d'Esaguy, Comissao Portuguessa, De Assistencia
Aos Judeus Refugiandos, Rua Rosa Arauho 12,
Lisbon/PORTUGAL.

Gentlemen,
We are certifying by this letter that Mr. David LEITNER
Formerly in Bratislava (Czechoslovakia), now somewhere in Hungary, is in possession of a valid and acknowledged affidavit for the purpose of immigration to USA.
We are now endeavoring according to the new regulations of July 1st 1941, to obtain in Washington the renewal of the acknowledgment of this affidavit for Mr. Leitner himself and at the same time for Miss Terezie Leitner, his daughter.
As there are no more American consulates anymore in Czechoslovakia and it is not certain how long Mr. Leitner and his daughter may be able to remain in Hungary, we shall be extremely grateful, in the interest of Mr. Leitner whom we know as a highly respectable personality, if you would try that a transitory stay in Portugal may be granted to Mr. and Miss Leitner in order to get his American Immigration Visa at the American Consulate in Lisbon.
Thanking you in anticipation, we are fully prepared to assist in the matter as efficiently as possible and remain.

Yours very faithfully,
AGUDAS ISRAEL WORLD ORGANISATION
Branch Office, New York,
PRESIDENT

On November 4, 1941, Opa received another letter from Rabbi Y Rosenheim, confirming that Mr. Masaryk had agreed to 'make every effort to assist your father and sister in obtaining visas to the United States. He will undertake that personally in Washington.' This too was refused, and the reason given was simply that Moishe Dovid Leitner had a hearing impairment and was unsuitable for a visa!

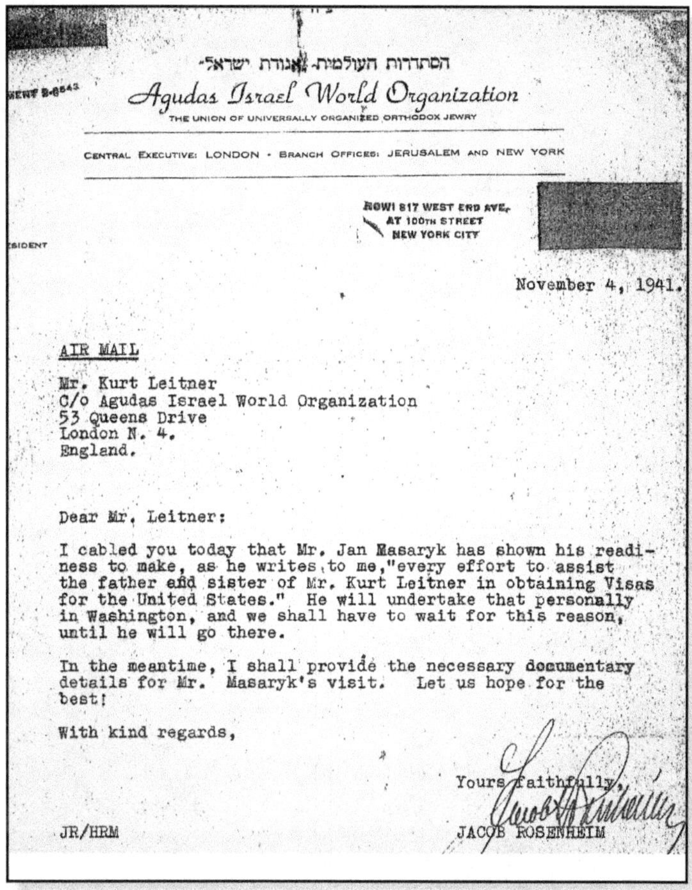

הסתדרות העולמית-אגודת ישראל

Agudas Israel World Organization

THE UNION OF UNIVERSALLY ORGANIZED ORTHODOX JEWRY

CENTRAL EXECUTIVE: LONDON • BRANCH OFFICES: JERUSALEM AND NEW YORK

817 WEST END AVE.,
AT 100TH STREET
NEW YORK CITY

November 4, 1941.

AIR MAIL

Mr. Kurt Leitner
C/o Agudas Israel World Organization
53 Queens Drive
London N. 4.
England.

Dear Mr. Leitner:

I cabled you today that Mr. Jan Masaryk has shown his readiness to make, as he writes to me, "every effort to assist the father and sister of Mr. Kurt Leitner in obtaining Visas for the United States." He will undertake that personally in Washington, and we shall have to wait for this reason, until he will go there.

In the meantime, I shall provide the necessary documentary details for Mr. Masaryk's visit. Let us hope for the best!

With kind regards,

Yours faithfully,

JACOB ROSENHEIM

JR/HRM

On June 3, 1942, Opa obtained a letter from Chief Rabbi Hertz, with a warm letter of recommendation for their favourable consideration for immigration, which was forwarded to the Queen at the Palace. He initially asked his sister-in-law to write to the Queen, as she was a British subject, and this, he hoped, would carry more weight, but this too was refused. Opa then took the next step and wrote to the Queen himself, but again received a negative reply on July 3, 1942.

TELEPHONE
AVENUE 5377
TELEGRAMS
CHIRABINAT, MAIDA, LONDON
CABLEGRAMS
CHIRABINAT, LONDON

OFFICE OF THE CHIEF RABBI,
4, CREECHURCH PLACE, ALDGATE.
LONDON, E.C.3

3rd June, 1942.

TO WHOM IT MAY CONCERN.

Mr. Kurt Leitner has, since his arrival in this country in April 1939 from Czechoslovakia, devoted all his time to the social and welfare work of the Federation of Czechoslovakian Jews. Mr. Leitner has been acting as secretary to the organisation.

Through his perseverance and hard work, assistance has been given to a large number of Czechoslovakian refugees.

I understand that Mr. Leitner has submitted an application to the Czechoslovak Ministry of Foreign Affairs for the emigration of his father DAVID LEITNER and his sister TEREZIE LEITNER and I wish to recommend this application for favourable consideration. I should be pleased if every assistance could be given to Mr. Leitner in this effort, especially as his family have been known as loyal citizens when in Czechoslovakia.

J. H. Hertz
CHIEF RABBI.

BUCKINGHAM PALACE.

July 3rd.1942.

The Lady-in-Waiting is commanded by The Queen to acknowledge the receipt of Mr. Leitner's letter and to express Her Majesty's regret that she is unable to accede to the request contained therein.

Mr. K.Leitner,
96 Queen's Drive,
London, N.4.

Any communication on the subject of this letter should be addressed to :—
THE UNDER SECRETARY OF STATE,
HOME OFFICE
(ALIENS DEPARTMENT),
P.O. BOX No. 100,
PADDINGTON DISTRICT OFFICE,
LONDON, W.2.
and the following number quoted :—
K.24741.

HOME OFFICE,
P.O. BOX No. ~~100~~, 2,
Bournemouth,
~~PADDINGTON~~
~~DISTRICT OFFICE,~~
Hants.
~~LONDON, W.2.~~

13th June, 1942.

Madam,

Your letter to Her Majesty the Queen has been referred to the Secretary of State by Her Majesty's Command, but the Secretary of State regrets that he has been unable to advise Her Majesty to issue any command thereon.

I am, Madam,
Your obedient Servant,

Mrs. M. Leitner,
96, Queens Drive,
LONDON, N.4.

David Turkel, as editor of the 'Judische Presse' in Vienna, attended the 3rd Kenessio where he worked closely with Opa. The Austrian Aguda later sent him to America to help facilitate emigration papers for some Austrian Jews, and over a period of three years managed to obtain more than 9000 visas that allowed Jews to leave Europe.

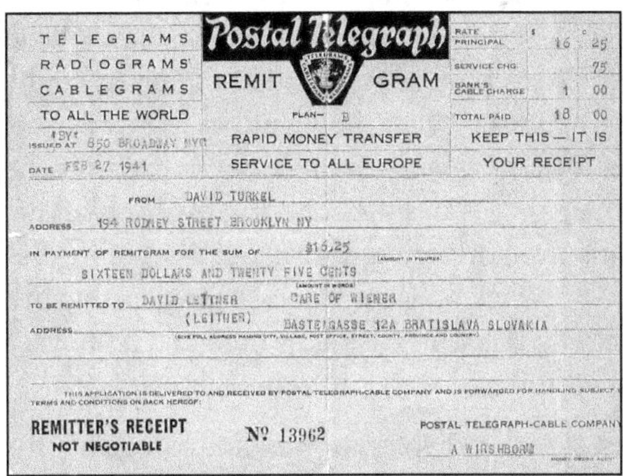

TELEGRAMS
RADIOGRAMS
CABLEGRAMS
TO ALL THE WORLD

Postal Telegraph
REMIT GRAM
PLAN— B
RAPID MONEY TRANSFER
SERVICE TO ALL EUROPE

	$	c
RATE PRINCIPAL	16	25
SERVICE CHG		75
BANK'S CABLE CHARGE	1	00
TOTAL PAID	18	00

KEEP THIS — IT IS YOUR RECEIPT

ISSUED AT *BY* 850 BROADWAY NYC
DATE FEB 27 1941

FROM DAVID TURKEL
ADDRESS 194 RODNEY STREET BROOKLYN NY
IN PAYMENT OF REMITGRAM FOR THE SUM OF $16.25 (AMOUNT IN FIGURES)
SIXTEEN DOLLARS AND TWENTY FIVE CENTS (AMOUNT IN WORDS)
TO BE REMITTED TO DAVID LEITNER (LEITNER) CARE OF WIENER
ADDRESS BASTEIGASSE 12A BRATISLAVA SLOVAKIA

THIS APPLICATION IS DELIVERED TO AND RECEIVED BY POSTAL TELEGRAPH-CABLE COMPANY AND IS FORWARDED FOR HANDLING SUBJECT TO TERMS AND CONDITIONS ON BACK HEREOF:

REMITTER'S RECEIPT
NOT NEGOTIABLE
№ 13962
POSTAL TELEGRAPH-CABLE COMPANY
A WIRSHBORD
MONEY ORDER AGENT

Copy of Postal Telegram confirming money transfer

In the meantime Opa used his diplomatic contacts with the Aguda and also the Czech Government in Exile and wired money, via America, to his father in Bratislava. In February 1941 he wired $16.25 (net) via his acquaintance David Turkel at 194 Rodney Street, Brooklyn, to his father, David Leitner c/o Wiener at 12A Basteigasse, in Bratislava. On Apri 7, 1941 he sent a further $13.25, on June 6, $22.25 and on October 15, another $11.25.

Since Opa's father and sister perished in the concentration camp and did not have their own burial plot or gravestone, their names were inscribed on Opa's own Matzeivo, as well as on the Matzeivos of his three brothers.

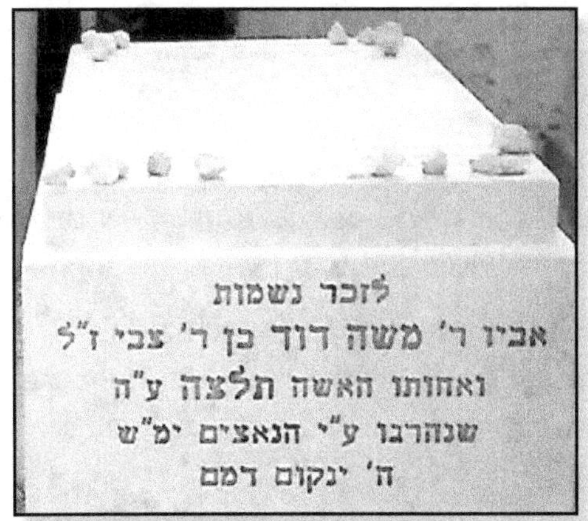

An inscription for his father and sister were incorporated into his own Matzeivo in 1988.

ELIYOHU HANOVI

Having heard directly from Reb Aaron of Belz 'that it was Eliyohu Hanovi who took you out' understandably made a lasting impression on Opa. Whenever he attended a Bris Miloh of a family member he would endeavour to wear his Shabbos clothes for the occasion, in honour of Eliyohu Hanovi who attends every Bris. For other Brisos that he attended, if there was insufficient time to change into Shabbos clothes, he would at least wear his Shabbos hat, and would then stand quietly, with his eyes fixed on the כסא של אליהו, that special chair that is designated for Eliyohu Hanovi, who might not be wearing his train driver's uniform, but was surely disguised in some other way. Nevertheless, Opa stood there silently with full attention, staring at that chair, just in case he would catch another glimpse of that angel who had miraculously saved his life.

This sensitivity and respect that he displayed was unique. After his petiroh, Mr. Akiva Moishe Adler asked Oma for the 'Kittel' which they needed to perform the 'taharoh'. Oma replied, 'Which one do you want? Opa had two'. To this Mr. Adler replied amazingly, 'I have served with the Chevra Kadisha for over 40 years and have never heard of anyone who had two Kittels; give me the one he used most recently.'

Oma explained that if Opa's Kittel got any stains on the first Seder night, he would put on a clean one for the second Seder! Since one pours out a special cup of wine for Eliyohu Hanovi, he wanted to look equally respectable on both nights.' This is something we only discovered after his death, as he never publicised it; for him this was nothing extraordinary.

After the Sedorim, however late we finished, Oma made sure to leave the table completely tidy, and only the כוס של אליהו was left on it. The room just had to look respectable for this esteemed visitor.

It is related that one year during the Pesach Seder, Rabbi Yissochor Dov of Belz sent his little grandson to open the door for 'Shefoch Chamos'cha'. Then the Rebbe asked the child, 'Did you see Eliyohu Hanovi?'

'Is it still possible to see him even in our times?' the young boy asked.

'There are those who can, but those who don't see him, and still believe he is there, are much greater,' was the Rebbes response.

Opa had both virtues; he had merited to see Eliyohu Hanovi himself, while at other times he firmly believed that he was there, and conducted himself accordingly.

CHAPTER 6
Life in London

LIFE IN LONDON

On March 30, 1939 the Home Office wrote to the secretary of the British Committee for Refugees from Czechoslovakia, that Opa should go to Prague to obtain his visa. On the following day Opa received confirmation from the British Committee for Refugees from Czechoslovakia exiled in London, that his permission had been granted to come to England, 'to train for future emigration'. This letter was addressed to him at Chodska 18, Prague XI, were he must have been hiding from the Nazis, or perhaps it was simply a forwarding address.

A.R.16

Any communication on the subject of this letter should be addressed to-
THE UNDER SECRETARY OF STATE,
HOME OFFICE
(ALIENS DEPARTMENT),
CLELAND HOUSE,
PAGE STREET,
LONDON, S.W.1,
and the following number quoted :-

L. 12608.

HOME OFFICE,
CLELAND HOUSE,
PAGE STREET,
LONDON, S.W.1.

31 MAR 39

30th March, 1939.

Madam,

With reference to your letter of the 10th instant, (HR/MZ) I am directed by the Secretary of State to say that Mr. Kurt Leitner should apply for a visa to the British Passport Control Officer in Prague to whom a communication is being sent.

The visa has been granted to enable Mr. Leitner to train for emigration.

I am, Madam,
Your obedient Servant,

S. G. Dunwater

The Secretary,
British Committee for
Refugees from Czecho-
Slovakia,
5, Mecklenburgh Square,
W.C.1.

D 4562946 10,000 D/d 137 1/39 P R P

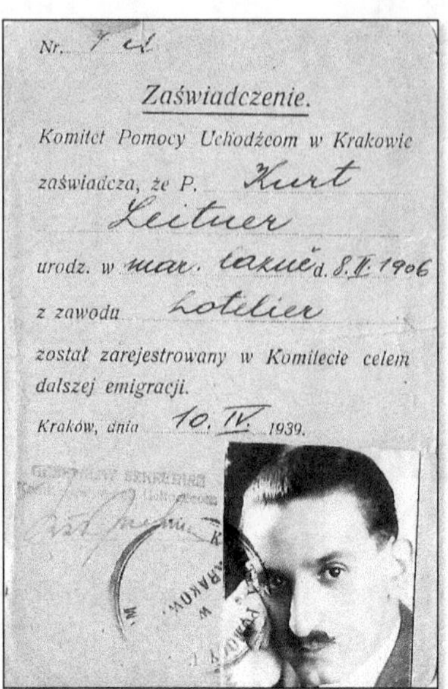

Nr. [illegible]

Zaświadczenie.

Komitet Pomocy Uchodźcom w Krakowie zaświadcza, że P. Kurt Leitner urodz. w mar. łaznie d. 8.[illegible].1906 z zawodu hotelier został zarejestrowany w Komitecie celem dalszej emigracji.

Kraków, dnia 10.IV. 1939.

Certificate for Jewish refugees, Krakow, valid until April 10, 1939

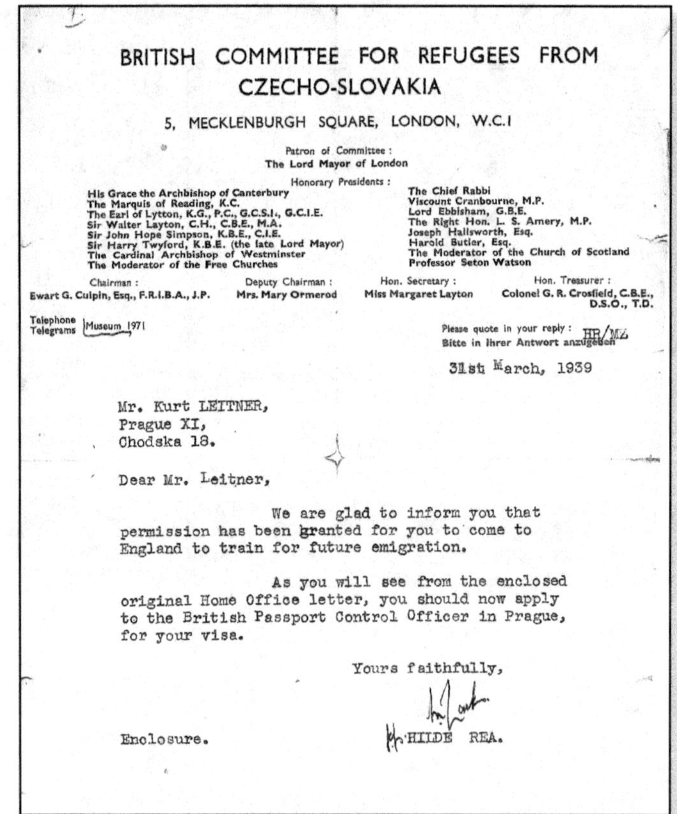

BRITISH COMMITTEE FOR REFUGEES FROM CZECHO-SLOVAKIA

5, MECKLENBURGH SQUARE, LONDON, W.C.1

Patron of Committee :
The Lord Mayor of London

Honorary Presidents :
His Grace the Archbishop of Canterbury
The Marquis of Reading, K.C.
The Earl of Lytton, K.G., P.C., G.C.S.I., G.C.I.E.
Sir Walter Layton, C.H., C.B.E., M.A.
Sir John Hope Simpson, K.B.E., C.I.E.
Sir Harry Twyford, K.B.E. (the late Lord Mayor)
The Cardinal Archbishop of Westminster
The Moderator of the Free Churches
The Chief Rabbi
Viscount Cranbourne, M.P.
Lord Ebbisham, G.B.E.
The Right Hon. L. S. Amery, M.P.
Joseph Hallsworth, Esq.
Harold Butler, Esq.
The Moderator of the Church of Scotland
Professor Seton Watson

Chairman : Ewart G. Culpin, Esq., F.R.I.B.A., J.P.
Deputy Chairman : Mrs. Mary Ormerod
Hon. Secretary : Miss Margaret Layton
Hon. Treasurer : Colonel G. R. Crosfield, C.B.E., D.S.O., T.D.

Telephone / Telegrams Museum 1971

Please quote in your reply : HR/MZ
Bitte in Ihrer Antwort anzugeben

31st March, 1939

Mr. Kurt LEITNER,
Prague XI,
Chodska 18.

Dear Mr. Leitner,

We are glad to inform you that permission has been granted for you to come to England to train for future emigration.

As you will see from the enclosed original Home Office letter, you should now apply to the British Passport Control Officer in Prague, for your visa.

Yours faithfully,

HILDE REA.

Enclosure.

The Chairman of the Federation of Czechoslovakian Jews made an application to the Home Office for permission to employ Opa as their secretary, which was granted on March 4, 1940. They however added to this letter a suffix, which stated ' I am to remind you that Mr. Leitner was permitted to land in the United Kingdom on condition of emigration and the Secretary of State would be glad to learn the probable date of his departure.' (This was in the middle of the War when one couldn't leave even if one wanted to!)

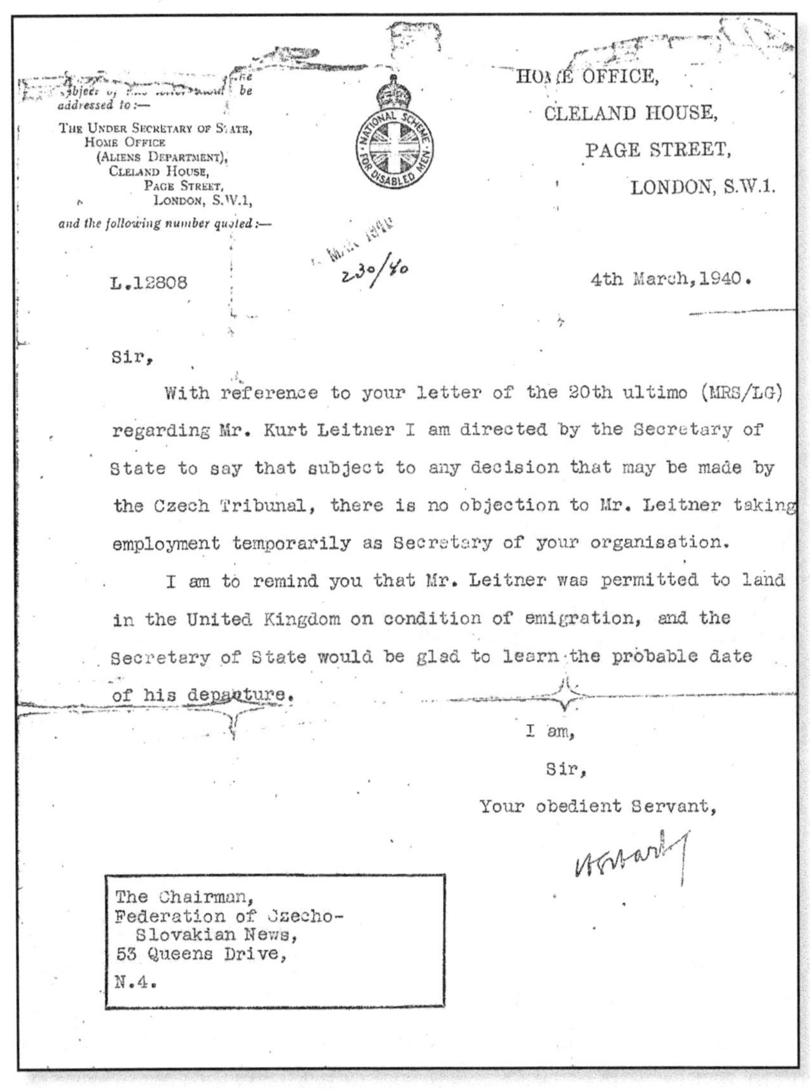

Any further communication on the subject of this letter should be addressed to:—

THE UNDER SECRETARY OF STATE,
HOME OFFICE
(ALIENS DEPARTMENT),
CLELAND HOUSE,
PAGE STREET,
LONDON, S.W.1,

and the following number quoted:—

L.12808

HOME OFFICE,
CLELAND HOUSE,
PAGE STREET,
LONDON, S.W.1.

4th March, 1940.

230/40

Sir,

With reference to your letter of the 20th ultimo (MRS/LG) regarding Mr. Kurt Leitner I am directed by the Secretary of State to say that subject to any decision that may be made by the Czech Tribunal, there is no objection to Mr. Leitner taking employment temporarily as Secretary of your organisation.

I am to remind you that Mr. Leitner was permitted to land in the United Kingdom on condition of emigration, and the Secretary of State would be glad to learn the probable date of his departure.

I am,
Sir,
Your obedient Servant,

The Chairman,
Federation of Czecho-Slovakian News,
53 Queens Drive,
N.4.

HATZOLOH WORK AND CONTACTS WITH CZECH PRESIDENT IN LONDON

Opa arrived in London just prior to the beginning of World War II, and seeing that he was a most efficient, organised and conscientious worker, and besides that, a bachelor without any family commitments, he was therefore the ideal person to help in the massive relief effort that was carried out by the Agudas Yisroel during these years. These relief operations are a rich, although tragic period in history, when the Aguda continued to organise shipments of food to the ghettos, despite government opposition. Opa was employed by the Agudas Yisroel and also by the Federation of Czechoslovakian Jews, but all other social work was done in a voluntary capacity.

Opa was an extremely well organised person. Also on a personal level, for example, when wearing a suit, every pocket was reserved for something specific, be it his pen, a diary, small change, his keys etc, and he never had to fumble around in his pockets to find something.

October 28, 1941 Czechoslavakian Jews; A Message of Loyalty

As part of his relief work on behalf of the Federation of Czechoslovakian Jews in London, Opa always ensured that he kept cordial relations with both the President's Office and the Consulate. In April 1941, as a gesture of goodwill and friendship, he sent them both a box of Matzos, a gesture that was acknowledged and 'greatly appreciated.'

President Benes received a delegation from the Federation of Czechoslovakian Jews on the occasion of the Czechoslovakian Independence Day. The Chief Rabbi as President of the Federation of Czekoslovakian Jews was represented by Vice President, Dr. I. Epstein, accompanied by Messrs. M.R. Springer, K. Leitner, and L. Singer. The delegation pledged the loyalty of the Czechoslovakian Jewry to the cause of the country which for twenty years has been an 'island of religious freedom in a Europe torn by racial hatred.' [The First Republic]

• On June 5, 1939, Mr. R. Springer confirmed that Mr. Kurt Leitner has been appointed as Hon. Worker at the Federation of Czech and Slovakian Jews. On July 6, Mr. R.W. Oppenheimer confirmed that Opa has been appointed as a Hon. Worker at the Orthodox Department at the Central Office for Refugees.

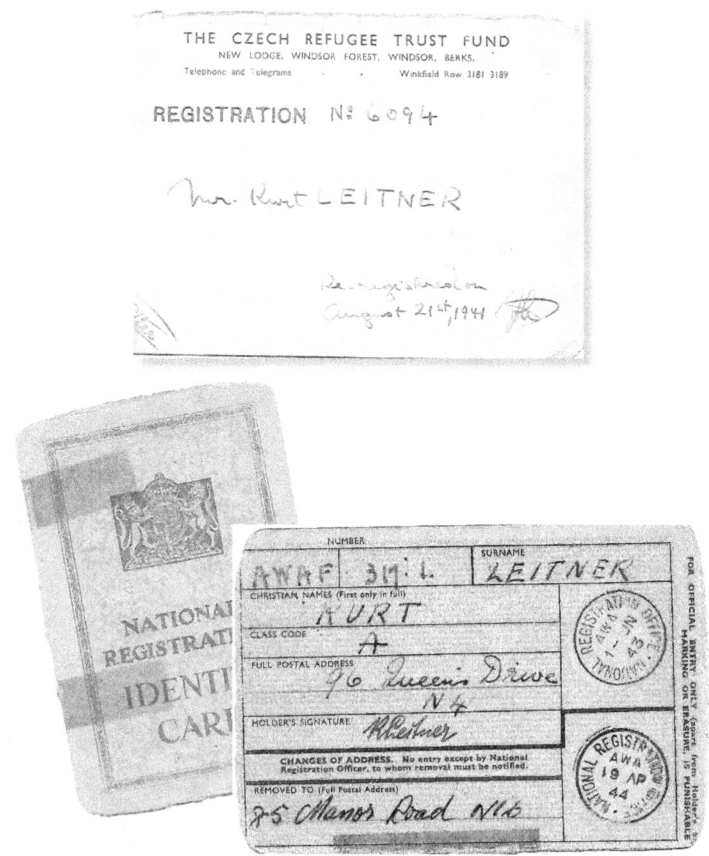

THE CZECH REFUGEE TRUST FUND
NEW LODGE, WINDSOR FOREST, WINDSOR, BERKS.
Telephone and Telegrams Winkfield Row 3181 3189

REGISTRATION No 6094

Mr. Kurt LEITNER

Re-registration
August 21st, 1941

NATIONAL REGISTRATI
IDENTI
CARD

NUMBER: AWAF 317 L
SURNAME: LEITNER
CHRISTIAN NAMES (First only in full): KURT
CLASS CODE: A
FULL POSTAL ADDRESS: 96 Queens Drive N4
HOLDER'S SIGNATURE: K Leitner
CHANGES OF ADDRESS. No entry except by National Registration Officer, to whom removal must be notified.
REMOVED TO (Full Postal Address): 85 Manor Road N16
FOR OFFICIAL ENTRY ONLY. MARKING OR ERASURE IS PUNISHABLE

Registration and Identity Card during his stay in London

The main relief operation in England during the war was masterminded by Mr. Harry Goodman and Rabbi Shlomo Schonfeld. They worked tirelessly in order to provide as much relief and help as possible to refugees in the U.K., and also sending much needed supplies to people who were still stuck in Europe. Opa worked closely with them, thereby forming a very close friendship with them.

Extracts from Opa's Police book whilst in London during the war includes:

1. Until March 27, 1940 he lived at 14 Lordship Park, London
2. From June 10, 1940 he lived at 22 Lordship Park, London
3. On April 21, 1941 Opa travelled overnight to Maidenhead on behalf of the Chief Rabbi's Emergency Council.
4. September 1941, permission was granted to work at the Pavillion Hotel in Buxton and then temporarily changed to Sommerford House, Terrace Road, Buxton.
5. On April 17, 1942 Opa was granted permission to be the Secretary of the Federation of Czechoslovakian Jews, based at 53, Queens Drive, London.
6. On April 18, 1944, he moved to 85 Manor Road, London.
7. On December 13, 1944 Opa was granted permission to travel for two nights to Cardiff, on behalf of the Chief Rabbi's Emergency Council.
8. On October 30, 1945 Opa was granted permission to travel from Liverpool to Chile.

Rabbi Shlomo Schonfeld's father, Rabbi Avigdor Schonfeld, established the Adass Yisroel Shul but unfortunately died on January 1, 1930, at the young age of 49, from blood poisoning caused by an infected cut on his finger, which today could have been treated quite easily with penicillin. His son, Shlomo, eulogised him, quoting from his father's previous Rosh Hashanah sermon. 'We do not just pray for life, but rather for a **purpose** in life' and that subsequently became Shlomo Schonfeld's motto in life.

Rabbi Schonfeld had learnt in the Nitra Yeshivah before the war, and through Hashgocho Protis became acquainted and friendly with Rabbi Michoel Ber Weissmandl. They later joined forces and became very active in their relief operations on behalf of the war refugees, and worked together with Mr. Julius Steinfeld, a member of the Schiffshul in Vienna, to arrange the 'Kindertransports' that travelled to London.

Julius Steinfeld

It was also a clear display of Hashgocho Protis that Rabbi Schonfeld had visited Marienbad frequently, and had noticed first hand Opa's exceptional organisational capabilities. Hence, when he arrived in London in 1939, Rabbi Schonfeld did not hesitate to rope him in, since he knew that he could rely on Opa as a trusted, capable and conscientious worker.

Initially, it was Rabbi Weissmandl who inspired Rabbi Schonfeld to establish the 'Ohr Yisroel' Yeshivah in London for boys aged 16-18, who were too old to be eligible for the 'Kindertransports'. For this purpose he first bought a large house at 109-111 Stamford Hill, and later at 65 Lordship Road, where Rabbi Babad, later the Rav of Sunderland, acted as their Rosh HaYeshivah.

German Jews never dreamt that the German 'Judenrein' policy would become a reality. Even Rabbi Yaakov Rosenheim was forced to leave Germany in 1935, and could never absorb the fact that 'his' Germany could descend to such despicable levels of inhumanity. The situation deteriorated rapidly after the Anschluss, as was reported in the New York Times.

'When Austrians woke up on March 12 1938, they discovered German troops marching through their streets in what became known as the Anschluss. Instead of displaying resistance, large crowds of Austrians greeted the Nazi invaders with raucous cheers and Nazi salutes, leaving little doubt that most were eager to join the Reich. Between the Anschluss and the start of the war some six months later, almost 100,000 Jews fled Austria.'

Soon after the Anschluss, American President Roosevelt called for an International Conference to discuss the 'refugee problem', which was held in the French town of Evian, from July 6-15, 1938, at which representatives from 32 countries and 25 voluntary organisations attended. Nazi Germany sent an official message to this conference that 'they would allow and assist mass Jewish emigration to any country that was willing to accept the Jews.' Although the detailed discussions held by Dr. Maximillian Landau with various governments, as reported a year previously at the Kenessio Gedoloh in Marienbad, were discussed at

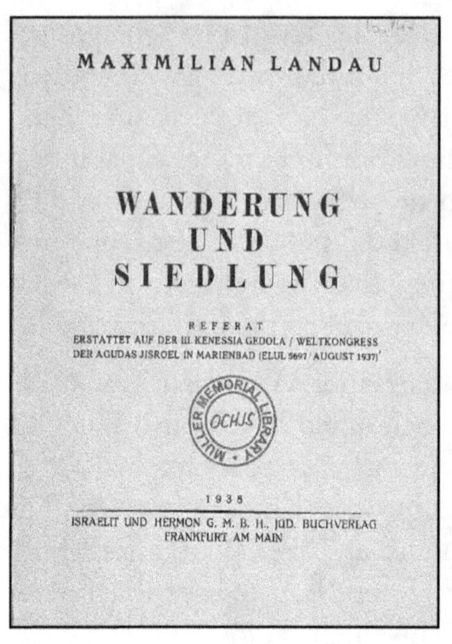

MAXIMILIAN LANDAU

WANDERUNG
UND
SIEDLUNG

REFERAT
ERSTATTET AUF DER III. KENESSIA GEDOLA / WELTKONGRESS
DER AGUDAS JISROEL IN MARIENBAD (ELUL 5697 / AUGUST 1937)

1938

ISRAELIT UND HERMON G. M. B. H., JÜD. BUCHVERLAG
FRANKFURT AM MAIN

Dr. Landau's speech at the 3rd Kenessio reprinted in 1938 for the Evian Conference

the Evian Conference, only the Dominican Republic agreed to take in 100,000 Jewish farmers that would help their economy. All the other nations might have shed crocodile tears for these Jewish refugees, but they had no more interest in them than did Germany. Many Western countries had been forced to accept large numbers of refugees as a result of World War I, that finished just about thirty years previously, but now refused to accept too many more refugees into their countries. Soon afterwards World War II broke out, and it might truly be said that it was a World War against the Jewish people.

Britain had placed strict immigration quotas for Palestine, in their eagerness to calm Arab riots against the implementation of the Balfour Declaration, and was likewise not eager to allow immigration into Britain. However, owing to public pressure on humanitarian grounds, Britain preferred to allow a limited number of refugees into their country, rather than relax their Palestinian quotas. So Britain became the 'first choice' for these asylum seekers and agreed to accept 50,000 refugees, as long as they had a legitimate job offer or a personal guarantee of financial support.

Soon after Kristallnacht Rabbi S. Schonfeld travelled to Vienna, and with the help of Mr. Julius Steinfeld arranged for three hundred children to come to England in a Kindertransport, arriving during the Chanukah school holidays. Rabbi Schonfeld made arrangements to convert three local schools into hostels where these children were put up, sleeping on mattresses on the floor, one next to another.

The **Health and Safety** Officer inspected one of these premises and voiced his disapproval at the overcrowded conditions. Rabbi Schonfeld was quick to reply and said, 'here it is **Healthier and Safer** than in Auschwitz.' That was the end of the conversation, and the inspector left, with nothing more to say.

Opa had an unusual genealogical talent which he used in helping to trace lost family members, sometimes matching up orphans with close relations, and sometimes by arranging their adoption into families of more distant relatives. Even later, when he attended the Daf Hayomi Shiurim, he was always fully conversant with the intricate discussions of the complicated inter-family relationships that are discussed in מסכת יבמות.

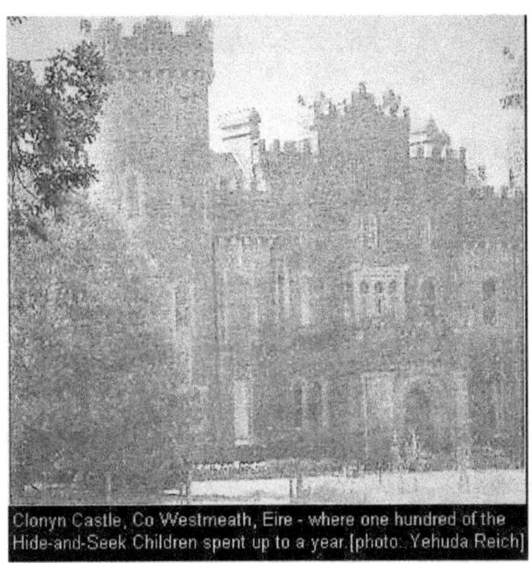
Clonyn Castle, Co Westmeath, Eire - where one hundred of the Hide-and-Seek Children spent up to a year.[photo: Yehuda Reich]

Clonyn Castle

Another Kindertransport from Poland was sent to Ireland, and the children stayed at Clonyn Castle near Dublin, which was generously donated for this purpose by a Mr. Levy from Manchester.

Rabbi Shlomo Schonfeld was responsible for raising the finances necessary for the continuation of his Kindertransports, and in 1940 the Charities Commission accounts for the Chief Rabbi's Religious Emergency Council showed an annual income of over £2,000,000. [The average living wage for a family at that time was £10 per week]. He achieved this by requesting small but regular donations, and in one of his mail shots that he sent to the public he wrote 'I am asking you for one pound per month to maintain orphans presently in Poland, whom I have arranged to take out from there.'

The German Blitz targeted London during 1940-1941 and nobody was safe. Some people hid in air raid shelters, and others used to hide in the underground stations of London, often sleeping there at night. Some people planned to return to their homes in the morning, only to discover that their houses had been bombed during the night, and new accommodation had to be found.

Rabbi Shlomo Schonfeld distributed Matzos to over 1200 Jews that occupied these air raid shelters, whilst the Aguda Report for this period confirms that Shiurim continued unabated in the shelters even during the Blitz. All these activities needed to be constantly updated, owing to the ever changing demographic nature caused by the effects of the bombings.

In March 1941, Rabbi Shlomo Schonfeld obtained permission to send fortnightly food parcels and religious requirements to any observant Jewish servicemen in Europe, providing for nearly 25,000 people in Her Majesty's Forces. For Pesach, too, he ensured that these servicemen obtained appropriate supplies, which were much appreciated.

Below are some excerpts of the gratitude expressed by these recipients:

> *'Your Pesach package was the nicest gift I received during my entire army life'.*
>
> *'You must have gone through a great deal of expense to ensure that I have a kosher Pesach and believe me, I can't describe how grateful I am.'*
>
> *'Were it not for you folk at home, the morale of the Jewish soldier would be very low. The Pesach parcel certainly stimulated my determination to continue to live and observe the laws of our Holy Torah.'*
>
> *'You have no imagination how much it means to us boys in the services to know that there is someone at home who remembers us on Passover'-- etc.*

Rabbi Schonfeld came up with the ideas for all these activities, but left it to Opa and others working with him to implement them. My father was extremely busy with the Hatzolo work, and was Rabbi Schonfeld's right hand man.

In 1942, Rabbi Shlomo Schonfeld requested from the British Government permission for the sole rights and import of 'Arba Minim' from Eretz Yisroel, which he was granted and then distributed throughout the country as well as to the Armed Forces.

In September 1941, Mr. Yehuda Hofmann, owner of 'Somerset House', a small kosher hotel in Buxton, invited Opa to come and help him over the busy Yom Tov period. He obliged and went to help there, but immediately after Yom Tov explained to Mr. Hofmann that he was needed in London. However, he suggested that he offer the job to his younger brother, Uncle Shurl, who lived in London, and was very capable and had been trained in the Hotel School in Marienbad. Mr Hoffman took his advice, and Uncle Shurl accepted the job.

At the end of the war, the British Government announced that any relief organisation that provided its own transportation would be allowed to conduct their independent relief activities immediately following liberation. Rabbi Shlomo Schonfeld then implemented the concept of the 'Synagogue Ambulance' that travelled to the camps and provided kosher food, medicines, religious articles and other services wherever required. These units could easily be converted from a Synagogue into an Ambulance and vice versa, as required.

The Synagogue Ambulance pictured below was donated by the Hebrew Congregation of Melbourne, (Australia), who were not directly involved in the war, but contributed by funding generously for the purchase and upkeep of this ambulance. A total of nine Synagogue Ambulances were purchased, funded by various communities worldwide whose countries were likewise not directly engaged in the war, but participated in the relief effort with their generous donations. These Synagogue Ambulances were employed for different concentration camps after the war, thereby providing urgently required rehabilitation to the persecuted in the now liberated camps. They were also involved in collecting information from camp inmates, who were trying to trace lost or missing relatives.

Consecration of the first Synagogue-Ambulance (12th November, 1944). Chief Rabbi Dr. J. J. Hertz, is in the front

The first shipment involved the distribution of 120,000 tins of kosher meat to various Jewish organisations in France, Holland, Czechoslovakia, Greece and Tripoli. A second shipment contained 500 tons of kosher supplies. The Chief Rabbi's Religious Emergency Council also shipped over 100,000 items of religious articles, including Tefillin, Mezuzahs and Tallesim. This was a gigantic operation, and required a very methodical organisation to ensure its success.

Telephone: STAmford Hill 1971. Registered under the War Charities Act, 1940.

CHIEF RABBI'S
RELIGIOUS EMERGENCY COUNCIL

Chairman: The Chief Rabbi of the British Empire.
The Very Rev. Dr. J. H. HERTZ, C.H.

Joint Hon. Treasurers:
OSCAR PHILIPP, Esq.
Rabbi HARRIS SWIFT.

Executive: Dayan H. M. LAZARUS, M.A.
Rabbi Dr. S. SCHONFELD, (Exec. Director)

Secretary: HENRY PELS, Esq

86, AMHURST PARK,
LONDON, N.16.

6-7-1945

TO WHOM IT MAY CONCERN

This is to certify that Mr.K.Leitner is an accredited representative of the above council.He has kindly undertaken to purchase quantities of foodstuff for despatch to the liberated concentration camps and to other needy persons in Europe.This arrangement is sanctioned by the Ministry of food the councel for British societies for relief abroad.

Executive Director.

Transcription:

Chief Rabbi's Religious Emergency Council, 86, Amhurst Park, London N.16.

Dated 6-7-1945.

TO WHOM IT MAY CONCERN

This is to certify that Mr. K. Leitner is an accredited representative of the above council. He has kindly undertaken to purchase quantities of foodstuff for despatch to the liberated concentration camps and to other needy persons in Europe. This arrangement is sanctioned by the Ministry of food the council for British societies for relief abroad.

Signed: Shlomo Schonfeld, Executive Director.

Extract of a letter received by Opa, written July 19, 1945 (Tisha B'Av) by Rabbi Shloime Baumgarten, who had gone to Bergen Belsen to bring relief, comfort, and above all, Yiddishkeit to the survivors of one of the most notorious of Hitler's concentration camps. The visit was organised by the Chief Rabbi's Religious Emergency Council headed by Rabbi Dr. Schonfeld, who travelled in a Synagogue Ambulance.

This is what Rabbi Baumgarten wrote to Opa, translated from the original German:

> ...I will forward information as I hear it and would like someone to keep a record of it. I am fasting very well; yesterday evening I said Eicha and organised a Minyan for men and women. There were 400 girls and women and 100 men. This morning – Tisha B'Av – there was again a Minyan but with fewer people. There were no Kinos available so we said Eicha again.
>
> You cannot imagine the amount of tears which we shed yesterday evening. The events far exceeded what the Midrash and Gemoroh tell us about the Churban of the Beis Hamikdosh. What is the significance today of the story of Chanah and her seven sons.... who were able to be Mekadesh Hashem? They would all have been happy to die like that. I hear, for instance, that Hungarian children before entering the gas chambers said Tehillim and Shema Yisroel out loud and called to each other that only minutes separated them from Gan Eden. A father whose son tried to escape was forced to hang his own son, and the Nazis jeered him with the words: 'Here, look at your offspring'. The father was not spared either.
>
> I request that before all this is filed, it should be recorded.
>
> The Taanis passed well. I was the guest of Baba Ungar, a cousin of the Lackenbacher Rov (Rav Chaim Ungar). She koshered everything and comes from a very Chassidic home. She told me that her father rose every night at one o'clock to learn Torah.
>
> As general information, I want to add that when the transports arrived in Auschwitz, the arrivals were selected. A few young able bodied people were sent to work and the others were despatched to the gas chambers. The remainder were re-selected daily i.e. those who looked weak and pale were sent to be gassed. From one transport, 300 able bodied women and girls were selected for work, only to be sent to the gas chambers the following day. These are only some examples of countless incidents.

In another letter Rabbi Baumgarten wrote from Bergen Belsen, he reported what he had witnessed (translated):

'I arrived here shortly before Shabbos, when two girls approached me, crying bitterly. Their mother had just died, and all they requested was that she should be buried in her own individual grave, rather than in a mass grave. I went to speak to the Burial Officer and ב"ה their wish was granted and I even spoke a few words at the funeral.

You walk through the camp and people approach you from all sides, as they all need encouragement and advice. My Tefillin are in use from morning until night. I wish I had hundreds more pairs here.

How can I describe the last Shabbos? I was asked to speak to about 200 people. They relate how one Kehilla after another was sent to Auschwitz. Every single person who survived is a separate miracle. These survivors have been a fortnight without bread, without a drop of water, and that was a common occurrence. Children of six years of age fasted for days and gave their slice of bread to their mothers.

I have visited the children's home and have arranged for a Bris Milo; the first in Bergen Belsen. In the evening I am speaking to the Beth Jaakov Group which has been active here since liberation…

We continued our work in and around Bergen Belsen, setting up many religious and welfare activities, including various Minyanim, kosher kitchens, Torah classes, Shechita and Mikvo'os.

Rabbi S. Schonfeld in army uniform

A fuller and more detailed account of the numerous rescue operations that were the brainchild of Rabbi Schonfeld and accomplished and assisted by Opa, can be read in an excellent book entitled 'Holocaust Hero' by David Kranzler.

All Aguda Relief work throughout the world was coordinated, and they worked closely together in order to maximise their overall accomplishments. Below is a telegram sent to London on October 8, 1944, which proved extremely important to the success in the Allied war effort at the time of the liberation.

On the October 8, 1944 a telegram was sent to Chief Rabbi Josef Hertz, at 1 Mulberry Street, London, England.

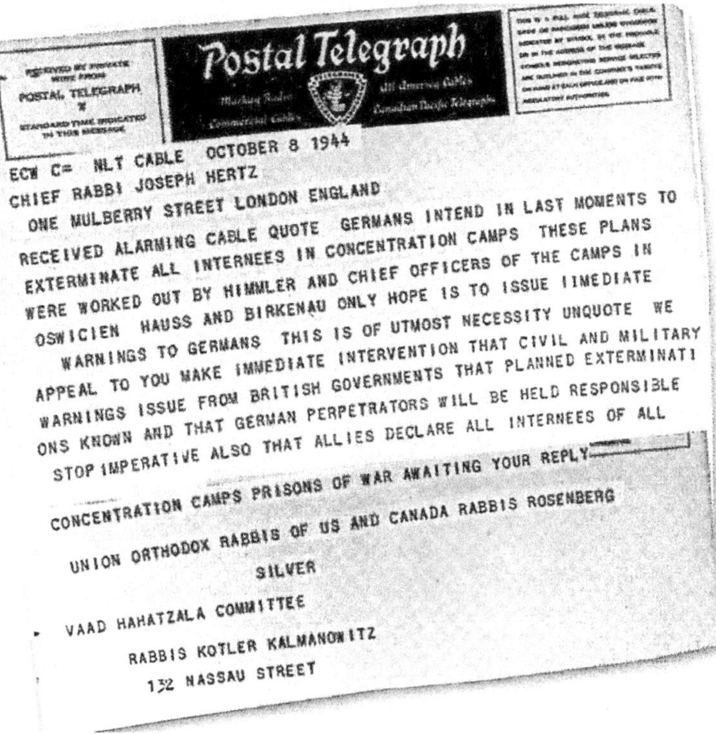

Postal Telegraph

ECW C= NLT CABLE OCTOBER 8 1944
CHIEF RABBI JOSEPH HERTZ
ONE MULBERRY STREET LONDON ENGLAND
RECEIVED ALARMING CABLE QUOTE GERMANS INTEND IN LAST MOMENTS TO
EXTERMINATE ALL INTERNEES IN CONCENTRATION CAMPS THESE PLANS
WERE WORKED OUT BY HIMMLER AND CHIEF OFFICERS OF THE CAMPS IN
OSWICIEN HAUSS AND BIRKENAU ONLY HOPE IS TO ISSUE IMEDIATE
WARNINGS TO GERMANS THIS IS OF UTMOST NECESSITY UNQUOTE WE
APPEAL TO YOU MAKE IMMEDIATE INTERVENTION THAT CIVIL AND MILITARY
WARNINGS ISSUE FROM BRITISH GOVERNMENTS THAT PLANNED EXTERMINATI
ONS KNOWN AND THAT GERMAN PERPETRATORS WILL BE HELD RESPONSIBLE
STOP IMPERATIVE ALSO THAT ALLIES DECLARE ALL INTERNEES OF ALL
CONCENTRATION CAMPS PRISONS OF WAR AWAITING YOUR REPLY

UNION ORTHODOX RABBIS OF US AND CANADA RABBIS ROSENBERG
SILVER
VAAD HAHATZALA COMMITTEE
RABBIS KOTLER KALMANOWITZ
132 NASSAU STREET

'Received alarming cable quote Germans intend in last moment to exterminate all internees in concentration camps. These plans were worked out by Himmler and chief officers of the camps in Oswicien Haus and Birkenau. Only hope is to issue immediate warnings to Germans. This is of utmost necessity'. We appeal to you make immediate intervention that civil and military warnings issue from British Governments that planned exterminations known and that German perpetrators will be held responsible. Imperative also that Allies declare all internees of all concentration camps prisoners of war. Awaiting your reply.

Union of Orthodox Rabbis of U.S. and Canada Rabbi Rosenberg – Silver

Vaad Hatzala Committee,

Rabbi Kotler - Kalmanovitz, 132 Nassau Street.

It is well recorded that as the end of the war approached, efforts were made at many concentration camps to destroy records, and either to murder the remaining prisoners or transfer them deeper into German territory before the Allies could arrive and liberate them. These transports were usually from places outside Germany, e.g. from Auschwitz, to camps inside Germany. One example of this are the three train loads of prisoners that left Bergen Belsen on April 10, 1945 to their destination of Theresienstadt, with 2500 prisoners on each train. With the information that had been received from the Vaad Hatzala in America, allied bombings prevented these trains from reaching their destination, and twelve days later arrived in a small town of Trobitz, from where they all escaped to freedom. Mrs. R. Masher ע"ה, who died in Manchester in 2017, was one of the survivors from Bergen Belsen who travelled on one of those trains.

Many Jewish families had entrusted their children into the care of non-Jewsish neighbours in an attempt to secure their safety, and these families were reluctant to release their foster children again after liberation. The idea of the Synagogue Ambulance was adapted by the American Aguda too, and after the war, Rabbi Silver, dressed in an American Army uniform and accompanied by two Americal soldiers, toured the Polish camps. Every Sunday morning, Rabbi Silver would enter the Polish churches and monasteries whilst they were in the midst of their prayers, walk up to the front, and flanked by his two 'bodyguards' would turn and face the crowds and slowly say one sentence, whilst scanning carefully the reaction on the faces of the children present. In a loud voice he called out the first Possuk of 'Shema Yisroel' and observed their reaction. Any positive reaction was sufficient proof that this child was of Jewish origin, and Rabbi Silver ensured that they left their non-Jewish foster parents.

As secretary of the Federation of Czechoslovakian Jews, Opa was instrumental in collating and publishing a booklet entitled 'The Persecution of the Jews in Nazi Slovakia'. In this booklet, the Czech Government in Exile in London used their diplomatic connections and smuggled out, via Switzerland, detailed letters from suffering Jews about their terrible conditions back in Europe. This was published in 1942, with the hope that this would get some reaction and assistance from the British Government. Rabbi Schonfeld also obtained direct information from Rabbi Weissmandl about many of the atrocities that were being carried out in Europe, which were conveyed to the British Government too, and demanded firm action.

The gruesome facts of the persecution are a small testimony of what actually occurred in Slovakia.

THE PERSECUTION OF THE JEWS IN NAZI SLOVAKIA

THE PERSECUTION OF THE JEWS
IN
NAZI SLOVAKIA

REPORTS AND DOCUMENTS

Bratislava, the Forked Jewish Street showing the Rococo House

With Messages from
DR. EDVARD BENES
(President of Czechoslovakia)
and
DR. JURAJ SLAVIK
(Czechoslovak Minister of the Interior)

Issued by the
FEDERATION OF CZECHOSLOVAKIAN JEWS,
53, Queen's Drive, London, N.4.
1942

FOREWORD

THIS booklet is an attempt to relate the story of the persecution and the mass expulsions of Jews from the puppet " state " of Slovakia.

Some 80,000 Jews lived in this land, in peace and contentment, particularly so, in the Masaryk-Benes period between Versailles and Munich, the years 1919 to 1939.

But their complete destruction has been decided in Berlin, not in Bratislava.

In the French Yellow Book on the causes of the war, there appears a report of M. V. de Lacroix, French Minister in Prague, transmitted to the French Minister of Foreign Affairs on February 7th, 1939.

" What appears to have most impressed Dr. Chvalkovsky, the Czechoslovak Foreign Minister, was the importance which Herr Hitler and Herr von Ribbentrop attached to the Jewish question, absolutely out of proportion to the importance assigned to other questions. The Foreign Minister of the Reich, as well as the Chancellor, are said to have stated emphatically that it was not possible to give the German guarantee to a State which did not eliminate the Jews."

After the last visit of " Prime Minister " Bela Tuka to Berlin, the official newspaper " Slovak " reported that Tuka was told in the German capital that the Jewish question must be regulated.

In this booklet, the manner in which this " regulation " is proceeding is reported. The majority of these reports are taken from news items appearing in Slovak newspapers.

For three centuries the Jews have lived in this Slovak land. They have farmed and tilled it; they have built industries and commerce. They have made it a centre of Jewish learning. Already more than 200 years ago the Yeshivah of Pressburg was famed. There were 59 Jewish elementary schools in the Slovakia of the wise President Masaryk, of which 35 used the Slovak language as the medium of instruction. The six theological colleges of Slovak Jewry were world renowned, attracting pupils from the four corners of the globe. Social institutions, welfare centres, hospitals, all these were firmly established.

And now, in the midst of this war for freedom, the Slovak Jewish communities have been destroyed. The men are being expelled, sent to concentration camps and to death in the mines. Their women-folk face direst distress. Their property has been " expropriated to the State "; more than 10,000 businesses have been " liquidated," and over 25,000 acres of farm-land confiscated.

This booklet relates from official sources how the sick are dragged from the hospitals, Jewish houses searched by day and by night, people dragged from their hiding-places, Jewish personal belongings stolen; even at the frontiers where they flee, guards are placed to turn them back and arrest them. We read how Jewish girls and women are destined to " special " camps: the men for an unknown destination, to death in the labour camps of occupied Russia.

A priest who intervenes is arrested: the Church is told it must not interfere. Synagogues are closed, and the property of the Jewish communities liquidated. A baptism " plot " is invented to arouse the docile population, denounced subsequently by the Apostolic Delegate.

As an appendix there are published extracts from letters smuggled out of Slovakia through Switzerland to this country. Their authenticity is unquestioned. They prove how in this hour of direst need the Jews of Slovakia have not lost their faith:

" The Lord is for me, I will not fear:
What can man do unto me? "

For we know that " the hands are those of Esau." We know that this vileness is inspired and directed from Berlin. We know that it will pass. And that in God's good time a free Czechoslovakia will be restored to a free Europe.

June, 1942. H. A. GOODMAN.

3

A Message from President Benes

THE Jewish problem, along with many othes relating to the reconstruction of the life of our State after the conclusion of the war, has greatly occupied my thoughts. It represents an important factor in our efforts to secure civic liberty and social justice in Czechoslovakia within the framework of the genuine and improved new order which, as a sequel to the chaos let loose upon the world by the insane Nazi experiment, is certainly destined to come into existence.

Great tasks await us. In the restored Czechoslovak Republic all sections of the population, in so far as they have shown themselves, and will show themselves in the future, as capable of aiding the work of the State, must receive due justice. Religious freedom is, of course, the first pre-supposition and foundation, and one which cannot be dispensed with by any properly organised state. We shall not depart in the least from the principles of true and honest democracy which we adhered to in creating our first republic. They led us to progress, peace and development. The Nazis, through the fact that they are today repudiating them, have turned Czechoslovakia into a hell. Their murderous emissaries destroy the works of human culture, introducing in their place the torture chambers of the Gestapo. They incite people to intolerance, to racial, religious and ideological fanaticism; they expel those who are not so cowardly as to accept their regime, or those who in their eyes have sinned only through the fact that they were not born of aryan parents, while at the same time they drive their own youth to the common grave of the battlefields.

But all this is only transitional. It will pass away, like everything which is in contradiction with the laws of humanity. The Czechoslovak State will be re-established, and with it its previous conception of democracy.

Hold on, therefore, to the end, and be sure that the renewed Czechoslovak Republic will have no other programme than the programme of religious tolerance of the first Republic of Masaryk.

Dr. E. BENES.

The Jews in Nazi Slovakia

THE attitude and methods of the present rulers of Slovakia, a country directed by the Nazis and administered by traitors, are opposed to the entire Slovak tradition, and differ diametrically from everything that the Slovak patriots were proclaiming and realising both at the time of the Hungarian slavery, and during the twenty years of the Czechoslovak Republic. This could easily be proved in all walks of national life as well as in all branches of the life of the State, but this appears unnecessary as the evidence in this case is plainly very striking. Instead of traditional Slav solidarity we perceive servility to the Germans, instead of democracy and tolerance nothing but Nazi totalitarianism and terror, instead of the freedom of conscience and of religious liberty, Gestapo methods and prisons. The same applies, of course, in a full measure to the Jewish question, and in Bratislava to-day they boast of their perversity.

After the last visit of Bela Tuka to Berlin the newspaper of the so-called President Tiso, " Slovak," stated that whilst Bela Tuka was in the Nazi capital he was told that the problem of co-existence of different national groups in Slovakia had been settled in a model way, and that the Jewish question also appeared to be regulated there better than anywhere else outside Germany.

It is a fact, however, that the co-existence of different national groups settled in such a highly satisfactory way signifies simply the hegemony of a small group of Germans

4

over the whole nation, and that the boast concerning the "regulation" of the Jewish question is a sad and infamous allegation that nowhere in the world, except in Germany, are the Jews more oppressed, tortured, robbed and persecuted than in Tuka's Slovakia.

I am not in possession of all data by which I could prove the shameful boast of the rulers of Bratislava, but let me just mention some facts of the last few months as announced by the Bratislava Broadcasting Station. On September 10th, 1941, the Bratislava Station announced that the council of ministers approved, after a prolonged deliberation, the Jewish Code as well as a regulation concerning a special levy on Jewish property. What provisions the Jewish Code contains appears only from some later remarks and from regulations which followed. The Code defines the term "Jew" exactly in the same way as is laid down in the Nuremberg laws, that is on the basis of the race. In the same way it defines the idea of the admixture of Jewish blood. Jews older than six years must have a visible mark on their clothes, this being in the form of a yellow star over the left breast. The Jews are not permitted to live in the centre of the towns, they are not permitted to employ women-servants below the age of forty, they are not permitted to own industrial enterprises, land and other real property, and they are not permitted to visit places of entertainment, theatres, exhibitions, etc.

The application of the Jewish Code is extremely severe. Jewish property which so far had not been confiscated was subjected to a 20 per cent .tax, the proceeds of which amounted to 600 millions of Czech Kronen. For the payment of this levy it was decreed that all Jews are jointly and severally liable. Jewish enterprises are being liquidated, which means that they are being taken without compensation. Up to November 1st, 9,620 Jewish firms were thus "liquidated" and, as reported from Bratislava, more than 400 millions of annual clear profit has been taken away from over 13,000 firms owned by Jews. Jewish house property to the value of 1,200 millions has been expropriated together with about 25,000 acres of land. Bratislava announced further that even the personal property of the Jews will be "aryanised," and that the Jews will be permitted to take with them to the Ghetto only objects of absolute necessity.

In Bratislava a Ghetto is being founded, but only for employed Jews. These Jews are now concentrated in certain streets and even there they can be given three months' notice to vacate the premises at any time. They are permitted to live only in old houses. This Ghetto is only a transitory arrangement as all Jews will be removed from Bratislava.

As soon as the authorisation to work is taken away from a Jew, he has to move together with his family to another Jewish centre. By the end of 1941, 70 per cent. of all Jews, that is 10,000 persons, had to move from Bratislava.

Special concentration camps for Jews are being created, and special labour obligations apply to Jews. Even Jewish intellectuals have to perform the most arduous tasks. Before concentration camps are created the Jews are permitted to settle only in the following towns: Trnava, Nitra, Zilina, Presov and Spisska Nova Ves. Jews are not allowed to buy milk and other food in the morning hours and must not do so in the open market, that is, outside licenced shops.

I have stated here an example of how the Jews are treated in the "free" Slovakia. These are sad facts and circumstances and no great fantasy is needed to realise them. Well known also is the brutality and the inconsiderateness of the so-called "Minister of Interior" Sano Mach, who carries out the anti-Jewish laws and regulations. Well known also, however, are his corrupt practices and we can easily judge the disinterestedness of his officials. The application of these laws and regulations could, to better advantage, be entitled: Larceny, robbery, terror and beastliness .

All, however, that is happening to our Jewish fellow-citizens in Slovakia is only temporary. Slovakia is a part of Czechoslovakia and it will remain in the hands of traitors and Nazi lackeys only until the victorious end

5

of this war. The words of President Benes will then equally apply to Slovakia as a part of Czechoslovakia: —

" The renewed Czechoslovak Republic will have no other programme than the programme of religious tolerance of the first Republic of Masaryk."

Dr. JURAJ SLAVIK.

The Old-New Synagogue, Interior

6

Law concerning the Jews of Slovakia

(Issued on September 9th, 1941: No. 186/41)

Marking of parcels and letters.

Every Jew or Jewish organisation, who sends a parcel, letter, etc., within the country, has to put a special sign (the Star of David) on it.

The penalty for the contravention of this law will be a fine of 100 Crowns to 1,000 Crowns, or imprisonment of 1—15 days'. (Paragraph 27-1).

Prohibition of slaughter of animals according to Jewish Rites.

The slaughter of animals of any kind according to Jewish rites is prohibited, as well as the cutting or the sale or the purchase of such meat. This also concerns the products of such meat.

The penalty for contravention of this law will be a fine of 100 Crowns to 10,000 Crowns, or a penalty of 1—15 days' imprisonment. (Paragraph 37-1/2).

Female Employees in Households.

It is prohibited to employ non-Jewish female staff in Jewish households. A household is considered Jewish if the majority of the members are Jews.

Charwomen, nurses and maids who do not sleep in the household are also included in this law.

The penalty for contravention of this law will be a fine of 500—50,000 Crowns, or 5—30 days' imprisonment. (Paragraph 41).

Legal Representation of Jews.

A solicitor may represent a Jew only if the law absolutely requires such legal representation, or if the Court considers it essential. Such representative must himself be a Jew. This regulation also concerns public notaries.

A non-legal representative of a Jew can only be another Jew of close relationship (husband, brother, etc.) to the person concerned. (Paragraphs 8 and 49).

Employment of Jews.

Everyone who employs a Jew on the day this Order comes into force must obtain special permission to do so by October 31st, 1941. No application will be considered after that date.

Any Jew between the ages of 16—60 who is not already in employment, or doing forced labour (Arbeitsdienst) must immediately take up any work ordered by the Minister of the Interior or his delegate. (Paragraphs 22, 43 and 258).

General prohibitions.

No Jew may carry any weapon.

No Jew will be permitted to fish.

No Jew may drive a Slovak vehicle. (Paragraph 51).

Passports and travel papers.

Passports or travel papers will be issued to Jews only by special permission of the Ministry of the Interior. Such papers have to be returned within eight days on arrival from another part of the country.

(The Order consists of 270 clauses).

7

I. Expulsions and Labour Camps

"The sword comes to the world for the delay of justice, and for the perversion of justice."
Ethics of the Fathers V.

Establishment of Concentration Camps in Slovakia.

The Slovak Minister, Sano Mach, recently strengthened the solution of the Jewish problem; he has forbidden the movement of Jews except to Jewish camps and Ghettos. As there is evidence that Jews recently purchased large quantities of textiles, he has ordered the restoration of these articles. The Jews are only allowed to retain a portion of their clothing. The Hlinka Guard and F.S. control the campaign. The Minister of the Interior has undertaken the final problem of the emigration and expulsion of Jews. Internment camps have been constructed in seventeen communes. A great deal of interest concerning the Jewish migration is being shown by the Protectorate. Jews in Slovakia are the bearers of enemy propaganda and spread rumours, and many Slovak Jews have recently become so insupportable that they are being sent to labour camps. An examination of Jews from sixteen to forty-five is being carried out in Pressburg, and those Jews fit to work are immediately despatched to labour camps. As many Jews disregard the decree ordering the wearing of the Star of David, this naturally gives rise to ill-humour amongst the population. The Minister of the Interior has put an end to this by ordering the Star of David to be increased in breadth to ten centimetres instead of six, and it must be visible to all. There are to be no exceptions, except for certain Jews employed by the State, whose families, however, are not exempt. The Minister of the Interior has apologised to the impatient public, stating that the Jewish problem will definitely be solved, and that Jews will be expelled from Europe .

(7th March. *Donauzeitung*, Belgrade).

Camps for Jewesses and Prostitutes.

The suggestion that Jewesses and prostitutes may be interned together in labour camps is made editorially.

"We have three kinds of labour camps, for Jews, for the anti-Social elements, and for vagabond gypsies. The problem of a camp for Jewesses and prostitutes is not yet solved."

(Sept. 7th, 1941. *Gardista*, Bratislava).

Fined for Selling Fish to Jews.

A Jew has been arrested for failing to wear the Star of David in public. Shocked at the incident, his wife attempted to commit suicide.

A woman fishmonger has been sentenced to one month's imprisonment and a fine of 10,000 Kr. for secretly selling fish to Jews, each one of whom has also been fined 1,000 Kr. and imprisoned for one day.

(Oct. 9th, 1941. *Grenzbote*, Bratislava).

Stars of David on Jewish Doors.

All Jewish households must indicate the fact that they are Jewish by displaying the Star of David, ten centimetres large, on the front door of their houses.

(March, 20th, 1942. *Donauzeitung*).

Reprisal Arrests.

Thirty-two Jews, suspected of "Communistic activities," have been arrested in Bratislava, according to a report from the Slovak capital quoted on the German radio.

Following the alleged shooting of a gendarme by "youths" in Bratislava, police and Hlinka guardsmen threw a cordon around the district affected, and the arrests were made as a reprisal.

(April 16th. *J. T. A.*).

8

All Jews will be Expelled.

The preliminary arrangements for the expulsion of Jews from Slovakia have been completed by March 25th, 1942. All Jews will be expelled from Slovakia. Jewish girls and unmarried women, and eventually women without children will be brought to production centres, where they have to carry out heavy but necessary work. According to the European New Order, special parts will be allotted for the settlement of Jews, where they will be able to live.

Jewish families will go together, and not be separated. Those who leave now will not be separated either, as their families will be brought to the same place. The actual settlement will be arranged shortly. Every Jew may take luggage of about 100lbs. with him out of Slovakia. The Jews who have been expelled lose their Slovakian nationality.

Baptised Jews will also be expelled. They will have the possibility to live in a Christian way.

(March 29th, 1942. *Slovenska Pravda*).

Grotesque Hide and Seek.

The police have arrested all Jews working at the Jewish centre (Judencentrale), and sent them to labour camps, under paragraph twenty-two of the Jewish Code, because it was discovered they had warned conscripted Jews who were willing to pay for the warning which enabled them to hide in time. Some Aryans who had assisted Jews were arrested with them. In Pressburg the Jews have started a grotesque game of hide and seek, but the police will know how to find them and punish them.

(March 22nd. *Grenzbote*, Bratislava).

Jews will be Deported Penniless.

Sano Mach, Minister of the Interior, ordered the Hlinka Guards to punish severely those interfering with the expulsion of the Jews. Particular severe punishment was threatened to those attempting to take material advantage of the expulsion. Bratislava radio announcing this order, revealed that some " swindlers, disguised as Hlinka Guards and provided with faked official identity cards," had confiscated property of deported Jews. This public warning had to be issued because large-scale robbery was carried out by members of the Hlinka Guard on their own account following last week's decree providing for the complete expropriation of Jewish movable property, including clothing.

Co-operating with the Hlinka Guards, Slovak Security Police have taken 3,000 Jews and Jewesses from the districts of Saris and Zemplin to labour camps. Presov and Michalovse, the main towns of these districts, were entirely evacuated of their Jewish population.

At a press conference Sano Mach declared that the Jewish problem in Slovakia must be finally solved by depriving the Jews of Slovak citizenship and deporting them penniless. " They will have to go as they have come. With bags and bundles in their hands." Mach announced at the time that measures had been taken to prevent the Jews from returning to Slovakia. It is believed that they will be deported to Eastern Poland and occupied Russia. Mach also declared that 18 Communist wireless transmitters, all operated by Jews, had recently been discovered and confiscated.

(March 29th. *Grenzbote*, Bratislava).

600 Jews sent to Labour Camps.

Police and Hlinka Guards have rounded up and sent to forced labour camps 596 Jews and Jewesses who have " been excluded from the economic life of Slovakia," it is announced by the Bratislava radio.

(April 6th. *J. T. A., London*).

Jewish Women in Hiding Deported.

There were rounded up and sent to the camp 96 Jewesses who had been hiding in an attempt to avoid deportation.

(April 6th, 1942. Bratislava Broadcast).

9

Jewish Hospital Patients to be Deported.

Medical commissions have been appointed by M. Sano Mach, the Slovakian Minister of the Interior, to sort out Jewish hospital patients for deportation, M. Mach declared that the hospitals are crowded with an unusually large number of Jewish patients, and that the commissions have been instructed to inquire into the " genuineness of their ailments."

Recently baptised Jews are to be included in the first batches of those to be deported, the Minister stated. At the same time he announced that the new measures will be applied to all those who are considered to be Jews under the Jewish Code.

(April 12th. *Gardista*).

32,000 Deported.
Slovak Parliament Approves.

The Slovak Parliament has approved a law of a constitutional character which gives the Government ample powers to expel Jews from Slovakia. Those expelled automatically lose their nationality, and their property will be confiscated by the State.

By this law the Slovak Parliament has sanctioned the work, already started, of ridding the country of the Jewish element.

Until to-day more than 32,000 Jews have been deported from Slovakia.

(May 16th. 1942. Bratislava broadcast).

1,600 " Evacuated " from Presov.

Sixteen hundred more Jews have been evacuated from Presov. All Jewish houses in the district have been searched by the police, and large quantities of textiles and other goods, allegedly hoarded by the Jews, have been confiscated.

(May 10th, 1942. Radio Paris).

Stopped at Frontiers.

The latest " Schwindlmanover " of the Jews, is an attempt to seek refuge in Hungary, state reports from Pressburg. According to Sano Mach, Minister of the Interior, this is in consequence of the latest law for the expulsion of Jews. There are arrests on the frontier every day. A Jew, Bruck, and his Aryan brother-in-law, were arrested in Precho by the Slovakian police for attempting to obtain transport into Hungary by bribery.

(May 1st. *Donauzeitung*, Belgrade).

Further Deportations of Slovakian Jews.

The deportations of Jews from Slovakia continue " according to plan," it is announced by the Slovakian Press Bureau.

Sixteen hundred Jews were deported during last week from the Trebisov and 2,000 from the Michalovce districts.

(May 24th. *Jewish Telegraphic Agency*, Stockholm).

Baptised Jews Deported but
Separately " Accommodated."

The Slovak Parliament has passed a resolution asking that the Government should take care that deported baptised Jews should be " accommodated " separately, and enjoy an opportunity of living in accordance with their creed.

(May 17th, 1942. *Grenzbote*).

Alarming Rumours Allayed.

Commenting on the expulsion law, the paper declares that it constitutes a reply to the people who are spreading alarming rumours to the effect that the anti-Jewish measures lack legal basis.

(May 16th. *Gardista*).

10

II. Expropriation of Jewish Property

"Wherefore should I fear in the days of evil when the iniquity of them that would supplant me compasseth me about, even of them that trust in their wealth, and boast themselves in the multitude of their riches."

Psalm XLIX.

Attack on "90,000 Enemies."

Slovakian Jews have been deprived of 6,000 houses, 12,300 business enterprises, and 500 "associations" (Vereine) during the past year .

A bitter attack on Slovakian Jews in an editorial in the same journal declares that "we must never forget that until the end of the war there will be 90,000 Jews in our country, that is to say, 90,000 enemies who are full of hatred. Daily incidents show that the Jews are planning, with Semitic hatred, for a Slovakian defeat.

"Whoever does not loathe Jews by natural instinct must be taught to do so, if necessary by the use of drastic methods."

(Feb. 1st. *Grenzbote*, Bratislava).

New Economic Blow to Slovak Jews.

An order requiring all Slovak partners in firms which still have Jewish partners, either active or "sleeping," to give immediate notice to the dissolution of the partnership.

The new order affects cases in which the Jewish owners of firms were compelled by a decision of the General Economic Office in Bratislava to take in non-Jewish partners. These newcomers are now enabled simply to expel Jewish partners and to establish themselves as full owners of the businesses into which they have been forcibly introduced.

(March 24th. *Slovak Official Gazette*).

Personal Property of Slovakian Jews Confiscated.

The entire personal property of the Jews in Slovakia has been confiscated under a new decree issued by the President of the Central Economic Office of Bratislava .

The property of the Jews is to be sold by public auction, and the proceeds will "go towards the solution of the Jewish Problem."

The decree was issued in connection with the deportation of the Jews of Slovakia to forced labour camps which is to take place during the next month under the supervision of the Hlinka Guard.

(March 31st. *Boersenzeitung*, Berlin).

Expropriations and Food Seizures.

Out of 12,000 Jewish firms, 9,935 have been liquidated with an average turnover of 1,184 million crowns, and 1,888 have been Aryanised with an average turnover of 1,465 millions. 8,000 Jews have already been sent to labour camps. No Jews, except those living there before 10th March, or those with a special permit, are allowed to enter Bratislava or Zilinia. Zilinia police seized 850kg. of unleavened bread which the Jews managed to bake in spite of the flour rationing.

(April 4th. *Review of Foreign Press*).

All Furs Confiscated.

Slovakian Jews had been forced to deliver up furs to the value of 4,062,000 crowns by March 15th. The number of furs confiscated was 21,889, most of them being delivered over to the military authorities.

Particularly valuable furs, to the value of 2,000,000 crowns, were auctioned and the proceeds given to the fund for Slovak soldiers .

(April 22nd. *Lidove Noviny*).

All Property Confiscated.

Mach announced at a press conference that 32,000 Jews out of a total of 90,000, have already been deported. By the end of May, the number deported will rise to 45,000. By the end of September the last Jew will have left Slovakia. Deported Jews lose Slovakian citizenship. The property of Hungarian Jews

11

living in Slovakia was confiscated. Negotiations will be started with Hungary about the houses and shares belonging to these Jews. It will probably be agreed that this property will be made over to members of the Hungarian minority in Slovakia. Landed property will be dealt with by the land office.

(May 13th. *Neue Tag*, Prague).

Never Happened Before.

From Berlin: Slovakia enacted the bills about the deportation of Jews with the approval of Parliament, a thing which has never happened before in any country. However, considerable restrictions were made; for instance, Jews who by March 14th, 1939, had become members of the Christian community are exempt from deportation, also those who married Christians and are still living with them. The President is entitled to exempt Jews from deportation for various reasons. These Slovakian laws show that Bratislava has attempted to solve the Jewish problem on religious principles.

(May 17th. *Social Demokraten*, Sweden).

Slovakian Minister of Commerce Hails Country's "Liberation from Jewish Influence."

Slovakia's "liberation from Jewish influence" was hailed by M. Medritsky, Slovakian Minister of Commerce, in a broadcast on the Bratislava radio.

In reviewing the anti-Jewish measures taken in Slovakia, the Minister spoke of the great changes which Slovakia's economic system had undergone as a result of the elimination of the Jews. Thanks to the liquidation of many Jewish businesses, he said, the Slovakian people have been finally liberated from Jewish influence.

(May 15th. *Jewish Telegraphic Agency*).

"Greatest Efficiency" in dealing with Jewish Problem in Slovakia.

The Jewish problem must be dealt with the greatest efficiency, M. Sano Mach, Slovak Minister of the Interior, declared in a speech to the Hlinka Guard over the Bratislava wireless. He announced that Jewish buildings, including 6,000 houses, are to be taken over. Stressing the necessity of continuing with the work of reconstructing the Slovak State, M. Mach appealed to the Hlinka Guard to fulfil the duty of the Slovaks towards Europe.

(May 21st. *Jewish Telegraphic Agency*).

Stolen Property of Exempted Not Returnable.

Parliament has passed a law on May 15th, stipulating certain exceptions to the Jew-deportation law. The number of Jews to whom these exceptions apply is not known: they will be temporary and strictly limited. Deported Jews lose their citizenship and their property will be confiscated.

Jews exempted from deportation are allowed to keep their goods and chattels, but cannot claim restitution of such goods confiscated before May 15th, 1942.

(May 17th. *Grenzbote*).

Expropriated Land goes to Leading Supporters of Present Regime.

The greater part of landed estate confiscated from the Jews in Slovakia was transferred to leading members of the Hlinka Guard, and other prominent supporters of the present regime, according to information reaching Czechoslovak circles in London.

Jewish-owned real estate in Slovakia confiscated, of which figures have now been published, show that so far 237 estates totalling 34,000 Katastraljoch (over 48,000 acres) have been distributed. Only 19,700 acres of land was given to 64 smallholders. The remainder passed into the hands of leading Slovakian Quislings.

(May 21st. *Jewish Telegraphic Agency*).

12

III. The Baptism "Plot"

" And He will teach us of His ways, and we will walk in His paths. For out of Zion shall go forth the law, and the word of the Lord from Jerusalem."
Isaiah II, 2.

Priest Arrested.

The Calvinist priest Puspas, who recently went to a house to baptise Jews, was arrested and put into a concentration camp. The Minister of the Interior, Sano Mach, has been concerned over the Jewish problem, since the papers have been reporting mass baptisms. In order to preserve victory at the front, it is necessary to regulate the Jewish problems at the home front in the most minute details, because the Slovak people desire liberation from Jewish exploitation and dissection. The Slovak public opinion refused to be weedled by appeals to pity which are nothing more than threats to labour. Nothing can save the Jews, not even the baptising priest. A correspondent of *Grenzbote* examined the Jewish baptisms. Forty Jews in the town of Freistadl paid 60,000 kronen for baptism, the wealthy Jews betraying the fact that they possess more liquid money than they are entitled to. The article concludes by saying that these Jewish baptisms represent an attack against the Slovak people and the culprits must be arrested. Competent authorities assure the public that similar matters will be eliminated.

(March 27th. *Donauzeitung*, Belgrade).

" The Jewish Influence in the Church."

The Volksgruppe Research Institute is investigating the Jewish influence in the Church, with the object of removing it from the dogma and life of the Churches and restoring relations between the churches and the people.

(March 27th. *Donauzeitung*).

" Insulting the Almighty."

It is rumoured in Slovakia that Jews will soon be dispossessed. Hundreds of wealthy Jews have been baptised to evade the regulations. The Volksdeutsche paper *Grenzbote*, demands the immediate prohibition of baptism since the present practice is insulting the Almighty.

(March 21st. *Donauzeitung*).

" A Jew Baptism Plot."

The pro-Nazi press, notably *Grenzbote* of March 26th, has been making a great feature of an alleged Jewish plot to escape the anti-Jewish laws, which condemn Jews to deportation to labour camps.

The Jews, these papers declare, are utilising the trick of wholesale conversion to Christianity to evade the law. Both Catholic and Calvinist clergy were said to be aiding and abetting this, and of course, for money.

In one town, the *Grenzbote* declared, 40 Jews paid 60,000Ks. for baptism, while one Protestant pastor baptised 36 Jews on one day at the rate of 1,000Ks. a Jew.

Unfortunately for them these papers were rash enough to name the places where these mass conversions were said to have happened, one of the districts being that of Tyrnau, where in addition to many of the past baptisms, " the Jesuits are at present preparing 120 Jews for baptism."

This specific declaration caused the *Katolicke Listy* to investigate, with the result that on April 5th it issued the following declaration:

" The Catholic Church does not exclude anybody who wishes to become a Catholic, but every priest who baptises an adult must be convinced that he whom he baptises has the necessary knowledge of the Catholic faith. . . . The time of preparation is five to ten months. The Apostolic administration of Tyrnau has officially declared that no Jew has been baptised in 1942, except for one Jewess on her death-bed, and furthermore, there is no mass preparation of Jews for baptism .

(April 25th, 1942. *Ministry of Information, Catholic Bulletin*).

13

IV. Persecution of Religion

"Not unto us, O Lord, not unto us, but unto Thy namesake give glory . . . wherefore shall the nations say, where then, is their God? But our God is in the heavens."

Psalm CXV.

Synagogues must be "Disguised."

Synagogues in Slovakia must have their appearance changed so that they shall resemble outwardly an ordinary building or dwelling-house, under the terms of a new order by the Nazi-controlled authorities of the country.

If this is not done, the synagogues will be confiscated and taken over by the State, it is learned in Czechoslovak circles in London.

(Feb. 20th, 1942. *Jewish Telegraphic Agency*).

All but on Jewish Communal Board Dissolved.

On April 1st, the eve of Passover, 60 Jewish community boards were dissolved; only one was left functioning.

At the same time all Jewish restaurants were closed by the Slovak police; the staffs were sent to labour camps.

(April 5th, 1942. *Jewish Telegraphic Agency*).

Rabbis Imprisoned.

Many Jews, including several Rabbis, have been imprisoned for spreading warnings about forthcoming anti-Jewish measures.

(April 6th, 1942. *Jewish Telegraphic Agency*).

The Statue of High Rabbi Löw (Löw ben Bezalel), a Masterpiece of Sculpture by Šaloun in the City Hall of Prague

14

V. The Church Protests

"For My house shall be called a house of prayer for all peoples."

Isaiah LVI, 8.

Penal Proceedings Against Pastor.

On April 12th, the Pastor of Vrbove, Jan Dado, who is a Czech from Holesov, has caused a scandal in the Church by preaching about the baptism of Jews, declaring that the Slovak Government has not the right to proceed against the Jews as it does.

The congregation was indignant and shouted: "White Jew, it is a scandal." The matter gave rise to penal proceedings against the Pastor.

(April 23rd, 1942. *Gardista*).

"Not in Accord with Humanity."

What is being done to the Jews of Slovakia is not in accordance with the principles of humanity, and even less with the principles of true Christianity.

(May 11th, 1942. *Evangeliky Posol Tatier*, quoted by *Gardista*).

Mach Replies to Catholic Objections.

Sano Mach, Slovak Minister of the Interior, dismisses the arguments of Catholic circles, who object to the anti-Jewish measures on the ground that the confiscation of Jewish possessions was contrary to the Christian principle of respecting honestly acquired property. "Jewish property was not honestly acquired. There may be exceptions, but in fulfilling the nation's destiny, exceptions must be disregarded."

(May 10th, 1942. *Gardista*).

Church Papers Protest.

At a course of Hlinka Guards commanders and storm troopers at Stola, Sano Mach, the Minister of the Interior, declared that the Protestant and Catholic ecclesiastic authorities approve of the deportation of Jews. While claiming that there was no reason for accusing priests of raising obstacles to the deportations, the Minister was forced to admit that some church papers had actually protested against the treatment meted out to the Jews of Slovakia.

(May 11th. *Gardista*).

THE VICTIMS WRITE

(These letters from Slovakia have been smuggled across the frontiers, into Switzerland, and then to London. The names of the senders and the recipients are personally known in London).

My Dear Ones,

Here we are waiting for the time of freedom. Oh, we are longing for it. I cannot describe how well off you are, there in liberty.

But we — we are prisoners in a mousetrap, humiliated, robbed of all our belongings, left with a few clothes and a place to sleep. One transport after another goes off into the unknown, to Poland, to Russia. There is no news of those who have been snatched away. We hear nothing, nothing at all.

Until August they will deport us all. At the frontier the people are passed on to the Gestapo in Poland. People are dragged from their houses at any time, day or night. On every house door, on every flat the names of all Jewish occupants are written, and beneath the yellow Star of David. Even the small children bear this sign. In the streets

From the Foreign Minister of Czechoslovakia

I would like to tell you how much I appreciate the work of the FEDERATION OF CZECHOSLOVAKIAN JEWS.

My and your ideals are identical in this great struggle, namely, return of international decency, religious freedom, and free Jews and free Czechoslovakia in a free Europe.

Carry on, and may God bless you.

Very sincerely,

JAN MASARYK.

The Task of the Federation of Czechoslovakian Jews

ON that tragic day of 15th March, 1939, when the armies of Hitler marched into Prague, there was formed in London an organisation to care for the interests of Czech Jewry, and to aid the refugees who already then were fleeing from the Nazi invader.

A group of Czech Jews and Anglo-Jewish friends gathered together, and under the presidency of the Chief Rabbi, Dr. J. H. Hertz, formed the FEDERATION OF CZECHOSLOVAKIAN JEWS.

In these three years the Federation has concerned itself with the problems of Czech Jewry, now unhappily dispersed throughout the world, or suffering beneath the Nazi yoke.

It has concerned itself with Czech Jewish children, interested itself for the well-being of the large number of Jews in the Czech armed forces, aided refugees on the Continent to find homes again, rendered services in innumerable directions wherever the need arose; its Case-Book represents every aspect of life and need of the refugee. All this work has taken place in constant co-operation with Czech Government offices, with the High Commissioner for Refugees, the Czech Refugee Trust Fund, and other representative bodies .

The Federation is at all times ready to help and advise, to intervene and to protect, Jewish refugees from Czechoslovakia.

One day ,when peace comes,. the great Jewish communities of Bohemia and Slovakia, of Prague and Bratislava, of Brno and Tyrnau, will flourish anew, and the Jews of Czechoslovakia will again take an honoured part in the life of that land of liberty, identified with the names of the leaders of freedom and democracy Thomas Garrique MASARYK and Edvard BENES.

"TRUTH MUST PREVAIL"

FEDERATION of CZECHOSLOVAKIAN JEWS

(To protect the interests of Czechoslovak Jews)

President:
The Very Rev. Dr. J. Hertz,
Chief Rabbi of the British Empire.
Vice-Presidents:
Dr. I. Epstein, Ph.D., D.Litt.
Dr. C. Dushinsky, F.R.Hist.S.
V. I. Gaster, Esq.

Chairman:
H. A. Goodman, Esq.
Treasurer:
J. Harris, Esq.
Joint Secretaries:
M. R. Springer.
K. Leitner.

53, QUEEN'S DRIVE, LONDON, N.4.
Phones: STAMFORD HILL 2173/5207.

In order to promote the ideology of Agudas Yisroel, Opa arranged the publication and distribution of the opening addresses that were given by Rabbi Yaakov Rosenheim at the Foundation Conference of Agudas Yisroel in Kattowitz in 1912, entitled 'What does Agudas Yisroel Want?' and his speech at the Kenessio Gedoloh in Vienna in 1923, 'Agudas Yisroel - Its Object and Realisation.'

(1)

OUR AIM:
To solve in the spirit of the Torah all problems which confront Jewry from time to time in Eretz Israel and the Diaspora.

מטרתנו:
לפתור ברוח התורה והמסורה את כל השאלות השונות אשר תעלינה יום יום בחיי כלל ישראל בארץ ישראל ובגולה.

SERIES OF ESSAYS
ON
AGUDAS ISRAEL
PUBLISHED BY THE
AGUDAS ISRAEL ORGANISATION OF GREAT BRITAIN
53, Queen's Drive, London, N.4.
5705—1944

What Does Agudas Israel Want?

An address by Mr. Jacob Rosenheim

delivered at the Foundation Conference at Kattowitz 5672—1912

My task is to outline briefly the idea and the programme of the Agudas Israel. I am confronted with a double difficulty. For some I shall be saying too much and for others too little. Too much, because the ideas which gave birth to the Agudas Israel are not artificially created and therefore do not manifest themselves as previously unknown revelations. They are in the air we breathe, and sound ordinary and obvious, like all truths. Too little, because only the principles of our Organisation can be indicated now; its objects may be traced on broad lines. The details and practice must and should emerge from the Organisation itself, which alone can extract from all the possibilities what is necessary and attainable.

We have assembled here at an historic moment to establish our Agudas Israel, at a moment of earnest, historic significance, quite apart from whether our work will immediately succeed to the full extent we hope or will remain a mere trunk, whether it will be completed to-day or to-morrow, by ourselves, or by our children and grandchildren.

For it is not an Organisation at the side of other organisations that we are setting up, not an Organisation to carry out a specific task, whose value comes to an end with the realisation of any particular object. Our aim is rather to revive an ancient Jewish possession; it is the traditional conception of Klall Yisroel —Israel's collective body, animated and sustained by its Torah as the organising soul—which through our Agudas Israel we seek to realise in the midst of the civilised world and with the technical means provided by civilisation.

CIVIL MARRIAGE BY PROXY

My parents were first cousins, and the two families were very close. My father was born in Marienbad, and lived there until 1938. My mother was also born there, but her family lived in Bad Gastein during the summer, 300 miles away, but the families often met in Marienbad.

They became engaged in 1938, but soon after their engagement the war broke out, and there was no possibility for them to get married. In the meantime Oma, together with her mother and sisters, escaped from Bad Gastein to Santiago de Chile, and Opa to London, a separation of nearly 10,000 miles. Thus began an engagement period that lasted 8 years, with very infrequent contact between them. Moreover, the Belzer Rebbe, Reb Aaron, had replied to Opa in 1939, 'I cannot recommend that you travel to Chile'. However, Opa was eager to get married, so he applied on humanitarian grounds for permission to allow Oma to come to England.

This permission was refused, as detailed in a letter received from the Czechoslovakian Ministry for Foreign Affairs on August 19, 1941: 'With regard to the case of Miss Hilda Kokisch, I regret that we are unable to take any action, as the British authorities grant entry into this country only to the wives or children of Czechoslovakian soldiers on active service here'.

His next option was to apply for a Civil Marriage by Proxy, and then re-apply for permission of entry for 'his wife'. Opa was hopeful that once he was 'officially' married, they would allow her to enter England.

When marrying 'by proxy' the bride and bridegroom legally get married on different days! Oma signed her marriage certificate in Santiago on January 21, 1943, witnessed by her two sisters, Theresa and Berta. However, before the process could be finalised, Opa had to obtain a written confirmation from the Chilean Consulate in London that a marriage 'by proxy' was legally acceptable in Chile, which he obtained on April 13, 1943. On May 3, 1943, Opa signed his Civil Marriage papers in front of John Arthur Dimond, the Notary Public in London, who confirmed their Civil Marriage to be complete.

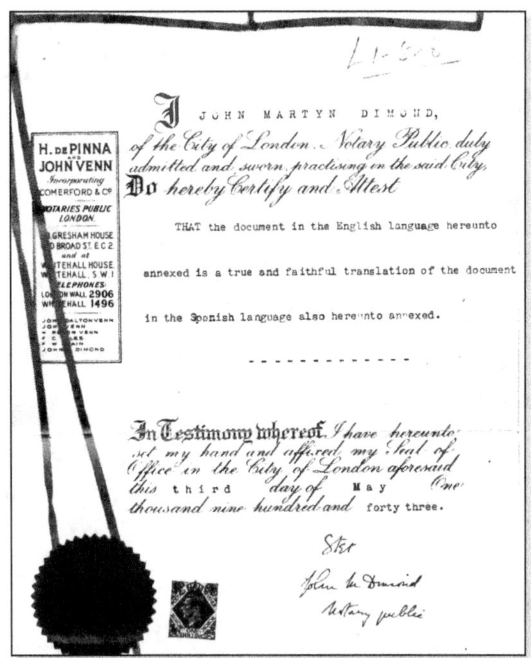
I JOHN MARTYN DIMOND,
of the City of London. Notary Public duly admitted and sworn, practising in the said City,
Do hereby Certify and Attest
THAT the document in the English language hereunto annexed is a true and faithful translation of the document in the Spanish language also hereunto annexed.

In Testimony whereof I have hereunto set my hand and affixed my Seal of Office in the City of London aforesaid this third day of May One thousand nine hundred and forty three.

John M. Dimond
Notary public

Civil Marriage Document.

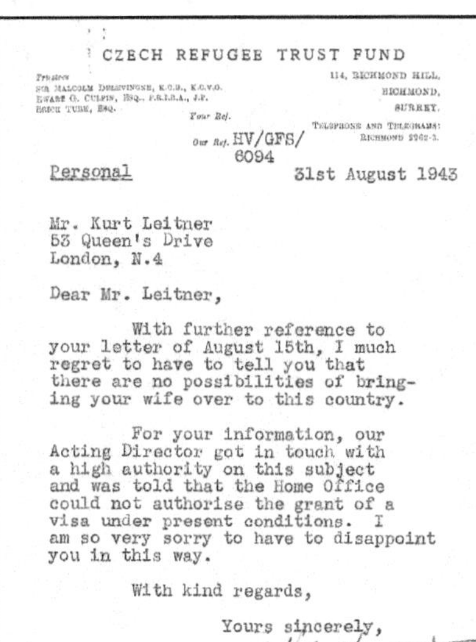
CZECH REFUGEE TRUST FUND

114, RICHMOND HILL,
RICHMOND,
SURREY.

Our Ref. HV/GFS/6094

Personal

31st August 1943

Mr. Kurt Leitner
53 Queen's Drive
London, N.4

Dear Mr. Leitner,

With further reference to your letter of August 15th, I much regret to have to tell you that there are no possibilities of bringing your wife over to this country.

For your information, our Acting Director got in touch with a high authority on this subject and was told that the Home Office could not authorise the grant of a visa under present conditions. I am so very sorry to have to disappoint you in this way.

With kind regards,

Yours sincerely,

H. VERSCHOYLE
Welfare Officer

P.S. I am returning to you the photostatic documents you enclosed in your letter to us.

Now that he was 'officially' married, Opa made another application to obtain permission for Oma to come to England, and was disappointed yet again, when he got a negative reply on August 31, 1943.

Opa was very upset and did not know what to try next. Oma had been refused permission to come to England, and Reb Aaron did not advise him to travel to Chile either. After further consultation with the Belzer Rebbe Opa received a reply on April 7, 1944 suggesting that both Opa and Oma attempt to come to Eretz Yisroel and settle there, and acknowledged his further donation of five pounds, as the letter below specifies.

Write the address in large BLOCK letters in the panel below.
The address must NOT be typewritten.

This form must NOT be rolled or folded.

Mist.
L. LEITNER
55 Queens Drive.
LONDON
N. 4

PALESTINE
PICTURE POST

77

17174

Write the message very plainly below this line.

Sender's Name and Address Rabbi A. Rokach
Jerusalem P.O.B. 1153.
Palestine

Date 3/III 1944.

[illegible]

Ch. A. Katz 183 Mullway Letchworth Herts

[illegible]

This space should not be used.

This transcribed:

P.O.B. 1153
Jerusalem
Palestine
7/March/1944

שוכט"ס לכבוד ידידנו היקר ירא ושלם המופלג וכו' ....

מוה"ר חיים ארי' נ"י לייטנער

אחדשה"ט

מכתבך עם הפ"נ 5 פונט הגיע לנכון ליד כ"ק אחי הה"צ מרן שליט"א ושמחנו לשמוע משלומך הטוב. כ"ק אחי שליט"א בירך שהשי"ת יציל את אביך היקר נ"י ואחותך תחי' מכל רע בכל מקום שהם ושתשמעו מהם בשורות טובות ובירך אותך בישועה בכ"ע בדבר השידוך השיב בזה"ל איני רוצה לומר דעה גדולה אבל אתה נכון הדבר שתיסע איה"ש לאה"ק וגם הכלה תבוא לאה"ק ושיהא בשטומ"צ.

תמחול להתראות עם ידידינו היקרים ה"ר חיים נטע נ"י כץ ועם ה"ר אלימלך נ"י רומפפלער ובאם תוכל לעזור להם בהשתדלות הסיוע לצורך קנין הבית לישב בה ולתורה ולתפילה ולעבודה זכות גדול יהי' לך

האדרעססא של ה"ר חיים נטע כץ היא כך:

.Ch. N. Katz 183 Mullway Letchworth Herts

והנני בזה ידידך דורש שלומך ומברכך שתשמע בשורות טובות בקרוב ושנזכה להתראות ולישועה ולגאולה בב"א

הק' מרדכי באאמו"ר זצוקלה"ה מבעלזא אבד"ק בילגורייא

On April 28, 1944, Opa received another letter from Belz which is self explanatory. It appears that Opa wrote to the Belzer Rebbe regarding a Shidduch suggestion on behalf of one of his friends, to which the Rebbe replied as written below.

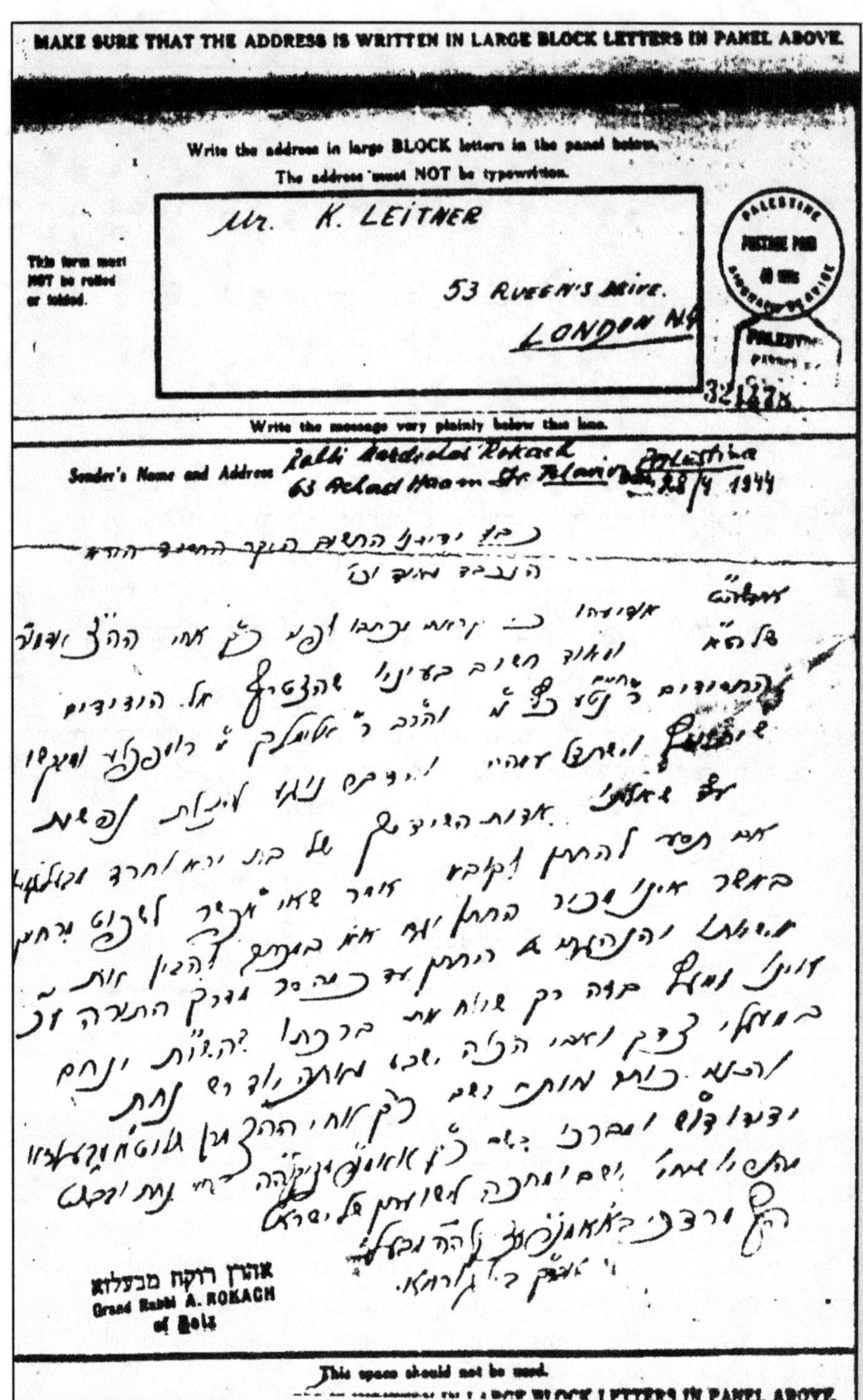

MAKE SURE THAT THE ADDRESS IS WRITTEN IN LARGE BLOCK LETTERS IN PANEL ABOVE

Write the address in large BLOCK letters in the panel below.

The address must NOT be typewritten.

Mr. K. LEITNER

53 RUEEN'S MIRE.

LONDON N4

This form must NOT be rolled or folded.

PALESTINE POSTAGE PAID

Write the message very plainly below this line.

Sender's Name and Address: Rabbi Aahdrolas Rokach, 63 Achad Haam Str. Tel Aviv, Palestina. Date 28/4 1944

אהרן רוקח מבעלזא
Grand Rabbi A. ROKACH
of Belz

This space should not be used.

MAKE SURE THAT THE ADDRESS IS WRITTEN IN LARGE BLOCK LETTERS IN PANEL ABOVE

This transcribed:

Rabbi Mordechai Rokach
63 Achad Haam Str Tel Aviv PALESTINE
28/4/ 1944

כבוד ידידנו החשוב היקר החסיד הירא הנכבד מאוד וכו'

אחדשה"ט

אודיעהו כי קראתי מכתבו לפני כ"ק אחי הה"צ אדמו"ר שליט"א ומאוד חשוב בעיני' שהצטרף אל הידידים החסידים ר' חיים נטע כץ נ"י והרב ר' אלימלך נ"י רומפפלער ומבקשו שיתאמץ וישתדל עמהם והדבר נוגע להצלת נפשות.

ע"ד שאלתו אדות השידוך של בת ירא וחרד מבעלגיען אם תסע להחתן לקובע אמר שאי אפשר לשפוט מרחוק באשר אינו מכיר החתן וגם א"א במכתב להבין את יראתו והנהגתו של החתן עד כמה סר מדרך התורה ע"כ אינו מייעץ בזה רק שולח את ברכתו שהשי"ת ינחם במעגלי צדק ואבי הכלה ישבע מאתה יודיש נחת.

והנני כותב וחותם בשם כ"ק אחי הה"צ מרן שליט"א מבעלזא ידידו דו"ש ומברכו בשם כ"ק אאמו"ר זצוקלה"ה רוב נחת ובש"ט מהוריו שיחי'

יושב ומצפה לישועתן של ישראל

הק' מרדכי באאמו"ר זצוקלה"ה מבעלזא אבד"ק בילגורייא

אהרן רוקח מבעלזא
Grand Rabbi A. ROKACH
of Belz

After his Civil Marriage Opa made an application on May 17, 1944 to Lloyds Bank, Finsbury Park, London, requesting permission to transfer an allowance of 5 pounds per month to his 'wife' as 'maintenance', incorporating the suggestion made by the Belzer Rebbe, that his wife would emigrate to Palestine, but this too was refused.

Opa then decided to ask Reb Shloime Baumgarten for advice since he knew the Kokisch family very well, as they had often spent time in their home in Vienna during the winter season, and Oma was very friendly with Reb Shloime's sister, also named Hinda. Opa had also had very close connections with Reb Shloime during his Hatzoloh work in London, and he promised to look into the matter and report back to him.

Reb Shloime then made some very discreet enquiries by a reliable relative of his who had also escaped to Chile before the war, and asked him two things. Firstly he wanted to know what facilities existed in Santiago for a young couple to set up a Jewish home, and also what the state of Yiddishkeit of the Kokisch family was, as they had now been in a strange environment, on their own, for the past six years. Were they still as steadfast in their Torah observance as they were before the war, or had things changed?

04571 FOR OFFICIAL USE ONLY

STERLING TRANSFER FORM (For payments NOT in respect of Imports).

DEFENCE (FINANCE) REGULATIONS.

APPLICATION TO TRANSFER STERLING TO A — (Delete lines not applying)

(A3) REGISTERED ACCOUNT

(A2) CHILE SPECIAL

(A2) CENTRAL AMERICAN ACCOUNT

(E) ACCOUNT OF A RESIDENT IN

Insert name of country in BLOCK CAPITALS (see note 1 overleaf).

TO Name and address of Bank to which application is addressed: LLOYDS BANK LIMITED, FINSBURY PARK BRANCH, 260, SEVEN SISTERS ROAD, LONDON, N.4. 65489

I/We the undersigned apply for permission to transfer the undermentioned sum:

Amount: £ 5 (say) Amount in words: Five Pounds per month

Name and full address of transferor (BLOCK CAPITALS): Kurt Leitner, 85, Manor Road, London, N.16.

Name of account to be credited (see note 2 overleaf)

Name and full address of beneficiary (BLOCK CAPITALS): Mrs. Hilde Leitner, Roberto Espinoza 891 Dep. 47 Santiago de Chile.

Name of Bank keeping above account (if applicable)

for the following purpose. (This Form must NOT be used in respect of payments for imports)

For partly support of maintenance to my wife, who is living in Chile. I have no possibilities to emigrate to Chile and my wife has no possibilities to come to England. Therefore I am forced to make this application to enable me at least partly to maintain and support my wife. If the bank of England is unable to grant my application I would suggest that I can submit a regularly monthly sum to Palestine and my wife

(full particulars must be stated: continue overleaf if necessary)

I/We declare that the above statements are true. Signature(s): KLeitner

Date 17/5/1944.

Stamp of Bank vouching for accuracy of statements and certifying signature(s) as valid on applicant's banking account: LLOYDS BANK LIMITED, FINSBURY PARK BRANCH, 260, SEVEN SISTERS ROAD, LONDON, N.4.

Stamp of Bank approving transfer, and date: FOREIGN EXCHANGE CONTROL THIS APPLICATION IS NOT ALLOWED 30 MAY 1944

Application for money transfer

I do not have the reply on record, but the fact that Opa was given permission to continue, implies that the answers to both questions were positive. This too shows the tremendous Mesiras Nefesh that the Kokisch family had for Yiddishkeit. A family without their father, who remained firm and unaffected in their standard of Yiddishkeit, while at first being housed in a non-Jewish home, and living in a city of assimilated Jews, is truly remarkable. It appears that this information was relayed to Reb Aaron of Belz, as further correspondence confirms. (See Chapter 10).

Opa then wrote to Reb Aaron stating that he had been engaged since 1938, and that his Kalloh had escaped to Santiago de Chile before the war, and there had been untold difficulties in obtaining immigration certificates to come to Eretz Yisroel. The Rebbe responded in a letter that was written on Erev Pesach (April 28, 1945)!

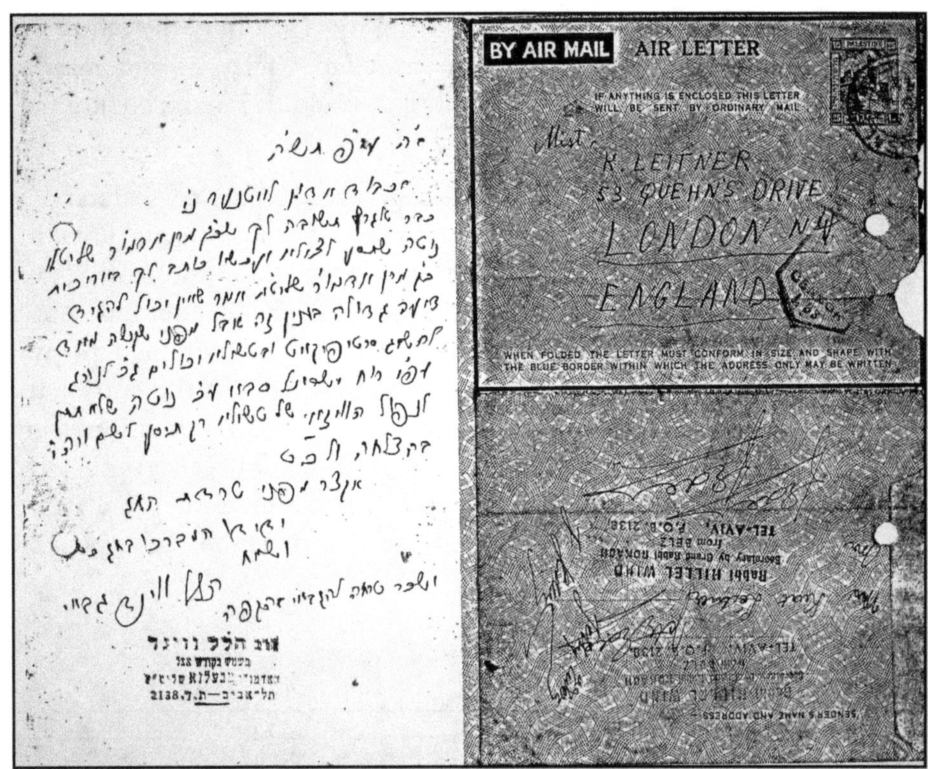

BY AIR MAIL AIR LETTER

IF ANYTHING IS ENCLOSED THIS LETTER WILL BE SENT BY ORDINARY MAIL

Mist. R. LEITNER
53 QUEEN'S DRIVE
LONDON N4
ENGLAND

WHEN FOLDED THE LETTER MUST CONFORM IN SIZE AND SHAPE WITH THE BLUE BORDER WITHIN WHICH THE ADDRESS ONLY MAY BE WRITTEN

Transcribed as:

ב"ה ער"פ תש"ה

לכבוד אדון לייטנער נ"י

כבר טלגרף תשובה לך שכ"ק מרן אדמו"ר שליט"א נוטה שתסע לצילא ועכשיו כותב לך באריכות כ"ק מרן אדמו"ר שליט"א אמר שאין יכול להגיד דיעה גדולה בענין זה אבל מפני שקשה מאד להשיג סרטיפיקאט ובטשילא יכולים ג"כ לנהג עפ"י רוח ישראל סבא ע"כ נוטה שלא תתן לנפול הוויזא של טשילא רק תסע לשם ויהי' בהצלחה ולכ"ט

אקצר מפני טרדת החג

ידידו המברכו בחג כשר ושמח

הלל וינד גבאי

ושכר טרחה להגבאי מהקפה

הרב הלל ווינד
בשמש בקודש אצל
האדמו"ר מבעלזא שליט"א
תל-אביב—ת.ד. 2138

Passport photo of Opa as a Choson, taken in London 1945

The only possibility remaining, therefore, was for Opa to travel to Chile and get married there, a task that would be impossible until after the war ended.

When Mr Springer, Opa's co-secretary at the Federation for Czechoslovakian Jews, informed him that his wife was seriously ill, Opa immediately requested her name and sent a letter to Reb Aaron of Belz, and his reply was received on July 15, 1945. At the end of the letter the Rebbe requested information about Opa's plans to move to Chile, always showing such care and fatherly interest. He also acknowledged a further donation of five pounds.

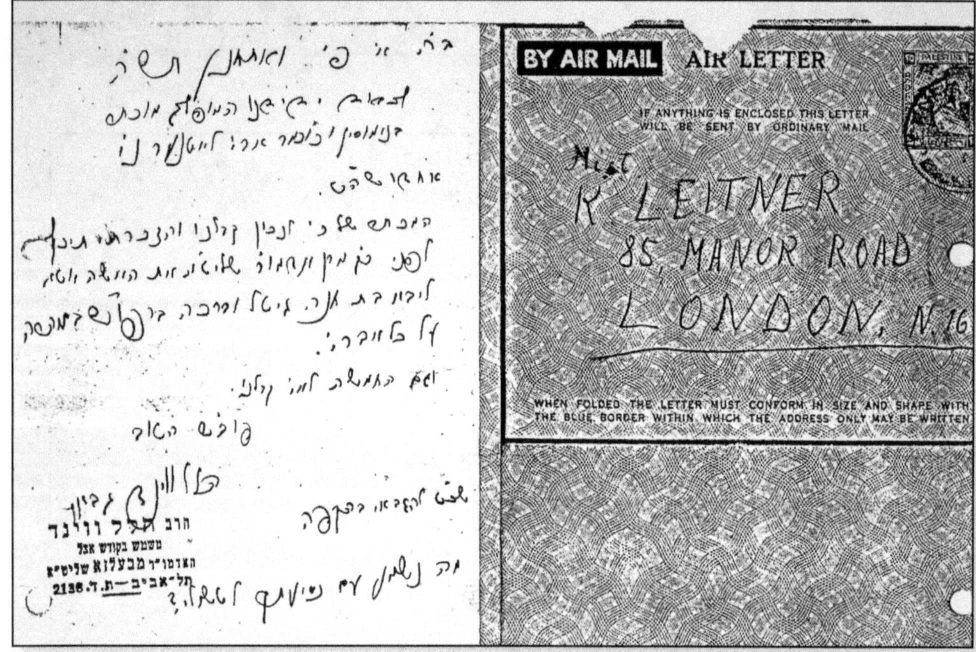
הרב הלל ווינד
משמש בקודש אצל
האדמו"ר מבעלזא שליט"א
תל-אביב—ת.ד. 2136

BY AIR MAIL AIR LETTER

IF ANYTHING IS ENCLOSED THIS LETTER WILL BE SENT BY ORDINARY MAIL

R LEITNER
85, MANOR ROAD
LONDON, N.16

WHEN FOLDED THE LETTER MUST CONFORM IN SIZE AND SHAPE WITH THE BLUE BORDER WITHIN WHICH THE ADDRESS ONLY MAY BE WRITTEN

This transcribed:

ב"ה א' פ' ואתחנן תש"ה
(15th July 1945)

לכבוד ידידנו המופלג מוכתר בנימוסין וכו' כמר ארי' לייטנער נ"י
אחדשה"ט

המכתב של כ' לנכון קבלנו והזכרתי תיכף לפני כ"ק מרן אדמו"ר שליט"א את האשה יוטא ליבא בת חנה גיטל וברכה ברפו"ש במהרה על כל אברי'.
וגם החמשה לא"י קבלנו

פוב"ש הטוב
הלל ווינד גבאי
שכ"ט להגבאי בהקפה
מה נשמע עם נסיעתך לטשילי?

הרב הלל ווינד
משמש בקודש אצל
אדמו"ר מבעלזא שליט"א
תל-אביב—ת.ד. 2138

PREPARATION FOR CHILE

In making preparations for his journey to Chile, Opa obtained many letters of thanks and good wishes from the numerous organisations that he was involved with in his Hatzolo relief work during his stay in London. Two of these letters were signed by Dayan Abramsky, with whom Opa had a very close connection.

Dayan Abramsky in his younger years

In order to collect funds for the 'Yalde Yisroel Fund', a fund that helped Jewish orphans, Opa had organised and distributed a unique 'pushka' box that was attached to a salt and pepper cellar which stood in the middle of the table during all meals. Their motto and aim was that each household would contribute just one penny before beginning their meal, which was appropriately called 'A Penny A Meal Fund'. Before starting their own meal they would thus remember and empathise with their less fortunate brethren. These small but regular amounts brought in substantial sums for the organisation, which were used to supply essential relief immediately after the war.

Joint Orthodox Jewish Refugees Committee.

Remember the position of our brethren on the Continent.

'Phone:
STAmford Hill
6688/9

53, QUEENS DRIVE,
LONDON, N.4.

Dear Sir/Madam,

We are writing to you at the moment when reports from the Continent tell us of the most terrible circumstances in which our brethren there find themselves

Already some months ago a scheme for the benefit of our brethren has been initiated and we would ask you to participate therein.

You will no doubt realize that while you and your friends are privileged to live a comparatively free life in Great Britain and are permitted to earn a living, many hundreds of thousands of our friends on the Continent are starving and subject to great privations and persecutions. Although at the moment there is little hope for direct relief we still feel that already now it is our duty to prepare for the day when we will be able to help. We would therefore invite you to join with us in the scheme by which 1d. should be donated at every meal we partake here. We would ask you to fill up the attached form to-day and also to interest three other people amongst your friends to do likewise and to post the attached slip without delay.

With many thanks in anticipation,

Yours faithfully,

H. Schwab — S. Baumgarten

H. L. SCHWAB. — RABBI S. BAUMGARTE

Remember what

your position would be.

THEREFORE JOIN OUR PENNY SCHEME WITHOUT DELAY.

A letter sent as a mail-shot inviting people to join the 'Penny a Meal Fund'

המפעל למען ילדי ישראל

MIFAL LEMAAN YALDE YISROEL

To maintain and support our Children in Palestine.

"YALDE YISROEL FUND"

53, QUEEN'S DRIVE,
LONDON, N.4.

Telephone: STAmford Hill 6658-9

17th January, 1944

Appeal Chairman:
Rabbi Dayan I. Abramsky.

Chairman:
Dr. A. Koppenheim.

Joint Treasurers:
Rabbi Dr. E. Munk, Ph.D.
B. Strauss, Esq.

Gen. Secretary:
K. Leitner, Esq.

Palestine Committee:
Rabbi M. Alter, (GER)
Rabbi M. Blau
Dr. I. Breuer
Rabbi J. Z. Dushinsky
Rabbi M. S. Friedman, (Sadagora)
Rabbi N. M. Friedman, (Czortkov)
Rabbi A. E. Finkel, (Mir)
Rabbi J. Kahaneman, (Poniwesh)
Rabbi M. Korelitz, (Wilna)
Rabbi I. M. Lewin, (Warszawa)
Rabbi S. Melcer, (Jerusalem)
Rabbi A. Schreiber, (Bratislava)
Rabbi J. Z. Soloweitschik, (Brisk)
Rabbi S. Sorotzkin, (Lutzk)
Rabbi J. A. Sher, (Slobotka)
Dr. M. Wallach, M.B.E. (Jerusalem)

PATRONS:
Rabbi S. Baumgarten
Dr. S. Ehrman, Zurich
Rabbi D. Feldman, Manchester
I. A. Goodman, Esq.
Rabbi J. J. Horowitz
Rabbi Dr. Leo Jung, New York
Rabbi Dr. Lewenstein, Zurich
Rabbi Dr. Mannes
. Mazur, Esq.
abbi S. Moskowitz
abbi S. Rabinow
abbi M.A. Rabinowitz, Sunderl'd
abbi M. E. Rogosnitzki, Cardiff
acob Rosenheim, Esq., New York
abbi Dr. S. Schonfeld, Ph.D.

TO WHOM IT MAY CONCERN

This is to certify that Mr. Josef Loebenstein is authorized by the above Campaign to collect funds on behalf of the Committee.

We would be much obliged if our contributors would kindly render Mr. Loebenstein every possible assistance in his work for us which he is doing in an honorary capacity.

This authorization is valid until June 30th 1944.

K. Leitner

K. LEITNER

Opa, as general Secretary, appoints Mr. J. Loebenstein as a collector for the fund.

Before Opa left for Chile, Dayan Abramsky wrote him a warm letter of recommendation, which described his efficient work for the cause.

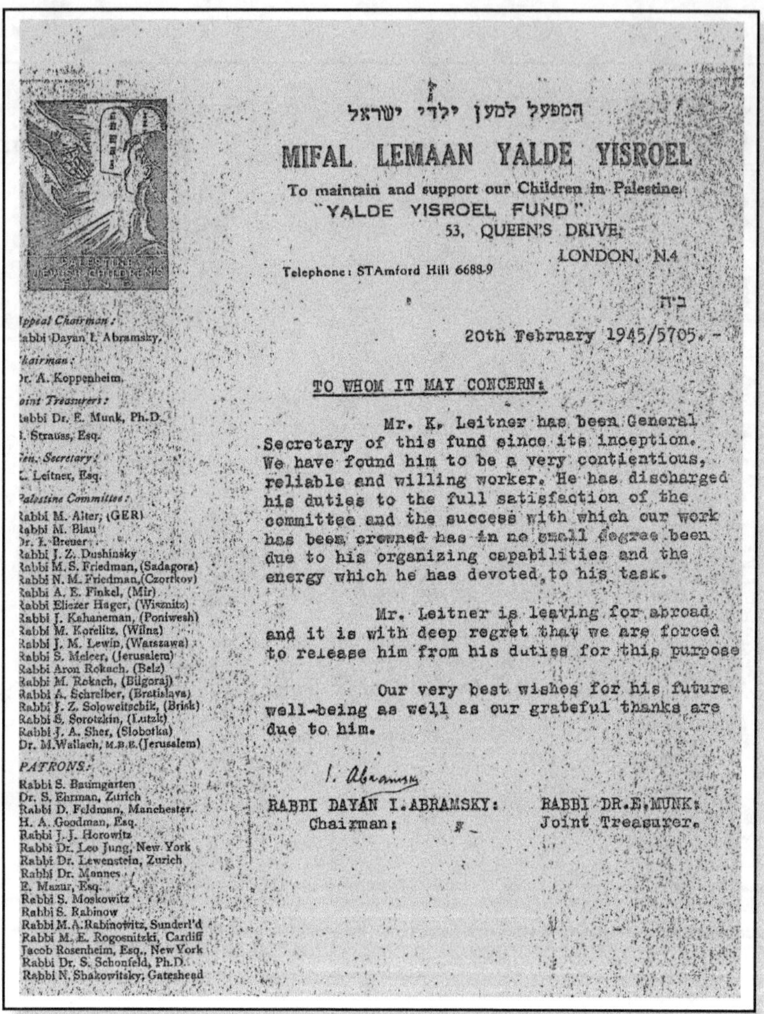

ב״ה

המפעל למען ילדי ישראל

MIFAL LEMAAN YALDE YISROEL

To maintain and support our Children in Palestine:
"YALDE YISROEL FUND"
53, QUEEN'S DRIVE,
LONDON, N.4

Telephone: STAmford Hill 6688-9

Appeal Chairman:
Rabbi Dayan I. Abramsky.

Chairman:
Dr. A. Koppenheim.

Joint Treasurers:
Rabbi Dr. E. Munk, Ph.D.
I. Strauss, Esq.

Gen. Secretary:
K. Leitner, Esq.

Palestine Committee:
Rabbi M. Alter, (GER)
Rabbi M. Blau
Dr. I. Breuer
Rabbi J. Z. Dushinsky
Rabbi M. S. Friedman, (Sadagora)
Rabbi N. M. Friedman, (Czortkov)
Rabbi A. E. Finkel, (Mir)
Rabbi Eliezer Hager, (Wisznitz)
Rabbi J. Kahaneman, (Poniwesh)
Rabbi M. Korelitz, (Wilna)
Rabbi J. M. Lewin, (Warszawa)
Rabbi S. Melcer, (Jerusalem)
Rabbi Aron Rokach, (Belz)
Rabbi M. Rokach, (Bilgoraj)
Rabbi A. Schreiber, (Bratislava)
Rabbi J. Z. Soloweitschik, (Brisk)
Rabbi S. Sorotzkin, (Lutzk)
Rabbi J. A. Sher, (Slobotka)
Dr. M. Wallach, M.B.E. (Jerusalem)

PATRONS:
Rabbi S. Baumgarten
Dr. S. Ehrman, Zurich
Rabbi D. Feldman, Manchester.
H. A. Goodman, Esq.
Rabbi J. J. Horowitz
Rabbi Dr. Leo Jung, New York
Rabbi Dr. Lewenstein, Zurich
Rabbi Dr. Mannes
E. Mazur, Esq.
Rabbi S. Moskowitz
Rabbi S. Rabinow
Rabbi M. A. Rabinowitz, Sunderl'd
Rabbi M. E. Rogosnitzki, Cardiff
Jacob Rosenheim, Esq., New York
Rabbi Dr. S. Schonfeld, Ph.D.
Rabbi N. Shakowitsky, Gateshead

20th February 1945/5705.-

TO WHOM IT MAY CONCERN:

Mr. K. Leitner has been General Secretary of this fund since its inception. We have found him to be a very contientious, reliable and willing worker. He has discharged his duties to the full satisfaction of the committee and the success with which our work has been crowned has in no small degree been due to his organizing capabilities and the energy which he has devoted to his task.

Mr. Leitner is leaving for abroad and it is with deep regret that we are forced to release him from his duties for this purpose.

Our very best wishes for his future well-being as well as our grateful thanks are due to him.

I. Abramsky

RABBI DAYAN I. ABRAMSKY: Chairman:

RABBI DR. E. MUNK: Joint Treasurer.

Opa received another letter from Dayan Abramsky, as President of the Keren Hatorah Committee, for his work on behalf of their organisation.

TELEPHONE: STAMFORD HILL 6688/9

קרן התורה

ב"ה

Keren Hatorah Committee

KEREN HATORAH RELIEF FUND

The World Fund for the Relief of Religious, Educational and Social Institutions

Chairman of Central Committee:
Jacob Rosenheim, Esq.

President:
Dayan Rabbi Abramsky

Executive:
Rabbi O. Abramson
Rabbi J. Horovitz
Rabbi Dr. J. Jakobovitz
Rabbi I. Margulies
Rabbi Dr. E. Munk
Rabbi Dr. D. Ochs
Rabbi S. J. Rabbinov
Rabbi Dr. S. Schonfeld
Rabbi A. J. Twersky
H. A. Goodman, Esq.
G. Heilpern, Esq
A. P. Landau, Esq.
D. Lichtig, Esq.
H. Pels, Esq.
Dr. M. Rottenberg
W. Schiff, Esq.

Patrons:
Chief Rabbi Dr. Hertz
Rabbi Atlas, Glasgow
Rabbi Hurwitz, Leeds
Rabbi Rabinowitz, Sunderland
Chief Rabbi Dushinsky, Jerusalem
Chief Rabbi Dr. Herzog, Jerusalem
I. M. Lewin, Jerusalem
Rabbi Dr. Kirzner, Cape Town
Rabbi Kossowsky, Johannesburg
Rabbi Dr. Jung, New York
Rabbi S. Schwab, Baltimore
Rabbi Silver, Cincinnati

Head Office:
53, QUEEN'S DRIVE,
LONDON, N.4

20th February 1945/5705:

K. Leitner, Esq.,
85, Manor Road,
London, N.16.

Dear Mr. Leitner,

It is with deep regret that we hear that you are leaving this country for South-America and we would express our very sincery wishes for a happy and prosperous future.

We are extremely grateful for all you have done for us during the past years in a honorary capacity. Your willing and constant help has been of great value to us and you have proved, to be an able and successful social worker. We can indeed ill-afford the loss of so contientious a worker as you have been.

We readily and warmly recomment you as a reliable and trustworthy person and feel sure that you will be successful in your new country of sojourn.

Yours sincerely.

I. Abramsky

RABBI DAYAN I. ABRAMSKY
Chairman:

Other letters of recommendations and gratitude for his superb social work were received on May 10, 1945 from The Office of the Chief Rabbi and signed by Chief Rabbi Hertz, from Mr. H. Goodman on behalf of Agudas Yisroel, Rabbi Springer on behalf of The Czechoslovakian Central Office of Orthodox Jews, the Secretary of the Board of Deputies of British Jews, Harris Lazarus on behalf of the London Beth Din, Mr. Lehman on behalf of the Joint Emergency Committee for Jewish Religious Education in Great Britain, and Kurt Sabatzky on behalf of the Jewish Search Centre for tracing missing Jews of Europe.

ORTHODOX JEWISH CHILDREN'S HOSTEL COMMITTEE.

35, LORDSHIP PARK,
LONDON, N.16.

Telephones: STAMFORD HILL 2173 and 5207.

Federation of Czechoslovakian Jews

TO PROTECT THE INTERESTS OF CZECHOSLOVAKIAN JEWS.

President:
THE VERY REV. DR. J. H. HERTZ,
Chief Rabbi of the British Empire.

Vice-Presidents:
DR. I. EPSTEIN, Ph.D., D.Litt.
DR. C. DUSHINSKY.

53, QUEEN'S DRIVE,
LONDON, N.4

TELEPHONE STEPNEY GREEN 4251.

צדקה ומרפא

REGISTERED WITH THE BOARD OF DEPUTIES

LONDON JEWISH HOSPITAL,
STEPNEY GREEN, E.1.

LONDON JEWISH

PADDINGTON 2776

THE GROUPS OF REFUGEES

Registered with the

CZECH REFUGEE TRUST FUND

Group Centre:
128 WESTBOURNE TERRACE,
LONDON, W.2

Chairman:
R. REITZNER

Hon. Sec.:
F. LOEVINGER

Your Ref.
Our Ref.

LONDON

GROUP - NICEM.

19-2-1945.

Beth Din, London

COURT OF THE CHIEF RABBI

בית דין צדק
דק"ק לונדון והמדינה

Telephone:
AVENUE 5377

4 CREECHURCH PLACE
ALDGATE
LONDON E.C.3

15th February, 1945.

To whom it may concern.

regret that you in-
to emigrate to South-

the group leader of
I wish to express to
th regard to Jewish

collaboration you
ful social worker.

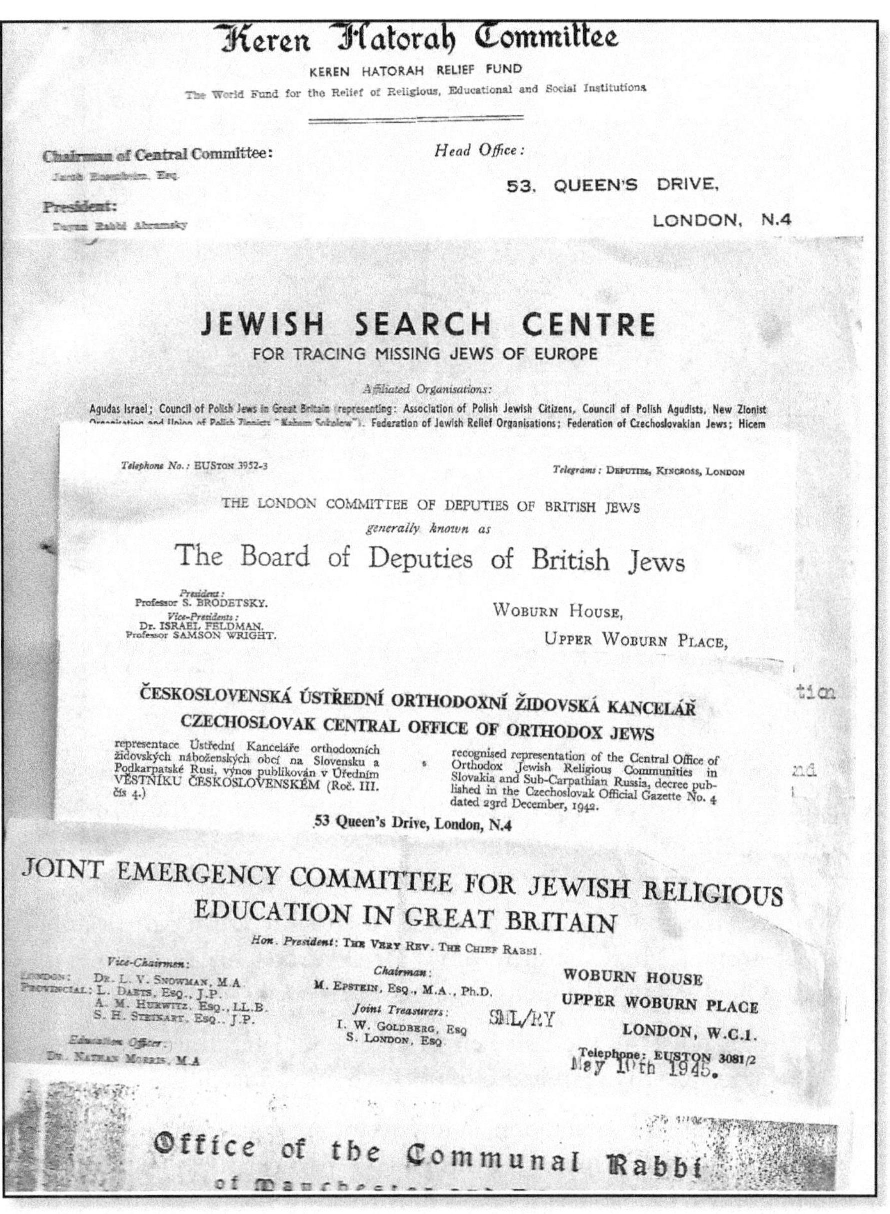

Keren Hatorah Committee

KEREN HATORAH RELIEF FUND

The World Fund for the Relief of Religious, Educational and Social Institutions

Chairman of Central Committee:
Jacob Rosenheim, Esq.

President:
Dayan Rabbi Abramsky

Head Office:
53, QUEEN'S DRIVE,
LONDON, N.4

JEWISH SEARCH CENTRE

FOR TRACING MISSING JEWS OF EUROPE

Affiliated Organisations:

Agudas Israel; Council of Polish Jews in Great Britain (representing: Association of Polish Jewish Citizens, Council of Polish Agudists, New Zionist Organisation and Union of Polish Zionists "Nahum Sokolow"). Federation of Jewish Relief Organisations; Federation of Czechoslovakian Jews; Hicem

Telephone No.: EUSTON 3952-3

Telegrams: DEPUTIES, KINCROSS, LONDON

THE LONDON COMMITTEE OF DEPUTIES OF BRITISH JEWS

generally known as

The Board of Deputies of British Jews

President:
Professor S. BRODETSKY.
Vice-Presidents:
Dr. ISRAEL FELDMAN.
Professor SAMSON WRIGHT.

WOBURN HOUSE,
UPPER WOBURN PLACE,

ČESKOSLOVENSKÁ ÚSTŘEDNÍ ORTHODOXNÍ ŽIDOVSKÁ KANCELÁŘ

CZECHOSLOVAK CENTRAL OFFICE OF ORTHODOX JEWS

representace Ústřední Kanceláře orthodoxních židovských náboženských obcí na Slovensku a Podkarpatské Rusi, výnos publikován v Úředním VĚSTNÍKU ČESKOSLOVENSKÉM (Roč. III. čís 4.)

recognised representation of the Central Office of Orthodox Jewish Religious Communities in Slovakia and Sub-Carpathian Russia, decree published in the Czechoslovak Official Gazette No. 4 dated 23rd December, 1942.

53 Queen's Drive, London, N.4

JOINT EMERGENCY COMMITTEE FOR JEWISH RELIGIOUS EDUCATION IN GREAT BRITAIN

Hon. President: THE VERY REV. THE CHIEF RABBI.

Vice-Chairmen:
LONDON: DR. L. V. SNOWMAN, M.A.
PROVINCIAL: L. DAVIS, ESQ., J.P.
A. M. HURWITZ, ESQ., LL.B.
S. H. STEINKART, ESQ., J.P.

Education Officer:
DR. NATHAN MORRIS, M.A.

Chairman:
M. EPSTEIN, ESQ., M.A., Ph.D.

Joint Treasurers:
I. W. GOLDBERG, ESQ.
S. LONDON, ESQ.

SML/RY

WOBURN HOUSE
UPPER WOBURN PLACE
LONDON, W.C.1.
Telephone: EUSTON 3081/2

May 10th 1945.

Office of the Communal Rabbi

Some thank you letters received before departure for Chile.

As the end of the war was approaching, preparations were put in place to enable Opa to travel to Chile. The first step was to obtain a letter from Rabbi Dr. Shlomo Schonfeld, which is self-explanatory, and paved the way not only for his journey to Chile but also to leave the option open for a return journey, if required.

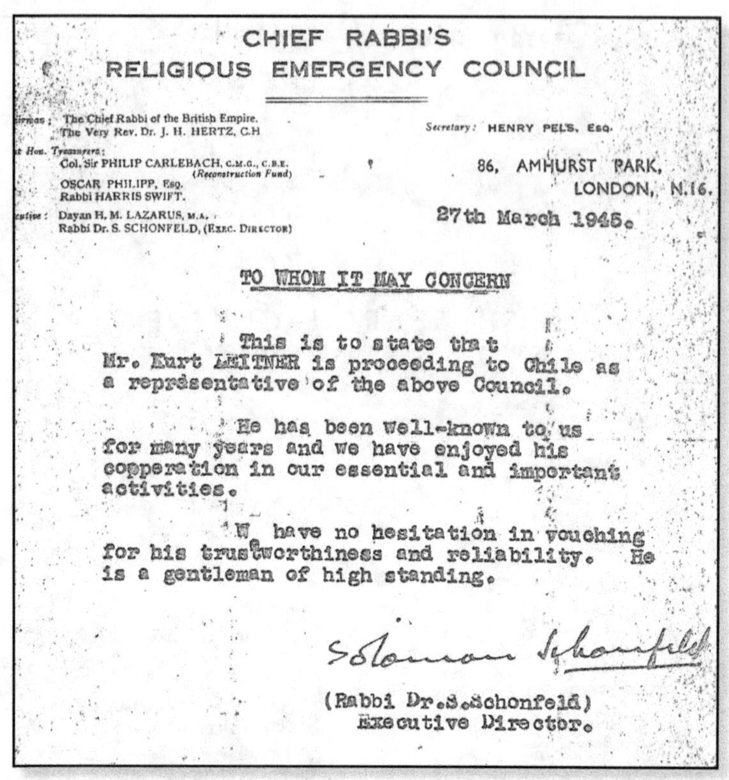

CHIEF RABBI'S
RELIGIOUS EMERGENCY COUNCIL

irman: The Chief Rabbi of the British Empire.
The Very Rev. Dr. J. H. HERTZ, C.H

Secretary: HENRY PELS, Esq.

t Hon. Treasurers:
Col. Sir PHILIP CARLEBACH, C.M.G., C.B.E. (Reconstruction Fund)
OSCAR PHILIPP, Esq.
Rabbi HARRIS SWIFT.

cutive: Dayan H. M. LAZARUS, M.A.
Rabbi Dr. S. SCHONFELD, (Exec. Director)

86, AMHURST PARK,
LONDON, N.16.

27th March 1945.

TO WHOM IT MAY CONCERN

This is to state that Mr. Kurt LEITNER is proceeding to Chile as a representative of the above Council.

He has been well-known to us for many years and we have enjoyed his copperation in our essential and important activities.

We have no hesitation in vouching for his trustworthiness and reliability. He is a gentleman of high standing.

Solomon Schonfeld

(Rabbi Dr.S.Schonfeld)
Executive Director.

On July 19, 1945 Rabbi Dr. Schonfeld sent a letter to the Minister of Information in which he wrote:

> We have arranged some months ago for the visit to Latin America of our co-worker, Mr. K. Leitner, who is travelling to Chile in the interest of the Chief Rabbi's Religious Emergency Council.
>
> He already possesses the Exit Permit (No. 42320) and Entrance Visa, but requires priority permission to obtain transport facilities.
>
> As Mr. Leitner is travelling on an important religious mission we venture to ask your support for this passage, particularly as the Exit Permit of Mr. Leitner elapses early in August.
>
> We should be grateful if you could kindly approach the Ministry of War Transport for some measure of priority for Mr. K. Leitner in connection with a steamer passage to Buenos Aires (en route to Chile). Thanking you in anticipation.
>
> Signed: Rabbi Dr. S. Schonfeld

On August 22, 1945, the following reply arrived from the Ministry of Information:

Telephone No.: EUSton 4321.
Telegrams :—"MINIFORM, LONDON."
In any further communication on this subject the following reference should be quoted :—
RC. 210

Your reference ....

MINISTRY OF INFORMATION,
MALET STREET,
LONDON, W.C.1.

22nd August 1945.

Dear Mr. Leitner,

Your letter of August 17th to the Director of Latin-American Division has been passed to me as I.shall be handling the arrangements for your priority sea passage to Buenos Aires. I note that you require a passage to leave after September 18th and I am communicating accordingly with the Ministry of War Transport and will advise you further as to the actual date of departure.

I understand you have been granted an Exit Permit to leave the United Kingdom and I presume you are taking the necessary steps to secure the Argentine and Chilean Visas.

Yours faithfully,

Communications & Broadcasting Division.

K. Leitner, Esq.,
85, Manor Road,
N. 16.

On October 20, 1945 Opa sent a telegram to Rabbi Yaakov Rosenheim, 2521 Broadway, New York that stated:

> 'Sailing: 1st November to Canada. - Will communicate from there. Thanks Greeting Leitner.

On the same day Uncle Fritz sent a telegram to KOKISCH at 891 Roberto Espinoza, Santiago de Chile, stating:

> 'Kurt on the way. Please communicate c/o Rosenheim 2521 Broadway New York 25. Greetings Fritz.

This was not only excellent news for Oma to be informed that her Choson was finally on his way after being engaged for close to eight years, but it also gave them advance notice to prepare for the forthcoming wedding.

On October 24, 1945 the Belzer Rebbe wrote to Opa and enquired if he had been successful in obtaining his visa to travel to Chile, and sent him his warmest ברכות for the future, and acknowledged his donation of five pounds.

BY AIR MAIL AIR LETTER

IF ANYTHING IS ENCLOSED THIS LETTER WILL BE SENT BY ORDINARY MAIL

Mr.
K. Leitner
85 MANOR ROAD
LONDON N. 16. ENGLAND

WHEN FOLDED THE LETTER MUST CONFORM IN SIZE AND SHAPE WITH THE BLUE BORDER WITHIN WHICH THE ADDRESS ONLY MAY BE WRITTEN

אהרן רוקח מבעלזא
Grand Rabbi A. ROKACH
of Belz

This transcribed:

ב"ה יום ד' פ' וירא תש"ו

(24/October/1945)

כבוד ידידנו היקר הנעלה ירא וחרד עוטה מעיל המדות המופלג וכו' כש"ת מוה"ר ק. לייטנער נ"י.
אחדשה"ט באהבה רבה.

מכתבו לנכון הגיע ליד כ"ק מרן אחי אדמו"ר שליט"א והתפלל בעדו ובעד משפחתו להשי"ת.
ויעזרהו השי"ת לקבל בשורות טובות. גם בירך אותו שהשי"ת ינחהו במעגלי צדק בדבר הנסיעה ואפשרות הנסיעה ובהצלחה ויצליח בכל עניני'.

כ"ק מרן אחי אדמו"ר שליט"א מבעלז מבקשו שיכתוב ויודיע תוצאות הדבר אם עלה בידו לנסוע למדינת טצילי.

הסך 5 פונט אשר שלח חודש תמוז נתקבל בתודה לכ"ק אחי שליט"א.

כ"ק מרן אחי אדמו"ר שליט"א מבעלזא מברכו שיוכל לחוג כלולת נשואיו בקרוב והנני מברכו שברכת צדיק תתקיים במהרה.

ידידו דורש שלומו המצפה לישועה קרובה

הק' מרדכי רוקח באאמו"ר מבעלז זצוקל"ה רב ואבד"ק בילגורייא

אהרן רוקח מבעלזא
Grand Rabbi A. ROKACH
of Belz

Before Opa left England he took out comprehensive travel insurance, and on October 30, 1945 additional insurance for his personal belongings.

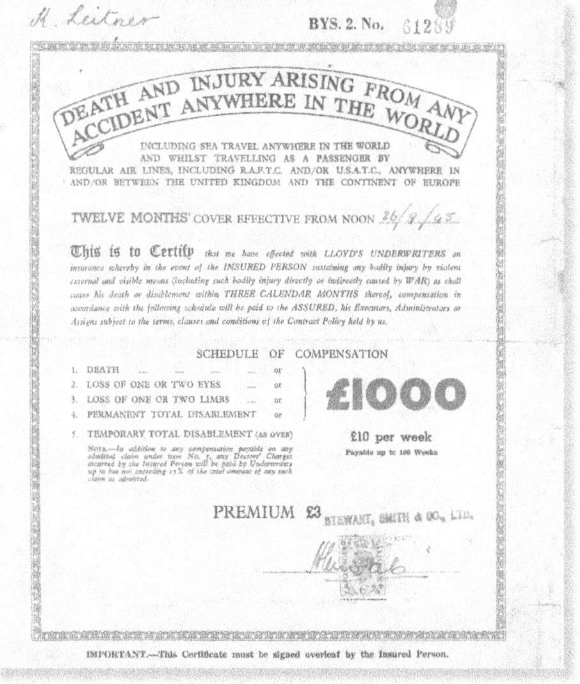

M. Leitner BYS. 2. No. 61289

DEATH AND INJURY ARISING FROM ANY ACCIDENT ANYWHERE IN THE WORLD

INCLUDING SEA TRAVEL ANYWHERE IN THE WORLD AND WHILST TRAVELLING AS A PASSENGER BY REGULAR AIR LINES, INCLUDING R.A.F.T.C. AND/OR U.S.A.T.C., ANYWHERE IN AND/OR BETWEEN THE UNITED KINGDOM AND THE CONTINENT OF EUROPE

TWELVE MONTHS' COVER EFFECTIVE FROM NOON 26/9/45

This is to Certify *that we have effected with LLOYD'S UNDERWRITERS an insurance whereby in the event of the INSURED PERSON sustaining any bodily injury by violent external and visible means (including such bodily injury directly or indirectly caused by WAR) as shall cause his death or disablement within THREE CALENDAR MONTHS thereof, compensation in accordance with the following schedule will be paid to the ASSURED, his Executors, Administrators or Assigns subject to the terms, clauses and conditions of the Contract Policy held by us.*

SCHEDULE OF COMPENSATION

1. DEATH ... ... or
2. LOSS OF ONE OR TWO EYES ... or
3. LOSS OF ONE OR TWO LIMBS ... or
4. PERMANENT TOTAL DISABLEMENT or

£1000

5. TEMPORARY TOTAL DISABLEMENT (AS OVER)

£10 per week
Payable up to 100 Weeks

NOTE.—In addition to any compensation payable on any admitted claim under item No. 5, any Doctors' Charges incurred by the Insured Person will be paid by Underwriters up to but not exceeding 15% of the total amount of any such claim as admitted.

PREMIUM £3 STEWART, SMITH & CO., LTD.

IMPORTANT.—This Certificate must be signed overleaf by the Insured Person.

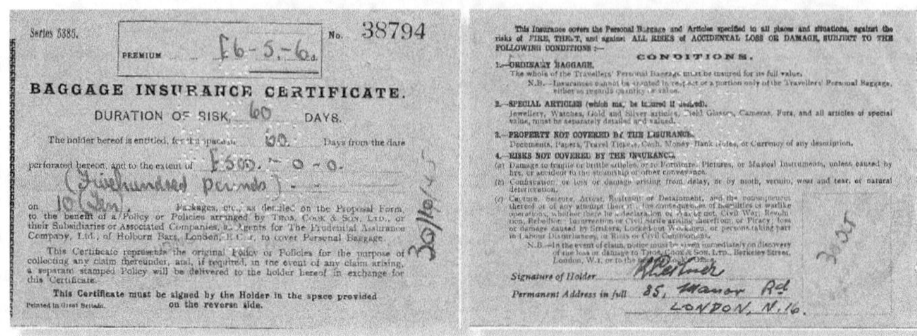

Series 5385. PREMIUM £6-5.-6d. No. 38794

BAGGAGE INSURANCE CERTIFICATE.

DURATION OF RISK, 60 DAYS.

The holder hereof is entitled, for the space of 60 Days from the date perforated hereon, and to the extent of £500.-0-0. (Fivehundred pounds) on 10 (Ten) Packages, etc., as detailed on the Proposal Form, to the benefit of a Policy or Policies arranged by Thos. Cook & Son, Ltd., or their Subsidiaries or Associated Companies, as Agents for The Prudential Assurance Company, Ltd., of Holborn Bars, London, E.C.1, to cover Personal Baggage.

This Certificate represents the original Policy or Policies for the purpose of collecting any claim thereunder, and, if required, in the event of any claim arising, a separate stamped Policy will be delivered to the holder hereof in exchange for this Certificate.

This Certificate must be signed by the Holder in the space provided on the reverse side.

Printed in Great Britain.

30/10/45

This Insurance covers the Personal Baggage and Articles specified to all places and situations, against the risks of FIRE, THEFT, and against ALL RISKS of ACCIDENTAL LOSS OR DAMAGE, SUBJECT TO THE FOLLOWING CONDITIONS:—

CONDITIONS.

1.—ORDINARY BAGGAGE.
The whole of the Travellers' Personal Baggage must be insured for its full value.
N.B.—Insurance cannot be granted in respect of a portion only of the Travellers' Personal Baggage, either as regards quantity or value.

2.—SPECIAL ARTICLES (which may be insured if desired).
Jewellery, Watches, Gold and Silver articles, Field Glasses, Cameras, Furs, and all articles of special value, must be separately detailed and valued.

3.—PROPERTY NOT COVERED BY THE INSURANCE.
Documents, Papers, Travel Tickets, Cash, Money, Bank Notes, or Currency of any description.

4.—RISKS NOT COVERED BY THE INSURANCE.
(a) Damage to fragile or brittle articles, or to Furniture, Pictures, or Musical Instruments, unless caused by fire, or accident to the steamship or other conveyance.
(b) Confiscation, or loss or damage arising from delay, or by moth, vermin, wear and tear, or natural deterioration.
(c) Capture, Seizure, Arrest, Restraint or Detainment, and the consequences thereof or of any attempt thereat; the consequences of hostilities or warlike operations, whether there be a declaration of War or not, Civil War, Revolution, Rebellion, Insurrection or Civil Strife arising therefrom, or Piracy; loss or damage caused by Strikers, Locked-out Workmen, or persons taking part in Labour Disturbances, or Riots or Civil Commotions.
N.B.—In the event of claim, notice must be given immediately on discovery of the loss or damage to Thos. Cook & Son, Ltd., Berkeley Street, London, W.1, or to the nearest Cook's Office.

Signature of Holder K Leitner

Permanent Address in full 85, Manor Rd LONDON, N.16.

On October 28, 1945 Opa received a telegram from Rabbi Yaakov Rosenheim in America which stated:

> 'We can have reservation boat Buenos Aires eight to ten days after your arrival here. -Valparaiso not possible. You need American Transit Visa at American Consulate London. Please advise us your arrival and name of ship.'

[Sailing to Valparaiso would have been simpler since Valparaiso is only 1 hour away from Santiago, but since this was not possible, the journey took much longer.]

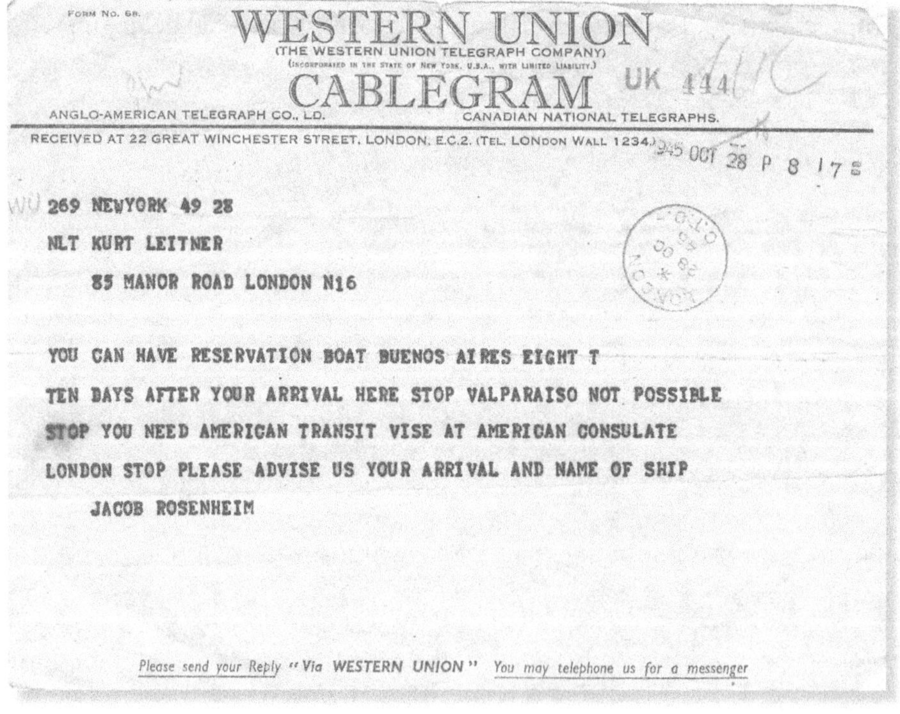

FORM No. 68.

WESTERN UNION

(THE WESTERN UNION TELEGRAPH COMPANY)
(INCORPORATED IN THE STATE OF NEW YORK, U.S.A., WITH LIMITED LIABILITY.)

CABLEGRAM UK 444

ANGLO-AMERICAN TELEGRAPH CO., LD. CANADIAN NATIONAL TELEGRAPHS.

RECEIVED AT 22 GREAT WINCHESTER STREET, LONDON, E.C.2. (TEL. LONDON WALL 1234.) 1945 OCT 28 P 8 17

WU 269 NEWYORK 49 28

NLT KURT LEITNER

85 MANOR ROAD LONDON N16

YOU CAN HAVE RESERVATION BOAT BUENOS AIRES EIGHT T
TEN DAYS AFTER YOUR ARRIVAL HERE STOP VALPARAISO NOT POSSIBLE
STOP YOU NEED AMERICAN TRANSIT VISE AT AMERICAN CONSULATE
LONDON STOP PLEASE ADVISE US YOUR ARRIVAL AND NAME OF SHIP
JACOB ROSENHEIM

Please send your Reply "Via WESTERN UNION" You may telephone us for a messenger

On October 31, 1945, Opa received a telegram from Rabbi Yaakov Rosenheim informing him that his host in Montreal was expecting him.

The Telegram reads:

> Kurt Leitner. Passenger Sydney Star Cunard Liverpool.
>
> Have wired Hartog Hartogsohn; 4667 St. Urbain Street Montreal. Safe Journey. Greetings Oppenheimer.

Charges to pay
s. d.
RECEIVED

POST OFFICE
TELEGRAM

No.
OFFICE STAMP

Prefix. Time handed in. Office of Origin and Service Instructions. Words.
44

From 344 11.0 LONDON T 17 To

KURT LEITNER PASSENGER SYDNEY-STAR CUNARD
LIVERPOOL =
HAVE WIRED HARTOG HARTOGSOHN 4667
ST-URBAIN-STREET MONTREAL SAFE JOURNEY GREETINGS =
OPPENHEIMER +

For free repetition of doubtful words telephone "TE 4667 + " or call, with this form at office of delivery. Other enquiries should be accomp... if possible, the envelope

Wt. 27501/P2570 50m. 9/44—McC & Co.Ltd—51-5162

On November 1, 1945 Mrs Erna Sanger, Uncle Shurl's mother-in-law, sent greetings for a safe journey from their hotel in Buxton direct to the boat, the Sydney Star. Opa had met her during his short stay in Buxton over Yom Tov in 1941. This was a very kind gesture on her part and was much appreciated by Opa.

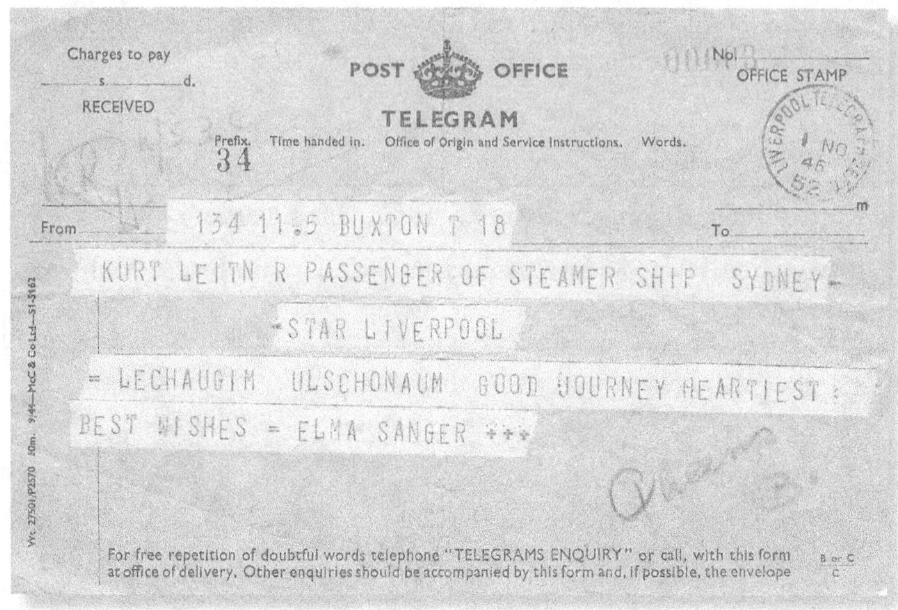

Charges to pay
s. d.
RECEIVED

POST OFFICE
TELEGRAM

Prefix. 34 Time handed in. Office of Origin and Service Instructions. Words.

No.
OFFICE STAMP
LIVERPOOL TELEGRAPHS
1 NO 46

From 134 11.5 BUXTON T 18 To

KURT LEITN R PASSENGER OF STEAMER SHIP SYDNEY-
-STAR LIVERPOOL
= LECHAUGIM ULSCHONAUM GOOD JOURNEY HEARTIEST :
BEST WISHES = ELMA SANGER +++

For free repetition of doubtful words telephone "TELEGRAMS ENQUIRY" or call, with this form at office of delivery. Other enquiries should be accompanied by this form and, if possible, the envelope

Wt. 27501/P2570 50m. 9/44—McC & Co Ltd—51-3162

(Telegrams were sometimes orally transmitted and this explains the many spelling mistakes. Costs of a telegram depended on the amount of words and were therefore kept to a minimum.)

Finally, on November 2, 1945, Opa boarded the Sydney Star, a cargo ship, on the first leg of his trip. The complete journey took him to Montreal in Canada a distance of 3500 km, then to Rio de Janeiro in Brazil via New York, and continuing on to Buenos Aires in Argentina, all in all a total of 9000 km from Montreal, and finally, to Santiago de Chile, another 1500 km.

Note that there were only 20 passengers on this cargo boat, [Opa is listed on line 15] and hence Opa received preferential treatment.

LIST OR MANIFEST OF ALIEN PASSENGERS FOR THE UNITED

S. S. Passengers sailing from , 2nd Nov , 19

The passenger manifesto for the Sydney Star, November 2, 1945. Opa is on line 15

The SS Sydney Star cargo boat on which Opa travelled to Canada on November 2, 1945

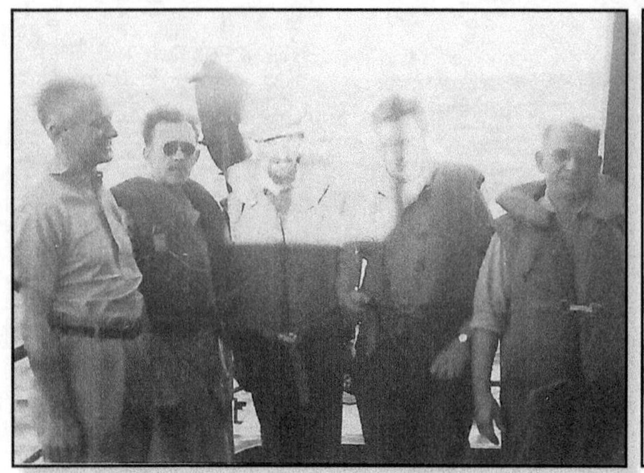

Opa (center) on the deck en route

En route to Canada

Opa left London on Friday, November 2, 1945, and arrived in Canada on November 10, which was a Shabbos. He didn't want to disembark on Shabbos as he would have had to take his luggage with him, and instead chose to stay on board until the following morning, as can be seen from his landing card. This was quite remarkable, considering that he was completely alone and in a strange country.

On November 9, 1945 Opa received the following welcome telegram from Mr. Hartogson, his host in Montreal:

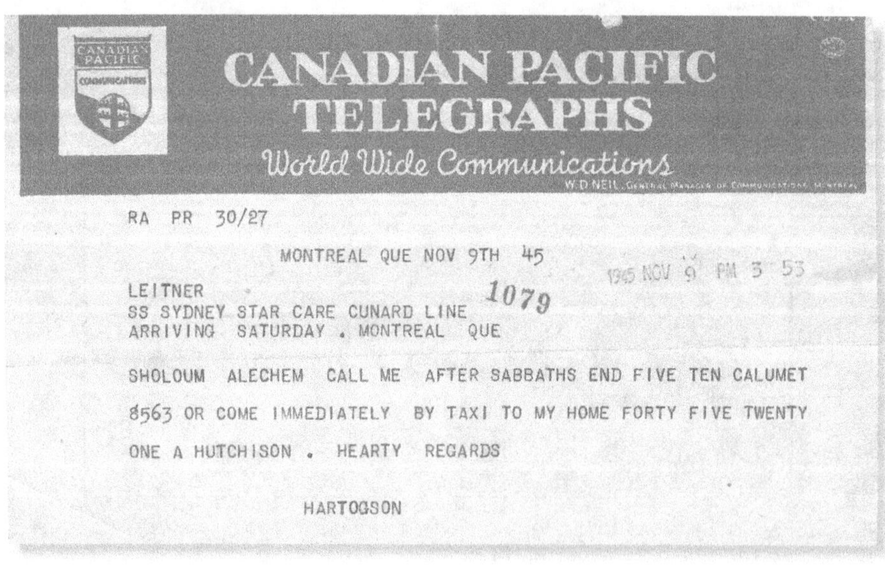

CANADIAN PACIFIC
TELEGRAPHS
World Wide Communications
W. D. NEIL, GENERAL MANAGER OF COMMUNICATIONS, MONTREAL

RA PR 30/27

MONTREAL QUE NOV 9TH 45

1945 NOV 9 PM 3 53

LEITNER
SS SYDNEY STAR CARE CUNARD LINE
ARRIVING SATURDAY . MONTREAL QUE

1079

SHOLOUM ALECHEM CALL ME AFTER SABBATHS END FIVE TEN CALUMET 8563 OR COME IMMEDIATELY BY TAXI TO MY HOME FORTY FIVE TWENTY ONE A HUTCHISON . HEARTY REGARDS

HARTOGSON

Montreal Que [Quebec] Nov 9, 1945 3.53 pm.
Leitner
SS Sydney Star Care Cunard Line
Arriving Saturday Montreal Que
Sholom Alechem Call me after Shabbos ends five ten. Calumet 8563 or come immediately by taxi to my home forty five twenty one Hutchinson.
Hearty Regards, Hartogson.

4/45. L.P. 15/161. B. 70

CUNARD WHITE STAR LIMITED.

LANDING CARD.

NAME Leitner Mr Kurt

MANIFEST No. LINE No. 15

ROOM No. BERTH

Cabin CLASS

BEFORE LEAVING THE VESSEL the holder must present this Landing Card to the U.S. Immigrant Inspector for endorsement.

NOV 11 1945

U.S. Immigrant Inspector

Front and back of Landing Card to enter Canada dated November 11, 1945

On Sunday morning Opa made his way to his host, Mr. Hartogson, where he stayed until his next ship was due to depart for Rio de Janeiro, Brazil, eleven days later. He first got to know Mr Hartogson during the Kenessio in Marienbad, and now had a chance to renew their friendship. Opa often spoke very highly about Mr Hartogson and his great hospitality.

Thanks to the various travel documents and crew pass we were able to follow my father's journey.

On November 22, 1945 Opa embarked on the second leg of his long trip on the 'Elko Victory', a cargo boat bound for Rio de Janeiro, Brazil. Since the boat had scheduled a short stop in New York, Opa had to obtain a transit visa before his departure from London. This second journey, which included Chanuka, lasted 16 days, and they docked on Shabbos, December 8, 1945. Like a few weeks before, Opa again chose to stay on the ship until the following day. There he received an official landing card that allowed him entry into Brazil, but only as a Transit passenger. The 'Elko Victory' belonged to the American Republic Liners and Opa continued on one of their company's ships to Buenos Aires, Argentina.

VOYAGE No. 4 DATE 11/22/45
MOORE-McCORMACK LINES, Inc.
CREW PASS AND MUSTER CARD
S. S. ELKO VICTORY
NAME KURT LEITNER
ART. No. ______ RATING PASSENGER
EMERGENCY STATION NONE
BOAT No. 2
BOAT STATION MAIN DECK, UNDER ASSIGNED BOAT
Initialed O.S.E.
(Signature of Crew Member)
6-38 *Keep This Card With You at All Times*

TRANS. 2. RIO DE JANEIRO AR DEC 8 - 1945
FIRST CABIN PASSENGER LANDING CARD
American Republics Line — STEAMER (VAPOR) (VAPOR) S/S ELKO VICTORY
VOYAGE No. (VIAGEM No.) (VIAJE No.) 4 — FROM (DE) (DE) New York
FIRST CABIN (CABINA DE PRIMEIRA) (CABINA DE PRIMERA) — MANIFEST NO. (MANIFESTO NO.) (MANIFIESTO NO.) R — PASSENGER NO. (PASSAGEIRO NO.) (PASAJERO NO.) 2
NAME OF PASSENGER (NOME DO PASSAGEIRO) (NOMBRE DE PASAJERO) Kurt Leitner
This card is to be retained by passenger and presented to Immigration Inspector on arrival at destination.

Crew Pass and Muster Card with Landing Card

From Buenos Aires Opa continued by train, where he travelled for three days, and passing over the snow capped Andes Mountain range to Santiago de Chile, where he finally arrived on Tuesday, December 25, 1945, almost eight weeks after having left London.

The Elko Victoria en route to Rio de Janeiro

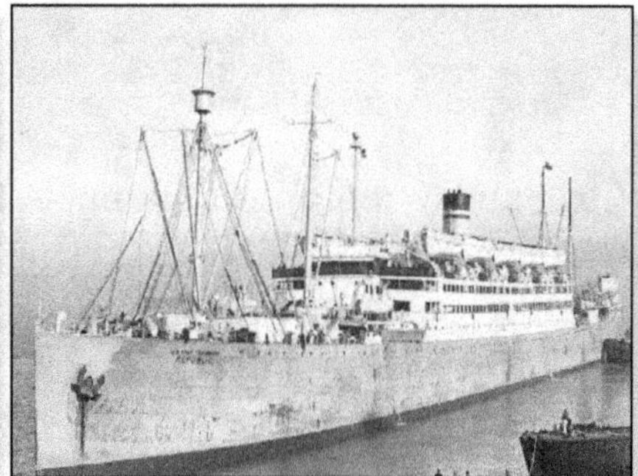

An American Republic Liner to Argentina

The Mountain Train across the Andes.

We can well imagine what a welcome he got in Chile, and how much both sides had to tell each other after a gap of nearly eight years!

CHAPTER 7
Santiago de Chile

CHILE

To gain some understanding of the sort of life that existed for the Yidden in Chile before and after my parents arrived there, and what they had to contend with, I will present a bit of Chile's historic background.

Chile is situated on the West Coast of South America, [sometimes known as Latin America]. Its land is sharply defined by the Pacific Ocean to the West and the Andes Mountain Range to the East. The stretch of land between these two physical barriers has an average width of eighty miles and is some 2800 miles long. (In order to visualise this, it can be compared to the distance between New York and Los Angeles) It extends from an utterly rainless desert in the North to the near Antarctic 'Tierra del Fuego' in the South. The language spoken is Spanish.

JEWISH CHILE

Jews began to settle in Chile as Marranos at the time of the Spanish Inquisition at the end of 1490, but then unfortunately assimilated with the local non Jewish society over the centuries. At the beginning of the 1900s, only about 100 people identified themselves as Jewish and lived in Santiago, the capital of Chile. However, a group of wealthy Orthodox refugees arrived in Chile in the late 1890s and got together to build the 'Chevra Kadisha Shul' with an adjoining Mikvah. These facilities served as the nucleus for the Orthodox Yidden in the years to come. From 1933 immigration soared, and a large number of people, mainly from Germany and Nazi occupied Europe arrived and by 1941 there were over 25,000 Jews there. This number continued to increase rapidly throughout the war years.

The Zionist propaganda machinery knew no limits, and South America was not spared either. With determination they set about spreading their Zionist ideology, which was organised via the United States of America, and despite World War II raging in Europe with the loss of millions of Jewish lives and the destruction of numerous communities, the Zionist Jewish World Congress sent a certain Rabbi J.X. Cohen (Associate Rabbi of the Free Synagogue) in 1941 to South America to survey all the Jewish Communities throughout the continent of Latin America. Regarding the situation in Chile, he remarked 'In Chile it may be said that Judaism and Zionism are identical; All Jews are Zionists.' Chilean Jewish life was centred in Santiago and based around the 'Circulo Israelita', a building which was erected in 1930 at a cost of $250,000, and accommodated numerous Zionist groups, the Women Aid Society, several youth groups and the 'Jewish Primary School' which was recognised by the Chilean Government and subsidized by it. This is the 'Jewish' Chile that greeted both the Kokisch family and Opa on their arrival!

Before the rise of Hitlerism in Germany, relations between Jews and Chileans were very cordial, unlike in the other South American Countries where Anti-Semitism was rampant. Chile was therefore named the 'Paradise of South America'

As a result of Rabbi Cohen's report about the Jewish communities of South America, a large Zionist Conference was organised in Montevideo, Uruguay, in July 1941, to identify all these communities with the Zionist cause, and to discuss what assistance they could be provided with in order to further their Zionist ideology.

Opa arrives in Chile and meets his Kalloh again after 8 years

When Opa arrived in Chile on the 25th December 1945, he was one of the few frum men in the city, but with his determination and charm, and with new immigrants arriving frequently, he soon found enough Orthodox Yidden who were interested in establishing their own Minyan and begin a new 'Austrittsgemeinde' in Santiago, which was appropriately known as the 'Chassam Sofer Minyan.' Although a small Orthodox Shul and Mikvah existed at the 'Chevra Kadisha Shul', it was not within walking distance from our house, and was therefore only accessible to us during weekdays.

Opa and Oma had to continuously swim against the tide, to ensure that Torah would be practiced even in this spiritually barren desert country of Chile. The Kitzur Shulchan Oruch was their Halocho Sefer, whose guidance they followed to the letter.

On January 14, 1946, one day before their Chasene, Opa sent Oma the following telegram:

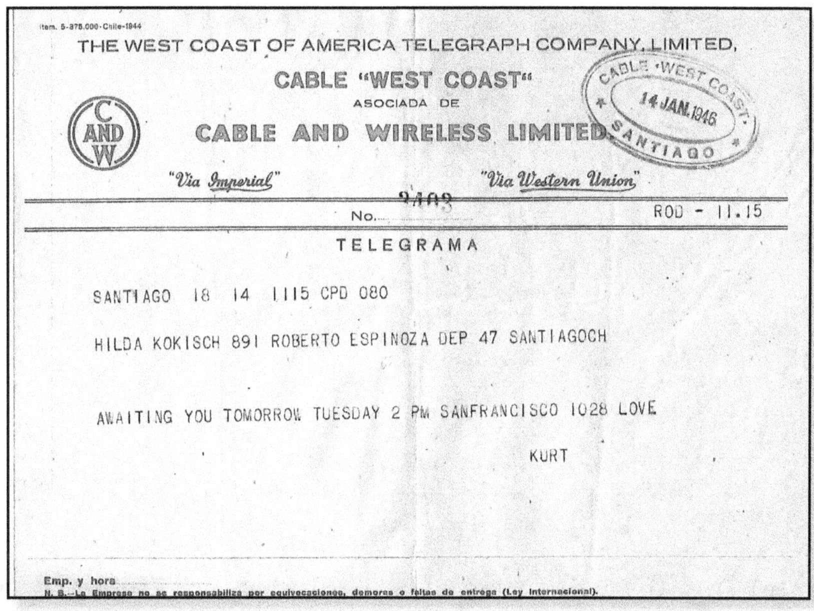

Item. 5-375.000-Chile-1944

THE WEST COAST OF AMERICA TELEGRAPH COMPANY, LIMITED,

CABLE "WEST COAST"

ASOCIADA DE

CABLE AND WIRELESS LIMITED

CABLE WEST COAST 14 JAN. 1946 SANTIAGO

"Via Imperial" "Via Western Union"

No. 9403 ROD - 11.15

TELEGRAMA

SANTIAGO 18 14 1115 CPD 080

HILDA KOKISCH 891 ROBERTO ESPINOZA DEP 47 SANTIAGOCH

AWAITING YOU TOMORROW TUESDAY 2 PM SANFRANCISCO 1028 LOVE

KURT

Emp. y hora

N. B.—La Empresa no se responsabiliza por equivocaciones, demoras o faltas de entrega (Ley Internacional).

The Chevra Kadisha Shul, where their Chasene took place, was at 1028 San Fransisco Sreet.

On their wedding day and also afterwards, they received many telegrams with Mazel Tov wishes from both family and friends.

Opa was 39 years old when he arrived in Chile and got married on the 13th of Shevat, on his 40th birthday. He went to the Chuppa alone; his mother had already died in 1934 in Marienbad, and he lacked information regarding his father, whether he was still alive or not. However, he was comforted by the knowledge that Reb Aaron of Belz was surely with him in thought and was sending him his ברכות on this momentous day, just like a father would bless his own son.

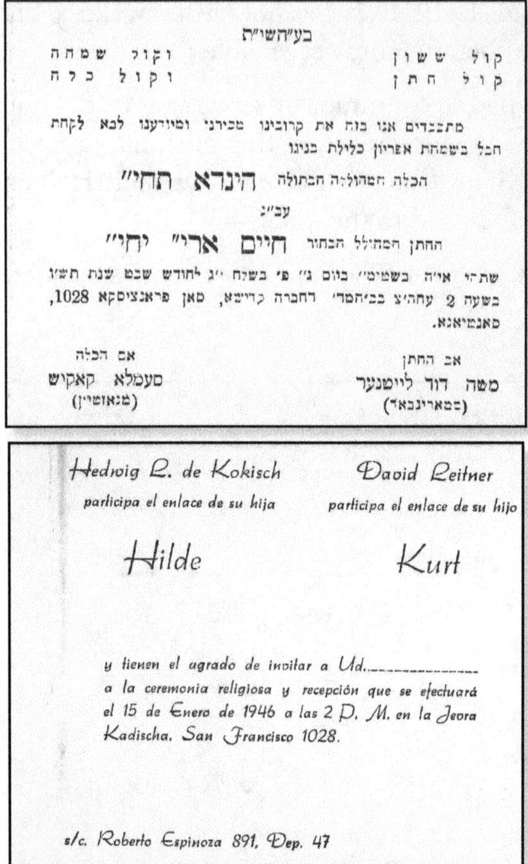

בע"השי"ת

קול ששון וקול שמחה
קול חתן וקול כלה

מתכבדים אנו בזה את קרובינו מכירנו ומיודענו לבא לקחת
חבל בשמחת אפריון כלילת בנינו

הכלה המהוללה הבתולה **הינדא תחי'**

עב"ג

החתן המהולל הבחור **חיים ארי' יחי'**

שתהי' אי"ה בשטומ"ו ביום ג' פ' בשלח י"ג לחודש שבט שנת תש"ו
בשעה 2 עחה"צ בבית חברה קדישא, סאן פראנציסקא 1028,
סאנטיאגא.

אב החתן
משה דוד לייטנער
(במארינבאד)

אם הכלה
סעמלא קאקיש
(מגאזשין)

Hedwig L. de Kokisch
participa el enlace de su hija

Hilde

David Leitner
participa el enlace de su hijo

Kurt

y tienen el agrado de invitar a Ud.______________
a la ceremonia religiosa y recepción que se efectuará
el 15 de Enero de 1946 a las 2 P. M. en la Jeora
Kadischa. San Francisco 1028.

s/c. Roberto Espinoza 891, Dep. 47

Opa and Oma's Wedding Invitation

Other Mazel Tov wishes received included one from his older brother, Uncle Fritz and family (the signature is an abridgement of their names Fritz Margit Judith Harry Monty).

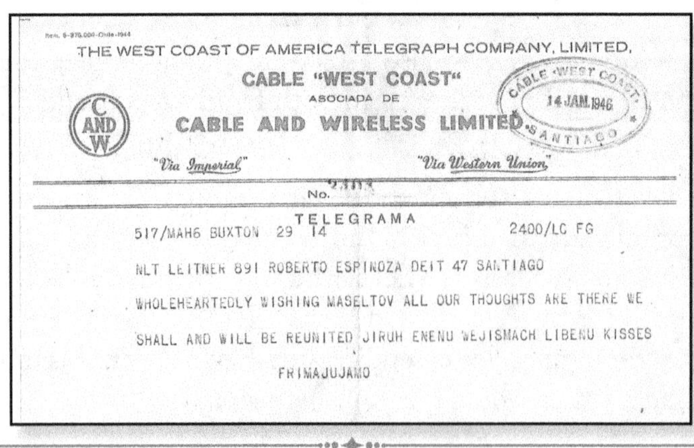

THE WEST COAST OF AMERICA TELEGRAPH COMPANY, LIMITED.
CABLE "WEST COAST"
ASOCIADA DE
CABLE AND WIRELESS LIMITED.
"Via Imperial" "Via Western Union"
CABLE "WEST COAST" 14 JAN.1946 SANTIAGO
No.
TELEGRAMA
517/MAH6 BUXTON 29 14 2400/LC FG
NLT LEITNER 891 ROBERTO ESPINOZA DEIT 47 SANTIAGO
WHOLEHEARTEDLY WISHING MASELTOV ALL OUR THOUGHTS ARE THERE WE
SHALL AND WILL BE REUNITED JIRUH ENENU WEJISMACH LIBENU KISSES
FRIMAJUJAMO

He also received a telegram from Uncle Shurl and family.

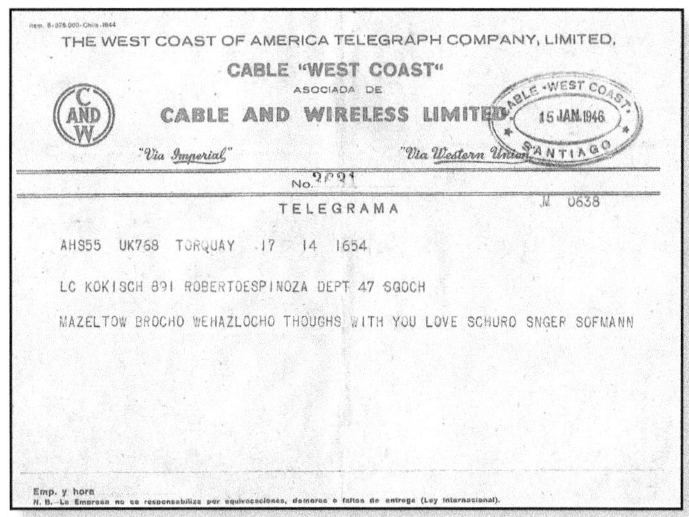

Item. 5-375.000-Chile-1944

THE WEST COAST OF AMERICA TELEGRAPH COMPANY, LIMITED.

CABLE "WEST COAST"

ASOCIADA DE

CABLE AND WIRELESS LIMITED

"Via Imperial" "Via Western Union"

CABLE "WEST COAST" 15 JAN.1946 SANTIAGO

No. 2791

TELEGRAMA M 0638

AHS55 UK768 TORQUAY 17 14 1654

LC KOKISCH 891 ROBERTOESPINOZA DEPT 47 SGOCH

MAZELTOW BROCHO WEHAZLOCHO THOUGHS WITH YOU LOVE SCHURO SNGER SOFMANN

Emp. y hora

N. B.—La Empresa no se responsabiliza por equivocaciones, demoras o faltas de entrega (Ley Internacional).

Rabbi Avrohom Goldberg

One of the guests at the wedding, Reb Avrohom Goldberg, the local Shochet, sent his wishes with the acrostics of חיים אריה and הינדא. It reads:

בה עסק לספר .. ולכל בני ישראל הי' אור
פה סאנטיאגו יע"א.

חדוה וששון תמיד באהליכם
יי' גם ברכה ישלח בעסקיכם
משמים הכריזו והסכימו לזווגיכם

אתם תהיו מאושרים כל ימי חייכם
רצונכם יעשה ה', וימלאו משאלותיכם
יהיו בשושנים סוגה דרכיכם

הי' זאת לאלפי רבבה, בזאת הברכה
יברכוך מלאכי המרכבה
נצח תפארתך ופארך
דתי המלך לא יסורו ממך
אשת חיל יאמרו על עליך אנשים ונשים וגם בעל

אברהם גאלדבערג ומשפחתו
שו"ב ומורה דפה

Good wishes from Rabbi A. Goldberg with acronym חיים אריה - הינדא

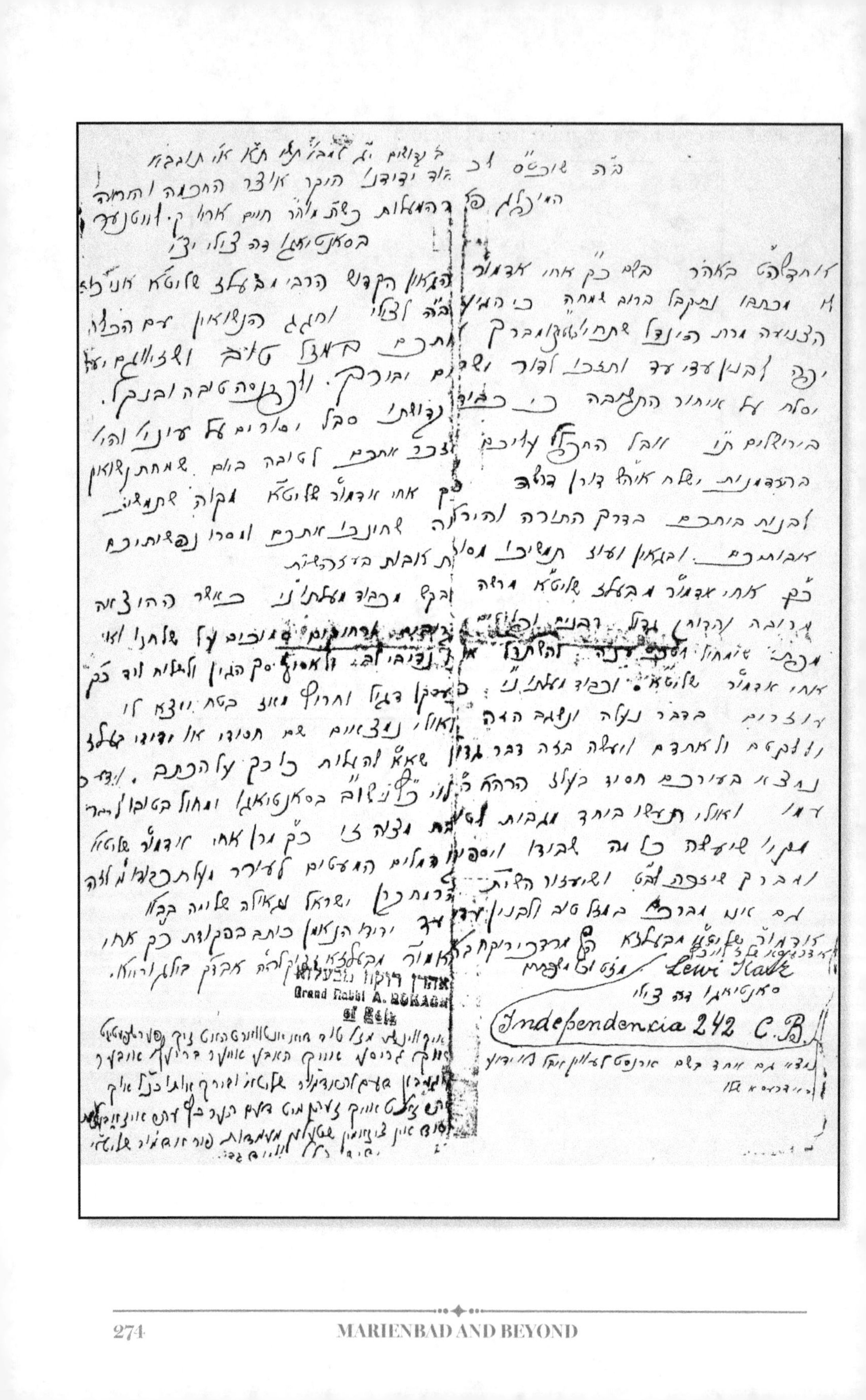

אהרן רוקח מבעלזא

Grand Rabbi A. ROKACH

of Belz

Lewi Katz

Independencia 242 C.B.

Transcribed:

ב"ה ב' קדושים י"ג למב"י תש"ו ת"א א"י תובב"א

(29/April/1946)

שוכט"ס לכבוד ידידנו היקר אוצר החכמה והיראה המופלג פאר המעלות כש"ת מוה"ר חיים ארי' ק. לייטנער בסאנטיאגו דה צילי יצ"ו

אחדשה"ט באה"ר

בשם כ"ק אחי אדמו"ר הגאון הקדוש הרבי מבעלז שליט"א אני כותב לו.

מכתבו נתקבל ברוב שמחה כי הגיע ב"ה לצילי וחגג הנשואין עם הכלה הצנועה מרת הינדל שתחי' בשטמ"צ ומברך אתכם במזל טוב ושזיווגם יעלה יפה לבנין עדי עד ותזכו לדור ישרים יבורך ולפרנסה טובה ובנקל. יסלח על איחור התשובה כי כבוד קדושתו סבל יסורים על עיני' והי' בירושלים ת"ו אבל התפלל עליכם וזכר אתכם לטובה ביום שמחת נשואין בהזדמנות ישלח איה"ש דורן דרשה כ"ק אחי אדמו"ר שליט"א מקוה שתמשיכו לבנות ביתכם בדרך התורה והיראה שחינכו אתכם ומסרו נפשותיכם אבותיכם ובגאון ועוז תמשיכו מסורת אבות בעזהשי"ת.

כ"ק אחי אדמו"ר מבעלז שליט"א מרשה לבקש מכבוד מעלתו נ"י כאשר ההוצאה מרובה והדוחק גדול רבנים ופליטים קרובים ורחוקים סמוכים על שלחנו ואי שימחול ויסכים בזה להשתדל אצל נדיבי לב ולאסוף סך הגון ולשלוח ליד כ"ק אחי אדמו"ר שליט"א וכבוד מעלתו נ"י העסקן דגול וחרוץ מאז בטח ימצא לו עוזרים בדבר נעלה ונשגב הזה ואולי נמצאים שם חסידי או ידידי בעלז וללקטם ולאחדם ויעשה בזה דבר גדול שא"א להעלות כל כך על הכתב וידע כי נמצא בעירכם חסיד בעלז הרה"ח ר' לוי כ"ץ נ"י שו"ב בסאנטיאגו ימחול בטובו לדבר עמו ואולי תעשו ביחד מגבית לטובת מצוה זו כ"ק מרן אחי אדמו"ר שליט"א מקו' שיעשה כל מה שבידו ויספיקו המלים המעטים לעורר מעלת כבודו נ"י לזה ומברך שיזכה לב"ט ושיעזור השי"ת [שתזכו] להרמת קרן ישראל וגאולה שלימה בב"א.

גם אני מברכם במזל טוב לבנין עדי עד ידידו הנאמן כותב בפקודת כ"ק אחי אדמו"ר שליט"א מבעלזא הק' מרדכי רוקח באאמו"ר מבעלזא זצוקלה"ה אבד"ק בילגורייא

אדרעססא של ר' לוי כ"ץ

סאנטיאגו דה צילי

Independencia 242 C.B.

נמצא גם אחד בשם ארנסט לעווין אבל לא

ידוע אדרעססא שלו

אהרן רוקח מבעלזא
Grand Rabbi A. ROKACH
of Belz

איך ווינשע מזל טוב דיא אנטווארט האט זיך פערשפעטיגט איך האבע אייער בריעף איבער געגעבען דעם להאדמו"ר שליט"א ובירך אותו כנ"ל אויך איהר זאלט אייך זעהן מיט דעם הער כץ עהר איז א בעלזער חסיד אין צוזאמין שטעלען מעמדות פיר אדמו"ר שליט"א ידידו הלל ווינד גבאי

In May 1946 Opa received a letter from Reb Aaron of Belz, together with a letter from his brother, Reb Mordechai, the Bilgorajer Rebbe. They acknowledged receipt of Opa's Chasuna invitation and sent him a warm and hearty Mazel Tov. Reb Aaron hoped for an opportunity to send him a wedding gift.

He apologized for the delay in sending his good wishes, but the Rebbe had been in Yerushalayim as he was suffering from an eye ailment and needed to recuperate there, where it was a bit cooler than in Tel Aviv. Reb Mordechai confirmed that Reb Aaron had davened for them on the day of their Chasuna! The Rebbe blessed Opa to merit to 'build a house of תורה ויראת שמים and continue to follow on the same path that his parents had shown him, and he should also merit good children that also follow in this path'. The Rebbe wished them פרנסה טובה ובנקל.

He also requested extra financial assistance. There were many new refugees arriving daily in Eretz Yisroel and were in dire need of financial help, many of which relied solely on the Rebbe for this. He informed Opa that there was a Mr. Levy Katz, also a Belzer Chossid, who lived in Santiago, and perhaps they could raise some money together.

After their wedding they first lived at 891 Roberto Espinoza but later moved to a small house at 185 San Isidoro were they remained for two or three years.

Opa's first effort for a Parnoso was an Import – Export enterprise, which was registered at the British Chamber of Commerce in Chile, as the letterhead shows. He had some good contacts abroad and tried importing various goods, but I don't know how successful this venture was. But one thing is certain. My parents were able to import all the Yiddishkeit and teachings that they saw at home in Europe and successfully build their home in Chile on those foundations!

AMEROPA

KURT LEITNER
REPRESENTACIONES – REPRESENTATIONS
SANTIAGO DE CHILE
SAN ISIDRO 185
CASILLA 9650 – TELEFONO 86743

MIEMBRO DE LA
"BRITISH CHAMBER
OF
COMMERCE
IN THE
REPUBLIC OF CHILE"

THE MATZO BAKERY

Opa arrived only a few short months before Pesach 1946, and his first priority was to procure Matzos for the approaching Yom Tov. He went to inspect an established local Matzo bakery but noticed that it needed some halachic improvements, which the owner was not prepared to carry out, as he found these unnecessary. The matzos were kosher 'bedi'eved', but improvements were definitely desirable. Therefore, soon after that first Pesach, my father made the owner of that Matzo bakery an offer to purchase his factory, which was so generous that he could not refuse. So now Opa was the proud owner of a Matzo bakery, and he set about making the necessary changes that would enhance the Kashrus of the bakery, and improve the taste of the Matzos. To this end he used the knowledge he had learnt from Rabbi Dovid Feldman in Marienbad and made very practical use of the Kitzur Shulchan Oruch.

Universally, all Matzos are made from the same ingredients, just flour and water, but they still don't all taste the same. The different qualities that are to be found with various manufacturers depend largely on the type of oven and its shape, and the heat generated within it. Opa therefore searched and ב"ה found an expert who built him a new custom made oven which enhanced the quality of his Matzos tremendously.

Opa was always particular to provide the best quality possible, whether in his catering business, at the Matzo bakery or in any communal work that he performed. He was eager to demonstrate to the non-orthodox Jewish population that they had no excuse for not eating kosher simply because of its inferior taste. They would eat and enjoy his Matzos because of their superior quality, despite them being Kosher and of a high standard of kashrus.

The factory employed about 35 Jewish people in total and operated for 5 months of the year. They produced excellent machine Matzos and supplied all of the South American Continent. Although the factory used machines for the actual baking, it was not fully automated, as it did not have conveyor belts etc. and much work was still performed by hand. His matzos can therefore best be described as 'machine hand Matzos'! The Matzos were ready and baked in record time, only 7 minutes after the water had been added to the flour. During Opa's first few years in Santiago their community did not have an official Rov who could arrange the supervision of the production, but nonetheless everything was done exactly as the Halocho stipulates. Everything was performed so scrupulously that even the 'Eida Charedis' would have given them a 'Hechsher' on their production. There were never any shortcuts.

The Matzo factory business card and letter headed paper
[*Note change of home address*]

One of the first requirements for the baking of Matzos is that the water used for making the dough must be cold, and this is achieved by drawing the water from a well on the afternoon before it is to be used, which is then left to stand overnight in a cold room, out of the sunlight. This is known as 'Mayim Shelonu' – water that has 'rested' overnight. Therefore Opa had to ensure that he had a sufficient suitable 'kosher' water supply to enable him to bake the full quota required for the following day. The use of metal barrels is also recommended, as the coolness of the metal helps to ensure the water contained therein remains cool.

קצור שלחן ערוך סימן קט:
אין לשין את המצות אלא במים שלנו הלילה דהינו שישאב אותם בין השמשות ויעמדו בתלוש כל הלילה וכו"

'Mayim Shelonu' water for matzo baking stored in the cool cellar in metal barrels

In those days, long before disposable goods became commonplace, many more items were re-used than today. For example, milk was sold in glass bottles, which after use had to be rinsed and returned to the milkman, who then returned them to the dairy where they were washed and sterilised, and then refilled. Similarly, the miller would use large cloth sacks made from a thick jute material for delivering the flour to the bakery. After use, these sacks would be returned to the miller for the next batch. The miller would of course have to wash and dry the empty sacks before he refilled them. That was the normal practice and quite ok for Chometz use. However, when this is done with flour used for Matzo baking suitable for Pesach, it creates a problem. There will always be some flour that gets stuck between the stitches of the seams of the bags, and if this flour gets wet as is very likely during the washing process, it woud be rendered as Chometz.

קצור שלחן ערוך סימן ק"ח ס" ו :

השקים שמשימים בהם את הקמח טוב לעשותן חדשים או לכל הפחות
להתיר את התפירות ולכבסן היטב היטב בחמין ובאפר ובשפשוף וחביטה

To avoid this problem, they had to open the seams of the sacks after they had been emptied of all the flour, undo the stitching of the side seams, wash these "bags" which were now big rectangular pieces of material, and when completely dry, stitch them up again. Since these bags were of unusually coarse material, they could not be sewn up on a regular sewing machine. Unpicking the seams was relatively easy, but stitching them up again was very tedious and required a heavy thread and very long sewing needle, a job that Oma undertook almost single handedly.

To ensure that the flour for the Pesachdig Matzos came only in their 'mehudar' bags, Opa printed his logo "a large Mogen Dovid inside a larger circle and the words 'Fabrica de Matzes–Kurt Leitner" onto the bags, and arranged with the miller that these sacks were to be used exclusively for his Matzo flour. Again, no shortcuts.

קצור שלחן ערוך סימן קי :
ראוי לכל ירא שמים שיהא הוא בעצמו עומד ומשגיח בעשית ואפית המצות שלו

Pictures of the Matzo bakery in progress

During the nine years that Opa lived in Chile, the Chilean economy was not very stable and inflation was high. With a suitable contact at the Chilean bank he was able to exchange any Chilean 'pesos' that he earned at the bakery into American Dollars, which acted as his hedge against inflation. Since much of the production was exported to other South American countries thereby bringing in foreign currency to Chile, these 'dollars' were not too difficult to obtain.

The bakery was very successful and during the nine year period that Opa owned it, turnover increased in real terms by over 50%.

Chilean currency 1000 pesos and 20,000 pesos

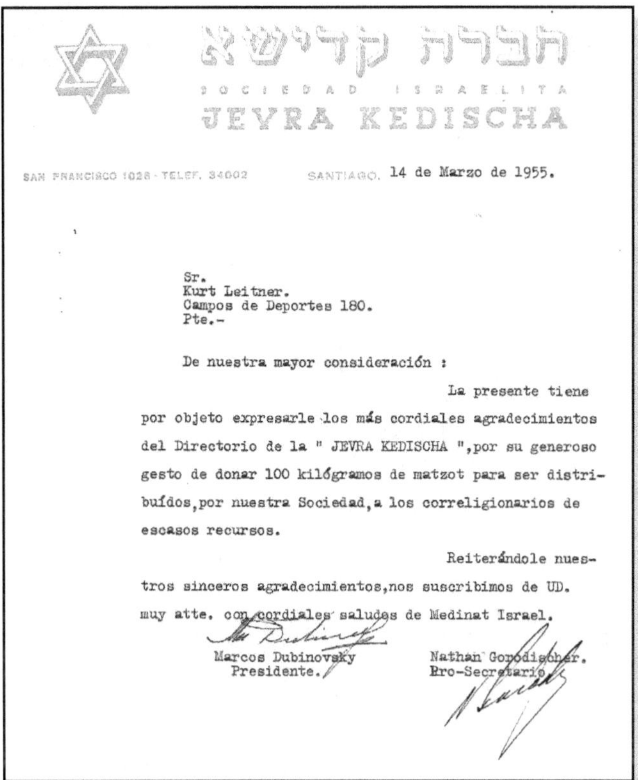

חברה קדישא

SOCIEDAD ISRAELITA

JEVRA KEDISCHA

SAN FRANCISCO 1028 - TELEF. 34002 SANTIAGO, 14 de Marzo de 1955.

Sr.
Kurt Leitner.
Campos de Deportes 180.
Pte.-

De nuestra mayor consideración :

La presente tiene por objeto expresarle los más cordiales agradecimientos del Directorio de la " JEVRA KEDISCHA ", por su generoso gesto de donar 100 kilógramos de matzot para ser distribuídos, por nuestra Sociedad, a los correligionarios de escasos recursos.

Reiterándole nuestros sinceros agradecimientos, nos suscribimos de UD. muy atte. con cordiales saludos de Medinat Israel.

Marcos Dubinovsky
Presidente.

Nathan Gorodischer.
Pro-Secretario.

The above letter acknowledges a donation of 100 kilo of Matzos which Opa had donated for distribution to the members of the Chevra Kadisha Shul for the Pesach prior to our departure.

Even whilst in Chile Opa continued his correspondence with Reb Aaron of Belz. At the end of 1946 he received a personal invitation for Reb Mordechai's Chassene, the Rov of Bilgorai, Reb Aaron's brother.

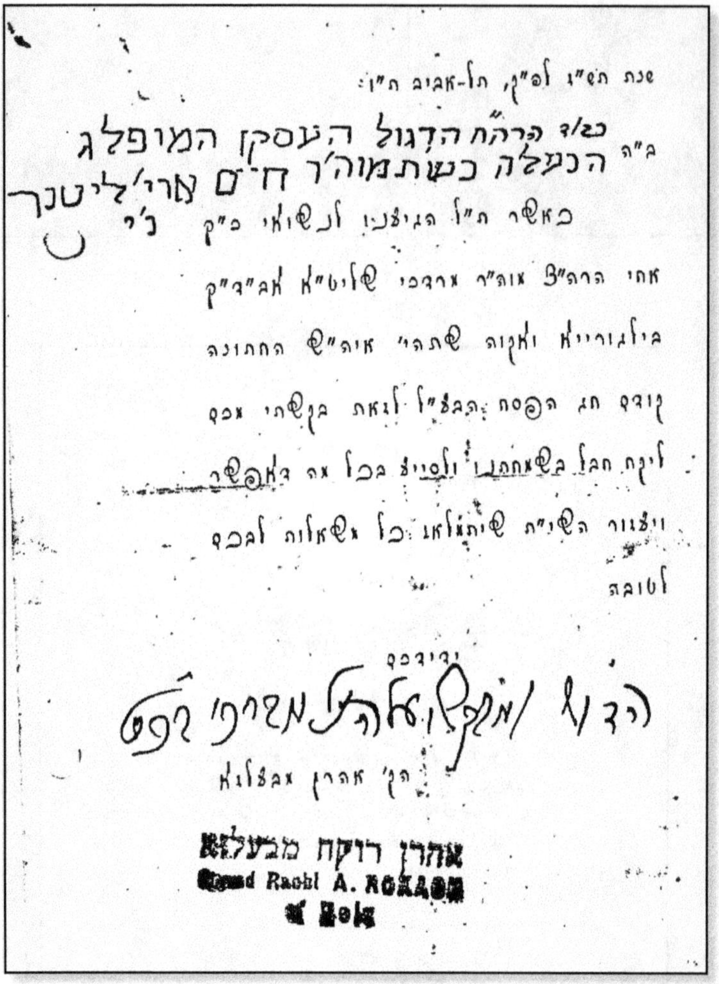
שנת תש"ז לפ"ק, תל-אביב ת"ו:
ב"ה כב'ד הרה"ח הדגול העסקן המופלג
הנעלה כשת מוה'ר חיים ארי' ליטנר נ"י
כאשר ת"ל הגיענו לנשואי כ"ק
אחי הרה"צ מוה"ר מרדכי שליט"א אבד"ק
בילגורייא ואקוה שתהי' איה"ש החתונה
קודם חג הפסח הבעל"ל לזאת בקשתי מכם
ליקח חבל בשמחתנו ולסייע בכל מה דאפשר
ויעזור השי"ת שיתמלאו כל משאלות לבבכם
לטובה
ידידכם
הדו"ש ומבקשו על הנ"ל מברכו בכט"ס
הק' אהרן מבעלזא
אהרן רוקח מבעלזא
Grand Rabbi A. ROKACH
of Belz

This transcribed as:

שנת תש"ז לפ"ק - תל-אביב ת"ו:

ב"ה כבוד הרה"ח הדגול העסקן המופלג הנעלה כש"ת מוה"ר חיים ארי" לייטנער נ"י

כאשר ת"ל הגיענו לנישואי כ"ק אחי הרה"צ מוה"ר מרדכי שליט"א אבד"ק בילגורייא ואקוה שתהי" איה"ש החתונה קודם חג הפסח הבע"ל לזאת בקשתי מכם ליקח חבל בשמחתנו ולסייע בכל מה דאפשר

ויעזור השי"ת שיתמלאו כל משאלות לבכם לטובה

ידידכם

הדו"ש ומבקשו על הנ"ל מברכו בכט"ס

הק" אהרן מבעלזא

A separate letter soon followed with regard to this Chasuna with a request for assistance:

Transcribed:

הנני פב"ש ידידנו העלה איש המעלה הנעלה מופלג רודף צדקה וחסד איש
כש"ת מוה"ר חיים ארי' נ"י לייטנער

כ"ק מרן אחי אדמו"ר שליט"א שואל בשלומו שולח לו מכתב חתונה מבקשו
למחול ולעשות מגבית לטובת הנשואין למצו' גדולה יחשב

מברכו בהצלחה בענייני הכלל ובעניני' הפרטיים

ידידו דו"ש באהבה מברכו בשמחת פורים

הק' מרדכי רוקח באאמו"ר זצ"ל מבעלזא אבד"ק בילגורייא

אהרן רוקח מבעלזא
Grand Rabbi A. ROKACH
of Belz

Apart from their work at the bakery, Opa and Oma applied for the franchise that was offered every year to run the catering facilities at the 'Bnei Yisroel Cultural Centre'. This was a large centre that also housed the 'Theodor Herzl Jewish school' that we attended. All catered functions were always managed together, since Oma felt it was important to be in the kitchen and make sure that everything was done as required for a kosher function. They ran this from May 6, 1952, until March 31, 1955. The Jewish community in Santiago was very happy with Leitner's catering and enjoyed the culinary delights, presentation and high quality service, and all this in the name of a strictly kosher catering!

If we were to encapsulate my parent's ethos and approach to life, I think the most accurate description would be that they displayed a conviction that כל ישראל בני מלכים הם – every Jewish person is to be treated as 'royalty' and with equal respect, irrespective of their personal religious observance. This was apparent in the way they treated the large spectrum of guests in Marienbad, Bad Gastein, Nice and San Remo (see Chapter 10), and is evident from the letters of recommendation received from their various employments and social work that they were involved in.

The following letter of recommendation [which is translated] needs no explanation – it is simply a Kiddush Hashem of the highest order:

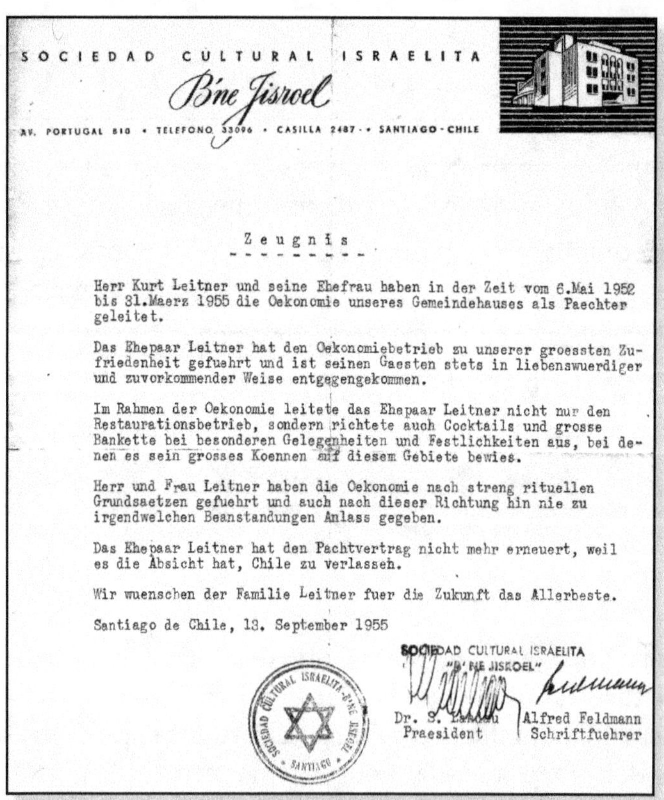

SOCIEDAD CULTURAL ISRAELITA

B'ne Jisroel

AV. PORTUGAL 810 • TELEFONO 33096 • CASILLA 2487 • SANTIAGO - CHILE

Zeugnis

Herr Kurt Leitner und seine Ehefrau haben in der Zeit vom 6.Mai 1952 bis 31.Maerz 1955 die Oekonomie unseres Gemeindehauses als Paechter geleitet.

Das Ehepaar Leitner hat den Oekonomiebetrieb zu unserer groessten Zufriedenheit gefuehrt und ist seinen Gaesten stets in liebenswuerdiger und zuvorkommender Weise entgegengekommen.

Im Rahmen der Oekonomie leitete das Ehepaar Leitner nicht nur den Restaurationsbetrieb, sondern richtete auch Cocktails und grosse Bankette bei besonderen Gelegenheiten und Festlichkeiten aus, bei denen es sein grosses Koennen auf diesem Gebiete bewies.

Herr und Frau Leitner haben die Oekonomie nach streng rituellen Grundsaetzen gefuehrt und auch nach dieser Richtung hin nie zu irgendwelchen Beanstandungen Anlass gegeben.

Das Ehepaar Leitner hat den Pachtvertrag nicht mehr erneuert, weil es die Absicht hat, Chile zu verlasseh.

Wir wuenschen der Familie Leitner fuer die Zukunft das Allerbeste.

Santiago de Chile, 13. September 1955

SOCIEDAD CULTURAL ISRAELITA
"B'NE JISROEL"

Dr. S. Landau
Praesident

Alfred Feldmann
Schriftfuehrer

SOCIEDAD CULTURAL ISRAELITA "B'NE JISROEL" • SANTIAGO •

COMMENDATION

Mr Kurt Leitner and his wife were the leaseholders for the food establishment of our community centre from May 6, 1952 until March 31, 1955.

Mr and Mrs Leitner have managed the catering business to our great satisfaction, and have always treated our guests with utmost kindness and courtesy.

Apart from running and managing the catering of the restaurant they have also organised receptions and big parties for special occasions and festivities, where they have proven their large expertise in this field.

Mr and Mrs Leitner have adhered to the strictly Orthodox traditions in respect of the food preparation and catering, and have never given any reason for concern.

Mr and Mrs Leitner have not renewed their contract because of their intention to leave Chile.

We wish family Leitner all the very best for their future.

Santiago de Chile, September 13, 1955.

Dr. S. Landau	Alfred Feldmann
President	Secretary

SOCIAL WORK IN CHILE

Soon after Opa's arrival he established a local branch for Agudas Yisroel, a Chilean branch for The Chief Rabbi's Religious Emergency Council, represented the Vaad HaYeshivahs, collected funds for the Belz institutions in Eretz Yisroel, and was responsible for bringing Reb Shlomo Halberstam of Bobov to Santiago in July 1949 on a fund raising campaign.

"Agudas Israel" aspira resolver todos los problemas judíos en consonancia con Torah y tradición

ההסתדרות הארצית „אגודת ישראל" בצ'ילי
AGUDAS ISRAEL DE CHILE
Roberto Espinosa 891 - Dpto. 47 - Tel. 80784 - Casilla 9478
SANTIAGO
OFICINAS CENTRALES: JERUSALEM — NUEVA YORK — LONDRES

מטרת אגודת ישראל היא:
לפתור ברוח התורה
והמסורה את כל השאלות
בחיי עם ישראל

Letterhead for Agudas Yisroel in Chile

Ramificación Chilena del
CONSEJO DE EMERGENCIA RELIGIOSA
del Gran Rabino del Imperio Británico.

FUNDADOR,
El difunto Gran Rabino, el muy Rev. Dr. José H. Hertz.

VICE-PRESIDENTE:
Dayan H. M. Lazarus
(Delegado del Gran Rabino)

PRESIDENTE
Dayan Dr. I. Grunfeld

SECRETARIO:
Enrique Pels

DIRECTORES:
Rabino Dr. S. Schonfeld
Rabino Kopul Rosen, M. A.

COMITE CHILENO:

PATROCINANTES:
H. E. M. Claude G. Bowers
(Embajador Americano)
H. E. M. John Hurleston-Leche, C. M. G., O. B. E.
(Embajador Británico)
H. E. Dr. Jan Havlasa
(Embajador Checoeslovaco)
Señora Gabriela Mistral
Dr. Natalio Berman B.

PRESIDENTE HONORARIO:
Gran Rabino Dr. Maguenzo

CONSEJO:
Señor Abraham Azerman
Señor Heymen Abramczyk
Señor Moisés Cimmerman
Señor Fernando O. Friedman
Señor José Francos
Señor Moisés Gertenhaus
Señor Isaac Goren
Señor Eugenio Hochman
Señor José Korniz
Señor Efraim Kohn
Señor Kurt Leitner
Señor Nuta Nebenschoss
Señor Profesor Dr. Julio Plaut
Señor Dr. Max Reinberg
Señor Osias Schupper
Señor Isaac Schwarz
Señor Jonas Wolf.

DIRECCION.
SECRETARIO HONORARIO:
Kurt Leitner
San Isidro 185 - Santiago de Chile
Teléfono 86743 - Casilla 9650

Religious Relief Committee in Chile – Hon. Secretary K. Leitner

Many of the names on the lower section of this notepaper were members of the Chassam Sofer Minyan.

ועד הישיבות בארץ ישראל

וזאת לתעודה

חבר נכבד

ועד הישיבות בארץ ישראל

Rabbi Zalman Sorotzkin

Rabbi I. Z. Meltzer (1870–1953)

Certificate from Vaad HaYeshivahs representative for Santiago signed by Rabbi Isser Zalman Meltzer and Rabbi Zalman Sorotzkin

Owing to the large proportion of Zionist sympathisers in Santiago and the fact that Opa had earned himself an excellent reputation as being honest and sincere in his Yiddishkeit, it was possible for him to solicit funds for 'Eretz Yisroel', and managed to send regular donations to the Vaad HaYeshivahs.

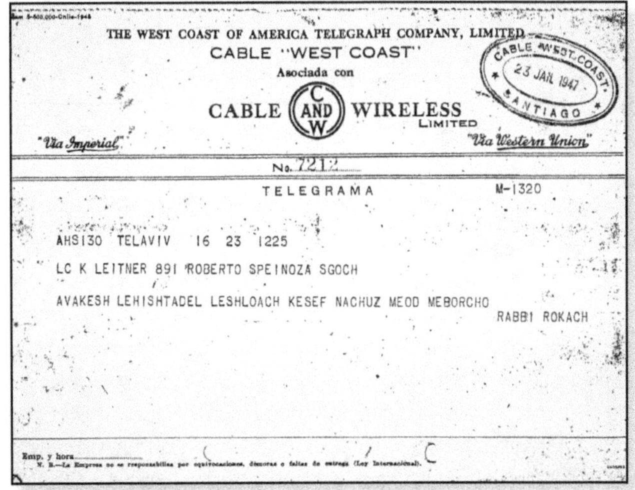

THE WEST COAST OF AMERICA TELEGRAPH COMPANY, LIMITED

CABLE "WEST COAST"

Asociada con

CABLE AND WIRELESS LIMITED

"Via Imperial" "Via Western Union"

CABLE WEST COAST 23 JAN 1947 SANTIAGO

No. 7212

TELEGRAMA M-1320

AHS130 TELAVIV 16 23 1225

LC K LEITNER 891 ROBERTO SPEINOZA SGOCH

AVAKESH LEHISHTADEL LESHLOACH KESEF NACHUZ MEOD MEBORCHO

RABBI ROKACH

Emp. y hora

N. B.—La Empresa no se responsabiliza por equivocaciones, demoras o faltas de entrega (Ley Internacional).

January 23, 1947. Telegram from Reb Aaron of Belz, requesting additional financial assistance

אהרן רוקח מבעלזא
Grand Rabbi A. ROKACH
of Belz

Letter sent February 24, 1947, transcribed:

ב"ה ד' פרשת תצוה תש"ז פה תל אביב (24th Feb 1947)

לכבוד ידידנו הרבני הנכבד העסקן החסיד המופלג איש תבונה ויקר רוח וכו'
מוה"ר חיים ארי' לייטנער נ"י

אחדשה"ט לפלא בעיני כ"ק מרן אדמו"ר שליט"א שלא הי' מכ' זה זמן רב שום מכתב וידיה משלומו ומבריאותו הטוב והנה נתתי לכ' טלגרם שכ' ישתדל לאסוף סכום הגון בשביל כ"ק מרן אדמו"ר שליט"א כי שורר דחקות גדולה ל"ע בבית כ"ק מרן אדמו"ר שליט"א והנה כעת שולח לכ' ר"פ חתונה בילעט מכ"ק מרן אדמו"ר שליט"א שעומד לפני חתונת אחיו הרה"צ מבילגורייא שליט"א וצריכים ע"ז הוצאות מרובות בפרט על ענין דירה וצרכי בית והלבשה שעולים בכאן להון רב ע"כ יראה כ' להזדרז במצות הכנסת כלה כזה ולשלוח תיכף כי מחכים ע"ז. והנה אודיע לכ' שכ"ק מרן אדמו"ר שליט"א מרגיש עצמו ב"ה טוב והשי"ת יעזור שיהי' בבריאות השלימות וגם הזכרתי את כ' לפני כ"ק מרן אדמו"ר שליט"א וברכו בברה"ג וי"ש ולפרנסה והצלחה בכ"ע וב"ב שיח' בברה"ג

ידידו המברכו בשמחת פורים וחג כשר
הלל וינד גבאי

אהרן רוקח מבעלזא
Grand Rabbi A. ROKACH
of Belz

A ROV FOR THE ORTHODOX KEHILO

The small Orthodox community in Chile had been looking to appoint a Rov for their Kehilo, and in July 1948 were looking forward to the arrival of a prospective candidate. Both sides were duly impressed and came to an arrangement early in 1949. The new Rov took up his position. Progress at last!

BOBOVER REBBE VISITS SANTIAGO

Opa was delighted to welcome the Bobover Rebbe, Rabbi Shloime Halberstam, who was visiting Santiago in July 1949 on a fundraising mission on behalf of the Bobover institutions of New York. As mentioned earlier, Reb Shloime and my father became close friends since they got to know each other as young boys in Marienbad, a friendship that they cherished throughout their lives, and Reb Shloime would refer to Opa as 'mein Jugendfreund' [friend of my youth].

My brother Shloime was born during the Bobover Rebbe's stay in Chile, and it is therefore not surprising that my father felt honoured to offer the Rebbe to be Sandak at the Bris.

Bobover Rebbe - Reb Shlomo Halberstam visits Santiago July 1949. Opa stands behind him to the left

Even in later years, whenever Reb Shloime came to London, Opa would try and visit him if possible. On one of these visits he persuaded his younger brother, Uncle Shurl, to come too, who had not seen Reb Shloime for over 40 years, and on entering the room, Reb Shloime greeted him immediately and called him by his first name, to the amazement of all those present!

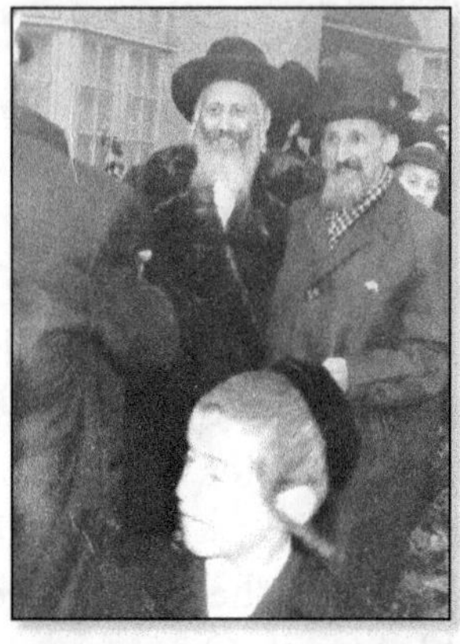

Reb Shlomo Halberstam (Bobover Rebbe), in London with Opa, Micha behind Opa

Opa greeting the Bobover Rebbe (London), my brother Shloime second from left

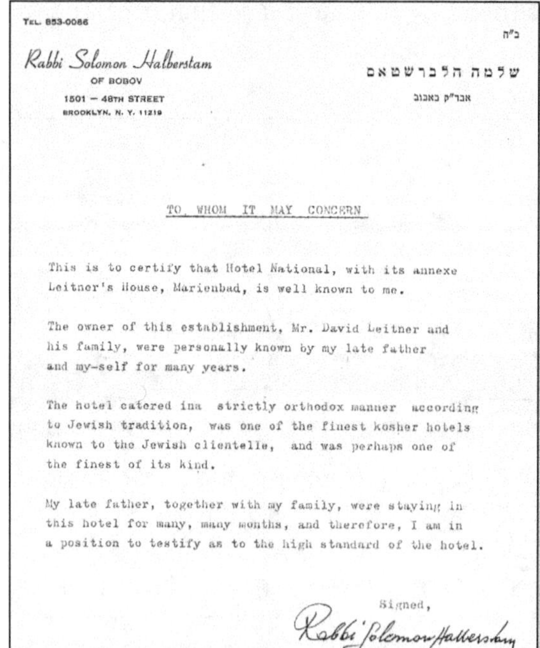

TEL. 853-0066

ב"ה

Rabbi Solomon Halberstam
OF BOBOV
1501 – 48TH STREET
BROOKLYN, N. Y. 11219

שלמה הלברשטאם
אבד"ק באבוב

TO WHOM IT MAY CONCERN

This is to certify that Hotel National, with its annexe Leitner's House, Marienbad, is well known to me.

The owner of this establishment, Mr. David Leitner and his family, were personally known by my late father and my-self for many years.

The hotel catered ina strictly orthodox manner according to Jewish tradition, was one of the finest kosher hotels known to the Jewish clientelle, and was perhaps one of the finest of its kind.

My late father, together with my family, were staying in this hotel for many, many months, and therefore, I am in a position to testify as to the high standard of the hotel.

Signed,

Rabbi Solomon Halberstam

Personal letter from the Bobover Rebbe confirming his stay in Marienbad.

Opa's personal interest in the Bobover institutions continued throughout his life, as these two letters demonstrate. In the early 1960s there were some negotiations between Bobov and Opa, with the view of Opa emigrating to Eretz Yisroel and managing the Bobover hotel in Bat Yam, an offer that he eventually declined.

Soon afterwards Mr. Porush opened the Central Hotel in Yerushalayim, and tried to convince Opa to manage it for him. Opa had earned himself a worldwide reputation in the Kosher hotel business, and his expertise was still remembered and in demand.

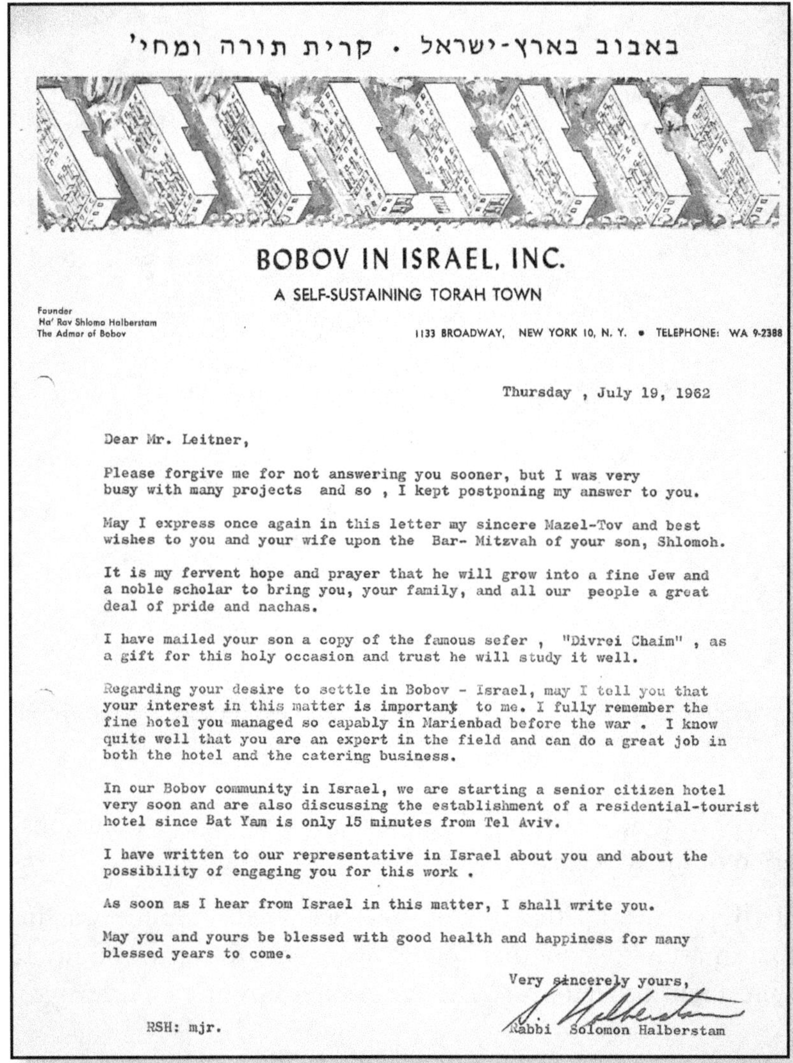

באבוב בארץ-ישראל • קרית תורה ומחי'

BOBOV IN ISRAEL, INC.

A SELF-SUSTAINING TORAH TOWN

Founder
Ha' Rav Shlomo Halberstam
The Admor of Bobov

1133 BROADWAY, NEW YORK 10, N. Y. • TELEPHONE: WA 9-2388

Thursday , July 19, 1962

Dear Mr. Leitner,

Please forgive me for not answering you sooner, but I was very busy with many projects and so , I kept postponing my answer to you.

May I express once again in this letter my sincere Mazel-Tov and best wishes to you and your wife upon the Bar- Mitzvah of your son, Shlomoh.

It is my fervent hope and prayer that he will grow into a fine Jew and a noble scholar to bring you, your family, and all our people a great deal of pride and nachas.

I have mailed your son a copy of the famous sefer , "Divrei Chaim" , as a gift for this holy occasion and trust he will study it well.

Regarding your desire to settle in Bobov - Israel, may I tell you that your interest in this matter is important to me. I fully remember the fine hotel you managed so capably in Marienbad before the war . I know quite well that you are an expert in the field and can do a great job in both the hotel and the catering business.

In our Bobov community in Israel, we are starting a senior citizen hotel very soon and are also discussing the establishment of a residential-tourist hotel since Bat Yam is only 15 minutes from Tel Aviv.

I have written to our representative in Israel about you and about the possibility of engaging you for this work .

As soon as I hear from Israel in this matter, I shall write you.

May you and yours be blessed with good health and happiness for many blessed years to come.

Very sincerely yours,

S. Halberstam

RSH: mjr.

Rabbi Solomon Halberstam

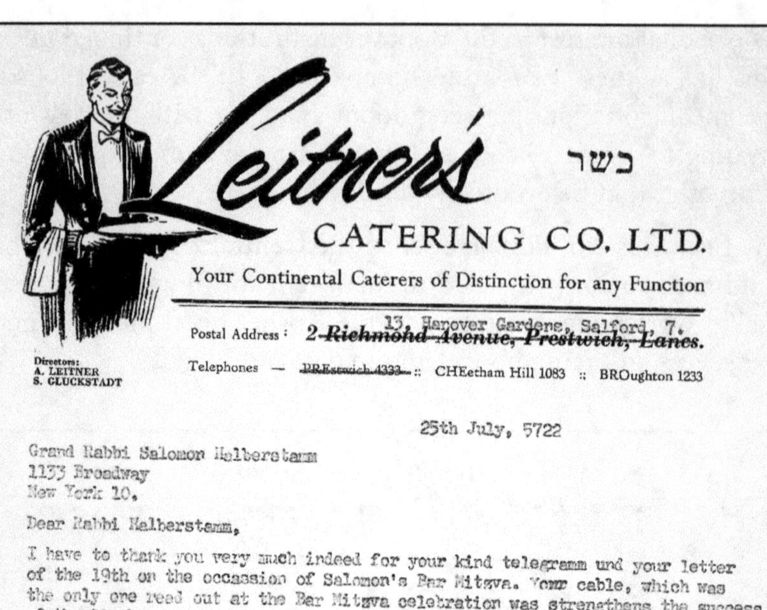

Leitner's כשר

CATERING CO. LTD.

Your Continental Caterers of Distinction for any Function

Postal Address: ~~2 Richmond Avenue, Prestwich, Lancs.~~ 13, Hanover Gardens, Salford, 7.

Directors:
A. LEITNER
S. GLUCKSTADT

Telephones — ~~PREstwich 4333~~ :: CHEetham Hill 1083 :: BROughton 1233

25th July, 5722

Grand Rabbi Salomon Halberstamm
1133 Broadway
New York 10.

Dear Rabbi Halberstamm,

I have to thank you very much indeed for your kind telegramm und your letter of the 19th on the occassion of Salomon's Bar Mitzva. Your cable, which was the only one read out at the Bar Mitzva celebration was strengthens the success of the Simche an appreciated by everyone present. May I therefore thank you once again for your thought, dear Rabbi Halberstamm.

Your letter, especially the last paragraph ist most interesting und we are looking forward to receive more news from you regarding your projects. In the meantime I am enclosing Copy of a letter from the Jewish Community in Santiago de Chile, which perhaps will be of some help for the manager in Israel.

If it is Hashgoche, than we will be delighted to settle town in Israel und let us hope, that we will be the right couple, to work for
Bobov in Israel
for your and our benefit.

I hope that you, dear Rebbe and all your family ar enjoing the best of health and thanking you in anticipation for further good news, I remain

as ever

Very Sincerely Yours.

(KURT LEITNER)

Correspondence with Bobov regarding the Management of Bat Yam Hotel

Opa kept in touch with Reb Shloime and sent regular donations over a period of many years.

When Opa gave up the catering business, Reb Shloime was instrumental in arranging another source of income for him, and my father became a rent collector for "The Freshwater Group of Companies."

Rabbi Solomon Halberstam
OF BOBOV
1501 – 48TH STREET
BROOKLYN, N. Y. 11219

שלמה הלברשטאם
אבד"ק באבוב

יום ב' פ' בהר בחקותי שנת תשל"ט לפ"ק ל"ב למב"י

תפארת גדולה ועטרת ישועה לכבוד
ידידי היקר הנגיד הנכבד
כש"ת מו"ה חיים ארי' לייטנער נ"י

ישא ברכה מאת ד' בעד פעלו הטוב אשר הרים
באהבה, ושלח מעות שבוע סך של חמשה פונט
ולעומת זה אביע לו ברכת תודה רבה, יברך ד' חילו
ופועל ידיו ירצה ויצליח בכל אשר יפנה ויהי' שבע רצון
ומלא ברכת ד' בבריאות השלימות ואורך ימים ישביעהו
ויראהו בישועתו כברכת נפש ידידו דו"ש באהבה רבה

הק' שלמה הלברשטאם

This transcribed:

שלמה הלברשטאם, אבד"ק באבוב

יום ב' פ' בהר בחקותי שנת תשל"ט לפ"ק ל"ב למב"י

תפארת גדולה ועטרת ישועה לכבוד ידידי היקר הנגיד הנכבד
כש"ת מו"ה חיים ארי' לייטנער נ"י

ישא ברכה מאת ד' בעד פעלו הטוב אשר הרים באהבה ושלח מעות שבוע סך של חמשה פונט

ולעומת זה אביע לו ברכת תודה רבה יברך ד' חילו ופועל ידיו ירצה ויצליח בכל אשר יפנה ויהי' שבע רצון ומלא ברכת ד' בבריאות השלימות ואורך ימים ישביעהו ויראהו בישועתו כברכת נפש ידידו דו"ש באהבה רבה

הק' שלמה הלברשטאם

Acknowledgement (from Reb Shloime Halberstam) for donations received. (One of many)

Although my parents waited many years until they could get married due to the outbreak of the war, they ב"ה merited five sons, all born in Chile.

Micha was born in January 1947 and was named מרדכי צבי: מרדכי after Omas father and צבי after Opa's grandfather, as they were still hopeful that Opa's father was still alive and had somehow survived the war. By the time that I was born in March 1948, there was still uncertainty about Opa's father, משה דוד, and they gave me only one of his names, Dovid. However, they called me Dada, for the sake of כבוד אב ואם, so as not to call me by my grandfather's name just in case he was still alive. Shloime was born in July 1949, and the Bobover Rebbe, who was his Sandek, suggested the name Shloime, which was also the name of Opa's maternal grandfather. Aaron was born in February 1951, followed by Binyomin in November 1953.

ENJOYING THE FAMILY IN CHILE

Enjoying his oldest son, Micha (1.1.1.3.1) born January 1947

MAKING PLANS TO EMIGRATE TO ENGLAND

Our family was ב"ה growing, business was very good, but Opa and Oma were very concerned about the lack of authentic Jewish education in Santiago, and that their children had no suitable friends to play with. They decided that for the sake of their Chinuch and for this reason alone, they had to 'pack their bags' once again and move away. My grandmother, Sima Kokisch, was living with us at the time, but unfortunately was too old and frail to join us on the long journey to England, and was also suffering from angina. Opa had to inform her of their plans, and although it was initially very difficult for her to accept, she fully understood their concerns and the need to take this bold step. In fact, she encouraged us to do so, and as sign of her approval, told Oma that when they leave Chile, she wants to give them her most precious possession as a gift - the Sefer Torah that they had brought with them from Bad Gastein. It was to accompany them on their next step of the journey, and should be given to Micha as his Bar Mitzvah present. This Sefer had been written in memory of her husband, מרדכי Kokisch, and Micha - מרדכי צבי - bore his name. As if by some prophetic vision, this was the only Bar Mitzvah of her grandchildren that was celebrated while she was still alive. As for herself, she would make arrangements and move in with her youngest daughter, Aunty Berty.

Sima Kokisch was niftar in August 1960, nearly five years after we had left, and by 1964 Aunty Berty and her family had decided to emigrate to Eretz Yisroel for the same reasons: the lack of authentic Jewish Chinuch. En route to Eretz Yisroel they made a few stops in Europe, a story that is described later in greater detail.

The Belzer Rebbe, Reb Aaron

Before Opa would move away from Chile, in fact before any major decision, he naturally consulted with Reb Aaron of Belz, and was adviced to preferably move to London, otherwise to America, but that he should only live amongst Orthodox Yidden. Whatever he decides to do should be with Hatzlocho, and the Rebbe acknowledged and thanked for a further donation of fifteen pounds.

Transcribes as:

לכבוד ידידנו הרה"ח המופלג המפורסם וכו' מוה"ר חיים ארי' לייטנער נ"י
מכתבו לנכון קבלנו באיחור רב וגם הסך 15 פונט לנכון קבלנו ומסרתי פתקא לכ"ק מרן אדמו"ר
שליט"א וברכו בבה"ג וי"ש ולפרנסה והצלחה בכ"ע ואודות הנסיעה אמר כ"ק מרן אדמו"ר
שליט"א אם אפשר ללונדון הי' יותר טוב ואם לאמריקא אז יהי' הדירה במקום שדרים חרידים ומה
שכ' יעשה יהי' בהצלחה
וזו' תחי' והיוצ"ח בבה"ג וי"ש ולגדלם בניקל ואך נחת וכ"ט וחמותו בבה"ג ושנה טובה ומבורכת
וכ"ט

ידידו הפוב"ש
הלל ווינד גבאי
פ"ש להרב ר' לוי כ"ץ שליט"א
פ"ש להרב ר' עמרם טובער שליט"א
הנ"ל

Whilst in Chile and thousands of miles away from his previous home in Europe, Opa kept up to date with the news, and regularly received the Jewish papers. After having been so involved with his social work in London he naturally wanted to stay abreast of what was happening in other parts of the world. Furthermore, when living at the other end of the world, one naturally gets a feeling of isolation, and these newspapers provided a useful way of keeping in touch and still feeling part of civilization.

On October 20, 1953, Opa wrote the following letter to Rabbi Dr. Schonfeld, a letter that says it all; his unique sense of humour, diplomatic skills and his Mesiras Nefesh for his children's Torah Chinuch are all apparent in this one letter.

Translation of this letter (which was written in German):

> בס"ד
>
> October 20, 1953
>
> Dear honourable Rabbi Schonfeld,
>
> Due to my 7 year absence from England I fear I may not be able to express myself adequately in English, and ask you to forgive me for writing in German. I hope I will have the honour to receive your reply, which can of course be written in English.
>
> I have read about your activities in various papers and articles, and I am familiar with the situation there. You will have also received my numerous regards, some in writing, others transmitted orally.
>
> I understand from a recent write-up in a newspaper that the "Union of Orthodox Hebrew Congregations" has discussed the idea of building its own strictly Orthodox Matzo bakery, which in turn prompts me to offer you my services. I have taken over a long established Matzo Bakery here in Santiago, which I've now been running for the past few years. With Hashem's help I have managed to increase the turnover over that of my predecessor by 50%, and without exaggerating I would consider myself an expert in this field.

It is my sincere wish to return to England, since my dear children, who are already at an age where they need to attend school, cannot receive the necessary Jewish education here.

Since you've used your valuable contact to help me get "priority" permission to emigrate, and the Home Office is aware of the fact that I had undertaken the journey to South America on behalf of the Chief Rabbi's Council, it should not be too difficult for you and your contacts to arrange the re-entry into England for me and my family, and permission to reside there. Apart from procuring permission for immigration I am not asking for anything, and will of course pay for all expenses in connection with the travel. It would, however, be of great help if upon my arrival I would find a place to use my Matzo baking expertise and options to earn a living.

In case that the project of the Matzo bakery would not materialise immediately, permit me to ask you all the same to arrange my immigration. I am sure that the British General Consul will attest favourably to my business here in Santiago.

I hope, my dear Rabbi Schonfeld, to receive your positive reply shortly, and send you and family Harry Goodman my best wishes,

Yours sincerely,

Kurt Leitner.

Rabbi Dr. Schonfeld replied immediately on October 30, 1953, confirming their interest in having their own Matzo bakery in London, but 'we have to find the funds to buy the premises and machinery and only then be able to appoint a manager. We might be able to obtain the required visas, if the present machinery could be brought to England.'

On November 24, 1953 Opa replied that he intended to sell the bakery as a going concern, and hence leave the machines in Chile. However, the Jewish Chinuch of his children was his first priority, and if that was the price he had to pay in order to get the required visas to come to London, then he would bring the machines with! He explained briefly what machines he owned, and that the Matzos were baked within a time span of seven minutes from the moment that the water was added to the flour! Since it was now already the end of November 1953, the Matzo baking season had already started in Chile, and all plans that would allow Opa to supply Kedassia with Matzos for Pesach would have to be put in place for the following year, with baking starting in late 1954, to be available for Pesach 1955.

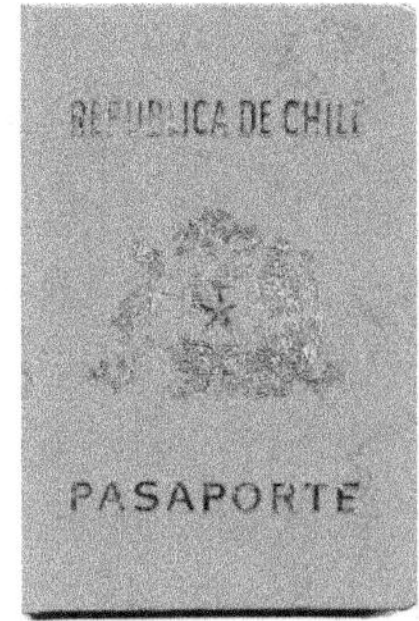

Rabbi Schonfeld advised Opa that when he subsequently would apply for a visa to come to England, he should do this with a Chilean passport and not with the original Czech one. [This would make it impossible for the authorities to trace his past history, especially since he previously entered England as a refugee. Bio-metric passports did not exist yet.]

Opa was in a very big quandary as to what to do. On the one hand he needed to take the machines with to London in order to secure his visas, but on the other hand he did not want to leave the Yidden in Chile without Matzo baking facilities either. Furthermore, if the machines remained in Chile he could sell the Matzoh bakery as a going concern. So what was he to do? The only solution was to have the machines copied and then to take one set with to England. The other set would then remain in Chile so that South America would not be left without Matzos. Opa had to find a way of duplicating these machines. In an open revelation of Hashgocho Protis, Opa's brother-in-law, Uncle Lutcho, owned a foundry that manufactured farm machinery, and was happy to oblige.

Every Sunday from then on, when the Matzo bakery was not in operation, they would dismantle one part of a machine and take it to the metal foundry where these components were copied. After that they brought them back, and the same evening assembled the original machine again, ready for the next day's production. For us it was always a treat to go with Opa to the foundry, where we had to wear goggles and could watch the colourful sparks emanating from the machinery, when they cut or welded two pieces of metal together.

The manufacture of a complete set of Matzo-baking-machines was a major expense but this did not deter my parents.

On July 11, 1954 Opa wrote to Rabbi Schonfeld, confirming that a box of his machine Matzos had been sent on March 17 via the British

Overseas Line, together with all the photographs of the machinery and their respective dimensions, as he had previously requested.

On July 21, 1954, Rabbi Schonfeld requested the names and contact details of two gentlemen in Santiago who could act as referees for their visa applications. Opa replied and submitted Rabbi Dr. Blum, 'Chief Rabbi of Chile' and Dr. Siegfried Landau, President of the 'Bnei Yisroel' Cultural Centre' [a signatory on the letter of recommendation above].

All was going to plan, until Rabbi Schonfeld wrote on January 17, 1955, that he had 'heard from the Home Office concerning your application for permission for you to come and manage the Matzo bakery'. Apparently the authorities do not like the way in which we propose to employ you fully for only three months a year. They feel that under our suggested contract you would most of the time be carrying on business more or less on your own, and you would not be classified as an ecclesiastical officer. We shall, therefore, have to return to the more definite proposal which you originally suggested, namely that we should buy your machinery and employ you in the usual manner.'

Initially, Opa requested a sum of £1500 for the machines, but he settled for £1000 in order to get the required visas. He was to receive a wage of £10 per week [for a family man with five children] for working at the bakery, in addition to a 5% commission on sales, and free accommodation above the bakery.

On July 28, 1955, Rabbi Dr. Schonfeld wrote to Opa to his address in Campos de Desportes in Santiago de Chile stating:

> 'Mr. H.A. Goodman has just telephoned me to say that the Home Office have now granted your visa. It is given on the understanding that you have the Chilean nationality. It will take a fortnight before the Home Office authorisation reaches Santiago, so please do not apply until then.'

Opa, who in the meantime had obtained Chilean citizenship, applied for a visa at the British Consulate in Santiago, which he received. However, his visa to England was only granted for an initial period of **six months**, but they still decided to sell most of their possesions in Chile and move to England.

On August 10, 1955 he informed Rabbi Schonfeld that he had booked passage to England on the only ship available, the 'Reina Del Pacifico' that was scheduled to depart on November 16 and would arrive in Liverpool on December 16, 1955. Since they would be travelling for such a long time, they would need a good supply of kosher food, and he enquired what tinned kosher foods were available in England.

Rabbi Schonfeld replied on August 24, 1955 that "as far as tins are concerned only Skrek could be relied upon, although they were not under Kedassia supervision."

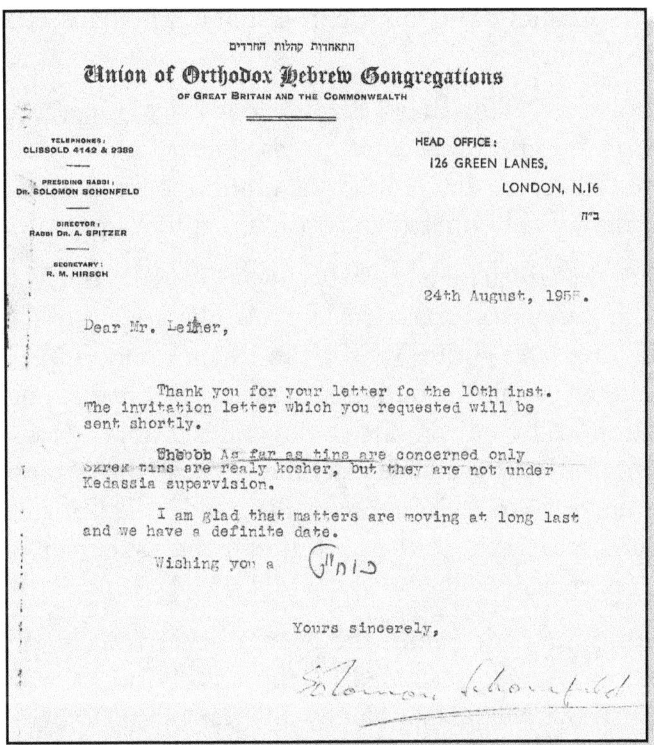

התאחדות קהלות החרדים

Union of Orthodox Hebrew Congregations

OF GREAT BRITAIN AND THE COMMONWEALTH

TELEPHONES:
CLISSOLD 4142 & 2389

PRESIDING RABBI:
DR. SOLOMON SCHONFELD

DIRECTOR:
RABBI DR. A. SPITZER

SECRETARY:
R. M. HIRSCH

HEAD OFFICE:
126 GREEN LANES,
LONDON, N.16

ב"ה

24th August, 1955.

Dear Mr. Leiner,

Thank you for your letter fo the 10th inst. The invitation letter which you requested will be sent shortly.

Shbbbb As far as tins are concerned only Skrek tins are realy kosher, but they are not under Kedassia supervision.

I am glad that matters are moving at long last and we have a definite date.

Wishing you a כוח"ג

Yours sincerely,

Solomon Schonfeld

My father then asked Rabbi Schonfeld for a letter (written on official letter-headed paper), inviting him to come to London as an expert Matzo baker, to set up their new bakery. This was necessary in order to avoid any queries from the authorities who might find it rather strange that after having obtained Chilean Citizenship only recently, he now wanted to leave the country together with his whole family. Such a letter of confirmation would provide him with a realistic alibi.

We arrived in Liverpool on Friday, December 16 and initially settled in Manchester, (our journey to England will feature in a chapter of its own), but soon afterwards we had to renew our visas, as the initial six months' permission was about to expire.

Kedassia had purchased premises on Wightman Road, London N8, which they intended to use as their Matzo baking facility. In the meantime our family was still living in Manchester, and my father's initial visa was granted on the grounds of being an expert Matzo baker, exclusively for use in the London Matzo bakery. The Home Office was not very happy, and asked for an explanation why Opa was living in Manchester and not doing his job in London, where his 'expertise' was so urgently required!

On November 19, 1956, Rabbi Schonfeld wrote to Opa, and suggested that he apply for an extension of his visa by writing to Mr. Gedalla at the Home Office, c/o the Advisory Committee for the Admission of Jewish Ecclesiastical Officers, and write the following:

> 'Since my arrival here I have been working with the Matzo bakery of the Union of Orthodox Hebrew Congregations. The bakery which we have at 395 Wightman Road, London N8, has had to be altered to suit the purposes of Matzo baking on a proper scale. Alterations have been carried out and it is hoped to conduct trial baking with the available machinery within the next few months. We do, of course, already bake the hand-rolled Shemura Matzo on a considerable scale and I attend the bakery in London for such purposes.
>
> During the period until the Matzo bakery can be put into full use, I have been seconded by the UOHC to their sister community, the Machzikei Hadass of Manchester, where I am acting as Administrator of the kosher food organisation. I am thus working in the spheres for which the Home Office granted me permission to come here. I should be grateful if you would kindly ask the Home Office to extend my permit for a further year.'

Opa wrote this letter the following day, immediately after receiving the letter from Rabbi Schonfeld, and received a reply from Mr. Gedalla on December 5, which is self explanatory. He was not very happy at all.

Telephone: ROYAL 4711 (2 lines) DG/PL. Telegrams: EISHEL, EDO. LONDON.

Advisory Committee for the Admission of Jewish Ecclesiastical Officers

COMMITTEE

CHAIRMAN: JAMES LAYTON. (Jews' Temporary Shelter)

DAYAN H. M. LAZARUS, M.A (Beth Din)

R. N. CARVALHO, M.A., B.C.L. (Jewish Memorial Council)

MAJOR B. DAVIDSON. (Liberal Jewish Synagogue)

H. GLEDHILL.

H. A. GOODMAN, J.P. Union of Orthodox Hebrew Congregations)

(Board of Deputies)

ABRAHAM MANN. (Federation of Synagogues)

H. PELS.

H. J. PHILLIPS, M.B.E., M.A. (London Board of Jewish Religious Education)

A. WINGATE. (United Synagogue)

DAVID GEDALLA, A.C.C.S., Hon. Secretary

IN YOUR REPLY PLEASE QUOTE: ADCOM/646/54.

YOUR REF:

63, MANSELL STREET, LONDON, E.1.

5th December, 1956.

K. Leitner, Esq,
15, Hanover Gardens,
Salford, 7.

Dear Sir,

I have your letter of the 20th November, and must at the outset point out that the permission granted to you to come to this country was to engage in the Matzo Bakery in London as Manager, and for no other purpose without the prior consent of the Home Office.

I am further to point out that you gave an undertaking to that effect, which is lodged with the Home Office.

Quite apart from that consideration, it might be difficult to agree that employment as an "Administrator of the Kosher Food Organisation" is ecclesiastical in the accepted sense of the term.

I am sending a copy of this letter to Dr. Schonfeld and would be glad to have his observations. Until then no request can be made for an extension of your permission to remain in this country. If, and when, we do feel able to recommend an extension, we shall of course need your passport (as well as those of your wife and family, if they have already arrived).

Yours faithfully,

DAVID GEDALLA,
Hon. Secretary.

c/c. to Rabbi Dr. S. Schonfeld.

Rabbi Schonfeld's reply from December 19, 1956:

> "When Mr. Leitner arrived, an attempt was made to install the machinery, but was stopped by the Sanitary Inspector as the premises did not meet with their requirements. They required the immediate carrying out of a number of costly and complicated improvements, before he would permit the baking to take place. We cannot be expected to spend the large sums of building improvement work requested by the Inspector, until we are satisfied that the machines are the correct ones and are capable to economically produce the quantities that we require. Thus you see

how the implementation of our agreement with Mr. Leitner has been complicated by circumstances entirely beyond our control.

Under the circumstances, we felt that Mr. Leitner's services should insofar as they were unused, be utilised in activities requiring such quasi ecclesiastical services as he could render. We therefore seconded him to our sister-organisation in Manchester where there was an urgent need for a supervisor manager for kosher food distribution. We felt that in such circumstances the Home Office would understand the difficulties in which we were placed and would raise no objection on Mr. Leitner temporarily performing a necessary function related to the kind of purpose for which his original permit was granted. We notified this to the Police in Manchester who noted it in his Police Registration Book.

Yours sincerely,

Rabbi Dr. Schonfeld"

Mr. H. Goodman then wrote a memo to Opa and advised him that, when making his application for his visa extension, all the family's passports should be sent by the Machzikei Hadass Office, and not privately.

On January 23, 1957, Mr. Gedalla confirmed that he had submitted the passport to the Home Office, together with an explanatory letter why Opa and his family were in Manchester. Shortly thereafter he obtained a one year extension for his visa.

A year later a similar correspondence took place, until the Home Office finally granted them permanent visas on May 27, 1960 and permission to remain in Manchester, and no further restrictions imposed.

Given indefinite leave to enter the
United Kingdom

Permanent permission stamped into their passports.

To cut a long story short, the Leitner family obtained their visas to remain in England, they resided in Manchester and not in London, and the Matzo baking machinery that they brought with from Chile was never ever used.

רבות מחשבות בלב איש ועצת ה' היא תקום

CHAPTER 8
Journey to England

OUR JOURNEY TO ENGLAND

Once the required visas to come to England were obtained, preparations began in earnest. The Matzo bakery had to be sold as a going concern, as well as the bungalow, all the furniture and household goods. Apart from this, we all needed summer and winter clothes for the 30 day journey to England. When we left Chile in November, it was summer, but it would be the middle of the English winter when we arrived, since the seasons are reversed when crossing the Equator. However, since it was summer in Chile, it would have been difficult to find warm clothing in the shops, and these had to be bought some months before.

Opa and Micha traveled to the port city of Valparaiso about three months before our departure, where they booked our journey, chose the cabins and ordered the necessary kosher food that would be sufficient for our forthcoming month-long journey. This would have to be procured in England and brought with on the boat's inbound journey to Chile, the only boat that sailed between Valparaiso and Liverpool. This boat, the 'Reina Del Pacifico' – 'Queen of the Pacific', was a large ocean liner that could accommodate up to 800 people on its three decks, offering first, second and third class accommodation. The ship belonged to the 'Pacific Steam Navigation Company', an English company from Southampton, who owned the sole rights to carry post from England to the Pacific countries en route. The entire journey from Valparaiso to Liverpool is over 12000 km.

Opa booked our cabins in the third class, with rooms next to the ship's engine room and large motors. During our long journey we somehow got accustomed to the monotonous churning noise that these motors made. [The cost of the entire journey for the family was double the amount of what Opa paid for his house in Hanover Gardens!] We also received special tickets that permitted us to re-enter the boat after disembarking at each port on the way.

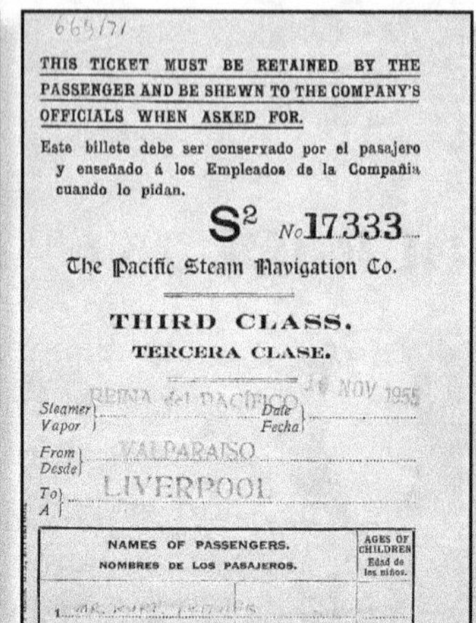
THIS TICKET MUST BE RETAINED BY THE PASSENGER AND BE SHEWN TO THE COMPANY'S OFFICIALS WHEN ASKED FOR.

Este billete debe ser conservado por el pasajero y enseñado á los Empleados de la Compañía cuando lo pidan.

S2 No 17333

The Pacific Steam Navigation Co.

THIRD CLASS.

TERCERA CLASE.

Steamer / Vapor: REINA del PACIFICO Date / Fecha: NOV 1955

From / Desde: VALPARAISO

To / A: LIVERPOOL

NAMES OF PASSENGERS. NOMBRES DE LOS PASAJEROS.	AGES OF CHILDREN Edad de los niños.

Permit to leave and re-enter the ship whilst en route

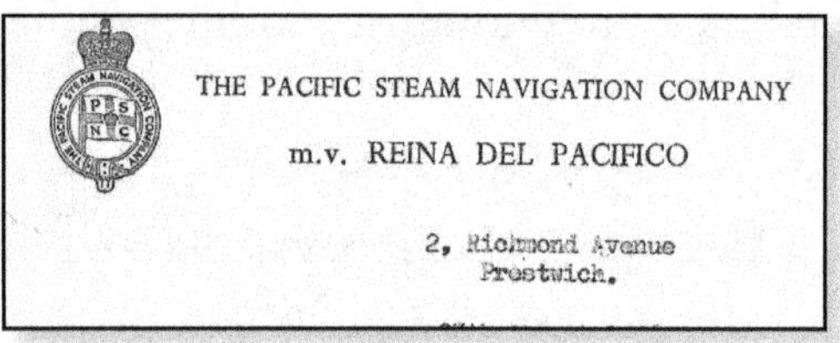
THE PACIFIC STEAM NAVIGATION COMPANY

m.v. REINA DEL PACIFICO

2, Richmond Avenue
Prestwich.

Official Letterhead from Ship

The newly manufactured Matzo baking machines were well wrapped and packed in a large wooden crate for shipping. Sufficient kosher food was ordered in advance to last us for a whole month. A large proportion of this food came from Skrek in London, who supplied tinned meat balls, ravioli and onion soup. So one day we might have had onion soup with meat balls for supper, and the next day ravioli and onion soup, in a regular pattern. We had of course an ample supply of Matzos, and sometimes we managed to procure some fresh bread and fruit en route, when the ship made a short stop.

November 16, 1955 was rapidly approaching, and a farewell reception was organised by the 'Chassam Sofer Minyan' that presented Opa with a beautifully inscribed silver 'Becher' and plate, which he was proud to use every Shabbos. The whole Minyan came to the Valparaiso port to wish us a safe journey, as seen below.

The farewell departure from Chile at Valparaiso

We left on Wednesday November 16, 1955 from Valparaiso, a port city some 50 miles from Santiago, and stopped en route at Antofagasta in Northern Chile, then in Lima, the capital of Peru, and later in Panama City. We then crossed the Panama Canal, traveling on to Kingston, the capital of Jamaica. There Oma bought us all straw peak-caps to protect us from the burning overhead sun, which we kept as a souvenir of this journey, and often wore during the summer holidays in England.

Whenever possible we tried to disembark at all stops. This was for two reasons. Firstly, it gave us the opportunity to purchase some fresh fruit and other permitted food supplies to add some variety to our menu, and a welcome change from the daily portion of onion soup. Secondly, it was interesting to take a small tour of these different cities, which made the journey more exciting. Keeping five boys occupied all day on a boat for a month was not an easy task, so these breaks were always welcome. After all, how many times can one enjoy playing 'snakes and ladders'?

The ship did not always dock at the port, and sometimes anchored off shore, when they lowered the life boats and we went ashore in these smaller boats.

OUR JOURNEY THROUGH THE PANAMA CANAL

Map of Canal

Entering the Canal *Flying Fish*

The Panama Canal is an artificial 77 km (48 miles) long waterway in Panama that connects the Atlantic with the Pacific Oceans, cutting across the Isthmus of Panama, and is a key conduit for international maritime trade. There are locks at each end that lift ships up to the central Gatun Lake, an artificial lake created to reduce the amount of excavation work required for the Canal, 26 m (85 ft) above sea level, and then lowers the ships at the other end. The original locks are 110 ft wide and 1050 feet deep, and ships built to this size are known as Panamax ships, as they are the maximum size that are capable of crossing the canal. Each crossing through the Panama Canal costs the shipping lines a fee, which is charged according to the size of their ship, but it is worth their while to pay these high fees as it shortens the journey by at least 8000 miles which would otherwise take them via the South Pole. Furthermore, such a passage was only possible in the summer, as the waters at the South Pole freeze during the winter. The entire journey through the Canal takes approximately 10 hours. Since its construction, over one million ships have benefited from its use. The Panama Canal has been appropriately named 'the world's greatest shortcut!'

Construction of the Canal first began in 1881 by the French, but they had to abandon it owing to major engineering problems, and many deaths caused by disease, when they had to cut through jungles and swamps. In 1904 the Americans took over the project, and completed it approximately ten years later, with the help of 43,000 workers.

One of the highlights of our voyage to England was no doubt the crossing of the Panama Canal, a truly unique experience. It was eleven days after we had departed Valparaiso, when the captain of the ship announced early on Shabbos morning that we were about to enter the Canal, and everybody was invited onto the top deck [1st Class] to view this spectacular crossing. Apart from outstanding views of the Isthmus of Panama, the opening and closing of the locks kept us all fascinated. We only interrupted our observations to go to our cabins to make Kiddush and have our Shabbos meal.

Crossing the Canal

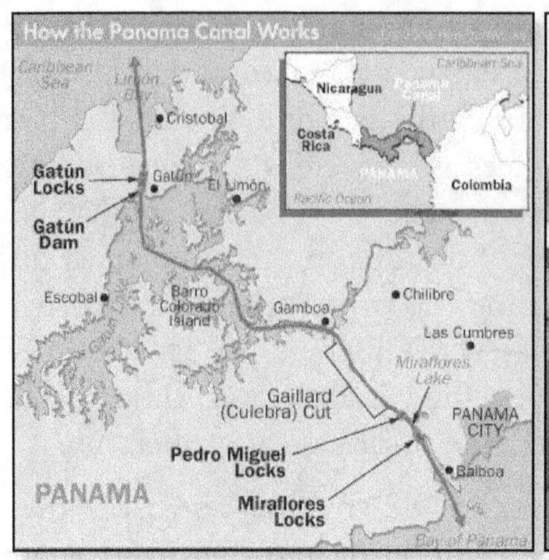

The complete route across the Panama Canal

A ship going through the locks on the Canal

We then crossed the Atlantic Ocean, a non-stop seven day journey, surrounded on all sides by nothing but sea. There was, however, one thing that interrupted this monotony: the sight of the 'flying fish' in one area of the Atlantic Ocean. We had already crossed the Equator, and the weather changed from being summer in the Southern Hemisphere to winter in the North, quite an adjustment. It was time to change from our summer clothing to warmer winter wear. We finally arrived at La Coruna in Spain, then continued on to Santander, from where we proceeded to La Rochelle in France. On our final leg of the journey we crossed the English Channel and stopped in Plymouth, and finally docked in Liverpool early Friday morning December 16, 1955, from where we travelled by car to Manchester.

The Reina Del Pacifico ran aground in 1957 and was replaced by the 'Reina Del Mar' [Queen of the Sea] which continued to serve the same route.

The Reina Del Pacifico was scheduled to arrive on the shortest Friday of the year, December 16, and Opa was naturally very concerned about Chillul Shabbos. He therefore asked his brother to write to the head office of the shipping line to inquire if we could remain on the ship until after Shabbos. He reasoned that by the time the ship docked in Liverpool, and us having been passengers of the third class, we would be the last to disembark and clear customs. After that it would be almost impossible to get to Prestwich, where Uncle Shurl lived, and make it in time for lighting Chanuka and Shabbos lights. The response that Uncle Shurl received prompted my father to take further action.

THE PACIFIC STEAM NAVIGATION COMPANY

(INCORPORATED BY ROYAL CHARTER 1840)

AGENTS FOR ROYAL MAIL LINES, LIMITED

TELEGRAMS: PACIFIC, LIVERPOOL 2.
TELEPHONE: CENTRAL 9251
TELEX: 62 - 230
ALL COMMUNICATIONS TO BE ADDRESSED TO THE COMPANY

PACIFIC BUILDING,
JAMES STREET,
LIVERPOOL 2.

REF. P:HW:PB.

7th December, 1955.

A. Leitner, Esq.,
2 Richmond Avenue,
Prestwich,
LANCS.

Dear Sir,

We acknowledge your letter of 6th December, and would advise that "REINA DEL PACIFICO", is expected to arrive alongside the Princes Stage, Liverpool, early on the morning of Friday, 16th December, for the purpose of landing passengers. It is difficult to say precisely when your brother and his family will land, but we think that they will have done so and had their baggage cleared through the Customs by no later than 9.30.a.m. or so.

In these circumstances, there would appear to be no reason to suppose that Prestwich will not be reached well before an hour before sundown on the Friday.

We would be unable, in any case, to allow your brother and his family to remain on board after the landing of the other passengers, and although no delay to the ship is envisaged it has occurred to us that if circumstances beyond our control, such as weather or other incidents unexpectedly arise to prevent the arrangements we have outlined being carried out, your brother may consider landing at Plymouth, where "REINA DEL PACIFICO" is due to arrive early a.m. on Thursday, 15th December, also for the purpose of landing passengers.

Yours faithfully,
THE PACIFIC STEAM NAVIGATION COMPANY.

HEAD OF PASSENGER DEPARTMENT.

He then went to speak to the ship's captain and explained his predicament, and after presenting the captain with a box of 'Cuban Cigars' that he had recently purchased, he agreed to 'do whatever possible' to help. The captain in fact travelled as fast as possible to try and oblige. We cannot forget the last leg of the journey, crossing the English Channel up to Plymouth and then to Liverpool, when the ship encountered very adverse weather conditions, and most passengers suffered badly from sea sickness. I remember that last night on the boat. The sea was so stormy, that in order to ensure the safety of our Chanuka lights, we had to place the Menoros in the sink that was filled with water. The ship rocked from side to side, which promptly sent all the plates flying off their storage racks in the kitchen and smashed onto the floor.

The next morning, the captain gave us permission to disembark **first**, and personally escorted us off the ship, much to the surprise of the first class passengers. Opa just took his Tallis and Tefillin and our most essential clothing required for Shabbos, and agreed with the customs officer that he would return as soon as possible, to clear the required customs formalities. It was a very short Friday and he couldn't wait. I think this was the first and last time that Opa willingly travelled out of town on a Friday, but this too was purely לכבוד שבת so that we could reach Manchester in time for Shabbos, and he really didn't have an option.

Uncle Shurl was waiting for us at the Liverpool docks that Friday morning, and with the help of Yaakov and Arthur Sanger kindly brought us all to Manchester. It was ראש חודש טבת – an appropriate time to make a new start.

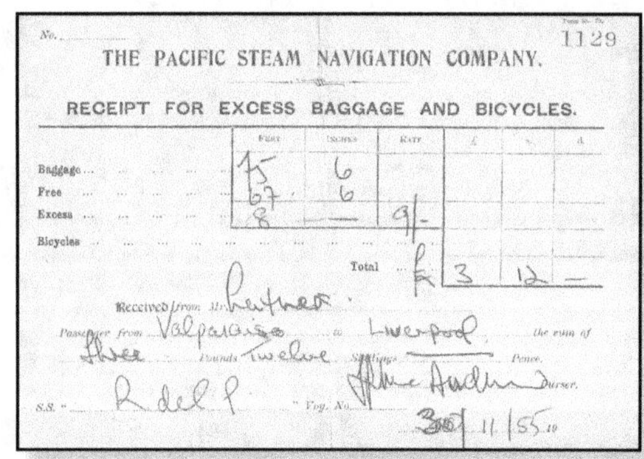

No. 1129

THE PACIFIC STEAM NAVIGATION COMPANY.

RECEIPT FOR EXCESS BAGGAGE AND BICYCLES.

	Feet	Inches	Rate	£	s.	d.
Baggage	75	6				
Free	67	6				
Excess	8	—	9/-			
Bicycles						
Total			£	3	12	—

Received from Mr. [illegible]

Passenger from Valparaiso to Liverpool, the sum of Three Pounds Twelve Shillings — Pence.

S.S. "R del P" Voy. No. Purser.

30/11/55

Receipt for excess baggage, paid two weeks after our arrival in Liverpool

CHAPTER 9
Manchester

ARRIVING IN MANCHESTER

The first Shabbos we stayed with Uncle Shurl and family at 2 Richmond Avenue in Prestwich, where they occupied only the top floor of the semi detached house, as an elderly lady lived on the ground floor. Some time later on, Uncle Shurl, as sitting tenant, was able to purchase the entire house. Before we arrived, Uncle Shurl had rented a house for us on 66 Northumberland Street, Salford 7, conveniently situated opposite the Machzikei Hadass Shul.

On that first Shabbos all eleven of us crowded into the few rooms and enjoyed the Shabbos meals in Prestwich. After the meal, Opa, Uncle Shurl and Johnny walked down to 66 Northumberland Street where they slept, whilst the remainder of the family slept at Richmond Avenue, sharing the bedrooms and converting the 'Vono' couches into beds. For family there is always room.

Soon afterwards we moved to Northumberland Street, but would often walk to Prestwich on Shabbos morning to visit Uncle Shurl and family. After a few months, Opa ב"ה managed to buy his own property, and we moved into 13 Hanover Gardens on Wednesday, October 31, 1956. The following Motzei Shabbos my mother wrote a letter to my grandmother in Santiago, describing the new house in vivid detail, and mentioned a few times how delighted they were with it. For the first time in their lives they lived on a street with Jewish neighbours and within walking distance of the local Jewish primary school. The children could even walk there by themselves, without having to cross any main roads. They were especially touched by a special Hashgocho Protis that occurred. On the day before they were meant to complete their house purchase, the mortgage lender wrote that owing to the house being over 40 years old, their mortgage would be 10% less than had initially been agreed upon. Oma mentioned further, how on that same day, her mother's letter had arrived from Chile, which included a very generous gift, the exact amount of the 10% that was needed for completion! She also related about the warm welcome they had received on the day that they had moved into their new home. Many members of the community had sent them food and flowers, and the Jewish neighbours had offered to look after the children after school, to allow Oma time to unpack. ...'We were truly overwhelmed, and we received so many flowers that I had to resort to using empty milk bottles for vases.'

Opa enjoying a bike ride on Hanover Gardens - watched by Micha

13 Hanover Gardens with Shabbos and Chanuka room

The following year, Opa bought a wooden garden shed which was adapted as a Sukko, and the roof operated by a pulley system. This Sukko stood permanently in our back garden, not too distant from the kitchen and back door of the house. Initially we would cut down rhododendron branches which we used for S'chach, but they were often infested and this disturbed our peaceful Yom Tov atmosphere. The following year, with the contacts that Opa had at Smithfield market, he was able to purchase bundles of pine leaves, which enhanced the Sukko tremendously. Not only were they not infested, but they also had a beautiful fragrance and were very decorative. In future years, he would also send a few bundles to the Manchester Rosh HaYeshivah to enhance his Sukko, his appreciation for כבוד התורה and a sign of friendship. The use of pine for S'chach has since become widespread.

Similarly, the Shuls were decorated for Shavuos with these rhododendron branches, which served their purpose, but did not enhance the decor. Opa surprised the community when he arranged with Rogers the Florist to decorate the new M.H. Shul with a beautiful display of colourful flowers and plants. This lent the Shul an aura of splendour and was a welcome enhancement that has continued ever since, and has been adapted universally in most other Shuls. To Opa this was a natural enhancement to the כבוד בית הכנסת and would remind him of the way he had decorated the stage at the Kenessio with flowers and plants.

M.H. Shul majestically decorated for Shavuos

FINDING A JOB IN MANCHESTER
Machzikei Hadass

When we arrived in Manchester, we only rented a house, since Opa intended to move to London and manage the Matzo bakery there, as stipulated in his visa application. However, there were genuine delays in the required building work at the bakery in London, and although Opa did travel to London several times to supervise their hand baking production, the machine Matzo baking never actually materialised. There were even two occasions when final plans to move to London were made, and each time something happened at the very last moment that prevented us from going.

The first one was on the morning when the removal firm 'Frank Hill' came to pick up all our belongings, and one of the children was found to have contacted measles, making travel impossible. On a second occasion we were affected by a very heavy snow storm. The front entrance of the house on Northumberland Street had three steps, and I remember that when attempting to leave the house and stepping onto the top step, the snow was so high that it covered and entered the top of our wellies (rubber boots). Trains were cancelled, roads were closed, and travelling was impossible.

In the meantime Opa applied for a job with the Machzikei Hadass Communities, and became their first full time secretary. The heimishe community was very small, and organised Orthodox Jewish life in Manchester was still in its infancy. Although there existed a large Jewish community that had come here from Russia in the 19th century, and many others from Eastern Europe at the turn of the 20th century, due to the difficult financial situation prevalent at the time, many drifted away from their true and authentic Torah way of life.

It was through the pioneering work of a few dedicated Askonim who had arrived as refugees from different parts of Europe that things slowly began to improve. Some arrived before World War II, and many more afterwards. By the time we arrived in December 1955, the Machzikei Hadass Shul was housed in an old building at 17 Northumberland Street on a large plot of land that had been purchased and donated to the community by Reb Avrohom Pfeffer. The building comprised of a large long and narrow room where the men davened, the depth of this room allowing for three rows of seats along its length, which was adequate for our requirements in those early years. Adjacent to this large room was a smaller room that was used for the ladies' Shul. There was also a separate room on the other side of the corridor that was used for a Cheder, in addition to a very primitive men's Mikvah. Rabbi Simcha Rapoport, the dedicated Shamash of the Shul, made sure that the Shul was always warm, maintaining the old coal stove that stood at the back of the Beis Hamedrash, and altogether kept the old building as clean and respectable as was possible. The upstairs of the building was 'out of bounds' and very dilapidated. Around the back was an old disused stable that was converted into a bakery for hand Matzos, which was well used by different groups to bake their Matzos.

The small community consisted mainly of new refugees who had recently arrived in England, and were trying hard to find suitable employment. Money was scarce, but everybody was happy and grateful to have survived the war and to be alive. Each individual had his own personal story, but they now had the opportunity to rebuild their own private lives as well as that of the Orthodox Kehilla.

The members of Machzikei Hadass davened Nussach Sefard, and those who wanted to daven Nussach Ashkenaz were given permission to form their own Minyan but still be affiliated with the M.H. This new Minyan became known as the 'Adass Yeshurun', a Minyan that followed the customs of the German Kehillohs. Initially they davened in the front upstairs room of 35a Northumberland Street, until they eventually built their own premises on Cheltenham Crescent, after obtaining restitution money from Germany.

Reb Berel Waldman had established a Talmud Torah Cheder at 11 Wellington Street, which included a Beis Hamedrash where the Chassidim davened together on Shabbos. Across the road to the Cheder, at 10 Wellington Street East, was the 'Shotzer Rebbe's Minyan' where we davened on Shabbos. This was a small, friendly Minyan, and Opa enjoyed the Chassidic warmth of the Tefillos and the Nigunim. He was often asked to lead the Kabolas Shabbos where he was able to sing the various Nigunim that he had heard in Marienbad from the different Rebbes. Opa was also the regular Baal Tefiloh for Yom Kippur Mincha, having a very pleasant and musical voice and an excellent 'Nussach Hatefiloh' which always delighted the congregation.

Opa was a member of M.H. and initially davened there, especially during the week. However, at one General Meeting it was decided, due to the ב"ה rapid growth of the Kehilo, to primarily allocate seats to the adults, as they could not ensure enough seats for all the children to sit near their fathers. Opa told them at this meeting that he understood their point of view, but if there wasn't enough space for his children, they would then be going outside, and he would not allow them to play outside during davening. He stated that he would continue paying his membership to M.H.Shul, but until a larger Shul was built and he would have seats for all his children near him, he would now become a member of the Adass Yeshurun, where his children could sit with him. Opa had, after all, had a yekkishe upbringing and would not feel out of place if he davened there. He left without bad feelings, but followed his conviction and knew his priorities.

The Old Machzikei Hadass Shul at 17 Northumberland Street and the ladies entrance

On one of his fund raising campaigns in Manchester, Rabbi Sholom Schwadron spoke eloquently and quoted the phrase כי ביתי בית תפילה, using this as the theme of his speech. In his usual humorous way he explained how well he had been received in people's homes during his fund raising campaign. He was happy to see that everybody was ב"ה living in decent and well appointed homes, some had wallpaper, and some even had carpets and chandeliers in their dining room. ...„Yet when I came to Machzikei Hadass for davening, I see this dilapidated building that needs to be supported externally to ensure it does not cave in. The lessons that are to be learnt from the phrase כי ביתי בית תפילה are that both our homes and the בית תפילה should be equally respectful and have a similar decor." The message hit home, and soon after, a building committee was formed and plans were drawn up for a new Shul. As a token of appreciation, Rabbi Schwadron was invited to attend the opening of the new Shul.

FOUNDATION STONE LAYING CEREMONY FOR THE NEW SHUL IN 1958 AT 17 NORTHUMBERLAND STREET

In June 1958, the Machzikei Hadass celebrated the foundation stone laying ceremony for the new, purpose built Shul that would be able to cater to the fast growing Orthodox community. This was located on land that they owned, adjacent to the old Shul, and when the new Shul was completed, the old one was demolished, and was later made into the present M.H. car park.

Seated Right to Left; (unknown), Reb Gedalia Rabinowitz, Reb Yisroel Ehrentreu, Reb Wolf Dresdner, Dayan Golditch, Reb Feivish Feingold speaking, Rav M.M. Schneebalg [Rov of M.H.], (unknown)

Right to Left: Rabbi Margulies, Dayan Golditch, Rabbi Yisroel Ehrentreu, Opa, Reb Feivish Feingold, Mr Pinchos Harris, Mr Leo Fulda, and Mr Bummi Heilpern in background [behind Mr. Harris]

The new Shul was dedicated on 17 Elul 1962, over 4 years after the foundation stone laying ceremony. This relatively long period was due to some complications that arose when the contractors dug the foundations. Whenever they returned after having dug up the ground, they noticed that the newly dug holes had started to fill up with water, despite there not having been any rainfall in the interim. They carried out some soil tests and discovered a natural spring of water below the Shul, which explained why water was coming up from the ground and filled these empty spaces. The architects decided to use a new building technique which included spreading a thick layer of concrete across the entire floor area, so that if there would be any settlement in the future, it would all occur simultaneously and not cause any cracks in the wall structure. They then erected a steel girder frame for the outer shell, a method that is fairly common today, but back in the 1960s was still a very novel and experimental technique.

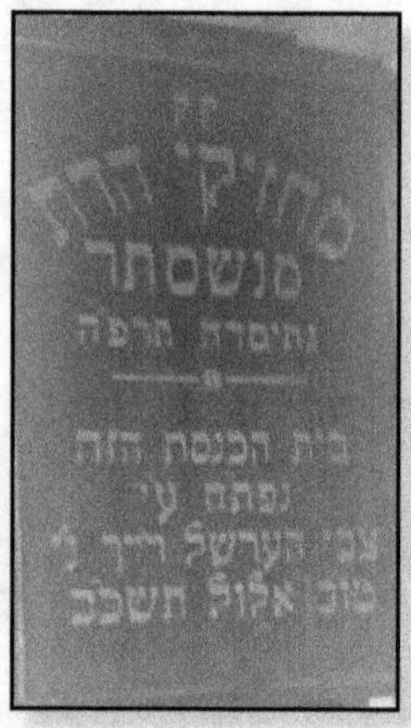

Plaque and New Shul, opened by the President, Mr. H. Reich on 17 Elul 1962

Mr. L.D. Brunner showing the children their new Sefer Torah. Binyomin Leitner and Binyomin Eckstein watching

A celebration dinner to mark the joyous occasion of the Shul's completion was held at the Higher Broughton Assembly Room, [a hall on Bury New Road, where McDonalds stands today] and was catered by Leitner's Catering.

ב"ה

קהלה קדושה מחזיקי הדת

The Executive of the

Machzikei Hadass Communities, Manchester

request the honour of your presence at the

OPENING OF THE NEW SHOOL

NORTHUMBERLAND STREET, SALFORD, 7

Sunday, 16th September, 5722- יום א' טר"ב אלול תשכ"ב

at 3.30 p.m.

followed by a

CELEBRATION DINNER

at the Higher Broughton Assembly Rooms,

Great Cheetham Street, Salford, 7

Reception 6 p.m. Dinner 6.30 p.m.

R.S.V.P. by return

Invitation for the Celebration Dinner on the Opening of the New Shul

The inauguration of the new M.H. Shul
L. to R. Mr. L.D. Brunner, Reb Hershel Goldstein (with tallis), Rav Dovid Schneebalg, Mr. Leibel Goldstein, Dayan Weiss, unknown, Rabbi Schwadron, Rav Boruch Hersh Dresdner, Manchester Rosh HaYeshivah Reb Y.Z. Segal, Rav Yossel Halpern, Mr Hershel Reich, Mr Menachem Rand

Later, when the new M. H. Shul was complete, Opa bought seven seats in total, one for Oma in the ladies gallery and six downstairs, but with a condition, as explained in the letter below.

ב"ה

בית הכנסת מחזיקי הדת

Machzikei Hadass Synagogue

LEGH STREET — NORTHUMBERLAND STREET
SALFORD 7

All communications to:
Central Office
Machzikei Hadass Communities
438 Bury New Road, Salford 7
Tel. BROughton 3571

Sivan, 5722.

Dear Member,

As you may be aware, the new building for our Shool is now complete and in a matter of a few weeks we hope to have the decorations finished and the seating installed and, B'ezras Hashem, the shool will be open for the Yomim Noroim.

It has been decided to sell the seats for £25 per couple, which will just cover their cost. You will appreciate that the sale of seats will be to members of the Synagogue only and will not be transferable. Your early remittance, which will assure you of a mokom kovua , will be appreciated.

Seats for children will be sold for a nominal sum of £5 per seat plus an annual rental of £1.1.0d.

Should members wish to donate articles for use in the Synagogue, the Committee will be pleased to hear their proposals.

Yours sincerely,

H. REICH. (Chairman.)

To Machzikei Hadass Synagogue.
Dear Sirs,
I would like to reserve for my wife and myself and 5 Children (boys) seats, under the conditions, that the 6 seats in the Men Shool should be in two following rows of 3 each starting on a corner, without any differenc to me, in which row you will reserve the ~~sixs~~ seats (even in the last two rows)
Please let me know your decision and confirmation.
Yours faithfully:

K.LEITNER.

6 seats

Invitation to purchase seats in the new M.H. Shul with Opa's reply

Opa was particular that his children would sit near him for davening, so that he could show them the correct place when necessary, and ensure that they would have the correct decorum and respect for Tefilla at all times. He therefore sat in the middle of the second row so that he could look after us during davening. It was sufficient for us to be aware that he was sitting behind us, if we needed any help. He would often quote the phrase 'זקנים עם נערים יהללו את שם ה' ' when one praises Hashem then that is done when parents and children daven together. Opa bought all of us our own Siddur and also a set of Machzorim, that he personally inscribed, so that we felt proud to come to daven. In the early 1960s when money was still very tight, to own your own Siddur and a full set of Machzorim was a true luxury.

I remember one Sunday afternoon arriving for Mincha, after having played football at the Aguda with some friends. Our shoes were obviously not very clean; Opa did not get annoyed but nevertheless sent us home to polish them first. Another time we arrived without wearing our ties, and the same thing repeated itself. This taught us to be dressed respectfully for Tefilla.

M.H. SECRETARY

Soon after his arrival in Manchester, Opa became the General Secretary of the Machzikei Hadass Community, a new full time job that had not existed previously. With this he had undertaken a mammoth task, namely to help build up an Orthodox Kehilla, a challenge that he was happy to accept and carry out to the best of his ability.

The community purchased premises at 438 Bury New Road, part of a row of retail shops where the Newbury Health Centre stands today. The ground floor was used for the M.H. Butcher shop, and Opa was given a room on the first floor to use as his office. He had a large chart on the wall, and entered the various weekly sales of M.H. milk and poultry. For some reason, Machzikei Hadass Communities was a separate entity to that of the M.H. Shul, and each one had different Askonim working for them. There was, however, sufficient pioneering work to keep everyone busy.

The aim of Machzikei Hadass was to become a fully fledged independent community, modelled on the principles of an 'Austrittsgemeinde', but at the same time adhering to the highest standards of Kashrus and being meticulous in all aspects of Halocho. Opa together with other Askonim was therefore responsible for organising, maintaining and constantly improving the services required for an Orthodox community, which included supplies of Matzos, kosher milk, kosher poultry and meat, Mikvah facilities, and Chevra Kadisha and Burial services. I will describe each of these individually in order to create a picture of what Manchester was like in 1955 when we first arrived. We cannot compare our situation today to what they had then, a picture that is quite unrecognisable.

MATZOS AND HAND MATZOS

The Machzikei Hadass had a facility at the back of their premises on Northumberland Street, which was converted into a hand Matzo bakery. This was used regularly by various groups starting soon after Purim until the afternoon of Erev Pesach. The first group to bake was the Manchester Yeshivah, when the whole Yeshivah baked over 350 lbs in one day. The last group was Rabbi Schneebalg's on Erev Pesach after midday, with many other groups using the facilities in the interim days, with baking taking place on most days.

The rear to the M.H with the entrance to the Matzoh Bakery on the left

Machine Matzos

The members of M.H. also needed machine Matzos, and Opa, being the expert in this field, set about finding a suitable factory. These matzos had to be made to the highest standard of Kashrus and at the same time be top quality. Until then M.H. had been baking machine Matzos

The M.H. Kashrus symbol

at a biscuit factory, where they also had a Matzo bakery. Opa went to inspect this bakery, and on his return reported his findings to Rabbi Dovid Schneebalg, the Dayan of Machzikei Hadass. Since M.H. wanted some extra 'hiddurim' that this Matzo bakery could not supply, it was decided to search elsewhere. Opa then travelled to Switzerland, and was extremely happy with the facilities offered by a Mr. Guggenheim of Zurich, where Machzikei Hadass subsequently baked their Matzos under their own Hashgocho. These Matzos were superb, and M.H. continued going there for a number of years until unfortunately, a devastating fire burned down the entire factory. For the next few years M.H. baked in Strassbourg and later went to bake at Ludmir's bakery in Yerushalayim, always relying on their own Hashgocho, under the personal supervision of Dayan Schneebalg.

KOSHER MILK

All fresh milk was sold in glass bottles, which were rinsed after use and returned to the milkman. A milkman delivered the milk to one's door every morning, using an electrically powered 'milk-float'. He would make his rounds early in the morning, and once a week would collect the money from his customers for the milk they had received.

Opa had to find a suitable farm that was not too far from Manchester, and who was prepared to supply the community with Kosher milk. The main inconvenience from the farmer's point of view was that he could not start the milking process in the morning until the 'Mashgiach' [supervisor] had arrived. The supervisor's job was to ensure that all the milk churns were empty before the milking began, to keep an eye on the entire milking process, to ensure that no milk from other animals was mixed in with the kosher cow's milk, and then supervise the filling of the bottes and sealing their tops. To seal the glass bottles he had to use a special tool that pressed pre-printed aluminium foil caps firmly over and around the top of the bottles. This foil had the M.H. name printed and embossed on it, and the Mashgiach would lock any remaining roll of foil into a secure cupboard at the farm, for use on the following day. Milking usually began at 5am, so the supervisor had to be willing and capable of rising early enough to reach the farm on time, irrespective of the weather.

The milkman would then collect the full bottles from the farm and deliver them to his customers. For the Pesach production the farmer could not use the regular recycled glass bottles, but had to supply new ones, and a different colour foil was used to seal them, so that the public knew how to differentiate between them.

It all sounds quite simple, but this had to be done every single weekday, and if the Mashgiach was not available for whatever reason, either unwell or on holiday, a replacement had to be found without fail. On occasions, Opa would drive the Dayan early in the morning to make an unannounced visit to the farm to ensure everything was fine. In those days, milk was only available from the milkman, and could not be bought from the kosher grocery shops.

I remember that once, on a cold winter morning, an M.H. member returned from Shacharis and picked up his two bottles of milk from his doorstep, and to his surprise found that one bottle contained frozen milk while the other one was liquid. He immediately telephoned the Milk Marketing Board who despatched an inspector to his home to investigate the matter. After defrosting the one bottle, he placed a hygrometer, [an instrument that measures density of a liquid] into each bottle, thereby confirming that the two milks had different densities, and a police raid was carried out at the milk farm. There they discovered that the farmer had fraudulently copied the aluminium foil and had his own separate roll. After the Mashgiach had left, he continued to fill more bottles, albeit with a mixture of different milks obtained from a variety of animals, and sealed these extra bottles with his own forged foil, and sold them as kosher.

A new farm had to be found, and ב"ה business continued.

KOSHER MEAT

Independent Shechita is one of the most valuable assets of an autonomous Kehilloh. The Slaughter of Animals Act of 1933 delegated the licensing of Shochtim to an appointed Rabbinical Commission, nominated by the Chief Rabbi and the Board of Deputies who were strongly against allowing independent Shechita in England, which had, until then, been unified and controlled by them. In 1954, shortly before we arrived in England, the government ended the post-war food rationing, which in turn created a greater demand for kosher meat consumption.

Initially M.H. was granted permission to only slaughter fowl, and after lengthy and protracted negotiations with the Chief Rabbi and the Manchester Shechita Board, M.H was given permission to open ONE butcher shop in Salford.

The facility for kosher poultry was organised by a certain Mr. Gardner who ran an efficient operation from premises located on Rigby Street, approximately where the Salford Community Hub stands today. This was well within the Jewish area and a convenient place for Kapporos before Yom Kippur, an extra display of true Hashgocho Protis. The M.H organised the Shochet and Mashgiach, and Mr. Gardner did the rest. For every bird that went through these premises, M.H. received an appropriate 'Hashgocho fee'.

Unfortunately, during the early years, there was a lot of friction between supporters of the Shechita Board and those of Machzikei Hadass. At a wedding, for example, only half the people ate the meat, and the other half didn't. If it was an M.H. catered affair, then people who supported the Shechita Board would not eat the meat or the chicken soup, only due to political reasons.

A constant competitive struggle existed between the Beth Din butchers and M.H. as each tried to increase their share of the kosher meat market. Up to this point in time, they would 'shecht' [slaughter] the chickens and the Mashgiach would check the innards, and pull out most of the feathers. The housewife would still need to 'Kasher' her chicken by salting it etc, and clean away the remaining feathers, a fairly unpleasant and smelly task.

M.H. was hugely successful when they produced their innovative 'Super Chick'. For the first time the housewife could purchase a 'ready koshered chicken'. Every chicken came packed and sealed in a colourful and pre-printed plastic bag, and all she had to do was open the bag and cook or roast the chicken, as desired. The poultry were supplied perfectly clean and already completely kosher, an operation that was supervised by Mr. Jochnovitz, who enjoyed an excellent reputation in Manchester for reliability in Kashrus. The housewives welcomed this pleasant innovation, which made their task much simpler, and at the same time helped boost M.H. sales of poultry dramatically, resulting in the graph on Opa's office wall taking a steep upward climb.

The slaughtering of cattle was much more difficult, as M.H. were refused a licence by the Shechita Board. However, with great determination, the M.H. executive overcame this hurdle too. Reb Yossel Halpern, who had himself previously been a qualified Shochet, was the President of the M.H. Community. Opa often remarked about him, that "he is such a clever man, but one thing he cannot understand. He simply doesn't know the meaning of the word 'NO' ". With an iron determination he lead the negotiations for the independent slaughter of cattle, and succeeded by negotiating with the Chief Rabbi of Ireland, a completely independent body to that of the British one, who agreed to grant them the necessary licence. From then on, Rabbi Chaim Katz, the Shochet for M.H., and the Mashgiach, would travel every Monday morning on the early flight from Manchester to Dublin on the KLM airlines, perform their job there, and return on the last flight that same evening. The meat was ferried across by boat and arrived the following day in Manchester, where it was delivered to the butcher shop to be 'kashered'. These weekly journeys to Ireland continued for several years, until eventually Dayan Abramsky, Senior Dayan under Chief Rabbi Brodie, used his influence and arranged that M.H. obtained their own licence for Shechita in England.

Dayan Abramsky, on arrival at the London Beth Din, found a similar grim situation to that which existed in Manchester with regards to his own butchers. He too saw the rampant ignorance and non compliance of Halacha that was prevalent amongst many butchers, Mashgichim, and the establishment in general, and had to fight extremely hard to make the necessary changes. He therefore fully understood and sympathised with the requests made by the Machzikei Hadass for their own Shechita.

Machzikei Hadass' only butcher shop on 438 Bury New Road was run efficiently by Mr. Klein, and Mr. Kornbluh, their full time Mashgiach. After the 1956 Hungarian Revolution, a new wave of Jewish refugees arrived in Manchester, and M.H. was fortunate to be able to employ Mr. Rebenwurzel, an expert in the production of processed meats. M.H. was then able to offer a range of different sausages, salami, worsht and cold-cuts, all of which helped the business expand, and the graphs on the office wall to climb even higher.

MIKVAH SEDGLEY PARK

One of the essential requirements of an Orthodox Kehilla is a Mikvah, and although an old Mikvah existed, it was in dire need of upgrading. So M.H. undertook to build, what was to be in those days, a most modern facility.

The foundation stone for the new Mikvah at Sedgley Park was laid on the 25 Iyar 5716 [May 6, 1956]. Mr. Moishe Grosskopf, head of the Mikvah Committee, worked extremely hard to raise the necessary finances for this project and organised many fund raising events in order to achieve his goal. Opa was also instrumental in obtaining funding as Restitution from Germany, considering that the majority of the Kehilo's members were European refugees from World War II.

L. to R. Mr Moishe Grosskopf, Dayan Abramsky, Mr Akiva Adler. Behind: Mr L.D. Brunner, Opa, Mr Harry Goodman.

Mikvah Building opened 11 Iyar 5717 (12/May/1957). M.H. President, Mr. Hershel Reich unveiling a plaque together with Opa

Accompanying Dayan Abramsky to the train for the return journey from Manchester after attending the opening

About six months after the Mikvah was opened, Mr. Grosskopf received a summons from the Bank to meet them ten days later to explain why he hadn't repaid the loan that was long overdue. Opa immediately informed Mr. Harry Goodman in London, who confirmed in a letter to Mr. Grosskopf that the M.H. Mikvah had made an application for Restitution Money from the German Government to which they were entitled to, and that he himself would be traveling to their next meeting in Rome in six weeks, and would report to the manager on any progress in obtaining this money. Mr. Grosskopf presented this letter to the bank manager, who agreed, for the meantime, to postpone any action being taken against M.H. for the repayment of the loan.

Opa, in his perfect German, and using his diplomatic skills, wrote a very strongly worded letter that was addressed to the Papal committee who administered the distribution of restitution money on behalf of the German Government. On arrival in Rome, Harry Goodman telephoned Opa and informed him that a copy of his letter had been passed on to every member at the meeting and that the M.H. Mikvah grant had been pushed up to the top of the agenda. Needless to say, they obtained the full grant that they had requested, to everyone's satisfaction.

CHEVRA KADISHA

As part of an independent Orthodox Kehilla it was essential to have an independent Chevra Kadisha and burial facilities. Shortly before we arrived in England, the Machzikei Hadass negotiated and purchased a section of the 'Beis Olam' from the United Synagogue at Phillips Park in Whitefield. Mr. Meir Gluckstadt, a stalwart member of the Adass Yeshurun, became the first president of the Chevra Kadisha, and Opa and many other members of this Shul joined his team.

It is a widespread 'Minhag' for the members of the Chevra Kadisha to make a 'Ta'anis' once a year, after which they have a 'Seudo' together, known as "the Chevra Seudo". On one of these occasions, Rabbi Gedalia Rabinowitz was honoured to be the guest speaker. At the end of his speech he finished by saying, 'Gentlemen, I want to finish off by giving you all my sincere Brocho, one simple Brocho that should suffice for all of you. You should all remain 'unemployed' at the Chevra Kadisha for many more years to come!'

Plaque marking entrance to MH Burial Plot

The land at Phillips Park Cemetery consisted primarily of clay soil, which could not absorb the large amount of rain common in Manchester, causing major water-logging to the plot. Adequate drainage was extremely expensive to install, and often, when a grave was dug, the bottom would soon fill up with inches of water, even before the actual burial took place.

In the early and mid 1970s there were demonstrations against the Israeli government, who had turned a blind eye, and perhaps even encouraged, autopsies to be carried out on the deceased, in the interest of promoting 'medical and scientific research'. There were frequent large protest marches and public rallies in many cities against these halachically forbidden practises, all of which were well reported in the international press. These protests soon spread to other countries and many Orthodox communities organised public rallies and speakers to protest against these acts, in the hope of putting pressure on the Israeli government to stop these autopsies and legislate against their legality. Machzikei Hadass had also made arrangements to organise a public event in protest, and had invited the popular 'Maggid', Rabbi Sholom Schwadron, who had agreed to come and speak at this event, which the organisers hoped would attract a large crowd.

When Opa heard about this, he voiced his strong opposition to such a demonstration rally. He stated emphatically, "that as long as you bury your members in water instead of soil, you have no right to criticise their lack of כבוד המת by performing autopsies. Put your own house in order first." He would not rest and did everything possible to cancel this planned protest meeting, which did not take place in the end. Opa kept on pressuring the community to install suitable drainage at the Phillips Park Cemetery, irrespective of the cost.

In the early 1980's, after the sale of Hotel Bristol in Bad Gastein, Oma and her two sisters bought burial plots on Har Hazeisim. After the purchase was complete, Opa again raised the drainage problem at an M.H. executive meeting, but when no plan of action was agreed on, Opa rose from his seat and informed the meeting that he was cancelling his membership with the Machzikei Hadass Burial Board and had bought plots in Eretz Yisroel. They then realised that he was very serious and meant business, leaving them all speechless. Steps were then taken to install adequate drainage.

But the story does not end there. Opa was niftar late Friday afternoon on 27 Ellul 5748 (1988) just at the onset of Shabbos. The following Sunday was Erev Rosh Hashonoh, and the earliest time that he could have been transferred to Eretz Yisroel for burial would have been Wednesday, some five days later. At the behest of the Rov of M.H. and the Belzer Rebbe, he was buried 'al tenai' [conditional] in Phillips Park and was to be transferred 12 months later to Eretz Yisroel. When burying 'al tenai' one ties two ropes on either end of the coffin to facilitate the ultimate exhumation. He rested temporarily in Manchester for a complete 12 months, and as strange as it sounds, that year was declared a year of drought, with very little rainfall – a very rare occurrence in Manchester. There was even a countrywide "hose pipe-ban", which forbade people to use fresh water for watering their gardens, washing cars etc, in an attempt to conserve as much water as possible.

Mr. Hertz Grosskopf, an active member of the M.H. Chevra Kadisha, confirmed that when the exhumation took place a year later, the coffin was completely dry and came out undamaged on the first attempt. Even the Home Office representative, who by law had to be present to witness the exhumation, was utterly surprised.

Subsequently the M.H. bought a second plot adjacent to the first one at Phillips Park, which was drained properly before being put into use. The drainage of this second plot was accomplished by my brother, Aaron, who organised the complete project in Opa's merit. Hashem repaid Opa for his powerful campaign for כבוד המת.

M.H. GENERAL MEETING 1958

The General Meetings of Machzikei Hadass were always well attended, and honoured with Dayan Schneebalg's presence. We can imagine that there was plenty to report, much to comment about and many constructive suggestions to be made for continuous improvements in our growing community. At one of these General Meetings, after everyone had given their respective reports, Mr. Brunner presented the 'Financial Statement' of the Kehilla and the meeting almost came to an end.

Then Opa got up to speak and said:

> 'Rabbosai, we have just heard the financial report, how much the Kehilla has spent on wages, how much was spent on gas and electricity, on repairs etc. Just two weeks ago there was a General Meeting at the Manchester United Football Club, and there, too, they announced how much they had spent on wages, how much on gas and electricity, repairs etc. Their figures might have been much higher than ours, but we are not a football club! We are a Jewish Community. Why is there no figure for the funding of Chinuch, no allowance for funding a Gemach, or a Kimcha De-Pis'cha Fund, a Loan Society? Let us not compare ourselves to a Football Club, we are an Orthodox Jewish Kehilla and should have different aspirations. There is room to improve, gentlemen.'

And with that the meeting closed with some food for thought. Would anything change? Only time would tell.

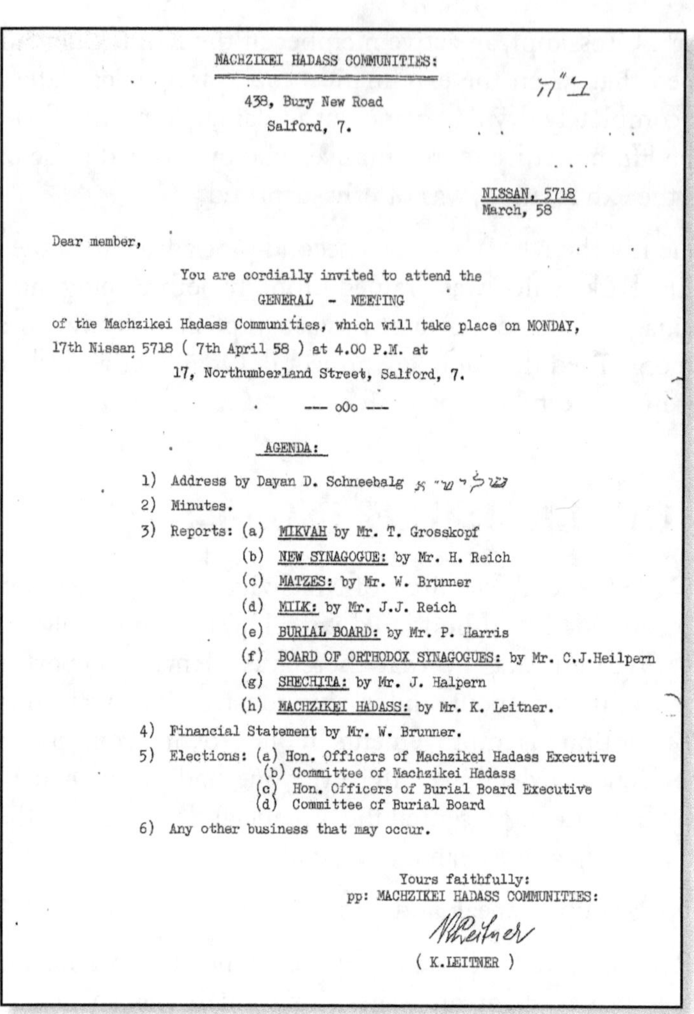

MACHZIKEI HADASS COMMUNITIES:

438, Bury New Road
Salford, 7.

ב"ה

NISSAN, 5718
March, 58

Dear member,

You are cordially invited to attend the
GENERAL - MEETING
of the Machzikei Hadass Communities, which will take place on MONDAY, 17th Nissan 5718 (7th April 58) at 4.00 P.M. at
17, Northumberland Street, Salford, 7.

--- oOo ---

AGENDA:

1) Address by Dayan D. Schneebalg שליט"א
2) Minutes.
3) Reports: (a) MIKVAH by Mr. T. Grosskopf
(b) NEW SYNAGOGUE: by Mr. H. Reich
(c) MATZES: by Mr. W. Brunner
(d) MILK: by Mr. J.J. Reich
(e) BURIAL BOARD: by Mr. P. Harris
(f) BOARD OF ORTHODOX SYNAGOGUES: by Mr. C.J.Heilpern
(g) SHECHITA: by Mr. J. Halpern
(h) MACHZIKEI HADASS: by Mr. K. Leitner.
4) Financial Statement by Mr. W. Brunner.
5) Elections: (a) Hon. Officers of Machzikei Hadass Executive
(b) Committee of Machzikei Hadass
(c) Hon. Officers of Burial Board Executive
(d) Committee of Burial Board
6) Any other business that may occur.

Yours faithfully:
pp: MACHZIKEI HADASS COMMUNITIES:

K. Leitner

(K.LEITNER)

Invitation to attend the M.H. General Meeting, signed by Opa.

Rabbi Dovid Scheebalg continued to lead the Kehilla until December 1964 after which he emigrated to Eretz Yisroel and settled in Bnei Brak. His son, Rabbi Menachem Mendel, who had been Rov of the 'Shteibel' in Kings Road, Prestwich, was appointed as his successor and moved into the heart of Broughton Park and settled in Broom Lane. He infused much vitality and chassidishe warmth into the expanding Kehilla. One of his early innovations was to invite all sections of the growing community to come to M.H. a half hour before the end of each Yom Tov, where everybody would dance together. Also the ladies would watch from the gallery to enjoy this beautiful sight. This small but growing community was built and maintained on unity.

At the Airport accompanying Rabbi D. Schneebalg on his departure for Eretz Yisroel -December 1964. Left to Right; Reb Berel Waldman, Mr. Werjuka, Reb Hershel Reich, Mr. Moishe Moskovitz, Reb Yeshaya Kornbluh, Dayan Scheebalg, Opa and Reb Chaim Feivel Scheebalg [the Rov's oldest grandchild] in the forefront

Reciting Birchas Hachamo 1981 outside MH with Rabbi Schneebalg wearing his Tallis and leading the proceedings

35A NORTHUMBERLAND STREET

During the war, the local Agudas Yisroel Relief Operations were carried out from 35a Northumberland Street, which then became the centre for all their youth activities. This too, was an old building, but it served its purpose then, and for many subsequent years.

THE ADASS YESHURUN

The Adass Yeshurun Ashkenaz Minyan davened in the upstairs front room at 35a Northumberland Street. It was a large Minyan comprised mostly of immigrants from the larger German cities, each with their own slight variation of Minhogim, but all using Nussach Ashkenaz. This Minyan was rather special and unique; as from all those who davened there very few ever came on time, most actually arrived early, well before davening started! There was no talking in Shul, the decorum was excellent. They had no official Rov at the time, but Rabbi Yehuda Roberg filled that role in an honorary capacity.

Rabbi Roberg was the Principal of Broughton Jewish Primary School, the school that we attended. In those years it was difficult to find sufficient suitable teachers for the Kodesh subjects, and although Rabbi Naftoli Freedman was a very popular Rebbe, he could only teach one class at the time. I remember when a boy once raised his hand to ask Rabbi Roberg an innocent question. "Why do you not employ Rabbi Freedman for four hours every day, and let him teach each class for one hour. Why does all the Kodesh have to be taught only as a first lesson every morning and you are struggling to find four different Rebbes?" This was a very sensible and constructive suggestion.

Rabbi Roberg, without batting an eye lid, took out a new stick of chalk from his draw, and started to write a string of noughts across a double blackboard that covered the front wall of the classroom, perhaps twenty noughts in total. He then asked the boy, 'What number is this?' to which he immediately responded, 'nought'. Rabbi Roberg then placed a single number 'one' in front of these noughts, and repeated the question, 'What number is this?' The boy struggled to answer, but eventually tried his luck and said, 'one hundred trillion'. Rabbi Roberg then explained: 'The difference is simple, if you place something of value at the front, then everything else, even the string of noughts, gains in value. That is why I want to have a Kodesh lessons for each class first thing in the morning, to place that 'one of value' at the front of each day, for every child and every class.

Rabbi Roberg practised what he preached: When everybody had finished davening and was busy taking off their Tefillin and folding their

Tallis, ready to go to work, Rabbi Roberg would turn around and learn one or two Mishnayos aloud. He wanted to put that 'One' in front that would add so much value to their day. This Shiur still continues to this day, over sixty years later, although it is given before davening.

In those days one could only find Sefard Siddurim in Machzikei Hadass, and likewise in Adass Yeshurun, there were only Ashkenaz Siddurim. As part of Opa's upbringing in הכנסת אורחים he always had both types of Siddurim available. If a visitor came to Adass Yeshurun who was used to daven Nussach Sefard, he would hand him a Sefard Siddur (especially reserved for visitors), to make him feel welcome. Likewise, the reverse was true, when he davened at M.H., he would keep a spare Askenaz Siddur available for any visitor. This was done discreetly, but was a most natural thing for Opa.

The German refugees, who were amongst the members of the Adass Yeshurun, were eligible to apply for a grant for compensation from the German Government which would allow them to rebuild their Shul that the Germans had destroyed in their home country. When this money came through, with Opa's assistance, an old dilapidated building with a large rear garden was purchased on Cheltenham Crescent. There they built a new Shul towards the back, and then demolished the old house which was unsafe for any further use. When the building was complete, the Adass Yeshurun moved out of 35a to their new and purpose built premises.

INAUGURATION OF ADASS YESHURUN SHUL AT CHELTENHAM CRESCENT, 1959

Opa is holding the 'Kokisch' Sefer Torah and Mr. Possenheimer the other one

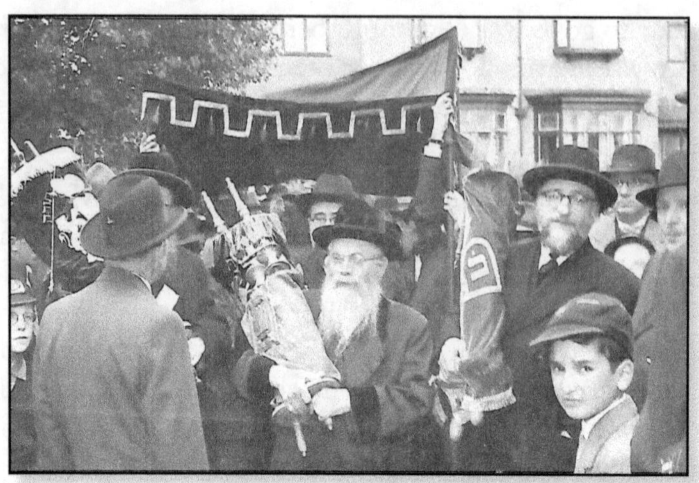

Rabbi Dovid Schneebalg holding the Kokisch Sefer Torah, entering the long path leading to the new Shul on Cheltenham Cresent, with Dayan Golditch to his right. My brother Aaron front right

REB GEDALIA'S SHIUR

The Aguda building, or 35a, as it was commonly known, was used primarily for Pirchim and Zeirim activities, which we shall describe more fully below. The front room upstairs that was previously used by the Adass Yeshurun did not remain empty for long as it was there that Reb Gedalia Rabinowitz gave a public, two hour long Gemoroh Shiur twice a week.

It is hard to imagine today that there was a time when there was only one main public Shiur for 'Baalei Batim' in Manchester, which took place just two evenings a week. Reb Gedalia's Shiur was extremely popular and attracted a large crowd. He would explain even the most difficult and intricate subjects with such clarity, that it was simply an act of self punishment not to attend.

Many people in Manchester during the 1960s-1980s earned their livelihood from selling purses, handbags and suitcases, while others traded as cloth merchants. Some had warehouses, and others would fill their vans with merchandise and travel to the surrounding towns and villages, to sell to vendors at numerous market stalls. Many of these travelling salesmen would not leave town on a Monday or a Thursday, in case, owing to traffic or adverse weather conditions, they would arrive back late for Reb Gedalia's Shiur. One of his Shiur participants was a solicitor, who often had reason to travel to London, but would only accept his assignment if there was a seat available on the Pullman (express train) that would arrive back in Manchester in time for him to attend the Shiur. If not, he would travel on a different day, or sometimes even decline the business altogether. That is how popular the Shiur was, and as it continued to grow and the room could not accommodate everyone anymore, they took down the partition between the front and back rooms to make room for the extra participants.

Due to a lack of finance these rooms had no heating, and during the long cold winter all participants sat there with their woollen coats and scarves, until eventually a gas heater on a meter was installed. A volunteer would stand by the door after the Shiur and collect contributions towards the heating costs. He also volunteered to come one hour before the Shiur and place the required money into the gas meter to make sure the room was warm before the Shiur began.

Reb Gedalia Rabinowitz speaking

So far they had Reb Gedalia, the Maggid Shiur, and suitable premises, and all that was required were the Gemoras to learn from.

After the war the refugees had very little money, and a large industry sprang up that allowed buying a variety of goods 'on approval' via 'mail order catalogues'. This worked as follows:

Many companies had a system where one could order almost any non-perishable item 'on approval'. Once the selected goods arrived and the customer was happy with the items, he paid for them in weekly instalments. Also Lehmanns, the big Seforim importer in Gateshead, offered a similar service. Many people did not own a complete Shas, and certainly could not afford to buy one outright. So they purchased a Shas 'on approval' and Lehmanns would send one volume at a time with the above conditions. As soon as the last payment for one particular Sefer was received, the next one was dispatched, and in that fashion one worked toward owning the complete set.

Reb Gedalia himself, the son of the previous Rov of Sunderland, was actually a business man. He worked as a cloth merchant, with a warehouse in the city centre, but in fact spent most of his days (and nights) learning. I remember going to pick up Opa from a Shiur in 35a one winter's night, and since I had arrived a few minutes early I went upstairs to wait, where it was warmer. Reb Gedalia said something so amazing, that I still remember it today, some 50 years later. He read out three words of Rashi relevant to the Gemoroh that they were discussing at that time, and said, 'Rabbosai, I spent six hours last night trying to comprehend what Rashi is trying to add with these three extra words!'

Nobody could fall asleep during his Shiurim. They provided the refugees with something spiritual that gave them renewed strength. After his move to Eretz Yisroel he became the Rov of Divrei Shir in Bnei Brak, where he continued to attract large crowds, with some people even travelling regularly from Yerushalayim just to attend his Shiur.

Perhaps apart from the actual Torah that Reb Gedalia taught, he imparted a constant and unspoken lesson to the Baalei Batim who attended his shiur. When Hashem gave the Jewish People the Torah on הר סיני the entire congregation was present, since the Torah belongs to everyone and all are obliged to learn it.

But Reb Gedalia was by no means the only Talmid Chochom who worked at some trade yet spent a considerable amount of time learning. To name a few, there was Reb Hershel Goldstein, who worked in the mornings and gave Shiurim at the Yeshivah's evening classes, as well as many other Shiurim from his home to accountants and solicitors; Reb Feivish Feingold, who was a cloth merchant but was asked by Dayan Schneebalg to deliver the weekly Pirkey Ovos Shiur in Machzikei Hadass; Rabbi Elimelech Zimet, who ran a manufacturing unit in town, but would give a daily Shiur at Manchester Yeshivah. They taught us that despite being business men it was possible to be a Talmid Chochom.

On Sunday afternoons we didn't have school and would go to Pirchim at 35a, also known as Aguda. There we used to play board games such as monopoly, chess, cluedo, table tennis, snooker, etc. all the time supervised by Madrichim from the Zeirei Agudas Yisroel. People had little money, and most families did not possess such a variety of games at home, so the Aguda filled this need and also gave them the opportunity to meet with other youngsters from different schools.

A Zeirei Agudas Yisroel meeting at 35a Northumberland Street–establishing RIAF (Russian Immigration Aid Fund). Left to Right: Mordechai Schwinger, Jeffrey Davies, Opa, Chaim Heilpern, Mr. Unsdorfer, Rabbi Efraim Margulies

The girls, incidentally, had a similar program, set up by Bnos Agudas Yisroel.

The Madrichim for the Pirchim, the Zeirei Agudas Yisroel, were older teenage boys who had learned in Yeshiva for a few years, and then went on to study for a profession or went into employment. They also had their own programs and activities at 35a, and enjoyed an annual summer camp.

Shabbos afternoon we would again meet at 35a, and enjoy 'Shabbos group'. The boys living in the Prestwich area would meet at Kersal Crag for similar activities, which was nearer for them. At these Shabbos groups we usually heard a short 'Vort' on the Sedra, a quiz, an inspirational story, and we would sing together and enjoy a bit of nash, too. The Pirchim also had a camp during the summer holidays, and an annual Mishnayos Siyum in the winter break. These activities were vitally important. On the one hand we associated and enjoyed being with Jewish friends, as many of us went to the non-Jewish grammar schools . At the same time it also gave us much encouragement and enthusiasm, and inspired us to increase our learning in our spare time.

During half-term holidays the Madrichim would often arrange outings to the countryside, or to some interesting stately home, or even to tour a factory. They took their responsibility seriously and saw these outings as excellent opportunities to inspire us, and teach us concepts of Emunah and basic halochos. I still remember one time, when our popular Madrich, Moishe Barron, told us to bring a packed lunch and meet at 35a at 10.30 in the morning. We went on a long ramble in the countryside, and when we stopped for lunch near a stream, he asked us to wash for 'hamotzi' but purposely did not bring a suitable cup with, because he planned to teach all the boys the Dinim of 'Tevillas Yodayim' - immersing one's hands in a stream, rather than pouring water over them from a cup. Previously we had no idea that such a concept even existed, and we learnt many more practical lessons on these outings.

Pirchim often organised a 'Shalosh Seudos' in the summer, first and foremost to mix with heimishe friends, and being inspired by a guest speaker. In the winter there would often be a table tennis tournament followed by 'Melava Malka', with plenty of stories of Gedolim and lively 'Zemiros'. This was in stark contrast to our life in Chile.

At 35a there was also a small 'office' with a Gestetner Stencil Printer. Every month we printed 'The Pirchim Monthly', a magazine which included interesting stories, a crossword and local Pirchim news. This magazine was edited by a Madrich, but the boys were encouraged to contribute articles, all of which helped to foster the 'community spirit' amongst the boys.

PIRCHIM CAMP

The summer camps were a major undertaking. A suitable boarding school was rented and boys between the ages of 9 -14 from all over England would enjoy an uplifting two weeks holiday. There was a camp Rov who spoke to the boys at meal times, and was also available for private consultation, if and when needed. He was also responsible for the Kashrus in the kitchen, the Eruv for Shabbos, etc. The Camp Leader worked closely with the Organiser who had to arrange all the outings, activities and food supplies. The Camp Leader would ensure that the boys came to davening, bentched together after the meals, and ensured that all the communal activities ran smoothly, and added to the great spirit of camp. Camp fees were not cheap, and for a family with more than one child of eligible age it was a struggle to send more than one child per year.

Reverend Wulwick, the Rov of Heaton Park Shul, contacted the head of the Zeirim every year after Pesach and gave him a large sum of money from his 'holiday fund'. He claimed that he had a wealthy uncle who gave him money annualy, to enable children to enjoy a 'kosher' holiday. This sum covered the expenses for 10 boys for the full two weeks in Aguda Camp, including their fares and spending money. Hashem always has His messengers!

PIRCHIM SIYUM

We arrived in Manchester on December 16, 1955, and on the 25th of that month, the Pirchim Mishnayos Siyum took place in Manchester, in the Broughton Jewish Primary School dining hall [presently Beis Menachem] on Park Lane. Our 'new' cousin from London, Harry [צבי אברהם] Leitner, whom we had not met before, was asked to speak on behalf of the London boys, so we felt this was a good enough reason to attend. The hall was full to capacity with 200 children and many men; the Rabbonim were seated on chairs at the front behind a row of tables, while everybody else, boys and parents, sat on the school benches! Opa came along with the three older boys, but being new in town had not secured any seats. Mr. Falk (who himself had attended the Kenessio Gedoloh in Marienbad and recognised Opa) very kindly came to his rescue and asked the people seated on his bench to move up slightly, thereby making an extra place for Opa. We boys sat on a nearby window sill and watched.

This was the first time that we saw such a large number of frum Jewish boys sitting together! We didn't understand any English but the sight of so many frum boys all wearing titzis and cappels, just like we did, was a sight to behold! We experienced a sense of belonging, all wearing the same Jewish uniform. This Siyum was to us 'like fresh water on parched lips'. For Opa it was perhaps the first time in 18 years, since the last Kenessio Gedoloh, that he saw Rabbonim sitting together at a table in support of a Torah activity. It must have brought back memories of that major event, with its hundreds of Rabbonim and thousands of delegates. This Pirchim Siyum could be aptly termed a gathering of some of the שירי כנסת הגדולה - but it was a step in the right direction. It was here that Opa first met the Manchester Rosh HaYeshivah, Rabbi Yehuda Zev Segal, to whom he became very attached, a friendship that he maintained throughout his life.

The Pirchim Mishnayos Siyum began in 1948 when the newly established Pirchei Agudas Yisroel of England planned an inter-city-football game between the members of the London, Manchester and Gateshead Pirchim groups. Rabbi Kohn of Gateshead mentioned that it was a very good idea to play together with other Orthodox boys, but that they should enhance their game and combine it with something spiritual, and suggested that the boys should complete Mishnayos Seder Moed. He too wanted to add the purposeful 'One' to these recreational activities. Thus began the annual Pirchim Siyum Mishnayos, alternating between these three towns. For many years it was a full week of activities, outings, swimming, and of course the inter-city football match, with the 'Farher' and the actual Siyum as its highlight. One local Madrich was appointed as the 'billeting officer' who arranged accommodation for those boys who were unable to make their own arrangements, and who might not have had family or friends in the host town. In Manchester, my brother Micha took on that responsibility for many years. The Siyum was a major undertaking, and the Madrichim worked tirelessly for a few months prior to the Siyum to ensure that everything would run smoothly.

For many years the ultimate responsibility for the whole organisation in Manchester was undertaken by Mr. Tevy Goldstein, who would form two committees, one consisting of Madrichim that were responsible to organise the activities for the entire week, including the inter-town football tournament. A second group would organise the actual Siyum celebration, as well as raising the entire budget to cover the week's events. Tevy was an amazing man, working quietly and efficiently, who always came up with some surprise that made each Siyum extra special. He knew how to get the boys excited, giving them much 'Cheshek' to increase their learning and give them something to remember.

In the early 1960s the Siyum was held on a Sunday evening at the Broughton Assembly rooms, a hall on Bury New Road at the junction with Great Cheetham Street, now occupied by the large McDonalds. The boys were asked to meet at Machzikei Hadass for Mincha and Maariv, dressed in their Shabbos clothes. They then lined up according to the Masechta that they had learnt. Plaques were distributed with the relevant Masechta which the boys had to hold up, whilst they marched, six across, down Northumberland Street and Bury New Road towards the Siyum Hall, and other boys lining the route with flaming torches, similar to those seen at a Hachnosas Sefer Torah today. To add to this special sensation, we had a police car escorting us with flashing lights at the front, side and rear of the long procession. The boys entered the hall in the order of the Masechta that they had learnt, and also sat accordingly on allocated tables, placing their placards into appropriate vases on the table.

Tevy Goldstein arranged for all the Rabbonim to enter the hall together, whilst the boys and the Siyum choir welcomed them with lively singing and clapping. A few years later, the Siyum had, for the first time ever, achieved that one boy was tested on over 1000 Mishnayos that he had learnt and knew by heart. This was very gratifying as this achievement was a direct result of the excitement and competitive spirit that the boys had witnessed at previous Siyumim. The atmosphere was electrifying as the chairman skillfully announced the winning boy's name and at that instant all the lights in the Siyum hall went out; only one spot light remained and followed the winning boy as he made his way to the stage to receive his prize – a complete set of ש"ס. Tevy Goldstein had draped a kitchen trolley with a white table cloth and placed the 20 volume ש"ס on it. The prize winner had to wheel this trolley right through the hall, illuminated only by the spotlight, while everybody stood up, clapped and sang for a good ten minutes. The results were instantaneous, as the following story, which I heard from the boy's father to whom it occurred, illustrates.

The father of the boy in question was a very respectable Rov in Manchester, who gave many Shiurim on a regular basis. He had a fourteen year old son, who, although did not misbehave, but nevertheless was a cause of concern to his parents. He would come home after school and had no other interest but to play for hours on end. He stored his toys and board games under his bed, and every night would stay up until late and play. Nothing wrong, one might say, but at the age of fourteen, and being a son of a Maggid Shiur, it was nevertheless a cause of concern to the parents.

This father told me that when this son came home from this Pirchim Siyum, where he had witnessed how much כבוד התורה was accorded to this young prize winner who had worked so hard to learn 1000 Mishnayos by heart, he put away all his toys that very same night and turned over a new leaf. That boy is today himself a grandfather and still learns diligently in a Kollel.

The highlight of every Pirchim Siyum held in Manchester was the Manchester Rosh HaYeshivah who would address the boys on their level, and in English. He usually related a moving story of the Chofetz Chaim, and in one of these earlier Siyumim he told the boys, 'My dear Pirchim, who are so fortunate to celebrate together the learning of Mishnayos. The aim of every boy in this hall should be to go to Yeshivah for at least one year when he finishes school.' That was the maximum one could expect in those early days! He would always encourage the boys to make a commitment to improve by taking only one small step at a time. He spoke about 'Emunah in Hashem' and the importance of saying and understanding the 13 אני מאמין that are printed in the Siddur after Shacharis. He suggested that the boys should just say one every day, slowly and with sincerity, rather than rush through all thirteen daily. I think that every boy in the hall accepted this simple and small step upon himself.

This was a far cry from the national anthem that we were accustomed to saying every morning in Santiago, and was appropriately replaced by our proclamation of אני מאמין באמונה שלמה at the start of every single day. Small steps taken regularly can lead a long way, and that was part of our new 'Chinuch' that we received in Manchester which was simply unobtainable in Santiago.

THE 1983 SIYUM IN MANCHESTER

The Pirchim Siyum in 1983 was held in Manchester for a whole week, and included a variety of activities. It was headed by my brother Shloime, as Chairman of the Siyum Committee. Each boy, on arrival, received a twenty page newsletter and program of the week's activities, in which Shloime, following Opa's footsteps, wrote the following foreword.

Dear Pirchim,

Welcome to Manchester and welcome to the 34th Siyum Hamishnayos.

Coming together, as we have, for a Siyum Hamishnayos of Pirchei Agudas Yisroel, requires us to think carefully over two points.

Firstly, we must remember during the whole Siyum week, that everyone, your hosts, the Baalei Battim of Manchester, other children, the policemen you see in the street, the coach drivers, know that you are here for a Siyum Hamishnayos. They all know that you have learnt a part of our Torah and are now celebrating this achievement. These people around you are watching you to see how you behave, how you greet people when you meet them, how you enjoy yourselves without being unruly, how you help your friends whenever possible. This you must be aware of at all times. The Kiddush Hashem you can create is tremendous – just by using your common sense!

Secondly, you must remember to which organisation you belong to.

As you will all know, The Agudas Yisroel was formed by the Tzaddikim of the past generation. Gedolim like the Chofetz Chaim, The Gerrer Rebbe, Reb Chaim Ozer Grodzenski, the Brisker Rov, with their great minds and greatness in Torah, found it important to set up an organisation so that we today can unite in Achdus under the banner of Agudas Yisroel. They gave of their time and effort to ensure that we today have Pirchei Agudas Yisroel.

To this organisation, founded by the greatest Gedolim of all time, do we belong.

We have to live up to their expectations.

The job of the Siyum Committee is to ensure that you have an enjoyable time here in Manchester during the Siyum week. We hope we succeed. Your job is to ensure that the Siyum is a Kiddush Hashem.

On behalf of the Manchester Kehilla, I thank you for coming and giving our town the opportunity of being hosts to this GREAT TORAH EVENT.

BeBirchas Torah V'Aguda

Signed: Shloime Leitner.

Pirchim Organiser and Siyum Committee Chairman

The Pirchim Siyum continues to be held in Manchester every three years, but unfortunately, owing to a lack of suitable manpower, it has been shortened from a full week to just a weekend.

The following year, 1984, the Siyum was scheduled to be held in Gateshead, and Avrohom Leitner, Micha's oldest son, was chosen to speak on behalf of the Manchester Pirchim boys. Opa travelled together with Micha to attend this Syium and give Avrohom some encouragement. After Avrohom's speech, the chairman, Rabbi Shamai Zahn, thanked him for his wonderful words. He then added "...we are privileged to have with us tonight his grandfather, Mr. Kurt Leitner, who had seen all the pre-war Gedolim annually in Marienbad and also at the 3rd Kenessio Gedoloh." Opa saw this as an opportunity to relate some stories of these Gedolim and of his memories of the 2nd and 3rd Kenessio, and spontaneously went on stage, took the microphone, and spoke to everybody's delight for over fifteen minutes. When he finished, Rabbi Zahn thanked the 'unscheduled speaker' for his interesting and unique speech.

Pirchim Siyum - Opa with grandsons (l. to r. Moishi, Avrohom)

Opa the unscheduled speaker 1984

PIRCHIM AND ZEIRIM

We were always encouraged to participate in Pirchim groups, outings and Siyum activities as we now had heimishe friends to be with, something that we sorely lacked in Chile. When we got older we were also encouraged to take a more active part in organising these events. We had to use our own initiative which helped us gain a lot of experience and discover our individual talents and capabilities.

One of the major fund raising events for Pirchim and Zeirim's general expenses was the 'Purim-Spiel'. They would put on an excellent play, performing at people's houses where they would be eagerly awaited, which enhanced and livened up their Purim spirits. Reb Mordechai

Sufrin, a Madrich and member of the Zeirim 'spielers', would perform with them, and after the set 'grammen' had been sung, would add personalised grammen for each individual household that they were visiting, which he composed on the spot, something that was always well received and appropriately rewarded.

When we were children, taking photos was not as easy as it is today, as there were no digital cameras. The camera could only be operated after a film, which was coated with a light-sensitive chemical, was inserted. After taking the photos, this film had to be taken out of the camera in a dark room and developed, using certain specialised chemicals, which then became the 'negative', so called because the picture was reversed. One then had to print and enlarge this negative onto photographic paper, and finally could hold the actual photo.

As Pirchim we also made a play and went to various families collecting funds. I remember how we once acted out a 'humorous Chupo', with a 'Choson and Kalloh', an acting Rov and a photographer, a job that was played by Shloime Chesner [later of Chesner Studios, London]. Just shortly before that Purim, Polaroid had announced their new 'Instant Photographic Camera' that could produce a ready photo thirty seconds after taking the picture. During the "dress rehearsal" on Taanis Esther at 35a, Shloime Chesner took pictures of the 'Choson and Kalloh'. Then on Purim, after our performance, he pretended to photograph them, as is normal at every Chassene, and thirty seconds later pulled out a perfect photo from behind his camera, much to everyone's amazement. People believed that they had witnessed the new Polaroid Instant camera in action, and marveled at the speed of its operation. However, when we performed at the last house, the householder noticed that the pattern of the wallpaper on the photo did not match that of his dining room, and realised what we had done. But after all, it was Purim!

Shloime and Dovid at the Purim Play with the "new Polaroid Instant Camera"

At Pirchim, we could use our talents and have our fun in a kosher way. We undertook to raise money for Chinutz Atzmai in Eretz Yisroel by organising the sale of 'milk tickets' that sold for 6 pence each [old currency – 240 pennies to a pound]. Each ticket covered the cost of one glass of milk, and displayed a picture of an Israeli boy enjoying a glass of nourishing milk. We printed a brochure containing a large selection of prizes, ranging from a pocket torch to an eight gear 26 inch bicycle, depending on the amount of tickets that each boy sold. The response was staggering, with the top boy in Manchester selling the equivalent of over 24,000 tickets!

Other money-raising events were used to sponsor and support orphans in the Sdei Chemed Children's Village in Rishon Le'Zion in Eretz Yisroel, which was established by Agudas Yisroel.

ENTERPRISE

We were very fortunate that our parents allowed us to develop each according to our abilities and encouraged us to carry out innovative projects in any field that we felt we could succeed in, provided it was legal and a suitable venture. Here are some examples:

Micha, with an aptitude for chemistry, used to make 'sherbet'. This was packed into little white paper bags and sold on Sunday afternoons at 35a. He named it 'Pirchim-ade' as all proceeds went to the Pirchim. This Pirchim-ade was a kind of sugary powder, and when poured into a glass of water, would produce a flavoured, sparkling lemonade. He also made a 'potato–stamp' by scooping out the surface of half a potato, and used it to print 'Pirchim-ade' onto each paper bag, thereby making it look more professional!

After his Bar Mitzvah, Micha wanted to develop his own photographic films. Boots the Chemist sold 'Developing Kits' together with all the required chemicals, but he still needed a dark room where this could be processed. There was an outhouse at 13 Hanover Gardens, which housed the washing machine and wringer (which squeezed the excess water out), and had a sink and a small window. Oma gladly encouraged Micha to convert this into 'his darkroom' which he could use every weekday apart from Monday, when she used to do the laundry. He covered the window with black paper to block out all natural light, and changed the bulb, that would only produce a deep red light which would not harm the photographic developing process. Micha started developing films in his spare time, and was soon joined by two of his friends. One of them later became a professional photographer, Shloime Chesner of Chesner Studios, London, and Micha later went on to study chemistry and took up his profession as an Analytical Chemist. This all started and 'developed' from the darkroom at the back of my parent's house.

When we arrived in England, the only kosher 'nash' item that was available in the shops was 'Vesop's Potato Crisps' under Kedassia supervision. Reverend Groundland undertook to compile a 'Kosher Sweet List' by corresponding annually with all the main confectionery manufacturers in England to verify their ingredients. These sweets were not under supervision, but were 'approved', and most people relied on this list, as Reverend Groundland made very thorough and extensive enquiries.

At the beginning of Elul we would cycle down to some confectionery wholesalers and obtain details and prices of a selection of 'approved' kosher confectionery, and then offer these to the Baalei Battim in time for Succos and Simchas Torah. This involved a lot of work, printing order forms, buying and making up the orders, delivering the goods, and collecting the money, but this too proved an excellent income for Pirchim.

In the early 1960s, philately [stamp collecting] was a major hobby which many children enjoyed. Boys would collect, buy, sell and swap stamps with their friends, and take pride in organising their collections in 'stamp albums'. Although Britain was the first country in the world to introduce postage stamps in 1840, by 1968, only 20 years after the establishment of the State of Israel, the Stanley Gibbons Stamp Catalogue contained more Israeli stamps than English ones. The Israelis printed a whole range of colourful stamps for every occasion. Jewish people worldwide felt connected to Eretz Yisroel, and these Israeli stamps became very popular with Jewish collectors, both adults and children.

Micha and myself set up a trading company of 'Mianda Philatelists [Mianda standing for **Mi**cha **and Da**vid] and used to purchase 18 sets of every issue of Israeli stamps, 12 of which we sold at a profit to two retail shops, one in Manchester and one in London, that allowed us to build up a large private collection of stamps at no cost to ourselves.

We also possessed a 'Fretwork Kit' which contained the normal carpentry tools and a fret saw with a set of blades. We were encouraged to construct wooden models, and Oma often took us to Piccadilly Gardens in Manchester to the Hobbies shop to choose suitable patterns and buy whatever we needed to produce these models. Oma also encouraged Micha to build a large bookcase from floor to ceiling which graced the Chanukah room.

We had a nice variety of activities in our youth, and were never bored with "nothing to do".

JEWISH SCHOOLING IN MANCHESTER

When we arrived in Manchester there existed a Jewish Primary School, know as 'Broughton Jewish Primary School' on Park Lane [present day Beis Menachem], with Nursery classes on Singleton Road, known as Latham House [present day Lubavitch] and a Kindergarten on Upper Park Road, named Cassel Fox [present day Tashbar]. These were some 15 minutes walk from our house, and this was the school that the five of us attended. Miss Schlesinger was the Headmistress and Rabbi Yehuda Roberg its Principal, in charge of the Kodesh lessons. He lived on Parkside Avenue just off Leicester Road, and would cycle to school so that he could use his bike to commute between these three buildings, with the school day beginning at 9am and finishing at 4pm.

The Jewish Day School in Prestwich had also been recently established, with Rabbi Ehrentreu as Principal. When we arrived, Opa also received a visit from their Governors, as they were eager that we attend their school. Every Orthodox child was a great asset to the schools, and every parent would choose which school he wanted his children to attend.

At the age of eleven every child had to take an entrance exam, and depending on the marks attained, one either went to a secondary or grammar school. The vast majority of frum children went to these non-Jewish schools as little existed by the way of Jewish Grammar education. [Jewish High School for Girls was established by Mrs. Ruth Royde in 1958 and was housed at the Shomrey Hadass Shul in Prestwich, and Manchester Jewish Grammar School was established for the boys at a similar time]. The non-Jewish High schools also began at 9 in the morning but finished at 3.30 in the afternoon. However, we got plenty of homework which would keep us busy for an hour or so, but we could choose when to do it during that evening. All children remained in secondary school for a minimum of five years and finished with the 'O' Level exams [today's equivalent of GCSE] in as many subjects as one was capable of. Many children continued for another two years and took three subjects to 'A' [advanced] level standard. It was therefore not uncommon for a boy to go to Yeshivah for full time learning only at the age of 17 or 18. Each of the five Leitner boys attended a different secondary school according to what was best for him.

After finishing our secular school at 3.30pm we then went to 'Cheder' from 5 until 6.30 where we learnt Limudei Kodesh [just one and a half hours a day!]. The Manchester Yeshivah had a large Cheder with over 70 boys attending, commonly known as 'the Yeshivah evening classes'. Since there was no school on Sunday we attended Cheder on Sunday mornings as well. The younger boys were taught by Rabbi C.B. Silbiger, who introduced us to Gemoroh in a very novel way. He would portray a lively discussion taking place between the differing opinions of the Tanoim and Amoroim mentioned in the Gemoroh, that often resulted in the class taking sides between themselves and discussing the point in question. This was his unique way to introduce us to תורה שבעל פה! Our time in Cheder was divided between Gemoroh, Chumash with Rashi, and Halocho. The middle class was given by Rabbi Efraim Margulies and the top class by Rabbi Hershel Goldstein. Rabbi Goldstein was himself a graduate of a Public school and had obtained high grades in his A level subjects before learning for many years in Yeshivah, both in England and in Chevron. He was therefore an excellent choice as Rebbe for the older 'academic' teenaged boys, many of whom were studying for their A-Level exams. On Sunday mornings, when we had three hours of Cheder, Reb Hershel, as he was fondly called, would give us an unseen passage of Gemoroh to prepare between ourselves, in order to acquaint us with 'Gemoroh logic'. Sometimes, as a treat, he would teach us a relevant chapter of Rabbi Dessler's 'Michtav M'Eliyohu', that added an extra dimension to our Torah education.

When we completed our secular education at school, we would go to learn 'full time' in Yeshivah, which is another story.

Manchester Yeshivah was extremely fortunate to have as its president Mr. Saul Rosenberg, who was very capable and extremely devoted, ensuring that the physical requirements of the Yeshivah were always provided for in the best possible way. He invented and adopted many schemes that both publicized the Yeshivah to the wider public in Anglo Jewry, and brought in the required finances for the Yeshivah's upkeep. One annual activity that the Yeshivah would arrange was a 'Prize-giving' with a prominent Guest Speaker which the majority of the local parents and many members of the public attended. This Prize-giving was for all the students of both the 'evening classes' and the 'full time' learners. Of course Mr. Rosenberg made sure that the people had to pay for the privilege of sponsoring a prize, and this left the Yeshivah with a financial surplus. He would collect sponsors in excess of the total number of boys attending the Yeshivah, so nearly everybody got a prize and some got even more than one.

I remember that I was scheduled to receive a prize and Reb Hershel asked me what Sefer I would like. The selection in the shops was not so big, and furthermore, I had been Bar Mitzvah and had already received most of what was of interest to me at the time, or what was available in the local shops. I had nothing on 'my wish list' so I discussed it with my mother. She suggested that I ask Reb Hershel and see what he recommended. So that is what I did, and soon after Oma enquired as to 'what did Reb Hershel suggest?' I was actually embarrassed to answer, because I was sure that Opa would object. He suggested I ask for a sefer by the name 'Mizrachi', and Opa being such a staunch Agudist, I was convinced that he would never agree. Oma simply said, 'If you asked your Rebbe, you must follow his advice.' Just straight forward 'Emunas Chachomim'. [The Mizrachi (1455–1525) is the first comprehensive commentary published based on Chumash Rashi and has no political connections].

Whilst on the topic of the Manchester Yeshivah's 'evening classes' I would like to continue with a short description of the 'Full Day' Program at Yeshivah. After all, we left Chile for the sake of our Yiddishe Chinuch, and the Manchester Yeshivah definitely played a major role in this, and therefore should form an integral part of this story.

The 'Full Day Yeshivah' comprised of about 80 boys, that were divided into six or seven different classes, as the need arose. The younger two Shiurim were given by Rabbi C.B. Silbiger, the first from 10 until

11.30 am. and the second followed on until 1pm. Rabbi Silbiger had the ability to explain the plain text of the Gemoroh with such clarity, that very often the boys would ask the questions that had bothered the Tosefos or the Maharsho. The middle two Shiurim were given by Rabbi Zimet who was a very big תלמיד חכם. The top two Shiurim were given by Reb Meir Zvi Ehrentreu, the Rosh HaYeshivah's oldest son-in-law, who appeared to us boys simply as 'Moishe Rabbeinu'. He was such a humble man, and yet he knew everything. Whenever he was asked a question he took out the appropriate Sefer from the book case, lifted his right finger to the correct height, and with his left hand would flick through the pages until he reached the page that contained the answer he required, and then dropped his right finger vertically down to the correct place. Spot on every time! The Rosh HaYeshivah would also give a Gemoroh Shiur, if and when required.

Rabbi Dubov, perhaps twenty five years older than the Rosh HaYeshivah, had originally lived in Russia under the Czar and would be in the Beis Hamedrash at least one hour before the beginning of Shacharis, already wearing his Tallis and Tefillin. He related that when he was in Russia, it was once announced that the wicked Czar Nicolai I would be visiting their small town the following month. Everybody got busy; they cleaned and decorated their houses, hung up flags on all the lampposts and swept the streets. When the scheduled day arrived, everybody donned their Shabbos clothes and stood outside on the pavement, at least one hour before the anticipated time. ב"ה the visit passed without any negative consequences for the Jewish inhabitants, but Rabbi Dubov related that after this visit he reasoned that if one can be ready one hour early for this wicked Czar, then להבדיל we should likewise manage to be ready for Hashem every morning! He sat at his place in the middle of the Beis Hamedrash and learnt Gemoroh with his favourite commentary, the Maharsho. He would often remain behind after Shacharis and wait for the Rosh HaYeshivah to share with him a new insight he had found that morning in the Maharsho. I still remember, after more than fifty years, how Rabbi Dubov's face would glow with excitement and his eyes would sparkle when he explained an innovative comment.

The Manchester Rosh HaYeshivah, Rabbi Yehuda Zev Segal, has become a world famous גדול, but what I want to describe here is how we, as boys in the mid 1960s, appreciated him. We saw in him a person

Manchester Rosh HaYeshivah

that although certainly a man of 'ראשו מגיע השמימה' – his aspirations were heavenly, but despite that, when it came to teaching the Talmidim, could transform himself into a סלם מצב ארצה – he had both feet on the ground and could talk to us on our level. He would coach and encourage us to begin to climb that ladder, one step at the time, and try and reach higher spiritual levels.

Looking up at the Rosh HaYeshivah from our vantage point on the ground level, we just saw the accomplishments of the teachings of Pirkei Ovos: שמעון הצדיק היה משירי כנסת הגדלה – הוא היה אומר על שלשה דברים העולם עומד על התורה ועל העבודה ועל גמילות חסדים. The world stands on three pillars: Torah, Tefilla and Gemillas Chesed, and to the Manchester Rosh HaYeshivah each one of these pillars was of equal importance, as he exerted as much effort and diligence in his Torah learning as he did into his Tefilla and into caring for others. A world that stands on three pillars will remain stable; it is only when one pillar is higher than the next that things begin to wobble and become unstable.

In Yeshivah we learnt the regular 'Yeshivah Messechtas' so what made Manchester so different and special? The answer might be that we had a varied programme, and each topic was equally important. We had a daily 'Mussar' Seder, a daily half hour for Chumash with Rashi on which we were tested on every week, and another half an hour for Halocho, thereby gaining a wider spectrum and appreciation for many different aspects of Yiddishkeit. Above all, however, the Rosh HaYeshivah and our Rabbonim taught by their example.

Every Shiur/class in Yeshivah had a private Shiur with the Rosh HaYeshivah once a week when he taught us Mishna Berura – Hilchos Shabbos, emphasising how important it was to revise these Halochos frequently and regularly.

As is common in most Yeshivahs and schools, after the Purim festivities it is hard to get boys to focus on serious learning for another week and a half until their Pesach holidays. At Manchester Yeshivah the daily learning program changed after Purim, and this provided a new impetus and excitement. The last Sunday in Adar was reserved for the Yeshivah to bake hand matzos at the Machzikei Hadass facility, and hence we concentrated on learning the relevant Halochos of baking. The older boys were responsible to organise the cleaning up of the bakery, which was last used on Erev Pesach of the previous year. Sometimes some repairs and improvements to the bakery had to be arranged, sufficient fire wood to be purchased, along with sheets of plain paper to bake on, sanding paper to clean the rolling pins after use, etc. In short, there was plenty to do. On the Thursday afternoon prior to baking we would travel by van to a facility in Altrincham to fetch מים שלנו, and the Rosh HaYeshivah accompanied us and gave us a Shiur on the way.

Baking started at 8am on Sunday morning, and everybody was there; the boys and all the Rabbonim, including Rabbi Dubov, despite his advanced age. What impressed me most was how the Rosh HaYeshivah would busy himself all day long. He inspected everybody's fingernails after every wash, checked the wooden rolling pins, observed the kneading, and constantly urged the boys to work fast, and all the time saying לשם מצות מצוה as he walked briskly through the bakery. On this one day we were taught how every phrase in the Mishna Berura had practical applications and was strictly adhered too, and this taught us how to put our learning into practise.

Baking finished at around 8pm, and then Rabbi Dubov would organise a lively 'Rekida' and serve some 'Vodka'. The happiness of having accomplished this beautiful Mitzvah together was evident on everyone's face. Each boy was allocated Matzos which he proudly took home, to be used at the Seder table.

The next day, before we departed for home, the Rosh HaYeshivah spoke to the boys about the importance of the Mitzvah of כיבוד אב ואם – honouring one's parents, and to use the opportunity whilst at home to perform this Mitzvah well.

FAMILY REUNION

Micha's Bar Mitzvah פרשת וארא תש"כ was the first occasion for Opa and Oma to make a 'grand family reunion' after the war, and many relations and friends took this opportunity and made a special effort to attend. The 'guest of honour' was of course Aunty Ernestine, who especially came from

Copenhagen. She was the youngest sister of Opa's father and Oma's mother, the only two surviving members of that generation, and was treated with much honour and respect. Whilst in Manchester she took the opportunity to speak to the ladies about the importance of being modestly dressed [Tznius] and finished her speech by reminding them 'that wearing a skirt that is sufficiently long to cover the knees is a minimum requirement, not a maximum!

At my Barmitzva some 14 months later, Oma was in her 'Ovel year' for her mother, so the Barmitzva Seudo was held at 13 Hanover Gardens, and after seeing how beautiful it was to make a Simcha at home, they made the other three Barmitzvas at home as well.

LEITNER'S CATERING

Both Opa and Oma were professional caterers, having attended and completed their 'Hotel School' and had previously worked as Hoteliers and in Catering, both in Europe and in Chile. However, the catering business they opened in Manchester was, in some way, a much more difficult task. Whereas previously they enjoyed the use of dedicated hotel or restaurant premises, where they cooked and served the food, their new catering business in Manchester necessitated them moving their entire inventory of pots, pans, plates, cutlery and foods from venue to venue as required for each function. Furthermore, in North Manchester, Jewish function halls did not exist yet, and one first needed to kasher the kitchen, ovens, work surfaces and stoves, before one could even begin cooking or heating up the food. In addition, one never knew how clean the kitchen equipment had been left from the previous event.

ב"ה Leitner's Catering soon became popular, especially amongst Yidden in the more affluent area of Didsbury, where the Wilbraham Road Shul had its own dedicated kosher kitchens for both meaty and milky, and its own small functions hall. Opa catered many functions there, which enabled him to leave his plates and crockery stored under lock and key, for an extended period of time. He also enjoyed a very cordial and friendly relationship with Rabbi Felix Carlebach, the Rov of the Wilbraham Road Shul, as many of the Carlebach family had frequently vacationed in Marienbad.

Opa's and Oma's integrity was such, that for all their catered functions they would only serve food that had been prepared to a standard of Kashrus that they themselves would be comfortable with. It was entirely irrelevant whether the client was observant or not, as their Kashrus was always of the highest standard. It was therefore self understood that Oma would always be in the kitchen overlooking the preparations and checking the vegetables.

When Opa and Oma began their catering business here in Manchester, the friction between the Shechita Board and M.H. was still very strong. To avoid any problems, they had a double supervision and both organisations were entitled to send supervisors to any of their functions. Due to their outstanding culinary provisions, the business soon became popular in all circles. The Orthodox clients were confident of their high standard of Kashrus, apart from the excellent reputation that had preceeded them from Marienbad, and the wider community was attracted by the professional presentation and excellent service.

The Royal Crown made from starched serviettes adorns the top table

Mr. S. Gluckstadt and Opa at the Royal buffet reception

On November 10, 1960, the 'Jewish Lads Brigade and Club' organised a dinner to celebrate the opening of their new Club House on Middleton Road in Manchester. Her Royal Highness, Princess Alexandra, was to honour the occasion with her presence. Leitner's Catering was engaged to cater for this special Royal function, a task that was performed to everybody's great satisfaction and delight. Uncle Shurl used his expertise in serviette design, and created a three-tiered crown that graced the top table, something that even the Princess marvelled at.

Three days later, Mrs. Cassel wrote a very complementary thank-you letter to my father and Mr. Gluckstadt, the chef, which is self explanatory. Opa then had a brochure printed to advertise Leitner's Catering, including this letter of thanks and a photo of the Royal 'serviette crown'.

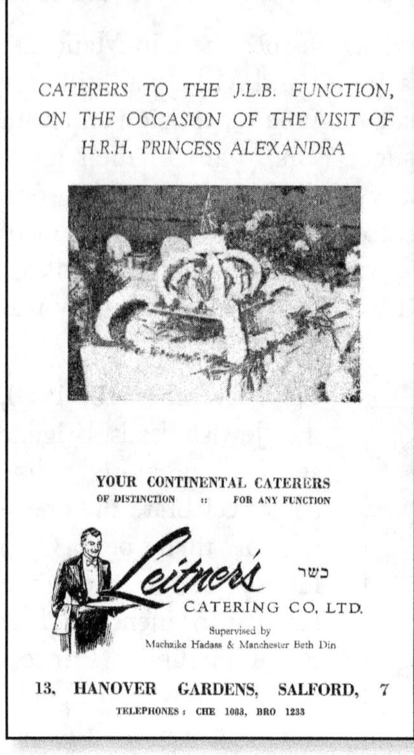

Front cover of the brochure

JEWISH LADS' BRIGADE and CLUB

FUNCTIONS COMMITTEE

Copy of letter received on the occasion of the visit of H.R.H. Princess Alexandra at the J.L.B. Banquet November 10th, 1960.

November 13th, 1960.

Mr. Leitner and Mr. Gluckstadt.

My dear Gentlemen,

It is my great pleasure to write to thank you for your help in connection with the opening of the new Henriques House at which the ceremony was performed by H.R.H. Princess Alexandra on Nov. 10th.

Praise cannot be high enough for the magnificent Buffet Luncheon, Afternoon Tea and Dinner you provided. The tables looked superb and your thought for detail was a great credit to you.

When I think of the limited facilities at your disposal, I can describe your achievements, only as miraculous. The success of the occasion was heightened by all you did for us.

I must also thank you for your co-operation, which you gave so fully and it was a great pleasure to be associated with you for such a notable event.

I wish you "Strength to Strength", which is the motto of the J.L.B.

Very sincerely yours,

Eileen Cassel.

Letter of thanks from Eileen Cassel

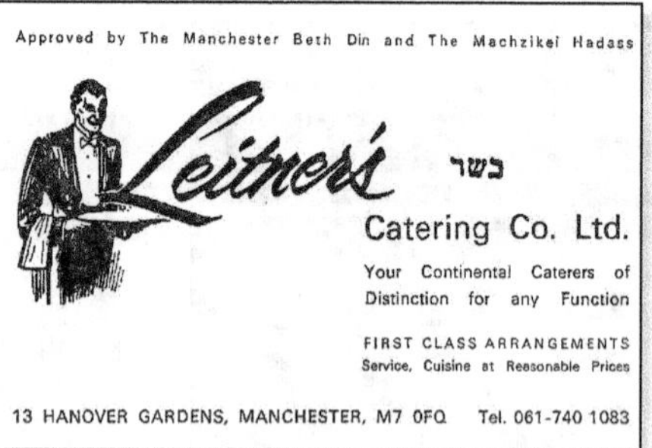

Leitner's Catering Business Card

Not only was Opa meticulous with regards to the standard of Kashrus for the food he served, he was also anxious to create the correct atmosphere at all of these 'Jewish' functions that he catered. Let me explain.

When asked to cater a Bar Mitzvah or Sheva Brochos that would take place on Shabbos, they would prepare and supply all the food and arrange the waiters/waitresses, but would never attend personally, since they did not want to leave the family alone on Shabbos, and taking the children with was not an option.

I remember one occasion when a non-orthodox wealthy family asked them to cater a Bar Mitzvah on a Shabbos in the Shul hall in South Manchester. Since the Rov of the Shul would be out of town that week and not be present to supervise, there was a possibility that some 'Chillul Shabbos' might take place. This was an 'English' family and Opa had reason to suspect that they would be tempted to switch on the kettle in order to serve 'a hot cup of tea' at their son's Kiddush on Shabbos morning. People would know that the food was supplied by 'Leitner's catering', and Opa did not want to be associated with a possible Shabbos desecration. When he explained the situation to his client, the Baal Simcha assured him that all would be fine. Despite that, Opa asked Shloime and me to walk to South Manchester early on Shabbos morning, a two hour walk in each direction, just to be present during the Kiddush and ensure that Shabbos was observed correctly!

At all their catered functions that took place on Shabbos for which Opa had hired the waiters, they were strictly forbidden from smoking in and around the premises, as they were employed for a Jewish function and had to show respect for the Jewish Sabbath.

The non-Jewish waitresses always had to come dressed respectfully. Some of the waitresses would be employed already in the afternoon to begin setting tables, whilst others came only later on to help during the function. I remember hearing about one occasion when one of the staff arrived one afternoon to start work, but did not adhere to the dress code that Opa requested. When he asked her to go home and change into something more appropriate, she took offence, and all the other waitresses present sided with her and marched out in protest, thereby leaving the hall with all the tables unset. Opa was not prepared to give in on a matter of principle, and went to the Manchester Rosh HaYeshivah to discuss the situation. He supported him fully and allowed some of the Yeshivah boys to help out that afternoon and evening, by setting the tables and serving the meal at the function!

All the waitresses had to apologise before they were employed again by Leitner's Catering.

After every function the Baalei Simcha were invited to the kitchen and offered any left over food. My father felt that this rightfully belonged to them, and if there were any complete gateaux or Oma's famous apple strudel left, these were generally gratefully accepted.

My parents ran a retail shop on 'Market Place' where they cooked and baked for all their functions. Machzikei Hadass wanted them to also sell bread under their Hashgocho, but they refused. There was an elderly couple, Mr. and Mrs. Vogel, who lived on Howe Street, and they made an income from supplying Challos and Bulkes for Shabbos, and Opa was not interested to encroach on their parnossoh.

The retail shop on Market Place, Bury New Road

REBUILDING TORAH WITH PRIDE

Opa spared no effort to personally witness the rebuilding of Torah institutions after the war. In 1961, before the M62 and M1 were built, a trip to Gateshead over the Pennines was no simple feat. He very much wanted us all to be present at the opening ceremony for the new Beis Hamidrash of the Yeshivah, and so we travelled in our Bedford van to Gateshead. My father would often quote the possuk: 'בנערינו ובזקנינו נלך כי חג לה' לנו... (שמות י:ט) – when we celebrate a spiritual event, the parents travel with their children to witness it together. This was a major Torah event for Anglo Jewry and Opa did not want to miss it, and was also eager that his children be present at this joyous occasion. The journey went smoothly, but when we reached the Yeshivah itself, we were informed that there was simply no room for the children to enter the building and only adults were to be admitted. Opa convinced them, that on the contrary, the children were the ultimate future of the Yeshivah, and they should and must be given first priority, and not asked to stay outside! He explained that he had moved all the way from Santiago, a distance of some 10,000 miles only for the sake of the Chinuch of his children, and would not accept that there was no room for the children. After consulting with the Rabbonim of the Yeshivah, benches were placed at the front of the Beis Hamidrash, and we children were given 'front seats'.

The new wing of Gateshead Yeshivah

Gateshead Yeshivah's new wing was opened on Sunday the 15 Elul 5721 [August 27, 1961] by Chief Rabbi Brodie, with Rabbi Moishe Swift as the guest speaker at the celebration Dinner. I remember when Opa went to greet Rabbi Brodie, and apologised in case he had been somewhat impolite in his numerous letters he had written to the Chief Rabbi regarding the application for a Shechita licence on behalf of the M.H. Community. Rabbi Brodie just smiled and dismissed the matter with a wave of his hand, saying, "Don't worry, I know you are employed as their secretary and have to obey their instructions!" They then exchanged a few kind words.

Opa had met the Ponevezher Rov, Rabbi Yosef Shlomo Kahaneman, at both the second and third Kenessio of Agudas Yisroel. The Rov travelled worldwide on behalf of his Yeshivah in Bnei Berak and numerous other Torah institutions that he set up after the war, and would also visit Manchester. Opa became one of his 'Netzivim', a way of providing financial support to the Yeshivah, in memory of his father and sister, for whom they learnt Mishnayos on their Yahrzeit. The Ponevezher Rov would make a point to personally visit each of these 'Netzivim' families, as they were refered to. Opa would receive the Rov at home at 13 Hanover Gardens, and Oma woud prepare him a warm drink and some of her fine baked goods, all served on our 'bone china' tea set. I recall one of these occasions, when Opa took the Rov to Mincha after his visit, and as they entered the Shul still a few minutes early, two men were talking together in the cloakroom. One mentioned that he had just been to the local Seforim shop and saw that they had reprinted the 'Aruch Hashulchan' authored by Rabbi Yechiel Michel Epstein, to which his friend remarked: 'the Aruch Hashulchan is a Shulchan Oruch back to front!' The Ponevezher Rov heard this sly remark, but did not react. That evening the community hosted a reception in his honour at Levi House on Bury Old road to which Opa took us children along, as an opportunity to meet this eminent pre-war Godol.

As the Rov got up to speak, he mentioned what he had heard that afternoon regarding the Aruch Hashulchan. He then related a very interesting episode about Rabbi Epstein, who unfortunately had become blind in his later years, and they arranged for Yeshivah Bochurim to learn with him, on an hourly cycle. 'I was one of those boys who was chosen to learn with Rav Epstein', said the Ponevezher Rov. 'We sat on opposite sides of the table; I had an open Gemoroh in front of me, whilst Rav Epstein said every word from memory. On one occasion, Rav Epstein introduced the Gemoroh's statement with אמר רבא, but I corrected him and said, 'I am sorry to interrupt but it states אמר רבה. Rav Epstein repeated this statement three times, and each time I corrected him. Despite me having the open Gemoroh in front of me, he was convinced that he was right. He exclaimed: 'It can't be אמר רבה! Please go and fetch my Gemoroh from the attic, the one I used to learn from in my youth, and we will check it.' I duly fetched his old Gemoroh, looked up the relevant passage, and confirmed what Rav Epstein had known all along! The Rov's message was clear, 'before anyone makes a remark about a Godol he has to appreciate his true greatness.' The message was taken.

L. to R. Dayan Weiss, Ponevezher Rav speaking, Dayan Golditch, Levi House 1963

MANCHESTER KOLLEL

It is hard to imagine Manchester today without a Kollel in town, but that was the case until 1964. As Hashgocho Protis has it, it was Dr. Rottenberg, the local G.P. of the community, who was the founder of the Manchester Kollel and had put much effort into its establishment. Because he was viewed by the general public as a 'working professional', they gave him their generous support and there was very little opposition to its establishment, and ב"ה many others have followed since, helping to create a vibrant Torah City that Manchester has now become.

VISIT TO ISRAEL FEBRUARY 1967

Opa's youngest brother, Uncle Erich (1.1.1.5), had been unwell for some time, and Opa made arrangements to go and visit him. I was recovering from a bad bout of flu and the Manchester Rosh HaYeshivah had advised Opa to take me with, as a good break and some sunshine would help me to recuperate. So the two of us went to Eretz Yisroel for 10 days and stayed with Uncle Lucho and Aunty Berty at Rechov Nechemiah in Bnei Brak, a visit for which Opa had planned a full and varied program. We first visited Uncle Erich in Herzlia, whom Opa hadn't seen for 29 years. We then

Oscar Gerstel (1.1.8.3) *Oscar Leitner* (1.1.3.2)

travelled with him in his small car to Haifa, taking the tourist route via Zichron Yaakov, where we stopped and enjoyed a guided tour of the Carmel Winery. In Haifa, Opa first went to visit the three Leitner cousins who lived together, and from there asked to be taken to the Kever of Oscar's mother, the wife of Max Leitner. We then went to see Oscar Gerstel and his family who had left Marienbad in the early 1930's.

Our next stop was Yerushalayim, to visit Dayan Abramsky who lived in Rechov Hapisga in Bayit Vegan. Opa's appointment was scheduled for 1pm, so we took the bus to the final stop at Mount Herzl, and then walked across sand dunes to our destination. There were only two buildings in the entire Bayit Vegan at that time, Yeshivah Kol Torah and the block of flats where Dayan Abramsky lived. Before we entered the building we had to empty our shoes from the sand that had accumulated in them! Opa was always very punctual, and at 12.55 rang the bell. The Rebetzen showed us into the Dayan's room, where the Dayan sat at a large table, writing his commentary on the Tosefta, and invited us to 'please sit down,' whilst he continued writing. At 12.58 his Rebetzen brought him a cup of Russian tea, while the Dayan opened his desk draw, took out a large piece of pink blotting paper and dried the ink off his writing. After that he cleared the table, and as he put everything back on the bookshelf he explained, 'this way I will know where everything is after dinner, when I need it again'.

He then excused himself and said 'I need to know what Hashem is doing in the world' and switched on the radio to hear the headlines of the 1pm news. Every minute was accounted for and not wasted! He then turned to us and spoke with Opa for about 45 minutes. Dayan Abramsky had had a very close and personal relationship with my father, both during the war years in the administration of the various relief projects, as well as being involved in trying to obtain the rights for Shechita on behalf of Machzikei Hadass in Manchester.

At the conclusion of that momentous visit Opa had arranged to meet Rabbi Itche Meir Lewin, a brother-in-law of the Gerrer Rebbe, whom he had known from the Kenessio Gedoloh in Marienbad. Reb I.M. Lewin was a member of the Knesset, and was happy to arrange for us a guided tour of the new Knesset parliament buildings.

The next day Opa had made an appointment to meet the Belzer Rebbe, who was still based in Rechov Agripas. Before he left England, Opa had prepared a whole album with photos and letters of interest and a detailed description of each item in the album, which he now presented to the Rebbe. When we entered the room, the Rebbe rang a small bell on his table as a sign for his Gabbe to come in.

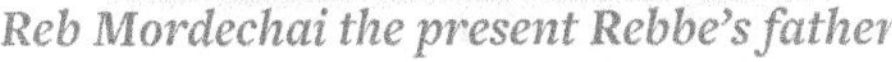

Reb Mordechai the present Rebbe's father

The present Belzer Rebbe

He motioned to him to bring a bowl of fruit, a request that was promptly fulfilled, but as soon as the Gabbe had left the room, the Rebbe rang the bell again, and when the Gabbe returned, the Rebbe said, 'for a 'Yekke' you also need plates and a knife and fork', a remark that reminded my father of his stay in Belz over Sukkos, when Reb Aaron had also insisted that Opa was given cutlery to eat with, as he was used to from Marienbad. Opa then spoke to the Rebbe for nearly 2 hours, relating all about his ancestors and Marienbad, and presented the Rebbe with the album of photos, which also contained a wedding invitation that he had received when Reb Mordechai, [the Rebbes' father] got married again in Eretz Yisroel. I just sat there and listened to the conversation, and was intrigued how the Rebbe, who was only 19 years old at the time, asked calculated and targeted questions. At one stage he wanted to work out how old Opa was, so he asked him a few questions. First he asked Opa how many siblings they were, and what they were called.

Then, after talking about another topic for a few minutes, the Rebbe asked 'who was the oldest' and then, after another interruption, asked how much older was his older brother. From this information he was able to calculate exactly how old Opa was, without having to ask him directly.

At the end of the visit, the Rebbe remarked, 'you knew my father better than I did!'

From there we went down the road and toured the Belzer Yeshivah.

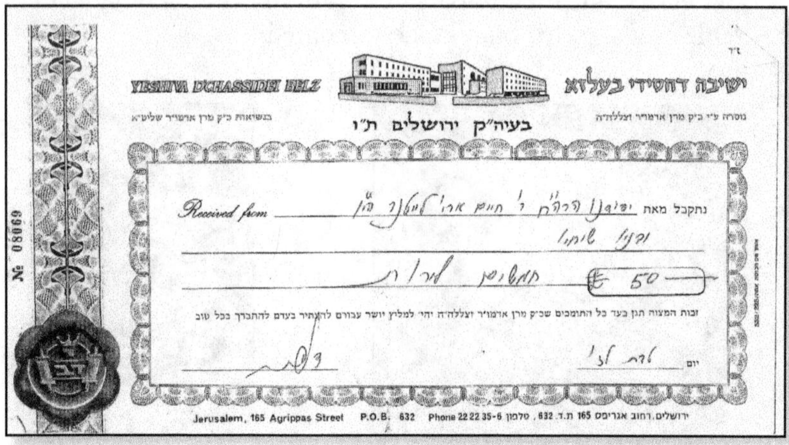
№ 08069

YESHIVA DCHASSIDEI BELZ — ישיבה דחסידי בעלזא

נוסדה ע"י כ"ק מרן אדמו"ר זצללה"ה — בנשיאות כ"ק מרן אדמו"ר שליט"א

בעיה"ק ירושלים ת"ו

Received from — נתקבל מאת

£ 50

זכות המצוה תגן בעד כל התומכים שכ"ק מרן אדמו"ר זצללה"ה יהי' למליץ יושר עבורם להעתיר בעדם להתברך בכל טוב

יום

Jerusalem, 165 Agrippas Street P.O.B. 632 Phone 22 22 35-6 — ירושלים, רחוב אגריפס 165 ת.ד. 632, טלפון

Receipt for donation to Belz Yeshiva
[*50 pounds were equivalent to five weeks wages for an average family*].

The Matzeivoh of Reb Aaron

Next came a visit to Har Hamenuchos, where Opa spent a considerable amount of time at the Kever of Reb Aaron of Belz, naturally a very emotional experience. He had last seen the צדיק in Belz 29 years before. He had saved his life, and at every crossroad had advised him which way to go and what to do. They had also corresponded together frequently, and he felt a very close attachment to him, like a son to this father. When we were finally ready to leave, Opa remarked 'we've lost a unique צדיק, but I am comforted by the fact that the Royal Dynasty of Belz is continuing, with a young Rebbe who will rebuild and expand Belz to its former glory.'

Opa had also arranged to meet up with some old acquaintances that he knew from Chile, and approximately 40 people met one evening in a flat in Tel Aviv, each one relating their stories of how they came to settle in Eretz Yisroel. They conversed mostly in Spanish, but I couldn't understand them as by that time I had forgotten most of it, except maybe a few words, such as 'pokito' – a little!

One of the more affluent visitors at the hotel in Marienbad had been Mr. & Mrs. Bart. Mr. Bart later became the first Governor of the Bank of Israel in 1948, but at the time of our visit to Eretz Yisroel in 1967 he was no longer alive. Opa made a point to visit his widow, who had built a large Old Age Home in her husband's memory. She was extremely touched that Opa had taken the trouble to visit her, and that he insisted in taking a tour of the Old Age Home.

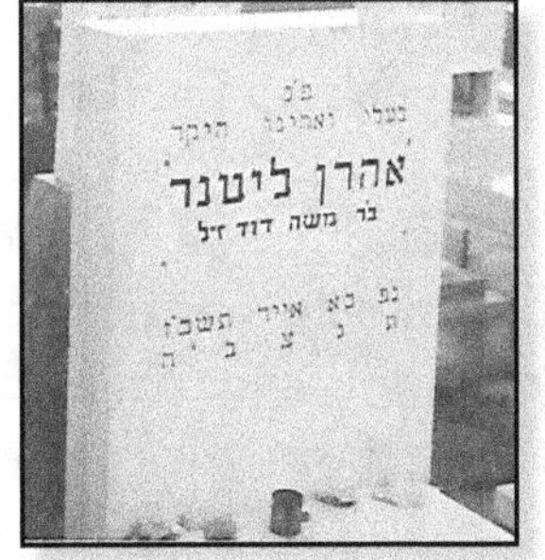

Erich Leitner (1.1.1.5), Herzliah

Uncle Erich died just four months later, on the day that the "Six-Day-War" broke out, in June 1967.

THE SHABBOS QUEEN

Opa and Oma not only kept Shabbos but they even kept Erev Shabbos too. This might sound a little strange, so let me explain. The Shulchan Oruch writes (Orach Chaim 251;1) העושה מלאכה בערב שבת מן המנחה ולמעלה אינו רואה סימן ברכה יש מפרשים מנחה גדולה ויש מפרשים מנחה קטנה.

Opa was always completely ready for Shabbos before מנחה גדולה and was already dressed for Shabbos. He then checked that the Shabbos table was laid, all place settings neatly arranged and nothing was missing. Once he had reassured himself that the table was indeed fit for a queen, he would sit down to have some dinner, and then go to the Shabbos room and learn the Sedra with the commentary of Rabbi S.R. Hirsch.

During the winter he would drive down to Salford Grammar School in Eccles about two hours before Shabbos, to fetch us and as many other boys that would fit into our Bedford van. This non-Jewish Secondary School had approximately 150 Jewish boys, out of a total of 700, and during the short winter Fridays the school would provide two double-decker buses to take the Jewish boys home, one and a half hours before the onset of Shabbos. Every Friday afternoon there would be two buses waiting outside the front gate of the school, plus the additional blue Bedford van, with Opa in the driver's seat.

The same happened on Chol Hamoed Sukkos: My father would come to pick us up at dinner time so that we could have our lunch in the Sukko. My mother always made sure that dinner was ready, and insisted that we washed for המוציא, make a לישב בסוכה and say ברכת המזון with יעלה ויבא. Opa would then take us back in time for the afternoon school bell.

At one of the parents evenings at the school, Mr Simms, the non-Jewish headmaster, asked Opa why he took the trouble to fetch his sons when the school already provided two buses for that purpose. Opa's reply remains as relevant today as it was in the 1960s. He explained to the headmaster the importance of Shabbos and its timely preparation. He spent an hour every Friday afternoon just so that his children could be home that little bit earlier than if they would have taken the bus, which inevitably needed to make frequent stops. This was a weekly lesson to demonstrate the importance of preparing for Shabbos and be ready well in time, thus allowing us to enter Shabbos in a relaxed atmosphere.

Opa had printed on his stationery 'Telephone will not be answered from Friday sunset until Saturday night' as he wanted a tranquil atmosphere to prevail over Shabbos at home, without the disturbance of the telephone's ringing.

Telephone will not be answered from Friday Sun Set until Saturday night

K. LEITNER

13 HANOVER GARDENS, MANCHESTER, M7 0FQ

Telephone: 061-740 1083

כולל שומרי החומות

לצדקת רבי מאיר בעל הנס זי"ע

There is an amazing story about preparing for Erev Shabbos that occurred to Opa's granddaughter and great grandson שלמה, and it is worth while taking a little break from reading this book and, if phoning from Eretz Yisroel dial 00972 39290707 and after the introduction and reaching 'personal stories', simply press 2 – 6 – 3 – 4#. The corresponding English number is 02033751580 and after the long introduction, again press 2 -6 -3 -4# and listen to Malki's incredible true story about the positive benefit of getting ready for Shabbos early. You will then appreciate why the acronym of **מזמור שיר ליום השבת** *spells out the word שלמה – the name of her son that is at the centre of this remarkable story!*

Every week we accept the holiness of Shabbos when we recite (Tehillim 92) that begins with **מזמור שיר ליום השבת**. *This is immediately followed by chapter 93, which happens to be the dedicated Psalm that the Levyim sang in the Beis Hamikdosh on a Friday. These two chapters appear to be in the reverse order, as Friday always preceeds Shabbos. Why recite the chapter referring to Shabbos, before the one dedicated for Friday? The lesson is simple; the quality and holiness that you will experience on the forthcoming Shabbos depends on your preparation for it on Friday.*

In fact we actually says this same sentiment in the phrase of Lecho Dodi every Friday night when we sing ;-

לקראת שבת לכו ונלכה כי היא מקור הברכה **מראש** מקדם נסוכה
To welcome the Shabbos, come let us go for it is the scource of blessing, from the beginning, from antiquity she was honoured.........

Apart from the actual meaning of these words, stressing the importance of proper preparations for Shabbos, the letters that follows those of the highlighted word ראש, in the alphabetical sequence, also spells out שבת!

Opa and Oma were particular not to go out of town on a Friday as this would not be conducive to a relaxed approach to Shabbos. I remember when I was looking for a job and searched the Daily Telegraph Monday Job supplement. My eye caught an advert that matched my qualifications and ambitions, and as a perk they were even offering subsidised interest rates on house mortgages, definitely an appeal to people looking to buy a house. I phoned the number advertised, and although the job was based in Manchester, all interviews were taking place at their Head Office in Leeds, which was located in an office block next to the Leeds train station. Interviews were scheduled to last only ten minutes, beginning in August. I booked the first appointment at 9.10am that would have allowed me to be back in Manchester by 10.30am the latest. I was really excited about this, but when I told Oma, she simply said, 'Friday morning we don't travel out of town.' I phoned back and cancelled the appointment.

OPA'S SOCIAL WORK IN MANCHESTER

Having developed a very close contact with Rabbi Shloime Baumgarten during the war years, Opa was appointed as the Manchester representative for 'Rabbi Meir Baal Hanes', a Tzedoko that was originally established by the Ksav Sofer, to aid the Orthodox community in Eretz Yisroel. Opa would often drive us around on Sunday afternoons, and at other times we went on our bikes, to collect the 'Pushkes' (Tzedoko boxes) that required empying. He took great pride in this work and made sure that any new member of the community or newly married couple received a Pushke and a gift of a 'Challoh' cover, embroidered with the Rabbi Meir Baal Hanes logo. All money collected was sent regularly to Rabbi Shloime Baumgarten in London.

In his later years, when he was less able to drive around, my father would invite the public to bring their Pushkes at a specific time to his house. After a few years, when even this became too strenuous, he appointed my brother Aaron to continue the collection, and informed the public of this new arrangement. This was about 10 weeks before he was niftar, and Aaron has continued to expand this collection ever since.

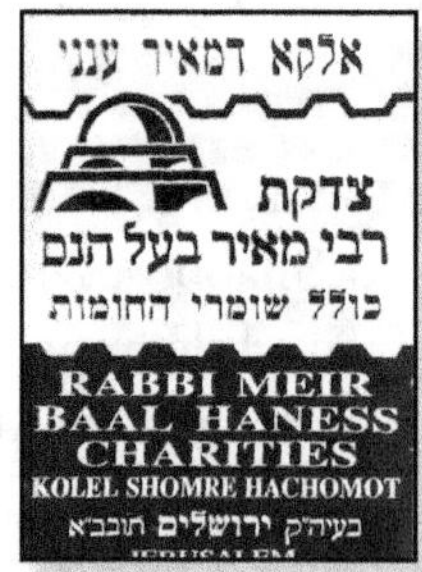

A Rabbi Meir Baal Haness Pushke

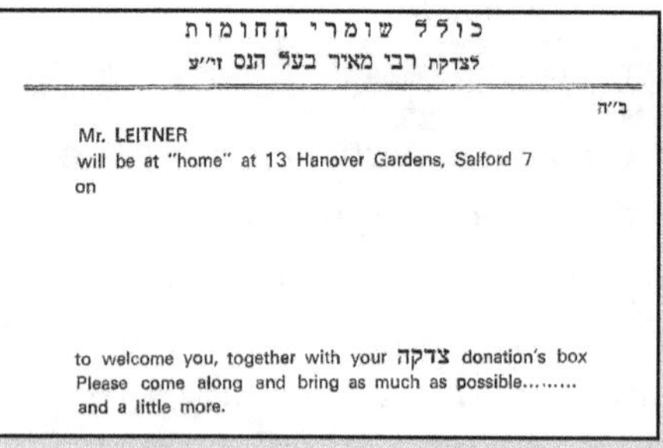
כולל שומרי החומות
לצדקת רבי מאיר בעל הנס זי"ע

ב"ה

Mr. LEITNER
will be at "home" at 13 Hanover Gardens, Salford 7
on

to welcome you, together with your צדקה donation's box
Please come along and bring as much as possible.........
and a little more.

Personal invitation card to bring the box to be emptied

Kolel Shomre Hachomoth
RABBI MAIR BAAL HANES CHARITIES
JERUSALEM Israel

כולל שומרי החומות
לצדקת רבי מאיר בעל הנס זי"ע
בעיה"ק ירושלם ת"ו

נר שם טוב

נזר גבאות קודש

GABAY APPOINTMENT

הון ועושר בביתו וצדקתו עומדת לעד

רודף צדקה וחסד ימצא חיים צדקה וכבוד

וזאת התעודה

ביד החבר ידידנו הנכבד

הר"ר חיים ארי' לייטנער נ"י

גבאי קודש ... מאנטשעסטער

הנהלת כולל שומרי החומות

Address KOLEL SHOMRE HACHOMOTH P.O.B. ... JERUSALEM Israel

Certificate of Appointment as Gabbe for Manchester 1962

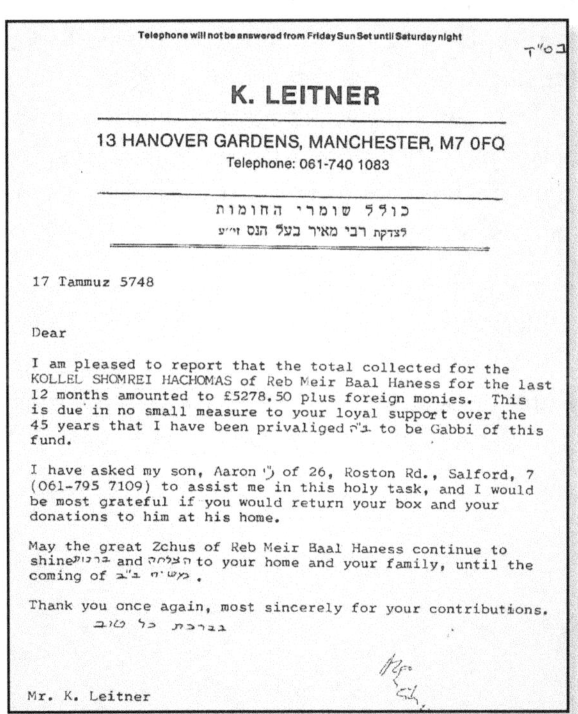
Telephone will not be answered from Friday Sun Set until Saturday night

בס"ד

K. LEITNER

13 HANOVER GARDENS, MANCHESTER, M7 0FQ
Telephone: 061-740 1083

כולל שומרי החומות
לצדקת רבי מאיר בעל הנס זי"ע

17 Tammuz 5748

Dear

I am pleased to report that the total collected for the KOLLEL SHOMREI HACHOMAS of Reb Meir Baal Haness for the last 12 months amounted to £5278.50 plus foreign monies. This is due in no small measure to your loyal support over the 45 years that I have been privaliged ב"ה to be Gabbi of this fund.

I have asked my son, Aaron נ"י of 26, Roston Rd., Salford, 7 (061-795 7109) to assist me in this holy task, and I would be most grateful if you would return your box and your donations to him at his home.

May the great Zchus of Reb Meir Baal Haness continue to shine ברכות and הצלחה to your home and your family, until the coming of משיח ב"ב.

Thank you once again, most sincerely for your contributions.

בברכת כל טוב

Mr. K. Leitner

Handing over to his son, Aaron, Tamuz 5748

When the Aguda building was finally demolished at 35a Northumberland Street, Opa had plans drawn up to build an Aguda centre known as 'The Harry Goodman House', but unfortunately had to abandon the project owing to a lack of interest from the community at large.

Private Social Work

With his contacts in applying for compensation and restitution from the Germans, which he successfully used to help Adass Yeshurun, M.H. Shul and Sedgley Park Mikvah, Opa also helped several individuals to obtain German pensions and compensation for loss of health.

RESTITUTION CLAIM

As early as May 28, 1947, Opa began, what was to become a major project, to try and get compensation for the loss of their property in Marienbad and restitution for the loss of income that this had caused. In response to a newspaper article by Dr. Rudolf Kuraz, the Consul of the Czechoslovakian Embassy in New York, promising fair treatment for all Jewish property claims, Opa requested the Consul's assistance in achieving this goal, and reminded him of Thomas Masaryk's motto; 'Truth must prevail'. In his reply, the Consul was very diplomatic, and only offered some assistance in trying to trace his father and sister, but avoided the issue of property restitution and compensation.

Opa exerted much time and effort over the years to try and get compensation and despite having copies of the Property Deeds and numerous letters of testimony from previous hotel guests, he never succeeded in obtaining any justice. There are two complete draws in the filing cabinet full of this futile correspondence.

Santiago, 28th May 1947.

H. E. Monsieur Dr. Rudolf KURAZ,
Czechoslovak General Consul
1790 Broadway
New - York 19.

His Excellency,

With greatest interest I am reading in the " Aufbau " an articel regarding your statement (Copy enclosed) and take the liberty to write to you in this respect. My name is KURT LEITNER, I am the son of ~~xx~~ Mr. David Leitner, who was proprietior of the famous " Hotel National " in Marianske Lazne till October 1938 when my whole family has to leave the town for racial and religious-political reasons. We wre leaving near Marianske Lazne from 1859 as loyal citizens, especially to the Czechoslovak Republic for which statement I am able to give proofs. My whole family declared themselves to the jewish nationality.

My father together with my sister, 3 brothers and myself went in 1938 to Prague. One brother emigrated to Palestine, two to England, and I went on the 23rd of March 1939, after the Nazis occupied Czechoslovakia through Poland to England, where I was working during the whole war for czechoslovak Refugees in England, in this connection I had several times discussions with H.E. Dr. Edurad Benes, H.E. Jan Masaryk and the whole Czechoslovak Government in Exil. For personal reasons I went to Santiago and we are drying to restituit our family property in Marianske Lazne, but I am sorry to state, till now without any result.

My father and sister were deported in 1942 from Bardijov to Poland and I don't know about their whereabouts.

Perhaps your statement reg. the Czechoslovak help for Jewish people will give me the right to apply to you for your kind assistance. I would like to mention, that all my brothers and myself stand 3 times before the recruiting officer of the Czechoslovak Government in England.

As Referenc I would like to mention:
M. Vanek, First Secretary of the Czechoslovak Embassy in London
H.E. Dr. Jan Havlasa, Czechoslovak Minister in Santiago de Chile.

With many thanks in anticipation for your kind assistans

I remain

YOURS VERY SINCERELY,

(K.LEITNER)

Encl.

Claims Department
Foreign and Commonwealth Office
Charles House 5-11 Lower Regent Street LONDON SW1Y 4LU

Telephone (01) 214-9151

K Leitner Esq
13 Hanover Gardens
MANCHESTER M7 OFQ

Your reference

Our reference GC/-CZECH

Date 15 November 1982

Dear Mr Leitner

Thank you for your letter of 10 November about the Foreign Compensation (Czechoslovakia) Order 1982 and the loss of property in Czechoslovakia owned by your late father.

It is a settled rule of international law that a State cannot take up a claim against another State unless the claimant was its national at the date of injury (and is so at the date of presentation of the claim). Reflecting this, so far as concerns the loss of property in Czechoslovakia, the Order in Council lays down that the claimant must be able to show that he was a United Kingdom national when the Agreement with Czechoslovakia entered into force (2 February 1982) and that the property of which he has been deprived was owned by a UK national at the time of deprivation. Claims in respect of property which was not owned by a UK national at the time of deprivation were not, and could not have been, settled by the Agreement with Czechoslovakia.

I am sorry I am unable to send you a more encouraging reply.

Yours sincerely

N A McGregor

A letter received on November 15, 1982 verifies his determination, even at his advanced age, to obtain justice

As late as September 1982, Opa wrote to his former colleague, Mr. Springer, to try to get some compensation for the Hotel in Marienbad. Unfortunately he was unable to help, as he was scheduled to undergo a serious operation in the near future. Opa confirmed that he had phoned the Gabbe in Belz, and the Rebbe had sent his wishes for a 'Refuoh Sheleimo bimheiro'. Opa asked to be kept informed of his progress, so that he could relate back to the Rebbe. This note was signed, 'Sincerely, old friend, K. Leitner.'

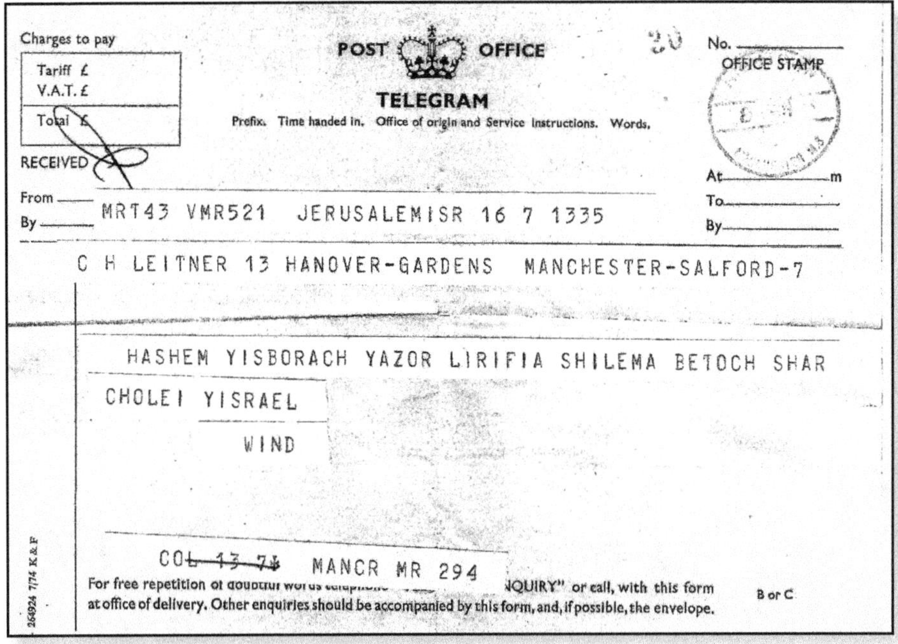

Charges to pay
Tariff £
V.A.T. £
Total £
RECEIVED

POST OFFICE
TELEGRAM
Prefix. Time handed in. Office of origin and Service Instructions. Words.

No.
OFFICE STAMP
At m
To
By

From
By
MRT43 VMR521 JERUSALEMISR 16 7 1335

C H LEITNER 13 HANOVER-GARDENS MANCHESTER-SALFORD-7

HASHEM YISBORACH YAZOR LIRIFIA SHILEMA BETOCH SHAR
CHOLEI YISRAEL
WIND

COL 13 7 MANCR MR 294

For free repetition of doubtful words telephone ... "ENQUIRY" or call, with this form at office of delivery. Other enquiries should be accompanied by this form, and, if possible, the envelope.

B or C

264924 7/74 K&F

Telegram received from Belz for a Refuoh Sheleimo

CHAPTER 10

Kokisch Family

KOKISCH FAMILY

Although Opa left many photos and letters that depict his life history, we don't have as much material about Oma's family. Nevertheless, from the little that we do have, and from the stories that we've heard, we've managed to get a picture of this part of the family which is just as inspirational and amazing. The Mesiras Nefesh that was displayed by both Oma and her parents, and the great Hashgocho Protis that they experienced throughout their lives, leaves us dutybound to follow their exemplary way of life.

Mordechai (Max) (2.1.1) Kokisch

Mordechai (Max) (2.1.1) Kokisch was the second son of שמואל (Samuel) (2.1) and מלכה (Amelie) Kokisch. Samuel Kokisch died on Febuary 20, 1882 at the young age of 48, and his wife died in a tragic accident in 1901, when she fell asleep in her rocking chair near the coal fire. Her clothes caught fire, resulting in her ultimate death three days later.

The Kokisch family had lived in various towns near Vienna for at least three generations. Oma's great-grandfather, Ozer Kokisch, and his son Shmuel (2.1) and grandson Mordechai (Max) (2.1.1) are buried in Vienna. Max Kokisch (2.1.1), my grandfather, married Sima (Hedwig) Leitner (1.1.4) on Lag B'Omer 1903 in Marienbad. Part of the year they lived in the Austrian resort of Bad Gastein, and during the winter they resided initially in Nice and later on in San Remo, both situated on the Riviera, where they ran kosher hotels. The Jewish population of France grew steadily after the Emancipation and it was not until the early 1900s that anti-semitism became a serious issue, after the false spy accusations that were levelled against Mr. Dreyfuss. It is more than likely that this prompted Max Kokisch to move from Nice (in France) to San Remo (in Italy).

Bad Gastein.

HOTEL AND RESTAURANT

MAX KOKISCH.

NEWLY BUILT with EVERY COMFORT in central position of this Spa.

(During the Winter at Nice, Rue Grimaldi, 8.)

Advert that appeared in the Jewish Chronicle 1900. The hotel is in Bad Gastein in summer and in Nice in winter. Both advertised on the same brochure and advert

A SHORT HISTORY OF SAN REMO

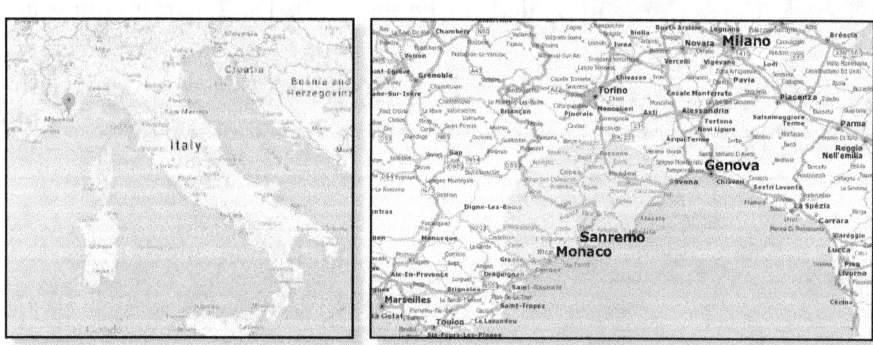

Location of San Remo on the Italian Riviera

From the middle of the 18th century San Remo grew rapidly due to the development of tourism, which saw the first grand hotels built and the town extended along the coast. Many notables vacationed there, amongst them the Empress Sissi of Austria [wife of Emperor Franz Yosef], Empress Maria of Russia, and

Emperor Nicholas II of Russia. The Swedish chemist, Alfred Nobel, made it his permanent home and occupied a luxury villa there.

The International San Remo Conference of April 19–26 April 1920, held not long after the end of World War I, was instrumental in gaining much publicity in the world press for the town with its excellent facilities, which led to an increase in tourism to the city.

San Remo's Mediterranean climate and attractive seacoast on the Italian Riviera made it a popular destination for tourists and European nobility. The city is famous for its production of 'extra virgin' olive oil, and is also known as the 'City of Flowers', another important aspect of its economy. It borders onto Monaco and the French Riviera, with a population of approximately 5000 people living in an area of 1000 square kilometers.

Hotel in San Remo

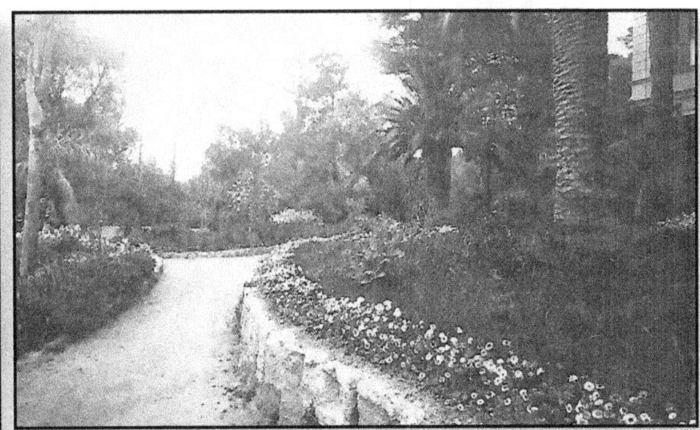

The Hotel in San Remo lined with palm trees

Oma and her sisters attended a non-Jewish school in San Remo. The Kokisch girls received a solid education at home and learnt to be proud of being Jewish. They were strictly forbidden to socialise with their non-Jewish classmates, and were taught to keep to themselves. Despite being younger than her classmates, Oma did very well in school, and her reports confirmed that she was top of the class and never marked late, nor did she ever receive any detention or other punishment work at school. Apart from all the regular subjects that are listed in their school reports there is also one called 'Table Manners'! There was just one note of criticism in the reports of the Kokisch sisters, namely their "lack of social skills by not interacting and playing with other classmates." They naturally followed their parents' instructions who forbade them from playing with the non-Jewish classmates. Going to a non-Jewish school meant also attending on Shabbos, which used to be a regular school day. They had to show up, but would merely sit in class and listen, and then spend all Sunday morning writing up the notes from the previous day.

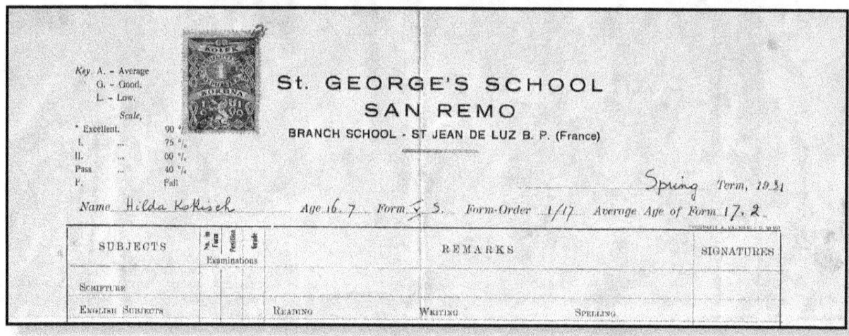

Key. A. - Average
G. - Good.
L. - Low.

Scale,
* Excellent. 90 %
I. ... 75 %
II. ... 60 %
Pass ... 40 %
F. Fail

ST. GEORGE'S SCHOOL
SAN REMO
BRANCH SCHOOL - ST JEAN DE LUZ B. P. (France)

Spring Term, 1931

Name Hilda Kokisch Age 16.7 Form V. S. Form-Order 1/17 Average Age of Form 17.2

SUBJECTS	No. in Form	Position	Grade	REMARKS			SIGNATURES
	Examinations						
Scripture							
English Subjects				Reading	Writing	Spelling	

Oma's School Report Spring 1931

A SHORT HISTORY OF JEWS IN AUSTRIA

Since the 12th century, Jews have had a mixed history in Austria, ranging from prosperity to pogroms and persecution. The Jewish Renaissance began in 1848 when the Jewish population was granted civil rights, partially due to their participation in the 1848 civil war, and were allowed to form their own autonomous religious communities. Unfortunately, Vienna became the centre of the Haskala and the granting of full citizenship in 1867 led to a large influx of Jews from many European countries. The Kokisch family also lived in Austria during this period.

The Jews became predominant in all spheres, and by 1930 half of Austria's doctors and dentists were Jewish as well as over 60% of the lawyers. Because of the freedom that the Jewish people were granted in Vienna, the Jewish population grew from 6200 in 1860 to 40,200 in 1870, and by 1938 it had reached 135,000. This open success gave rise to anti-semitism which, unfortunately, also grew rapidly.

A BRIEF HISTORY OF BAD GASTEIN

The name 'Bad' meaning 'spa', reflects the town's historic health resort. Thanks to the special qualities of the waters of Bad Gastein, it became a fashionable resort in the 19th century, and was visited by European Monarchs as well as the affluent members of the population. This spa town lies in the Austrian state of Salzburg and is most famous for the Gastein Waterfall, which is part of the well known Tauern National Park, covering an area of over 1800 square kilometres and enjoys most stunning natural beauty. Bad Gastein, 1083 metres above sea level, is situated about 100km from Salzburg. It has a total of 18 natural springs that provide 5 million litres of water at 45 degrees centigrade per day. The population numbers approximately 4000 people and occupies an area of 170 square kilometres. The accessibility and popularity of Bad Gastein was enhanced by the completion of the Tauern Railways in 1909 that transverses the Austrian Alps, and provides frequent connections to Vienna, Linz and Salzburg. [Vienna is about 4 hours by train and Marienbad 5 hours from Bad Gastein]. It was Marie Curie who discovered that these spa waters contained radon, a radio active element, which resulted in 'radon therapy' that began in the town, as a cure for arthritis.

Being situated at over 1000 metres above sea level, the town soon became popular for its winter sports and alpine skiing.

The Gastein waterfall 1083 m above sea level

General view of Bad Gastein

Oma was always grateful at the special Hashgocho in having learnt in school that Bad Gastein was 1083 metres above sea level. This same number later became her phone number at 13 Hanover Gardens, namely BROughton 1083!

My grandfather, Max (מרדכי) Kokisch, was a professional Hotelier. He found a piece of land near the Gastein Waterfall which appealed to him as an ideal spot on which to build a kosher hotel. There were stunning views of the waterfall and the entire mountainous surroundings. He consequently had an architect draw up plans which were submitted as a Planning Application to the local Council in Salzburg. Bad Gastein was slowly developing into a holiday and therapeutic resort, and this would be the ideal place for Jewish holiday makers to enjoy the kosher facilities. The Planning Application was refused, and the Council was not even ashamed to state the reasons for their refusal. It was plain and simple. 'The Application is refused as we do not want Jewish property owners in the town centre'.

Max Kokisch was naturally very upset, but there was little he could do to change their decision. We always believe גם זו לטובה – everything is for the best, and this disappointment was to be for their ultimate benefit. He thus learnt his lesson, and saw how welcome he really was in Bad Gastein in particular, and by the Austrians in general. He subsequently instructed his family to always be in possession of a foreign passport irrespective of the country they would reside in, to facilitate any eventual escape, should the need arise, and thus they all obtained Polish passports.

In the meantime he continued to look for another piece of land and ב"ה soon found one on the outskirts of the town, just opposite the entrance to the National Nature Reserve, on a busy crossroad. It also enjoyed fabulous views, although maybe not as stunning as the previous site. He submitted a new planning application which was approved, and then set about building 'Hotel Bristol', a 50 bedroom kosher hotel that was completed in 1907. There were no other resident Jewish families living in Bad Gastein, and my grandfather relied on the holiday makers for a Minyan, which was never a problem. As the hotel brochure shows, it was an elegant and strictly kosher hotel, and offered in-house therapeutic baths and plenty of grounds for walks, a sure combination for a relaxing holiday. Although Bad Gastein also developed into a winter resort, which offered winter sports facilities and included some of Europes longest ski slopes on these Austrian Alps, my grandfather's hotel was not open during the winter months.

Hotel Bristol belonged to the 'Association of Jewish Hoteliers and Restaurants', who published a pocket 'Luach' that could be personalised for each hotel, to be distributed to their patrons. This was a very useful and comprehensive booklet, and provided a lot of essential information, as these sample pages, taken from the 1929 calendar, demonstrate:

Eintritt der Nacht am Ausgang der Sabbate, Fest- u. Fasttage im Jahre 5690
Beginn am vorhergehenden Abend: im Winter etwa 1 Std., im Sommer etwa 1½ Std. früher.

Datum 1929	Sabbat Fest- und Fasttage	Berlin	Breslau	Hamburg	Köln a. Rh.	Königsberg i. P.	Leipzig	München	Budapest	Prag	Wien
5.10.	א' דר"ה	6,16	6, 2	6,31	6,42	5,49	6,20	6,24	5,54	6,11	6, 5
6.10.	ב' דר"ה	6,14	6,—	6,28	6,40	5,46	6,18	6,22	5,52	6, 9	6, 3
7.10.	צום גדליה	6,12	5,58	6,26	6,38	5,44	6,16	6,20	5,50	6, 7	6, 1
12.10.	האזינו	6,—	5,49	6,13	6,29	5,32	6, 5	6,10	5,40	5,57	5,51
14.10.	יום כפור	5,55	5,43	6, 9	6,23	5,27	6, 1	6, 6	5,36	5,53	5,47
19.10.	א' דסכות	5,45	5,33	6,—	6,13	5,16	5,51	5,57	5,27	5,43	5,38
20.10.	ב' דסכות	5,43	5,31	5,58	6,11	5,14	5,49	5,55	5,25	5,41	5,36
26.10.	שמיני עצרת	5,32	5,20	5,45	6,—	5, 1	5,38	5,46	5,16	5,31	5,27
27.10.	שמחת תורה	5,30	5,18	5,43	5,58	4,59	5,36	5,44	5,14	5,29	5,25
2.11.	בראשית	5,19	5, 8	5,31	5,48	4,47	5,26	5,35	5, 5	5,19	5,16
9.11.	נח	5, 8	4,58	5,19	5,38	4,35	5,15	5,26	4,58	5,10	5, 7
16.11.	לך לך	4,58	4,50	5, 9	5,30	4,24	5, 6	5,17	4,48	5, 1	4,58
23.11.	וירא	4,51	4,40	5, 2	5,20	4,16	4,58	5,10	4,43	4,54	4,51

28

The times of begining and end of Shabbos and Yom Tov in various European cities

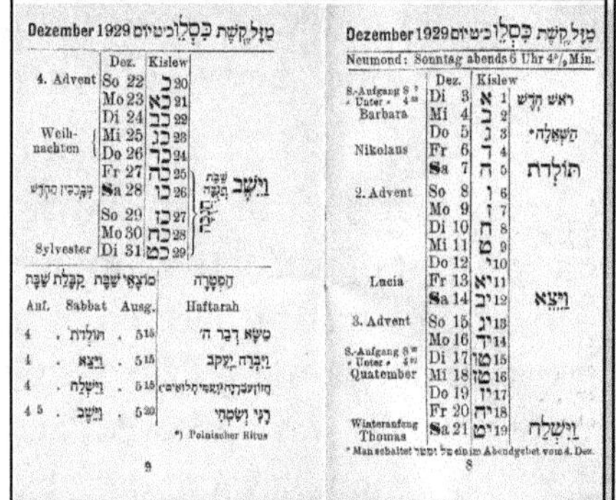
Dezember 1929 מזל קשת כסלו כ"ט תש"ץ

Hebrew/English calendar with weekly Sedra and Haftorah

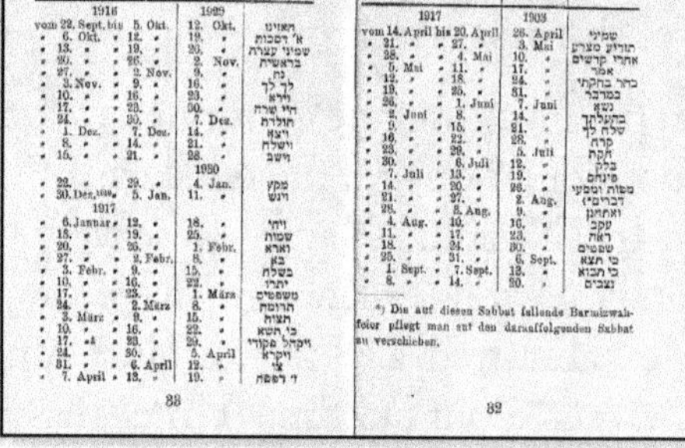
Barmizwah-Tabelle

für die Knaben, die zwischen dem 22. Sept. 1916 und 14. Sept. 1917 geboren wurden.

Barmitzvah calendar for boys born in 1916/17

During the winter my grandparents would move to a different location and continue managing a kosher hotel there. Initially they lived in Nice at 8 Rue Grimaldi, just five minutes from the promenade, and later moved to San Remo, which also lies on the same coast line, on the Italian Riviera, where they ran the kosher hotel until 1931.

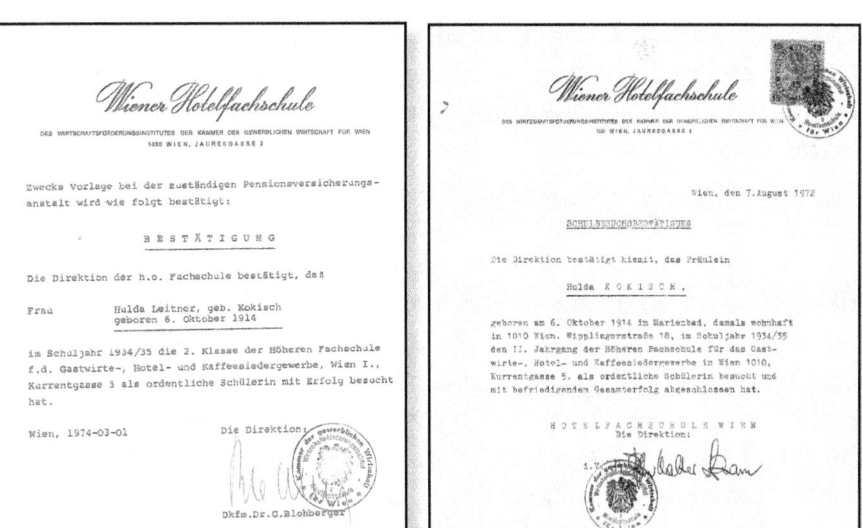

Wiener Hotelfachschule

DES WIRTSCHAFTSFÖRDERUNGSINSTITUTES DER KAMMER DER GEWERBLICHEN WIRTSCHAFT FÜR WIEN
1030 WIEN, JAURESGASSE 3

Zwecks Vorlage bei der zuständigen Pensionsversicherungsanstalt wird wie folgt bestätigt:

B E S T Ä T I G U N G

Die Direktion der h.o. Fachschule bestätigt, daß

Frau Hulda Leitner, geb. Kokisch
geboren 6. Oktober 1914

im Schuljahr 1934/35 die 2. Klasse der Höheren Fachschule f.d. Gastwirte-, Hotel- und Kaffeesiedergewerbe, Wien I., Kurrentgasse 5 als ordentliche Schülerin mit Erfolg besucht hat.

Wien, 1974-03-01

Die Direktion:

Dkfm.Dr.G.Blohberger

Wiener Hotelfachschule

DES WIRTSCHAFTSFÖRDERUNGSINSTITUTES DER KAMMER DER GEWERBLICHEN WIRTSCHAFT FÜR WIEN
1030 WIEN, JAURESGASSE 3

Wien, den 7.August 1972

SCHULBESUCHSBESTÄTIGUNG

Die Direktion bestätigt hiemit, das Fräulein

Hulda K O K I S C H ,

geboren am 6. Oktober 1914 in Marienbad, damals wohnhaft in 1010 Wien. Wipplingerstraße 18, im Schuljahr 1934/35 den II. Jahrgang der Höheren Fachschule für das Gastwirte-, Hotel- und Kaffeesiedergewerbe in Wien 1010, Kurrentgasse 5. als ordentliche Schülerin besucht und mit befriedigendem Gesamterfolg abgeschlossen hat.

H O T E L F A C H S C H U L E W I E N
Die Direktion:

Certificates to confirm Oma's completion of The Hotel School in 1934/5,

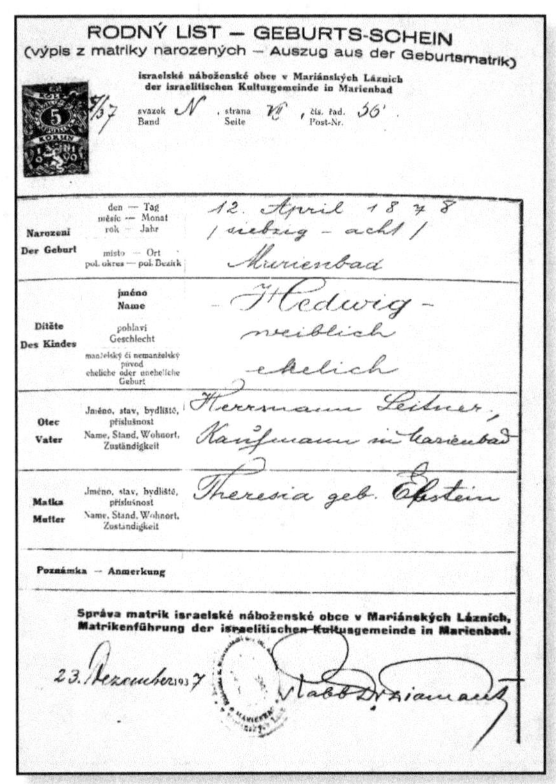

RODNÝ LIST – GEBURTS-SCHEIN
(výpis z matriky narozených – Auszug aus der Geburtsmatrik)
israelské náboženské obce v Mariánských Lázních
der israelitischen Kultusgemeinde in Marienbad

7/37 svazek Band N , strana Seite VII , čís. řad. Post-Nr. 56.

Narození / Der Geburt	den — Tag, měsíc — Monat, rok — Jahr	12. April 1878 / siebzig – acht /
	místo — Ort, pol. okres — pol. Bezirk	Marienbad
Dítěte / Des Kindes	jméno / Name	Hedwig
	pohlaví / Geschlecht	weiblich
	manželský či nemanželský původ / eheliche oder uneheliche Geburt	ehelich
Otec / Vater	Jméno, stav, bydliště, příslušnost / Name, Stand, Wohnort, Zuständigkeit	Herrmann Leitner, Kaufmann in Marienbad
Matka / Mutter	Jméno, stav, bydliště, příslušnost / Name, Stand, Wohnort, Zuständigkeit	Theresia geb. Epstein
Poznámka – Anmerkung		

Správa matrik israelské náboženské obce v Mariánských Lázních,
Matrikenführung der israelitischen Kultusgemeinde in Marienbad.

23. Dezember 1937

Rabb. Dr. Diamant

Birth Certificate of Hedwig (Sima) Kokisch' (1.1.4) April 12, 1878

Oma and her sisters also attended a non-Jewish Primary school in Bad Gastein and each day they would take their packed lunches for dinner. Aunty Reisel, Oma's older sister, noticed that Peter, one of her classmates, always just stood in a corner of the dining room while everybody else was enjoying their lunch. This was a daily occurrence, a fact that puzzled her, and she took the courage to ask him for an explanation, but Peter was reluctant and just too embarrassed to reply. After questioning him several times, Peter admitted that his father worked hard all week and received his wage packet on a Thursday evening. However, on his way home, he passed the local pub, and before he arrived home that evening, a large portion of his weekly wage had been spent. Hence his family had insufficient money to provide their children with a daily lunch, and he went hungry. Reisel took pity on him and very kindly shared her own lunch with him. When she came home after school, her mother noticed that she was unusually hungry. Reisel explained what had transpired, and from then on her mother gave her permission to take two daily lunch packets to school, so that she could discreetly provide one to that unfortunate boy. Peter was extremely grateful for this act of kindness, which continued throughout their school years.

It is remarkable that it was a Kokisch girl, about whom the school report had complained that they 'lacked social skills and care' that showed so much compassion for a non-Jewish classmate, unlike any other of Peter's twenty non-Jewish friends!

Hotel Bristol - BAD GASTEIN KOSHER HOTEL

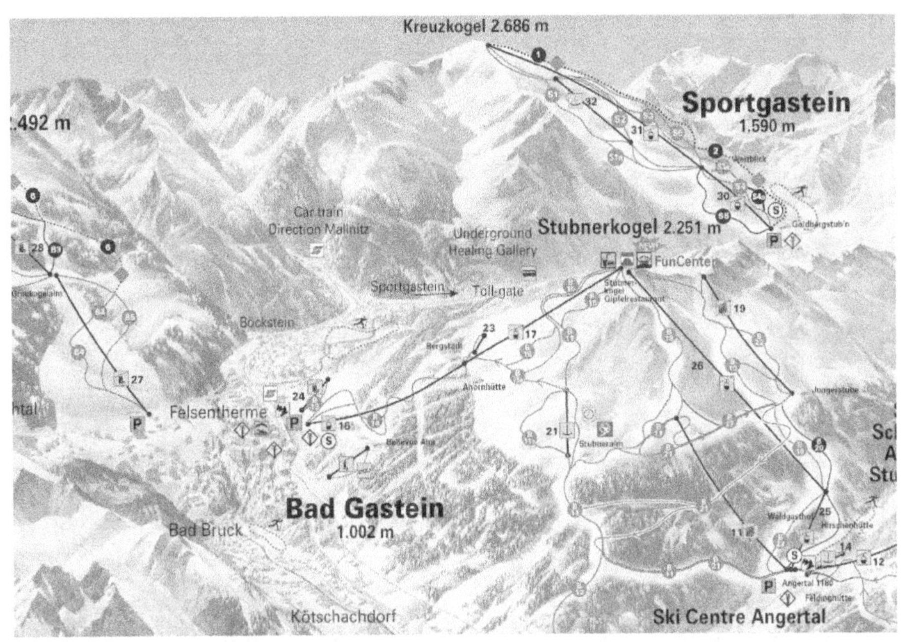

Ideal for Winter Sport in Bad Gastein Region

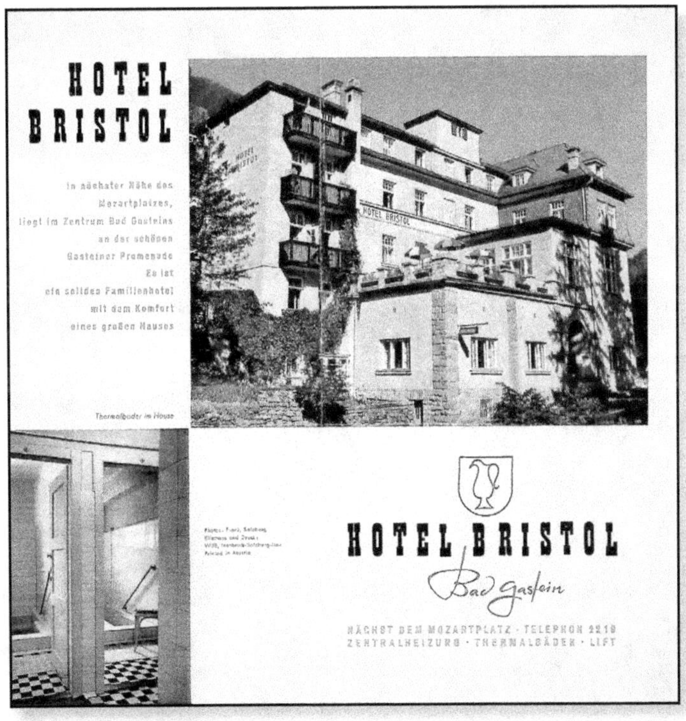

The Hotel Brochure showing the In-House thermal baths, Bad Gastein

BAD GASTEIN liegt 1080 Meter über dem Meere und ist dank seiner Thermalbäder, der reinen Bergluft und seines weltberühmten gesunden Klimas ein Ferienort, der wirklich neue Kräfte schenkt.
Seine schönen Spazier- und Wanderwege, die Lifts auf die Berge erschließen die Schönheit der hochalpinen Landschaft bis auf 2500 m.
Bad Gastein verfügt über alle Sommer- und Wintersportanlagen.

Die schöne, große Halle ist unseren Gästen reserviert, während die herrlich gelegene Terrasse alle Bequemlichkeiten der Erholung bietet

Alle Zimmer sind wohnlich eingerichter und haben fließendes kaltes und warmes Wasser

Part of the hotel brochure, Bad Gastein

The hotel lounge, Bad Gastein

The hotel dining room, Bad Gastein

Max (Mordechai) Kokisch was Niftar suddenly in his sleep in 1930, and soon after my grandmother sold the hotel in San Remo, whereupon the family continued to operate only the hotel in Bad Gastein during the summer. During the winter they would rent a flat in Vienna, where they became acquainted with Rabbi Yosef Baumgarten of the Schiffshul. They enjoyed the Jewish life there and made new friends, something that they had sorely missed in Bad Gastein, San Remo and Nice.

In 1931, at the stone setting for מרדכי Kokisch in Vienna, he was eulogised by Reb Yonas Rosenfarb. This 'Hesped' is a living testimony of the integrity and sincerity of my grandfather, and grants us a glimpse into his life:

(translated from German:)

> 'Chazal say: Avrohom composed Tefilas Shacharis, Yitzchok Tefilas Mincha, and Yaakov Tefilas Arvis /Maariv.
>
> Avrohom's life was like Shacharis, a morning, material and spiritual awakening and rising up. Everything was a beginning for him. Avrohom, the son of Terach, an idol worshipper, was the first who recognised Hashem. He left his father's house, and climbed step by step to honour and riches. He never relied on his

own strength and wisdom, but put all his hope onto Hashem, and his Tefiloh was therefore a Shacharis, the Tefiloh for the morning.

Yitzchok's life was filled with happiness and well-being from the beginning. He inherited everything from his father; his name, riches and honour. He associated with princes and kings, for him the sun shone at midday. He was not proud, did not boast about his success, he always relied on Hashem, his Tefiloh was therefore a Tefilas Mincha, a Tefiloh said in the afternoon.

Yaakov's life was 'Evening', shrouded in darkness, a chain of suffering, even before his birth he had to fight with Esav. But he did not dispair and never lost hope, but relied solely on Hashem. His Tefiloh was therefore Tefilas Arvis, a Tefiloh for the evening.

Dovid Hamelech said in Tehilim: 'Kos Yeshuos Eso u'veshem Hashem Ekro', also by suffering and sorrow I call on Hashem's Name. We say the Brocho of Shehecheyonu by good tidings, and likewise by ח"ו bad tidings 'Boruch Dayan Ho'emes'. Everything is Hashem's will, and we have to accept it.

We can say the same about the niftor, Reb Mordechai Kokisch. I knew him for several years. He was a true Yerei Shomayim. He experienced several phases during his life, morning, midday and evening, but always remained a 'Maamin' and 'Baal Bitochon', he always trusted in Hashem. He was humble and his whole growth was that of Shacharis and Mincha. He did not know pride, did not become conceited because of his wisdom or enterprises. He always attributed his successes to Hashem. Also when he experienced times of 'Arvis' he never despaired or lost hope, he always relied and trusted in Hashem.

There are people who at first sight create a favourable impression, but after some time show their true colours. But an honest person who is straight in every aspect, gains the respect and love of others. The more time that one spends in the company of such a person the more one is convinced of his sincere character, and the niftar would fit this description. He was called Mordechai.

מרדכי is referred to in Megillas Esther as 'איש יהודי', a person and a Yehudi in the fullest sense.

The term איש, when referring to the deceased Reb Mordechai Kokisch, best describes the impeccable good nature of this man in his inter–personal relationships with other people. He was also well liked and respected in non-Jewish circles. As a יהודי he was pious and a ירא שמים (G-d-fearing), and respected Rabbonim and Talmidei Chachomim. Whenever he had spare time he quenched his thirst with learning Torah. In San Remo we had the opportuntiy to frequently sit together and learn, and I admired his joy when we discussed Torah.

Chazal teach that a man's character can be recognised by three things and one of them is 'Bekiso', with his purse. Reb Mordechai Kokisch could be termed a real Baal Tzedoko. Whoever approached him for a donation would not go away empty handed. He gave 'Besever Ponim Jofes', with a friendly countenance, since giving Tzedoko with a smile is of much greater value.

We have come together here to put up the Matzeivo. It has 2 purposes, one is for the benefit of the niftar that one should not forget him, and one for the family left behind. In this case we honour the Niftar, because we do not need the Matzeivo to remind us of the Niftar, as he will remain with us as unforgettable, he lives on in all our hearts. Like the Chachomim say, 'Tzadikim bemisom keruyim chayim'. Pious Yidden are seen as alive after their death. Chazal say further 'Yaakov Ovinu lo mes', just as his children lived, he lived as well. When a person leaves frum yiddishe children he lives forever, because they continue his life's work and are following in his path. Reb Mordechai did not die, he lives in a much better world and has nachas, because he did not live in vain. He left behind children that Jewish parents can be proud of, children who are Yerei Shomayim, are Maaminim and have good character traits.

Yaakov Ovinu had twelve sons. They were all Tzadikim, but only Yosef merited to be called "Yosef HaTzadik". All the others lived near their illustrious father and were not tempted to do anything but keeping Torah and Mitzvos. It was therefore easier for them to reach the status of Tzadikim, unlike Yosef, who was many years in a strange country among idol worshippers, far from Torah and

> a moral way of life. But he did not become influenced and remained firm and loyal to Torah and Hashem'.
>
> Reb Kokisch's children spent years in places where there were no Yidden, and did not become influenced from their foreign surroundings. Such children are a credit to the house of Yaakov. This is how Shlomo Hamelech described (Shir Hashirim) 'Keshoshano bein hachochim, like a rose amongst thorns, ken raayosi bein habonos', likening to you, a Yiddishe daughter.
>
> Your late father should be a Melitz Yosher for your choshuva, pious mother, for the children, for your houses. You should not know of further sorrow, there should be happiness and joy in your house. May the time come soon of והשיב לב-אבות על-בנים ולב בנים על-אבותם פן-אבוא והכיתי את-הארץ חרם. Omen

Sima Kokisch continued to run Hotel Bristol on her own, but they soon began to feel the rapid rise in anti-Semitism in Europe which was a great cause of concern.

For example, the Jewish Telegraphic Agency reported on October 7, 1932:

> The District Court today lifted the ban against the appearance of the Gazetta Warswaska, the organ of the anti-Semitic National Democratic Party (Nazi Party) which had previously been banned by the Government in Poland.

On October 9, 1932, just two days later, it was reported in the press:

"The Walls of Bad Gastein, the famous Austrian resort, were plastered with anti-Semitic posters and the inscription 'Judaea Verecke! Judaea Perish!' stared all visitors in the face, declared Mr. Morrison, a prominent Zionist communal worker. Prompt action, however, was taken by the liberal minded leaders of the Bad Gastein community, and the realisation in particular, that Jewish visitors would leave the resort, led to the prompt removal of the objectionable posters. The view was expressed that the present phase of anti-Semitic movement in Central Europe, 'is more menacing than ever before.'

The Jewish population of Austria clearly saw 'the writing on the wall,' and tried to secure visas to any country possible. The Kokisch family at this time included Sima and her four daughters, all possessing Polish passports, as Max Kokisch had advised, and they too frantically tried to obtain the required visas to enter a foreign 'friendly' country. They left no stone unturned, but all attempts appeared futile, as they were not alone in their search to obtain entry visas, and there were only limited immigration quotas available.

ERNST LEITNER (1.1.5)

Before we can continue with this narrative we have to sidestep and focus on Ernst Leitner, who was Hashem's Shliach in providing assistance that enabled Oma and her mother and sisters to escape and reach Santiago de Chile.

Ernst Leitner (Yaakov), a son of Herman (1.1) (צבי) Leitner, and brother of Moishe Dovid (1.1.1) and Sima Kokisch-Leitner (1.1.4), was born on January 19, 1880. He deserves a special mention because of his connections and assistance that he provided for the entire family. He lived in Berlin and unfortunately remained a bachelor, but kept excellent contacts with every member of the family.

In March 1938 Austria was annexed by Nazi Germany in the 'Anschluss', and by May 1938 Jews had lost nearly all of their civil liberties and rights. Those with foreign passports were allowed to emigrate if they were fortunate enough to find a country that would accept them. Approximately 130,000 Jews were fortunate to leave Austria, but those who possessed Austrian citizenships found it impossible to leave the country. The only solution at that time was if they could get a visa that would allow them to enter and settle in a foreign country, which was an almost impossible task, as nearly every country had imposed strict quotas for issuing visas to foreign nationals.

Jewish Telegraphic Agency reports Thursday July 27, 1939 from a report received on the previous day from London:

At least 70,000 Jews, representing half of the population of Bohemia and Moravia, must emigrate from the "Protectorate" within a year, as ordered by the Gestapo. Hundreds of Jews lined up yesterday outside the Maisel Street Shul in Prague to apply for emigration permits.

Police in Pilsen ordered the display of signs 'Jewish Enterprise' in the German and Czech languages in all Jewish shops. Spas and other health resorts in the 'Protectorate and in Sudetenland' are facing economic ruin, whilst the Marienbad spa management applied for the second time to the Nazi district leader for modification of the regulations regarding Jewish visitors.

On July 26, 1939, 1000 Jews from Vienna left for Italy where they planned to stay only long enough to obtain permission to enter the USA, Britain or any other country. Every emigrant had to deposit upto $50 each in an Italian bank for their future living expenses, money that was collected by various Jewish charities abroad. Despite Italy's official anti-Semitic policy, the group was guaranteed to be well received as their financial deposits would help replace the empty coffers caused by the collapse of that year's tourist trade.

Shmuel Kokisch died at the young age of 48, on Feb 20, 1882, when Max Kokisch was only 9 years old. Max had an older brother, who was 15 years old at the time of his father's death, and decided to leave home. He lost all contact with the rest of the family and unfortunately with Yiddishkeit too. Today, we don't even have a record of his first name and refer to him simply as 'Bechor Kokisch'.

Nobody even knew where he lived apart from Uncle Ernst in Berlin, who kept an informal contact with him. Early in 1938 Sima wrote to her brother in Berlin to enquire of "Bechor's" whereabouts, in the hope that he might be able to procure visas for them, wherever he was. Uncle Ernst replied that all he knew was that he had moved to Santiago de Chile some time ago, but did not know his address, since he hadn't had any correspondence from him for a number of years. Sima, in desperation, wrote a letter to this brother-in-law in Santiago, and described the very serious situation and grim outlook in Europe. She asked him if there was a possibility of obtaining five visas to enable them to come to Chile, for herself and her four daughters. Despite not knowing his address she nevertheless put her trust in Hashem and addressed the letter to:

Mr. Kokisch,

Santiago de Chile.

Although this was a very incomplete address, the letter ב"ה eventually arrived at the correct destination after some delay!

A reply was sent from Family Kokisch in Chile on June 21, 1938, in which they wrote that their father ['Bechor Kokisch'] was unfortunately not alive anymore as he had died in 1923, but shortly before his death he disclosed to his wife and children, 'You should know that I am Jewish and I have family living in Europe. I ask of you, as my last wish, that should they ever request some help from you, to please do everything possible to assist them. He then explained that his Jewish family have different laws and customs; they will only use their own dishes and will also not eat from our food. Do not take any of this unaccustomed behaviour personally, it is simply part of their religion.' His family confirmed that they would carry out his wish, and shortly afterwards he passed away. The wife of Bechor Kokisch died on March 21, 1939, just shortly before Sima Kokisch and her daughters arrived in Santiago.

When they received my grandmother's letter fifteen years after their father had died, they immediately went into action to secure the necessary visas to enter Santiago. A letter dated October 19, 1938 from the Chilean Consulate in Santiago, confirmed that applications had been received for their entry visas, and the relevant visas would be granted to them at the Chilean Embassy in Vienna, whom they should contact. The Kokisch family in Chile also wrote that they would be welcome to stay with them at their home in Santiago and added, 'We are not wealthy, but whatever we possess we will gladly share with you'. What more could they expect?

Of course they signed off with their full address:

Doktor Humberto Kokisch
Gran Avenida 2594
Santiago
Chile (Sud América).

Doktor Humberto Kokisch,
Gran Avenida 2594,
Santiago de Chile. (South America)

As soon as they had received the good news that visas were available for them, they sent their passports to the Jewish Community in Salzburg, where they were registered, who forwarded them with the relevant documents to the authorities in Vienna. The situation for all Jewish people was bleak and was getting worse by the day. Family Kokisch now felt trapped in Bad Gastein, since they didn't even have their passport with them. They enquired repeatedly from the Jewish Community in Salzburg about their papers and documents, and on November 6, 1938, [just 3 days before 'Kristallnacht'] finally received the following information:

Israelitische Kultusgemeinde
Salzburg
Lasserstraße 8, Telephon 1073/8

Salzburg, 6. NOVEMBER 1938

Zahl: 326/938

LIEBWERTE FAMILIE KOKISCH !

BETREFF: KORRESPONDENZ.

Nochmals wiederhole ich den Bescheid, den mir hier der betreffende REFERENT bezüglich Ihrer Pässe gegeben:„Die Pässe sind von hier an die POLIZEI - DIREKTION WIEN, ABTEILUNG für Ausländer geschickt worden"

Meines Erachtens wollen Sie bei der POLIZEI-DIREKTION WIEN I. Schottenring gefl. diesbezüglich anfragen. Wiederum füge ich hier die für Sie bei mir eingelangte Korrespondenz bei.

Indem ich Ihnen glückhaften Erfolg unter Gottes gnädigem Beistand bei allen Bemühungen u. Besrebungen wünsche, verbleibe ich mit herzlichen Grüssen meinerseits und seitens meiner Lieben

zu weiteren Hilfsdiensten stets bereit

7 BEILAGEN

PS: Bitte um Empfangsbestätigung.

This transcribes:

Israelitische Kultusgemeinde
Salzburg
Lasserstrasse 8, Tel 1073/8

Salzburg
November 6, 1938

Number 326/938
Re Correspondence.

Dear Family Kokisch, נ"י

Again I repeat the information that was given to me by the Official in respect to your passports. The passports were sent from here to the Police Department's Foreign Office in Vienna.
I think you should ask for them at the Police Department Vienna 1, Schottenring.
I enclose again all the correspondence for you which was sent to me.
With my sincere wishes that 'ה Loving Kindness bless you with happiness and success in all your undertakings and efforts.
I remain with best wishes from me and my dear ones, and will gladly help if you need anything else.

Dr. D.S. Margulies,
Rabbi for the City and County of Salzburg.

7 enclosures
P.S. Please confirm receipt thereof.

The general situation for the Austrian Jews was desperate and much relief was arranged at the Schiffshul. This soon became the central meeting point for obtaining help, spearheaded by Mr. Julius Steinfeld, who later worked closely with Rabbi Dr. Schonfeld in London in organising his 'Kindertransports'.

On the Friday night of November 9, 1938, unprecedented violence erupted that was targeted against Jews and their property in Germany and Austria, which appears to have been set off by Germany's anger at the assassination of a German Official in Paris by a Jewish teenager. In the space of just two days, many hundreds of Shuls were burnt down, over 7000 Jewish businesses were looted, Jewish cemeteries vandalised, and schools and homes were destroyed while the local police and fire service simply stood by and watched. This Friday night became known universally as 'Kristallnacht,' [the 'Night of the Broken Glass,] to commemorate the shattered glass that littered the streets. The morning after the pogrom, some 30,000 German Jews were arrested for the simple 'crime' of being Jewish and sent to concentration camps. Nobody was safe.

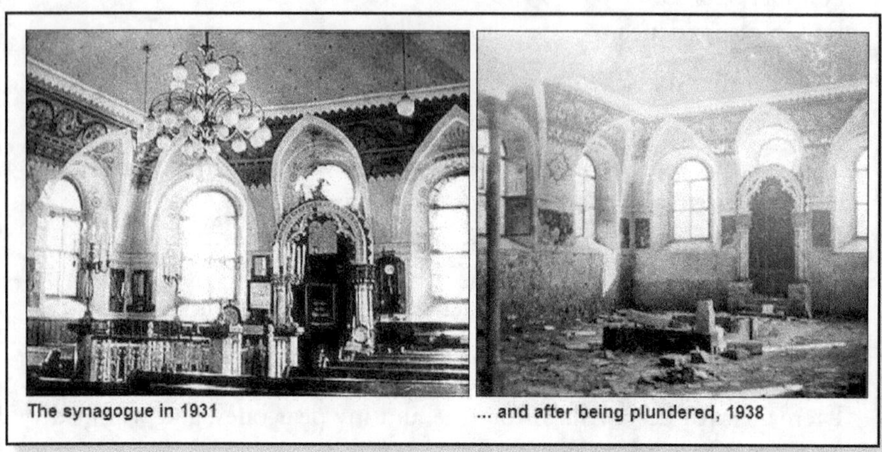
The synagogue in 1931 ... and after being plundered, 1938

The effect of Kristallnacht on a typical Shul

November 10, 1938 was a Shabbos, and as Sima and her four daughters sat around the Shabbos table enjoying their Shabbos meal in Hotel Bristol, they heard the dreaded sound of loud knocking on the front door. The winter season had already begun and there were no guests at the hotel. Two armed uniformed Gestapo stormed in, and with rifles at the ready, one of them screamed, 'Pack your belongings! We are fetching you in an hour.' This was their usual practice, a command to trick the Jews into taking their valuables with them, making it easier for the Germans to confiscate them later, without having to search the entire house.

Sima, however, had the presence of mind to rise gracefully from her chair and calmly exclaim:

'I am sorry, but today is Shabbos and we cannot travel. Come back tomorrow.'

The German officer was fuming. What a nerve! How dare this Jewish lady answer back! He went red in the face, turned around, and together with his colleague stormed out of the hotel, making sure to slam the door behind them. When they arrived back at the police headquarters the sergeant in charge noticed their angry looks and demanded an explanation. They told him about this cheeky Jewess who had dared to answer back; such audacity was previously unheard off; she had made it clear that they refused to travel on Shabbos.

The inquisitive sergeant then enquired, 'Who was this woman that made you so angry?' The reply was soon in coming, 'Family Kokisch of Hotel Bristol', to which the sergeant simply replied, 'Leave them alone today, and fetch them tomorrow', much to the surprise of the two Gestapo policemen.

The sergeant in charge was none other than Peter, that very same school boy who years earlier had enjoyed his daily lunches, with compliments of the Kokisch family of Hotel Bristol. Hence his command to 'leave them alone'; this was a small reward for the exceptional kindness that he had received from them. What Hashgocho Protis!!

However, Sima Kokisch could not know if the Gestapo would actually return within the hour as they had promised, so she called the resident non-Jewish caretaker and instructed him to take a large laundry wicker basket and line it with tablecloths, and place the hotel's Sefer Torah, all the Chumashim, Siddurim, the Poroches and all the Shul's valuables into it. She also instructed him to remove the Mezuzahs from all the doorposts in the hotel, and fill the remaining space with their silver cutlery, candlesticks, and other valuables and essential possessions. He was then to seal the basket and transport it to a warehouse in a different section of the town.

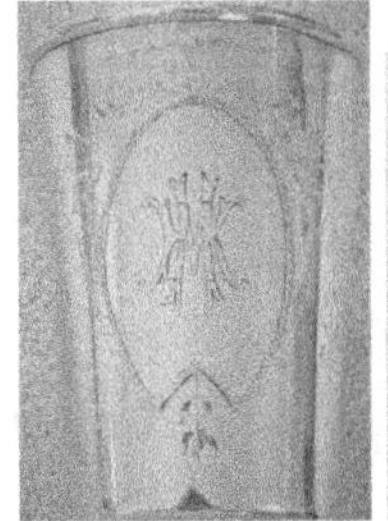

Max Kokisch's (MK) personalized Kiddush Becher, Besomim holder and Havdoloh Plate that originated from Hofmann in Frankfurt

When this was completed, they continued their Shabbos meal, and were pleased that there were no further disturbances that Shabbos. In the meantime, if they were to come back, they would find nothing of value left at the hotel. The Gestapo did, however, return on the following day with plans to transport them to the station, en route to the concentration camps. On arrival at the station, the Gestapo soon realised that they had just missed the last connecting train.

Hotel Bristol was situated on the towns' outskirts and travel to the station took longer than if they would have lived in the city centre. Now Sima realised the special Hashgocho Protis of not being granted their original planning application to build a hotel in the city centre, which would have been close to the train station, and would have resulted in their instant deportation!

Looking back at this remarkable turn of events we can conclude: The Kokisch family were saved thanks to their kindness in saving Peter from going hungry, and bringing him sandwiches every day. This is just as שלמה המלך writes: "שלח לחמך על פני המים כי ברב הימים תמצאנו" (קהלת יא:א)- "Send your bread upon the waters, for after many days you will find it. That was the direct result of their חסד".

Seeing that they had "missed the train", the Gestapo then took the Kokisch family to the police station, where they were kept overnight in a police cell. They had taken the only valid papers that they possessed, which were a letter from Santiago, confirming that the visas were available at the Chilean Embassy in Vienna, and their confirmation letter of November 6, received from the Rabbinate in Salzburg, that proved that their passports had been sent to Vienna. Early on Monday morning, Peter, the Officer in charge, confirmed with Vienna that their visas to enter Chile were valid, and released them from prison, instructing them to travel immediately to Vienna to pick up their passports and visas. Once they reached Vienna they still had to wait for over a month until eventually they were in possession of their valid passports and visas!

From Vienna they travelled together to Strasbourg (France), but Reisel went to Switzerland to benefit from the pure air, since she suffered from a chronic attack of bronchitis. Their Chilean visas were only valid for twelve months, so they were eager to finalise their travel arrangements as soon as possible. Furthermore, the general situation in Europe was very tense, with daily reports of anti-semitic incidents, which pushed them even more to leave as soon as possible. From France they travelled to Holland, taking with them the large laundry baskets with their most valuables possessions.

Oma often described the generosity of the Dutch Yidden who had been extremely helpful in arranging all the necessary travel documents and procuring sufficient kosher food for their 13000km journey to Santiago, which included large quantities of hard cheese and salami that would keep reasonably well without a fridge. They had planned to take a ship that was to arrive in Valparaiso on March 24 1939, eleven days before Pesach. Reisel remained in Switzerland for a while, and then had to pick up her visa at the Chilean Consulate in Paris. She travelled only some time later on, by herself, and arrived in Santiago on June 8, 1939.

The Polish passport with the Chilean Visa, issued in Vienna

As Hashgocho Protis would have it, there was a Professor on board the cargo ship to Chile who gave them some lessons in Spanish, so that when they arrived they knew some elementary Spanish, the language spoken in Chile, and were not completely at a loss in their new surroundings. Incidentally, Aunty Berty had actually taught herself some Spanish during their stay in Vienna. The ship had to make an unscheduled stop in Panama City, after one of the Jewish passengers had died en route, and they were all given permission to attend the funeral at the Jewish cemetery.

It is interesting to point out that soon after the war, and without any lengthy legal restitution and compensation procedures, the Kokisch family got their property back in Bad Gastein, after which they appointed a manager who ran the hotel, until it was eventually sold in 1980. Uncle Alex, the younger brother of Max Kokisch, as early as 1948, travelled to Salzburg, and was actively involved in the restitution claim, and one year later they got the property back, as well as compensation for loss of income for the intervening years!

Looking back, the Kokisch family did not lose out, having shown true Mesiras Nefesh for keeping Shabbos (**'I am sorry, but today is Shabbos and we cannot travel. Come back tomorrow').** They took their valuables with them to Chile, and their property they got back soon after the war. In 1948, Uncle Alex (2.1.2) wrote to Sima Kokisch in Chile, (his sister-in-law), that he had made a thorough inventory of all the hotel property, and apart from a few blankets that were missing, everything else was intact. All the furniture was in perfect order; all the hotel linen, kitchen utensils and machines etc. were all there. Hence their entire possessions were left intact, in the merit of their Mesiras Nefesh for Shabbos. What a powerful lesson for life!

The Kokisch family in Chile were waiting for my grandmother and family at the port in Valparaiso on their arrival on March 24, 1939, just 11 days before Pesach, and took them to their flat in Santiago, where they kindly allocated them one large room for them to share. Their laundry basket that had accompanied them from Bad Gastein doubled up as their table and cupboard, whilst this single room was to be their temporary bedroom and dining room combined. It was only a small flat, and they were given the largest room!

When they arrived they found a postcard waiting for them, which had been sent by a relative from Germany by the name of 'Epstein', wishing them all the best for the future in their new location. [The wife of Herman Leitner (1.1) was a nee Epstein.]

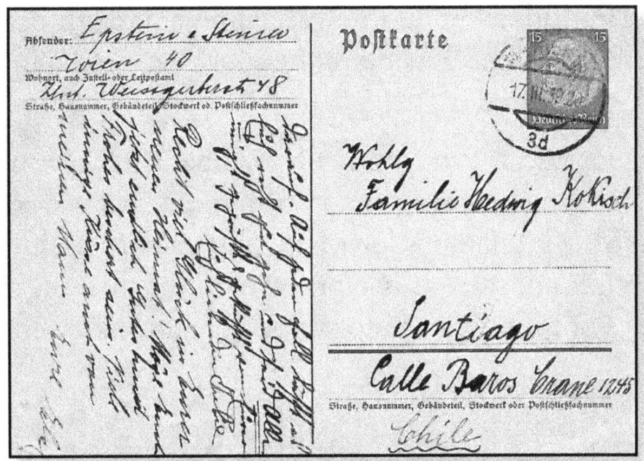
Absender: Epstein e Steiner
Wohnort, auch Zustell- oder Leitpostamt
Straße, Hausnummer, Gebäudeteil, Stockwerk od. Postschließfachnummer
Postkarte
Wohlg.
Familie Hedwig Kokisch
Santiago
Calle Baros Arane 1245
Straße, Hausnummer, Gebäudeteil, Stockwerk oder Postschließfachnummer
Chile

Sent on March 17, 1939 to Chile

Let's picture this scene: They had arrived in a strange country; they did not understand too much Spanish, and could not accept any food or drink that they were offered. Yet Sima and her four daughters had each other for company, and encouraged and strengthened each other, which enabled them to remain steadfast in their observance of Shabbos, Tznius and Kashrus. They were fortunate that Rabbi Amrom Tauber had also recently arrived from Austria, who was a big תלמיד חכם and acted as their Rov and spiritual mentor. In the early 1950s, when a few more frum families had arrived, Rabbi Tauber even began a Daf Hayomi Shiur in Chile. This not only enhanced the Torah learning, but it also provided the new immigrants with a feeling of being connected to all the other thousands of Yidden worldwide who learnt the same page in the Daf Hayomi program. Rabbi Tauber remained in Santiago until 1960, after which he moved to London.

Oma told me that for their first Pesach in Chile, they 'kashered' their glass plates by a special process called 'wassering'. The perfectly clean glass dishes were immersed in a bath of cold water for three days, but changing the water every 24 hours. After that they were ready to be used on Pesach. Matzos they had brought with from Holland, and wine was home-made by boiling raisins in water.

During their first few years they had to manage with sardines, kippers and other kosher fish that were locally available, but had to forgo eating meat since there was no reliable Shochet there. Everything else was freshly cooked and prepared at home. Even soft cheese was home-made by placing full fat milk in a special muslin cloth bag, which was hung on the clothes line outside in the sunshine, producing soft cheese whenever they required it.

Their home soon became the centre for Orthodox refugees who arrived in Santiago, who found hospitality and warm meals that were always available. Herman Struck, a famous Jewish graphic artist, was a frequent visitor to the Kokisch home, and as an appreciation for their regular kindness, gave Oma two of his original autographed pictures as a wedding present.

'Ost Jude' and 'Rabbiner' both signed by Herman Struck

Initially, the Kokisch girls tried to find suitable employment in Santiago, but all businesses were open on Shabbos. Since they obviously would not work on Shabbos, they were forced to find a new job every single week. This went on for a few months, until they decided that the only long term solution would be to become self-employed, and they planned their next enterprising venture.

Santiago enjoys a Mediterranean climate and most available ladies' clothes did not meet their standards of Tznius. The alternative was to sew their own clothes, which then gave them the idea of taking this a step further. They decided to open a small factory, making ladies blouses and other accessories. Between the four sisters they shared many talents and pooling together they turned this into a successful enterprise. The business developed, and soon they had earned enough money that allowed them to move into their own rented accommodation. Oma was happy when by 1943 the business had improved sufficiently, that they were able to buy their own commercial 'Singer' sewing machine, a real luxury in those days.

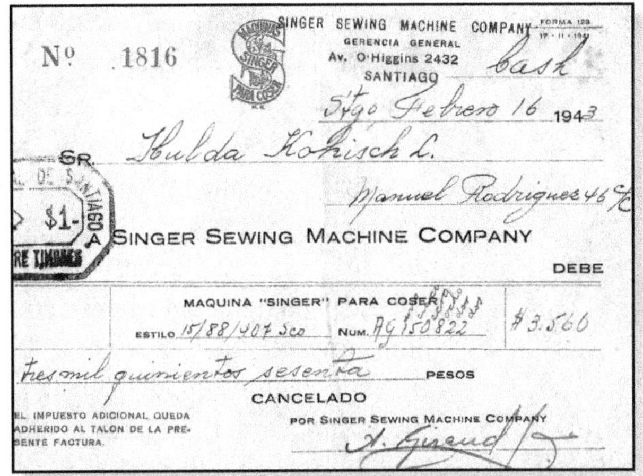

Nº 1816

SINGER SEWING MACHINE COMPANY

GERENCIA GENERAL
Av. O'Higgins 2432
SANTIAGO

Cash

Stgo. Febrero 16 1943

SR. Hulda Kokisch L.

Manuel Rodriguez 465

A SINGER SEWING MACHINE COMPANY

DEBE

MAQUINA "SINGER" PARA COSER	
ESTILO 15/88/407 Sco NUM. AG150822	$3.560

tres mil quinientos sesenta PESOS

CANCELADO

EL IMPUESTO ADICIONAL QUEDA ADHERIDO AL TALON DE LA PRESENTE FACTURA.

POR SINGER SEWING MACHINE COMPANY

A. Giraud

Receipt of Purchase of Industrial model Singer Sewing Machine

Reisel Kokisch, Oma's sister, had suffered from bronchitis since birth, and spent a month recuperating in Switzerland, while the rest of her family went to Chile. She followed them a few months later.

Even after they settled in Santiago, she often spent time at the seaside town of Constitucion, just south of Valparaiso, as the sea air proved beneficial for her medical condition. In a letter from January 26, 1945, written to her mother, she enquired about a certain type of thread that she had found in a local shop which she wanted to use. She wanted confirmation that there wouldn't be any problem with Shatnes! It is truly commendable how particular they were in keeping every Mitzvah under all conditions. Sadly, Aunty Reisel died in Santiago on ראש חדש אדר in 1950 at the age of 42, and is buried there.

AUNTY BERTY (1.1.4.4)

Aunty Berty, Oma's younger sister, was born in Bad Gastein in 1919, where she went to school, and in 1939 emigrated to Chile with her mother and sisters. Opa and Oma were first cousins, and incidentally, so were Aunty Amelie and Uncle Poldi. However, for Aunty Berty, living in the spiritual desert of Santiago in the late 1940s, her Shidduch came from a different source.

יעקב אלעזר Kahan was a Hungarian Bochur who had learnt in the Galanter Yeshivah and was later conscripted into the Hungarian army

חתן Kahan as a יעקב אלעזר

until 1936. He then escaped to Southern France and lived there for about 6 years, until the German invasion. After that he made his way to Tangiers, but struggled financially. One brother had managed to escape to Santiago de Chile in 1938, and invited him to come and work in his foundry, where he manufactured farming equipment. In February 1948 Yaakov Elozor (Uncle Lucho) the 'Yeshivah Bochur', travelled to Santiago where some time later he got engaged to Aunty Berty. This, too, was open Hashgocho Protis, that a frum Yeshivah Bochur should move to Chile, and become a suitable match for Aunty Berty. During their engagement period they discovered that they had actually met once before, a *chance* encounter in a French restaurant in early 1939.

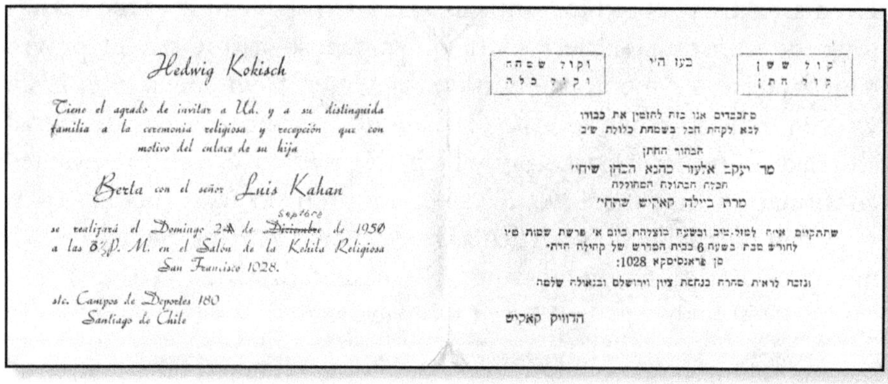

Hedwig Kokisch

Tiene el agrado de invitar a Ud. y a su distinguida familia a la ceremonia religiosa y recepción que con motivo del enlace de su hija

Berta con el señor Luis Kahan

se realizará el Domingo 24 de ~~Diciembre~~ Septiembre de 1950 a las 8½ P. M. en el Salón de la Kehila Religiosa San Francisco 1028.

stc. Campos de Deportes 180
Santiago de Chile

קול ששון קול חתן — בעז״ה — וקול שמחה וקול כלה

מתכבדים אנו בזה להזמין את כבודו
לבא לקחת חבל בשמחת כלולת ש״ב

הבחור החתן
מר יעקב אלעזר כהנא הכהן שיחי׳
עב״ג הבתולה המהוללה
מרת ביילה קאקיש שתחי׳

שתתקיים אי״ה למזל-טוב ובשעה מוצלחת ביום א׳ פרשת שמות ט״ו
לחודש טבת בשעה 6 בבית המדרש של קהילת חרדי׳
סן פראנסיסקא 1028:

ונזכה לראות מהרה בנחמת ציון וירושלם ובגאולה שלמה

הדוויק קאקיש

Aunty Berty's wedding invitation 1951 ראש חודש אלול

After Aunty Berty got engaged and the wedding invitations were already printed, she caught pneumonia and the wedding had to be postponed, as can be seen on the above invitation, where the dates had been altered.

Before we emigrated from Chile, Oma's mother moved in with Aunty Berty where she lived until she was niftar on August 16, 1960, and was buried in Santiago. During the Shiva for my grandmother, Aunty Berty received a phone call from Aunty Ernestine in Copenhagen, Sima Kokisch's youngest sister and only surviving sibling. Her memorable and comforting words included …'You have lost your only mother and at the same time I have lost my only sister. We can therefore cry and mourn together.'

Aunty Berty had three children, the oldest, Moishe, was born in 1952, Sarita in 1954, and Avrohom in 1956. Although they employed Rabbi Avrohom Goldberg, the Shochet, as a private Rebbe to teach their children after school, the atmosphere in Santiago was not conducive for raising a frum family, and they too began to make plans to emigrate, for the same reason that had prompted Opa and Oma earlier on.

Although the Jewish School had tried to be more accommodating and introduced some extra Jewish topics in the curriculum, they also appointed a 'Vaad HaChinuch' to advise the Governors on ways to introduce more authentic Yiddishkeit into the school. Uncle Lucho would often joke and say, they are not a Vaad HaChinuch but 'weit von Chinuch' [far removed from Chinuch]. They therefore decided to follow our example, and made arrangements to emigrate. By this time, the Jewish Agency, who were eager to promote Jewish immigration to Israel, offered very attractive incentives that included free travel to Israel on a national carrier, tax free allowances on new machines and goods purchased abroad, and generous mortgage loans for the purchase of new homes in Israel.

Oscar Gerstel (1.1.8.3) had left Marienbad and emigrated to Eretz Yisroel in 1933. When he got married, he settled in Haifa and got a very high position at the "Zim" Shipping Company that was based in the port city of Haifa. Apart from various cargo boats, Zim also owned a luxury ocean liner, the 'Theodor Herzl', which sailed from Buenos Aires, Argentina, to Haifa, with a stop over in Naples, Italy. Thanks to his connections at the shipping company, Oscar Gerstel was able to arrange that family Kahan had sufficient reliable kosher food for the journey, which made it much easier than Opa and Oma's arrangements some nine years earlier, who had to organise and provide their own food. In 1964, the Kahans flew to Buenos Aires, and then boarded the Theodor Herzl liner bound for Naples. The bulk of their luggage had been sent ahead to Haifa, while they continued on to Paris, to visit Aunty Amelie and tour the city, where they stayed for about three weeks. From there they went to Copenhagen for a 3-day visit to Aunty

Ernestine (Rebetzen Winkler) and then came to Manchester, where they spent 8 weeks with us.

Thus they were able to participate at Aaron's Bar Mitzvah, and then spend Pesach with us, together with Aunty Amelie and Uncle Poldi.

That Pesach was a very special Yom Tov, as the three sisters, brothers-in-law and cousins were re-united once again. After Yom Tov the three Kokisch sisters travelled together to Vienna, to visit their ancestors' קברים. The Kahan family ultimately settled in Bnei Brak, and many years later moved to Rechov Sorotzkin in Yerushalayim. Uncle Lucho and Aunty Berty are both buried near Opa and Oma on Har Hazeizim, in the Cohanim's section.

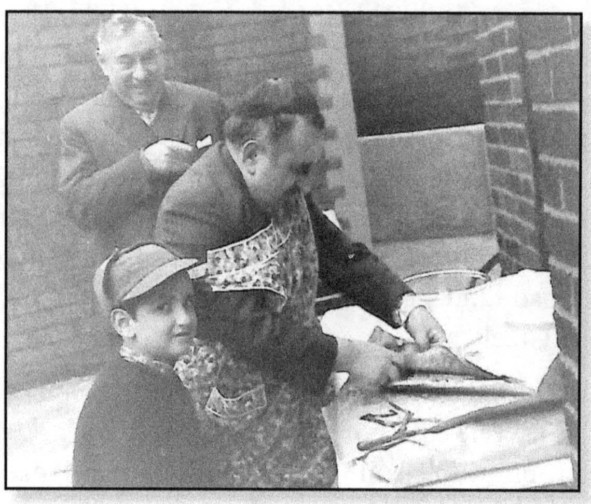

Erev Pesach at 13 Hanover Gardens; Uncle Lucho preparing the fish for Yom Tov. Uncle Poldi behind and Avrohom Kahan watching

CHAPTER 11

Nostalgia

POSSESSING A SIXTH SENSE

There were times that we experienced strange occurrences that indicated that Opa and Oma both possessed a 'sixth' sense, a special gift and guidance from Above.

The Manchester Rosh HaYeshivah advised Opa, "ב"ה you have five boys living in town, who will soon be getting married, and you will get five daughters-in-law. It is alright to invite your children to move into your home for a Yom Tov, or a short period of time, but your daughters-in-law, like all other women, enjoy their own kitchens. Although you have a large house, it is inadvisable to ask them to share accommodation with you on a long term basis." Opa took the Rosh HaYeshivah's advice to heart, and Hanover Gardens, after having served as a very happy home, was referred to as 'The Headquarters' once we were married.

Every Friday night after Maariv we would make a detour on the way home and go to 'the headquarters' to wish Opa and Oma a Good Shabbos. Of course we visited them during the week as well, but Friday night we all met at the same time, and Opa and Oma always looked forward to these weekly family reunions.

It was on a Friday night when we came to wish a good Shabbos; Opa hadn't been feeling too well and had stayed at home. Since he was at home, he still wore the Belzer Kameioh that he had received from Reb Aaron, and whilst we were all present in the room, he suffered a stroke. We called the Hatzoloh doctor who arrived promptly, but the situation was serious; Opa had become paralysed on one side of his body, and as he lay on the floor he 'swallowed his tongue', thereby blocking his airway and restricting his breathing. At that instant, Oma, who was standing nearby, emitted a loud scream, upon which Opa opened his mouth and the tongue was released, to everybody's relief and the doctors' amazement.

Every Rosh Hashono and Yom Kippur, before we start the Mussaf prayer, the Chazan says a short Tefilloh quietly which begins with הנני העני ממעש and then, about half way through, the Chazan says a few words in a loud voice: ותגער בשטן לבל ישטינני – "and scream at the Soton so that he should not accuse me." That is exactly what Oma did subconsciously, and succeeded with her loud scream to revert the situation. Opa was taken to Crumpsall Hospital by ambulance, and the following morning we davened nearby at the Manchester Yeshivah, and then walked the short distance to the hospital. We inquired at the reception to find out which ward Opa was in, and were told, much to our surprise and disbelief, that he had been discharged and taken home. We then went to Hanover Gardens, and indeed he was sitting up in the Shabbos room, as if nothing had transpired, he was still wearing the Belzer Kameioh.

Opa had suffered a total of five strokes, but ב"ה none of them left any visible permanent damage.

Another amazing incident transpired on September 20, 1974. Opa was at that stage semi-retired and did not need to daven with the 7.30 am Minyan as he had done in the past. He would join the Minyan that began at 8 o'clock or sometimes a little later. ב"ה some of us were already married and Opa and Oma merited having grandchildren. As happens quite often, these new arrivals would be born during the night, and it was quite possible that by the time Opa went to Shul, the good news would have spread. To make sure that Opa heard the good news from his children and not from someone outside his family, we would pass his house on the way home from the hospital and drop a note through our parents' letter box, wishing them Mazel Tov on their new grandson or granddaughter. In this way we were guaranteed that Opa had received the good tidings directly from his children, before he went to Shul. Of course we would then call or visit a little later in the morning and celebrate together.

Early one Friday morning I dropped a note through my parents' letter box, telling them about the birth of our new baby girl, and on Shabbos I got an 'Aliyoh' and named our baby Gittel, after Opa's mother.

After Shabbos Opa told me about a dream that he had had on Thursday night; he had seen his mother and sensed that a baby girl had been born that would be named after her, Gettie Leitner. He got up and made a note of the time 1.10am, the exact time that the birth occurred! He put the note into an envelope and sealed it!

On Motze Shabbos Opa handed me a sealed manilla envelope that contained a note in his handwriting, on which he had written, 'Gettie Leitner 1.10 am'.

BELZ IN MANCHESTER

Although Opa had been an active member of Machzikei Hadass and davened there daily, in his later years he was happy to be able to go to the new Belzer Beis Hamedrash on Broom Lane, which opened in 1982, and was a lot nearer. Two years later they were delighted to welcome the Belzer Rebbe in their new premises.

Opa enjoyed witnessing the rapid expansion of this vibrant מקום תורה and was always proud to participate in their activities. My brother Aaron would fetch him daily, and take him to the Daf Hayomi Shiur that was given in Belz, and as a token of appreciation for this kindness, Aaron received Opa's set of Shas Gemoroh after he was niftar.

However, Opa still went to Adass Yeshurun when he wanted to daven Mincha and Maariv a little earlier, and it was on one of those occasions that the following episode occurred.

One summer evening Opa came to daven at Adass Yeshurun, and despite it being very warm he wore a coat. He made his way to his seat, when he was approached by Dr. Wilks, who offered to help him take off his coat and hang it up in the cloakroom. Opa was already in his late 70s and Dr. Wilks thought that it was perhaps too difficult for Opa to take off his coat unassisted, but Opa politely refused. After davening he went over to Dr. Wilks to thank him for his kind offer and explained that he was used to wearing a 'gartel' for davening, a custom that is not followed in Adass Yeshurun. He therefore preferred to wear a coat, and wear his gartel inconspicuously underneath it, without openly contravening the customs of the Shul whilst upholding his own personal custom.

Opa was extremely proud of being associated with the new Belzer Beis Hamedrash, and would often sit and recite Tehillim or learn from a Sefer. Owing to his large repertoire of stories of the pre-war Gedolim, Opa was often asked to speak at functions.

A small reception was arranged in Belz, to honour a supporter who had dedicated a room in the building. Soon after the new building was purchased on behalf of Belz in Manchester, my brother Binyomin undertook to build a spacious men's Mikvah in the cellar, which he still manages, and ensures that it is always clean and respectable.

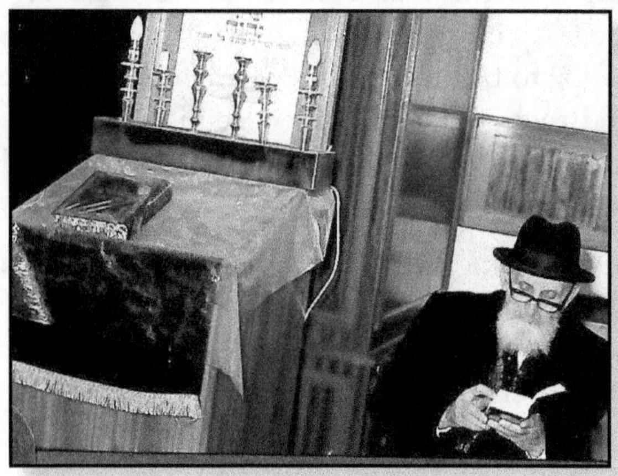

Opa learning in Belz Beis Hamedrash

Opa Speaking at a Seudo in Belz

י סיון תדש"מ - *Even Hapino commemorative coin*

Opa kept up with the growth of Belz worldwide with much interest, and was delighted to learn about the plans to build a new Beis Hamedrash in Yerushalayim, and was proud to own a coin that was issued to commemorate the stone laying ceremony.

When Opa and Oma felt that looking after a large five bedroom house was becoming too much for them, but were reluctant to move, my older brother Micha worked hard to obtain a grant that allowed them to convert the house into two flats. In this way they could use the ground floor for themselves, and rent out the first floor. The previous wash-room [ex photographic studio] was transformed into a bathroom, and the Shabbos room became their bedroom. They did not have to compromise on living space, as they still enjoyed a spacious and cosy ground floor flat.

Towards the end of his life, as Opa became more housebound, and on the recommendation of Meir Heilpern, Oma engaged Mr. Josefovitz to spend time with Opa on three afternoons per week. This gave Oma the freedom to go shopping, visit the grandchildren, or simply enjoy a break and relax. Mr. Josefovitz, a Holocaust survivor who came to England through the efforts of Rabbi Dr. Schonfeld, was a staunch Munkatcher Chossid, who had been a frequent visitor to Marienbad. Thus Opa and Mr Josefovitz immediately found much common ground to reminisce, and would spend time either learning or talking together. Opa always looked forward to these visits, and Mr. Josefovitz enjoyed coming too.

After Opa had bought the plots on Har Hazeizim in 1980, and received written confirmation from the Chevra Kadisha, he gave each of us a copy of the receipt, together with a detailed map showing the exact location of the plots. Also enclosed in this envelope was another letter of 'instructions' as his 'Will and Testament' which only included the following:

1. He should be carried out of the house through the French windows of the Shabbos room and not through the front door.
2. He should be carried out by his five sons and his nephew, Johnny Leitner [his other nephew, Anthony Kahan is a Cohen].
3. They should carry his coffin to the Belz Beis Hamedrash, where a Hesped should be said.
4. He should be buried on Har Hazeizim in the allocated plot, as per enclosed map.

There were no financial matters mentioned at all.

In February 1988 Oma started feeling unwell and weak, and went to Dr. Ebbing, who referred her to a specialist. She couldn't find the exact cause of the illness and decided to perform an exploratory operation. Oma was admitted to Crumpsall Hospital shortly before Purim of that year, and merited Hashgocho Protis, that Miss Feingold, a friendly Jewish nurse, was working on her ward during her stay and looked after Oma extremely well.

Soon after Purim, the operation was performed, and as soon as Oma had recovered from the anaesthetic, the surgeon, accompanied by nurse Feingold, came to her bedside. The doctor then told Oma the full truth of what she had found, and was very blunt about the prognosis, exclaiming in a cold tone, 'You have less than seven days to live!' With that she simply walked away, making her way to the next patient. Miss Feingold was shocked, but there was nothing she could do, and was duty bound to follow the doctor to the next patient. After completing her rounds on the ward, Miss Feingold returned to Oma and asked her, 'Did you hear what the doctor had said? You didn't show any reaction at all. You never even blinked an eyelid!' Despite her weakened condition, Oma replied without hesitating, 'I've been through so much in my life, and Hashem has always helped me, so what is the point in worrying?' That was a truly remarkable statement, remaining so calm after hearing such a grave prognosis. Once again this confirmed Oma's strong Emuno despite her compromised health and showed how Oma had perfected herself in the Mitzvah of תמים תהיה עם ה' אלקיך – ' You shall be wholehearted with Hashem, Your G-d.' The concept of תמימות – simple faith, is actually not so simple to achieve. It takes a special person, whose faith in Hashem is unequivocal, to achieve 'temimus'. It requires one to live a life of acquiescence; to ask no questions; to believe that everything is for the good; to maintain wholesome belief in Hashem that everything that occurs in one's life is Divinely orchestrated. This 'simple faith' is what guided Oma and was the yardstick by which she lived.

There was little the hospital could do, and they were prepared to discharge Oma very soon afterwards. It was now shortly before Pesach, and we knew that Oma could not go to her house for the time being. Since Opa had already been staying with us shortly after Oma was hospitalised, we arranged that Oma would come, too. We had given Opa the front room, which became his bedroom, and for Oma we made a 'bedroom' in our dining room/Shabbos room, where we sectioned off a part with a Mechitza. She needed her own space in order to recuperate, as Opa sometimes had trouble sleeping at night. To make her feel more at home and as comfortable as possible, we had brought her own bed from her house.

Oma was discharged from hospital on a Monday morning, close to פסח. She arrived by ambulance at about midday, and was helped down the path and into the house. As she walked slowly towards her bed that was prepared for her in the dining room [sorry I meant the Shabbos room], and still feeling rather weak, she decided to sit down for a while. One of my daughters had been revising some נ"ך and had left מלכים ב' on the table. As Oma sat by the table, catching her breath for a few minutes, she opened this sefer at Perek 20, and was instantly drawn to the first three Pessukim there:

> בימים ההם חלה חזקיהו למות ויבא אליו ישעיהו בן אמוץ הנביא ויאמר אליו כה אמר ה' צו לביתך כי מת אתה ולא תחיה: ויסב את פניו אל הקיר ויתפלל אל ה' לאמר: ------- ויבך חזקיהו בכי גדול:
>
> ' In those days Chizkiyohu became critically ill, when Yeshayo the son of Amoz the prophet came to him, and said to him, "So has Hashem said, 'Give orders to your household, for you are going to die and you shall not live.' And he turned his face towards the wall and prayed to Hashem, saying,... And Chizkiyohu wept profusely."

ישעיהו had just left the palace and was commanded to go back and inform חזקיהו immediately:

> שמעתי את תפלתך ראיתי את דמעתך ---- והספתי על ימיך **חמש עשרה** שנה.....
>
> ...I have heard your prayers; I have seen your tears..... and I will add fifteen years to your life.

Reading the above gave Oma just what she needed: she found solace and guidance of what she should do. Shortly after that she asked my brother Shloime to buy her a Siddur with clear print and good English translation, and davened as never before. This 'chance' discovery that Oma found in the words of the Novi was 'Hashem's way to demonstrate 'Hashem has always helped me, so what is the point in worrying'.

Because Oma's bed was in our dining room, she could participate with the Seder night as much as she managed. All the family helped in caring for both Opa and Oma, and came regularly.

ב"ה through the power of hers and our Tefillos her health improved, and shortly before Shovuos they moved back to Hanover Gardens. In August of that year Opa and Oma were well enough to enjoy a full day's outing to the seaside at St. Annes.

Hoshana Raba 5747 was an unusually warm day, and the back door at my parents' house was left open so they could enjoy the fresh breeze. Opa went to get ready for Yom Tov, and when he came out of the bathroom, he noticed that his weekday trousers had been tampered with. To his shock he discovered that the 'Belzer Kameioh' was gone, and so was his Kiddush cup that he had received from the Chassam Sofer Minyan in Santiago before his departure. Nothing else was missing or had been touched, but Opa was extremely upset. The Kameioh that Reb Aaron of Belz had given him was a priceless treasure and irreplaceable.

When the present Belzer Rebbe heard about this after Yom Tov, he sent Opa another Kameioh, which provided Opa with a degree of comfort. It is no secret, but Opa was niftar on the 27 Elul of that same year, on the Yahrzeit of the 'Sar Sholom', the first Belzer Rebbe.

The new Belzer Kameioh

The first night of Rosh Hashono 5749 was on Sunday September 11, 1988. Every family member in town had been to visit Opa and Oma on Friday to wish them a כוח"ט. Relatives who were learning in local Yeshivahs and Seminaries as well as all the sons, who would normally have visited on Friday night after davening, had reason to come in during the day, too. One great-niece who was learning in the Manchester Seminary had also been to visit, and Opa had wished her a good Yom Tov and said 'Ich fahr heint aveck' [I am going away today]. The poor teenager was shocked and thought Opa might have been confused. Unfortunately she was soon to understand the true meaning of this remark.

Opa didn't feel well on Erev Shabbos and went to lie down in the Shabbos room, which was now his bedroom.

אליהו הנביא ascended to heaven in a chariot of fire (מלכים ב פרק ב י"א) and so on that Friday night, just as Oma finished lighting her Shabbos candles and came back to the bedroom, she noticed Opa's pale complexion and understood that he had also ascended to heaven, like the flicker of the wick of her Shabbos lights.

Opa was niftar at the onset of **Shabbos** and left instructions that he must be carried out from his worldly 'Headquarters' through the doors of the '**Shabbos** Room'. Opa who had been so scrupulous throughout his life to ensure that Shabbos was honoured and kept with total devotion, not only for himself, but also for his family and employees in all circumstances, took this final opportunity to stress and convey to us all his 'Shabbos legacy'.

As mentioned earlier, Opa was niftar late Friday afternoon, Ellul 27, 5748, a day that is commemorated in Belz as the Yahrzeit of the first Rebbe, the Sar Sholom.

Since Sunday was Erev Rosh Hashono there was no possibility of bringing him to Kevuroh in Eretz Yisroel. The earliest day that this could have been accomplished would have been Wednesday, five days later. At the behest of Rav Schneebalg and the Belzer Rebbe, he was buried 'al tenai' [temporarily] in Phillips Park, to be transferred to Har Hazeizim twelve months later. As Opa was buried on Erev Rosh Hashono, we only sat 'shiva' for a few hours. We didn't have much time to absorb this heavy loss, and going to Shul that Rosh Hashanoh evening was a stark contrast to our emotions. The Brocho of מחי'ה המתים took on a new and powerful meaning.

The Belzer Rebbes had always been very close to Opa, and soon after Rosh Hashono we received a very comforting letter from the present Rebbe.

Oma spent Sukkos with Binyomin and his family, and then returned to her own home. She was ב"ה feeling much better, but was happy that one of the older granddaughters slept by her at night.

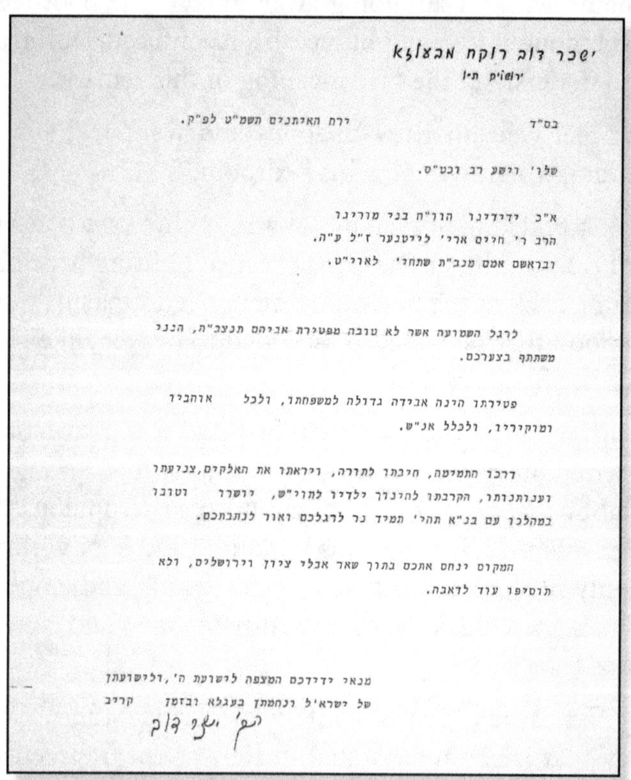

ישכר דוב רוקח מבעלזא
ירושלים ת"ו

בס"ד ירח האיתנים תשמ"ט לפ"ק.

שלו' וישע רב וכט"ס.

א"כ ידידינו הרו"ח בני מורינו
הרב ר' חיים ארי' לייטנער ז"ל ע"ה.
ובראשם אמם מנב"ת שתחי' לאוי"ט.

לרגל השמועה אשר לא טובה מפטירת אביהם תנצב"ת, הנני
משתתף בצערכם.

פטירתו הינה אבידה גדולה למשפחתו, ולכל אוהביו
ומוקיריו, ולכלל אנ"ש.

דרכו התמימה, חיבתו לתורה, ויראתו את האלקים, צניעתו
וענותנותו, הקרבתו להינוך ילדיו לתורי"ש, יושרו וטובו
במהלכו עם בנ"א תהי' תמיד נר לרגלכם ואור לנתבתכם.

המקום ינחם אתכם בתוך שאר אבלי ציון וירושלים, ולא
תוסיפו עוד לדאבה.

מנאי ידידכם המצפה לישועת ה', ולישועתן
של ישראל ונחמתן בעגלא ובזמן קריב
הק' יששכר דוב

Letter received from the Belzer Rebbe

SEFER TORAH

Sima Kokisch had owned a Sefer Torah which was written in memory of her late husband, מרדכי Kokisch. This Sefer had accompanied them from Bad Gastein to Chile, and then came with us to England in 1955. Initially it was used by the Adass Yeshurun Minyan, but when it was urgently required by another Minyan a few years later, it was loaned to them. One rainy Shabbos afternoon at Mincha, someone got an "Aliyoh' and water dripped from his hat onto the open Sefer Torah'. Unfortunately, the Sefer Torah was rolled up and returned to the Oron Hakodesh before the parchment was completely dry, and as a result of this became permanently damaged. Oma was naturally devastated and showed the Sefer Torah to various Sofrim to see if it could be repaired, but to her dismay it remained possul.

After Opa was niftar, Oma decided to write a short will with instructions how we should divide the inheritance.

She wrote just a few points:

1. From the rental income from Hanover Gardens, we should have a Sefer Torah written, and on completion should place it in the Belzer Beis Hamedrash on Broom Lane, where Opa was an active and proud member in his later years.
2. Any gifts that any of her children had ever given to them should be returned to that specific family.
3. She allocated to each of her children items of value of which there was only one.

For example the Kiddush cup, the candlesticks, Opa's Shas, etc. In this way everybody got something unique. (The remainder of the household goods were listed, and if anyone had a specific need for something, would state his preference. All other things were equally shared out, after having made five piles and then drawn lots.)

Each grandchild received a personally inscribed Sefer Tehilim.

בס"ד

ספר תהלים זה

קבלתי מזקנתי ע"ה

ביום שלפני הסתלקותה

ויה"ר שאמירת הפרקים

יהא לתועלת ולעילוי נשמתה

ונשמת זקני ע"ה

גיטל לייטנער שת"י

יום היאצ"ט של זקני כ"ז אלול תשמ"ח

יום היאצ"ט של זקנתי ה' אייר תשמ"ט

Personalised inscription for each grandchild

As mentioned before, from the
of the house I would like
that you have a Sefer Tora witten
with the Belzer Rovs guidance
for the Belzer Beth Hamedrash in
Manchester, for my perents לע"נ sister
Papis Perents: Sister לע"נ and Papis לע"נ
name.

Part of Oma's Will regarding the Sefer Torah.

This reads:

As mentioned before, from the [rent] of the house I would like that you have a Sefer Torah written with the Belzer Rov's guidance for the Belzer Beth Hamedrash in Manchester, for my parents לע"נ , sister, Papi's parents לע"נ, sister לע"נ and Papi's לע"נ name.

Shortly before she was niftar she called me to her room and asked me specifically to make sure we have the Sefer Torah written as soon as possible. 'She would be very embarrassed to meet her mother in the next world, having a guilty conscience that her Sefer Torah was now unfit for use. Please replace it as soon as possible!'

In December 1988 Oma was unwell again, and after a short stay in hospital moved back in with us at 10 New Hall Road, and again all the family helped care for her. Shortly after Pesach she was again admitted to hospital, by which time she was having problems with her breathing, and was more comfortable sleeping in a sitting position on an armchair. Again, the kind Jewish nurse, Miss Feingold, brought her a special 'Parker Knoll' armchair from another ward, and Oma felt much more comfortable. When the hospital wanted to discharge her, Oma felt that she could only come home if she would have a similar armchair. Between us we decided to find the identical chair, but the problem was that Parker Knoll only made furniture to order. The stockist in Manchester only had samples of various chairs and fabrics from which customers could order, but these samples were not for sale. By pure Hashgocho Protis, Stockton's on Ancoats Street had one Parker Knoll chair stored away in the back of a railway arch, which they were pleased to sell to us. This particular armchair had been made for a customer some months before, but was never collected. The chair was delivered at the same moment as the ambulance brought Oma home, early Friday morning.

On Sunday morning, Oma expressed her wish to 'bentch' her grandchildren, and in order of age gave each one a Brocho. However, after bentching the first few children she grew too weak and bentched all others together. ב"ה she completed this task, and finished with the parting message to them all, 'Torah lernen is the ikker' [Torah learning is the main thing]. She was niftar on Wednesday morning ה' אייר תשמ"ט just eight months after Opa, sitting on the Parker Knoll armchair.

She was brought to Eretz Yisroel for Kevuroh, and the Levayo began from outside Aunty Berty's [Oma's youngest sister] house at 9b Sorotzkin, Yerushalayim, and continued on to Har Hazeizim, where Oma was buried next to Opa's reserved kever, and her sister Aunty Amelie.

ארונה בא

בצער רב ובכאב מודיעים אנו על פטירת
אמנו הצנועה והחשובה מנב"ת

מרת הינדא לייטנר ע"ה

בת הר"ר מרדכי קוקיש ז"ל
אלמנת הר"ר חיים אריה לייטנר ז"ל
ממנצ'סטר — אנגליה
ארונה יגיע מלונדון בטיסה 016 אל על
היום יום חמישי ו' אייר תשמ"ט, וההלויה בשעה 6
לערך מרחוב סורוצקין 9ב', ירושלים להר הזיתים

המשפחה המתאבלת

הקמת מצבה

להורינו היקרים
הר"ר **חיים אריה** ז"ל (KURT)
מרת **הינדא** ע"ה (HILDA)

לייטנער

ממנצ'סטר-אנגליה

תתקיים אי"ה מחר יום רביעי כ' באלול
בשעה 4.00 בהר הזיתים גוש חדש ד'
אוטובוס יצא מבנייני האומה בשעה 3.30
ויעבור דרך רח' סורוצקין 9ב' בשעה 3.40
המשפחה

The newspaper announcement in the Israeli Hamodia

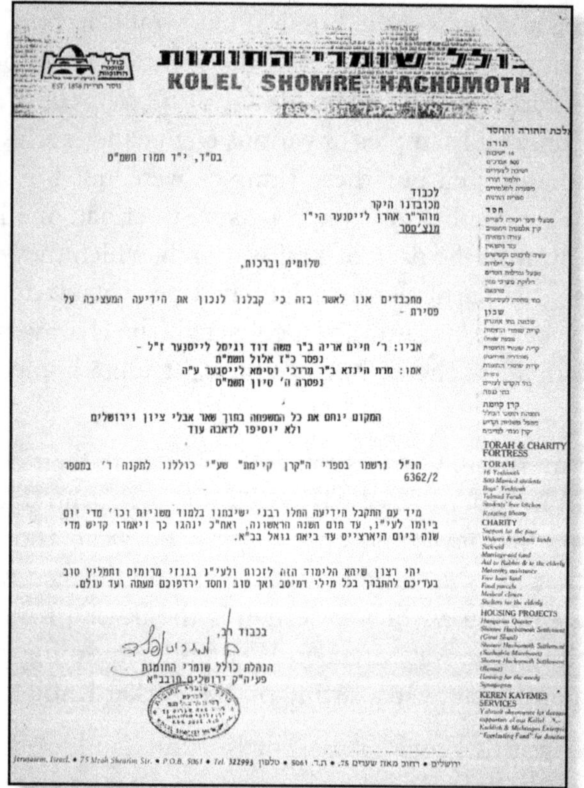

כולל שומרי החומות
KOLEL SHOMRE HACHOMOTH
EST. 1858 נוסד תרי"ח

בס"ד, י"ד תמוז תשמ"ט

לכבוד
מכובדנו היקר
מוהר"ר אהרן לייסנער הי"ו
מנצ'סטר

שלומים וברכות,

מתכבדים אנו לאשר בזה כי קבלנו לנכון את הידיעה המעציבה על פסירת -

אביו: ר' חיים אריה ב"ר משה דוד וגיטל לייסנער ז"ל -
נפסר כ"ז אלול תשמ"ח
אמו: מרת הינדא ב"ר מרדכי וסימא לייסנער ע"ה
נפסרה ה' סיון תשמ"ט

המקום ינחם את כל המשפחה בתוך שאר אבלי ציון וירושלים
ולא יוסיפו לדאבה עוד

הנ"ל נרשמו בספרי ה"קרן קיימת" שע"י כוללנו לתקנה ד' במספר 6362/2

מיד עם התקבל הידיעה החלו רבני ישיבתנו בלמוד משניות וכו' מדי יום ביומו לעי"נ, עד תום השנה הראשונה, ואח"כ ינהגו כך ויאמרו קדיש מדי שנה ביום היארציים עד ביאת גואל בב"א.

יהי רצון שיהא הלימוד הזה לזכות ולעי"נ בגנזי מרומים ותמליץ טוב בעדיכם להתברך בכל מילי דמיטב ואך טוב וחסד ירדפוכם מעתה ועד עולם.

בכבוד רב,
[signature]
הנהלת כולל שומרי החומות
פעיה"ק ירושלים תובב"א

TORAH & CHARITY FORTRESS
TORAH
16 Yeshivoth
CHARITY
HOUSING PROJECTS
KEREN KAYEMES SERVICES

Jerusalem, Israel. • 75 Meah Shearim Str. • P.O.B. 5061 • Tel. 322993 טלפון • 5061 .ת.ד • 75 ירושלים • רחוב מאה שערים

Condolence Letter received from Kolel Shomrei Hachomos (Reb Meir Baal Haness) July 1989

As mentioned earlier, Opa was buried in Manchester 'al tenai' and 12 months later, on September 19, 1989, was transferred to Har Hazeizim. After the kevuroh we had to sit Shiva again for one day, and then organised the two Matzeivos, to be unveiled one week later. It was suggested that we use a firm situated behind the old 'Tachana Merkazit' [bus terminal] in Yerushalayim. Hashgocho Protis had led us to this firm, whose owner had been a resident of Marienbad, and provided us with the most efficient and hassle free service!

The 5 brothers at the Kevorim of Opa and Oma, 1989

פ נ
חלוץ לכל דבר מצוה לקלות וחמורים
ירא אלקים מעודו ונודע בשערים
יעיל בסדור כנסית אגודת הגבורים
מקורב לצדיקי בית בעלזא
שלשלת האדמו"רים

אוד מוצל מאש ע"י איש רוכב בסערים
רודף להצלת אחיו מצפרני הארורים
יד עניים לקופת רמבעה"נ בהידורים
הפליא בחסד של אמת
והעמיד דור ישרים

ה"ה העסקן הוותיק
ר' **חיים אריה** ז"ל
בן ר' משה דוד לייטנער ז"ל
מעיר מאריענבאד
ואח"כ במאנשעסטער במדינת אנגלי'
נפטר בשם טוב
כ"ז אלול תשמ"ח לפ"ק
ת.נ.צ.ב.ה

פ נ
אשה צנועה תמימה
כל כבודה בת מלך פנימה
מצוינת בבטחונה ומופלאה באמונה
זהירה בדיבורה ובכל מדה נכונה
עמדה לימין בעלה כל ימיה
והדריכה ביתה בדקדוק המצוות
מסרה נפשה למען חינוך בניה
וזכתה לדור ישרים ההולכים בדרכי'

מרת **הינדא** ע"ה
בת ר' מרדכי קוקיש ז"ל
אשת ר' חיים אריה לייטנער ז"ל
ממאנשעסטער באנגלי'
נפטרה בשם טוב
ה' אייר תשמ"ט לפ"ק
ת.נ.צ.ב.ה.

The inscriptions on Opa and Oma's Matzeivos on Har Hazeizim.

During that week in Eretz Yisroel we commissioned a Sofer to write the new Sefer Torah לע"נ our parents ע"ה. We were honoured that this Sofer was recommended to us by the Belzer Rebbe himself, who personally wrote the first letter, and on completion, the final letters too.

The Belzer Rebbe שליט"א writing the final letters, with the Sofer standing to his right, and Binyomin behind

The Hachnosas Sefer Torah took place on November 22, 1993. The procession started from Machzikei Hadass and made its way to Belz on Broom Lane, accompanied by a very large crowd and lively dancing and music.

The new Sefer together with the Kokisch Sefer en route from M.H. Shul to Belz on Broom Lane.
1st picture Shloime Leitner
2nd picture L. to R. Micha; Binyomin and Aaron Leitner

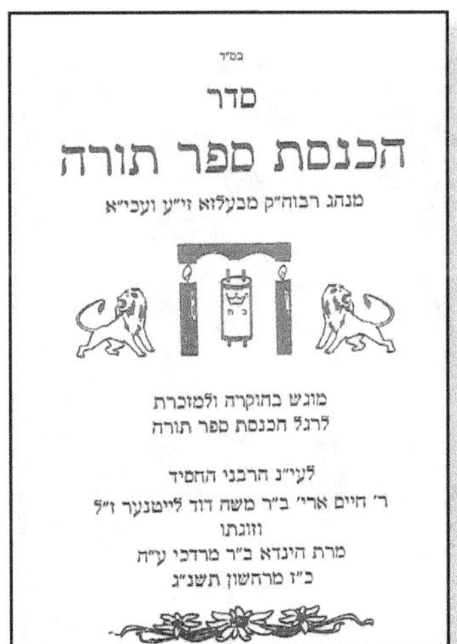

בס"ד

סדר

הכנסת ספר תורה

מנהג רבוה"ק מבעלזא זי"ע ועכי"א

מוגש בהוקרה ולמזכרת
לרגל הכנסת ספר תורה

לעי"נ הרבני החסיד
ר' חיים ארי' ב"ר משה דוד לייטנער ז"ל
ווזגתו
מרת הינדא ב"ר מרדכי ע"ה
כ"ז מרחשון תשנ"ג

The front cover of a three page souvenir

Together with the Sefer Torah the family also donated a new Poroches, with Opa and Oma's names embroidered on it, and a cover for the Bimah with the names of Uncle Poldi and Aunty Amelie, who didn't merit to have any children. Shloime, with his artistic talents and expertise in woodwork, had the top of the Oron Hakodesh decorated to look like the original design of the roof of the Belzer Beis Hamedrash in Belz.

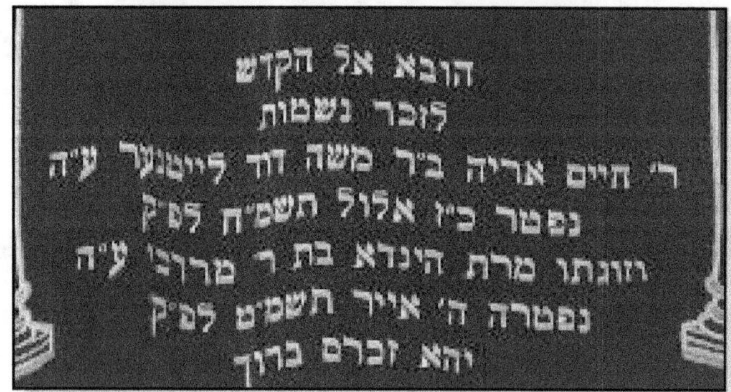

The new Poroches in memory of Opa and Oma in Belz Beis Hamedrash with inscription highlighted

The Belzer Rebbe also participated in this joyous occassion by sending us his warm greetings.

ישכר דוב רוקח
קרית בעלזא
ירושלים ת"ו

בס"ד

כ"ו חשון שנת תשנ"ג לפ"ק.

שלו' וישע רב וכט"ס, אל מע"כ ידידינו הנכבדים והנעלים, נדיבי לב רודפי צדקה וחסד, בני ידידנו הבלתי נשכח, הרה"ח מוה"ר חיים ארי' לייטנר ז"ל, ולכל אנ"ש מתפללי השטיבעל במנשסתר יצ"ו, כל או"א בשמו הטוב יבורך, הי"ו.

לרגל שמחת הכנסת הספר תורה על ידי המשפחה שיחיו, יהי רצון שיהיה לע"נ אביהם תנצב"ה, ולא ימישו ד"ת ומצותיה מזרעם.

ולכל המתפללים, שיזכו להגדיל תורה ולהאדירה מתוך רוב נחת וכ"ט.

הכו"ח בפקודת הקודש
אליעזר וינד
משב"ק

A personal letter from the Belzer Rebbe for the occasion

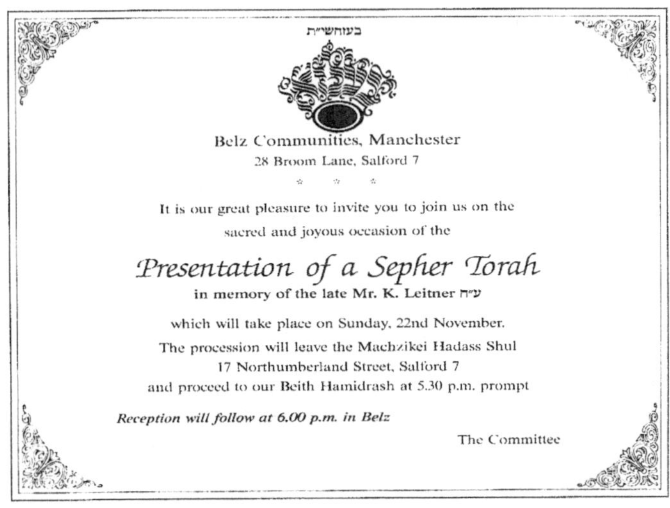

בעזהשי"ת

Belz Communities, Manchester
28 Broom Lane, Salford 7

It is our great pleasure to invite you to join us on the sacred and joyous occasion of the

Presentation of a Sepher Torah
in memory of the late Mr. K. Leitner ע"ה

which will take place on Sunday, 22nd November.
The procession will leave the Machzikei Hadass Shul
17 Northumberland Street, Salford 7
and proceed to our Beith Hamidrash at 5.30 p.m. prompt

Reception will follow at 6.00 p.m. in Belz

The Committee

Personal invitation for the Hachnosas Sefer Torah

The close connection with the Rebbes of Belz has ב"ה continued with the present Rebbe too, and it is gratifying to note that on the Thursday evening (ב' אלול תש"ע) of the week of Shiva for our brother שלמה ישיעה we received a phone call at approximately 11pm from the Belzer Rebbe himself, who spoke to each of the Aveilim individually. On this same day, the Rebbe had celebrated the Bris of a grandchild, and it was already 1am in Eretz Yisroel!

SOME NOSTALGIC MEMORIES

Below is an article written by Micha that was printed in the "Pirchim Monthly" August 1991, and will provide some background to what Jewish life in Santiago was like, as seen through the eyes of our oldest brother, who remembers the most of those early years.

THIS IS CHILE - MICHA RECOLLECTS:

Quien gano?

My brothers and I would spend Shabbos afternoons with our faces against the railings at the bottom of our garden, watching the crowds, thousands strong, making their way back down the wide avenue that was our street. "Quien gano?" (Who won?), we would ask. The crowds were returning from the weekly football match held at the stadium at the bottom of our street - the tree lined avenue known as Campos de Desportes. Most of you would probably never have heard of Chile, let alone find it in an atlas! I was born there!

Chile is a long thin stretch of land along the west coast of South America, some 2800 miles long and no more than 111 miles wide. The Pacific Ocean flanks the entire west of the country whilst the Andes, a range of snow capped mountains, flanks the east and divides Chile from its immediate neighbour, Argentina. The upper end of Chile is a desert, lying near the Equator, whilst the southern tip reaches almost to the South Pole. I lived with my family in Santiago, in the capital,

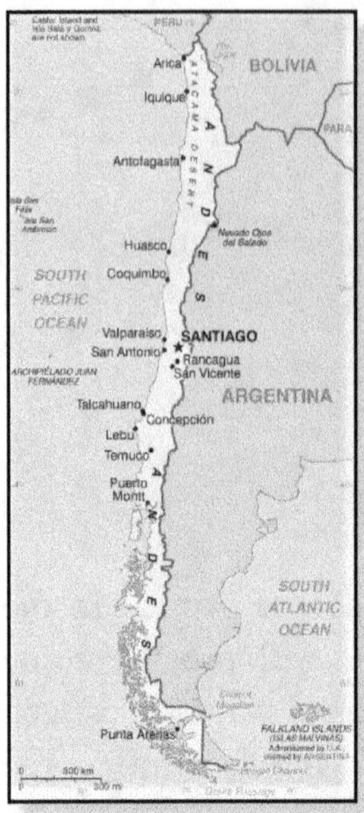

Map of Chile

situated near the middle of the country, some 50 miles from the sea, and with a climate similar to that found in Eretz Yisroel. The weather is very warm most of the year, and snow is non existent in the winter months of June – September.

We lived in the affluent part of the town, near the Football Stadium and around the corner from the Presidential Palace. I remember going for walks on Shabbos mornings with my parents past the Palace, and sending regards with the guard at the gate for the President. I wonder now if he ever received them. Our home was a large bungalow surrounded on three sides by spacious gardens, which grew the most delicious fruits, such as grapes and oranges and other more exotic fruits, the names of which I have now forgotten.

My parents ran a Matzo factory 5 months of the year and the kosher restaurant 12 months of the year, 6 days a week, where they also catered for all the Jewish functions in town.

Santiago in the 1950's contained maybe 20 heimishe families from amongst thousands of unfortunately "Freier Yidden". The Yiddish community was made up of refugees who had managed with Yad Hashem to escape to Chile, where unfortunately most of them quickly forgot their Jewish roots, and assimilated amongst the non-Jews. That made the remnants of undiluted Yiddishkeit cling together even more and encouraged each other not to forsake the traditions of their youth. Minyan was in our house on Shabbos. On weekdays [the children] we davened alone, watched by the tender loving eyes of our grandmother, who lived together with us. To give you an idea of what Yiddishkeit was really like in Santiago, you have to realise that we went to the only Jewish school in Santiago. And what a school that was! My brothers and I were the only boys who wore a cappel at all, in a school of several hundred children.

I remember how each morning the entire school lined up in rows in the large playground when 'Puro Chile', the Chilean national anthem, was sung by all, followed by the raising of the Chilean flag to the top of the mast; and then we sang the 'Hatikva', the Israeli national anthem followed by the raising of the Israeli flag to the top of its mast. In order to ensure that we did not become too influenced from the Chevra at school, my parents' imbibed us with a long list of rules that had to be strictly adhered to. For example, under no circumstances were we ever allowed to accept sweets or a biscuit from another child at school – these were definitely treife. I remember when we arrived in Manchester in December 1955, as a boy of nine years old; I could simply not understand why all the children in Broughton Jewish Primary School ate 'treife' biscuits, including the so called frum children.

When my parents explained that those biscuits were kosher I could not understand at all how other people's biscuits could be kosher. I had grown up to believe that all biscuits are treife (like bacon) and that was that. The only Yiddishkeit I remember learning in Chile was from home and from a private Rebbe - very little from school itself. My parents clung to their true Yiddishkeit with a tenacity that is rare to find these days, despite numerous difficulties. My mother arrived in Santiago together with her mother and sisters in late March 1939 – and with the close proximity of Pesach they had simply no idea how they were going to manage. But manage they did! They lived for months with a non-Jewish family - who spoke only Spanish and my mother's family mainly German. Yet my mother often told me how the non-Jewish family accommodated them and bent over backwards to supply them with all their needs, understanding full well, that as Yidden they could not and would not even drink a glass of cold water from untoiveled Keilim.

Micha, wearing a cap, with his school class

Kosher milk was not delivered to the doorstep in Santiago as we take for granted in Britain, and kosher food in general was very rare to find. I remember my Aunty from Paris [Aunty Amelie] (1.1.3.1) sending us occasionally parcels of kosher food - what a treat! Kosher Swiss cheese and Kosher Swiss chocolate – imagine that – what a Yom Tov, but never a kosher biscuit. The Esrog came each year by post from Europe or Eretz Yisroel. What a lot of stamps on the box to add to our collection.

At the time when my brother Aaron was born, there was no Mohel to be found in Santiago. My parents were frantic. What should we do? The nearest Mohel was in Buenos Aires in Argentina, a distance of nearly 900 miles, and they simply didn't have the money to pay for his trip, what would they do? In the end they decided they would sell the silver candelabra – a priceless piece with sentimental value; being one of the only articles my father managed to smuggle from Marienbad during his escape from the advancing German Army into Czechoslovakia. Yes – they would sell the candelabra to pay for the Mohel's ticket. But ב"ה -Hashem listened to their Tefillos and a local Mohel turned up at the last moment. Thus the Bris took place bizmano, and the candelabra remained in the family as an heirloom. That sort of Mesiras Nefesh for the sake of a Mitzvah is rare to find these days. When I was 8 years old, my parents decided that time was up! They simply couldn't stay in the treife atmosphere of Chile and expect their five boys to grow up to be Ehrliche Yidden. The only solution was to emigrate, but where to? My mother's choice was Eretz Yisroel but my father would not hear of it! He wanted London where he had been during the war years working for Agudas Yisroel in their Hatzolo work. Besides, he had two brothers there, who no doubt would help us settle down. And so my parents decided to emigrate to England and to settle in London.

Departure was set for November 16, 1955. Three months previously my father took me to Valparaiso to meet the ship, the 'Reina Del Pacifico' (the Queen of the Pacific) that would take us to England on its next voyage. We boarded the ship, where my father got down to business – choosing the cabins that would be reserved for Family Leitner – and booking all the kosher food that would be required to satisfy our needs during the 30 day trip to Liverpool – since the kosher food would have to be sent from London on the ship's return trip from England. To pay for this expensive journey, my parents sold everything they had in Chile, a lovely bungalow, all its furniture and the goodwill of a very successful Matzo factory. By the time the date of our departure arrived, November 16, 1955, my parents had spent practically all their money and all that was left was the shedding of parting tears from my dear loving grandmother, who we never saw again, my uncle, aunt and cousins, who some years later also emigrated to Eretz Yisroel, from our maid Chuana and from Mr. Felix Bonne, an elderly bochur who lived in our house. Thus my parents left behind in Chile everything they possessed – apart from their most treasured possessions- their 5 little boys – and set sail on a journey into the unknown and to a hopefully more secure future in Yiddishkeit. What happened on the journey and when we arrived in England is a story for another day.

SOME OF MY OWN MEMORIES FROM CHILE:

I remember...

The majority of the population in Santiago was poor, and perhaps owing to the hot Mediterranean weather did not work too hard, and those people who did find work, did not do so for very long hours either. The most popular word in Chile was 'manana' – meaning 'tomorrow' in Spanish. If you asked anybody to do a job for you, he would initially say, 'manana' perhaps – tomorrow but never today. Hence they had little in the way of financial earnings.

I remember the local bus service offered a three class system of travel; first, second and third class. As the weather was usually very hot, the windows on the bus were always open, and for safety reasons they all had metal bars across their apertures. The first class travellers would board the bus and were entitled to take a seat. The second class passengers were allowed to stand inside the bus, whilst the third class ones stood outside and held on to the metal bars with both hands. When the bus moved they simply lifted their legs, and at the next bus stop, they could enjoy a little rest, until the bus was ready to leave again. Needless to say, there were always less fare paying passengers on these buses.

A typical Chilean bus

Another recollection that stayed with me:

I Remember...

Opa was always particular in the way he dressed, being extremely immaculate and neat. The only time I remember Opa walking in the street in his shirt sleeves and without a jacket was the day after Yom Kippur in Chile. It was a hot summer's day and Opa walked along the main dual carriageway with an assistant carrying a large ladder. Opa had obtained permission from the local council to prune some of their 'palm trees', as he needed a 'Lulov' for Succos. When he found what he wanted, he leaned the ladder against the tree and climbed up to reach the central branch that would be suitable as his lulov, whilst his assistant held the ladder. He also cut a few more Lulovim for other members of the Chevra Kadisha Shul.

I Remember...

The three older Leitner boys attended the only 'Jewish' school in Santiago. This was a large school with approximately 400 Jewish children, but we were the only three boys who wore 'cappels' and 'tzizis'. The school was run by two representatives that had been especially sent from Israel. The State of Israel had only just been established in 1948, and they had very little money for their own requirements. However, despite that, the Israeli government, in their eagerness to uproot authentic Yiddishkeit and spread their Zionist ideology throughout the world, found sufficient funds to send 'shluchim' to different countries whose sole aim was to ensure that Zionism was the only Jewish topic that was to be taught to the younger generation. That was priority number 'ONE'. Believe it or not, the only Yom Tov that was taught, spoken about and celebrated in our 'Jewish' school in Santiago, was that of the 5th of Iyar – Israeli Independence Day. No Rosh Hashonoh, no Yom Kippur, no Shabbos, not even Purim was ever mentioned. Once a year, they made a large party for the entire school, on the 5th of Iyar, and what a fancy party that was!

Our parents always had to be one step ahead, so Oma offered to bake all the cakes for this party, in order to ensure that her boys, and the rest of the school, had kosher food to eat, an offer that was graciously accepted. I still remember that Oma made a large cake and decorated it with chocolate cream, and then with the prongs of a fork, inscribed a pattern of a large Mogen Dovid on it, as the most appropriate decoration for this special occasion.

However, our early genuine Torah education came from home, and every Shabbos morning after Kiddush we would all take a long walk in the nearby park, and Opa would tell us about the Sedra, ask quiz questions and discuss some Dinim in connection with that particular time of year. He would share with us his vivid memories of the Gedolim he had met in Marienbad, and how fortunate we were to be frum Yidden, who had Hashem's Torah to guide us. Later on, Opa employed the local Shochet, Rabbi Avrohom Goldberg, who would come to our house in the afternoons and give us some private Kodesh lessons.

I Remember...

I remember seeing my grandmother many an evening relaxing at home, and enjoying knitting clothes for the grandchildren, or crocheting a variety of decorative mats and tablecloths. Before we left Chile in 1955, she gave Oma a hand crocheted white tablecloth that is nearly eight feet long.

I Remember...

As our family grew, Opa decided to move to a larger dwelling, and viewed a large bungalow on 180 Campo de Desport. This occupied a corner plot with large gardens and plenty of fruit trees. But before my parents signed for the house, they invited my grandmother, Sima, to come and view the property and give her approval. Since she was living with us, they wanted her to choose a bedroom for herself. After looking around the bungalow together with my parents, they wanted to know what she had thought of it, as they greatly valued her opinion. She was very much in favour of what she saw and quickly pointed out the advantages of the various rooms, with comments such as, 'at this fireplace you can burn your Chometz', 'in this corner of the garden you can build your Sukko' etc. Her straightforward and practical yiddish outlook taught my parents a valuable lesson: A Jewish home is built on the foundation of its spiritual suitability.

This lesson they remembered all their lives, and later on in Manchester, when they eventually bought their own house on Hanover Gardens, it was really a unique home. A large five bedroom house, nestled on a quite street, that enjoyed a front and back garden. But it remained a very unique house, the only house that neither had a dining room nor a lounge! Our 'dining' room was always referred to as the Shabbos room, as this was the place where we enjoyed our Shabbos meals, and Shabbos being the focus and highlight of the week. The lounge was known as the Chanukah room, which had a large bay window facing the street and that is where we lit our Menoras.

I Remember...

The "Chassam Sofer Minyan" davened in our house on Shabbos and Yom Tov, as it was too far to walk to the "Chevra Kadisha Shul" where Opa davened during the week. On Erev Yom Tov a large lorry would bring about 50 chairs and several tables, which were needed to accommodate the many people who would come to join the davening on Rosh Hashanah and Yom Kippur. Some of these 'Mispallelim' would only come for Kol Nidrei and Yizkor, and some just for Maftir Yona! At these times all of us children slept in one bedroom, and the rest of the rooms would be used for davening. I also remember that we filled several large tins with sand on Erev Yom Kippur, and then stuck large

25-hour candles into them. A non-Jewish man stayed there overnight to make sure that it did not become a fire hazard.

I Remember...

In 1948 Aunty Amelie (1.1.4.1) got married to her first cousin, Leopold Deutsch [Uncle Poldi] (1.1.2.2) and went to live in Paris. She naturally corresponded frequently with her elderly mother and family in Santiago, and even made the long journey to visit them, but there was little possibility for speaking on the phone. The communications network as we know it today was then practically non-existent. Let me explain what it was like to make a long distance phone call between Santiago and Paris in the early 1950's.

an early telephone of the 1950s

If one needed to phone anywhere outside one's own local district, one could not simply dial the required number directly, but had to go via an 'operator'. The operator would request one's own telephone number, the country and district that one wanted to call, and the correct number. The operator then connected the appropriate cables manually from one exchange to another, and finally dialled that number. Once this connection was made, one could speak to one's acquaintance. This sounds simple and relatively uncomplicated. But when one wanted to speak to someone from abroad, for instance from Santiago to Paris, as was the case here, then the same procedure occurred but 100 times more often. Each city between Santiago and Paris had their telephone operators, and each one connected to its neighbouring one, a rather lengthy procedure. I remember that in Elul 1954, my grandmother and Oma wanted to speak to Aunty Amelie in Paris to wish each other a כתיבה וחתימה טובה. The phone call was 'booked' through the operator, and it took nearly 15 hours until the final operator in Paris connected their call, and they were finally able to speak to each other. During this period our phone was engaged and could not be used for any other calls. It could also happen that after waiting those 15 hours to be connected, the operator would come on the line and announce, 'sorry no reply', or 'sorry telephone is engaged' and one had to try again the following day. Apart from this rather complicated system, there was also a large charge to cover the many hours of trying to establish a connection, even if one later only spoke for a very short period of time, or perhaps not at all! Despite the difficulty in speaking across continents, people still made the effort to talk to their loved ones and hear their voices.

I Remember...

In order to obtain kosher milk, one normally goes to a farm for milking. The farmers would supplement their cows' feed with food in the form of pellets, which are made from processed grains of 'Chometz'.

To avoid any doubt of Chometz, Opa arranged to go to a large farm one day before Erev Pesach, where the cows grazed naturally on vast expanses of grassy fields. The milk from these cows was sure to be Chometz-free, as they had definitely not eaten any Chometz. The farmer then saddled his horse and went with a long lasso to round up some cows from the field, and Opa proceeded to supervise the milking for Pesach, which yielded enough milk for our family and other members of the Chassam Sofer community. They filled a full milk churn and then distributed it as required.

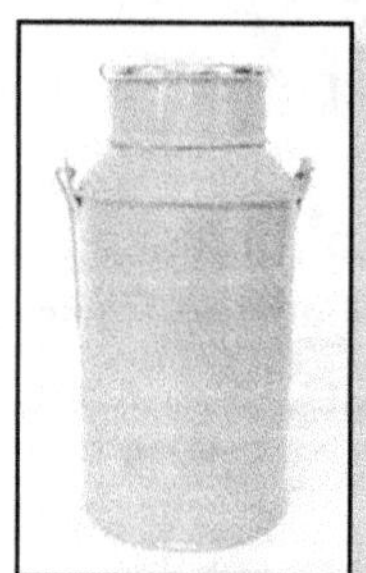

A typical milk churn and farmer with lasso catching his cow for milking

An amusing memory...

One of our earliest memories after our arrival in England was seeing 'Double Decker' buses, something we had never seen in Santiago. Our excitement grew, when a few weeks after our arrival we were given permission to travel on one. We made our way upstairs and were delighted to sit at the front and watch all the cars overtake us. Apart from the driver there was also a conductor on the bus who would go from one passenger to another and collect the fares. When you were nearing your destination and wanted to get off at the next stop, you had to press a red button (this system is still used today), on which it said 'PUSH ONCE'. Our knowledge of English was still very minimal, and we read the 'PUSH ONCE' sign as if it was Spanish, as ONCE in Spanish means ELEVEN. Being very obedient children, we pressed the button ELEVEN times, much to the annoyance of the driver, who stopped the bus even before the next official stop, and made us get off immediately! We definitely learned one new English word that day!

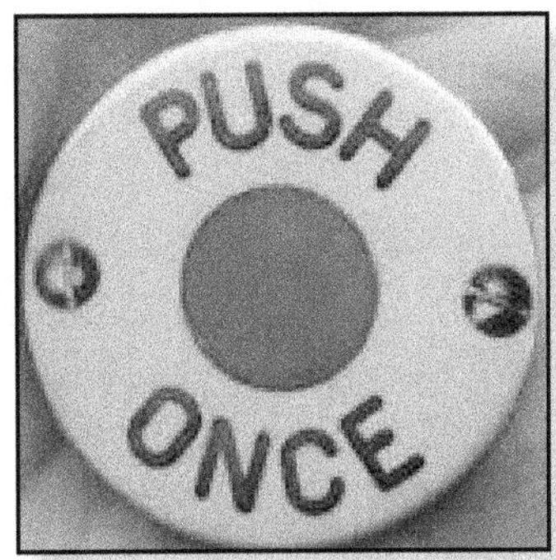

The Stop Button on the bus – Push ONCE

CHAPTER 12

The Leitner Family

UNCLE FRITZ (שלמה) LEITNER (1.1.1.2)

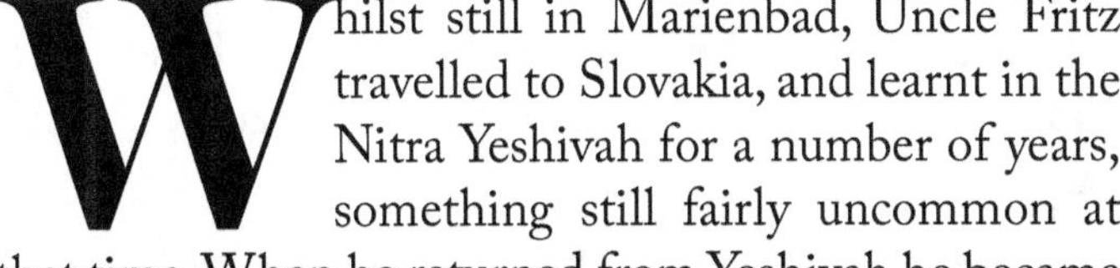

Whilst still in Marienbad, Uncle Fritz travelled to Slovakia, and learnt in the Nitra Yeshivah for a number of years, something still fairly uncommon at that time. When he returned from Yeshivah he became apprenticed as a dental technician, and worked in this capacity both in Marienbad and later on in London, too.

When the Leitners had to leave Marienbad in September 1938, Uncle Fritz travelled with them to Prague, where, soon after, he became engaged to Malka (Margit) Wiener from Pressburg, a granddaughter of Rabbi Avrohom Herzl, the famous Maggid of Pressburg.

They escaped to London with the help of Rabbi Dr. Shloime Schonfeld, whom he knew from the Nitra Yeshivah, and got married in Bournemouth in early 1939, just before the outbreak of the war. Their oldest daughter, יהודית – Judith, was born on February 8, 1941 [Opa's birthday] followed by צבי אברהם – Harry, April 26, 1942 at Windsor Hospital. Whilst Aunty Margit was in hospital, she received a visit from the Queen Mother, which made headlines in the national papers: 'Queen Mother visits Jewish Refugee in Hospital'.

They then moved to London, and initially lived in Queens Drive and later moved to 19 Lordship Road, N16. After the "Battle of Britain" began, London was especially hard hit with regular enemy bombs falling almost nightly, and they were forced to evacuate. Uncle Shurl, (see below) who was working at the kosher hotel in Buxton, invited his older brother, Uncle Fritz, to join him. Uncle Fritz accepted the offer, and moved there with his family where they stayed for almost 10 years.

Buxton is a small town, about 1 hour away from Manchester, and has been a favourite holiday resort ever since the Romans built their famous bath houses there, using the natural Buxton Springs, reminiscent of Marienbad in many aspects. Uncle Fritz became the bookkeeper for the hotel, and also worked as a dental technician for a local denture manufacturer. He was also responsible to 'shomer' the milk every morning, so that the customers at the hotel could enjoy kosher milk. One Shabbos they hosted the family of Reb Tuvia Weiss, and it was on that particular Shabbos morning that Uncle Fritz made an announcement during lunch, that 'unfortunately the gas flame had blown out, and there will not be any Cholent this Shabbos'. On an occasion soon afterwards, Rabbi Weiss spoke and praised Uncle Fritz for being strict about keeping the laws of Shabbos correctly, and not looking for any leniencies.

Their next two children were born in Manchester, as there were no suitable facilities in Buxton, Monty – (יהודה מרדכי שמעון) born July 28, 1944 and their youngest daughter Gitty (גיטל) born March 28, 1946.

Mr. and Mrs. F. LEITNER, of Somerford House, Private Hotel, Buxton, extend their cordial כתיבה וחתימה טובה wishes to you and your family. Although we are closing down after Sukkoth for the winter months, we shall be delighted to see you again in Buxton for next Pessach or during the Summerseason.

42, Northfield Road, London, N.16 STAmford Hill 5121	Somerford House, Buxton Phone: Buxton 373

Rosh Hashono Greetings from Mr. & Mrs. F. Leitner

After the war, Family Hofmann sold the Buxton hotel to Uncle Fritz, who later converted it into a guesthouse, catering for long-term residents. During this period Uncle Fritz hired Rabbi Wagschall as a Rebbe for his children, who travelled regularly to Buxton to teach them some Yiddishkeit, since they all attended a non-Jewish school there. When they were short of a Minyan for Shabbos, Uncle Fritz would pay for boys to travel from Manchester or London to spend the weekend in Buxton.

During this time, the daily running of the guest house was managed by Aunty Margit, while Uncle Fritz rose early to shomer the milk and then continued his work as a dental technician. For the sake of the Chinuch of his children and on the advice of Reb Aaron of Belz, they moved to London, and the Buxton property was converted into flats and rented out.

At first Uncle Fritz lived at 42 Northfield Road in Stamford Hill, where he continued working in his profession. He then became self employed and established a Linen Hire Company, which is still a family run business today. Later they moved to 143b Upper Clapton Road, in close proximity of their youngest daughter, with a Minyan across the road, and the convenience of a bus stop outside the front gate. Uncle Fritz was niftar on 17 Teves 5748/ 7 Jan.1988, just a few months before Opa. Aunty Margit later moved to Schonfeld Square and was niftar on 9 Sivan 5759/ 24 May 1999.

Uncle Fritz together with Opa enjoying each others' company at a Simcha

UNCLE SHURL (ישעי׳ה/ARTHUR) LEITNER (1.1.1.4)

Uncle 'Shurl' as he was commonly known, was born in Marienbad on August 16, 1907. After he graduated from high school he continued his education and took a Hotel Course. Being extremely talented with his hands, he specialised in 'table decoration', learning how to make stunning masterpieces from starched cloth serviettes (napkins) that adorned the tables and added much to the decor at every event. In Marienbad, apart from helping in his parents' hotel during the high season, he also ran a small hardware store in an annex on the ground floor, which was demolished in Feb 1938.

In September 1938, when the Leitners were forced to leave Marienbad, Uncle Shurl made his way from Prague to Paris, were he stayed for a few months. In the early 1940's he wanted to go to England, and walked all the way to Calais, a journey that took approximately three weeks, walking at night and hiding and resting during the day. We can only imagine what he looked like after this ordeal. On one occasion, after he had found a suitable barn to rest, he stopped to put on his Tefillin and daven, before lying down to rest. However, his rest was short lived, as he had been spotted by a neighbouring farmer who alerted the police, who promptly arrested him on suspicion of sending secret Morse Code messages to the enemy! When he showed them his Tefillin and explained that these 'black boxes' were not Morse Code Transmitters but a religious article that Jewish people wear during prayers, they apologized and released him.

He reached Calais just before the "Battle of Dunkirk", when thousands of Allied troops were evacuated to safety across the English Channel, over a period of nine days. This was just before May 10, when Germany invaded Northern France. Uncle Shurl got onto one of these boats and arrived in England, where he stayed in a 'Displacement camp' for Jewish Refugees in London. Shortly afterwards he managed to locate his older brother, Uncle Fritz, who was already living in London at that time, and was given permission to join him. When he arrived at their house, they didn't recognise him. They were naturally very suspicious, since they had no idea that he had arrived in England, and given his appearance after the difficult three week trek, it did nothing to dispel their concerns. However, it did not take long to confirm that he indeed was their brother and they welcomed him with open arms.

Serviette decorations by Uncle Shurl at a function by Leitner's Catering in Leicester Hall

Soon after he got to London he found employment in a factory that manufactured batteries. He came home every evening completely covered in black carbon dust, the main ingredient of these batteries, but he was happy to have some sort of income, and that was his first priority. In early 1942, Mr. Yehuda Hofmann, who owned 'Sommerford House', a small kosher hotel in Buxton, heard that one of the Leitners from Marienbad was living in London, and invited him to come and help him manage the hotel. Uncle Shurl gratefully accepted the job and remained there until after the war. In 1943 he was joined by Uncle Fritz and his family, who had to get away from London due to the heavy shelling.

Uncle Shurl got married in Buxton on the 4th night of Chanukah 1944 to Rosie Sanger, a daughter of Erna Sanger, nee Hofmann.

After the war, Family Hofmann together with Uncle Shurl and Aunty Rosie, moved to the south of England where they bought the Sandringham hotel in Torquay, after having sold the hotel in Buxton to Uncle Fritz.

Marquetry hand-made by Uncle Shurl *Uncle Shurl in Torquay June 1947*

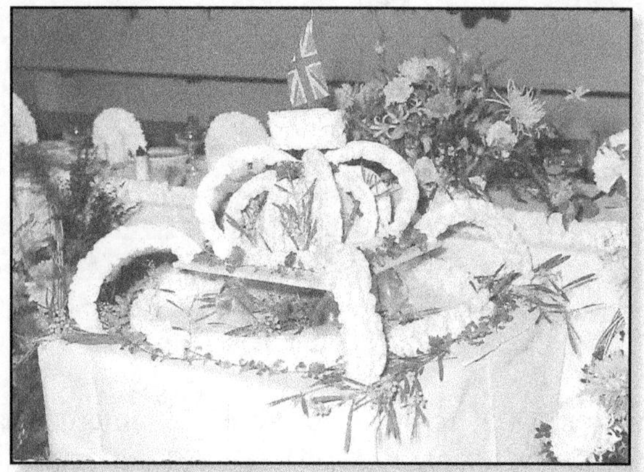

Uncle Shurl's Royal 3-tier Crown made entirely from starched serviettes

Uncle Shurl and Aunty Rosie were soon blessed with their children; Johnny born in January 1946, and Gettie in August 1947, while the family lived in Torquay. In 1949 they moved to Manchester, and initially lived at 140 Waterloo Road, before moving to 2 Richmond Avenue, Prestwich, where they occupied only the top floor of the house.

In a letter that Aunty Rosie wrote to our grandmother in Chile dated November 6, 1955, just ten days before our departure, she described how much they were all looking forward to welcome us in England. Also Johnny and Gettie added a couple of welcoming words to us [in English].

When Aunty Rosie was hospitalised at the Hammersmith Hospital in London W12 in June/July 1956, Uncle Fritz and his family cared for her and brought her kosher meals every single day for almost three months. These daily trips were quite time consuming, an hour's journey in each direction, having to take several buses, in addition to the time spent with the visit itself.

On June 7, 1956 Aunty Rosie wrote again, but this time from the Hammersmith Hospital in London. Despite her being stuck in hospital for a lengthy time, Aunty Rosie wrote to Sima Kokisch, just to confirm how well the Leitners had settled down in Manchester, and how her own children were delighted to have their new cousins for company!

Rabbi Schneebalg sitting, and Opa (r) with Uncle Shurl (l)

For as long as Uncle Shurl lived in Prestwich, he was a member of the 'Steibel' on Kings Road, a Minyan that was headed by Rabbi M.M. Schneebalg, where Uncle Shurl and the Rov became very close friends. Johnny celebrated his Bar Mitzvah there, and has remained their loyal and regular Baal Koreh and Baal Tefilla throughout the years.

Uncle Shurl travelled to Eretz Yisroel in 1949 with the view of emigrating there, but received a message via the police to return home, as his wife had taken ill, and he was needed at home. After Aunty Rosie was niftar in 1959, Uncle Shurl remained at Richmond Avenue, and only much later moved to Midfield Court in Salford, to be near his daughter Gettie.

UNCLE POLDI (״יהודה ארי״ה/LEOPOLD) DEUTSCH (1.1.2.2)

Uncle Poldi's parents were Adolf (אברהם) Deutsch and Sophie (יסכא) nee Leitner (1.1.7) and ran a guest house in Wiesbaden, Germany.

After his schooling in Wiesbaden he was employed by Beer, Sondenheimer & Co, a large chemical company in Frankfurt, from April 1917 until the summer of 1930, when the company closed that laboratory. However, they testified to his high quality of work and his experience and expertise as an analytical chemist of ferrous metals. He had studied at the universities of Frankfurt, Wiesbaden and Berlin, under the famous professor of chemistry, Professor Fresenius, becoming a world expert in his field.

When the Gestapo came to power, they were aware of his exceptional talents, and wanted to capture him so that he could help them in their war efforts. A keen chemistry student would be invaluable in developing new and more lethal poisonous gases and explosives, and they put out a search warrant for him.

Adolf (Avrohom) Deutsch (Uncle Poldi's father)

Uncle Poldi (1.1.2.2) and Uncle Alex (2.1.2)

Uncle Poldi escaped to France, and in October 1940 wrote to his Kokisch cousins in Chile, requesting them to try and obtain visas for himself, his sister and parents, to join them in Chile, but was unsuccessful. He was getting desperate since he could not find suitable employment without giving away his whereabouts, which in turn would have resulted in being found by the Germans. He confirmed later that during this period of austerity they survived thanks to the food parcels sent by Aunty Ernestine from Copenhagen.

When the Germans occupied Northern France, Uncle Poldi escaped with his sister and parents to Nice, in the south of France.

It is with thanks to הקב"ה that the family ties were so strong, that all those who had earlier on enjoyed close bonds and were now scattered around the globe, didn't spare any effort to try and trace each others' whereabouts, enquire about their welfare and provide the required assistance whenever possible. There are dozens of letters on file which testify to this family unity, from which I have chosen a few excerpts.

> On January 15, 1942, Uncle Poldi wrote to Aunty Ernestine in Copenhagen:
>
> … 'Last week we received your letter dated December 23, 1941 which made us very happy. [This letter arrived 3 weeks later]. We thank you for the two food parcels that arrived on January 7, but the other two have not arrived to date. We are very grateful for every single parcel that reached us, as this helped sustain us in these difficult times.'…
>
> During the many years of World War II and also for some time after that, food was rationed and food parcels were at a premium. Uncle Poldi suggested that in future all parcels should be sent 'recorded delivery' and that his family would receive a letter with the tracking number. With this in hand they could then check with the Post Office to find out if anything had been received for them, and the Post Office would hopefully be less likely to withhold it from them.
>
> This idea was later adopted and proved successful in ensuring that parcels actually arrived at their desired destination.
>
> On April 15, 1942, Uncle Poldi confirmed…that he had received the postcard from Copenhagen on Feb 23, 1942, and the two registered parcels from February 12 had arrived, too, much to their delight, for which he thanks them profusely…
>
> On April 16, he wrote again to Copenhagen, to thank explicitly for the large box of essential Pesach supplies that had just arrived.

He adds that he has received news from the family in Chile, that all is fine…

On June 29, 1942 Uncle Poldi wrote to Aunty Ernestine in Copenhagen. His letter was written in Nice, France but was sent from Geneva, Switzerland:

…'We received your postcard of June 19, and today we were extremely happy to receive the 5 parcels you sent us. This coincided with the homecoming of my dear Papa from hospital after a successful eye operation. ב"ה he can see again and can even go out and go for a walk by himself! This is after suffering from total blindness for three years, which incapacitated him so much that he was unable to eat by himself…

…All the food you sent was extremely well received by all, and was very tasty. Poldi.'

The Germans invaded Northern France in April 1940, and Southern France, including Nice, in November 1942, by which time Uncle Poldi had to go into hiding, whilst the remainder of the family (parents and sister) escaped to Geneva.

He was hidden by a non-Jewish lady in a small attic room, who provided him periodically with kosher food which kept him alive throughout the remainder of the war. From his attic window he would observe the Gestapo below patrolling the streets. This small attic was so cramped, that after the war was over and he was able to come out of hiding, he had to learn how to walk again. Throughout his life he would often suffer from nightmares because of his ordeals that he suffered during the war years.

But ב"ה he survived, and in June 1948 married his first cousin Aunty Amelie (1.1.4.1), Oma's oldest sister, and settled in Paris, while his parents and sister remained in Geneva.

Mr. Sam Levy was very friendly with family Deutsch and on the day after the Chassene wrote to Sima Kokisch in Chile. He wished her a hearty Mazel Tov for her daughter's wedding and described the whole event in great detail, since she unfortunately could not attend in person.

The Chassene was further enhanced by the presence of Aunty Ernestine Winkler, [Sima Kokisch' youngest sister] who came as a representative of all the family in Chile.

Uncle Poldi was an active member of the 'Rue Cadet' Shul in Paris, officially known as 'Adass Yereim'. Rabbi Dr. Eli Munk was the Rav of the Shul who was a native of Paris but had studied for the Rabbinate at the renowned Hildesheimer Rabbinical Seminar in Berlin, and also took his Doctorate Degree at Berlin University. Uncle Poldi was extremely close to Rabbi Munk, and Aunty Amelie was very friendly with his daughter, Amelie Munk, who later married Rabbi Jackobovitz, who became the Chief Rabbi of "The British Empire and Commonwealth." Uncle Poldi assisted Rabbi Munk in raising large sums of money for the Paris Mikvah and other important projects.

Rabbi Hildesheimer

Their home on 80, Rue Rene Boulanger, was part of a large and somewhat unusual housing complex that filled a whole cul-de-sac. It extended along both sides of the road, with blocks of flats, five storeys high, on either side, with a small alley between. An estimated 200 families lived there, all sharing the same address. This cul-de-sac was enclosed by a large door, and the first flat on the ground floor on the left belonged to the 'concierge' – a sort of caretaker. On the wall of his entrance there were rows and rows of small cubby-holes, where all the post and messages were left for the occupants. Uncle Poldi was fortunate that he lived on the fourth floor of the first block and also had his business at the same address, which was further down this alley, on the second floor.

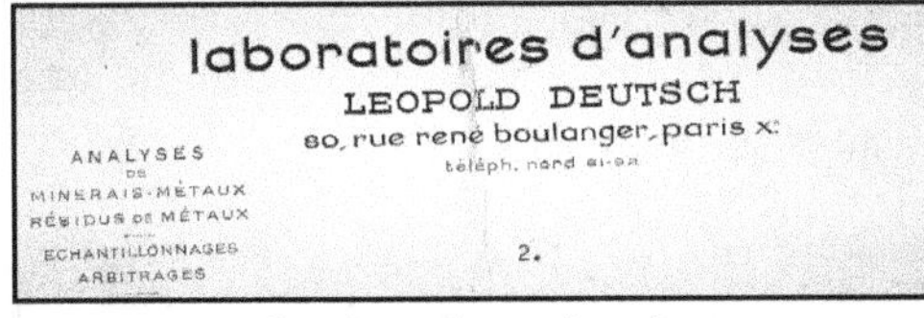

laboratoires d'analyses
LEOPOLD DEUTSCH
80, rue rené boulanger, paris x:

ANALYSES DE MINERAIS-MÉTAUX
RÉSIDUS DE MÉTAUX
ÉCHANTILLONNAGES
ARBITRAGES

2.

business letterhead

Owing to his expertise in chemistry, he opened an 'Analytical Chemistry' Service which soon became famous for analysing metals. He really would have preferred to be employed by another laboratory, but since this would most likely have conflicted with keeping Shabbos, he decided to become self-employed.

Uncle Poldi (1.1.2.2) in his lab in Paris.

The following episode is another manifestation of his Mesiras Nefesh for the sanctity of Shabbos.

A brief explanation of his job in analysing metals serves as the background to this story:

When a metal merchant wants to sell a ship-load of metal to a manufacturer, he wants to be sure that he is getting the correct item. Raw metal never comes in a pure state; it is always mixed with dross and impurities. For example, if the merchant has 20,000 tonnes of aluminium ore which he states is 85% pure, he will fix his selling price accordingly. The buyer will need to send in an analytical chemist to sample the shipment and analyse it to verify that the percentage of metal is correct, and also that it is the exact grade of metal that he requires. If, however, the analytical chemist only finds 25% metal content, the buyer will naturally only agree to pay a much lower price. From a purchase of 20,000 tonnes one only needs to take a small sample from many different places to obtain a statistical accurate measure of its contents. The total sample taken from such a large consignment may weigh only 500 grams, but nevertheless has to be representative of the total.

Uncle Poldi was an expert in how to take samples from a large consignment, and his expertise was highly sought.

One of his larger clients was negotiating purchasing a complete merchant shipment of metal that was due to arrive in Hull, an English port city about 80 miles from Manchester. The boat was scheduled to dock on a Thursday morning in the middle of November. This was perhaps the biggest job he had ever received from one of his main customers in France, and would net him a handsome fee. Uncle Poldi travelled to Manchester and stayed with us, while he waited for news of the exact time that the ship was scheduled to dock. When the ship was delayed due to heavy fog, I remember Uncle Poldi sitting next to the phone in the corridor, eagerly and nervously awaiting further instructions from Hull.

In the mean time no one coud use the phone, and if we needed to make a call, we had to go to the nearest phone-box. Eventually we heard that the boat was scheduled to arrive on Friday midday, and Uncle Poldi was required to be in Hull to carry out his urgent sampling, a job that would take several hours, and perhaps even more than a day. Although he had been looking forward to this assignment and the promise of a large profit, he refused to go at this point, as it would most certainly interfere with Shabbos.

I am grateful that I did not know much French to understand all that this client said, but his tone of voice spoke for itself to get the gist of the conversation. To say that he was not very impressed with Uncle Poldi's refusal to get to Hull immediately is an understatement, and he made it quite clear that this was a very big contract, and he was not prepared to lose it. He said he could not afford to delay the boat at dock, and pay the extra 'parking fees' that were payable to the Shipping Authorities for every extra hour the boat sat in the dock. To add to his aggravation, the port was closed on Sunday which meant that he would have to wait until Monday before he could sample the merchandise.

The client had little choice but to try and find another chemist that would analyse his consignment at short notice. However, when he was unable to find anyone else, he requested that Uncle Poldi get there on Monday and carry out his work on the following day. He also got him to understand that he would not use his services anymore after that! Uncle Poldi travelled to Hull and spent nearly two days taking samples, which he then took to Paris to analyse. In the meantime, the boat was sitting in Hull and clocking up parking fees!

The merchant maintained that his merchandise contained 85% metal content, whereas the analysis found only 30%, an unusually large discrepancy. The seller accused Uncle Poldi of incompetence, and demanded a second analysis by a different company. This was done, but they also came to the same conclusion and result, that there was indeed only 30% metal. The unscrupulous seller had melted down the metal ore and added water to the molten metal, ensuring that when it solidified it would add plenty of extra weight to his merchandise without any extra metal content. I don't know if the buyer ever bought this merchandise, but Uncle Poldi received a sincere apology from his French client and a handsome reward, and needless to say he remained his client for the rest of his career, too.

During a casual conversation, Uncle Poldi related this episode to Rabbi Munk in Paris, who was so impressed that he bestowed on him the 'Chover' title, as a public acknowledgement for the Mesiras Nefesh that he displayed to observe Shabbos under such trying circumstances.

Although Uncle Poldi suffered a great deal of anxiety during the war, he always managed to cheer other people up. He and Aunty Amelie came to all our Barmitzvas and Chassenes, and often also came for Yom Tov. Uncle Poldi's visits were always eagerly awaited as he delighted us with humorous sketches, some played out as a one-man-show, and some together with us children. He also composed amusing 'grammen' for each Simcha.

Uncle Poldi acting out his play and also organised a children's performance

Uncle Poldi's older sister had been looking after her elderly father in Geneva, and only got married at a later stage in life, and continued to live in Geneva.

ת'נ'צ'ב'ה

Adolf Deutsch

1867-1955

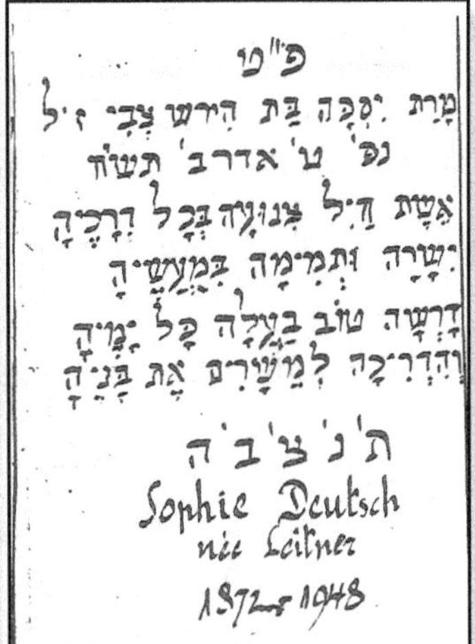

Inscription on the Matzeivos of Adolf Deutsch and his wife Sophie (1.1.2) *nee Leitner, both buried in Geneva*

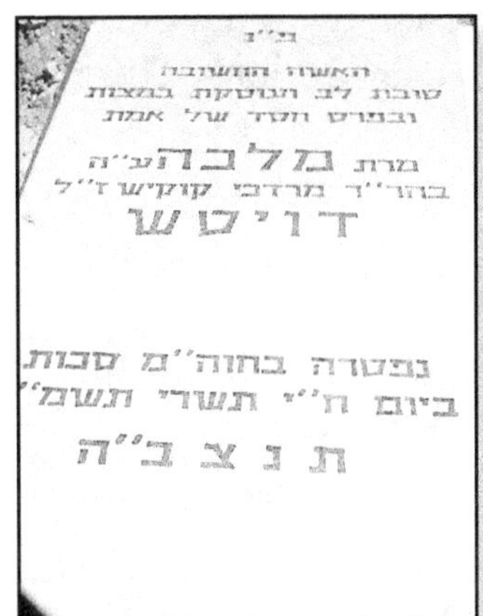

Matzeivos of Uncle Poldi (1.1.2.2.) *and Aunty Amelie* (1.1.4.1) *on Har Hazeizim*

UNCLE ALEX (אלכסנדר) KOKISCH (2.1.2)

Uncle Alex Kokisch was the younger brother of my grandfather, Mordechai (Max) Kokisch. He had been a successful soldier in the Austrian Army during World War 1, and received several medals for bravery, but despite that, both he and his wife suffered in Theresienstadt during World War 2. Below are extracts of a letter he wrote from Vienna to my grandmother, his sister-in-law, Sima Kokisch in Chile, on December 6, 1945 that vividly describes their experiences.

(translated fairly literally to portray their feelings)

> …'As I am now sitting on a chair by the table, enjoying good electric lighting, I recall all the suffering and misery that we endured. It is a real miracle that Hedwig (his wife) was able to endure all this. However, from the 30,000 or more inmates that were in Theresienstadt, I had the privilege ב"ה of being together with Hedwig throughout the entire three years! Apart from that, we ב"ה received a weekly food parcel from Anny (1.1.7.2), and also some from Hedwig's cousin, that kept us alive and saved us from starvation. Another miracle was that they never transported us to Auschwitz, considering that from the 15,000 Yidden from Vienna only a few survived the fate of those who were sent to the crematoriums. The gas chambers in Theresienstadt were operational and we were slated to be gassed on May 15, 1945, but ב"ה the Russians liberated us on May 8, and we were saved.
>
> Nevertheless we suffered a lot, but the worst was the fear of being sent on a 'transport' at any time, which meant certain death. But even without this we still endured much and constant suffering. Many different diseases and illnesses including typhus and dysentery were our daily fare.
>
> For seven years we were denied freedom. For four years [1938-1942 in Vienna] we endured all types of restrictions. No permission to use a tram, no access to public parks, and no visits to places of interest. We had a nice flat at Rudolf von Altplatz – and this was also an exception, because the Nazis came all the time to view the 'Jewish flat'. We lived in constant fear, and then, one day the inevitable happened. We were evicted and had to look for new accommodation, and even then we lived in constant fear of being deported to Poland.
>
> On October 2, 1942, some 1200 men, women and children were put up in a transit camp at Malzgasse, and slept on straw. After two days we were taken on a transport. The next morning we

arrived at Auschwitz, and with our luggage on our backs and driven on like a herd of cattle we had to walk to Theresienstadt without stopping. On arrival, everybody tried to find a little space to rest on the brick floor, where the dust was 10cm high. Already the entry into this building was awful. Two corpses lay in the corridor, which we had to pass over, and they were only removed some 36 hours later. In this way we spent the first three days on the floor at house Q609, but again ב"ה Hashem helped us. The brother of our old neighbour in Vienna had already been in Theresienstadt, and he arranged for both of us to be housed in Q313.

Theresienstadt was a town designed with streets running along vertically and horizontally. The street names were prefixed with either a Q (Querstrasse – horizontal lane) or with an L (Langstrasse – vertical lane). The original occupants of the town had been sent away, and it was now occupied by 30,000 – 60,000 Jewish prisoners, from Czechoslovakia, Hungary, Austria, Germany, Holland and Denmark. At Q313 we got a room of 14 square metres, which we shared with another 3 couples. Our place was close to the door, on the floor, with mattresses which had seen better days! If one of the occupants wanted to leave the room at night, as often happened, we had to pull our covers over our heads, since the door led onto a very draughty corridor. Nevertheless we were together, unlike the majority of the people, where men and women were separated, and the husbands had to go to the other end of town to see their wives.

In the morning we received some black coffee, or rather dark coloured water, which was mostly not even warm. At dinnertime we received mainly potato and some sauce, and in the evening, coffee, but there was sufficient bread. Later on, our rations improved as we received food parcels from Anny every Friday or Shabbos. This bolstered our morale and was tangible proof of her love and devotion to us. She saved her own rations of sausage and cheese from the food parcels that she herself had received from her parents in Czechoslovakia, so that she could send them to us. This was our Yom Tov; to open the weekly parcel and spread these 'delicacies' out on the bed. We were allowed light until 9 pm, unless we were punished with a 'no-light ban'. We also had a small cooker in our room. In this manner one day followed the next, one week and another week, one month after another, for almost three years.

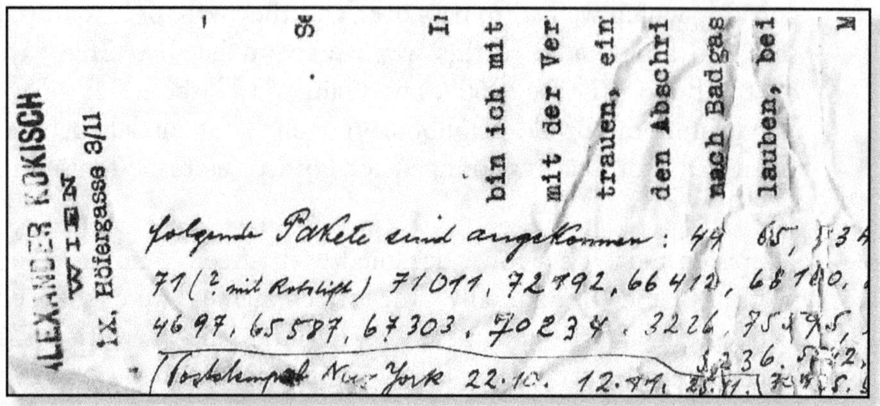

ALEXANDER KOKISCH
WIEN
IX, Höfergasse 3/11

bin ich mit
mit der Ver
trauen, ein
den Abschri
nach Badgas
lauben, bei

folgende Pakete sind angekommen: 49 65, 534
71 (? mit Rotstift) 71011, 72792, 66412, 68100,
4697, 65587, 67303, 70234. 3226. 75475,
3236.
(Poststempel New-York 22.10. 12.44. 25.11.

A record of the recorded parcel numbers on the side of the letter

Finally the day of our liberation arrived, but this too was not easy. We travelled in cattle trucks for 3 days and 4 nights from Theresienstadt to Vienna, and what awaited us on arrival was also unpleasant. But ב"ה the most important thing was that we were free. We were free to breathe again, free to attend Shul again after seven years of seclusion, free to go for a walk, and free to use public transport.

...We frequently saw Louise Leitner (see 1.1.3) and her three children in Theresienstadt, and they too lived together the entire time they were there. Twice during their stay they were scheduled to be deported to Poland, but ב"ה their names were deleted from the transport list at the last moment. They are now in Prague and are living in 11 Veletrizni, Prague 7.

...Have you heard anything from Uncle David, Reisel, Uncle Isidor and Thea, or from Family Deutsch?

With kindest wishes,

Alex.

The four Leitners left Prague and emigrated to Eretz Yisroel, where they were interned by the British Mandate in the infamous Atlit detainee camp. They claimed that the situation that awaited them at this detainee camp was even worse than what they had experienced and endured in Theresienstadt, and they categorically refused to stay there under such conditions!

In May 1947, Uncle Alex wrote to Chile, firstly to thank them for having received more than 30 food parcels during the war years which were sent from Santiago. He also confirmed that he had recently visited the cemetery in Vienna, and that all the Kokisch gravestones were intact and well maintained. He added that as of September 1946, they also received food parcels from the Agudas Yisroel that even contained a special delicacy – 'gefilte fish'.

A typical internment camp.
The inscription below was written on the back of the photo:
In this ancient house which is being used as a repatriation home, people are living like animals, together with young children, they simply refused to sleep at this internment camp, as the conditions were even worse than those experienced in Theresienstadt.

BEN ZION (בן ציון) LEITNER (1.2.2.1)

Ben Zion Leitner's father was Zvi, a brother of Gottlieb Leitner, owner of the Goldene Schloss Hotel in Marienbad.

On one of Rabbi Josef Shloime Kahaneman's (Ponevezer Rov) visits to Marienbad, he advised Zvi Leitner (1.2.2) to send his two sons to Yeshivah and get a Torah education, instead of accepting their place at Rome University. ב"ה Zvi Leitner took the Rov's advice, and the two boys initially went to Kelm and later to the Mirrer Yeshivah. Ben Zion and his brother Yechezkel both miraculously escaped with the Mirrer Yeshivah to Shangai, and were the only two surviving members of that part of the family. Whilst in Shangai, Ben Zion informed Reb Chazkel Levenstein one morning, that he had had a very disturbing dream the previoust night, and asked for some guidance. Reb Chazkel replied, 'Keep this day as your father's Yahrzeit'!

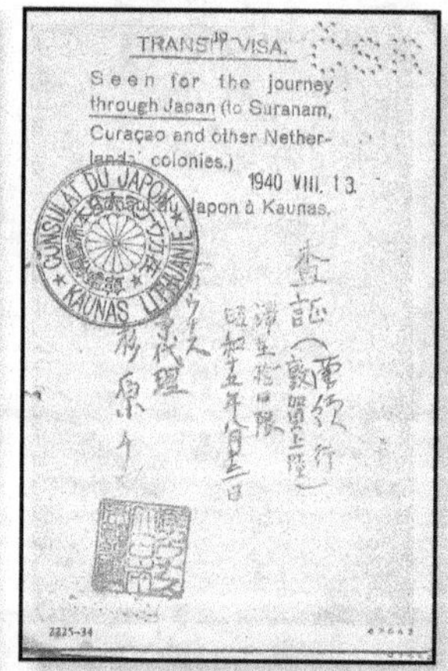

Pages of Ben Zion Leitner's (1.2.2.1) passport with transit visa through Japan

After the war Ben Zion went with the Mirrer Yeshivah to America, where he subsequently got married. Some time later on they emigrated to Eretz Yisroel and settled in Bnei Brak at 5, Rechov Baal Shem Tov. Ben Zion was very active in many communal projects. He was instrumental in the rescue of Jewish children from Christian missionaries, was a founder member of the Petach Tikvah Girls Seminary, and administrator for the 'Ohr Hachayim' Institutions in Bnei Brak.

Ernst Leitner (1.1.5) was a very successful businessman who owned two large 5-storey houses on 41 and 43 Solmsstrasse in East Berlin. They comprised of a total of 40 luxury flats that were all rented out, and covered an area of 591 square metres. Ernst was niftar in Berlin on August 27, 1941, and was buried there in the Jewish cemetery on Herbert Baumstrasse 45. It is worth noting that despite having died in Berlin in the middle of the war, in a town occupied by the Nazis, he nevertheless merited to be buried in the Jewish cemetery and have a Matzeivo erected the following year. For the record, he lies in the B2 section of the cemetery, second row, gravestone number 106276.

After the war the family sold his properties and the proceeds were distributed to all the 26 heirs in October 1966. Max Maimon (husband of Anny Maimon (1.1.7.2), who was a successful businessman and living in London, wrote to Opa, advising him that there exists a system named 'Property Dollars' which allowed British citizens to buy and sell property abroad, that would entitle them to an additional 28% over the normal exchange rate for German Marks! Opa was grateful for this information, and in fact received this extra amount for his share of the inheritance.

41 and 43 Solmsstrasse East Berlin (first two blocks)

In November 1966, Ben Zion Leitner wrote to Opa and suggested that a suitable memorial plaque be arranged for Uncle Ernst, who had died as a bachelor. Opa was very much in favour of this idea, and wrote to all the heirs of Uncle Ernst, and enclosed a copy of Ben Zion

Leitner's letter. He also added that Ben Zion's mother, Selma Leitner, had always looked after Uncle Ernst, and especially during his final stay in hospital she cared for him with great devotion. [In fact Selma Leitner was in charge of the Bikur Cholim of the Jewish Community in Berlin.] Together, the family dedicated a room at the Kol Torah Yeshivah in Yerushalayim with a donation of $1000, a substantial sum in those days.

לעילוי נשמת

יעקב בן מוה"ר צבי לייטנר ז"ל

נפטר ד' אלול תש"א, בברלין

ת.נ.צ.ב.ה.

הונצח ע"י קרוביו בארץ ובחו"ל

Plaque at Kol Torah Yeshivah Jerusalem a dedication for Ernst (Yaakov) Leitner

It had always been assumed by the larger Leitner family that Ernst Leitner's Hebrew name was Aaron. As was so common at that time in the Ashkenaz communities, people were often called by their secular names and their (real) Jewish names were not commonly used and sometimes not even known, even to close family members. It was only after Uncle Ernst' was niftar, that Aunty Ernestine (Winkler), his youngest sister, insisted that his Jewish name was Yaakov and not Aaron.

Another seeming error or discrepancy came to light with regards to משה דוד Leitner's father, Opa's grandfather. Opa always thought that his grandfather was called צבי. However some of the family's Matzeivos referred to him as צבי הירש while others inscribed his name as הירש צבי! Furthermore, the correct Jewish name of Oma's mother was סימא and not סעמל as inscribed on her tombstone.

RABBI & MRS. B. Z. LEITNER
5, Baal Shem Tov Street
Benei-Brak

בן־ציון ובלה לייטנר
רחוב בעל שם טוב 5
בני־ברק
טל. 7-20252

בס״ד

27.11.66.

Lieber Kurt!

Wir haben uns sehr gefreut mit Johnnie's Besuch und danken sehr für die Grüsse die wir von Euch bekommen haben. Uns geht es ב״ה gut. Du weisst wahrscheinlich dass wir einen Sohn bekommen haben. Der Bris war schon vor drei Wochen.

Von Kahane haben wir gehört, dass Ihr in Berlin verkauft habt, und Oscar hat mich angerufen um zu fragen was man tun kann, um den Namen des Onkel Ernst Selig zu verewigen. Ich glaube, am angebrachtesten wäre es, ein Zimmer in "KOL TORA" auf seinen Namen zu nennen: das sind wir seinem Andenken schuldig. Es wird eine Bronztablette mit seinem Namen über den Eingang des Zimmers angebracht, und so wird sein Andenken, da er doch leider kinderlos dahingegangen ist, auf ewige Zeiten in würdigster Form und durch das Sechut vom Limmud Hatora geehrt. "KOL TORA" ist Dir bekannt, auch Tante Ernestine und alle wissen, dass KOL TORA ihre Verpflichtungen gewissenhaft und würdevoll ausführt, und sind sicher mit dieser Art von Verewigung einverstanden.

Mit herzlichen Grüssen an Deine l. Familie auch von Bella und den Kindern unbekannterseits

Dein

Ben Zion

Meine Lieben,

Anbei Copy of Schreiben von Ben Zion Leitner, Wollt Ihr bitte entweder mir (13 Hanover Gardens, Manchester - Salford 7) oder direkt an Ben Zion Eure Stellungnahme mitteilen, damit endlich diese Ehrenschuld an Onkel Ernst sel. unsererseits gedeckt wird. - Ich moechte nur betonen, dass Ben Zions Mutter Frau Selma Leitner, diejenige war, die Onkel Ernst sel. bis zum letzten moment gepflegt hat und im Spital mit Essen versorgte. -

Beste Gruesse allseits

Kurt

(KURT)

Letter from Ben Zion Leitner (1.2.2.1) with Opa's comments

This translates:

Dear Kurt, לאי"ט
27.11.66

We were very happy with Johnny's visit and thank you very much for your kind regards. ב"ה we are well. You'll probably know that we had a baby boy. The ברית was three weeks ago.

From Kahan we heard that you've sold Berlin, and Oscar called me to ask what we can do to perpetuate the memory of Uncle Ernst. I think the most appropriate thing would be to dedicate a room in 'Kol Torah' in his memory – we owe it to him. They would affix a bronze plaque with his name above the entrance to the room, and the Zechus of Limmud Hatorah will be a very befitting perpetuation of his memory since he unfortunately died childless. 'Kol Torah' is well known to you, and Aunty Ernestine as well as everyone else knows that 'Kol Torah' carry out their obligations conscientiously and honourably.

With best wishes for your dear family, also from Bella and the children, whom you've not met.

Yours,

Ben Zion

Opa appended his reply to the above letter:

My dear Cousins לאי"ט,

Enclosed is a letter from Ben Zion Leitner. Please let me know (13 Hanover Gardens, Manchester-Salford 7) or write to Ben Zion directly, what you think of it, so that we can repay our debt of honour to Uncle Ernst ע"ה. I just want to mention that it was Mrs. Selma Leitner, Ben Zion's mother, who brought Uncle Ernst ע"ה food to the hospital and cared for him until the very end.

Best Regards to All,

Kurt

CHAPTER 13

Hakaras Hatov

THE SANTIAGO MIKVAH

Oma's mother and sister are both buried in Santiago, and since we arrived in England in December 1955, none of the Leitner's have ever gone back there to visit their graves. We also didn't know what condition their Matzeivos were in, and if the cemetery was well maintained or overgrown.

Opa and Oma often dreamt about having them reburied in Eretz Yisroel, and made serious enquiries as to how to bring this to fruition. The reason was of course that the family could visit their graves frequently, apart from the spiritual aspect of being buried in Eretz Hakedosha. They knew that it wasn't a simple matter, very costly too and they would also have to find a reliable person to undertake to do the job properly. Despite that, Opa went several times to discuss this possibility with Dayan Yitzchok Weiss (Minchas Yitzchok) who, after giving it some serious thought, advised them not to proceed.

Dayan Y. Weiss

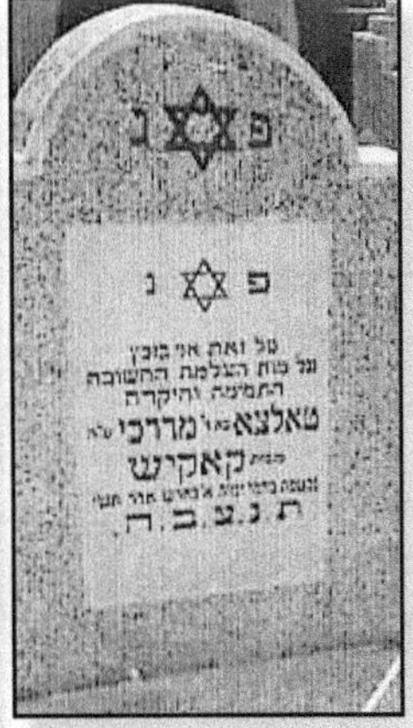

The two Kevorim in Chile - סעמל בת צבי *(Sima)* (1.1.4) - טאלצא בת מרדכי (1.1.4.2)

About fifteen years ago, Micha, as the oldest grandchild, felt that he should perhaps pay a visit, despite the distance and expense involved, but was advised not to go. But he didn't want to leave it at that and wanted to find out the state of the graves. He therefore called Rabbi Yitzchok Shaked, the Rov of the Orthodox community in Santiago, to enquire if he would be able to obtain pictures of the gravestones of both his grandmother and aunt. Some time later two photos arrived via e-mail, confirming that the gravestones and inscriptions as well as the cemetery were well maintained. Micha telephoned the Rov in Santiago to thank him for his services, and asked about the, 'Jewish Chile' where he was born, what progress had been made, how the Kehila was faring, and if there was anything that he might want from him.

Rabbi Shaked was quick to respond. "Yes, we need money, and plenty of it too, to build a new Santiago Mikvah!" The Rov explained that the Orthodox population had now moved to a different area, and the area where the old Mikvah stood was a rather run-down, unsavory area of town. They really needed to build one nearer to where they lived, and he therefore had begun a campaign to build a new, modern Mikvah. He was still short of $120,000 to complete this project.

So Micha undertook to help in whatever way he could, and sent out, bi-annualy, 7000 appeal letters to Yidden in London, Manchester and Gateshead, requesting donations for this worthy cause, 'The Santiago Mikvah Appeal'. This went on for three or four years, and all the funds that came in were promptly wired to Chile.

One evening Micha received a phone call from a friend who informed him that a wealthy acquaintance of his was seriously interested in helping to complete the Santiago Mikvah project. He wanted to know all the details, where they were holding at present, and how long it would take to complete the project. He also asked to see photos and get more details so that he could respond to this wealthy gentleman.

Micha immediately contacted his Mikvah project manager in Santiago, Mr. Ady Magendzo. He requested all the relevant information and stressed that it was needed urgently! This was on a Monday. When Micha called his contact in Chile, he was told that only the previous night the community executive had attended a meeting regarding the Mikvah and had decided, due to a lack of funds, to postpone the entire project for six months and put everything on hold. The shell of the building had already been built but they still required another $45,000 to complete the interior of the rooms and add all the fixtures, which would take another three weeks to complete, once they had the funds.

Micha got Ady to send him all the above information by e-mail, and by the next day managed to get an appointment and meet with the wealthy donor. Another day passed, and the entire amount of $45,000 was wired to Chile, with one condition: that the work be completed within three weeks.

On Shabbos morning the Rov made a public announcement. Only last Sunday evening the executive decided, due to a lack of funds, to postpone the Mikvah project for 6 months – and the following day they received a phone call from the other side of the globe requesting full details of the Mikvah project. By the Thursday of that same week they were in receipt of the entire sum, which would now allow them to complete the Mikvah within three weeks. This announcement and clear Hashgocho Protis was met with great excitement, and brought many of the ladies to tears. The Rov then made a special משברך for their British Friends that had enabled the project to reach completion so speedily.

Three weeks later, the community in Santiago had a state of the art Mikvah and celebrated this with a commemorative dinner to mark this very special event. Amongst the many guests they also welcomed the Israeli Ambassador to Chile and a Jewish Minister of the Chilean Government, who graced the event with their presence, as the new Santiago Mikvah became a reality. They also wanted Micha to fly over for this dinner, but instead he wrote them a speech which was read out, relating this wonderful story of Hashgocho Protis. His speech concluded with a very powerful message: 'All the thousands of kilometres of land and sea that separate us physically cannot diminish the bond of friendship that exists between Yidden.' Opa and Oma dreamt of reburying their close relations in Eretz Yisroel, a dream that never materialised, but it is in their merit that Santiago got a new Mikvah instead.

Construction of the Santiago Mikvah

This Mikvah was built with the assistance of our friends in England from MANCHESTER, LONDON AND GATESHEAD.
May the זכות of the use of this Mikvah bring spiritual and material blessing to all those who helped complete this project.
Nissan 5767

The plaque at the entrance of the Mikvah:

THE SANTIAGO EXPERIENCE

18 DECEMBER 2005

Fifty years after we arrived in England, Micha, single handedly, arranged and funded a magnificent event to commemorate this special milestone in the Leitner history. He invited all the Leitner descendants to a catered סעודה that was held at the Crumpsall Shul Hall, at which 90 family members attended. The hall was fittingly decorated with pictures of Chile and the Matzo bakery, the tables were adorned with Chilean and British Flags, and everything was meticulously planned with the entire family deriving much inspiration from the event.

As the family made their way to the entrance, a welcome surprise awaited them. Yossi, my son, had parked his car at the hall's entrance bearing specially made number plates to mark this special occasion!

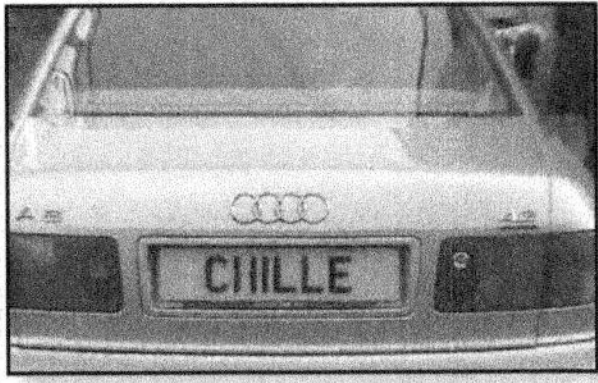

The appropriate car number plates to commemorate this special occasion

The proceedings were opened by a short introduction by Micha who welcomed everybody, and was immediately followed by a Siyum conducted by my son, Mordechai Meir, after which we were able to recite Kaddish together, as a fitting tribute to our dear parents. Then Aaron spoke, outlining the life in Chile and the sacrifice that Opa and Oma had made in leaving their luxurious life behind. He finished by making another Siyum Messechta. Aaron composed some grammen for this special occasion, which gave us a glimpse into Opa and Oma's past and achievements.

בצאת Opa and Oma from Europe – were well known Askonim,
בצאת Opa and Oma from Chile – also were busy Askonim.

בצאת Opa and Oma from Europe- left an elderly father behind.
בצאת Opa and Oma from Chile – also left an elderly mother behind.

בצאת Opa and Oma from Europe – lived away from the big centres of Yiddishkeit.
בצאת Opa and Oma from Chile – also lived away from the centres of Yiddishkeit.

בצאת Opa and Oma from Europe – left behind their comfortable homes,

בצאת Opa and Oma from Chile – also left behind their comfortable homes.

בצאת Opa and Oma from Europe – they left quickly
בצאת Opa and Oma from Chile – they left with a plan.

בצאת Opa and Oma from Europe – they left because they had to,
בצאת Opa and Oma from Chile – they left because they wanted to.

בצאת Opa and Oma from Europe – they left at night,
בצאת Opa and Oma from Chile – they left בעצם היום הזה.

בצאת Opa and Oma from Europe – was Mamesh Pikuach Nefesh,
בצאת Opa and Oma from Chile – was with Mesiras Nefesh.

בצאת Opa and Oma from Chile – meant leaving behind a Mother, Mother-in-law, who was also an Aunty.

בצאת Opa and Oma from Chile – meant giving up a good parnossoh.

בצאת Opa and Oma from Chile – meant selling a prestigious and a spacious bungalow with beautiful gardens.

בצאת Opa and Oma from Chile – meant moving away from a country with a warm climate.

בצאת Opa and Oma from Chile – meant saying goodbye to all the things they had and may never have again.

בצאת Opa and Oma from Chile – meant turning their backs on their own future in order to give US children a proper future.

This was followed by a lively chorus of בצאת ישראל ממצרים.

Shloimi, Micha's son, then presented a slide show that vividly recapped both the life in Chile and our subsequent journey to England.

Then it was my turn to express שבח והודאה to הקב"ה.

...At the end of the שמונה עשרה we express our thanks to הקב"ה for everything that He has done for us, with the words 'Modim Anachnu Loch' and end this same paragraph with the words of 'Al She'anachnu Modim Loch, Boruch Kel Hahodos'. The obvious question is why repeat this phrase again at the end? The answer is that we begin with words of thanks for everything that Hashem has done for us, but end off with a special mention of thanks, for giving us the opportunity that allows us to express this gratitude to Hashem. We are assembled here together to express openly 'Modim Anachnu Loch' to הקב"ה for all the חסדים that He has shown us, but at the same time we express extra thanks for giving us this unique opportunity in which to express this gratitude in public.

...we also have tremendous הכרת הטוב for the great Mesiras Nefesh of our parents for the sake of our חינוך.

...We shake the Arba Minim in all six directions when we say the Possuk of הודו לה' כי טוב כי לעולם חסדו -. With the word הודו we shake the לולב in forward direction, whilst with the word Hashem we do not shake it at all; with the word כי we shake the לולב to the right, and with the word טוב we shake it towards the back. What is the significance of this? If one wants to see the true goodness – the true טוב in anything, then one needs to look back and examine its history, similar to the lulov that is shaken towards the back when mentioning the word טוב. We can all "shake" our heads in admiration as we look back and appreciate this טוב that has resulted from our parents' decision to leave Chile 50 years ago, and at the same time contemplate what might have happened if they would not have taken this momentous step! We are gathered here today to relate and retell in public that טוב – by looking back and contemplating the consequences of their Mesiras Nefesh, and follow their example as to how to lead our lives. This Possuk of 'הודו לה... ends with the words ...כי לעולם חסדו that has the same gematrioh as חיים ארי'ה!

...The תורה shows us how to express feelings of gratitude in 'פ ביכורים, that begins by first revisiting the difficult period in history with the words of ארמי אבד אבי. We therefore need to begin by mentioning this most difficult epoch of Jewish History that both our parents lived through – namely that of World War II. With great ס"ד they were both able to escape and were spared the fate of the millions of Kedoshim. Each in their own miraculous way was forced to leave their home with few worldly possessions, and start anew in a completely foreign land, which they succeeded in doing without compromising or deviating in the slightest from the dictates of the Shulchan Oruch. Oma arrived in Santiago in early 1939, whilst Opa came in 1946, after having spent the war years in London.

...Opa decided to leave Chile despite his financially comfortable life, because he was more interested that his children and grandchildren should be שומרי תורה ומצוות and appreciate what שמע ישראל means. With the state of Jewish education that was available to us in Santiago, this would have been very doubtful. שמע ישראל is a proclamation that incorporates a person's total Emuna in Hashem, which we are obliged to reconfirm every morning and evening. Chazal stress the importance that Shema should contain a total of 248 words by adding the six words contained in the Possuk of 'Boruch Shem Kevod Malchuso Leolom Voed' and repeating the three words of 'Hashem Elokechem Emes' at the end. The number 248 corresponds to the number of positive Mitzvahs, which every male member of Klal Yisroel is obliged to keep. Many of these Mitzvahs, however, do not apply to ladies. Rabbi Yehuda Hachosid poses a very interesting question. If Chazal found it so important that the שמע should contain a total of 248 words, why does the Torah itself omit nine of these words, thereby necessitating Chazal to insert them?

Rabbi Yehuda Hachosid points out that the actual text of שמע that is written in the Torah contains only **239** words, a number that corresponds to the gematria of the word **ברזל** – iron. Iron is a metal that represents unyielding strength, one with which to express our total Emuna in Hashem in all situations. ברזל is also the acronym of **בלהה רחל זלפה לאה** , the four wives of Yaakov, as the strength of one's Emuna in Hashem is ingrained and taught to the next generation by the mothers of Klal Yisroel. The שמע therefore only contains 'ברזל' words.

Oma's mother lived with her in Chile, and for her to agree that we move away for the sake of our Yiddishkeit required perhaps an even greater Mesiras Nefesh. She could have found plenty of excuses and Kibbud Em would have been a very plausible one. Oma knew that once she moved, she would more than likely never see her mother again. She not only agreed with Opa, but took an active and positive role in all the preparations and arrangements that were necessary for this to come to fruition. Furthermore, it was Oma's mother herself who ultimately gave her consent to this move and displayed this positively by presenting them with her most precious possession. She fully appreciated that we were emigrating only for the sake of Yiddishkeit, so she gave us her own Sefer Torah that had been written in memory of her husband, and was miraculously saved from the hands of the Germans. This was her way of showing her approval to this extremely difficult, personal and emotional decision.

Iron, when in the wrong environment, can become rusty and deteriorate. These ladies of iron that were so special and different, were made from very superior iron – like 'Stainless Steel', that remained unaffected, untainted and unchanged by its surroundings. It was these ladies of ברזל, ladies of stainless steel and possesing an iron-strong character and determination that formed the basis of our upbringing and Emuna.

...it is well known that when red hot iron is placed into a contrasting cold bath, it hardens the metal. Similarly, when parents and grandparents forego their natural feelings of motherly love and respect for each other only for the sake of Torah and Yiddishkeit, then that will strengthen our Emuna, in the same way that iron is strengthened into steel. Our entry permit to England was a container full of pieces of iron – in different shapes and sizes that comprised of the Matzo baking machinery. These numerous pieces of ברזל is our parents' ירושה (inheritance) to us, an heirloom that should be our strength in Emunas Hashem and adherence to the Shulchan Oruch in all circumstances.

...I once heard Rabbi Tuvia Weiss describe his escape from the horrors of World War II. What gave him the courage to continue with life and cling to Yiddishkeit upon arriving in London alone, a refugee, and after having lost all his relatives? The answer was one simple and sincere thought. He asked himself, why has Hashem singled me out from my entire family and kept me alive? Is it so that I can enjoy life and its luxuries? Surely I have been spared in order to accomplish a loftier goal. This simple thought in Emuna gave him the impetus to become what he is today, and this same thought was the backbone of our parent's entire philosophy to life. They were saved from amongst six million others who did not survive the atrocities of the war, in order to be instrumental in rebuilding Yiddishkeit, a mission that they accomplished with distinction.

...In the תפילות of ראש השנה we mention the phrase of 'באין מליץ יושר – The Meforshim explain that the word יושר is made up from the acronym of 'יתגדל **ו**יתקדש **ש**מה **ר**בא". It is therefore a special merit for both Opa and Oma that we were able to combine this special event with סיומים, where קדיש was recited in their merit. May they continue to be מליצי **יושר** and their lives serve as an inspiration to all the family, עד ביאת גואל צדק.

CHAPTER 14

Leitner Family Tree

LEITNER FAMILY TREE

Herman צבי *Leitner*

Moishe Dovid משה דוד *Leitner*

Max מרדכי *Kokisch*

In previous generations, especially amongst the Ashkenazi communities, it was not uncommon for Jewish people to have a secular name apart from their Jewish names. When writing this family tree I have, in the first instance, used the secular names, and, where known, placed their Hebrew names too. This was done to simplify tracing the people mentioned to the numerous documents that are on file.

The father of Yoachim [Chaim Aryeh] Leitner was Avrohom Leitner whose Matzeivo was found in Drumol (number 23).

Yoachim Leitner - חיים אריה
d. 21/Jan/1889 Drumol
י"ט שבט תרמ"ט

(1.1) Herman Leitner b. 1834 d. 12/Oct/1918	**צבי** נ. תקצ"ד מ. ז' חשון תרע"ט
(1.2) Edward Leitner b. 29/Dec/1839 d. 03/Jun/1910 Drumol [There are two Yechezkel Leitners buried in Drumol. One with grave number 22, died 14/Jan/1833.]	**יחזקאל** נ. כ"ב טבת ת"ר מ. כ"ה אייר תש"ע

(1.1) Herman Leitner - צבי
b. 1834 d. 12.Oct.1918 Drumol.
נ. תקצ"ד - מ. ז" חשון תרע"ט

Theresa Epstein טאלצא
b. 31/Jan/1842 d.2/April/1897 Drumol
נ. כ" שבט תר" ב - מ. כ"ט אדר ב" תרנ"ז

(1.1.1) Moishe Dovid Leitner b. 2/Dec/1869 died in the camps, Yahrzeit kept same date as his father.	**משה דוד** נ. כ"ח כסלו תר"ל מ. ז' חשון תש"ב
(1.1.2) Sophie Leitner – (Yiska) b. 1872 d. 20/Mar/1948. Buried in Geneva	**יסכא** נ. תרל"ב מ. ט' אדר ב' תש"ח
(1.1.3) Max Leitner b. 18/Jul/1874 d. 6/Apr/1917 Buried in Marienbad on Erev Pesach.	**מאיר** נ. ד' אב תרל"ד מ. י"ד ניסן תרע"ז
(1.1.4) Hedwig Leitner (Sima) b. 12/April/1878 d. 16/Aug/1960. Buried in Santiago de Chile	**סימא** נ. ט' ניסן תרל"ח מ. כ"ג אב תש"כ
(1.1.5) Ernst Leitner b. 19/Jan/1880 d. 27/Aug/1941 Buried in Berlin	**יעקב** נ. ו' טבת תר"מ מ. ד' אלול תש"א
(1.1.6) Ernestine Leitner (Esther) b. 5/March/1882 d. 12/Dec/1976 Buried on Har Hazeizim Jerusalem	**אסתר** נ. י"ד אדר תרמ"ב מ. כ' כסלו תשל"ו
(1.1.7) Isidor Leitner b. Prague 8/June/ 1884 d. 27/Jul/1942 in the camps.	נ. ט"ו סיון תרמ"ד מ. י"ג אב תש"ב

(1.1.8) Berta Leitner (Baila)	**בילא**
Emil Leitner b. 20/April/1876 d. 08/May/1882 age 6 Buried in Marienbad	נ. כ"ו ניסן תרל"ו מ י"ט אייר תרמ"ב
Helene Leitner b. 16/March/1886 d. 07/Apr/1887, age 13 months Buried in Marienbad	נ. ט' אדר ב' תרמ"ו מ. י"ג ניסן תרמ"ז

(1.1.1) Moishe Dovid Leitner - משה דוד

b. 2/Dec/1869 (Drumol) died in the camps, Yahrzeit 7th Cheshvan

נ. כ"ח כסלו תר"ל - מ. ז' חשון תש"ב

Married on 21/May/1901 ג' סיון תרס"א

Gittel Schopflocher Furth (Germany) גיטל בת שלמה

b. 12/July/1871 d. 29/July/1934

נ. כ"ג תמוז תרל"א - מ. י"ז אב תרצ"ד

[buried in Marienbad – Matzeivo removed by Germans in 1939]

Parents of Gittel Schopflocher (from Furth)

Father: Salomon (from Furth) - שלמה

b. 14/Jan/1824 d. 05/Apr/1903 נ. י"ד שבט תקפ"ד - מ. ח' ניסן תרס"ג

Mother: Sara (nee Goetz) שרה

b. 08/Aug/1835 d. 22/May/1908 נ. ג' אלול תקצ"ה - מ. כ"א אייר תרס"ח

(1.1.1.1) Theresa Leitner (Tolze) b. 12/Feb/1903 d. 9/Aug/1942 in the camps Theresa had a twin sister who died at birth and is buried in Marienbad, name unknown.	**טאלצא** נ. ט"ו שבט תרס"ג מ. כ"ו אב תש"ב
(1.1.1.2) Siegfried (Fritz) Leitner (Shloime) b. 9/Apr/1904 d. 7/Jan/1988 had a twin who died at birth and is buried in Marienbad, name unknown.	**שלמה** נ. כ"ד ניסן תרס"ד מ. י"ז טבת תשמ"ח
(1.1.1.3) Kurt Leitner (Chaim Aryeh) b. 8/Feb/1906 d. 9/Sep/1988	**חיים אריה** נ. י"ג שבט תרס"ו מ. כ"ז אלול תשמ"ח
(1.1.1.4) Arthur (Shurl) Leitner (Yeshaya) b. 16/Aug/1907 d. 10/Apr/1982	**ישעיה** נ. ו' אלול תרס"ז מ. ט"ז ניסן תשמ"ב
(1.1.1.5) Erich Leitner (Aaron) b. 3/Jan/1909 d. 31/May/1967	**אהרן** נ. כ"ט שבט תרס"ח מ. כ"א אייר תשכ"ז

(1.1.2) Sophie Leitner (Yiska) יסכא
b. 1872 d. 20/Mar/1948
נ. תרל"ב - מ. ט' אדר ב' תש"ח

Avrohom Deutsch from Wiesbaden אברהם
b. 1867 d. 7/Dec/1955.
נ. תרכ"ז - מ. כ"ב כסלו תשט"ז

(1.1.2.1) Theresa Deutsch (Tolze) b. 1893 d. 29/June/1985	**טאלצא** נ. תרנ"ג מ. י' תמוז תשמ"ה
(1.1.2.2) Leopold Deutsch Y(ehuda Aryeh) d. 31/Mar/1983	**יהודה אריה** מ. י"ז ניסן תשמ"ג

(1.1.3) Max Leitner (Meir) - מאיר
b. 18/Jul/1874 d. 6/Apr/1917
נ. ד' אב תרל"ד - מ. י"ד ניסן תרע"ז
(buried in Marienbad on Erev Pesach)

Louis (Breindle) Bloch from Falkenau ברינדל

(1.1.3.1) Berta Leitner b. 22/Jan/1905	**ברתה** נ. ט"ז שבט תרס"ה
(1.1.3.2) Oskar Leitner b. 24/Dec/1907 d. 11/Jan/1999	**אריה** נ. י"ט טבת תרס"ח מ. כ"ג טבת תשנ"ט
(1.1.3.3) Theresa (Reisel) Leitner b. 22/May/1912 d. 14/Sep/2013	**טלזה (ריזל)** נ. ו' סיון תרע"ב מ. י' תשרי תשע"ג

(1.1.4) Hedwig Leitner (Sima) - סימא
b. 12/Apr/1878 d. 14/Aug/1960
נ. ט' ניסן תרל" ח - מ. כ"ג אב תש"כ

Married in Marienbad on Friday (Lag Ba`omer) 15/May/1903 - י"ח אייר תרס"ג

Max Kokisch from Brody – מרדכי
b.09/Apr/1871 d. 30/Jul/1930
נ. י"ח ניסן תרל"א - מ. ה' אב תר"צ

(1.1.4.1) Amelie Kokisch (Malka) b. 1904 in Bad Gastein d. 16/Oct/1981.	**מלכה** נ. תרס"ד מ. י"ח תשרי תשמ"ב

(1.1.4.2) Theresa Kokisch (Tirza Tolze - known as Reisel) b. 1908 in Nice d. 18/Feb/1950	**תירצה טאלצא** נ. תרס"ח מ. ראש חודש אדר תש"י
(1.1.4.3) Hilda Kokisch (Hinda) b. 6/Oct/1914 in Marienbad d. 10/May/1989	**הינדא** נ. י"ח תשרי תרע"ה מ. ה' אייר תשמ"ט
(1.1.4.4) Berta Kokisch (Baila) b. 22/May/1919 in Bad Gastein d. 11/Nov/1996	**בילא** נ. כ"ב אייר תרע"ט מ. כ"ט חשון תשנ"ז

(1.1.5) Ernst Leitner (Yaakov) - יעקב

b. 19/Jan/1880 d. 27/Aug/1941

נ. ו' טבת תר"מ - מ. ד' אלול תש"א

He was a bachelor, buried in Berlin.

(1.1.6) Ernestine Leitner (Esther) - אסתר

b. 5/Mar/1882 d. 12/Dec/1976

נ. י"ד אדר תרמ"ב - מ. כ' כסלו תשל"ז

Married in Marienbad on September 9, 1913 ז' אלול תרע"ג

Rabbi Dr. Michoel Sholom Winkler רב מיכאל שלום

b. 5/Jul/1863 (Jerusalem) d. 25/Jul/1932 buried in New York

נ י"ח תמוז תרכ"ג - מ. כ"א תמוז תרצ"ב

(1.1.6.1) Menashe Winkler b. 12/Apr/1919	**מנשה צבי** נ. י"ב ניסן תרע"ט
(1.1.6.2) Efraim Winkler b. 29/May/1921 d. 12/Feb/2014	**מאיר אפרים** נ. כ"א אייר תרפ"א מ. י"ב אדר א' תשע"ד

(1.1.7) Isidor Leitner

b. Prague 8/June/ 1884. Died in concentration camp 27/Jul/1942

נ ט"ו סיון תרמ"ד - מ. י"ג אב תש"ב

Regina Gerlitz (Warsaw)

Died in concentration camp 27/Jul/1942

מ. י"ג אב תש"ב

(1.1.7.1) Theresa Leitner b. 22/5/1912 d. 27/Jul/1942 Died in concentration camp	נ. ו"סיון תרע"ב מ. י"ג אב תש"ב
(1.1.7.2) Anny Leitner	

(1.1.7.3) Herma Leitner	
(1.1.7.4) Marion Leitner	
(1.1.7.5) Mimi Leitner	
(1.1.7.6) Lisl Leitner	
(1.1.7.7) Benny Leitner	

(1.1.8) Berta Leitner בילא

Emil Gerstel - מרדכי

(1.1.8.1) Leopold Gerstel	
(1.1.8.2) Adolf Gerstel	
(1.1.8.3) Oscar Gerstel (due to illness later changed to חיים אריה) b. 3/Jan/1903 in Marienbad d. 6/May/1965 in Haifa	**אריה** נ. ד' טבת תרס"ג מ. ד' אייר תשכ"ה
(1.1.8.4) Edward Gerstel b.12/Dec/1911	**יחזקאל** נ. כ"א כסלו תרע"ב

(1.1.1.1) Theresa Leitner (spinster) (Tolze) - טאלצא
b.12/Feb/1903 d. 9/Aug/1942 in concentration camp
נ. ט"ו שבט תרס"ג - מ. כ"ו אב תש"ב

(1.1.1.2) Fritz (Siegfried) Leitner (Shloime) - שלמה
b. 9/Apr/1904 d. 7/Jan/1988
נ. כ"ד ניסן תרס"ד - מ. י"ז טבת תשמ"ח

Margit Wiener from Pressburg - מלכה בת אברהם
d. 24/May/1999
מ. ט' סיון תשנ"ט

(1.1.1.2.1) Judith Leitner b. 08/Feb/1941	**יהודית** נ. י"א שבט תש"א
(1.1.1.2.2) Harry Leitner (Tzvi Avrohom) b. 26/Apr/1942.	**צבי אברהם** נ - ט' אייר תש"ב
(1.1.1.2.3) Monty Leitner (Yehuda Mordechai Shimon) b. 28/Jul/1944 d. 08/Sep/2011	**יהודה מרדכי שמעון** נ. ח' אב תש"ד מ. ט' אלול תשע"א

(1.1.1.2.4) Gitty Leitner b. 28/Mar/1946	**גיטל** נ. כ"ה אדר ב' תש"ו

(1.1.1.3) Kurt Leitner (Chaim Aryeh) - חיים אריה
b. 08/Feb/1906 d. 09/Sep/1988
נ. י"ג שבט תרס"ו - מ. כ"ז אלול תשמ"ח

Married in Santiago on 15/Jan/1946 י"ג שבט תש"ו

(1.1.4.3) Hinda (Hilda) Kokisch from Bad Gastein הינדא
b. 06/Oct/1914 d. 10/May/1989
נ. י"ח תשרי תרע"ה - מ. ה' אייר תשמ"ט

(1.1.1.3.1) Micha Leitner (Mordechai Tzvi) b. 19/Jan/1947	**מרדכי צבי** נ. כ"ז טבת תש"ז
(1.1.1.3.2) David Leitner (Dovid) b. 20/Mar/1948	**דוד** נ. ט' אדר ב' תש"ח
(1.1.1.3.3) Salomon Leitner (Shloime Yeshaya) b. 12/Jul/1949 d. 06/Aug/2010	**שלמה ישעיה** נ. ט"ו תמוז תש"ט מ. כ"ו אב תש"ע
(1.1.1.3.4) Aron Leitner (Aaron) b. 04/Feb/1951	**אהרן** נ. כ"ח שבט תשי"א
(1.1.1.3.5) Benny Leitner (Binyomin) b. 03/Nov/1953	**בנימין** נ. כ"ה חשון תשי"ד

(1.1.1.4) Arthur (Shurl) Leitner (Yeshaya) - ישעיה
b. 16/Aug/1907 d. 10/Apr/1982
נ. כ"ו אלול תרס"ז - מ. ט"ז ניסן תשמ"ב

Married in Buxton on 14/Dec/1944 כ"ח כסלו תש"ה

Rosa Sanger from Frankfurt-am-Main רבקה
b. 13/Jul/1920 d. 03/Feb/1959
נ. י"ז תמוז תר"פ - מ. כ"ג אדר א' תשי"ט

(1.1.1.4.1) Johnny (Harold) Leitner (Yom Tov) b. 30/Jan/1946	**יום טוב** נ. כ"ח שבט תש"ו
(1.1.1.4.2) Getty Leitner (Gittel Ruth) b. 21/Aug/1947	**גיטל רות** נ. ה' אלול תש"ז

(1.1.1.5) Erich Leitner (Aaron) - אהרן
b. 03/Jan/1909 d. 31/May/1967
נ. י' טבת תרס"ט - מ. כ"א אייר תשכ"ז
—— 1st ——
Kato Schreiber
—— 2nd ——
Carla (Karoline) Hohenberg
b. 28/Feb/1916 Vienna נ. כ"ד אדר א' תרע"ו

(1.1.2.1) Theresa Deutsch (Tolze) - טאלצא
b. 1893 d. 29/June/1985
נ. תרנ"ג - מ. י' תמוז תשמ"ה

———

Emil (Elimelech) Lubelski - אלימלך בן שלמה חיים
b.1903 d. 29/July/1986
נ. תרס"ג - מ. כ"ב תמוז תשמ"ו

(1.1.2.2) Leopold Deutsch (Yehuda Aryeh) - יהודה אריה
d. 31/Apr/1983 מ. י"ז ניסן תשמ"ג

———

(1.1.4.1) Amelie Kokisch (Malka) - מלכה
b. 1904 in Bad Gastein d. 16/Oct/1981
נ. תרס"ד - מ. י"ח תשרי תשמ"ב

(1.1.6.1) Menashe Winkler - מנשה צבי
b. 12/Apr/1919 נ. י"ב ניסן תרע"ט

———

Esther Rivkah Besbroda - אסתר רבקה
b. 12/Feb/1920 d. 03/Oct/2010
נ. כ"ג שבט תר"פ - מ. כ"ו חשון תשע"א

(1.1.6.1.1) Michoel Sholom b. 31/Oct/1944	**מיכאל שלום** נ. י"ד חשון תש"ה
(1.1.6.1.2) Gershon b. 12/Mar/1949	**גרשון** נ. י"א אדר תש"ט
(1.1.6.1.3) Yaacov b. 13/Jan/1953	**יעקב** נ. כ"ו טבת תשי"ג
(1.1.6.1.4) Dov Eli b. 19/Jun/1955	**דוב אלי** נ. כ"ט סיון תשט"ו

(1.1.6.1.5) **Shoshana** b. 25/Sep/1960	**שושנה** נ. ד' תשרי תשכ"א

(1.1.6.2) Efraim Winkler - מאיר אפרים
b. 29/May/1921 d. 12/Feb/2013
נ. כ"ד אייר תרפ"א - מ. י"ב אדר תשע"ג

Chaya Sompolinsky - חיה
b. 10/Aug/1923 d. 01/May/2015
נ. כ"ח אב תרפ"ג - מ. י"ב אייר תשע"ה

(1.1.6.2.1) Golde Winkler b. 30/Sep/1944	**גלדה** נ. י"ד תשרי תש"ה
(1.1.6.2.2) Yerith Winkler b. 28/May/1946	**יראת שרה** נ. כ"ז אייר תש"ו
(1.1.6.2.3) Michoel Winkler b. 05/Apr/1948	**מיכאל אלחנן** נ. כ"ז אדר תש"ח
(1.1.6.2.4) Rosa (Tirza) Winkler b. 23/May/1951 d. 13/Sep/2013	**תרצה** נ. י"ז אייר תשי"א מ. ח' תשרי תשע"ד
(1.1.6.2.5) Avrohom Eliyohu Winkler b. 23/Oct/1956	**אברהם אליהו** נ. י"ח חשון תשי"ז
(1.1.6.2.6) Shula Winkler b. 19/Jul/1958	**שולמית** נ. י"ג תמוז תשי"ט
(1.1.6.2.7) Shimshon Winkler b. 03/Feb/1961	**שמשון** נ. י"ז שבט תשכ"א
(1.1.6.2.8) Gila Rachel Winkler b. 27/May/1967	**גילה רחל** נ. י"ח אייר תשכ"ז

(1.1.7.2) Anny Leitner

Max Maimon

(1.1.7.3) Herma Leitner

Adolf Klein

(1.1.7.4) Marion Leitner

Mr. Harley

(1.1.8.3) Oskar Gerstel
b. 3/Jan/1903 נ- ד" טבת תרס"ג

Reisel Adler from Munich

(1.1.8.3.1) Bea Gerstel b.7/June/1937	נ. כ"ו תמוז תרצ"ז
(1.1.8.3.2) Micha Gerstel b. 01/Sept/1938	נ. ג" אלול תרצ"ח

(1.2) Edward Leitner (Yechezkel) - יחזקאל
b. 29/Dec/1839 d. 03/Jun/1910 Drumol
נ. כ"ב טבת ת"ר - מ. כ"ה אייר תר"ע

Marie Leitner
b. 05/Oct/1836 d. 09/Oct/1912
נ. כ"ד תשרי תקצ"ז - מ. כ"ח תשרי תרע"ג

(1.2.1) Gottlieb Leitner (Yechiel) b. 1885 d. 10/Dec/1928	**יחיאל** נ. תרמ"ה מ. כ"ז כסלו תרפ"ט
(1.2.2) Herman Leitner	
(1.2.3) Fanny Leitner	
(1.2.4) Sophie Leitner	
Edward and Marie Leitner had other children who died as infants. Their names were:	
(1.2.5) Emanuel Leitner b. 18/July/1874 d. 26/Dec/1874	נ. ד" אב תרל"ד מ. י"ח טבת תרל"ה
(1.2.6) Berta Leitner b. 25/October/1877 d. 25/Nov/1877	נ. י"ט חשון תרל"ח מ. י"ט כסלו תרל"ח
(1.2.7) Mina Leitner (a twin of Berta) b. 25/October/1877 d. 02/Feb/1878	נ. י"ט חשון תרל"ח מ. כ"ט שבט תרל"ח
Emanuel, Berta and Mina were all buried in Marienbad.	

(1.2.1) Gottlieb Leitner (Yechiel) - יחיאל
b. 1885 d. 10/Dec/1928
נ. תרמ"ה - מ. כ"ז כסלו תרפ"ט
[he is buried in Marienbad – Matzeivo removed by Germans in 1939]

Dora Adler
b. 05/May/1884 נ. י' אייר תרמ"ד

(1.2.1.1) Emil Leitner	
(1.2.1.2) Malchem Leitner b. 24/Mar/1901	נ. ד׳ ניסן תרס״א
(1.2.1.3) Martha Leitner b. 06/Jun/1914 d. 11/Mar/1998	נ. י״ב סיון תרע״ד מ. י״ג אדר תשנ״ח
(1.2.1.4) Ruth Leitner	

(1.2.1.2) Malchem Leitner
b. 24/Mar/1901 נ. ניסן תרס״א

Dr. Oesterreicher

(1.2.1.3) Martha Leitner
b. 06/Jun/1914 d. 11/Mar/1998
נ. ו' סיון תרע״ד - מ. י״ג אדר תשנ״ח

Rabbi Michael Munk

(1.2.1.4) Ruth Leitner

Mr. Sheingarten

(1.2.2) Herman Leitner - צבי

Selma Goldschmidt רבקה שרה בת ר׳ יוסף

(1.2.2.1) Ben Zion Leitner b.09/Jun/1919 d. 13/Aug/2010	**בן ציון** נ. י״א סיון תרע״ט מ. ג׳ אלול תש״ע
(1.2.2.2) Yechezkel Leitner	**יחזקאל**

(1.2.2.1) Ben Zion Leitner - בן ציון
b. 09/Jun/1919 d. 13/Aug/2010
נ. י״א סיון תרע״ט - מ. ג׳ אלול תש״ע

Bella Kaufman from Stuttgart Germany - בילא בת ר׳ יהושע
b. 06/Jun/1928 d. 07/Jan/2018
נ. י״ח סיון תרפ״ח - מ. כ׳ טבת תשע״ח

(1.2.2.1.1) **Tzvi Yehoshua Leitner** b.1948 d. 19/Dec/2010 [married Miriam Fishbein]	**צבי יהושע** נ. תש"ח. מ. י"א טבת תשע"א
(1.2.2.1.2) Selma Leitner [married Yitzchok Fuchs]	**רבקה שרה**
(1.2.2.1.3) Devorah Malka [married Dovid Joselovski]	**דבורה מלכה**
(1.2.2.1.4) Miriam Nechama [married Yehoshua Blumenfeld]	**מרים נחמה**
(1.2.2.1.5) Naftoli Moishe [married Chana Tziporah Weiss]	**נפתלי משה**

(1.2.2.2) Yechezkel Leitner - יחזקאל

Sarah Friedman - שרה

(1.2.2.2.1) **Tzvi**	**צבי**
(1.2.2.2.2) **Yosef**	**יוסף**

(1.2.3) Fanny Leitner

Mr. Adler

(1.2.4) Sophie Leitner

Dr. Rosenberg

There is also a record of stillborn twins, Gottlieb and Edward Leitner, who died 23/Feb/1936 ל' שבט תרצ"ו, but no further details known.

KOKISCH FAMILY TREE

Amelie Kokisch (מלכה), the wife of שמואל Kokisch, died in a tragic accident in 1901, when she fell asleep near the coal fire, sitting in a rocking chair. Her clothes caught fire resulting in her ultimate death, some three days later.

(2.1) Samuel Kokisch שמואל -
b. 1834 d. 20/Feb/1882
נ. תקצ"ד - מ. א' אדר תרמ"ב
Buried in Vienna Gate 1 gravestone 6-22-49

מלכה Malka

(2.1.0) The oldest son has been named simply as `Bechor Kokisch`.	
(2.1.1) Max Kokisch (Mordechai) b. 09/Apr/1871 d. 30/Jul/1930	**מרדכי** נ. י"ח ניסן תרל"א מ. ה' אב תר"צ
(2.1.2) Alex Kokisch d. 14/Dec/1962	**אלכסנדר** מ. י"ז כסלו תשכ"ג

(2.1.1) (Mordechai) Max Kokisch - מרדכי
b. 09/Apr/1871 d. 30/Jul/1930
נ. י"ח ניסן תרל"א - מ. ה' אב תר"צ

Married in Marienbad on Friday 15/May/1903 Lag Ba`omer. י"ח אייר תרס"ג

(1.1.4) (Sima) - Hedwig Leitner סימא
b. 12/Apr/1878 d. 14/Aug/1960
נ. ט' ניסן תרל"ח - מ. כ"ג אב תש"כ

(1.1.4.1) Amelie Kokisch (Malka) b. 1904 in Bad Gastein d. 16/Oct/1981	**מלכה** נ. תרס"ג מ. י"ח תשרי תשמ"ב
(1.1.4.2) Theresa Kokisch (Tirza Tolze known as Reisel) b. 1908 in Nice d. 18/Feb/1950 in Chile	**טאלצא תרצה** נ. תרס"ג מ. ראש חודש אדר תש"י
(1.1.4.3) Hilda Kokisch (Hinda) b. 06/Oct/1914 in Marienbad d. 10/May/1989	**הינדא** נ. י"ח תשרי תרע"ה מ. ה' אייר תשמ"ט
(1.1.4.4) Berta Kokisch (Baila) b. 22/May/1919 in Bad Gastein. d.11/Nov/1996	**בילא** נ. כ"ב אייר תרע"ט מ. כ"ט חשון תשנ"ז

(2.1.2) Alex Kokisch – אלכסנדר
d. 14/Dec/1962 מ. י"ז כסלו תשכ"ג

Hedwig
d. 06/Jun/1955 מ. ט"ז סיון תשט"ו
Both are buried in Vienna, door 4 gravestone 14a-2-43

(1.1.4.1) Amelie (Malka) Kokisch - מלכה
b. 1904 in Bad Gastein d. 16/Oct/1981
נ. תרס"ד - מ. י"ח תשרי תרמ"ב

(1.1.2.2) Leopold Deutsch (Yehuda Aryeh) - יהודה אריה
d. 31/Apr/1983 מ. י"ז ניסן תשמ"ג

(1.1.4.3) Hilda (Hinda) Kokisch הינדא -
b. 06/Oct/1914 in Marienbad d. 10/May/1989
נ. י"ח תשרי תרע"ה - מ. ה' אייר תשמ"ט

Married in Santiago on 15/Jan/1946 י"ג שבט תש"ו (on Opa's 40th birthday)

(1.1.1.3) Kurt Leitner (Chaim Aryeh) חיים אריה
b. 08/Feb/1906 d. 09/Sep/1988
נ. י"ג שבט תרס"ו - מ. כ"ז אלול תשמ"ח

(1.1.1.3.1) Micha Leitner (Mordechai Tzvi) b. 19/Jan/1947	**מרדכי צבי** נ. כ"ז טבת תש"ז
(1.1.1.3.2) David Leitner (Dovid) b. 20/Mar/1948	**דוד** נ. ט' אדר ב' תש"ח

(1.1.1.3.3) **Salomon Leitner (Shloime Yeshaya)** b. 12/Jul/1949 d. 06/Aug/2010	**שלמה ישעיה** נ. י"ט תמוז תש"ט מ. כ"ו אב תש"ע
(1.1.1.3.4) Aron Leitner (Aaron) b. 04/Feb/1951	**אהרן** נ. כ"ח שבט תשי"א
(1.1.1.3.5) Benny Leitner (Binyomin) b. 03/Nov/1953	**בנימין** נ. כ"ה חשון תשי"ד

(1.1.4.4) Berta Kokisch בילא -
b. 22/May/1919 in Bad Gastein d. 11/Nov/1996
נ. כ"ב אייר תרע"ט - מ. כ"ט חשון תשנ"ז

Lucho (Yaakov Elozor) Kahan יעקב אלעזר בן משה צבי
b. 11/Jul/1908 d. 27/Jan/1995
נ. י"ב תמוז תרס"ח - מ. כ"ו שבט תשנ"ה

(1.1.4.4.1) Moishe Kahan b. 27/Jul/1952	**משה** נ. ה' אב תשי"ב
(1.1.4.4.2) Sarita Kahan (Soroh Tolzeh) b. 11/Jun/1954	**שרה טאלצא** נ. י' סיון תשי"ד
(1.1.4.4.3) Avrohom Kahan (Avrohom) b. 25/Jun/1956 d. 8/Sept/2003	**אברהם** נ. ט"ז תמוז תשט"ז מ. י"א אלול תשס"ג

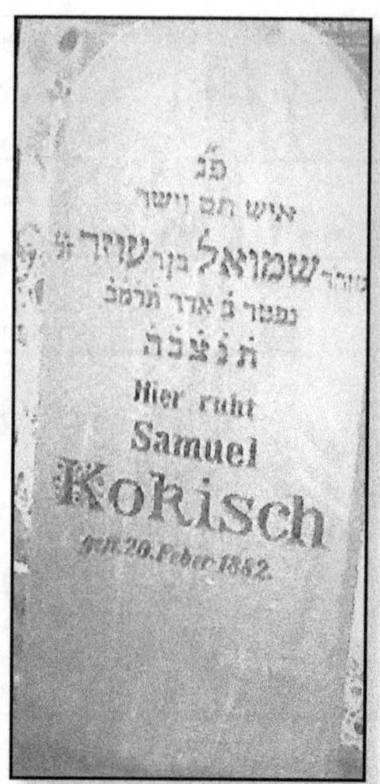

Shmuel ben Ozer Kokisch, Oma's grandfather

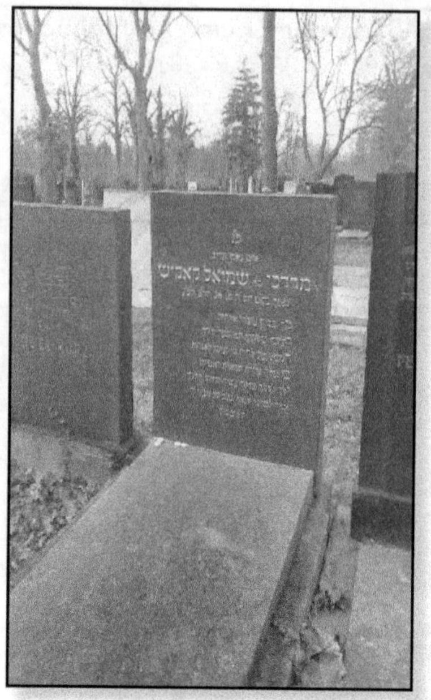

Mordechai ben Shmuel Kokisch Oma's father buried in Vienna

In Vienna there is also a gravestone for:

Sara Kokisch died at age 68 on March 27, 1940 (י"ז אדר ב' ת"ש) Door 4, gravestone 20a-26-54.

b) Berta Kokisch died at age 19 on October 22, 1882 (ט' חשון תרמ"ג) Door 1, gravestone 5b-3-23

c) Chaim Rudolf Kokisch died at age 48 on July 19, 1918 (י' אב תרע"ח) Door 1, gravestone 19-51-38a

There is a letter on file from Uncle Alex Kokisch who wrote that his great-grandfather, Ozer Kokisch, used to spell his name with an ‚e' and not with an ‚i', hence spelling it as Kokesch. This might be of interest and significance for anyone who tries to research the Kokisch/Kokesch ancestry even further back.

CHAPTER 15

Yahrzeits

THE LEITNER FAMILY YAHRZEIT INDEX

	תשרי	
ח' תשרי	Rosa Bamberger (Winkler) (1.1.6.2.4)	תרצה בת ר' מאיר אפרים
י' תשרי	Reisel Leitner (1.1.3.3)	טאלצא בת ר' מאיר
י"ח תשרי	Amelie Deutsch (Kokisch) (1.1.4.1)	מלכה בת ר' מרדכי
כ"ד תשרי	Mirel Leitner (wife of Edward) (1.2)	מירל
	חשון	
ז' חשון	Herman Leitner (1.1.)	צבי בן ר' חיים אריה
ז' חשון	Moishe Dovid (1.1.1) Exact Yahrzeit unknown and kept as his father's, above.	משה דוד בן ר' צבי
כ"ו חשון	Esther Rivkah Winkler (Besbroda) (see 1.1.6.1)	אסתר רבקה
כ"ט חשון	Berta Kahan (Kokisch) (1.1.4.4.)	בילה בת ר' מרדכי
	כסלו	
י"ז כסלו	Alex Kokisch (2.1.2)	אלכסנדר בן ר' שמואל
י"ט כסלו	Berta Leitner (1.2.6)	
כ" כסלו	Ernestine Winkler (Leitner) (1.1.6)	אסתר בת ר' צבי
כ"ב כסלו	Avrohom Deutsch	החבר ר' אברהם בן ר' יצחק
כ"ז כסלו	Gottlieb Leitner (1.2.1)	יחיאל בן ר' יחזקאל

כ"ט כסלו	Mina Leitner (1.2.7) (twin of Berta -1.2.6)	
	טבת	
י"א טבת	Tzvi Yehoshua Leitner (1.2.2.1.1)	צבי יהושע בן ר' בן ציון
י"ז טבת	Siegfried Leitner (Fritz) (1.1.1.2)	שלמה בן ר' משה דוד
י"ח טבת	Emanuel Leitner (1.2.5)	
כ' טבת	Baila Leitner (wife of Ben Zion 1.2.2.1)	בילה בת ר' יהושע
כ"ג טבת	Oscar Leitner (1.1.3.2)	אריה בן ר' מאיר
	שבט	
י"ט שבט	Yoachim Leitner	חיים אריה בן ר' אברהם
כ"ו שבט	Uncle Lucho (Kahan) (see 1.1.4.4)	יעקב אלעזר בן ר' משה צבי
כ"ט שבט	Mina Leitner (1.2.7)	
	אדר א'	
י"ב אדר א'	Efraim Winkler (1.1.6.2)	מאיר אפרים בן הח' ר' מיכאל שלום
כ"ג אדר א'	Rosa Leitner (Sanger) (see 1.1.1.4)	רבקה בת ר' יום טוב
	אדר ב'	
א' ראש חודש אדר	Reisel Kokisch (1.1.4.2)	תרצה טאלצא בת ר' מרדכי
ב' אדר	Samuel Kokisch (2.1)	שמואל בן ר' עוזר
ט' אדר ב'	Sophie Leitner (1.1.2)	יסכא בת ר' צבי
י"ג אדר	Martha Munk (Leitner) (1.2.1.3)	מלכה בת ר' יחיאל
כ"ה אדר ב'	Rifka Leitner (wife of Shloime (1.1.1.3.3)	רבקה בת ר' יצחק משה הלוי
כ"ט אדר ב'	Therese Leitner (nee Epstein) (see 1.1) - (wife of Herman צבי Leitner)	טאלצא
	ניסן	
י"ג ניסן	Helene Leitner (sister of Moishe Dovid)	
י"ד ניסן	Max Leitner (1.1.3)	מאיר בן ר' צבי
ט"ז ניסן	Arthur Leitner (1.1.1.4)	ישעיה בן ר' משה דוד
י"ז ניסן	Leopold Deutsch (1.1.2.2)	הח' ר' יהודה אריה בן הח' ר' אברהם

	אייר	
ד' אייר	Oscar Gerstel (1.1.8.3)	חיים אריה בן ר' מרדכי
ה' אייר	Hinda Leitner (Oma) (Kokisch) (1.1.4.3)	הינדא בת ר' מרדכי
י"ב אייר	Chaya Winkler (Sompolinsky) (see 1.1.6.2)	חיה בת ר' שמשון
י"ט אייר	Emil Leitner (brother of Moishe Dovid)	
כ"א אייר	Erich Leitner (1.1.1.5)	אהרן בן ר' משה דוד
כ"ה אייר	Edward Leitner (1.2)	יחזקאל בן ר' חיים אריה
	סיון	
ט' סיון	Margit Leitner (see 1.1.1.2)	מלכה בת ר' ישעיה
ט"ו סיון	Hedwig Kokisch (wife of Alex 2.1.2)	
כ"ט סיון	Yoachim Leitner	חיים אריה בן ר' אברהם
	תמוז	
י' תמוז	Therese Lubelski (Deutsch) (1.1.2.1)	טאלצא בת הח' ר' אברהם
כ"א תמוז	Rabbi Dr. Michoel Sholom Winkler	החבר ר' מיכאל שלום בן הח' ר' מנשה
כ"ב תמוז	Emil Lubelski (see 1.1.2.1)	אלימלך בן ר' שלמה חיים
	אב	
ה' אב	Max Kokisch (2.1.1)	מרדכי בן ר' שמואל
י"ג אב	Isidor Leitner (1.1.7)	?? בן ר' צבי
	Regina Leitner (Gerlitz) (1.1.7)	
י"ג אב	Theresa Leitner (daughter of Isidor Leitner) (1.1.7.1)	
י"ז אב	Gittel Leitner (Schopflocher) (see 1.1.1)	גיטל בת ר' שלמה
כ"ג אב	Hedwig Leitner (Kokisch) (1.1.4)	סימא בת ר' צבי
כ"ו אב	Theresa Leitner (1.1.1.1)	טאלצא בת ר' משה דוד
כ"ו אב	Shloime Leitner (1.1.1.3.3)	שלמה ישעיה בן ר' חיים אריה
	אלול	
ג' אלול	Ben Zion Leitner (1.2.2.1)	בן ציון בן ר' צבי
ד' אלול	Ernst Leitner (1.1.5)	יעקב בן ר' צבי

ט' אלול	Monty Leitner (1.1.1.2.3)	יהודה מרדכי שמעון בן ר' שלמה
י"א אלול	Avrohom Kahan (1.1.4.4.3)	אברהם בן ר' יעקב אלעזר
י"ג אלול	Ciona Leitner	צעשא סערקא בת ר' מאיר יהודה
כ"ז אלול	Kurt Leitner (Opa) (1.1.1.3)	חיים אריה בן ר' משה דוד

CHAPTER 16
Visitors Book

INDEX OF SOME RABBONIM THAT VISITED MARIENBAD

Albin Rabbi Yitzchok (Warsaw)
Alter Rabbi Avrohom Mordechai (Imrei Emes of Ger) (1866 – 1948)
Alter Rabbi Pinchos Menachem of Ger (1926-1996) (Pnei Menachem)
Alter Rabbi Yisrael (1895-1977)
Altman Rabbi Dr. (1878-1944)
Atlas Rabbi (Glasgow UK)
Auerbach Rabbi Dr. (Halberstadt)
Babad Rabbi (London)
Barantschik Rabbi J.
Bamberger Rabbi L. (Mainz) (1904-1980)
Baumgarten Rabbi Yosef (Vienna)(1864-1933)
Baumgarten Rabbi Shlomo (1904-1992)
Bengis Rabbi Reuben Zelig (Lithuania/Jerusalem) (1864-1953)
Birnbaum Rabbi Nathan (1864-1937)
Blau Rabbi Moishe (Yerusalem)
Bloch Rabbi Avrohom Yitzchok (Telse) (1891-1941)
Bloch Rav Eliyohu Meir (Telse) (1894-1954)
Bornstein Rabbi Dovid (Sochachov)
Boyaner Rebbe (Cracow) (1878-1951)
Breslauer Rabbi (Furth)
Breuer Rabbi Yitzchok (1883–1946) (Jerusalem)
Breuer Rabbi Shlomo Zalman

Breuer Rabbi Josef
Breuer Rabbi Refoel
Broda Rabbi Yacov (Myjava)
Buxbaum Rabbi Yehoshua (Galant) (1877-1944)
Cahn Rabbi L. (Fulda)
Carlebach Rabbi H. (Baden)
Carlebach Rabbi Josef Tzvi (Hamburg) (1883-1942)
Carlebach Rabbi Naftoli (Berlin) (1889–1967)
Cohen Rabbi H. (Berlin) (1884-1972)
Cohn Rabbi H.A. (Berlin) (1881-1948)
Danziger The Alexander Rebbe (1880-1943)
Deutsch Rabbi Moishe (Yugoslavia)
Deutscher Rabbi Moishe (1878-1941)
Deutschlander Rabbi Schmuel (Leo) (1889-1935)
Dubin Rabbi Mordechai (Riga) (1889-1956)
Dushinsky Rabbi Josef Tzvi, (Jerusalem) (1865-1948)
Eckstein Rabbi Moshe L. (Sered)
Eis Rabbi Chaim Yisroel (Zurich) (1876-1943)
Ehrentreu Rabbi J. (Frankfurt)
Ehrentreu Rabbi E. (Munich) (1854-1927)
Ehrmann Rabbi Dr. Shloime (Frankfurt)
Emanuel Rabbi Yitzchok (Hamburg)
Epstein Rabbi Mordechai (Slabodka) (1866-1933)
Erlich Rabbi Menachem Mendel
Falk Rabbi A. (Hamburg)
Feldman Rabbi Dovid (Leipzig/ Manchester)
Fisch Rabbi (London)
Frei Rabbi Meir (Shuran)
Friedensohn RabbiEliezer Gershon (1899-1943)
Friedman Rabbi Moishenu (Boyaner Rebbe – Cracow) (1841-1943)
Friedman Rabbi Avrohom Yacov (3rd Rebbe of Sadigur) (1884–1961)
Friedman Rabbi Yisroel (Chortkov)
Friedman Nachum Mordechai (1874-1946) 3rd Rebbe of Chortkov
Friedman Rabbi Yosef Sholom Mordechai (4th Rebbe of Sadigur) (1897-1979).,
Friedman Rabbi Alexander Zusha (1897-1943)
Friedman Rabbi Yitzchok (Husyatin)
Fuerst Rabbi Yeshia (Vienna)
Gelenter Rabbi Fishel (Berlin)
Goodman Mr. Aron (Harry) (London) (1898–1961)

Gottesmann Rabbi Yacov (Romania)
Greineman Rabbi – see Rabbi Karelitz
Gutterman Rabbi Aaron Mendel (Radzyminer Rebbe) (1860-1934)
Hager The Vishnitzer Rebbe [Ahavas Yisroel] (1860-1936)
Hager Rabbi Chaim Meir (Imrei Chaim of Vishnitz) (1888-1972)
Hager Rabbi Boruch (Seret Vishnitz) (1895-1963)
Hager Rabbi (Damezek Eliezer) (1895-1945)
Halberstam Rabbi Benzion (Bobov) (1874–1941)
Halberstam Rabbi Shloime (Bobov) (1907-2000)
Halberstam Rabbi Shayele (Tchechov)
Halberstam Rabbi Yechezkel Shraga
Halstoch Rabbi Yacov (Ostrawa)
Herskovitz Rabbi Alexander (Zagreb)
Hertz Chief Rabbi (England) (1872-1946)
Herz Mr. Mosi (Lucern)
Heshel Rabbi Avrohom (Novominsker Rebbe) (1907-1972)
Heshel Rabbi Y.M (Kopishnitzer Rebbe) (1888-1967)
Hirsch Rabbi (Holland)
Hirschhorn Rabbi Tzvi (Jaworzne)
Horowitz Rabbi Yonason (Yerusalem)
Horowitz Rabbi Yacov (Frankfurt) (1873-1939)
Horowitz Rabbi Mordechai (Romania)
Horowitz Rabbi Tuvia (Sanok)
Horowitz Rabbi Alter Yechezkel (Dzikov) (1879-1943)
Hurwitz Rabbi Shimon Tzvi (1864-1942)
Jacobson Rabbi Wolf Selig (Copenhagen) (1896-?)
Kahan Rabbi Kalman (Fulda) (1910-1998)
Kahane Rabbi Moses(Romania)
Kahaneman Rabbi Josef Shloime (Ponevez) (1886-1969)
Kalish Rabbi Shimon (Amshinov) (1882-1954)
Kalmanowitz Rabbi Avrohom (1887-1964)
Kanal Rabbi Yitzchok Meir (Warsaw)
Karelitz Rabbi Chaim Shaul (Palestine) (1912-2001) (Greineman)
Karelitz Rabbi Meir (1877-1955)
Katz Rabbi Reuven (Chust / Petach Tikva) (1870-1954)
Katz Rabbi Yaakov Tzvi (Holland)
Klein Herman Rabbi (Berlin)
Klein Rabbi Avrohom Yitzchok (Nurenberg) (1870 -1951)
Kohn Rabbi Dr. Pinchos. (Ansbach) (1867–1941)

Kornitzer Rabbi Josef Nechemia (1880-1933)
Kotler Rav Aaron Kotler (1891-1962)
Kunstadt Rabbi Boruch (Fulda) (1885-1967)
Kurtzman Rabbi Dovid (Krakow) (1865 – 1942)
Landau Rabbi Efraim (Bucharest) (1880-1950)
Landau Dr. Maximillian
Landau Rabbi Pinchos (London)
Landau Rabbi Avrohom Avigdor (Strikover Rebbe) (1917-2001)
Langer Rabbi Mordechai (1894-1943)
Lau Rabbi Moshe Chaim (Pietrokova) (1892-1942)
Leibovitz Reb Boruch Ber (1862–1939)
Lebowicz Rabbi Markus (Romania)
Levin Rabbi Channoch Tzvi,(Bendin) (1870-1935)
Levontin Rabbi Zalman Dovid (1856-1940)
Lewenstein Rabbi Tuvia (Zurich)
Lewin Rabbi Itzchok Meir (Bendin) (1893-1971)
Lewin Raw Aaron (1879-1938)
Liberson Rabbi Yitzchok Gedalia (1903-1982)
Lichtig Rabbi (Hamburg) (1873-1937)
Luria Rabbi Yitzchok (Tiberias)
Margulies Rabbi Yisroel Aryeh (Premishlan/London) (1903-1982)
Marilus Rabbi Eliezer (1853-1945)
Meier Rabbi Jacov (1856-1939)
Melchior Rabbi (Copenhagen) (1897-1969)
Merzbach Rabbi Tuvia (Darmstadt) (1900-1980)
Mett Rabbi (London)
Meyer Rabbi Dr. Seligman–(Regensburg)
Michalski Rabbi Michoel (Karlsruhe)
Mintzberg Rabbi Leib (Lodz)
Munk Rabbi (London) (1899-1978)
Munk Rabbi Eli (Berlin) (1867-1940)
Munk Rabbi Ezra (Berlin) (1867-1940)
Munk Rabbi Eli (Paris) (1900-1981)
Ollenberg Rabbi S.(Berlin)
Oppenheim Rabbi Dr. (Frankfurt)
Orleans Rabbi Yehuda Leib (Cracow) (1900-943)
Pappenhein Rabbi Binyomin Wolf (1848-1938)
Pappenheim Rabbi Kalman (Vienna)
Pardes Rabbi Schmuel Aaron (1887-1956)

Perlmutter Rabbi (1843 -1930)
Petuchovski Rabbi Marcus (Berlin) (1866-1926)
Plotzky Rabbi Meir Don (1866-1928)
Portugal Rabbi Zissie (Romania) (1989-1982)
Porush Rabbi Moishe (Palestine)
Posen Rabbi Yaacov (Frankfurt) (1852-1932)
Pruskin Rabbi Pessach (1879 -1939)
Rabinov Rabbi S. (Belgium)
Rabinowitz Rabbi Nosson Dovid (Biale Rebbe)
Rabinowitz Rabbi Eliyohu Akiva (Poltaverrov)
Reich Rabbi Koppel (Budapest) (1839-1929)
Reicher Rabbi Yeshia (Romania)
Rokach Rabbi (Sassover Rebbe/London) (1910-2003)
Rokeach Rabbi Yissochor Dov (Belz),(1854- 1926)
Rokeach -Rabbi Aaron (Belz) (1877-1957)
Rosenheim Rabbi Yaacov (5/ Nov/ 1870 – 3/Nov/ 1965)
Rottenberg Rabbi M. (Antwerp) (1872-1944)
Rottenberg Rabbi Yaacov (Kozowa) (1909-1990)
Rubin Rabbi (London)
Safrin Rabbi Yakov Moshe (Komarna) (1861-1929
Safrin Rabbi Shalom (1893-1937)
Safrin Rabbi Chaim Yacov (1892-1969)
Schachnowitz Rabbi Selig (1874 – 1952)
Schenkolewski Rabbi Meir (New York)
Schlesinger Rabbi M. (Frankfurt) (1898-1948)
Schlesinger Rabbi M. (Eisenstadt)
Schneebalg Rabbi Dovid (Romania) (1893-1968)
Schonfeld Rabbi Avigdor (1880-1930)
Schonfeld Rabbi Dr. Shlomo (1912-1984)
Schub Rabbi (Vilna)
Schwab Rabbi Shimon (1891-1965)
Shapiro Rabbi Meir (1887 – 1933)
Shkop Rabbi Shimon (1860-1939)
Sienkiewicz Rabbi H (Jerusalem)
Silberstein Rabbi Issaiah (Waitzen) (1857-1930)
Silver Rabbi Eliezer (1882 – 1968) (Cincinnati)
Snyders Rabbi Yaacov (Bratislava/ Basle) (1905-1984)
Sofer Rabbi Akiva (Daas Sofer) (Pressburg/ Jerusalem) (1878–1959)
Sofer Rabbi Avrohom Schmuel Binyomin (Kesav Sofer)

Sofer Rabbi Simcha Bunim (Shevet Sofer)
Sofer Rabbi Shloime (1853-1930)
Sofer Rabbi Shimon Sofer (1850-1944) (Erlau)
Soloveitchik Rabbi Chaim (Brisk) (1853–1918)
Soloveitchik Rabbi Yitzock Zev (Brisk) (1886 -1959)
Sorotzkin Rabbi Zalman (Slutz/ Yerusalem) (1881–1966)
Spira Rabbi Chaim Elazar Munkatcher Rebbe (1871 – 1937)
Spira Rabbi Yisroel (Blushover Rebbe (1889 – 1989)
Spitzer Rabbi Dr.Schmuel (Hamburg) (1872-1934)
Steiner Rabbi Avrohom (Kerestir)
Sussman Rabbi (Budapest)
Taub Rabbi S.Y (Modzitzer Rebbe) (1886-1947)
Teitlebaum Rabbi Yoel, (Orshiva/ Satmer)
Teumim Rabbi Shimon Frankel (Skovin) (1876-1942)
Turkel Mr. David (Vienna/ New York)
Turkel Rabbi Lippa
Ungar Rabbi Shmuel Dovid (Nitra) (1885–1945)
Wasserman Rabbi Elchonon Bunim (Baranowitz) (1875-1941)
Wassermann Rabbi M. (Bresslau)
Weber Rabbi Kalman
Weiss Rabbi Shimshon Refoel (Wurzburg)
Weiss Rabbi Yitzchok (Spinka) (1875- 1944)
Weissmandl Rabbi Michoel Ber (Nitra) (1903-1957)
Wesel Rabbi Benzion (Turda)
Winkler Rabbi Dr. Michoel Sholom (Copenhagen) (1863-1932)
Witkin Rabbi Hillel (Palestine)
Wittenberg Rabbi Shimon (Latvia)
Wolkin Rabbi Aron (Pinsk) (1865-1942)
Ziemba Rabbi Menachem (1883–1943)
Zirelsohn Rabbi Yehuda Leib (Kishinev) (1860–1941)